The Mammoth Book of

ROARING
TWENTIES
WHODUNNITS

Also available

The Mammoth Book of 20th Century Ghost Stories
The Mammoth Book of Arthurian Legends
The Mammoth Book of Astounding Word Games
The Mammoth Book of Battles
The Mammoth Book of Best New Horror #11
The Mammoth Book of Bridge
The Mammoth Book of British Kings & Queens
The Mammoth Book of Cats
The Mammoth Book of Chess New Edition and Internet Games
The Mammoth Book of Comic Fantasy II
The Mammoth Book of Dogs
The Mammoth Book of Dracula
The Mammoth Book of Endurance and Adventure
The Mammoth Book of Egyptian Whodunnits
The Mammoth Book of Eyewitness History 2000
The Mammoth Book of Fantastic Science Fiction (1970s)
The Mammoth Book of Future Cops
The Mammoth Book of Fighter Pilots
The Mammoth Book of Haunted House Stories
The Mammoth Book of Heroes
The Mammoth Book of Heroic and Outrageous Women
The Mammoth Book of Historical Detectives
The Mammoth Book of Historical Whodunnits
The Mammoth Book of the History of Murder
The Mammoth Book of Humor
The Mammoth Book of Eyewitness Battles
The Mammoth Book of Eyewitness WWII
The Mammoth Book of Jack the Ripper
The Mammoth Book of Killer Women
The Mammoth Book of Life Before the Mast
The Mammoth Book of Literary Anecdotes
The Mammoth Book of Locked-Room Mysteries and Impossible Crimes
The Mammoth Book of Love & Sensuality
The Mammoth Book of Men O'War
The Mammoth Book of Movie Detectives and Screen Crimes
The Mammoth Book of Murder and Science
The Mammoth Book of Road Stories
The Mammoth Book of New Sherlock Holmes Adventures
The Mammoth Book of Nostradamus and Other Prophets
The Mammoth Book of Oddballs and Eccentrics
The Mammoth Book of Private Lives
The Mammoth Book of Pulp Fiction
The Mammoth Book of Sex, Drugs & Rock 'n' Roll
The Mammoth Book of Soldiers at War
The Mammoth Book of Sword & Honor
The Mammoth Book of Tasteless Lists
The Mammoth Book of Terror
The Mammoth Book of True War Stories
The Mammoth Book of True Crime (revised)
The Mammoth Book of Unsolved Crimes
The Mammoth Book of War Diaries and Letters
The Mammoth Book of The West
The Mammoth Book of The World's Greatest Chess Games
The Mammoth Encyclopedia of The Unsolved

The Mammoth Book of

ROARING
TWENTIES
WHODUNNITS

Edited by Mike Ashley

CARROLL & GRAF PUBLISHERS
New York

Carroll & Graf Publishers
An imprint of Avalon Publishing Group, Inc.
245 W. 17th Street
NY 10011
www.carrollandgraf.com

AVALON
publishing group incorporated

First published in the UK by Robinson,
an imprint of Constable & Robinson Ltd 2004

First Carroll & Graf edition 2004

ISBN 0-7867-1416-6

Printed and bound in the EU

Contents

Copyright and Acknowledgments

Foreword: The Crazy Age

MIKE ASHLEY

We do love to apply nicknames to things, even decades. The Swinging Sixties, the Gay Nineties (or was it the Naughty Nineties?) and, of course, the Roaring Twenties. And aren't those two words evocative. You need scarcely utter them than our mind's eye conjures up visions of the jazz age, the charleston, country-house parties, the first talkies and, of course, those "bright young things". A decade of excitement, energy, eccentricity, fun and freedom – a complete release after the horrors of the Great War, and total gay abandon for the terrors yet to come.

Because, as we know, it wasn't all fun. The 1920s was a time of great hardship in Britain – the Jarrow March, the General Strike, the fear of communism and revolution. In America there was prohibition and the rise of gangsterism.

It was a decade of extremes, and it's out of extremes that the stories emerge. The 1920s saw the start of the Golden Age of the detective story. In Britain it was during this decade that Agatha Christie's Poirot and Miss Marple first appeared and, even more typical of the period, Dorothy L. Sayers's Lord Peter Wimsey. In America that role was taken by S.S. van Dine with his detective Philo Vance, but the 1920s also saw the rise of pulp fiction and the hard-boiled school led by Carroll John Daly and Dashiell Hammett. The one was a rebellion against the other, showing that even in crime fiction, there were extremes.

In this anthology I wanted to encapsulate those extremes. I wanted a selection of stories that not only showed the fun, the froth and the frolics of the 1920s but also the hard, violent and vicious underbelly. Above all I wanted the stories to reflect that unreality of the decade: a period when, rather like the "swinging sixties", people threw caution to the wind and lived life to the full, regardless of what was round the corner.

I also wanted the stories to show the exciting "newness" of things in the twenties. The movies were all the rage, with film stars the new celebrities, and by the end of the 1920s you could hear them as well. There was the radio and the first communication revolution with the growth of the telephone. And there was a travel boom, with the growth in the motor car and commercial airlines. With the 1920s we entered the era of the gadget, with mass production and a booming economy.

That's what you'll find here. From Annette Meyers's Greenwich Village partygoers to Robert Randisi's beauty pageant, from Marilyn Todd's murder in the artworld to Gillian Linscott's death in Britain's first telephone booth, from Hulbert Footner's "Bright Young Things" in the world of crime to Mat Coward's murder before the Communist revolution, these stories cover every facet of life in that mad decade.

So, let's party . . .

– Mike Ashley

Timor Mortis

ANNETTE MEYERS

Annette Meyers is probably best known for her series about corporate headhunters Xenia Smith and Leslie Wetzon, set amongst the wheeling and dealing of Wall Street and Broadway. Annette is well qualified to talk of the theatrical world as she worked with Hal Prince on the Broadway Productions of Fiddler on the Roof, Cabaret *and* A Little Night Music. *With her husband Martin, writing under the joint alias of Maan Meyers, she has produced a historical mystery series chronicling the Tonneman family down the generations in New York, starting with* The Dutchman *(1992). Annette introduced her poet-detective Olivia Brown in her 1999 novel* Free Love, *set amongst the arty set in Greenwich Village in the 1920s. The follow-up novel was* Murder Me Now *(2001). Here's the latest adventure.*

Greenwich Village is our enclave, our village, and we rarely venture east of Washington Square Park, unless of course it is for one of our fancy dress balls, which we hold at Webster Hall on Eleventh Street near Third Avenue.

The costume balls were inaugurated before the Great War by *The Masses*, an irreverent magazine to which everyone in the Village contributed short stories, poetry, drawings, essays and humor. The purpose of the balls was to pay off the magazine's persistent debts with the admission charged. The focus of *The Masses* was anti-war, and the government, in the midst of the Great War, had shut it down. Although *The Masses* has not survived, costume balls continue for the benefit of one or another of our Village institutions.

It was said that when our own Floyd Dell, one of the editors of *The Masses*, first approached the proprietor of Webster Hall about the cost for rental of the space, the proprietor asked, "Is yours a drinking crowd?"

To which our Floyd replied, "Hell, yes."

And the proprietor said, "You can have it for nothing."

You might very well ask, "What of Prohibition?"

The truth is, things are hardly different now, even with Prohibition. The bar at the costume balls is as crowded as before, perhaps even more so. The costume balls are our playground, and play we do, dancing and drinking till we greet a new day in Washington Square Park.

There may be hundreds of ways to die, and certainly, I've seen more than a few in my curious life, but to come to a costume ball riding naked on a white horse and have one's breast pierced by a feathered arrow is more than anyone's imagination – even mine – could ever contemplate.

But let me not get ahead of my story.

If you were a stranger in Greenwich Village and chose to begin your acquaintance in front of my sliver of a house on Bedford Street, whether you turn to the right, or left, you would soon be lost among our crooked, winding streets, streets that cross one another and take new names, or just stop never to resume, or resume as if nothing has happened several blocks away.

In the hour just before dawn, when the sky begins to

surrender darkness to threads of pink, my Village appears the painted set of a play about to begin. Innocent and pure. And all of us who make our home here are, for the moment, innocent and pure. In thought, if not in deed.

Corruptible? Well, of course. This is life, not a play. Perhaps we're naive to think we can live in art. And then again, what exactly does corruptible mean?

It began on one of those wicked March days when a person is seduced by the surprising silky air at midday, only to be viciously betrayed by afternoon. I was on my way home to Bedford Street wrapped in disagreeable thoughts, my head down against the wind, otherwise I might have seen her.

I'd come from a very unsatisfactory meeting with Mr Harper about my first book of poems, *Embracing the Thorns*, during which he, for all his promises, presented me with the most penurious of contracts. And he was, in fact, talking in terms of a year from now as, he said, they would prefer more from me than a slim volume of verses. Indeed. Indeed!

So I was hardly in fine fettle when, with some persistence, my friend Edward Hall eventually managed to get my attention. The taxi he was riding in pulled up beside me and he called, "Oliver!"

My determined stride suspended, out of the corner of my eye, I caught an odd flurry of color, blues on the wing, a human butterfly, before the apparition faded into the entrance of a shop.

"I've been trying to get your attention for two blocks," Edward continued. "You look like a dark cloud."

"Dark cloud? My dear Edward, I'll have you know I'm a thunderstorm, a tornado cloaked in a hurricane, a –"

"Enough, Cyrana!" He opened the door and pulled me into the cab, and with some aplomb, planted a tender kiss on my lips. "Come along and you can tell us all about it."

My artful abductor, I saw at once, was not alone in the taxi. On his other side sat a small, finely dressed gentleman, his exophthalmic eyes as bright and curious as a chimp's. His exquisite hands rested on the silver head of his walking stick.

"Oliver, may I present Michael Walling?"

I reached across Edward to shake hands with Michael Walling, whose name I'd recognized, Walling House being a well respected press. Edward is currently at *Vogue*, and when editors meet with publishers not their own, there's no telling what their meeting is about.

"Charmed," Michael Walling said, brushing my fingers with his little mustache.

"We're off to the Lafayette," Edward said. "Why don't you join us?"

"I wouldn't want to intrude," I said, modestly, but bestowing on publisher Walling my most brilliant smile.

"I should be delighted if you would join us, Miss Brown. I am a great admirer of your work."

The Hotel Lafayette and the Brevoort Hotel are the two best hotels in the Village, each insinuating its own continental flavor. They are situated almost back to back; the former, on University Place and Ninth Street, is where Gene O'Neill stays when he comes down from Provincetown. The Brevoort stands at Fifth Avenue and Eighth Street. In its basement is an informal café, the perfect place for merrymaking. Both locations are patronized only when we are in the money, which sad to say, isn't often. So I was not going to turn down an invitation to one or the other.

I've known Edward Hall longer than anyone else in the Village. At *Ainslee's*, he was the first editor to buy my poems. And for a short time we were lovers. When *Ainslee's*, like *The Masses*, went the way of other small magazines and journals, Edward moved on to *Vogue*, where – lucky me – he's continued to buy my poems. And although I knew that he'd like his early place back in my affections, for my part romantic passion is fleeting. My passion is for my work. But our friendship remains, and I treasure it.

As for Michael Walling, he could well have walked out of the previous century, an odd little man in a well-tailored suit and vest, not a wrinkle on him except around his eyes, where wrinkles lay like folds of draperies. His wide mouth was made wider yet by very prominent teeth and the thin mustache with waxed tips. He handed his spotless gray fedora and his silver headed walking stick to the doorman and suggested we take tea in the Game Room.

I'd been only once to the Lafayette's quaintly ornate Game Room, where after dining at the restaurant, a man, or nowadays a woman, could come for a cigar and cognac and French coffee. The ceiling is lofty, the room large yet somehow intimate, with tall windows facing the street. Mirrored walls reflect marble-topped tables lit by green shaded lamps. And of course French magazines and newspapers are available in a corner rack, and domino and chess players are encouraged by reserved tables. In style and grace, the Game Room was a perfect match for our host.

"So do tell us, Oliver, why you are a tornado cloaked in a hurricane," Edward said slyly. We'd settled in over little bread and butter squares, short bread and tea, rather churlishly delivered by an ancient waiter with a sibilant accent, more Balkan than French.

I shook my cigarette holder at Edward and told him in my most severe voice. "You are making fun of me, Edward."

"No, I swear —"

"My dear Miss Brown," Mr Walling broke in, "I cannot speak for Edward here, but I for one would like to know what caused your unhappiness. And, if you'll allow me to be your champion, I shall try to make things right."

"Well, thank you, Mr Walling, sir." The short bread could not have melted more sweetly in my mouth. "You are a gentleman, as opposed to Edward-here." I leaned toward him so he could light my cigarette when he lit his.

Edward laughed. "Forgive me, Oliver. Do tell your story."

I related my disappointment with Mr Harper and the postponement of my book, growing more and more impassioned, my hands moving with my words. Edward captured my hand in his, terribly contrite, as well he should have been.

Mr Walling set down his teacup, which he'd been holding but not sipping from during my narration. "Miss Brown, I am shocked at the cavalier way you are being treated by one of my publishing colleagues, and I do hope you will not think all publishers are the same. Do you have a contract?"

I removed the thin envelope from my pocket. "I have not signed it, but I'm afraid I must." As I sighed, I caught Edward's eye. "What else is a poor writer to do?"

"You might," Mr Walling said, taking charge of my other

hand, "consider allowing me to publish your first book of poetry. It would be an honor."

"Mr Walling!"

"Michael," said he.

"Michael, I am quite overwhelmed."

"You would have a fine presentation, Oliver." Edward's enthusiasm was contagious. "Do consider it."

"I see a slim volume bound in black cloth, the title and your name in gold lettering. Deckle-edged paper, of course." Walling looked deep into my rather spectacular, if I do say so myself, green eyes. "We would be prepared to offer you an advance of five hundred dollars, and we can publish when you're ready. What do you say, Miss Brown?"

I could hardly believe my good fortune. A beautiful book from a respected publisher, and a five-hundred-dollar advance. What did I say? I said, "If you'll pardon me for a moment." I took Mr Harper's mean contract to the fireplace and threw it in. The fire flared around the paper for a moment and held, as if reluctant to consume it. Whether it was an aberration, or an omen, I couldn't have cared less. I turned my back on it and gave my new publisher my consent.

We shook hands and Michael's nod to our surly waiter produced clean teacups filled with mediocre champagne, but still champagne. As the afternoon faded, the well showed no sign of running dry, and I noticed the waiters begin to scowl and grumble as more and more tables came to be occupied by decorous people.

"Do you care for archery, Miss Brown – Olivia – if I may?" my host asked.

"Olivia, of course, Michael. And as for archery, I must confess I know very little about it, but I have been known to be arch." Edward's hand squeezed my right thigh.

"Well, that can be rectified." Michael smiled at me but took the subject no further, except to say, "You must meet Clara. Perhaps Edward can bring you round next week to one of Clara's evenings."

"Well, I –" Now my left thigh got the squeeze, and I played with the wicked thought that I might press my thighs together and introduce my two suitors to one another. I rose instead and put an end to it. "I'd be delighted, Michael." Clara Walling is an artist of sorts, a woman with money who had prevailed upon her husband to buy one of the great white townhouses in Washington Square, so she could be closer to her quarry. She enjoys collecting young artists and writers and then showing them off to her Uptown friends. I'd heard about Clara Walling's evenings, and I am probably the only clever girl in Greenwich Village who's never been.

"I must be on my way," I said, "I have a costume to prepare."

"Costume?" Michael said.

"The Ball, tomorrow night," Edward said, becoming animated.

"Oh, yes, of course. That's what Clara's been working on all week. I'd quite forgotten."

"You must come, too, Michael," I said. "I'll save a dance for you."

"Then how could I not?" was Michael's gallant reply.

"We're trying to raise money to start a modern magazine," Edward said.

Edward had made the arrangements and we advertised our ball as a Feather Ball, the costume left to the attendees' imaginations.

I took my leave, but Edward followed me. I thought, oh, dear, I am going to have to be firm with him that there could be nothing between us.

"Oliver." He looked down at me with besotted eyes.

"Edward, dear, you know—" I was resigned that this was to be our eternal relationship. His devotion, my friendship. Still, his devotion was to be treasured. Some day I would be old and gray and there would always be Edward to tell me how much he loved me.

"Please pretend we are lovers," he said.

"Pretend? But Edward, you know we can only be dear friends."

"Oh, I know that, Oliver. But I'd like old Walling to think otherwise, because it's Clara and I who are lovers."

Well, I guess that told me.

I left Edward and Michael, surely two characters right out of Moliere, to discuss whatever it was I'd interrupted, and headed home, my feet fairly skimming the sidewalk, assisted by champagne and good news. The sun had receded, leaving behind a pale, mustardy twilight.

My Edward and Clara Walling. I had to laugh. You see, nothing is permanent. For all that, I couldn't wait to meet La Belle Clara in person.

As I approached Fifth Avenue, I saw someone among a fuzzy cluster wave to me. What was his name? Frank something or other. Calls himself Franz, wears a frayed cloak and a grimy crimson Byronesque tie. Claiming to be a writer, he's always on our fringe. I hardly knew him. And now didn't want to know him, as he has begun to conduct guided tours of Greenwich Village for tourists who want to view bohemians and visit our saloons and coffee houses. Our little enclave is being invaded. It's no wonder so many of us are sailing for Paris.

I pulled up short, changed direction and once again I caught a momentary glimpse of vivid color, blues, butterfly wings aflutter. I turned back but the vision was gone.

By the time I reached 73½ Bedford Street and home, the promise of spring was but a distant memory. The afternoon had turned chill and a punchy little wind flicked at my cloak with impudent disdain.

Home is the three-storey red brick house that had come to me from my great aunt Evangeline Brown, the black sheep of the Brown family. She'd chosen to live in Greenwich Village in a Boston marriage with Miss Alice. In fact, I never even knew of her existence until she died and left me her house. The duplex on the second and third floor was available for me, but as to the ground floor, a codicil to her will stated that the tenant in that flat was to live there rent free for the rest of his life. This tenant, I learned from the little brass plate next to his door, was one H. Melville, Private Investigations, Confidentiality Assured.

This is how I met Harry Melville and learned that my mysterious great aunt Evangeline, or Vangie, as Harry called her, had run a private investigation business and that he had been her assistant. As I am of an inquisitive nature, I saw no reason not to carry on the family business. And I think Harry, though he will protest, secretly relies on my help, from time to time, on his cases.

I'd just reached the gate, thinking about a lovely martini, when the front door opened and there was Harry himself, and shockingly attired, by which I mean no soiled trousers, but a real suit, looking for all the world like a customer's man from

Wall Street. That is, he would have were it not for his long hair, which he wears, pulled back with a rubber band into a ponytail.

"Perfect timing." He took hold of my arm, turned me about and walked me away from my lovely martini.

I confess I began whining, which is not my nature at all. "Where are we going? I was so looking forward to a lovely martini."

"You'll have your lovely martini if you come along with me."

"Aha! A bribe. Why would you have to bribe me? Is this a new client? I would love a new client."

"Not this one," he said.

Now that was intriguing. Who was this difficult client and why, if the client was so difficult, was Harry on his way to see him. "So why didn't the new client come to you, or has he heard that the springs in your sofa are lethal?"

Harry didn't respond, except for a squeeze of his fingers on my elbow, all the while propelling me back from whence I'd just come. He was in one of his dark moods, I could tell, so I stopped asking questions. When we arrived at his destination, the Brevoort, he guided me through the door to a seat in the lobby and told me to wait.

I didn't see why he was being so mysterious, but I was intrigued by his change of costume from seedy Village bohemian private detective to Wall Street broker, a profession for which he has neither use nor admiration. Or so I'd always thought.

Through the lobby of the slightly shabby, if expensive, continental Brevoort passes a mix of transients, residents and visitors, complementing the shabbiness of the lobby. I reached into my pocket for my pencil and notepad.

"Come along, Oliver." Harry pulled me from my chair and I dropped my pencil. And, Good Lord, here was another shock. Harry was wearing real shoes, not his usual scuffed sandals.

We entered an elegant, intricately carved elevator and went to the third floor. As Harry steered me down the corridor and stopped in front of a door, I decided I'd had enough of the mystery.

"You had better tell me the name of our client so I don't look the complete fool."

His jaw tightened. "A distant cousin," he said.

"Mine or yours?"

He didn't see the humor. He knows I have no relatives whatever, only dear Mattie, my friend and companion who lives with me at 73 ½ Bedford Street. He looked down at me and actually growled, "Let it be." He pressed the bell on the side of the door and in a short time, the door opened.

"Harry. Come in."

Harry stood in front of me so our client didn't notice me at first, but silence and I are often at loggerheads. You see, even with Harry blocking my view, which is easy as I'm a bit of a thing – Amy Lowell was impossible to obscure. To say she is vast would be a horrific understatement.

She responded to my gasp with a grudging, "Oh, I see you've brought *her*. You might as well come in, too, Olivia." She stepped aside, but there was little space in the small room as she took up most of it. She was wearing a flowing gown of multi-shades of purple, making of herself a floral mountain.

Amy Lowell is an established poet who does not suffer fools gladly. Her sharp wit and scathing tongue are well known in poetry circles. She is one of the Boston Lowells and unlike us the slovenly bohemians of Greenwich Village, Miss Lowell is a very proper person. Very proper and very enormous. You may think me cruel, but I have been on the receiving end of Miss Lowell's scathing wit and I'm still bleeding from the carving. She has let it be known in no uncertain terms that my morals are disreputable and that my poems, superficial, tainted with left wing concepts, not to mention feminist causes. As she tarred the great poet Elinor Wylie with the same brush, particularly condemning Elinor's several marriages, I take no heed of the opinions of Miss Amy Lowell. Well, hardly any.

Truly, she brings out the very worst in me, not the least because she worked furiously trying to keep women from the Vote. She criticizes feminists and has so many staid and stuffy conventional opinions, she might as well be a banker. Yet her poems are often even more sensual than mine and she lives openly in a Boston marriage. She is nothing but a judgmental snob, not to mention hypocrite.

Last month, at a reading in Philadelphia, when I was told that Amy Lowell had been their speaker the previous year, I couldn't help responding flippantly, "Therefore, I deduce that your program plan is one year a fat girl, next year a thin girl.''

"Distant cousin?" I now said dubiously as I took one of the two chairs in the tiny drawing room. My scruffy old Harry a Lowell? Certainly not.

Harry sat in the other, held the crease in his trousers and crossed his leg over the other. What was his design?

"Harry's mother was a Lowell," said the largest poet of our generation, male or female, looking down her nose at me from where she sat taking up the entire expanse of the sofa.

I produced a sound something like "eeek," and waited for Harry to disprove her.

"What is it, Amy?" Harry said, passing over my open-mouthed astonishment.

"Fania. She's run off again." She clipped a big Manila cigar, struck a match and lit the tip, proceeding to make unpleasant sucking sounds until she filled the little room with intense fumes.

"I thought she was being cared for," Harry said.

"She's very sly."

"Who is Fania?" I asked when I got over my shock about Harry being a Lowell.

"A distant cousin," Harry said.

"Another one?"

"Her dear dead mother married *a foreigner*," Amy Lowell said, as if that explained everything.

"What do you mean by *she's being cared for*?"

"The family keeps watch over Fania, for her own good." Lowell shifted her weight on the sofa and the poor sofa groaned.

"For her own good?" I directed my question to Harry.

"Fania has a mania," Harry said. "A paranoia."

"Freud! You give me Freudian diagnoses!" Lowell's explosion almost blew me right off my chair. "You see, it's that fraud, that madman's theories that have destroyed this delightful child."

I have to admit that I couldn't have been more surprised as Harry has never admitted to any real interest in the Herr Doctor, whose influence has seduced almost everyone we know into analysis. Not me, of course. I'll have none of it.

"Paranoia?" I asked. I put a cigarette into my ebony holder.

Harry came over and gave me a light from his cigarette. He remained standing.

"Fania is afraid of dying," Amy Lowell said, hand on her enormous bosom, calming herself.

"Most people are afraid of death, don't you think?"

Harry took his silver flask from his breast pocket and had a long swallow. I shot him a pleading look but he ignored it. How I could have used a good swig of gin. And hadn't he promised me a lovely martini for coming with him?

"Fania's way of dealing with her fear is eccentric," said Amy, sending another cloud of pungent smoke into the already dense air.

"How so?"

"For a time she hides in her rooms, too fearful to even venture into the gardens. Then she disappears and contrives to embarrass the family by her flagrant behavior."

"She tempts death," Harry said. "Her last adventure was a leap off the Cambridge Street Bridge. She broke both of her legs, but she lived."

"Naked," Amy Lowell said, "She was naked."

Horrors, I thought. At least to a Boston Lowell. "It seems to me she's trying to die, not that she's afraid of death."

Harry said, "She says her friend suggested it."

"Well, what kind of friend would do that, I'd like to know?"

"Fania," Amy Lowell said, drawing deeply on her cigar, "has an imaginary friend."

"Imaginary?"

"At least no one has ever seen her," Harry said.

"Does this friend have a name?"

Harry looked at his cousin, who said, "Camilla. Camilla Faye."

"And you're sure there's no such person?"

Amy Lowell gave me a not at all tolerant look, as if no sane person would ask such a ridiculous question.

I said, "I suppose it would be terribly expensive for the family to hire a full-time companion."

"Fania is a very wealthy young woman," Amy said. "If something were to happen to her, the money would leave the family."

"And go where?"

"To her unworthy father."

Dear, dear, I thought, perhaps Fania has reason indeed to fear death.

"Do we have any idea where she may be?" Harry said.

"I've had to take time from my speaking engagements to come here because she's been seen in the city. I want you to find her before she does something dreadfully embarrassing."

"You mean like dying?" I asked in my sweetest tone.

Thus arrived the moment Harry decided it was past time to leave. For my part, it couldn't have been a minute too soon.

As he held the door for me, the woman mountain called him back while waving me off imperiously. I was standing at the elevator fulminating when Harry caught up to me.

"She told you not to bring me, am I right?" I accused.

He grinned at me and loosened his tie, opened his shirt collar. We walked into Washington Square Park and sat on a bench as the meager sun cantered westward. Harry took off his jacket, though there was a definite chill in the air.

"It's hard to imagine that those lovely poems come from that immense barrel of flesh."

Smirking, Harry offered me his flask, at long last, and I finished off what little gin was left.

"And what could possibly be so secret that she had to whisper for your ear only?"

"That Fania has mutilated herself," he said, with a total lack of concern.

"Callous fellow!" I imagined dreadful things consisting of wounds and scars of the ear and nose variety. "Mutilated? In what way?"

"She has shaved her head and painted her scalp blue."

"Ah, an original. I would like to meet this Fania."

We smoked our cigarettes in silence. Harry appeared to be thinking, but one never quite knows with Harry. He could have been enjoying the waning light or the slim ankles of the college girls in their short skirts who strolled by.

"So you're one of those Lowells, are you?" I said.

"An accident of birth."

"You might have mentioned it in passing."

"It's not a part of my life."

"Now it is. Have you considered that poor Fania Lowell may not have a mania?"

"The Boston doctors diagnosed it. Aggressive behavior in fear of death."

"*Timor mortis*," I murmured, a poem forming in my mind.

"And her name is not Fania Lowell. It's Fania Ferrara."

"You Lowells do hide out under peculiar names," I said. "Melville. Ferrara. What next?"

We made a detour to the Hell Hole, once known by the gracious but incongruous name of The Golden Swan. It is an Irish saloon, the damp smell of beer ingrained in the wood of the sawdust-covered floor and disreputable tables. A thug named Lefty Louie tends bar, ready to throw out anyone who doesn't belong. The place is a favorite of Tammany bosses, gangsters, pimps, gamblers, and all sorts of low lifes, including artists and writers, Gene O'Neill being one, and the notorious Village street gang, the Hudson Dusters. The Dusters claim the Village, south of Thirteenth and west of Broadway, as their territory. They cluster in houses below Horatio and around Bethune on Hudson Street.

Harry steered me past the bar entrance on the corner of Sixth Avenue and Fourth Street, with some sort of mumbled explanation which I could not hear because of the thunderous passage of trains overhead on the Sixth Avenue El. They don't allow women, not even me, in the Hell Hole's gents-only Front Room, where above the doorway hangs the original wooden sign featuring a tarnished golden swan.

We girls are consigned to the so-called Family Entrance, a half glass door on Fourth Street. It leads to the Back Room, dreary and gas lit, smelling of mildew and fermentation, not to mention smoke, more from the blustery potbellied stove than from our cigarettes.

"Why don't I just run along home," I said, churlishly. I didn't like being consigned to the widows' closet.

Harry chucked me under the chin. "Impatience doesn't suit you."

Even after Harry brought me a chary cup of gin, I was not a happy creature sitting there among the piteous Irish widows weeping into their mugs of beer. The shouting and laughter from the Front Room drifted into my dreary spot. I took out my pencil and my little pad and wrote: *Timor Mortis*.

I was playing with a fair phrase when my nostrils were assaulted by an acrid, albeit familiar odor. The tenor of the room altered, almost with a concerted shudder. Standing over me was Red Farrell, one of the Hudson Dusters. The few weeping widows in the room cringed and kept their eyes in their beer mugs.

For some reason – another thing Harry has never shared – the Dusters are totally loyal to him. They have, in fact, watched over me when my life was in danger, and they treat me as some kind of mascot. But I admit, they take getting used to and if I didn't have this strange relationship with them, they would scare me half to death.

"Olwer!" Red Farrell doffed his tatty wool cap, releasing a conflagration. He's nothing short of a terror to behold. His ear is partially chewed. A scar runs down the left side of his face from his brow to his scraggly goatee. His eyes are pale blue, the pupils tiny black dots. The acrid smell was coming from the dark weed clenched between his teeth.

The Dusters call me Olwer because when Harry introduced us, he was recovering from a bad beating; he'd tried to say Oliver, and it had come out Olwer. They just assumed that's my name.

"Mr Farrell," I said. "How nice to see you again."

"Sherlock wants youse." The Dusters call Harry Sherlock, I suppose for obvious reasons. His breath made my eyes tear. I drank the rest of my gin and put my pad and pencil in my pocket.

"Olwer!" If Red Farrell is only terrifying, Ding Dong, the Dusters' leader, who was standing on the street next to Harry grinning at me through discolored teeth, is far worse. His smashed nose is but a small part of the picture. He was wearing a long, dark green velvet jacket, baggy trousers, an aviator silk scarf that had once been white. His derby was squashed down on his head almost to his bushy brows, which hung in wiry threads over his beady eyes.

"Mr Ding Dong," I said, flattered that he had come out of his lair to greet me. "You are looking well."

"Youse too, Olwer." He tilted his head at Red Farrell, the motion enough to send Red back into the Hell Hole.

I glanced at Harry, who seemed pleased.

"Have you seen our lady of the blue head?" I asked.

Ding Dong's hand made a circular motion near his ear. "Nutters, walkin' round lookin' like dat." He nodded to us and went back inside the Hell Hole.

Harry had an engagement, probably with his mysterious Uptown inamorata, but after I bemoaned the loss of the martini he'd promised, I suggested he soothe my hurt feelings with one of the bottles of gin I knew he had sitting with the cake of ice in his bathtub. I'd heard his bootlegger deliver in the dead of last night, so I was secure that he would come across.

Hugging the cold bottle to my breast, I climbed the stairs to my flat and found my dear, sweet Mattie at tea in my narrow little kitchen with her betrothed, Detective Gerry Brophy, whom we had met when we first came to live in the Village.

"Don't bother, Gerry," I said as Gerry struggled to his feet.

"Olivia." He was a going-to-orange redhead with loads of freckles and blue eyes that all but disappeared when he smiled, which he was doing at the moment.

"Olivia, tea?" Mattie said, her face flushed from the kettle, and maybe a little more.

"Something stronger, I think. Something purely medicinal, Gerry." I carried the bottle into our parlor and fixed myself the longed for martini. Is there nothing better than the tang of gin on the tongue? I came back into the kitchen. "Oh, Gerry, have you possibly heard about a new girl in the Village with a blue head?"

"Blue hair, you say?"

"No hair. A blue scalp."

He shook his head. "No, I can't say I have."

"I have," Mattie said. "I saw her in Washington Square the other day. Dancing under the arches, dressed as a butterfly, she was."

"You never mentioned it," I said. But perhaps I too had seen her earlier in the day, the flare of blue behind me, like the wings of a butterfly.

"Olivia, this is the Village. Everyone is a little strange."

"'Cept thee and me," I said, passing her my glass. She took a sip and passed it along to Gerry, who inhaled the fumes, good cop that he is, and passed it back to me and I finished it. "We must celebrate. Walling House is going to publish my first book of poems."

"What happened to Mr Harper?" Mattie asked.

I slipped a cigarette into my holder and bent to get a light from Gerry. "He went up in smoke."

Webster Hall is an auditorium suitable for social functions. For us it is the perfect place for dancing, with boxes overlooking our dance floor and the bar next door that keeps our whistles wet. Amid flying feathers, Kendall held me close as we spun round the floor, colliding now and then with other spinners, releasing more feathers into the air, until it was as if we had burst a multitude of pillows. I, still languid from making love, buried my face in the hollow of his chest. He is an old friend of Harry's, from the Great War. Kendall and I are, regrettably, only sometime lovers because he works in Washington for the Secret Service as a cryptographer. Still, I think it is the sensuality of anticipation that makes a long distance affair work well for us.

A girl in a feathered tutu that was disappearing with each movement danced by with a masked man in a white robe, on which someone had stenciled feathers. The costumes varied from original to extreme, though there were more than enough Robin Hoods and Little Johns. I myself wore a delicious green feather boa, which Mattie and I had found amid elegant clothing in one of the attic trunks that had belonged to Miss Alice, the love of my great aunt Evangeline's life.

The Victrola music would start and stop when whoever was winding it went off to refill his glass. But it didn't matter because we could hardly hear over the noise of the revelers and we made our own music anyway.

Yet, something disquieted me. A foreboding. I couldn't seem to put my finger on it, this sense that things were off kilter. A whiff of evil in the air. I pushed the presentiment away. We always have fun at our balls.

The dance floor had gotten crowded with inebriated Pierrots, street urchins, Robin Hoods of every size and shape, sheiks, and artists and their models. We could hardly move, my derriere pressed to that of a Hun in full regalia, feathers like a wreath atop his pronged helmet.

I saw Harry at a distance, up in one of the boxes, his arm round Norma Millay. The only concession he'd made to a costume was a huge Indian feather sticking out of his ponytail.

"Let's go upstairs," I said, trying to get Harry's attention. The other boxes were beginning to look like love nests.

"Go ahead," Kendall said, dropping a welcome kiss on my parched lips. "I'll get the gin." Tall as he is, he got lost in the feathered sea almost immediately.

As I made my way to the stairs, waving off first knight, then tramp, and finally a drunken caveman who pawed my breasts and tried to plant a gin-tainted kiss somewhere on my face, a creature costumed as a brilliant bird bumped me sharply and what seemed to me deliberately.

My Irish temper might have gotten the better of me had not the double doors to the street sprung open revealing the prancing hoofs of a white stallion. The revelry came to a stunning halt. Its rider, an apparition in multi-colored feathers, urged the stallion forward. Something like lightning flashed through the air. A simultaneous gasp filled the hall. The apparition's breast turned crimson. The stallion reared; its rider slid to the floor.

No one moved. Finally, I pushed my way to the injured person, but Harry, the Indian brave, was already there, on his knees beside the still feathers. When I peered through the gathering crowd, I saw a feathered arrow rising from the motionless crimson breast. What I had initially thought were feathers, were shredded bits of colored silk, like butterfly wings.

With tenderness most unlike him, Harry brushed the silken shreds from the face of the dead girl, the girl who had ridden in on the white horse, and I saw a flash of vivid blue.

Fania Ferrara was no longer missing.

By the time the police arrived, four coppers in midnight blue, the hall had emptied out, the bar next door shuttered, and the owner of the Victrola had disappeared with it as well. All that remained were scores of dirty glasses nestled among the feather carpet, and poor dead Fania, her breast dark with clotted blood surrounding the feathered arrow. And of course, Harry, Kendall, and I.

You well may ask what happened to the white stallion. It was last seen cantering up Third Avenue, sprouting wings and taking flight, according to an inebriated fellow clinging to one of the iron struts of the El.

Harry, who'd been holding Fania's white hand, stood. The copper with the most size and the triple chin spilling over his tight collar gave Harry the once-over. "You know her, Melville?"

"Her name is Fania Ferrara, Grundig," Harry said.

Grundig looked round the big hall, took in the evidence of liquored revelry and the feathers. "And I suppose you four were the only ones here."

One needn't respond to a purely rhetorical question.

"You better get Kilcannon." Grundig sent one of the other cops off to find this Kilcannon. Averting his eyes from Fania's nakedness, he then introduced himself as Sergeant Marcus Grundig, took our names, and suggested we wait for the inspector outside the hall. "This is no place for a lady," he said.

I suppose he meant me.

"Olivia?" Mattie's voice pierced my stupor.

I had a beastly hangover, and Kendall, before he left for Washington, had asked me to marry him, spelling for me the end of our affair. I'd sent him off with my usual I'll-think-about-it. I explained to him that my work comes first, that I have no desire to be either wife or mother, but he didn't seem to hear me.

"Olivia."

"You're shouting."

"I'm not shouting."

I peered out from under the bedclothes. The room was swirling and dipping. I ducked back into the cozy darkness.

"Olivia. You'd better drink this."

I peered out again. The room began to calm itself. Mattie was holding a steaming cup in a saucer.

"I need a cigarette."

She set the cup down on the little table next to my bed and lit one for each of us. "What happened last night?"

"How do you know anything happened?"

"Gerry was here this morning with an Inspector Kilcannon. They wanted to see Harry but Harry didn't answer his door."

"We were all upset last night." I took a sip of the hot black tea. My hand was shaking so that a portion went into the saucer. Mattie took charge of it.

"The ball ended badly. Harry's missing cousin Fania was shot dead with a feathered arrow."

"Dear God," Mattie said. Then: "Harry has a cousin?"

"Harry has more relatives than you would believe. He was terribly upset about Fania."

"I should think so."

"We'd better see how he is."

"Not just yet," Mattie said. "Inspector Kilcannon is in the parlor. And I saw Harry leaving when I brought the milk in."

"We talked to the Inspector last night, or this morning, it was. Told him everything we knew. What else can he want?"

Mattie went down to entertain Kilcannon while I washed my face and wrapped myself in the green patterned Japanese kimono I'd found in the attic. My head was throbbing. The tea hadn't helped. I knew just the thing that would cure me and it was in the parlor. Fresh air would have to do. I opened the window. Coming down Bedford Street were Ding Dong, Red Farrell, and Kid Yorke. Knowing they wouldn't be happy to meet up with Kilcannon, I leaned out of the window. They didn't see me. I looked round for something to toss and there was my feather boa. I sailed it out the window and it landed auspiciously on Kid Yorke's derby.

"Hey, Olwer," Kid Yorke wrapped my green boa about his scrawny neck.

Red Farrell and Ding Dong looked up at me.

"Coppers in my parlor," I stage whispered.

They took off with such speed that only a few green feathers fluttered to the street where they had stood only moments before.

Kilcannon, napkin across his knee, was having a cup of tea and a piece of Mattie's shortbread. He was what they call Black Irish, a descendant of the Spanish Armada sailors who jumped ship and married Irish girls: hair jet black, skin tone olive, and the sharp blue eyes of his Irish ancestor. He was thick torsoed without being fat, and had a fine black mustache. In vocation and style, he was as far from any of us here in the Village as you could get. But he was a fine-looking man, and I like fine looking men.

As I waltzed into my parlor, trying to avert my eyes from the liquor cabinet, Kilcannon got to his feet, dislodging the napkin. "Ah, Miss Brown. I hope you'll forgive me for disturbing your work." He set down his teacup and seemed suddenly speechless in my presence.

Mattie choked back a giggle and left us.

"I want to do everything I can to help find who killed Fania." I motioned for him to sit and I sat opposite, taking care with the folds of my kimono before realizing I'd forgotten to put on shoes. I waited for him to ask me whatever it was he wanted to ask, but he was definitely distracted by my bare toes. "Inspector?" I tucked my feet up under me.

The olive skin on his cheekbones flushed. "Perhaps you know where I can find Mr Melville?"

"He's probably gone to the Brevoort to break the news to his cousin Amy Lowell, who came down from Boston yesterday to try to find poor Fania."

"Then I'll be heading in that direction." He rose, almost reluctantly.

I joined him at the door to my parlor. "Have you any more information about who could have done this?"

"Only that there were at least a dozen Robin Hoods and a few Little Johns, all with bows and arrows, and even some Indian braves, say like Melville."

I admit to getting a bit huffy. "Harry didn't have a bow or an arrow and he would never have harmed his cousin."

Kilcannon didn't react. "So Miss Ferrara was staying with Mr Melville while she was visiting the city?"

Was that the point of his visit? "No. He had no idea she was even here until his cousin Amy told him Fania had run away and was somewhere in the city. She asked Harry to try to find her before –" Oh, dear, I thought, now I've done it.

"Before?"

"I think you should talk with Harry, or Miss Lowell, about Fania, as I only know a few bits and pieces, second hand." I shut up after that and as soon as Kilcannon left, I had my taste of gin.

A short time later, Harry returned to his flat, and not long afterward, Ding Dong and Red Farrell joined him. There was no sign of either Kid Yorke or, alas, my feather boa.

I stood in the doorway with my glass of gin. Red Farrell was stretched out on Harry's dilapidated sofa; Ding Dong sat cross-legged on his cluttered desk. Harry lit a cigar.

"What do you know?" I asked.

"She weren't on da street," Red Farrell mumbled without removing the derby from his face. "She were wid some rich people what has a private saloon on da Park."

My knuckles went white on the door jam. "I know them. Everyone knows them. Not a saloon, Mr Farrell, a salon. Harry?"

Harry nodded. "It appears that Fania was befriended by Clara Walling."

The drawing room was white, white walls, white rugs; the damask draperies were white, the chairs and sofas covered in white velvet, the chandelier, white porcelain. Our hostess was an imposing older woman, perhaps in her mid-thirties. A brazen silver streak marked her otherwise dark brown hair. She wore a gown lush in pattern and the color of burgundy, made even more outstanding as she was posed in front of a white marble fireplace.

She greeted me with, "My dear Olivia Brown, I'm so glad to meet you at last. I've been telling Edward for the longest time that he must bring you –"

"I always respond to invitations when I receive them," I said, smiling away a pinch of tartness. I did not like Clara Walling.

She locked arms with me. "I'm sure you know most everyone here. Edward, do get Oliver – if I may – some champagne."

I dipped my head. "Olivia," I said. I took the fluted glass from Edward. My friends call me Oliver. Clara Walling would not be my friend.

"Perhaps you don't know Jack Dempsey." She was taking the high ground, as if we were in competition. Maybe we were, if she and Edward had become lovers. "He's standing in front of the bay window with Lincoln Steffens and –" She rolled her peculiar pale hazel eyes – "all those girls. You're safe," she continued, touching my red tresses with what I thought to be too much familiarity. "Jack only likes dark-haired girls."

"Bother," I said. "What a disappointment." I was saved by the arrival of Hart Crane and Allen Tate, followed by that notorious lecher Max Bodenheim. Every starving poet, not to mention writer and artist, turned up at Clara Walling's Evenings because she served a sumptuous feast at midnight, a groaning board of ham and turkey and imported cheeses, and the very best of French wines.

As I greeted my friends, I drifted toward the new heavyweight champion who liked only dark haired girls. I do love a challenge, don't you know.

"Oliver!" Lincoln Steffens spotted me – he stood well above everyone but Dempsey. Greeting me with a wet kiss and arm round my shoulders, he pressed his way to the side of the champ. "Champ, meet our resident girl poet, Oliver Brown."

Dempsey's an enormous slab of a man with dark, intelligent eyes. My tiny hand entered a maw of muscle. It was not at all an unpleasant sensation. "Oliver?" he said. His voice was gruff, almost shy. I didn't think he was terribly comfortable in this setting.

"My friends think Oliver suits me better than Olivia."

"I like Olivia," the Champ said, my hand still lost in his.

The dark hair girls round him stirred uneasily. I smiled.

Then, wouldn't you know, Michael Walling appeared at my side, apologized to the Champ and whispered in my ear, "Clara likes her guests to circulate and meet other people." And I was rather unceremoniously plucked from the Champ's presence.

In that brief moment, as Michael took my arm and steered me away from Dempsey, my eyes met Clara's amid the crowd – there must have been close to two hundred people. She did not like me any more than I did her.

Who was Clara Walling? Where had she come from?

After Harry and I discovered Fania's connection to Clara Walling, I toddled off to *Vogue* to talk with Edward, ostensibly about the half dozen poems they were buying. He took me to lunch at the Waldorf. We talked about the death of the girl, Fania Ferrara.

"I'm not sure we should plan any more balls," he said.

"We're just attracting too many people from outside, and we don't know who they are."

"Michael is such a dear man," I said, moving the corned beef hash round my plate. The Waldorf was Uptown proper, which meant, no alcohol. "I'd heard last year that his press was in financial difficulties, but he was so reassuring."

"It's Clara, her money, you know. First husband was an oil man, died and left her a fortune. You'll love her. She's amazing."

I would reserve judgment, I thought. "How did Michael meet her?"

"He'd gone to see a writer in St Louis, and there she was. A hot-house rose among field flowers."

Oh, Edward, I thought, what has she done to you?

He continued, not noticing my horror at his poor metaphor. "Clara had always wanted to live in the Village. She had such a drab and boring existence in St Louis."

When I got back to Bedford Street, Harry was in a funk, feet up on his desk, drinking rye whiskey from the bottle. He told me Kilcannon had just left. The police had talked with Clara Walling. She firmly denied knowing Fania.

"Ding Dong could be mistaken," I said.

Harry looked dubious. "They don't miss much."

I agreed. I reported what I'd learned from Edward.

It turned out that one of Harry's Princeton chums was from St Louis. "Family publishes *The Post-Dispatch*," he said. "I'll get him on it."

We made a plan. I would go to Clara's Evening with Edward and see what I could glean.

So here I was, not gleaning very much. I slipped past Hippolyte Havel, one of our resident raving anarchists, who held his champagne glass up high and yelled, "Goddam bourgeois pigs!" then embraced me, blubbering, "Not you, Oliver, never you."

When a waiter offered more champagne, I was one of many who held out empty glasses. Beside me stood a girl about my age in a flowing silken dress of shades of blue. Her small face was almost hidden by the fullness of her hair, black with glints of gold and she had black gypsy eyes, touched with kohl. She looked vaguely familiar.

"You're Olivia Brown, the poet, aren't you?" she said in a child-like voice.

"Guilty," I replied, taking a hearty swallow of champagne. The room was extraordinary, the ceilings high and molded with cupids and love knots, but it was beginning to undulate. I wondered if we were nearing buffet time as I was more than a little tipsy and I had work to do. "What a beautiful room," I said. The girl was staring at me expectantly over her fluted glass.

"Yes," she said. "My aunt has exquisite taste."

Oliver, my dear, I told myself, you live under a lucky star. I turned my radiant smile on her. "Your aunt?"

"Clara. Yes. She's invited me to stay while I'm studying painting at the Art Students League."

"How very interesting . . ." I said. We were becoming manipulated by the crowd of hungry artists. It was nearing midnight. "In all this," I waved my hand, "I've missed your name."

At this moment the butler slid open the doors to the dining room and we were caught in the forward surge and as we became separated, I heard her say, "Camilla Faye."

Tipsy I may get, but I never forget a name. Camilla Faye was strung across my brain flashing in red neon. Camilla Faye is the name of Fania Ferrara's alleged imaginary friend.

I, being a mere slip of a girl, couldn't get near the table, but bohemian tour guide Franz, without his moth-eaten cloak, clad in sackcloth and sandals and his filthy crimson Byronesque tie, tried to feed me from his plate of sliced ham and turkey. He stared at me with lascivious eyes.

I edged my way to the open doorway Edward and I had passed through earlier. A maid directed me up the broad marble staircase to a bathroom, second door on the right of the wide corridor. The staircase, no longer marble, continued upward to a third floor.

There were three other doors off the corridor.

The master bedroom, first door on the left, was obviously Clara's, a true boudoir, lace and ruffles. A spot of color on the chaise brought me into the room. It was the remains of a brilliant bird costume.

Michael's bedroom was across the way, first door on the right, next to the bathroom.

After a quick peek, I passed both, as this was not in the plan. I opened another door, looking for Camilla Faye's room, but it was a wood paneled library. Books always seduce. Yes, there were books shelved floor to ceiling. But under glass was a gun cabinet, and beside it, also behind glass, a cabinet filled with archery equipment. Both cabinets were locked.

I left the library and slipped down the servants' stairs at the end of the hall. I heard moaning, male and female, and thumping. I peered into the kitchen. The moaning was coming from the scullery where china was scoured and washed, but where the scullery maid had a better idea of how to use her time.

No one was in the kitchen, at least for now. At any moment someone could be here. The kitchen was warm and steamy, the outside door slightly ajar. I moved quickly, hoping it wouldn't squeak as I opened it.

It did squeak but the noisy celebration from the scullery obstructed it. Harry, distinguished in clean corduroys, a flannel shirt, black beret, and an ascot of tiny fleurs-de-lis on a faded blue field, was waiting just as we'd planned. "Any problems?"

"You may thank the lovers in the scullery, bless them." I led him up the back stairs, pointed out Clara's room and Michael's and the library, where Harry wanted to have a look at the archery equipment. But we heard people talking on the stairs and made it into the bathroom in the nick of time, locking someone out. Whoever it was gave the door a few pounds, complained querulously, then quit. Harry turned the water taps on full. I noted they were gold.

"What else do you know?"

"Camilla Faye is a real person."

"Bloody hell."

"Clara Walling is her aunt."

"Ah, poor Fania." Harry's eyes were moist. "We let her down."

"Nobody believed her."

"We all had other lives to lead."

"But am I mistaken, Fania thought this Camilla was her friend?"

"She trusted her. They went on adventures together, so she said."

Someone pounded on the door. "Oliver, are you in there?"

"Good heavens, wouldn't you think Edward would be busy with his inamorata?"

"See if you can use your wiles and lure him away," Harry said.

"I've been looking everywhere for you, Oliver," Edward said, hand on my waist.

I walked him firmly toward the stairs. "I couldn't get near the banquet table and I'm so hungry," I said, giving him a hint of a kiss under his chin.

"Well, we'll remedy that at once," he said.

Edward left me to share a sofa with Max Eastman and John Sloan, who kissed me fondly and then went back to discussing the implications of the Sacco and Vanzetti case. I would have joined in but Camilla Faye strayed past and I went after her.

I touched her arm. "Camilla, I'm sorry we weren't able to continue our conversation. Do you know we have a mutual friend?"

She gave me half a smile, indeed a cautious smile.

"I am new to the city," she said, moving away from me. "I would be surprised to hear we know someone in common."

"Oh, but we do," I replied, at my most guileless. "Fania Ferrara."

Camilla shook my hand from her arm. "I know no one by that name."

She fled and I didn't follow her. Instead, I had another glass of champagne and asked a maid for my cloak, and as Edward had quite disappeared and Harry could take care of himself, I headed home, thoughts jumbling round my brain.

If Camilla Faye had befriended Fania Ferrara, what was her purpose? And what had Clara Walling to do with this?

As I neared my house, I saw a Western Union boy park his bicycle against my gate and walk to my door. He was carrying a telegram.

I rushed the rest of the way. "Is that for me?"

"It is if your name is Harry Melville," he said, smartly. "Which it is not."

"How do you know it's not?"

"Because you're Olivia Brown the poet and I saw your picture in the paper."

Well, I ask you, how can one argue with fame?

Harry opened his door. "Ah, good," he said. He tipped the Western Union boy a dime and took the telegram. "Come on in, Oliver. Here's what I've been waiting for." He opened the telegram.

I sat gingerly on the arm of his sofa. I know better than to try dodging the springs. "Well? Am I never to know what it says?"

Harry folded the telegram and put it in his pocket and headed for the door.

"Where are you going?"

"I called Kilcannon and told him to meet me at the Walling house." He was out the door before I got to my feet.

"Wait, Harry, I'm coming with you."

He looked back in time to see me trip over the thick roots of an old tree that were breaking through the sidewalk near Sixth Avenue, then waited for me to catch up. "You need a keeper," he said.

"Just tell me what the telegram said."

He unfolded the telegram. "Born Claire Kerr. St Louis. Good family. Sent to Florence to study art. Parents die while she's in Italy. Marries into old but impoverished Italian family. Becomes Clara. Finds that her inheritance comes to nothing because of her father's unfortunate investments." He tugged at my hand. "Don't slow down."

"Ah," I said, "impoverished Italian family. That would be the Ferraras?"

"Yes. There is a child. Camilla." He took a drink from his flask and passed it to me.

I was grateful beyond belief. "The plot thickens."

"Here's what I think happened. Walk, Oliver. Fania's mother Louisa arrives in Florence to see the museums. She meets Ferrara, who's a charming cad, and falls for him. She doesn't know he's married and he and Clara decide it's not in their best interest to tell her. Louisa's wealth is obvious. When Louisa returns to Boston, Ferrara follows her, probably with Clara's approval."

We were rushing across Sixth Avenue against the light. Harry held up his hand like a traffic cop. A town car screeched to a halt. "Bloody hell," Harry yelled. "You want to kill us?" Further sharp words were exchanged.

I tugged on Harry's sleeve. "Let's go. Finish the story."

Safely back on the sidewalk, Harry said, "Where was I?"

"Ferrara follows Louisa Lowell to Boston."

"Yes, and marries her, much against the family's wishes. Louisa dies when Fania's born. Ferrara returns to Clara in Italy, leaving Fania to the Lowells."

"But Clara is no fool. Fania is an heiress."

Harry nodded. "Clara makes plans to come back to the States, but the War intervenes and they must wait."

"So she sends Camilla to Boston to befriend Fania, somehow."

We turned the corner onto Washington Square.

"Yes, And Clara goes home to St Louis in the guise of a wealthy widow. She opens the family house, and tries to find a way to Fania's inheritance. Then by chance she meets Michael Walling."

I laughed. "He thinks she's got money, she thinks he's got money. A perfect relationship."

"Clara sees it as her opening to come East and help Camilla eliminate Fania."

"So Michael and Clara marry. And all the while Ferrara is waiting in Florence for his inheritance. These are nasty people, Harry."

The Walling house was dark.

We were too late.

Ding Dong came out of the park when he saw Harry. "Dey just got a taxi. Da old lady and da goil."

"Bloody hell."

"Poor Michael," I said.

"Da steamship line," Ding Dong said.

Harry reached into his pocket. "They can't go anywhere without these." He had two passports.

"Dey won't get far anyways."

"How so?"

"Kid Yorke slashed da tires." Ding Dong's nose twitched as if he detected an odd smell. He faded into the dusky park.

And Kilcannon rounded the corner with Gerry Brophy.

Clara and Camilla Ferrara were arrested for Fania's murder, though neither admitted being the deadly archer. And had Ferrara's marriage to Louisa Lowell been legitimate, Ferrara might have inherited a fortune. But as it was, even had Clara blamed the plot entirely on her husband, the evidence wasn't strong enough for the Italian authorities to either charge him or return him to America.

As for me, having lost both lover and publisher, I went back to my work.

Dialogue with Butterfly

Poor butterfly circling round my head,
"Oh, joy, oh joy," I hear you cry.
Poor lovely creature, don't you know
That you are doomed to die?

You flutter softly near my heart,
Which wounded, still lies bleeding.
"However short my life," you say.
"Mortal love's more fleeting."

Brave New Murder

H. R. F. KEATING

Harry Keating has been writing crime fiction – and writing about crime fiction – for forty years now, so hardly needs any introduction. He is best known for his series about Inspector Ghote of the Bombay C.I.D., but he has written much else besides, including several historical mystery novels. This includes a series written under the alias Evelyn Hervey about Victorian governess Harriet Unwin who first appeared in The Governess *(1984). Here he turns his attention to the early years of the 1920s and how the old world had to come face to face with the new.*

Perhaps it was the glory of England returning after the grim days of the Great War. Or perhaps it would prove, after all, to be something quite otherwise. It was the day of the first post-war Eton and Harrow match, that annual event, more social than sporting, which in the years up to 1914 had brought together in one place, Lord's cricket ground, almost all the Upper Ten Thousand. There, on the excuse of watching the next generation bat and bowl, as many of them had themselves in past years generation after generation, they had come once more to parade themselves in the sunshine, to assert their status once again. And in the Pavilion and in beflagged tents, dark blue and light, to have luncheon.

Now at the beginning of a new decade all seemed to be as it once had been. Yet before a single ball had been bowled after the lunch interval, murder was to splatter an ugly blot on the fair surface of the day.

At the time that it took place none of the nine or ten thousand spectators, in whose ranks the late conflict had cut such a swathe, knew, of course, that it had happened. It was only in the days succeeding the match that the news of it came to dominate every conversation. During the interval they had, as was the custom in "the old days", strolled about on the grass in front of the Pavilion, the gentlemen in tall shining silk hats, their womenfolk twirling bright parasols in dresses and hats as elaborate and striking as money could buy, if here and there could be seen a skirt that allowed stockinged calves to be fully in view.

"I had hoped," the Bishop of Cirencester, the Right Reverend Dr Pelham Rossiter, remarked, catching sight of one young lady so dressed, "that no such indication of the dreadful decline in the country's morality would be seen here today of all days. But it was, I fear, a hope destined to perish."

"My dear bishop," his companion, Wilfred Boultbee, the well-known City solicitor, replied, "I can see the day when ladies without even hats will be admitted at Lord's, and heaven knows what depravities will go along with that." His full grey moustache sank to an even lower angle than habitually.

The two of them wandered on, gently digesting their shares of the lobsters and pigeon pies, the salmon mayonnaise and tender lamb that had been provided after the long years of wartime deprivation in all the abundance of the milk-and-honey days of yore. The last bubbles of champagne gently eructated behind their firmly closed lips.

Just a few yards away a rather less elevated conversation was taking place between two other people soon to be caught up in the murder.

"God, what a fearful bore a day like this is," Julia Hogsnorton, daughter of the Earl, exclaimed to the Hon. Peter Flaxman, immaculate in beautifully brushed tall hat, tailcoat fitted to the twentieth of an inch over broad shoulders, pale spats just visible at the ends of black-and-white striped trousers, thin dark moustache trimmed to a nicety. "I can't imagine how you can stand it."

"My dear girl, I stood it for four years before the war, and even enjoyed it then, in a way. Nice to show one is one of the world, you know. So I don't find it impossible to enjoy it all again today. Since the fools with money are prepared to lay it on for me, and those Jewish Scotsmen are prepared to provide me with some cash, I'm happy to take advantage of their kindness. It's better than Flanders fields."

"Not that you spent much time slogging through the mud there, flinging yourself down in it each time a shell landed. Or not if what you told me one drunken evening was true. An A.D.C. somewhere well behind the lines, wasn't it?"

"Fortunes of war, old girl. Fortunes of war. But, talking of drunken evenings, shall we go back to the tent? I seem to remember unopened bottles lurking somewhere in the background."

"Oh, all right. But it can't go on for ever, you know, this relying on the gods and the moneylenders. A lady begins sometimes to feel uncomfortable in circumstances like that."

"Well, you'll have to put up with circumstances like that, unless you can suggest a way I can unclasp old Boultbee's tight fists."

He walked on, at a slightly faster pace than before.

Unpleasant revelations were, too, manifesting themselves now to the older moral couple digesting their luncheon.

"Bishop, excuse me," Wilfred Boultbee said abruptly. "I think I really must – Well, I think I should return to the luncheon tent. My soda-mint lozenges. I had them on the table, preparatory to taking one as I customarily do after any meal, but somehow I failed to see them as I left. But now I feel the need, acutely. You know my weakness of old, since we were at school even. A digestion that – how shall I put it? – that frequently fails to digest."

"I remember. Indeed I do. What was it we called you? Belcher Boultbee. Yes, that was it. Old Belcher Boultbee."

His richly reverberant episcopal laugh rang out.

But Belcher Boultbee was immune to it. He had suddenly spotted something, or rather someone, yet more irritating to himself than a young woman showing her calves.

"Bishop," he said, "let's, for heaven's sake, step out. I see that French fellow's heading back to the tent, chap young Flaxman insisted on bringing to luncheon. I had hoped, once we'd eaten, he would have the decency to remove himself. It seems he has not."

"I'll step out, if you want, though I must confess I found our foreign friend – What did Flaxman say he was called? The Comte de – de somewhere. I found him agreeable enough."

"Oh, agreeable," the City solicitor replied. "Yes, he's all of that. It's what you might call his stock-in-trade. And, for all that title of his, trade is what he's about. I happen to know rather more about the fellow than he'd like to think I do."

"Very well, let's get there before him. Perhaps he'll sheer off if he sees us. For myself perhaps I'll take just one more glass of champagne. And you can consume your soda-mint lozenge."

A more modest version of the rich episcopal laugh could be heard as they hurried on.

Equally making their slow way towards the tent where they had lunched were the last two members of the party whom the murder was deeply to concern, Peter Flaxman's cousin, Captain Vyvyan Andrews – they were both distantly related to Bishop Rossiter, the host – with his wife, Mary. Their conversation, too, was not as placidly reminiscent of the past days of glory as it might have been. But they had better reasons for lacking in joie-de-vivre.

"We should never have agreed to come," Vyvyan Andrews, pale-faced to the point where his fair, once military moustache seemed almost to have vanished away, in his borrowed tailcoat and slightly stain-marked silk hat, was saying in a bitter under-tone. "Never, never. I told you. But you would do it."

"But, darling, it was because – Well, because I hoped it would do you good, cheer you up."

"Cheer me up. You're pathetic, pathetic. How can you believe all I need is to be cheered up, as if I was having a bad cold, or a bit of a belly-ache? But I'm not sniffling and snuffling. I'm ill. Ill. My whole inside's been gassed out, and I'll never be the same again. Never."

He came to an abrupt standstill, plunged his hand feverishly into the top pocket of the frayed and ancient tailcoat, pulled out, not a silver cigarette case, but a crumpled packet of gaspers, fumbled one into his mouth.

His wife, ever alert, opened her handbag, extracted a box of matches, lit one and held it, in both hands for steadiness, to the up-and-down jiggling tip of the cheap cigarette.

Stolidly watching the little scene some dozen yards away, PC Williams thought enviously for a moment of the man who could light up whenever he wanted. On duty, keeping a benevolent eye – an eye, to tell the truth, a good deal more benevolent than that of the Bishop of Cirencester – on the nobility and the gentry strolling in the sunshine, no hope for him of the pleasure of tobacco for many hours to come. Especially since he was also keeping a less benevolent eye on the free seats not much further off where a small number of members of the proletariat, not top-hatted though equipped with squashy low-brimmed head-wear, awaited the resumption of play.

But then, taking in how much that feverishly puffed-at cigarette must be meaning to a man with uncontrollably trembling hands and twitching facial muscles, PC Williams abruptly found envy was not at all what he was feeling.

"I can't even hold down a job," he could make out Captain Andrews' raised voice saying. "Not even when I manage to get one. Having to depend on my wife going out to work. Yes, on you working, and working for a pittance. And you talk of cheering me up."

"Darling, I don't mind going out to work. I'm only glad Mr Boultbee found me something to do in his office."

"Yes, a piece of charity. From that tight-fisted monster who's our trustee. And what are you there? A filing clerk, a filing clerk."

"But, darling, Mr Boultbee – and I know he does treat the family trust as if it was his private fortune, not a penny to be spent from it except under duress – does need someone to file away the documents in that office, and it should be someone who's responsible enough to handle things which could be terribly important. So you can't really say I'm being paid out of charity. You know you can't."

"All I know is that day after day I feel terrible. I wish to God Jerry had put me out once and for all. Yes, I do."

He gave his wife, in her sad imitation of the de rigueur extravagant hats and dresses of the strolling ladies of the Upper Ten Thousand, a look that was not far short of being one of hatred.

"Darling," she said, "let's go in and sit down. Perhaps some champagne . . ."

When PC Williams had safely seen Captain Andrews and his long-suffering wife, closely followed by the Hon. Peter Flaxman with his lady-of-the-moment and the dandified figure of the French count, enter the isolated little pavilion-like tent, from which earlier he had been able all too clearly to hear the clink of china, the popping of corks, he did not hear again, as he had expected, the murmur of smooth conversation and occasional discreet laughter. Instead, there was a ear-piercing shriek and then voices raised in sharp questioning.

A moment later he found himself summoned with a single imperious gesture by Peter Flaxman. And, still helmeted, as he stooped to enter the tent in his turn, he saw Wilfred Boultbee, City solicitor, trustee of the estates of a dozen of the noblest and richest families in Great Britain, frigid moralist, lying slumped across the long-ago cleared lunch table, his right hand clutching a large white table-napkin. At the solicitor's side there was standing, distraught and utterly unbishop-like for all his purple vest and immaculate dog-collar, the Right Reverend Dr Pelham Rossiter.

Williams immediately took charge. He noted names, even those of the caterers. He examined the scene, as much of it as there was to be examined, an empty round table with gilt chairs still more or less in their places, a side table on which there remained four or five bottles of champagne together with a dozen or so of wide-brimmed glasses. He ascertained that Wilfred Boultbee was indeed dead and that near the hand clutching, as he was to say later, "with demonic strength" that napkin, there was a worn little tin in which there rested four flat white soda-mint lozenges. He suggested that Bishop Rossiter should sit in a chair in the corner.

"You'll be better off resting, your – your Grace," he said, thereby showing he had taken in at a glance the purple vest. "It must have come as a shock to you. Quite a shock."

Then, looking at the deflated, trembling man, he decided that, if ever any evidence untainted by afterthoughts was to be obtained it had better be before the bishop was taken away to recover.

"Sir, your reverence, my lord, could you just tell me what happened? You'd not been in the tent here for as much as a minute – I happened to notice you arriving with – That is, I happened to notice you arriving – before I heard that loud cry, anguished it was, yes, anguished."

"Very well, I–I'll try."

He managed to look up.

"I–I–I – He took one of his lozenges, soda-mint lozenges. We'd come back for . . . Old Belcher for once forgot – He took one from – from that little – that tin he has. And – and – one crunch and – and he gave that terrible cry and was dead. I–I know very well when a soul has gone to the Great Father of us all. My sad task, clergyman . . . Often at the bedside . . ."

"Thank you, your Rev – Grace, my Lord. That was most helpful."

PC Williams consulted the big silver watch from his pocket, pulled out his notebook, wrote ponderously for a little. Then, stepping to the door of the tent, but not a foot further, he blew his whistle to call for assistance.

So it was that at noon next day Detective Inspector Thompson, shrewd-faced, grey-haired, upright, found himself standing in front of the Commissioner of the Metropolitan Police, summoned to give an account of his investigation of an affair all but dominating that morning's newspapers from the stately *Morning Post* down.

"I'm afraid it's going to be a nasty business, sir," he said. "Baffling, the *Daily Mail* called it."

"I dare say it did, Inspector. But you're a Scotland Yard officer and we are not baffled at Scotland Yard. I require you to bring the matter to a conclusion in the shortest possible time. Damn it, man, from what I understand the possible suspects inside the locked gates of Lord's cricket ground comprise almost every member of the Upper Ten Thousand, Dukes and Earls and Cabinet Ministers among them. Unless – certainly the best possible outcome – you find your man is some disgruntled person from the free seats."

"Not any chance of that, sir, I'm sorry to say. The luncheon tent in which the tragedy occurred was under the eye all morning of PC Williams, from the Albany Street station, a man I once had under my command. A thoroughly reliable fellow. If anyone unauthorized entered that tent at any time Williams will have see them. I can promise you that."

The Commissioner puffed out a huge sigh of relief.

"Well, that would seem to eliminate the majority of the spectators," he said. "The Cabinet Ministers along with the riff-raff from the free seats."

He sat in thought for a few moments. Then looked up, eyes bright with hope.

"The waiters," he exclaimed. "There'll have been two or three of them at least in that tent, and you get some pretty dubious characters among such people nowadays with so many unemployed about, a good many of them resentful and un-disciplined."

"Looking into them was one of my first tasks, sir. And I can say with assurance that both of them – they numbered only two, as a matter of fact – have been vouched for. Elderly men, in service with the catering firm in question from before the War and too old to have been called to the colours."

The Commissioner, who was in full uniform, picked up his leather-covered swagger-stick from the desk in front of him, appeared to give it a close scrutiny and then replaced it.

"Tell me, Inspector," he said. "Have I got the situation right? Mr Boultbee died as the result of – ha – ingesting what appeared to be a common soda-mint lozenge – Good God, I take the things myself on occasion – but which had been treated with a poison. Do we yet know what particular substance it was? Eh? Eh?"

"No, sir, we don't. None of the four remaining mints in the tin have proved to be other than what they ought to be, and – And we shan't know precisely what was in the gentleman's stomach until further tests have been carried out. But, as you will know, sir, it is by no means impossible for a determined murderer to get hold of what they need. A visit to some chemist's shop at a distance, a false signature in the Poisons Book, it's altogether too easy."

"Yes. Very well, Inspector. I suppose our man – Unless, by God, it's a woman. Poison's a woman's weapon, you know. There were ladies present, weren't there?"

"Yes, sir. Miss Julia Hogsnorton, younger daughter of Earl Hogsnorton—"

"Well, I don't believe . . . No, perhaps we should bear that young lady in mind. Now I come to think of it, I've heard she's rather wild like a lot of young women these days. What they're calling the post-war generation. But who was the other lady there?"

"Mrs Mary Andrews, sir, wife of Captain Vyvyan Andrews, who was also present of course."

"Hm. Anything known, eh?"

"No, sir. A thoroughly respectable lady, sir. However, there is one circumstance that may be relevant."

"Well, let's hear, man. Let's hear it."

"Mrs Andrews is employed in the office of Mr Boultbee, sir. She works as a filing clerk. Something of a sinecure post, sir, I've gathered. Captain Andrews is one of the casualties of the War, sir, a victim, as I understand from his doctor, of neurasthenia arising from his experiences in the trenches and no-man's-land."

"Hm. You seem to have covered a good deal of ground in the last twenty-four hours, Inspector."

For a moment the Commissioner looked at his comparatively junior officer with an air of interest.

But it was for a moment only.

"Very well. So much for the female element. Species more deadly than the male, eh? Rudyard Kipling said that somewhere just last year. We shouldn't forget it. But who were the gentlemen present at the time?"

"Well, sir, there is, I suppose, the Bishop of Cirencester . . ."

"Ha. Bit of an awkward thing here. I know Rossiter pretty well. First met him, as a matter of fact, on the day of an Eton and Harrow match long ago. He was playing for Eton, a pretty fair bat, and I was, of course, an Harrovian. And, by golly, I took his wicket. Clean bowled him."

Inspector Thompson watched the Commissioner of the Metropolitan Police chuckling.

"I think, sir," he said eventually, "that the Bishop can be safely discounted. He did, of course, according to PC Williams's very thorough evidence, go into the empty tent with Mr Boultbee. But it was apparent to Williams, from the loud cry of agony he heard from where he was stationed not far away, that the poisoning occurred almost as soon as the two of them had entered. And the Bishop was certainly in a state of almost total collapse when Williams saw him immediately afterwards."

"Very well, I can take it then I shan't have to bowl him out again."

"No, sir. I don't think we will need to interview him further. He returned, with his chaplain, to Cirencester by the first possible train and there took to his bed at the palace."

"Ha, poor old Rossy, bowled over if not bowled out, eh? But let's get on with it, Inspector. Let's get on with it. We neither of us have time to spare today. So have you found out anything about the remaining gentlemen?"

"Yes, sir. I have. If we're to go by motive alone, there is a good deal of suspicion attaching to the Hon. Mr Peter Flaxman. And with the confusion there was in the tent as they all left after lunch, which my inquiries have shown must have been when the poisoned lozenge must have somehow put there for Mr Boultbee to take, it looks as if we may well have to rely simply on what motives the – er – suspects might have."

"Young Flaxman, eh? Then spit it out, Inspector, spit it out. May as well hear the worst."

"Mr Flaxman is a gentleman of limited means, sir, but considerable expectations, as I learnt from the late Mr Boultbee's junior partner. It seems Mr Boultbee was one of the trustees of a considerable fund which will come to the two beneficiaries, the cousins Peter Flaxman and Vyvyan Andrews, only when they attain the age of thirty. Neither will, in fact, do that for some five years yet."

"Ha, the root of all evil."

"Yes, sir. So we are told. And at Mr Boultbee's office I managed to gather that both gentlemen have applied since the Armistice for advances on their expectations, something which their trustees are permitted to make. However, it seems the three other trustees relied entirely on the advice of the late Mr Boultbee. And that advice has consistently been that no disbursements should be made."

"I hope, Inspector, that you brought no improper pressure on to Mr Boultbee's junior partner. You seem to have acquired a good deal of information which I should have thought was confidential."

Inspector Thompson looked steadily at the Commissioner.

"No, sir," he said, "there could, of course, be no question of that."

"I'm glad to hear it. So we appear to have arrived at a point where two of the people, and perhaps their ladies, who could have placed a poisoned lozenge into the cachou-box in which Mr Boultbee kept his supply of soda-mints were—"

"Excuse me, sir," Inspector Thompson broke in, with not a little daring, "but it is as well perhaps to have things entirely clear. Mr Boultbee, so his partner happened to mention, lost several years ago the silver box he carried his lozenges in, and – his partner indicated that he had, what shall I say, a certain mean streak – he refused to replace it but used instead a battered little tobacconist's tin that had once contained snuff. My informant indicated that people used to joke about that."

"Rather poor taste on his part, Inspector, if I may venture to say so."

"Perhaps it was, sir. However, it may be helpful to know about it if it comes down to trying to discover exactly what happened at that table when the lunch party set off for a stroll."

"No. No, wait, Inspector, you've forgotten something. Important, you know, to keep every thread in your hands."

A little frown gave added force to the rebuke.

"The French gentleman, sir? The Conte de Charvey. I have made inquiries about him. It seems he was a slight acquaintance of Mr Flaxman's and had put him in the position of being unable to withhold an invitation to the match."

"Had he indeed? A trifle suspicious that, eh? French fellow wanting to watch cricket. Unless, of course, he's one of those froggies who seem to think the game is one of the secrets of British power. As I suppose it is, come to think of it."

"Yes, sir. However, I also learn from the late Mr Boultbee's partner that Mr Boultbee knew something to the Count's disadvantage. I have had a word with Fraud, and apparently they've been keeping a sharp eye on him."

"Fraud, eh? Why haven't they informed me that a character of this sort has come to our shores? Eh? Eh?"

"I'm sure I couldn't say, sir."

"No. I dare say not. But . . . But do you think the fellow may have needed to get rid of someone who had come to learn too much about some underhand business of his? That sort of thing?"

"It always could be, sir. But one ought perhaps to bear in mind that the murderer would need to have known Mr Boultbee's habit of taking one of those soda-mint lozenges shortly after his every meal. But while all of the other four persons under consideration might well have been aware of that, it's scarcely likely that a stranger such as the Count would be."

"Yes. Yes, Inspector, I take your point. Good man, good man. Yet, let me remind you, we shouldn't put our French bad hat altogether out of the picture."

"No, sir. No, of course not. I will bear him in mind throughout the investigation."

"Hah. Yes. Yes, Inspector, you speak blithely enough of *throughout the investigation*, but let me tell you once again: this is a matter which has got to be cleared up in the very shortest of times. All right, this PC Wilkins, Watson, whatever, whom you seem to have such faith in, would appear, thank goodness, to have eliminated the hundreds of extremely distinguished persons who might conceivably have committed this appalling crime. But nevertheless the yellow press will, if they get half a chance, hope to draw public attention to – Well, to even the highest in the land. So action, Inspector, action."

"Yes, sir."

When Inspector Thompson left the Commissioner's office he had little hope that any amount of action would see the case concluded quickly enough to suit his chief. But, in the end, action proved to be what was needed. Directed more or less to go back to Lord's, where by night and day a police watch had been kept, he made his way into the luncheon tent, everything there still preserved just as it had been when PC Williams had entered. Though convinced that it was only in the motives of the four people most likely to have committed the deed that the solution must lie, he nevertheless stood looking down at the stained white cloth of the table. A blank sheet.

Or was it?

Wasn't there something there that somehow differed from Williams' minutely accurate description?

For more than a few minutes he stood there puzzling. What was it that seemed somehow wrong?

Is it, he asked himself, the mere absence of that little tobacconist's snuff tin from which the one deadly lozenge had, by chance surely, been plucked by that tight-fisted City solicitor? Nothing more than that? The tin itself, of course, had been sent to the fingerprint bureau at the Yard, and within an hour a report had come back to say that someone had scrupulously wiped the little shabby article clean of any possible clue as to who had flipped it open, taken out one lozenge – Wilfred Boultbee, so careful of other people's money, was very likely to have kept count of his supply of the miraculous means of combating the intolerable pangs of indigestion – and added that one deadly other.

No help there.

And then . . . Then it came to him. What was missing from the scene as he looked at it now was an object PC Williams had described well, if with a touch of honest Welsh hyperbole. In the dead man's hand, he had said, there had been a soiled white table-napkin clutched *with demonic force*. It had been, almost certainly, taken away with the body when it had gone for medical examination. But why had it been there on the table at all? It must have been left when the guests had risen from their places to go and stroll outside.

But – could this be what had happened? – had someone still had it, perhaps in their hand, after all the debris had been cleared away by the waiters? And had they then let it fall on the table in such a way that it covered up Wilfred Boultbee's little battered old tobacconist's tin? That could, if what Williams quoted to me from his notebook had it right, have accounted for the unusual circumstance of the dead man forgetting to take a lozenge immediately after eating.

But which of them was it? Who had picked up that napkin, dropped it so as to hide the little tin, and then, of course, subtly urged Wilfred Boultbee out of the tent before he had gathered himself together enough to remember he had not taken a lozenge?

Well, if that is what happened, one thing is clear. It's very unlikely to have been one of the women. I can hardly see either of them – I can hardly see any lady – taking that rigid man by the arm and laughingly leading him off. So it must come down to one of the two cousins, each with motive enough. Because, as I tried to make clear to the Commissioner, the French count, whatever he's up to in England, could not possibly have known about Wilfred Boultbee's poor digestion. So which of the two is it? Which?

Captain Andrews, the ruined man? The victim of the carnage which the civilized nations of the world have inflicted on one another? A man, you might say, with nothing to live for. Had he, as a last wild bid to acquire a decent income, murdered his tight-fisted, implacable trustee? A bid to free his wife from the daily toil of grubbing together enough to make their lives possible? Easy enough to feel sympathy for a man who had done more than give his life for his country, a soldier who had given all that made life bearable, had been left with the prospect of years ahead carrying round with him the body that the War had gassed out? Yet, if he has been driven to the last extreme of murder, he has to be brought to trial for it. Let judge and jury find what extenuating factors they can.

So, the Hon. Peter Flaxman? What about that typical example of the new, pleasure-devoted, careless world that seems to have come into being in the wake of all the horrors and deprivations of the years between 1914 and 1918? Is he a new breed, and a by no means pleasant one? A breed of self-seeking, hedonistic young people, uncaring of all below them in the social hierarchy? And is that, when you come down to it, what brought about the demise of a man altogether opposed to such a way of life? An old man who, you could say, represented all the virtues, all the strict morality, of an age on the verge of extinction?

Which of those two men is it – all but certain that one or the other of them put that deadly lozenge into Wilfred Boultbee's little tin – who in truth conceived that deadly scheme? Isn't the balance, however unfairly it might seem, equal between them? Each with the same obvious motive, each with opportunity enough, each offered the same easy means of finding a solution to their problems?

So which?

And only one answer. Startlingly plain, once one ceases to look at the human complexities and turns a steady gaze on the simple facts.

Captain Andrews, poor devil, has hands that constantly tremble, shake to the point, as Williams vividly recalled for me, of hardly being able even to hold a cigarette when he desperately wants to inhale the tranquillizing smoke. I cannot for a moment see Captain Andrews carrying out that little necessary piece of legerdemain under the starched white table-napkin.

So, if it isn't the one, it must be the other. Simple. Appallingly simple.

Right, I'm off to see the Hon. Peter Flaxman in his rooms in the Albany.

Or do they insist you have to say just *Albany*?

Whichever. It's there that I'll arrest the murderer of Mr Wilfred Boultbee, City solicitor, repository of a thousand secrets and tight-fisted representative of an age that's going, going, gone.

So Beautiful, So Dead

ROBERT J. RANDISI

Robert Randisi is disarmingly prolific with over 350 novels to his credit. Most of these are westerns but he has also written many private-eye novels, starting with his series featuring ex-boxer turned P.I. Miles "Kid" Jacoby, who first appeared in Eye in the Ring *(1982). Randisi founded the organisation the Private Eye Writers of America in 1981 and, with Ed Gorman, co-founded the magazine of the mystery field,* Mystery Scene, *in 1985. He also finds time to edit anthologies whilst with his partner, Christine Matthews (who also appears in this volume), he has started a series about husband-and-wife sleuths Gil and Claire Hunt.*

Occasionally Randisi will cross over his western and detective enthusiasms. The Ham Reporter *(1986), set in 1911, teams up Bat Masterson with Damon Runyon to solve a mystery. Masterson also appears in the following story, which is based around real events. Randisi tells me, "The facts about the Miss America Pageant are true. Val O'Farrell was real. He was described in two Bat Masterson biographies as a police detective, and as one of the top private detectives of his day. Bat Masterson died about 5 weeks after the events at the Pageant, sitting at his typewriter. The gangster Johnny Torrio is also mentioned. He had a young apprentice he later sent to Chicago – Al Capone."*

1

V al O'Farrell looked down at the dead girl with a gut wrenching sadness. So beautiful, so dead.

"What a body, huh? Why would anyone want to cancel the ticket of a babe like that? And pluggin' her in the head, too. Jeez, how you gonna figure that?"

O'Farrell turned to look at Detective Sam McKeever.

"What?" McKeever asked. "She's a babe. Hey, she's lyin' there naked under a sheet, what am I supposed to do, not look?"

"No," O'Farrell said, "she's used to bein' looked at."

"Like most beautiful young dames, huh?"

"This one more than some," O'Farrell said. "She's supposed to be one of the contestants at that new Beauty Pageant out in Jersey."

"Yeah? No kiddin'?" McKeever said. "I heard they was gonna let them wear these new skin tight bathing suit things."

"Tight and skimpy."

"You seen 'em?"

"Not yet."

During the beauty pageant in Washington D.C. last year the contestants had worn long stockings and tunic bathing suits. However, Atlantic City's first contest was going to be something really different and special because the censors had seen fit to lift their bans on bare knees and skin tight suits. It remained to be seen if the idea would fly.

"Hey," McKeever said, "you better get out of here before the boss shows up. You ain't a cop no more, you know."

"Oh, I know."

O'Farrell had retired from the force two years ago, in 1919, and had opened his own detective agency. He'd been on the "inside" so often, though, while on the job that he catered to a pretty high class clientele, these days. He went from being the best dressed cop in town to the best dressed shamus.

"How'd you know to come up here, anyway?" McKeever asked.

"I was supposed to pick her up and take her out to Jersey."

"You knew her?"

"Yeah."

"Maybe you better tell me about it, Val," McKeever said,

folding his arms, and O'Farrell did. He laid it out for the detective just as it had happened . . .

2

Vincent Balducci had come into his office two days before with flash and confidence bordering on arrogance. Most of the flash came from the sparks he was wearing in a couple of rings.

"I've got a job for you, Mr O'Farrell," he'd said, after introducing himself. He said his name like O'Farrell was supposed to know who he was. He did, but he didn't tip his hand – not yet.

"How did you get my name, Mr Balducci?"

"You were referred to me by a mutual acquaintance," Balducci said. "His name is not important. He said you used to be a cop, an honest cop – or as honest as they get around here. He said you were thorough and you wouldn't gouge me on your fee just because I'm rich." Balducci looked around O'Farrell's well furnished office. "I'm thinkin' the last part is probably right."

"All the parts are right, Mr Balducci," O'Farrell said. "Why don't we get to the point of the visit?" O'Farrell motioned him to his visitor's chair.

"All right." Vincent Balducci said, seating himself. He laid his coat over his lap. O'Farrell noticed it had a velvet collar. He laid a matching hat atop it. His hair was dark – too dark to be natural – and shiny, combed straight back. "Yes, why don't we. Do you know who I am?"

"I read the newspaper," O'Farrell said. The year old New York Times already had an archive of stories on Vincent Balducci, a millionaire "philanthropist". What that generally meant to O'Farrell was that the man had a lot of money and didn't know what to do with it.

"That will save us some time, then," Balducci said.

That was when Balducci told O'Farrell about Georgie Taylor. He was married, he said, but it was a loveless, sexless marriage that was entered into for convenience. Naturally he needed a friend outside his marriage. When he met Georgie he knew she was the one.

"But she's younger, right?" O'Farrell asked.

"Uh, well, yes," Balducci said, "quite a bit younger. I am sixty-five and she is, uh, twenty-five."

"You look good," O'Farrell said. "I had you pegged for fifty-five."

"Thank you," Balducci said, "I try to keep myself in shape."

And he did a fine job. Except for his obviously dyed hair and some lines on his face, he did look younger than he was. He was tall, fit, and he moved like a younger man. O'Farrell sneaked a look at his own growing paunch. He was fifteen years younger than the millionaire, but they probably looked the same age. He decided not to think about that.

"Lots of married men have dames on the side, Mr Balducci," he said to the man. "Where do I come in?"

"Have you heard about this beauty pageant in Atlantic City this weekend?"

"I heard something about it," O'Farrell said. "Is that the one with the new bathing suits?"

"Yes," Balducci said. "One of the major sponsors is the Atlantic City Businessman's League, of which I am a member."

O'Farrell was starting to get the drift, but he let the man go on.

"I've entered Georgie in the pageant."

"You didn't guarantee she'd win, did you?" O'Farrell asked. "You're not going to tell me that the fix is in, are you?"

"Uh, no," Balducci said, "that, uh, that part is not your concern."

So maybe the fix was in. But okay, the client is always right. That wasn't his concern.

"Fine."

"Georgie is very beautiful, and talented, and she has a big career ahead of her."

O'Farrell almost asked, "As what?" but bit his tongue.

"But I think she might be in danger."

"From who?"

"Well . . . an old boyfriend, other contestants . . . my wife . . ."

"Does your wife know about Georgie?"

"Not exactly. She knows that I have . . . friends on the side, but she doesn't know about Georgie . . . specifically."

"All right," O'Farrell said, "go on."

"The contest kicks off with a gala event taking place at the Atlantic City Yacht Club on Friday. Among others, my wife will be there. I want you to escort Georgie."

"Be her date?"

"Er, as it were, yes – and protect her."

"We've never met— "

"I will take you to her apartment on Beekman Place for an introduction," Balducci said. "After that it will be up to the two of you to plan your Friday evening."

"Mr Balducci," O'Farrell said, "today is already Wednesday and I haven't got a thing to wear."

"On top of a thousand-dollar fee," Balducci said, taking the comment completely seriously, "I will buy you a new wardrobe and pay all other expenses for the night. I would send you to my tailor, but there's no time, so you can simply shop in the best men's stores available."

O'Farrell was a man who enjoyed good clothes. He knew where to shop. Even while still in the employ of the New York City Police Department he used to dress better than any other detective – regardless of rank – leading to speculation that he was on the take. It was only the fact that everyone knew how scrupulously honest he was that kept anyone from believing that.

"All right," O'Farrell said. "When and where do I meet the young, uh, lady?"

"Tonight, if you're free," Balducci said. He leaned forward and placed a slip of paper on the desk. "Come to that address at eight p.m. I'll make the introductions."

O'Farrell leaned forward and picked up the paper, glanced at it, then put it in his shirt pocket.

"I'll need an advance."

"Of course," Balducci said. He took a wad of cash out of his pocket. No checks, no paper trail.

"Five hundred now? And a hundred for clothes?"

"Better make it two for clothes," O'Farrell said.

Balducci didn't hesitate. He peeled off seven-one-hundred dollar bills and placed them on O'Farrell's desk.

"Will that do?"

"That's fine." O'Farrell left the cash where it was.

"I'll see you tonight, then."

"I have some more questions."

Balducci stood up. He shot his cuffs and looked at his watch. "I'll answer the rest of your questions tonight. Right now I have another appointment."

O'Farrell walked his new client to the door.

"Eight o'clock, then," Balducci said, and left.

After Balducci was gone O'Farrell picked up the seven one-hundred-dollar bills and rubbed them together. He turned and looked out his second floor window down to Fifth Avenue, where a chauffeur was holding the back door of a Rolls Royce open for Vincent Balducci. He probably should have asked for more money. A guy who rides in a Rolls and is dizzy for a young dame probably wouldn't have squawked about it.

3

O'Farrell presented himself at the Beekman Place address at seven-fifty-five. He paused out front to look up at the place. It was only five storeys, but Beekman Place was not an inexpensive address. Each apartment was occupied by money – or, as in this case, paid for by someone with money.

He was wearing one of the new suits he'd bought that afternoon. It was September and the weather was still mild so he'd bought one brown linen and one blue pinstriped. He was wearing the linen. The pinstriped was for the night at the Yacht Club.

The young doorman announced him and he was allowed up to the third floor. When he rang the doorbell, the door was opened by Balducci, himself. O'Farrell had been expecting a butler, or at least, a maid.

"Come in," the man said. "Georgie is still getting dressed."

O'Farrell entered and closed the door behind him. He followed Balducci down a short hall until they entered a plushly furnished living room.

"I've made a pitcher of martinis," his host said. "Would you like one?"

"Sure."

"Olive or onion?"

"Olive, please."

Balducci poured out two martinis, put olives in both, and then handed one to O'Farrell.

"I was expecting a servant to answer the door," the detective said. "Maid's night off?"

"No servants," Balducci said. "It's bad enough the doorman knows me and see me coming here.

O'Farrell understood.

"Ah," Balducci said, looking past him, "here's Georgie now."

O'Farrell turned. He didn't know what he'd expected to see, but Georgie took his breath away. She was tall and slender, but with a proud thrust of breasts. Her dark hair was piled high atop her head, leaving her pale shoulders bare in a powder blue gown that bared both shoulders, but was high-necked. Since 1919 hems had been rising and, currently, it was not unheard of for them to be six inches from the floor – affording a nice view of ankle – but Georgie's gown was full length. It was her eyes, however, that really got O'Farrell. They were violet, the most amazing color he'd ever seen, and they were great big eyes. When she blinked he thought he could feel it inside.

She was pretty enough to be a Ziegfeld girl. O'Farrell wondered why Balducci didn't just use his pull to get her that job, rather than put her in some silly pageant?

"Georgie, this is Val O'Farrell, the private detective I hired to protect you."

"To hide me, you mean," she said, tightly. She was smoking a cigarette, took a moment to remove a bit of tobacco from her tongue with her thumb and pinky while appraising O'Farrell. Flashes of light on her fingers attested to the fact that Balducci didn't mind sharing his love of diamonds. He still had his rings on. "Well, he's big enough for me to hide behind."

"I just want him to protect you, darling," Balducci said.

O'Farrell suddenly realized how dressed up the two of them were and what it meant. Balducci's suit easily cost five times what his own new suit cost.

"Are you folks going out to dinner?" he asked.

"We all are," Balducci said. "I thought it would be a good opportunity for us to get acquainted."

"Don't let him fool you, Mr Detective," Georgie said. "He just wants to use you as a beard, that way if anyone sees us together he can say I was your date. He's become an expert at hiding me."

"Georgie . . ."

"Oh, all right," she said, "I'll be a nice girl. Mr O'Farrell, would you care to join us for dinner?"

"Well, I don't—"

"Please," she said. "Vincent will be paying the bill."

"Well," O'Farrell agreed, "when you put it that way . . ."

The only chink in Georgie Taylor's beautiful armor was her voice. It was high pitched, almost a whine, and marred what was otherwise a perfect picture. O'Farrell knew nothing about how this beauty pageant was supposed to be run. He wondered if it called for the girls to actually speak?

Dinner was a tense affair at a nearby restaurant that O'Farrell suspected was below Balducci's usual dining standards. Even Georgie had lifted one side of her lips and sniffed when they entered. For his part, O'Farrell found his steak delicious.

For a dinner where they were supposed to be getting acquainted – actually, he and Georgie – Vincent Balducci did most of the talking. O'Farrell spent more time looking at Georgie than listening to his client.

Later, when they returned to the apartment house on Beekman Place, Balducci stopped in the lobby and said, "I'm not coming up."

"Why not?" Georgie asked.

"Because you two need to talk," Balducci said. "I want you to spend some time together and really talk, this time." He turned to face O'Farrell. "Georgie has all the details about the party at the Yacht Club Friday night. I won't see you again until then. I'll, uh, have my wife with me, so if we come face to face we will just be meeting. Do you understand?"

"Perfectly."

"My dear," Balducci said. He leaned over to kiss Georgie but she imperiously presented him with nothing but a cheek. "I'll see you soon."

"Yes," she said, quietly. Then she looked at O'Farrell. "Well, come on, then."

The building had an elevator, but Georgie preferred to walk, which O'Farrell had discovered on their way down. He, in fact, had a distrust of elevators and had walked up when he first arrived. This was something he had shared with his friend, the great Bat Masterson. Masterson, a legend of the old west, now lived in New York and not only had a column in *The Morning Telegraph*, but was a Vice-President of the newspaper. In his mid-sixties, the old western lawman still had more faith in a horse than an elevator, and almost never used a telephone if he didn't have to. O'Farrell liked to think of himself as someone who had been born too late. He should have been with Bat on the streets of Dodge City, with a gun on his hip.

Georgie opened her door with her key and marched right to the sideboard. She was dragging her mink stole behind her and just let it drop to the floor. O'Farrell bent, picked it up and deposited it on a chair.

"I need a drink," she said. "Join me?"

"Why not, but if you don't mind I'll have bourbon."

"A man after my own heart," she said. She poured bourbon over some ice cubes in two glasses and handed him one. She sipped herself, clunked the glass against her teeth and eyed him over the rim.

"After this we could go to the bedroom and fuck our brains out," she offered. "Or we could take the drinks with us and go in now."

"Somehow," O'Farrell said, "I don't think that's what your boyfriend had in mind when he said he wanted us to get better acquainted."

"You don't think so?" she asked, raising her eyebrows. "Why else do you think he sent us up here alone? Come on, I saw the way you were lookin' at me in the restaurant."

"We're supposed to talk about Friday night," he said, "about the beauty pageant."

"Beauty pageant," she said. She held her glass tightly and let her other arm swing loosely about. He didn't remember how many drinks she'd had at dinner, but she certainly seemed drunk now. "What a crock! What a stupid idea. Marching around in bathing suits while a bunch of lecherous old men decide who the winner will be."

"I wasn't aware that the contest would be judged by a panel of old men?"

"Oh, it's not, but you know what I mean." She finished her drink and poured herself another.

"You don't think you can win?"

She turned around quickly, sloshing some bourbon onto her wrist. She took a moment to lick it off, a move O'Farrell found particularly erotic, especially since she kept those violet eyes on him the whole time. He shifted his legs, his position in his chair, but it didn't help.

"Of course I can win," she said. "I've got the looks, don't you think?"

"Oh, definitely."

"I just don't have the voice," she said, candidly. "I'm no dummy, I just sound like one. I know that when the contestants start to speak – to answer questions – my voice is going to be a liability."

O'Farrell was impressed. The girl had no illusions about herself or, apparently, her situation.

"And Vincent doesn't love me," she said. She wiggled the fingers of one hand at him, the light playing off the sparks. "He owns me, like one of these diamonds. It sounds odd. He just wants to have me on his arm to show me off, but then he never takes me out. I can't explain it. All I know is he's not here tonight and I really want it. Whataya say?"

"Look, Georgie—"

She did something with the top of her dress and it fell to her waist. Her breasts were beautiful round orbs with tight pink nipples. She would not have made a good Ziegfeld girl, after all. Too big. She stared at him with those big violet eyes and poured the rest of her bourbon over her bare chest. One ice cube fell to the floor while another disappeared into her dress.

Why not? he thought, coming to his feet. When would he ever get a chance like this again? He had to find out where that second ice cube had gone.

4

They spent the next morning getting acquainted over breakfast because they really didn't do much talking during the night. When O'Farrell asked her about the doorman she told him not to worry. The doorman liked her and wouldn't say a word to Balducci about O'Farrell staying the entire night.

"So who would want to hurt you?" he asked her over steak and eggs at a diner around the corner. He was wearing his linen suit again, but had left the silk tie off this morning, preferring to stow it in his jacket pocket. Georgie was wearing an angora sweater with a pin in the shape of the letter "G", and a skirt with a fashionable six inch hem. The sweater molded itself to her breasts. Her golden hair was pulled back in a ponytail. She wasn't wearing as much make up as the night before and looked much younger. But those eyes . . . made up or not, they popped.

"That's another one of Vincent's fantasies," she said. "Nobody wants to hurt me. I don't need a bodyguard – although I certainly needed you last night, didn't I?" She ran her toe up his leg.

"Just answer the question and stop playing footsie under the table, young lady."

"Ooh, Daddy," she purred, "scold me some more."

Somehow, after spending the night with her, her voice didn't seem quite as whiney or annoying. She sure had more than enough other qualities to make up for it – although some of those qualities certainly would not be seen by the judges.

"Georgie," O'Farrell said, moving his leg, "be serious."

"I am serious," she said. "Nobody wants to hurt me. Vincent thinks everyone wants what he's got. Well, if no one knows he's got me, what's the problem?"

"Someone must know," O'Farrell said, "somebody who works for him but knows when to make excuses for him."

"Sure, they know he's got someone," she said, "but not who it is."

"Look," O'Farrell said, "Balducci is paying me to protect you, and that's what I'm going to do."

"And more, I think," she said.

After breakfast O'Farrell walked Georgie back to her building and said he had to go home to change.

"Aren't you afraid someone's gonna attack me?"

"I think what Vincent wants is for me to escort you to the beauty pageant, and protect you," O'Farrell said, "starting with the party at the Yacht Club. So I'll pick you up here – what time is the party?"

"The festivities start at three," she said. "I'm supposed to be there at noon, though."

"Noon?"

"I'm part of the show, after all," she said, archly.

"How many contestants are there?"

"There were supposed to be a lot, but we ended up with just twelve. Some folks – sponsors – are really upset about it."

"Twelve beautiful girls, huh?" O'Farrell said. "All right, then I guess I'll pick you up here at ten. I assume Balducci will supply transportation?"

"He'll have an automobile here to take us over to New Jersey. Probably a Rolls."

O'Farrell made a face. He still preferred horses, but it was a long way to Atlantic City.

"Okay," he said. "I'll see you then."

"What about tomorrow?" she asked. "Don't you want to see me tomorrow?"

"I don't think—"

She came closer to him.

"After everything we did to each other last night you can wait two days to see me?"

"Hey, Georgie," O'Farrell said, "you're the one who said that what we did last night was just sex."

"Well, yes," she said, touching his lapel, "but it was good sex, wasn't it?"

"It was great," he said, "fabulous. You're a wonderful gal, but you belong to my client."

"That didn't seem to bother you last night?"

"Last night I gave in to bourbon and a pair of gorgeous . . . eyes."

She smiled. "You think my . . . eyes are gorgeous?" she asked, pausing suggestively exactly where he did.

"You know they are." Behind Georgie, O'Farrell could see the doorman watching him. A different one today than last night, but another young man, this one eyeing Georgie appreciatively – not that O'Farrell could blame him.

"You sure this doorman is not on Balducci's payroll?"

"I'm this sure," she said. She slid her hands around his neck and gave him a kiss that could have melted the soles of his shoes. Her tongue fluttered in his mouth and she bit his bottom lip lightly before stepping back and smiling at him.

"Okay," she said, wiggling her fingers at him, "see you the day after tomorrow, Lover."

5

But Friday, when he went to pick her up, there was no answer at the door. He went down to ask the doorman if he'd seen Georgie Taylor that morning. This was the same doorman who had watched her kiss him goodbye the other day.

"No, sir," the man said. "I haven't seen her today, at all."

O'Farrell studied the man for a moment, then took a ten out of his wallet.

"What's your name?"

"Henry, sir." Henry was a young man in his late twenties. He was eyeing the ten in O'Farrell's hand hungrily.

"Tell me, Henry, has Miss Taylor had any visitors since I was here?"

"No, sir."

"Not Mr Balducci?"

"Well, yes sir," Henry said. "He came by last night. I didn't know you meant him."

"Did he stay the night?"

"No, sir," Henry said, "He left after a few hours."

"Okay . . . anyone else?"

"No, sir," the doorman said. "She hasn't had anyone else upstairs since you left the other morning – uh, except for Mr Balducci."

"Did she go out at all since then?"

"Oh, yes sir," Henry said. "I saw her go out yesterday. She did some shopping and came home with a few bags. She stayed in after that – at least, as long as I was on duty."

"How many doormen are there, Henry?"

"Three, sir," Henry said, "but only one other – Leslie –" he said the name with a wry grin " – has been on duty since you were here. He worked yesterday afternoon and evening as well as the, uh, evening you arrived."

"I'd like to find out what he knows, Henry," O'Farrell said.

"I could ask him when I see him."

"No," O'Farrell said, "I'd like to find out as soon as possible. Could you call him? There'd be ten in it for him, and a second ten for you."

The promise of twenty bucks sent Henry to the phone to call Leslie. He asked the second doorman the same questions O'Farrell had asked him, and hung up shaking his head.

"Leslie says he never saw anyone go up to Miss Taylor's apartment, and he never saw her leave."

O'Farrell went over it in his head. So she'd only been out once all day Thursday, didn't go out at all anymore on Wednesday when he left her, or any time Friday morning until now. Balducci was the only person seen going up.

"Is there a back door, Henry?"

"Yes, sir," the doorman said. "It's kept locked. Tenants don't use it, and don't have a key. It's access to an alley where we throw out the trash, sometimes take deliveries."

"So you have a key, in case of deliveries."

"Yes, sir."

"Any deliveries since I left here Wednesday morning?" O'Farrell asked.

"No, sir."

O'Farrell gave Henry the twenty dollars and then took out another twenty.

"Henry, have you got a key to Miss Taylor's apartment?"

"Yes, sir," the doorman said. "Do you think something's happened to her?"

"Let's just say I have a bad feeling."

Henry waved away the second twenty and got the key . . .

"We found her like this," he told McKeever.

"Well, you've got each other to vouch for that," the detective said. "Is there anything you haven't told me?"

There was. He'd left out the part about having sex with his client's girl, and spending the night. He only hoped Henry had left that part out, too.

"No, that's it."

"That pretty much jibes with what the doorman told us. Well, you better scram, Val. The Lieutenant's gonna show up soon and he ain't gonna like it if—"

"Too late," the police officer on the door said.

O'Farrell and McKeever both turned in to see Lieutenant Mike Turico enter the room.

"Well, well," Turico said when he saw O'Farrell. "Guess you musta forgot you ain't a cop no more, O'Farrell."

"Hello, Mike."

Turico approached O'Farrell and felt the texture of wide lapel of the private detective's blue pinstriped suit . . .

"Turnin' private musta really paid off for you, Val," he said. He looked down at the matching Fedora O'Farrell was holding.

"I'm doin' okay, Mike," O'Farrell said, "Thanks for askin'."

"Bet the swells really like you in this outfit." He touched O'Farrell's red silk tie, straightening it. Without looking at McKeever he asked, "Who let him in here?"

"He just walked in, boss," the detective said. "You know how Val is."

"Yeah," Turico said, "I do." He stepped back from O'Farrell, jerked his thumb at the door and said, "Blow."

"Nice to see you again, too, Mike," O'Farrell said. The two had not gotten along when they were both police detectives, and it was no different now. Turico had always resented how O'Farrell got the high profile cases, but O'Farrell had a reputation for getting results, and Turico didn't. Naturally, Turico had risen to the rank of Lieutenant, since rank had more to do with who you knew than getting results.

Turico moved to inspect the body and McKeever followed O'Farrell to the door.

"Sam, sorry to bust in on you like this."

McKeever waved his apology off.

"Forget it. If the boss is gonna chew me out it's gonna be over this or somethin' else. But just between you and me, Val, you got a personal interest in this?"

"My client pays the bills for this place," O'Farrell said. "I met the girl. I liked her."

"Ah," McKeever said, "the sugar daddy. You got an idea where I can find him?"

"You can get his address from the manager of the building," O'Farrell said. "I don't have it on me. And he's got an office downtown somewhere. If the manager can't help you, let me know."

"McKeever," Lieutenant Turico yelled, "get your ass over here."

"Gotta go, Val. You gonna look into this?"

"I'm not sure, Sam."

"Well, let me know, huh?" McKeever said. "Turico might be here, but this is my case."

"I'll stay in touch." As he went out past the uniformed policeman he patted his arm and said, "See you, Ed."

Did he have a personal interest? Goddamn right, he did.

6

O'Farrell was still dressed for the Yacht Club party when he approached Bat Masterson at his desk at *The Morning Telegraph*. The old lawman turned newspaperman made a show of covering his eyes.

"I'm blind! I'm blind!" he cried, then dropped his hands. "Damned if you ain't the prettiest man I ever did see, O'Farrell."

"Cut it, Bat," O'Farrell said. "You're not the only one who can get all duded up."

"'All duded up'?" Bat asked. "I don't think I've heard anyone say that since Wyatt Earp back in ninety-nine."

O'Farrell rushed on, afraid that his friend would start telling one of his stories which would end with him taking a replica of his old gun out of his desk drawer. O'Farrell usually enjoyed Bat's stories, but he had no time for them today.

"Bat," O'Farrell said, sitting down across from his friend, "what's the skinny on the beauty pageant out in Atlantic City?"

Bat sat back and smiled broadly. Approaching his late sixties, both his waist and his face had filled out some, but when he smiled like that it took years off him.

"I know I'm one of the judges," he said.

"How'd you get that job?"

"Hell, they just up and asked me," the old gunman said. "Who am I to say no to judging a bevy of beauties?"

"Who asked you?"

"Some fella from the – what's it called – Atlantic City something—"

" – Businessman's League?"

"That's it. Said they needed artists to judge and I qualified
'cause I'm a writer. You believe that? I never been called an
artist before."

"Or a writer."

"You want me to shoot you?"

"Sorry."

"What's your interest?"

"I'll tell you," O'Farrell said, "but you've got to keep it
under your hat for a while."

"That's a hard thing to ask a newspaperman to do, Val, but
okay. For you I'll do it."

O'Farrell fed him the whole story, and Bat listened in
complete silence . . .

"What do you want me to do?" Bat asked.

"I wanted to find out what you knew about Balducci, and
about the pageant."

"Like what?"

"Like are they on the up-and-up, both of them?"

"As far as I know the pageant is," Bat said.

"Does that mean that Balducci isn't?"

"There's been talk that Balducci is in bed with a, uh, certain
criminal element."

"Like what?"

"Well, some of the crime reporters have been wondering if
he's in with this new Mafia," Bat said. "They wonder if he's not
involved with the giggle juice trade and other illegal activities."

"You sound like you're being real careful with your language.
Why would a rich man like him want to run liquor with the
mob?"

"Well," Bat said, "this new breed of – what do they call 'em –
gangsters is a lot different from the bad guys of my day. You
can't tell by white hats and black hats anymore, Val. And who
knows why rich men do what rich men do?"

"Okay, so Balducci might be in bed with the Mafia," O'Farrell said, "but the pageant is on the level?"

"As far as I can tell," Bat said. "I wouldn't have agreed to be
a judge if I thought different.'

"How are you getting out there?"

"They're sending a car for me."

"What time?"

"Around five, I think. Do you want to ride with me?" Bat asked.

"Yes, I would," O'Farrell said. "I think if I walk in with you I'll be able to get around easier."

"Fine," Bat said, "meet me here around quarter to five and we'll go look at some girls. What will you be doing until then?"

O'Farrell stood up. "Trying to find my client before the police do."

7

O'Farrell knew more about the Mafia and Johnny Torrio – which were natural offshoots of Paul Kelly and his Five Points Gang – then he wanted to let on to Bat Masterson. Friend or no friend, it wasn't wise to let a newspaperman know all that you knew. However, he'd met Vincent Balducci and didn't see him as a gangster. It was more likely he had some connections – crooked and lucrative – to Tammany Hall.

O'Farrell was unable to locate Balducci that morning and into the afternoon. He wondered if the police were having the same problem? At least he knew that the man was supposed to be at the Yacht Club in Jersey that evening.

He decided to make one more stop before meeting Bat Masterson to go to New Jersey. There were still some things he needed to know, and his buddy Sam McKeever would have the answers.

O'Farrell had decided not to change his clothes after leaving Bat Masterson, so when he returned to the offices of *The Morning Telegraph* he was still dressed for the Yacht Club party.

He met Bat in front of the building as a boxy, yellow Pierce Arrow Roadster pulled up. He and Bat got in and the driver pulled away and headed for New Jersey.

"Find your man?' Bat asked.

"No."

"Think he's in hidin'?"

"I doubt it," O'Farrell said. "Men with his money – and his connections – rarely go into hiding, even if they are suspected of murder."

"And is he?"

"He's on the list," the detective said, "since he was paying the bills for the girl."

"And what's your interest in this, Val, other than him bein' your client?"

"I met the girl and liked her, Bat," O'Farrell said. "She shouldn't have died like that."

"Like what?" Bat asked. "If you told me how she died I forgot."

"She was shot, once, in the temple."

"Any chance of suicide?"

"The word I got from the cops was that she was shot from close range, but there was no gun at the scene."

"Well, that rules out suicide – unless someone removed the gun."

"Too complicated," O'Farrell said. "I've found, in my experience, that the simplest answer is usually the right one. Once you start factoring in 'what ifs' you just complicate things, and muddy the waters."

"What about the gangster angle?"

"That muddies the waters," O'Farrell said, as if it was a perfect example of what he had been talking about. "I'm looking for a clean, simple solution."

"You're gonna solve this thing?"

"Bat," O'Farrell said, "I think I already have."

When they pulled up in front of the Yacht Club there were many other vehicles arriving, as well as those which had already arrived. More Pierce Arrows, Rolls Royces, even some sporty Stutz Roadsters.

O'Farrell and Bat were dropped right in front of the Club. A tent had been erected nearby to accommodate all the guests for party, and there were plenty of boats in the water to be involved, as well.

In fact, festivities seemed to have already begun, as not only were the contestants delivered to the docks by boat, but a man dressed as King Neptune, as well. Neptune arrived on a barge surrounded by twenty women in costume, and twenty black men dressed as Nubian slaves.

Once King Neptune and his subjects were on the docks the

second barge brought the beauty queens in. There were eleven of them, O'Farrell knew, because Georgie Taylor would have been the twelfth. Apparently, her death had gone unreported to pageant officials, who had not had time to replace her, or they'd been surprised when she hadn't arrived and had gone ahead with eleven.

The contestants were allowed to wear their new risqué bathing suits on the barge, showing lots of skin, but were then whisked away to don something more appropriate for the party.

"Well," Bat said, when the girls were gone, "it won't be easy judging the most beautiful out of that lot, tomorrow night. I'd better find the officials and ask them what they want me to do."

"I'll see you inside the tent, then," Val O'Farrell said.

"Better stick with me, Val," Bat said, "at least until I get you introduced to someone in the know."

That was wise, O'Farrell knew. On his own he might end up being kicked out before he could find Vincent Balducci.

"Good idea."

8

The pageant officials pinned a button on Bat's lapel that identified him as a judge, and agreed to give O'Farrell some sort of a guest button. So armed, both O'Farrell and Bat joined the party in the tent.

There was a stage with a big band on it, playing their hearts out while a male and female singer alternated songs. Guests in various stages of dress were filling a dance floor, or milling about holding champagne glasses or martinis or wine, all of which was being circulated by uniformed waiters. Money had been paid out, whether it was for a license, or just a bribe, but the giggle juice was flowing freely.

The men were wearing expensive suits and, in some cases, tuxedoes. The women flaunted jewelry – rings, bracelets, even tiaras – and the fashions of the day, in some cases their six-inch hems flying even higher while they danced the Charleston, the Shimmy, the Fox Trot or even the Black Bottom. It seemed as if many of the women who were young enough to care thought they had to do something to compete with the bathing beauties. Indeed, O'Farrell realized that some of the women on the dance floor were the contestants, themselves. He could imagine Georgie out there dancing among them, and it made him angry – angrier than he'd been since he first discovered her body.

A male singer started to sing "My Time is Your Time," and couples moved in closer to dance together.

"See him?" Bat asked.

"Who?"

"Your client?"

"Not yet."

"I see somebody you know," Bat said, pointing to Detective Sam McKeever of the New York Police Department, who was fast approaching with another man in a suit and some uniformed New Jersey police in tow. Right on time.

"Val," McKeever said, "this is Detective Willoughby, of the Atlantic City Police."

"What did you find out?" O'Farrell asked McKeever, after tossing Willoughby a nod.

"She was killed sometime Thursday night. Both doormen have alibis," McKeever said. "They were both seen on duty by other tenants."

"They could have slipped away long enough to kill her," Bat offered.

"You're muddying the waters again, Bat," O'Farrell said. "There are three logical suspects for this crime."

"And you've cleared the doormen?" Bat asked, looking at McKeever.

"Yeah," McKeever said, then, "Hey, you're Bat Masterson."

"At your service," Bat said.

One of the uniformed police said to the others, "That's Bat Masterson."

O'Farrell saw Bat's chest inflate until another officer said, "Who's he?" and a third said, "Newspaperman, I think."

"Did you manage to keep this from Lieutenant Turico?" O'Farrell asked.

"Yeah, but he ain't gonna like it."

"I wanted you to get the collar," O'Farrell said.

"Wait a minute," Bat said. "You said there were three logical suspects—"

"Well," McKeever said, "four, but I'm clearin' Val, here."

"Okay," Bat said, "so if you've cleared Val, and the two doormen, that leaves—"

"There he is," O'Farrell said cutting Bat off. He started to push through the crowd, causing several people to spill their drinks.

"Follow 'im," McKeever said to the other cops, and Bat followed them.

O'Farrell was faster than they were, though, and was not being careful about who he bumped. As he got closer Vincent Balducci turned and saw him coming towards him. The millionaire was impeccably turned out in a black tuxedo, and was holding a champagne glass. He was chatting with some people – one of whom was a matronly lady covered in jewels that did nothing to hide the fact that she was *not* one of the contestants. He frowned when he saw O'Farrell coming towards him, then saw something in the detective's face he didn't like. He turned and started pushing through the crowd. O'Farrell increased his speed, leaving McKeever and Bat and the other police to struggle through the crowd behind him.

The band started playing an up tempo number and people started doing the Charleston, again. Balducci was trying to run, now, and as he burst out onto the dance floor a heavyset woman trying to keep up with the music slammed into him with her hip and sent him flying across the floor. He bumped into a man whose arms and legs were flailing about in an obscene caricature of the dance and they both fell to the floor. The man shouted, but Balducci – in excellent physical condition – jumped up and began running again. He got a few steps when a slender but energetic girl in a flapper's dress banged into him with a sharp-boned hip and knocked him off balance. He managed to stay on his feet and finally made his way across the dance floor to the exit next to the bandstand.

O'Farrell, following in his wake, managed to avoid all the traffic Balducci had encountered and was right behind him.

It was dark outside. Balducci headed for the marina. O'Farrell wasn't even sure why the man was running, but he took his .45 from his shoulder holster just the same.

The millionaire ran to the end of a dock, then turned to face O'Farrell.

"You can't shoot me!" he cried out, waving his hands. "I'm not armed."

"Why would I want to shoot you, Vincent?" O'Farrell asked. He holstered his gun. "In fact, why are you running from me?"

Balducci was sweating so much that some of the dye from his hair was running down his forehead.

"Wh – why were you chasing me?"

"Was I?" O'Farrell asked.

"You came at me . . . the look on your face . . . I thought . . ."

The man was too fit to be winded from running. He was out of breath for another reason.

Suddenly, there was a small automatic in his hand. O'Farrell cursed himself for holstering his gun.

"I – I didn't mean to," Balducci said. "She told me about the sex . . . and I just went crazy . . . it wasn't my fault."

"Is that the gun?" Georgie had been shot at close range with a small caliber gun. "Where'd you get it?"

"It was hers," he said. "I gave it to her for protection. I – I never thought she'd try to use it against me."

"You must have frightened her."

"She . . . she was mine! She wasn't supposed to be with anyone else."

O'Farrell felt badly about that. Maybe if he hadn't slept with Georgie she'd still be alive now. or maybe it would have happened later, with someone else.

"Come on, Vincent," O'Farrell said. "If you shot her by accident, then you're not going to shoot me deliberately."

"You know," Balducci said, "you know . . . I knew it when I saw your face. I – I can't let you tell anyone."

O'Farrell wondered where the damned police were? And where was Bat Masterson? He was wondering how close he'd get to his gun if he tried to draw it now.

"Vincent—"

"I'm sorry," Balducci said, "I had no idea it would come to this when I hired you. I'm so sorry . . ."

Balducci tensed in anticipation of firing his gun, but before he could there was a shot from behind O'Farrell. A bullet struck Balducci in his right shoulder. He cried out and dropped his gun into the water, then fell to his knees and clutched his arm. O'Farrell turned to see Bat Masterson standing at the end of the dock with an old Colt .45 in his hand. He turned to check that Balducci was neutralized, then walked over to Bat.

"Thanks, Bat."

"I still got it," Bat said.

"Where'd you get that?"

"Hey, all the guns in my desk aren't harmless replicas, you know."

Behind Bat, Sam McKeever came running up with the other policeman.

"Damned Charleston," he said. "How'd you get across that dance floor without slamming into somebody?"

"I'm graceful."

"Did he do it?"

"He did it," O'Farrell said. "He confessed. I'll testify, but I don't think I'll have to."

The other detective, Willoughby, waved at his men and said, "Go get him."

"You'll need divers," O'Farrell told both detectives. "The gun fell in the water when Bat shot him."

"The same gun?" McKeever asked, surprised.

"Yeah," O'Farrell said, "for some reason he was carrying it around. He said he gave it to her for protection."

The uniformed police helped Balducci to his feet and started walking him off the dock. When they reached O'Farrell and the two detectives they stopped.

"I'm sorry I slept with her, Balducci," O'Farrell said. "It just happened, but she shouldn't have died for it."

Balducci's mouth flopped open and he said, "You slept with her, too?"

As they marched him away McKeever said, "One of the doormen. Apparently he went up there when Balducci wasn't around."

"So he didn't know about me and her," O'Farrell said.

"He does now," McKeever said.

"And so do we," Bat said.

"You dog," McKeever said.

"I wonder if his money will be able to buy him out of this?" Bat asked.

"Don't matter to me," McKeever said. "My job's just to bring 'im in."

Bat and McKeever started after the other policemen. Let them rib him, O'Farrell thought, bringing up the rear. It wasn't his fault she was dead. That's what counted. Now he could be sad for her, and not feel any guilt.

"There would have been murder"

IAN MORSON

*One of the believed threats of the 1920s was a communist
revolution in Britain. There was considerable social unrest
which manifested in, amongst other things, the General Strike
of 1926. When I first conceived this anthology I had not given
much thought to the rise of communism, so I was surprised to
receive not one, but two stories based on that theme. Fortunately both were ingenious stories and totally different. See
Mat Coward's for the other one. Ian Morson is best known
for his series about medieval Oxford academic and detective
William Falconer, who first appeared in* Falconer's Crusade
(1994).

Sunday afternoon, 22 April 1923.
The British Empire Exhibition site

"It looks like murder, Inspector."

"Superintendent, if you please." James O'Nions's retort
was short and abrupt. He was particularly sensitive about his
new rank. It had taken him long enough to attain – too long, in
his opinion – so he was at pains to correct his sergeant's albeit
natural error. Sergeant Banks blanched at his mistake. He knew
how thin-skinned his guv'nor was about his recent elevation.
But he had been calling him inspector for so long, it was
difficult to get out of the habit. Still, he was quick to mumble
his apologies.

"Sorry. Superintendent."

He returned to contemplating the charred remains in the hole at the foot of the tower. O'Nions, meanwhile, was scanning the almost completed building. The new Empire Stadium rose steeply above them with its two massive white towers breaking up the long and imposing façade. Many had commented favourably on the exterior, but O'Nions was not impressed. He thought the towers resembled nothing more than giant pepperpots. But then, he was in a bad mood. He hated being called out on a Sunday. Or rather Mrs O'Nions hated him being called out, and that was enough for him to hate it too. The Sunday roast would not keep, and nor would her temper.

The site in Wembley was still a hive of activity, even with the Cup Final less than a week away. For between the new stadium and the main road stretched out the bustling building site that was to become the British Empire Exhibition the following year. Large ferro-concrete pavilions had already begun to spring up across the area, and the whole affair was attracting a great deal of attention at home and abroad. Which was why Special Branch in particular had been called in to peer down a hole at a partially burned body at the foot of one of the stadium's towers.

O'Nions voiced his contempt for the new structures.

"They look like oversized garages. Either that, or redundant aeroplane sheds."

"Sorry, sir?"

"No matter, Banks, you would not understand. Get down there and tell me what you can see."

Sergeant Banks stared wide-eyed down the slippery clay embankment. All he could see was a vision of a Belgian trench, that the curled-up body did nothing to dispel. He squeezed his eyes shut, and shook his head to clear away the noise of the whiz-bang in his skull. Reluctantly, he scrambled down into the hole that had been due to have been backfilled that morning. Until that is, the workman given the job had peered into the tower's footings, and spotted a suspicious bundle. The sides of the hole were steep, and the red clay smeared all over the seat of the police sergeant's trousers. Now he knew why his guv'nor had stayed up top. He was never one to get his best brown boots dirty. Banks gulped back the bitter taste in his mouth as he examined the grisly remains, blackened and curled up in a ball.

The posture made it look as though whoever it was had tried to protect himself from the flames. There was a scattering of white powder on the body too. He reached out a hand to touch it.

"Don't touch, Banksie. It's probably quicklime. Give you a nasty burn, can that."

Banks nodded his thanks to O'Nions's timely warning. He also hoped the familiar tone from above meant that his guv'nor's irritation at his gaffe was forgiven. So he deemed it now safe to speak. He bent over the body and looked closely without touching anything. "Looks like there's no head, guv'nor. Nor hands neither. They didn't want us to know whose body it was. Going to be a hell of a job identifying it."

Superintendent O'Nions just grunted, and Banks wondered if he already had some idea of the body's identity. The guv'nor was brilliant at what Banks called "leaps of deduction". Guesswork, some of his detractors would call it, but not the sergeant. O'Nions, for his part, didn't disabuse his sergeant of his assumption of uncanny powers. He quite relished a bit of hero worship. The trouble was, he hadn't the faintest idea which of the three missing men it was.

Two weeks earlier, Hampstead

Albert Potter was deep in the conundrum at the core of the book he was reading, when Rosalind, his wife, entered the study that evening. Some years older than he was, she was causing him concern. This very morning she had said something very curious.

"I feel as though I am packing up," she had suddenly said over the toast and marmalade, "so that I am ready to depart when the time comes."

That was all, nothing more. And she had refused to elaborate, leaving the room with some dirty dishes in her hand, and an unspoken errand on her mind. Thinking about what on earth she meant made Albert shudder. They hadn't any trip abroad planned, had they? So, the pronouncement sounded more ominous than that. He had therefore been quite distracted when, on entering the study, Rosalind spoke only to announce an unexpected guest.

"Darling. Junius has called. He says it is most urgent that he speaks to you."

"Didn't you tell him I was – er – working on the book?"

Rosalind raised an elegant and well-plucked eyebrow. The accusation inherent in that slightest of gestures pierced Albert to the heart. She knew the slim volume of fiction in his hand was in no way going to contribute to their massive joint project on the history of the Poor Law. Crushed by the silent rebuke, Albert sighed and gracefully accepted defeat. Reluctantly, he put the newly published murder mystery aside, and stood up to welcome his fellow MP.

Fellow MP. It had a good ring to it.

Albert Potter still felt like a new boy in his first term at a public school. Elected a Labour MP for North Battersea in November 1922 at the age of sixty-three, even after six months he wasn't used to this change in his status. A noble status at odds with his physical form. At five foot four inches, and with a large head whose size was further exaggerated by his prickly bush of hair, which was greying now, he had never been patrician in dimensions. He had also soon learned that the longer-serving Members of Parliament, including many in his own Party, had cruelly christened him 'Tadpole'. Well, one day he would show them he was no tadpole, but a frog with a pretty loud croak.

The man who Rosalind showed in was small-framed with slicked-down black hair, and dark brown, bloodshot eyes framed with long, almost feminine lashes. His elegant suit, with the most stylish of cuts, fitted his lithe form perfectly. More spectacular were his aristocratic features, which were carved into a face of the darkest brown, almost teak-like hue. Junius Premadasa had been born in Ceylon to a very wealthy Sinhalese family, and had been sent to Britain in 1905 for an education. Despite his background, Premadasa, soon after leaving Oxford, had eagerly dabbled in first the Communist Party and then the Labour Party, eventually becoming an MP for the latter in West Ham, South. Today, his normally elegant demeanour was shattered by an obvious distress.

Albert self-consciously pushed the popular novel with its lurid yellow wrapper further under the cushion of his chair.

"Why, Junius! What is the matter?"

The same day. The Grapes public house, Battersea

No-one would have given Harry Rothstein a second glance. His stringy frame was clad in dusty, patched working clothes, matching most of the clientele of the pub. And his drawn, sun-reddened face was typical of an out-of-doors labourer drained of all energy by a full day's toil. He looked as if he had dropped in the pub straight from a building site. Which indeed he had. But Harry Rothstein was more than an anonymous member of the proletariat. He was one of Moscow's secret weapons. Not that that helped him make any more sense of the letter in his pocket. That is, he could understand what was written in the document, but the exhortations themselves were extraordinary, inconceivable. He was used to Moscow using such words as *cadres*, *vanguards*, and *comrades*. That was normal, and it was left to him to translate them into euphemisms the fellow Party members of his branch were more comfortable with. But this took the biscuit.

As soon as he had got the letter, he had confided in Prem, who happened to be in the local Party office. The elegant, little black man was a virulent anti-imperialist, which is what had brought him into the Party despite his social standing. But at first, even he could not believe his eyes.

"They're mad."

Premadasa poked a long, aristocratic finger at the letter. "Listen to this. 'Stir up the masses of the unemployed British proletariat.' And . . ." His dark eyes slid down the page seeking out another phrase. "Here it is . . . 'a successful rising is required in any of the working districts of England.' Fat chance, old man."

Harry Rothstein always marvelled at the black man's command of English vernacular. Except the words were oddly out of place expressed in such cultured tones. He sighed. "Doesn't Moscow know that our members are still British first and foremost?"

"Apparently not, if this letter is to be believed." His big, brown eyes clouded over at that moment, as he gazed into some far Parsee distance. How he squared his religion with his Communist beliefs, Rothstein wasn't sure. The black man was an enigma. So he wasn't surprised at Premadasa's next utterance. "However, there is something we can do about it."

"Like what?" Harry Rothstein thought he could not feel any more downhearted. But Premadasa's proposal weighed him down like an albatross round his neck. Such a risky action, and at the FA Cup Final, too. Reluctantly, Harry had made a telephone call, and then resorted to The Grapes. Where he managed to down three pints in quick succession without his sense of foreboding lifting.

Boleyn Football Ground, West Ham

Tommy Fields slung his kitbag over his shoulder and, without a word to the rest of the team, slipped out of the dressing room at Upton Park. He had played badly in the training session today, and the manager, Syd King, had given him a peculiar look as he changed out of his sweat-stained kit and back into his street clothes. He pulled on his thick roll-neck pullover, still not sure whether he would be included in the team for the Cup Final against Bolton Wanderers. Being a Lancashire man, there had been some muttering from other West Ham players about his loyalties. Hufton, the goalie, had dived at his feet during training, and somehow got tangled in his legs. Fields had fallen awkwardly, feeling a sharp pull to his left ankle. He had limped for the rest of the session.

As he exited the football ground, he saw an omnibus pulling away from the stop at the corner. He knew he would be late if he didn't catch it, and sprinted down the road in pursuit. The pain in his ankle returned, shooting up his leg, and he stumbled, almost falling. The conductor saw the fit-looking man stumble, and held out a helping hand. With his aid, Fields managed to haul himself on the rear platform, still clutching his kit-bag of muddy gear. The conductor, a stringy man with yellowing teeth peered at him, a frown on his pinched features. Then recognition dawned as he put a name to the handsome, broad face, topped with its unruly quiff of blond hair. Fields knew what was coming next.

"Tommy Fields, ennit? Yeah, course it is. I hope you can run a sight better than that down the wing on Saturday next. I've got a wager on the Hammers."

Fields allowed a thin, polite smile to cross his lips, as he slumped in the hard wooden seat. He still wasn't used to being recognized, and didn't know how to cope. It hadn't been long since he had been just another worker in a Lancashire boiler-making factory. Professional footballer and recognition were both virgin territory to him. Football – the people's game. Sometimes he wished he was back at the factory, despite the better money he earned as a footballer. Except the factory had closed down now, and lots of his mates were out of work. And here was the bus conductor, moaning about a little bet on the result of a football match.

"You think you've got problems, mate," he muttered.

The Grapes

Harry was surreptitiously reading the letter again, when a man slid on to the worn red plush of the bench next to him. Harry took in the well-built torso, and the broad features.

"Tommy Fields, as I live and breathe! Glad you got my message. Let me buy you a pint."

Harry should have been happy to see his old friend again. But he knew what he was about to ask of him. He didn't like to use people's weaknesses, even for the best of causes. And this was far from a good cause in Rothstein's mind. But he knew he was committed. He rose from his seat to get the drink. Fields pushed his kit-bag under the seat, and laid a hand on Rothstein's arm.

"Just tell me what you want, Harry. I'm in a hurry."

Rothstein looked hesitant to him, as if what he was about to say was too much to ask a friend he had not seen in over a year. His hesitation made Fields suddenly concerned, and not a little sickened. Harry Rothstein did not like making himself beholden to anyone. Nor did he like using people. But it looked like he was going to. Hadn't he got enough problems?

Harry looked closer into Fields' own eyes. Saw the doubt.

"Let's add a chaser to the beer. You're going to need one. Then maybe we can help each other."

Some days later, Scotland Yard

"Have you read this, Banksie?" Superintendent O'Nions was waving a sheet of duplicated paper in the air, as he stormed into his office. Sergeant Banks stood respectfully in front of his guv'nor's desk in the at ease posture that came naturally to the old soldier. He waited in silence. From long experience, he knew that O'Nions's question did not require an answer. He was going to be told what was in the missive whether he wanted to know or not. And O'Nions did not disappoint him.

"This is a circular message from BT." The initials were all that was necessary to identify the autocratic head of the CID. The sergeant knew what was coming. BT's obsession with the Labour Party and its links with those hotbeds of revolution, the Trade Unions, always coloured his thinking of late. Some would say clouded it. Banks thought himself lucky that there was no longer any record of his participation in the Police Strike of 1918. He had O'Nions to thank for that. It was a tie that bound the two men uneasily together.

O'Nions slumped behind his desk, cocking his feet on the battered surface.

"Listen to this. He reminds us that in the War, we saw the rise of Pacifist Societies, and that now Pacifism, anti-Conscription, Homosexuality and Revolution are all now inextricably mixed." He poked a finger at the slender sheet, quoting from it. " 'The real object of these people is the ruin of their own country.' "

As O'Nions read from the memo, Banks could hear the capitals dripping off the page. BT was very fond of capitals. Probably because his own men identified him by two of his own.

"Very interesting, sir," he murmured noncommittally. It was best to keep his feelings to himself, until he saw how his guv'nor was going to respond. You never knew how he would take one of BT's memos. O'Nions read silently through the rest of the screed, finally summing its contents up for his sergeant.

"He wants all his officers – and that includes me, Banksie – to bear in mind the following organizations in their investigations." O'Nions flicked the thin sheet over his desk, and Banks caught it before it fluttered to the floor. Where it would have nestled with several other sheets of a similar origin. He ran his eyes over the list of suspect organizations. Predictably, it included the usual Trades Unions. Especially those lined in the so-called Triple Alliance, that is, the Miners, Transport Workers and Railwaymen. Also on the list were such august and, in Banks's eyes, totally ineffectual bodies as the Fellowship of Reconciliation and the Council for Civil Liberties. Banks realized he too was beginning to think in words with capital letters. He preferred one of his own for the missive. Barmy – with a capital B. Despite his lowly status, and common exterior, Banks was a thoughtful man. He knew working people were still warweary and disillusioned, resentful of the new hedonism of the rich. But in a mood for revolution? Even those out of work were too close to the horrors of trench warfare and poison gas to even contemplate the violence that revolution, and street fighting would engender.

"It's daft, guv'nor."

"Of course it is, Banksie. File it with the rest of the rubbish."

Just as the sergeant went to drop the memo on the floor, the big, black telephone jangled on O'Nions's desk. The heavy-set man yanked the receiver off its cradle. Banks watched as his guv'nor spoke quietly into the mouthpiece, listened in his turn, then slowly replaced the receiver. He could see a gleam sparkling in the guv'nor's piggy eyes. Was this going to be another leap of deduction? O'Nions in fact was experiencing a revelation. But it was not one of deduction, but naked ambition.

"Here. Give me back that memo, Sergeant."

He took the thin sheet from his perplexed assistant, and scanned it more carefully this time. He suddenly realized that, if he could link the phone call to any of this Red Peril stuff (decidedly in capitals in his mind), the post of superintendent would be nothing. The sky would be the limit. His heavy brown boots clattered to the ground.

"Come on, Banksie. We're going to have a little chat with someone I know."

Albert Potter was worried. Worried and confused. It had been four days since the perturbed Junius Premadasa had burst in on him. Four days in which Albert had been unable to discover anything and now, to cap it all, Premadasa had disappeared. It was not as though at the time, the Sinhalese had exactly made clear what it was that concerned him. When Rosalind had ushered him in, Albert had at first offered a drink, but the Sinhalese had declined.

"No thank you, Potter. I do not want a drink."

Albert blushed, wondering if he had offended some religious proscription of the man's. He knew so little about Ceylon and its customs. Premadasa had until now seemed so European in his ways that Albert hardly considered him anything other than a fellow Englishman. He been to Oxford, after all. Now, he realized he didn't know the man at all well. He did know he was a member of the Communist Party, though. Maybe he could recover from the drinks embarrassment by asking Premadasa about the situation in Moscow.

"Tell me. Have you heard about the state of Comrade Lenin's health?"

It was more than a polite enquiry. Potter had actually become acquainted with a little man then calling himself Richter many years ago in London. He had been about Potter's height, and sporting a similar goatee beard. But unlike Potter, whose head was topped with a wiry thatch, Richter had already been completely bald. It had been a matter of some surprise for Albert to later identify the quiet and polite Mr Richter as the outspoken Chairman Lenin, the charismatic leader of the Soviet revolution. He knew that recently, Richter – he would always think of him as such, not as the Man of Iron – had suffered a mild stroke.

Premadasa looked no more pleased by Albert's enquiry than he had done by the offer of alcohol. His eyes narrowed, and his brow furrowed with a worried frown. His full lips pursed into a disapproving moue.

"And why would I know anything about Lenin that you can't read in the papers yourself?"

"I . . . er . . . I." Albert was nonplussed. He appeared to have put his foot in it twice in as many minutes. Maybe he should just keep his mouth shut. For a moment both men sat in silence, their heads bowed. Albert's new approach seemed to work. Suddenly, Premadasa groaned, and patted Albert on the knee.

"I'm sorry, old friend. I'm a little frazzled at the moment."

Potter noticed once again, how much Prem liked his little anglicisms. "I think I will take you up on that drink."

"Of course, what would you like?" Albert was fully prepared to play it safe and offer tea. But Premadasa pre-empted him.

"Whiskey, please. A large one."

Potter poured a generous measure, and with the drink in his hand, Premadasa became a little more emboldened.

"It was quite prescient of you to speak of . . . our mutual friend. Moscow has been figuring quite large in my thoughts recently."

"The poor man *is* ill, then."

Premadasa shook his head.

"I don't really know, old man. And even if he were dead, the Comintern wouldn't tell us. No, it's a more pressing matter than the state of one man's health." He hesitated, unsure what to say next. Then he managed to marshal his thoughts. "But closer to home, you might say."

"Home." Albert meant it as a question, but Premadasa clearly took the comment as an affirmation of Potter's understanding. A big tear squeezed itself from his big brown eyes, and he nodded eagerly.

"Yes. I knew you would understand. You know how the land lies at present. But it's entirely unfair of them to make such demands. You do follow my meaning."

Albert nodded sagely, wishing he had the first idea what the other man was referring to. He was beginning to frame a polite question that would not reveal the full depth of his ignorance, when Premadasa suddenly rose, and held out his hand. Bewildered, Albert got up from the sofa too, and took the proffered appendage.

"Excellent," said Premadasa, a smile lighting up his formerly clouded features. He sort of squinted with one eye in a grotesque manner, and Albert realised he was essaying a complicit wink. "Now you will pass on my concerns to that friend of yours."

"Friend."

Once more, Albert fell into the trap.

"That's right. That friend of yours. The one with the funny name. Tell him what I have said, but please . . ."

"Yes?" Now Albert was utterly lost. As lost in a fog as he had been that time in the Alps, when he nearly fell off the edge of the glacier near Zermatt.

"Please. No mention of my name. It could prove fatal."

With that, Junius Premadasa had turned on his heels and exited the room, leaving Potter with a puzzle and an untouched glass of his best whiskey. He watched at the window as Premadasa climbed into the driving seat of his car, and sped off. Potter was surprised that Thambyah, his constant manservant, wasn't there to drive Junius. He had followed his master all the way from Ceylon. Premadasa must have really wanted to keep his visit secret.

Now, four days on, he was still none the wiser. But at last he had decided to take some action. It had taken nearly that long for Albert to work out to whom Premadasa was referring when he mentioned the friend "with the funny name".

"Darling, Mr O'Nions is here."

Albert Potter was abruptly brought back to the present by the mellifluous tones of Rosalind. Who still had not explained her doom-laden utterance of four days earlier to him. That morning of Premadasa's arrival, and subsequent sudden disappearance. Why had Albert not seen immediately that he had meant O'Nions? Well, he was here now. But what was it that he was to tell the superintendent? Before he could properly marshal his thoughts though, the man himself entered Albert's study.

It had been a number of years since the two men had met, and Albert saw that the passage of time had not been kind to O'Nions. His face had become bloated and florid, and his hair, once the brown bowler was removed, appeared to have fled his brow. The obvious weight he had put on his girth – the result of too many Sunday roasts at home, no doubt – pressed down on his fallen arches. And as the man strode into the room, his hand outstretched, Albert noted a heavy gait where before the man had been nimble on his pins. He also took in the familiar brown boots, and surmised that O'Nions's elevation to Superintendent had not improved his sartorial choices any. He still had a presence, however, and as he shook the man's hand, Albert almost missed the quiet, intense little man who dogged his master's heels. Until O'Nions introduced him.

"This is Sergeant Banks, Mr Potter. Banks, this is Mr Albert Potter. He's . . ."

"A member of the Fabian Society, and a Labour MP, sir."

Albert smiled modestly. It was so invigorating to be recognized, especially by Special Branch. It made him feel a desperate character. O'Nions quickly shattered his cherished assumptions.

"Of course. You would know him." He turned to Albert again. "Bolshie Banks, we call him in the Force. On account of his leftish leanings."

Albert could see the sergeant stifle a grimace. Whatever sort of joke his boss made of his politics, Banks clearly took them seriously. Unusual for someone in Special Branch. Albert shook his firm, callused hand, and was about to enquire of the man's leanings, when O'Nions interrupted.

"Potter, you said you needed my help."

"Yes, Superintendent. I have a request to make of you. But I don't quite know if any of what I have to say will make sense." He was thinking of Premadasa's cryptic remarks, wondering how to express them. "I have a . . . friend, who shall remain nameless. He feels the government needs to be aware of, shall we say, unpleasant moves afoot in his world that . . ."

O'Nions cut across Albert's hesitancy.

"You're talking about some gang of ex-officers and homosexuals in the army and navy, sprinkled with some undergraduates at Oxford and Cambridge, no doubt. Wetting themselves at some new orders from Moscow."

Albert Potter winced at the detective's forthrightness. He glanced at the man's sergeant, looking for sympathy. There was none on offer.

"Parlour Bolsheviks, we call 'em, sir." It was Banks's hard response that shocked Albert most. He had thought Banks more sympathetic. Discomfited by both men's frosty faces, he felt himself between a rock and a hard place. Surprisingly, O'Nions features reformed themselves into a smile. A venal leer of a smile, but a smile nevertheless.

"I think we are in a position to help each other, Mr Potter."

"Oh? How is that, O'Nions?" Albert wasn't sure whether he should feel relief or concern at O'Nions's oily come-on. On balance, he thought concern.

*　　*　　*

The Grapes was a pub for hard-drinking men and loose women, and Harry Rothstein found the atmosphere intoxicating. Without even taking a drink. He loved the place, and the people who frequented it. His people. He looked round the smoke-laden bar at the faces surrounding him. The men he saw were young, but already bore the lined faces of people made old before their time by war and unemployment. The rosy faces of the women were painted on, and hardly hid their pinched nature, caused by the vicissitudes of their trade and their hard, fast life. Of course, respectable women would not be seen dead on their own in a public house. So it was obvious what these women were up to. Not that Harry Rothstein condemned them, drinking and smoking and laughing edgily with their potential clients. He himself was a whore to Moscow, wasn't he? Taking money from an increasingly impoverished Bolshevik government, while pretending to pleasure their desires. And he couldn't stop. Their money paid for his weakness. The recordings he bought, and played in private on the portable gramophone in his solitary lodgings.

He had become fascinated by the new sound of jazz when he had heard the music of the Original Dixieland Jazz Band. The live music had filtered through to the hot, stinking kitchens of the club where he had worked washing dishes as a boy. Its sweet abandon stirred something in his youthful heart. The other workers called it rubbish, the stuff the toffs cavorted to. So he had kept his decadent enthusiasm to himself. Over the years, as his collection grew, so did his scholarly interest in the music. But he never lost the sense of excitement when he played the precious shellac to himself.

A burst of harsh laughter from a group of men in the corner of the bar broke into his reverie. Suddenly he saw everything around him differently. All he could see now was a mood of desperate determination. As though everyone was clamouring to beat the greyness of their lives, if only for a brief moment. He took another pull at his pint, and patted the left breast pocket of his jacket. The letter in his inside pocket felt like a heavy weight against his chest. He knew he would have to do something about it. But first he had a meeting with a new recruit.

He had been surprised to get a message about him from Albert Potter of all people. Potter was Labour, and the Labour

Party was going respectable. It didn't approve of the Communist Party any more. But he was prepared to see the man for Potter's, and old times' sake.

Right on cue, a small, neat man slipped through the heavy, brass-handled doors of the pub, and looked cautiously around. His clothes were clean, if a little worn round the edges, and he wore a black bowler squared soldier-like on his head. A tattered copy of a newspaper stuck up from his right-hand jacket pocket. He crossed over to the bar, and examined the coins in his pocket carefully before ordering a drink. He was obviously out of work. Harry watched for a while, and marvelled how inconspicuous the man seemed. He just blended into the background. Just the sort of man he needed, as long as he measured up. Harry wormed his way through the noisy throng, and squeezed in beside the newcomer at the bar. The man was sipping at his pint. Harry waved his empty pint glass in the air, and got a refill. He turned to his target.

"Can I see your paper, chum?"

"Sure." The man pulled out his copy of the *Daily Herald* and passed it to Harry. "If you like your news straight from Moscow."

Harry chuckled. The Establishment saw the *Herald* as the cats-paw of the Reds. "What other sort of news is there?"

Sergeant Banks stuck out his callused hand. "John Banks. You must be Harry Rothstein."

Banks was surprised how easy it was to get into Harry Rothstein's offices. He could have walked in off the street, and would have been welcomed with open arms. The nerve centre of the Communist movement in this part of London was nothing more than a small, dingy shop-front in the East End. Old advertising boards filled the walls, curling slowly into oblivion. The scarred mahogany counter still stood in place, and a cheerful young girl with auburn curls sat behind it. She was bashing the keys of an old typewriter that, from her muted curses, was proving an uncooperative agent. Pamphlets were strewn across the rest of the counter. There was clearly no intention to hide any seditious material.

"Hello, Amy. I'm just taking this gentleman into the back for a chat."

Banks strode up the counter, and stretched a friendly hand across its surface towards the girl. "John Banks."

"Amy Clark." The girl clasped his hand, returning his frank look. Then she returned to her battle with the ancient machine. Not only was the literature openly available, so were the names of the staff apparently. Rothstein raised a flap at the end of the counter, and held it open for Banks.

"This way."

As Banks passed under the raised flap, he saw a large framed photograph of a familiar face in the corner of the shop. On a shelf below were laid out some cheaply bound books with lurid red titles inscribed on them. Banks could see the titles included "Where to Begin", "Tasks of the Revolution", and "What are our Masters thinking about?". Seeing what the new recruit was staring at, Rothstein felt a little embarrassed. The instruction from Moscow recently had been to institute "Lenin Corners" in their office. When completed, he had stood back, thinking it would only need a few candles to distinctly resemble a shrine to that other famous bearded man. The one with the bleeding heart. It made him feel uncomfortable. Banks could see Rothstein's unease and, saying nothing, followed him through to the back of the shop.

Rothstein's office was a clutter of papers, pamphlets and books. They were piled everywhere, including the only desk and on both of the two chairs in the tiny room. Rothstein hurried to shift papers from one of the chairs, making new drifts of revolutionary didactic in the process. Banks reckoned his boss BT ought to see the room for himself. If the Revolution was being organized from here, then he might change his mind about the Red Peril. An old safe, the green paint peeling from its sides, stood in one corner. A Victor. Opening it would present no problem to Banks. But then, if it was names Special Branch wanted, it wouldn't take too much effort. Banks could see stacked on the shelf behind Rothstein's head a set of battered wooden drawers labelled 'Members' and with letters on each drawer. But Banks had a specific job to do, and it didn't involve rocking the boat. He was here to find out what had scared Potter's anonymous friend.

Rothstein settled in the creaky chair behind the desk, motioning Banks to the other.

"So, you're an ex-serviceman, then."

Banks grinned self-consciously. "Is it that obvious?"

"From your manner, and the set of your hat, I would say so."

Banks fiddled with the brim of his bowler, now cradled in his lap. He wanted Rothstein to get comfortable with him, let him feel he knew him. Banks had long ago found he had a knack of making people think he was deferring to them. An outward show of deference had kept him out of trouble in the army, and in the police force. His only outward expression of his true feelings – supporting the Police Strike – had brought him trouble in triplicate. It had earned him a nickname, got him into trouble, and also in debt to his guv'nor at one fell swoop. Constraint was his watchword now. And with Harry Rothstein his diffidence paid off again.

It was not long before the man took him for granted, and talked openly in his presence. Within a couple of days he was a fixture in the shop. And on flirting terms with Amy Clark.

"If things were different, I would be asking you out, Amy Clark. Unless, that is, you and Mr Rothstein are . . . ?"

Amy smiled gently, and blushed. "Mr Rothstein has other . . . interests, Mr Banks. If what were different?"

"If I had a job. No, when I have a job. And it's John, by the way."

Amy blushed and continued pounding the typewriter keys. "The railways are just not taking anyone on, Mr B . . . John. I understand that."

His "cover" story was that he was a railwayman, unemployable because he was a Trades Unionist. Amy was being kind to him, saying there were no jobs available. He moved closer to her, rearranging the piles of pamphlets on the shop counter. It was a quiet evening, and Harry had dropped in on his way from work earlier to check if there were any messages. There weren't, and he was glad to be persuaded to leave it for one night. It provided Banks with an opportunity to poke around, and ask Amy some questions.

"Harry works in the building trade, doesn't he?"

"Oh yes. He's started working on those new buildings that are going up to house the Empire Exhibition next year."

"At Wembley?"

"Yes." Amy sounded really proud that Rothstein was involved with the construction of the new-fangled exhibition halls fashioned from tons of concrete. The fact that they were being built to bolster up the fading notion of Empire, seemed not to have occurred to her. Banks could see the naïve enthusiasm of the girl would not stretch to perceiving the conflict in it for a member of the Communist Party. But he wondered why Rothstein should agree to be involved in such a piece of pointless make-work for unemployed servicemen. He was about to dig deeper, when the bell on the shop door rang, and two men walked in.

One was wearing a blue serge suit with a waistcoat and a cap on his head. In his hand he gripped a wooden walking stick by the shaft. So Banks could see that the handle was of cheap metal, in the form of a dog's head. The other man, a little younger, wore a shabby grey suit and a trilby hat. Banks would have gauged the older man's age to be around twenty-seven or twenty-eight. The one in the grey suit looked a little nervous at the sight of Banks, whom he clearly did not expect to be in the shop. The other man, however, put on a jaunty air, and swaggered into the centre of the shop floor. He was still gripping his stick as though it were a cudgel.

"Hello, Amy. Is Rothstein in the back, then?"

He had a slight accent, a colonial twang that Banks couldn't quite place.

Amy looked hesitant. "I'm sorry, you've just missed him. He's gone home."

"Then we'll see him tomorrow evening. At the Grapes. Will you tell him?"

He stared, not at Amy, but straight at Banks as he spoke. Daring him to get involved. In any other situation, the policeman would have been pleased to pull him in. But the strong arm of the law was not what was required here, and Banks dropped his gaze with a slight shrug of his shoulder. None of my business, it said. When the door had slammed behind the two men, he looked across at Amy. She let out a sigh, almost as if she had not breathed since the men had entered.

"Who were they?" he asked. She frowned, as if embarrassed for witnessing Banks's own humiliation. Or for his obvious curiosity.

"Mr Marsh, and Mr Brown. Brown's the one with the stick. They're new recruits, but I not sure about them. I do know Harry seems a bit cagey when they are around. I'm glad he wasn't here tonight. I don't like them"

"William Thomas Marsh and Jack Alfred Brown," averred O'Nions, shuffling through the slim files on his desk. "Both ex-servicemen, both drawing their twenty-nine shillings' dole. Brown's South African, and served with the South African Heavy Artillery until his discharge in 1917."

"Which explains the accent." Banks silently rebuked himself for not recognizing it in the first place.

"Marsh was in the Navy. Dismissed the service in 1920. Nothing suspicious about Brown, except for petty pilfering. In fact, I wouldn't have put either down as revolutionaries on the evidence of their police files. Forget about them."

Banks nodded, but reserved judgement. In 1919, there had been evidence of Soviet incitement of sailors to go on strike and seize British ports. Of course, it had all been nonsense, and nothing had happened. But Marsh had been drummed out of the Navy the following year. In his business it didn't pay to be too sceptical. However, he moved on to more significant matters.

"There is the letter. That could be what got Potter's friend all skittish."

"What letter's that? Who from?" O'Nions was a little annoyed that his sergeant had been holding back information.

"Amy Clark told me about it. It was delivered by hand about a week ago. Rothstein's hardly let it out of his sight ever since. Apparently, he read it in his office, and emerged as white as a sheet. Amy thought it might have been bad news about Comrade Lenin."

O'Nions shot Banks a black look, irritated by his use of the Bolshie epithet.

"I'm just reporting what she said, guv'nor." Banks went on, determined to have a dig at his boss. "But it wasn't. About *Comrade* Lenin, that is."

"What was it about, then?" grumbled O'Nions. Even though he knew Banks was deliberately needling him, getting back in what small way the sergeant could for his hold over him, he remained calm. He needed Banks's undercover skills more than the sergeant realized. He needed him to find this letter.

"I don't know, and nor does Amy."

"Then you better get back to your little lady-friend, and get your hands on it." O'Nions leered. "The letter, that is. Meanwhile, I will talk to Mr Potter. See if I can winkle out his friend's name from him."

Tommy Fields looked at the end of his tether. Harry couldn't believe it. The man was due to play in a Cup Final soon, and he was downing drinks like there was no tomorrow. Harry conveniently forgot how many pints he had drunk to drown his own problems.

"What's the matter with you, Tommy? Can't you see people are looking? They know who you are. If it gets back to Mr King that his shining example of the finest aspect of the people's game, his well-honed athlete, is no more than a falling-down drunk, you'll be off the team."

Tommy drained the dregs of the pint glass in front of him, and lit another cigarette. A sneer painted itself on his bleary features.

"Harry 'All-men-are-equal' Rothstein, just listen to him. He can quote the Communist Manifesto till it comes out of his arse, but he still calls the bosses Mister. You might as well be touching your forelock at the same time. If *Mister* King wants me out of the side, then that's that."

Harry's face flushed at the footballer's scornful comments. He had always thought Tommy was a fellow socialist at heart. He'd even thought to ask him to help set up a football side to tour the Soviet Union. That would really have got him in well with Moscow. Maybe after this business was all over. At the moment, he felt like pushing his fist in the man's red and bloated face. But he was a patient, loving man, was Harry Rothstein. And besides, he needed Tommy.

"Of course you must be in the side. Otherwise how can you help me? Anyway, you're the best winger I've seen in years. Ted Vizard's got nothing on you."

The mention of Bolton Wanderer's outside-left seemed to rouse Fields from his morose demeanour. He narrowed his bleary eyes, and leaned closer to Rothstein.

"Tell me how important I am again . . ."

"Sorry, mate." Rothstein's mood suddenly changed. "Gotta go and have a pee. Tell you about it later."

He slid out from behind the heavy table, and began elbowing his way to the lavatories. Tommy stared gloomily at his empty glass, as his friend made his way through the crowded, smoke-filled bar. A man in a worn, blue serge suit stepped over his outstretched feet on his way to the rear door. The stick he clutched in his hand smacked against Fields's ankle, but the footballer was too far gone to care. A pinched-faced man in a grey suit sat down beside the footballer, and gave him a friendly pat on the shoulder. Neither saw the slim, unassuming man with the bowler hat set square on his head step carefully past also going towards the lavatories.

"I am beginning to sniff out a Communist conspiracy here, Potter."

Albert Potter, seated opposite O'Nions in the latter's office, could not help himself. He smiled involuntarily, squinted through his pince-nez spectacles at the Special Branch man, and then allowed the guffaw welling up in his chest to burst forth. O'Nions's face turned a dangerous shade of puce at the laughter, and Albert realized he was not joking. Suppressing the continuing urge to titter, he shook his head in disbelief. He had heard of the Head of the CID's obsession with the Red Peril, but had not realized it had infected the pedestrian mind of the Superintendent too.

"Really, Superintendent. You must see that the British Communist Party is nothing more than a bunch of well-intentioned radicals on the one hand, and airy-fairy intellectuals on the other. The first lot are so pig-headed they'll never do as Moscow tells them. And the second – well, you said so yourself – they're Parlour Bolsheviks. Quite harmless."

He sat upright in the hard chair O'Nions had placed him in, wishing he hadn't agreed to meet the man on his home ground. The back of the chair pressed uncomfortably into his spine, and he felt he was under interrogation.

O'Nions leaned closer, his ham fists splayed out on the surface of his desk. This was not what he wanted to hear. He would have to play his trump card.

"Are you saying Junius Premadasa is harmless? That speech he made in Hyde Park recently was downright seditious. Pity the Defence of the Realm Act has lapsed. During the War, I could have had him picked up from the street, and imprisoned before the day was over."

"How did you . . . ? When did you hear . . . ?" Albert Potter paled, and sank in his uncomfortable seat. He thought Junius's friends had managed to keep his little indiscretion secret. Precious few had heard him on his soap-box anyway. It now seemed news had got to Special Branch. He wondered who else had got wind of the speech. And how did O'Nions know that the unnamed friend he had referred to at the beginning of this business had been Premadasa?

The truth was, O'Nions hadn't known. But the fact that Junius Premadasa, MP and prominent member of the British Communist Party, had not been seen for several days in his usual haunts, had made him a prime candidate. He was the Parlour Bolshevik of all Parlour Bolsheviks. O'Nions leaned back in his chair, and positively basked in his own reflected glory. His little trick had worked. Potter had confirmed his suspicion.

"Good job he's done a bunk, Potter. Otherwise, I might have been inclined to pull him in for a little talk anyway." O'Nions focused his beady little eyes on Potter, causing beads of sweat to prickle on his forehead. "You don't know where he is, do you?"

Albert gulped, and shook his head. Why did O'Nions have this uncanny knack of making you feel you were lying to him, even when you weren't?

"That's a shame, Potter, but maybe you could ask around. It might be safer for him if he were in protective custody. There's some nasty customers out there, you know."

Banks stood at the urinal contemplating the pattern on the ornate green tiles in front of his face. He relieved himself of the beer he had had to consume while observing Rothstein's meeting with the well-built man he hadn't immediately recognized as Tommy Fields. It was the red, bloated face that had put him off. The man had obviously been drinking even before his session with Harry Rothstein. But the blond quiff had been familiar, and it was not long before Banks had placed it. West

Ham was his team, after all, and a blurry photograph of Fields had been in the local paper when he had signed on for the Hammers. What was the man doing looking so out of sorts with only days to go to the Cup Final? It was just at that juncture that Rothstein had rocketed out of his seat and made a dash for the lavatories. Banks had made his move, and had almost bumped into someone. He immediately identified the man with the walking stick as the South African Brown. He was also making a beeline for the lavatories. Banks gave it a few seconds, and followed.

Peering cautiously round the door of the urinals, he was surprised to find neither Rothstein nor Brown there. He was walking down the row of toilet cubicles pushing on doors, however, when a figure emerged from the last one. It was Brown, who rushed past him without showing any signs of recognition. Banks told himself that Brown's presence was just a coincidence. Except for one thing. There was no flushing sound from the end cubicle from which Brown had emerged. What had he been up to? With his own bladder bursting, he unbuttoned, and contemplated the matter of Rothstein's disappearance. It wasn't too difficult to engineer. The lavatories were outside the back of the pub, and it was easy to clamber over the wall in the yard, and disappear down the alley into the darkness. Had he been meeting Brown, or escaping him?

And where did Fields fit in to this? Banks suddenly thought of the Wembley site where Rothstein worked, and the great stadium where the Cup Final would shortly be played for the first time. With Fields in the West Ham team. He buttoned up, and hurried out of the lavatories. Maybe he could learn something by having a word with Tommy Fields. He pushed his way back through the growing crowd in the public bar to where Fields had been sitting. But Fields had disappeared too. And by the look of the upended glasses on the table still dribbling beer across its surface, he had gone either in a hurry, or by force.

Sunday evening, 22 April 1923.
The British Empire Exhibition site

By now the British Empire site had taken on an other-worldly appearance. A borrowed arc light glaringly illuminated the hole in the ground with a stark white light. Equally impenetrable shadows contrasted with the brightness wherever the lamp failed to shine. Two elongated shadows hovered against the wall of the west tower like wingless angels. Superintendent O'Nions and Sergeant Banks peered into the pit, where the pathologist was about his gory business.

"If you hadn't kept losing all the bloody suspects, Sergeant Banks, we might know whose body this was!"

Banks could see the sweat running down O'Nions's florid face. The man was yanking at the stiff, old-fashioned collar he had taken to wearing since his elevation to Superintendent. Poking his fat fingers in between collar and flesh, attempting to relieve the pressure. Banks still favoured a soft-collared shirt, though he was still obliged to wear a tie. The weather had turned sultry, almost tropical, but officers were still expected to dress respectably. His guv'nor's collar looked as though it was tightening round his fleshy neck, strangling him. Either that, or O'Nions was visibly swelling in front of his eyes. Too many undisturbed Sunday roasts, and too much sitting on his fat arse in the office, probably. Banks was glad he still worked out in the streets. He was glad, too, that he was well removed from the obsessions of the higher ranks. He preferred having O'Nions between him and BT's obsession with the Red Peril.

The trouble was that O'Nions knew he was not dealing with the pressure from above very well. He needed results to please BT, and just when he wanted them most, all the prime movers had gone to ground.

"With so much damage to the body, how are we going to know if it's Rothstein, Fields or Premadasa we have down there."

"Or some tramp, guv'nor."

O'Nions snorted in derision at the sergeant's remark.

"Who accidentally cut off his own head and hands, before setting himself alight?"

"I can maybe answer your question, Superintendent."

The voice drifted up from down in the pit.

"What's that, doctor?" O'Nions was sceptical that, if he couldn't work out whose body it was, then some bloody pathologist would have no chance. He was confounded by the reply.

"The body. Would it help to know that he wasn't English. From the skin colour – where he isn't burned, that is – I would say he was from the sub-continent. Indian, perhaps. Or Sinhalese."

O'Nions face coloured at the pointed nature of the doctor's retort. He turned away into the darkness.

"That settles it, then. Rothstein or Fields must have done Premadasa in because he spoke to Potter. You'd better find that letter."

"But guv, if I lift it, Rothstein's going to know who took it. Then I won't be incognito, and able to hang around him any more."

O'Nions nearly blew his top. "As far as we know, Rothstein doing a bunk probably means you are no longer incog-bloody-nito. And if you don't get your hands on that letter, there's precious little point in you hanging around anyway. Unless you fancy getting little Amy in the family way."

Banks tried hard to meet O'Nions's leer with a cold stare. It was the best he could do, because his guv'nor had read all the way to his very soul as usual. Banks was sweet on Amy Clark, Bolshie politics notwithstanding.

"So, get out there with some real coppers. Turn the place over, and find that letter."

Banks shuffled his feet, but could think of no excuse to avoid what his boss had commanded. "Yes, guv."

O'Nions let his sergeant leave the scene of the crime, before adding his own gloss on the command. "And if you can't find it, I'll have to bloody fake it!"

The room where Harry Rothstein had gone to ground was grey. Grey walls, bare, grey floorboards, grey mattress on the rickety bed. The bed-bugs on the mattress were probably grey as well. Harry imagined that in this dingy part of London, by the docks, nothing much had changed since Victorian times. For sure, the single cold water tap out in the back yard, shared by several inhabitants of the tenement, had been placed there when the old Queen was on the throne. Then, it had been a new and hygienic amenity. Now, it spoke volumes about the crumbling Empire she had ruled over, and how much of it still lingered on at home. A country fit for heroes to live in? Come the Revolution, maybe.

He smiled at his own foolishness, and sank wearily on the damp, stained mattress.

Going to earth sounded an appropriate definition of his actions in the circumstances. The dingy hovel he had rented was located in a warren of back-to-back houses crumbling down towards the chaos from which they had grown. The maze of streets would be bewildering to the outsider. Through their narrow confines scuttled little grey-faced creatures that hardly resembled Rothstein's fellow men. A forgotten underclass who rooted for their sustenance from amidst the detritus of others. It was the fear of all working men that they could tumble back into this hellish pit at any time.

"That's what separates me from you, Mr Premadasa," muttered Rothstein to himself, as he fumbled for his cigarettes. "You might spout the language, but when your back's against the wall, there's always a bolt-hole for the likes of you. What can I fall back on? A bloody great hole."

He looked around the room at the peeling wallpaper, and the threadbare curtains that, when drawn, failed even to cut out the yellowish flicker of light from the gas-lamp outside in the street. He struck a match, and lit his cigarette, inhaling the smoke deep into his lungs. He couldn't waste his time worrying about Junius Premadasa. But as for Tommy Fields, that was another matter altogether. He was relying on his friend, and all that held them together was Tommy's little weakness.

Rothstein prised open the cap on the bottle of beer he had bought, and took a swig straight from the neck. He belched as the fizzy brew hit his stomach. He normally didn't like drinking bottled beer – it left a sour taste in his throat. But he wasn't going to risk being seen in his usual haunts for the sake of a pint of draught. He did miss his old, scratchy portable gramophone though. What he wouldn't give for the sound of the ODJB playing *Tiger Rag* right now. He conjured the sound in his head, and capered round the shabby confines of the room, imitating the fruity trombone glissando.

"Hold that tiger . . . brrrrm, hold that tiger . . . brrrm, hold that tiger . . ."

He stopped suddenly, and stood stock still, his heart pounding. He was sure he had heard something. He heard it again. A scratching, rustling sound from outside his door. He laughed.

"Pull yourself together, Harry boy. In a place like this, if it isn't the mice it's the cockroaches." He took another pull on his bottle of beer, and essayed another little caper. He waved a finger in the air in imitation of the dance moves of the smart set he had seen on the silver screen. "Hold that cockroach . . . brrrrm . . ."

Rothstein sucked deeply on the stub of his cigarette, and stubbed it out on the cracked saucer on the floor beside his bed. He breathed the blue smoke out through his nostrils, contemplating his options. He knew what he should do, but didn't know yet whether he could. Only time would tell. But that didn't prevent the feeling of dread, and of guilt, that permeated to his very soul. He reached out for the packet of cigarettes. There was a scratching at his door, and he rolled off the bed.

O'Nions could scarcely contain his excitement. He now had some evidence to show BT that would have the old man licking his lips. He held the letter in his trembling fingers, and scanned it once again.

Instructions to British Communist Party

Executive Committee,
VERY SECRET
Third Communist International.
Presidium.
29 March.
To the Central Committee,
British Communist Party.
Moscow.
Dear Comrades,

"Dear Comrades," he murmured. The phrases rolled off his wet lips like plump sturgeon giving up their roe. "It is indispensable to stir up the masses of the British proletariat . . . a successful rising . . . to count upon the complete success of an armed insurrection."

He sat back in his chair, and plonked his boots on the battle-scarred edge of his desk. This letter, linked to Rothstein, along with Premadasa's seditious speech in Hyde Park would give him sufficient ammunition to convince his boss of a plot, which was aiming to reach its culmination soon. The problem was, he needed to come up with a target. He had some ideas on that, but he wasn't about to tell Banks. Let the sergeant run around chasing shadows. This would be his own personal triumph.

The gambling club hadn't changed much in forty years. Since the day that Billy Orwell had invested the proceeds of his prize-fighting days into the shabby building in the East End that had become his goldmine. Downstairs you could first dance with cheap women, and then upstairs, the rolling chemin de fer tables would conclude your expensive night. As many as sixty men were playing at any one time including shop-keepers, artisans, and gentlemen fond of slumming. And if your gambling desires were not sated, there was always the tape machine relaying racing information right into the premises. Old Billy still presided over this empire, his aging and battered features, crudely rearranged by other fighters' bare fists, beaming over his customers' eagerness to part with their hard-earned cash.

John Banks sidled up to the narrow door in the alley wall that suggested nothing of the pleasures that lay within. But Orwell's club did not need to advertise to draw in the gambling addict from the working classes. Indeed, the very opposite was the case. The exterior was so modest as to be downright invisible. Those who needed to, knew where to go. And how to gain access.

Banks tapped on the Judas-slitted door, which slid back revealing a pair of suspicious eyes. It was his informant, a former pugilist called Attey.

"Is he still here?"

Jack Attey worked for Orwell, but was in debt to Banks for being kept out of jail over the little matter of beating up a prostitute. He had been the first to respond when Banks put the word out about the names involved in the case. The pug-faced man nodded nervously, and quickly opened the door to let the policeman in. Banks slid past Attey, and made for the stairs up to the gaming room. He declined the offer of services from a heavily-scented blonde girl who hung around the landing, and strolled inconspicuously into the smoky fug of the chemmy tables. It took him a while to spot his quarry, but eventually he saw him. Tommy Fields was staring disconsolately as a pile of money was raked away from in front of him. Banks eased into the seat beside Fields, resting a firm hand on his shoulder.

"Can I buy you a drink, Tommy?"

Fields turned his dulled eyes on to the inconspicuous, little man at his side. The last thing he wanted was some eager football fanatic at his shoulder.

"Do I know you?"

"Does it matter? You need a drink, and I'm offering one."

Fields shrugged, and acquiesced to the man's offer. He was all done in, despite his physique. Banks thought he looked defeated. He pulled the day's *Daily Herald* out of his pocket.

"You're not in the team, then."

Fields scanned the West Ham team named for tomorrow's Cup Final. Hufton, Henderson, Young, Bishop, Kay, Tresadern, Richards, Brown, Watson, Moore, Ruffell.

"It doesn't look like it, does it?"

The card game continued around them as Banks whispered in the footballer's ear. "It could be worse."

"How?"

"You could be in jail."

Crowds of men were already beginning to pour out of the Metropolitan Railway station at Wembley Park, and it was only morning. The Cup Final between West Ham and Bolton Wanderers was four hours off. It was a similar situation at the Great Central Railway station at Wembley Hill, and Wembley station on the London and North Western Railway line. The site of the Empire Exhibition was witnessing a steady stream of capped and raincoated figures making their way towards the new stadium. To Albert Potter, standing at one of the upper window of the stand, it resembled a busy line of worker ants scuttling inexorably towards their target. The two white towers of the stadium sparkled in the late morning sunlight. From behind Potter, Sir Charles Clegg, President of the Football Association, tremulously voiced everyone's concerns.

"Does this look like a crowd of fifty thousand to you?"

That had been the attendance at the last Cup Final at Stamford Bridge.

"Don't worry, Sir Charles," said Potter confidently. He was

a board member of British Empire Exhibition Inc, and felt the
need to reassure the FA Committee members standing around
him in their plush overcoats and bowler hats. In fact he was
more than a little worried himself. But that was because Superintendent O'Nions had asked to see him on site in a few minutes
time. "We had a full infantry battalion marking time on the
terraces yesterday. They're as solid as a rock. Besides we can
accommodate over one hundred and twenty thousand."

Relieved, the committee members chuckled through their
luxuriant white moustaches. A hundred and twenty thousand.
Such a large figure for the Cup Final was inconceivable. Potter
slipped out the room, and left the gentlemen to their refreshments. In the long concrete corridors below the stand, his
footfall echoed hollowly. They were windowless and lit only
by electric light. He turned a corner, and at the farthest end of
the long corridor that ran the length of the stand, he could make
out two figures. As he approached, the larger one resolved into
O'Nions. He was pacing agitatedly up and down under the full
glare of a lamp. Beside him, slightly in shadow, stood the slim,
impassive figure of Sergeant Banks. His face gave nothing away.

"Ah, Mr Potter, good. The King is not due until two o'clock.
So we have time to conclude this matter. Banks tells me he has
arranged for Fields to do as he was instructed, and leave the
outer door to the changing rooms open. Rothstein is no doubt
going to slip in that way and carry out his plans."

"You don't really think that Harry intends to kill the King,
do you?" Potter was shocked at O'Nions's interpretation of
Harry Rothstein's intentions. He could imagine Harry trying to
harangue the crowd, to appeal to their working class sentiments,
to boo and hiss the King like some music-hall villain. That
degree of protest he thought Harry quite capable of. But
murder? Never.

O'Nions shook his head at Potter's naivety. "I have seen the
instructions from Moscow. There can be no doubt what Premadasa and Rothstein planned."

"And the steam shovel?" This was Banks, daring to question
his own boss in front of Potter. "Fields told me that Rothstein
planned to use the steam shovel from the building site for
something. What's he going to do? Brain the King with it?"

O'Nions face went puce at such impertinence. His future

career depended on his handling of this affair, and he wasn't going to let a Bolshie police sergeant interfere. He wished he had left Banks hanging out to dry during the Police Strike. Once a Red always a Red. Shame, he would have made a good policeman. Through gritted teeth, he told Banks to go and check on the uniformed police allocated to the King's protection. There were five hundred constables on site, and most of them were on that detail. Banks shrugged, and disappeared round the corner. Potter was left dealing with an embarrassing silence. He tried to break the ice.

"I could have done with some of those constables on the exhibition site today. We have been taking delivery of some exhibits for the Ceylon Pavilion. A bit early, but they had to come all the way by sea, and better they arrived early than late. That's what I say. Nevertheless, it's a headache, when you realize their value . . ."

He knew he was burbling, and O'Nions was paying him no attention. He decided to leave the superintendent to his plotting.

"I'll just go and see how . . ."

Potter followed Banks down past the players' changing rooms, and out on to the approach road to the new stadium. After the hollow silence of the concrete underworld, the noise and bustle outside assailed his senses. The crowds were even larger now, thousands of men milling around like a human whirlpool. And he was in danger of being sucked in. His head spun, and he almost pitched over. A strong hand grasped his upper arm, and pulled him to one side. It was the hand of Sergeant Banks.

"There's going to be a lot of people here today, Mr Potter. And the police aren't going to be of much use."

They watched as the press of people at the back of the crowd forced those at the front closer to the turnstiles. There was a trickle feeding through each turnstile, but the crowd outside was like a river in spate. Already some men were clambering over one turnstile gate simply to escape the suffocating pressure. The man at the turnstile was helpless.

"How are we going to spot Rothstein in amongst all these people?" groaned Potter.

"Do you really think he's going to sneak in and kill the King?"

"Don't you, Sergeant Banks?"

"I don't know, Mr Potter. But what I do know is that the guv'nor is basing everything he's got on two things. What Tommy Fields told me, and that letter. The problem is, I don't know where he got the letter from."

Potter looked confused. "Didn't he tell me that you found out about the letter?"

"Yes, I did. But I never managed to lay my hands on it." Banks gloomily contemplated the moment when he burst into the shop in the East End with two uniformed constables in tow. Amy Clark had looked shocked at first, then had fixed Banks with a censorious stare. He could see the disappointment in her eyes, as he went through the shop and office with a fine tooth comb. For the first time, he felt shabby doing the job he loved.

"The thing was, there was no letter there."

The two men watched on helplessly as the tide of men surged through the broken turnstile. Two policemen appeared round the edge of the crowd, and tried to restore some sense of order. It was like trying to bail out the North Sea with a bucket.

"But the fact is, it did exist." Potter still could not believe that O'Nions had faked evidence. "And there is still a danger to the King. Though how any assassin is going to make his way through this . . . mob . . . I don't know." He sighed. "To think I came here today as a diversion from my troubles at home. You see Rosalind . . ."

Banks suddenly turned to face Potter, a gleam in his eyes. "Did I hear you say as I left just now, that there was going to be a delivery of some exhibits to one of the pavilions today?"

"Yes. A consignment of pearls to the Ceylon Pavilion. If the van is able to get through this crowd. Quite valuable too, I understand. "

"How valuable?"

"They are insured for a million pounds."

"A million . . . Come on."

"Where?"

Banks was already pulling out his warrant card and flashing it at the two overwhelmed constables, who looked glad to be given other orders. The sergeant looked over his shoulder at Potter.

"The Ceylon Pavilion. It's just as you said. This assassination plot is Red Peril scare nonsense. It's just a sideshow."

Potter was beginning to understand, but Banks still spelled it out.

"A diversion."

The speech-making in the Chamber of the House of Commons was dulling Potter's senses. The debate on the debacle at the Wembley Stadium when over two hundred thousand people turned up, and nearly kyboshed the whole match, droned on incessantly. Only Potter knew that the real excitement had been witnessed by only a handful of people, and had taken place way across the site at the Ceylon Pavilion.

Potter had been soon left behind by the younger, fitter Banks and his two constables. They disappeared from sight, but he trotted on past one of the unfinished constructions that was to be India's Pavilion. The building was made of steel and fibrous plaster and was already flanked with minarets hundred feet high. In front of the pavilion was a sunken courtyard surrounded by an open colonnade. As he rounded the half-finished building, he was met by the most bizarre of sights. Hong Kong intended to reproduce one of its native streets. There were already twenty-four shops on one side of the road, and on the opposite side of the road there was a large Chinese restaurant. Down the middle of the road, lumbering towards the Ceylon Pavilion, rumbled a huge contraption designed to shift vast quantities of earth with its scoop. Closing up behind this bulldozer were the two uniformed constables. Their presence seemed to flush out two desperate-looking men advancing behind the steam shovel on foot. They were soon tackled by the constables and arrested. In the meantime, the shovel ploughed on its way, the driver not having seen or heard the apprehension of his fellow criminals. Potter reckoned that if it was Harry Rothstein in the cab, he was clearly intent on smashing down the main doors to the pavilion to get to the pearls. Potter could see Banks skirting round the rumbling, hissing monster to get in front of it.

Stumbling over the builders' rubble still littered along the Oriental street, Potter came up behind the machine as Banks stepped into the road. He stood with an arm thrown out in front of him like some constable on point duty. The machine clattered to a stop a bare few feet from him . Banks called up into the cab, where sat a mufflered figure with a flat cap pulled over his eyes.

"It's over, sir. Please climb down."

The machine seemed to give an almost human sigh, and the engine died. The figure still sat slumped in the shaped metal bucket of a seat. Potter was about to beg Harry to give himself up, when Banks called out again.

"Mr Premadasa, sir."

Potter couldn't believe his ears. Junius was dead. He had seen the body. So he could hardly believe his eyes, when the figure swung elegantly down from the cab of the machine, and doffed his cap in a mocking salute. Potter looked into the dark brown eyes of Junius Premadasa.

"Junius! But then, whose body . . . ?"

It was Banks, of course, who supplied the solution.

"I think you'll find, Mr Potter, that that was the gentleman's missing chauffeur. Who was also Sinhalese, was he not, Mr Premadasa?"

Premadasa raised a patrician nose to the skies.

"A necessary sacrifice. Now, I believe you would like to handcuff me, sir."

As he spoke these words, there was a mighty roar from the stadium behind them. Someone had scored.

In the Chamber, Mr J. Jones rose to his feet to speak.

"May I say that as far as the crowd were concerned they were good-humoured . . ."

Potter scarcely heard the rest of the eulogy to the assembled mass of football supporters. Who, he had only learned later, had gladly allowed a policeman on a white horse to organize them along the touchline. And then had supplied the King with three rousing cheers. Premadasa would have been mortified at their loyalty.

It turned out that he had organized the jewel heist to coincide with the Cup Final in the hope that all the other problems would divert the police, and that he could slip away in the crowd. While Tommy Fields and Harry Rothstein were sucked into a fake Communist plot, he and his accomplices, Marsh and Brown, would steal a million pounds' worth of pearls. And embarrass the Imperialist exhibition into the bargain. Funds and principles both satisfied, Premadasa would be able to disappear. He was already dead after all. Banks had guessed some of it, when he tracked Rothstein down to his bolt-hole. Harry had denied all participation in Prem's murder. Had assumed he was indeed still alive. But Prem's interest in the steam shovel, and the building site seemed incompatible with his ostensible plot to rouse into action the "proletarian army of the unemployed". Banks had all but figured it out then. Potter had inadvertently supplied the key. But with the hushing up of the whole affair – "for the sake of the Empire" – he could tell noone of his pivotal role. So it was with a sense of irony that he silently listened to the standing MP's final remarks.

"If it had not been for the conduct of the police, especially of the officer who was mounted on the white horse . . ." Here, laughter and cheers. ". . . and the good humour of the crowd . . ." Cries of hear, hear. ". . . there would have been murder."

Someone

MICHAEL COLLINS

*Michael Collins has been writing about his one-armed sleuth
Dan Fortune for nearly forty years, in fact for even longer if
you count the stories featuring Slot-Machine Kelly, a pro-
totype for Fortune, who appeared in short stories way back in
1962. The introductory Dan Fortune novel,* Act of Fear
*(1967) won Collins the Edgar Award for that year's best first
novel. There have been eighteen other Dan Fortune novels
since then plus many short stories, most of which will be found
in* Crime, Punishment and Resurrection *(1992) and Fortune's World (2000). Recently Collins has been reflecting on
Fortune's past and origins, and in the following story, which
sweeps us through the 1920s, we learn about Fortune's father
and how young Daniel came into the world. At first glance
you may not think about this as a whodunnit, but just ponder
a while on who's the victim and that will make you wonder
how, why and who.*

My father came to know Owney Madden, Arnold Rothstein, Mayor Jimmy Walker, and wealthy playboy Robert Jacob (Bobby) Astor, in 1923, and it changed his life, and
mine.

In 1923 the country was full of bounce. The war was over,
Europe was exhausted, but America was richer and stronger,
and then came 16 January 1920. Congress passed The Volstead
Act, Prohibition, and overnight the bounce turned into a binge.

The country became one big alcoholic party as the money rolled in. It was, as Ernest Hemingway wrote, as if life were a long leave from the front of a war not yet over. (How true that was they could not have known then, but in a short twenty years, they and their sons would be called once more to the front.)

Warren Harding was president, and whether the country reflects the president, or the president reflects the country, Harding was the perfect president for the times. On the golf course or at the poker table he vigorously enforced playing by the rules, while personally ignoring the rules of the nation with his boozing, on and off the golf course, his women, his gambling, and his turning a blind eye as his cronies pillaged the country's coffers culminating in Teapot Dome. It was anything goes, and have a drink on the house.

Kasimir Nikolai Fortunowski was born at the turn of the twentieth century in May, 1900, the only son of Tadeusz Jan Fortunowski, a Polish Lithuanian farm boy who read Marx and Lenin, was branded a dangerous agitator by the Tsar of all the Russias, and forced to run from the tsar's domains in 1892.

All that I learned from my step-grandmother, old Tadeusz's second wife. Much of the rest of this story my mother told me later in our shabby apartment on Manhattan's Lower East Side on those rare nights after school when she was at home with nothing to do but stare at the wreck of her life. Some of it I watched happening on my own with that peculiar insight children have before they turn into teenagers and see little but themselves.

Kasimir Fortunowski enlisted in the US Army the day he turned eighteen. Seven months later he returned home, having seen, as a song of the time tells us, the wonders of Paris, London, and the castles of the Rhine. He had also come to know men from all across America who were not named Kasimir or Nikolai or Fortunowski. Within a year he changed his name to Casey Nicholas Fortune, and after he found he had no chance of getting the white-collar work he thought he should have, joined the New York City Police Department.

Old Tadeusz Jan refused to speak to a man named Fortune, or to anyone who worked for the bosses as all policemen did. This did not bother my father who intended to be part of a newly confident America, and wanted nothing to do with the old country or the past of his father.

For Casey Fortune the party began in a blind pig on Fifty-Sixth Street off Tenth Avenue. He had done only average in his police training, so ended up walking a beat in Hell's Kitchen. Three years later he was still walking that beat. The blind pigs and higher class speakeasies were raided regularly when the powers-that-be decided to flex their muscle for someone's benefit, but between raids the off-duty policeman needed a drink or two to unwind from a bad day or to drown his sorrows the same as anyone else.

My father was in this mostly Irish blind pig that night, off-duty and minding his own business, when he sensed trouble at his end of the bar. It wasn't much: a slightly raised Irish-accented voice; the twitch of a shoulder; other Irish voices beginning to murmur like a low C-pedal in a symphony. Not enough to alert the bartender or the door-muscle, but they didn't have the advantage of recognizing the accent of the second voice that belonged to the large man with the twitchy shoulder.

Without a heart beat's hesitation, Casey Fortune whirled, knocking over his ersatz-Scotch and his beer chaser, and had the big man's arm in an elbow-breaking hold before anyone could blink. He quickly removed the pistol from the man's waistband, dropped it into his pocket, and flashed his badge. "Police. Everyone just go on about your business."

Without another word he hustled his prisoner out of the bar, with the man swearing in Polish at Americans, Irish, and the police all the way to the street. Once outside he marched his arrest to the nearest call box and phoned in the incident. Soon a trio of patrol cars and the paddy wagon appeared, the prisoner was shoved in, a detective took my father's report without comment, and, of course, padlocked the now all-but-empty blind pig.

As all this went down, my father noticed a man standing in the shadows some fifty yards away calmly watching the entire show. On the small side, the man was expensively dressed in a conservative dark blue suit and what had to be a cashmere topcoat against the late spring chill. Perhaps most impressive were the man's homburg and black shoes so well shined they reflected even the weak light of the street lamp a half block away.

Once the blind pig had been locked down, and the still-swearing prisoner carted away, everyone left and the street was deserted once more.

The well-dressed man came out of the shadows and approached Casey. "That was fast thinking, laddie. Prob'ly stopped a riot inside the pig, a wagon load of broken heads, and a bundle of my money. But what made you grab that guy? None of my people noticed anything wonky."

The moment the man moved closer and opened his mouth, Casey Fortune didn't have to ask who he was. No cop in New York did. Owney Madden, the biggest brewer in the city, king of the Eastside and a lot of the Westside, especially Hell's Kitchen where he had grown up to lead the Gopher gang, the lilt of his native Leeds and Liverpool still in his voice.

"You should tell your door muscle to screen who they let in a lot more carefully, and you'd still have that blind pig."

"Oh, that. Don't worry about it, kid, it'll be open for business tomorrow mornin'. You 'aven't answered my question."

Casey shrugged. "I recognized the guy's Polish accent, and saw his shoulder move to get ready to draw a pistol. A Polack with a pistol who walks into an Irish saloon and starts mouthing off is looking for trouble. The fastest way to end it was to grab his gun and hustle him out before anyone got really riled up."

Madden stared at Casey and slowly nodded. "'Ow long you been a patrolman over 'ere?"

"Three years."

At that Madden looked thoughtful. "Well, thanks again, kid. You're pretty smart. Buy yourself a decent drink on me," and peeled a hundred off a roll as thick as his wrist.

Casey hesitated. Madden laughed. "Go on, kid, it's naught but a drink, an' you can spend it in one of my joints if you want and call it a drink on the house."

Still laughing, the dapper little man turned and walked briskly east. As if by magic, a big black Packard appeared. Its rear door opened, Madden got in, and the car vanished into the night.

Casey Fortune walked the few blocks to his fourth floor walkup on Fifty-Second off Ninth Avenue still holding the hundred and feeling half exhilarated and half guilty. Had he taken a bribe from one of New York's most notorious gangsters? Or had the owner of a business establishment on his beat simply thanked him for doing his job well?

He thought about it most of the night. He was still thinking about it in the morning as he walked his beat. It was about ten a.m. when he passed where all the action had taken place last night, and found the blind pig open and operating exactly as Owney Madden had said it would. He had his answer. Madden was bribing someone a lot higher in the NYPD than he was, and a hundred-dollar drink was only a thank you.

The expensive Scotch was the first real whisky my father had had since being overseas in the war, and made him think of those great manor houses of England he had seen from the distance, and of the people who lived in them.

Less than two weeks later, Casey Fortune found himself suddenly promoted to detective because of his clever and decisive work at the blind pig, and transferred to a plum midtown beat full of speakeasies, most of them owned and/or supplied by Owney Madden.

Five minutes after he was off duty the first day on the detective squad, Casey appeared in the plush speakeasy Madden used as his headquarters when he was down from Harlem. He quickly spotted the Englishman at a far corner table with three other men, and recognized one of them: Jimmy Walker, the Tammany leader. Casey held a hundred out to the bartender. "Send your big boss over there a drink of his best Scotch."

The bartender curled a lip in scorn. "Boss don't take drinks from customers."

Casey flashed his new shield. "He will from me."

The badge did not really impress the bartender, but he was unsure enough of just who this cop might be that he poured the Scotch from a special bottle, and nodded the waitress to Madden's table. She raised an eyebrow, but she went. From the bar Casey saw Madden frown angrily at the drink placed in front of him, and then look toward the bar. Casey raised his shield case in salute.

Moments later the waitress returned in something of a trance, as if in shock. "Boss says you should join him."

Casey picked up his beer and threaded his way among the tables to Madden and his friends. A waiter materialized with an extra chair, and he sat down. Madden waved around the table. "Boys, you're lookin' at maybe the smartest honest cop in New York: Casey Fortune." He pointed at each of his companions. "Our future Mayor Jimmy Walker you 'ave to know, Arnie Rothstein, and Bobby Astor. We're all crooks but the one you got to watch out for is Bobby. He's legal."

Walker was as slender and innocent looking in person as he was in the news photos that plastered the newspapers every day. He gave Casey a perfunctory nod, and scowled at Madden, obviously not appreciating the joke. Bobby Astor, the black sheep playboy of the very proper Astor clan, lounged in his chair as if he had no spine. Under six feet, Astor wasn't much taller than Madden, and almost as slender as Walker. But he had two of the shrewdest, most calculating eyes Casey Fortune had ever seen.

Arnold Rothstein was the most famous gambler in New York, if not the country. But he was far more than that. In fact, as Meyer Lansky himself said later, Arnold was king of the Jewish underworld. Gambler, bootlegger – the fine Scotch Casey and Madden were drinking almost certainly came in on one of Rothstein's boats – and narcotics financial overlord. But above all, he was a "banker." With his impeccable family connections, and legitimate real estate businesses, he could arrange loans from banks and then finance gangsters no bank would do business with. Rothstein was the money man. He was also educated, dashing, handsome, and dressed better than Madden. In fact, Charley Lucky himself said it was Arnold who taught him to dress well, use the proper knives and forks, made him presentable in the legitimate business world.

Rothstein's hooded eyes studied Casey carefully, as if he were making entries in a ledger. Only Bobby Astor smiled, and said, "Too bad there aren't more like detective Fortune, Owney. Then you wouldn't have to pay off anyone, would you?"

Casey Fortune had no idea what Astor meant by that, and from the looks on the faces of the others, neither did they. Except, Casey felt, maybe Madden.

The four resumed their discussions of new Broadway shows they might invest in, how soon before the 1926 election should

Walker start his campaign for Mayor, and what investments Bobby Astor could steer them to. Casey said little, but he didn't feel bored or shut out. Far from it. These men were all rich, one way or another, all were important, all commanded respect, and all seemed to genuinely like each other – to a point. There was an aura of isolation about all of them that would forever preclude any genuine friendship.

It puzzled Casey, and he returned to his walk-up that night still thinking about that strange isolation like an invisible wall around each of them.

Over the next few years Casey had little time to think about that odd isolation. His midtown precinct was full of speakeasies, hotels, expensive apartments, actors' rooming houses, theaters, restaurants where booze was always under the table, gambling houses, floating poker and blackjack and craps games, and more private games in hotel rooms than there were police in the precinct. Gangsters owned half the property and they were always fighting over it.

A substantial part of the city government and the NYPD, from the top down, were on the take, but for the most part, along with the honest higher ups, the rank and file of patrolmen and detectives did their day-to-day jobs of solving and stopping the daily low-level street crime and ordinary murders, and raiding the speakeasies, brothels, gambling houses, and floating games whenever the higher ups had a point to make, or some politician needed to demonstrate how hard he was on crime.

Everyone knew the raids were hopeless, useless, and pointless. As long as Prohibition existed, nothing was going to stop the gangsters killing each other, or the gamblers gambling, or the nationwide binge. The public wanted a party, and there was too much money to be made in giving it to them to stop it.

So Casey Fortune arrested his murderers, solved his burglaries, collared his crooked gamblers, and remained on good terms with Owney Madden and his friends. No one asked him to do anything illegal, offered him a bribe to look the other way, or tried to buy him out lock, stock and barrel. Sure, they poured him free drinks, served him dinner on the house, shared tips on the horses, gave him free passes into any theater, and slipped him a few hundred now and then in appreciation for doing his job well and turning unwanted trouble away from their doors. They did that for every cop.

By sheer chance, for Casey they did something more. They gave him his wife, and me, my mother.

Handsome, charismatic, exciting, daring, well-dressed, and with perfect manners, Arnold Rothstein attracted the ladies in droves. He cultivated the image of the playboy gambler, ready to bet on anything and party all night, to cover his real activities and power in the Jewish Mob, and hence in the city.

On this particular night in 1925, my father was enjoying a free dinner in one of Rothstein's restaurants, when Rothstein himself swept in with five women, one on each arm and the others trailing close behind. Or two were close behind the gambler, the fifth seemed to be hanging back and not at all happy, looking around as if not sure what she was doing there. More of a girl than a woman, and yet Casey sensed a strength in her. She was not going to pretend she was having a ball with the dazzling Arnie. Casey sensed something else too – she was from out of town, and had not been in the city for long. It was there in a certain wariness, her evening dress not quite in the latest fashion, a shade less daring.

Just as the group reached the ornate curtains that Casey and every other cop in midtown knew hid the corridor that eventually led to the guarded door of the casino section of the restaurant, the woman put her hand on the shoulder of the woman in front of her and began to whisper urgently. She was still whispering as the entire party disappeared behind the curtains. Casey went back to his lobster dinner, but the woman stuck in his mind. It wasn't only that she was beautiful with a great body, it was a certain openness, honesty, he had sensed in her. She wasn't someone who played games.

He couldn't understand why a woman like that would trail around after Rothstein, so maybe he was wrong in his assessment. Then she suddenly reappeared through heavy curtains looking flushed and angry. As fast as he had pounced on the looking-for-trouble Polack in the blind pig, Casey left his table to intercept her half way across the restaurant toward the door.

He flashed his shield. "Anything wrong, Miss?"

"If you count unwanted pawing as wrong."

"Depends on how far the pawing went."

"Not that far," She sighed and shrugged. "My own fault, I suppose. When Janet, that's my friend who lives in the city, said I should come with her to meet this famous gambler, it sounded like fun. It wasn't." She gave a small shiver, and then turned on a dazzling smile. "Thanks for coming to rescue me anyway."

Casey took the plunge. "Have you eaten dinner?"

"Not a bite, and I'm famished."

"Then join me. I've just started, and it's on the house for my date too."

She hesitated less than a second. "Well then, I guess I'm on my first date in the city."

Things moved quickly after that. They found they hit it off, had a lot in common, and she was, basically, a Midwestern girl who wanted home and hearth, love and children. Fun, yes, but stability more. She liked a lot about the long party that was Manhattan in 1925, but she also liked a solid detective with a good job and a sure pension later. Being a friend of Owney Madden and his cronies, Casey was in a position to offer both.

They were married less than five months later. Madden insisted on throwing the reception in one of his Harlem Clubs, and with the help of Bobby Astor found them a nice three-bedroom apartment in Chelsea that Casey could almost afford on his salary. Madden squeezed "wedding presents" out of a lot of people, all in cash, to help make up the difference, and Bobby Astor advised them to put the cash into stocks and bonds and watch it grow. That's how you got to be an Astor. A year later I was born: Daniel Tadeusz Fortune. (The Tadeusz was for my step-grandmother who had moved into the third bedroom soon after my grandfather died.)

Life was good for Casey, thanks largely to Owney Madden, and Bobby Astor, especially Bobby Astor, who, being in a legitimate business and an Astor, was untainted by crime. The apartment was a steal, my mother turned out to be a lot more eager in bed than in public, his investments were paying and growing handsomely. He took my mother out to dinner, to the theater, dancing, and clubbing. My step-grandmother took care of me, told me stories of the old countries and my grandfather. Time passed easily, Casey made first grade, I grew.

Then came 4 November 1928.

Casey was never sure later why he decided to drop into the speakeasy on Fifty-Sixth Street next to the Park Central Hotel that night. He recalled he'd worked late on a nasty homicide, but had called it a night at ten and headed home. He had even called to tell my mother he was on his way. Something had to have caught his interest, or aroused his suspicions, to sidetrack him, and he found himself in that particular speakeasy. Whatever had brought him there must not have worked out because he recalled having only two beers before leaving a few minutes before eleven.

The single gunshot echoed muffled from the Park Central Hotel. As Casey ran toward the sound, two shadowed figures came out of the service entrance of the hotel. One collapsed in the entranceway, the other hurried away toward an alley across the street. Casey reached the service entrance. The man on the ground was Arnold Rothstein! A patrolman was already running from the opposite direction. "Take care of Rothstein," Casey shouted to the patrolman. Call an ambulance, and call in!" and plunged into the dark alley.

He reached to draw his revolver.

"I wouldn't do that, kid."

Stray light from a window in the building to Casey's left picked out the face of Owney Madden, and the two-inch barrel of a Colt Detective Special aimed at Casey.

"I heard Rothstein'd been welshing," Casey said. "Over three hundred grand, but I never heard any of it was your money, Owney."

"You think I'd shoot Arnie over the nicker? He was a friend. You don't shoot a friend over nicker."

"What do you shoot a friend over?"

"Business, kid. Times're changing, prohibition ain't lastin' forever. Lansky tried to talk to Arnie, but he wouldn't listen. He was always a gambler at heart, a showboat, a loner. He wasn't never goin' to fit in the new organization Meyer, Charley Lucky, me, and some other guys 'ave in mind."

Casey nodded to the Detective Special. "What now? You going to shoot me too? Am I a matter of business, too?"

"Everything's business, kid. So you tell me. Do I have to shoot you?"

There in the darkness of the alley, patrol cars and the ambulance arriving out on Fifty-sixth Street behind him, Casey battled inside himself. For five years Owney Madden had been a friend. Much of what he had he really owed to Madden. Yet Owney had never asked him to do anything illegal, never pressured him, never bribed him, never used him, and somehow he knew that if he said Owney did not have to shoot him the gangster would believe him and trust him. Something Lansky, Luciano, even Rothstein never would. They would have shot him already.

Finally, Casey said, "I won't keep quiet if another guy is convicted of shooting Rothstein."

"Fair enough, kid."

Madden grinned, lowered his pistol, and vanished into the darkness. Casey never heard a door open or close, but he knew Madden was gone, and he knew he would say nothing even if Rothstein died, and, somehow, he felt good.

Madden, a gangster and a killer, took his word, knew he was a man of honor.

The arrival of a large package soon after did not make Casey feel better, but it didn't make him feel worse. He'd made his decision without any promise of money. But the money was nice, and Bobby Astor was happy to invest it all in the best blue chip stocks. Casey and my mother began to think of an even better apartment in a better area. Maybe even the Upper East, or Central Park West. Perhaps private school for me.

A year later the dreams ended, the party was over, if not the booze. Only now the drinking was half hearted at best, and at worst to drown sorrows, to get through the desperate nights and days. Black Monday, the stock market crash, that signaled the beginning of the Great Depression. The flow of money, built on nothing more than the sand of optimism and straw of arrogance, slowed to a trickle.

My father lost everything we had, and on his salary alone we couldn't afford the spacious Chelsea apartment. My mother tried to get a job, but she had never worked in her life except on a farm, knew nothing but homemaking, and the unemployment lines got longer and longer. No one in business or government seemed to have any idea what to do.

Madden slipped Casey a few bucks, but even gangsters had lost in the crash, and lost even more as the flow of customers slowly dried up and blind pigs, speakeasies, breweries, and bootleggers started to shut down. To top it off, the Seabury Commission investigating Mayor Jimmy Walker to find out where all his money had come from began to turn up the corruption in the NYPD, and everyone came under scrutiny down to beat patrolmen. Casey couldn't risk taking any more money from Madden.

That was when we moved to the five floor walk-up on East Ninth Street near First Avenue, and my father started to brood. Not instantly, or constantly, but gradually increasing over time as he went about his job in this changed world where a robber could turn out to be no more than a man out of a job trying to put food on the table or pay the rent. It became a more ambiguous world for a cop, where it was sometimes hard to tell who was the victim.

Madden also lost a bundle in the crash, but it didn't bother him too much. "Just shows you a bloke should stick to what he knows. I'm a gangster, I make my money outside the law, and that's what I do. Only we gangsters got to change. We got to get organized. Irish, Jews, and Italians. We got to cooperate instead of fightin'. There's always something illegal people want: gambling, women, the hard drugs. We'll always make plenty of money."

He brooded about Jimmy Walker, who, unable to explain where all his money had come from, was forced to resign as Mayor, but skipped the country with all his loot and did not return until he was safe from prosecution, and later was appointed by Mayor LaGuardia as arbiter to help solve garment district disputes. And through it all, the accusations and investigations of his corruption, he was the well-paid president of a music record company.

But he brooded most about Bobby Astor. Nothing happened to Bobby Astor because of the crash. He had as much ready cash as ever. At first, Casey couldn't understand this. He knew that Bobby had invested heavily in all the same stocks he had advised Casey to buy. Only later did it transpire that Bobby had been tipped that certain major companies were on the brink of going under, and with half the nation overextended buying on low margins, the whole financial structure was on the verge of collapse. He immediately began to sell short, covering his possible losses, and when the collapse came, his profits and losses more-or-less canceled out and he even made a few bucks.

What Casey didn't understand was why Bobby hadn't warned him.

"Wouldn't work, old man. Too many people start selling short the market gets the wind up, and crashes before I'm covered. I had to be very careful and space my transactions over a fair period of time. Warning you would have been extremely bad business."

I was four when disaster struck both the nation and my family. Too young to understand, but not too young to feel, and I felt my father's bitterness. Somehow it was not the same as what my mother felt. She was afraid and angry, given to despair, partly by our changed circumstances and partly by my father's brooding. Only my step-grandmother seemed unchanged. She had lived through it all before.

Prohibition ended, the high rollers were gone, Arnold Rothstein was dead, Bobby Astor straightened out and took over one of the family businesses, and Owney Madden closed most of his midtown operations and concentrated on Harlem. The years passed, my mother eventually got a job as a sales clerk in a department store, and I grew up.

I was ten or eleven when I finally could put words to what I had sensed as a four-year-old. My mother's reaction had been, and was, fear, anger and hate for Bobby Astor and Jimmy Walker and Owney Madden. My step-grandmother expected the betrayal and inhumanity, it was always the way of the rich and powerful. But my father's brooding came from being a sucker, an honest cop who trusted friends. For not understanding the world and playing the angles the way the rich, the corrupt, and the crooked did. For being no one, nothing.

"I'm not nothing," I told him with my ten- or eleven-year-old hubris. "I'm me."

"Are you now, Danny?" His voice became gentle then. He put his hands on my shoulders and sat me down facing him on the couch. But his eyes were not gentle. He wanted me to understand what he understood. "Let me tell you a story. Do you remember the gambler Arnold Rothstein?"

"I've read about him. He got shot because he lost a lot of money in a card game and wouldn't pay. The police suspected a couple of the other players, but only charged one of them, and he was acquitted. So no one knows who did it."

"I know who shot him, Danny, and it wasn't about gambling." He told me the story of that night on Fifty-sixth Street and in the alley. "I thought Owney took my word I wouldn't turn him in because he trusted me as a friend, and an honest man." He laughed, and now the bitterness was back. "But it wasn't that at all. He knew he didn't have to kill me. He knew the chances of anyone being convicted for the death of Rothstein were nil – too many important people were deep into Rothstein's activities, they couldn't risk anyone talking. He knew even if I did report what I saw that night, nothing would come of it. Too many "legitimate" bigwigs were involved with Owney. There were no other witnesses. No one would listen to me. I was a nobody, a nothing."

The breaking point came in 1938. Casey had been the lead detective in a Park Avenue homicide investigation into the beating to death of a young man's fiancée. His family was old, wealthy, and important. Hers wasn't. The boy was acquitted. Next day Casey got up, kissed my mother, hugged me, and left for work.

He never came home.

He didn't show up at the precinct either, or turn in his badge and guns.

When he didn't report for three days, the NYPD put out an APB, but with three days' start in 1938, as long as he didn't try to use his badge or his guns, they were not going to find him except by luck. No credit cards then, no computers, no Internet.

I never saw him again, and I hated him for it.

My mother tried to hold us together. She worked longer hours, his precinct took up a collection for us and, although Casey had not put in his twenty years, he had a pension coming, and his Lieutenant, a man named Gazzo, talked the higher-ups into approving its payment to his wife. I got odd jobs to help out. But not too long after, my step-grandmother died, and without her I went wild.

My mother couldn't stand being alone night after night, and all the men she knew were cops. There were a lot of cops, and eventually Lieutenant Gazzo himself who was kind to her. My foray into petty crime ended the day I fell into the hold of a Dutchman ship while looting it with my buddy Joe Harris and lost my left arm.

In the hospital I had plenty of time to think. Of how my father finally saw the world, and of how my grandfather had always seen it. For my father, in the end, there was only power, wealth, and dominance by each individual who could achieve that by any means, legal or illegal. Every man for himself. That was the odd isolation he had sensed that first night at Owney Madden's table with Rothstein, Jimmy Walker, and Bobby Astor. Friends, but business was business.

For my grandfather the world was everyone on earth working together to achieve the fullest human potential. Community. No one growing rich and powerful on the sweat of others. No human being exploiting another human being.

The war came, and I tried to enlist. Naturally, they turned me down. One-armed soldiers are produced by war, not sent to fight one. I joined the merchant marine. After the war I continued to ship out. Long voyages give you plenty of time to read, and there were a great many things I wanted to learn, question I needed to ask. From time to time I stayed ashore and went to various colleges and universities. I never got a degree, that wasn't what I was studying and learning for. Eventually I landed back in Chelsea, got a one-room office with a window on an air shaft, and put my name on the door: Dan Fortune, Private Investigator.

Why? Because I still had a lot of questions: Why we do what we do; why do we believe what we believe; why do we make the laws we make. Who was the criminal and who was the victim?

It took me years to finally understand my father. How he felt trapped, his life over, and he had nothing, was no one. He ran, not away from us, but towards being "someone". Whether he achieved it or not, legally or illegally, I don't know. What I do know is when I finally came to terms with his need, I knew I would never be like him. I would follow the dream of my grandfather, old Tadeusz, not that of my father.

And my mother? She died young. Still unable to be alone, still lost. One of the victims.

Kiss the Razor's Edge

MIKE STOTTER

I wanted one story in this book that looked at the vicious underside of the gangster's world, not in America but in Britain, in London's East End. And I knew the man to do it. Mike Stotter was born and bred in the East End, treading the same steps as his fictional characters in "Kiss the Razor's Edge" but with less violence – he also boxed for East London and became Junior All London Champion Runner Up, a short-lived affair, a weak nose preventing him going any further. Mike has worked at various jobs ranging from BBC TV through to Asset Management. His short stories have appeared in various anthologies including, The Best of the American West *(Vols 1 and 2),* Desperadoes, Future Crimes *and* The Fatal Frontier. *Mike was the editor of* Shots Magazine, *which he continues on his website devoted to the genre,* < www.shotsmag.co.uk > .

Blood.
  You'd expect to see blood in a boxing match. It stands to reason, doesn't it?

Whenever Billy Griggs fought there was blood. Usually the opponents. And the fight tonight didn't look as if it was going to break the mould. Billy was sixteen years old and stood just shy of six feet. This was going to be his first fight in the lightweight division, having fought these last six months at light flyweight. His opponent was Whirlwind Washington who boxed out of

Camberwell. He was five feet seven and had been around a bit. But Billy had him outreached and out-classed. Griggs had wanted to be called Billy the Kid, after the Old West killer but his second christened him Billy "Fast Hands". Not that exciting but it went down well with the punters.

Mile End Road, Thursday evening and back to the Crescent for his second fight of the week. A special request from his new promoters. All the old faces were there. Up in the gallery were his vociferous fans from the streets. They were the ones who couldn't afford the shilling or two bob seats, but supported him each time he turned out. Second row down, the bookies and the fight fans stood shoulder to shoulder swapping tales and anecdotes, giving it the big 'un. Talking about boxers like they were prize horses: "He ain't got the legs," or "Got to keep his left up or he'll become a cropper," or "If he gets a second wind after round three, he'd knock the bloke's block off." It was par for the course. And, naturally, in the front row were the toffs. Out for the evening to see a "bit of a scrap". All dolled up to the nines, puffing away on huge cigars and some of them in top hat and tails.

The arc lights came on and cut through the tobacco smog. When Billy stepped through the ropes the audience were up on their feet as one, shouting and cheering him on. He was the local boy done good. The name of Billy Griggs was found on the lips of most men when it came to talking about sport down the pub. A boy wonder at sixteen and by all accounts could be a great fighter, as good as Jack Dempsey. An exaggeration or not, a lot of people put their week's wages on him. There were doubters, naturally. He wasn't a top-liner, hadn't gone the whole fifteen rounds but his promoters had confidence in him. His normal wage was four pounds a fight, which made him the top wage-earner at home but to cap this his promoters were happy to give him a fiver for this match. At this rate, Griggs thought to himself, he could go on forever.

Round two: Griggs got his first professional black eye when he dropped his guard and walked into a straight right jab.

"You gotta get yer distance right," his second, Tommy Martin said out of the corner of his mouth. "Get yer shoulder behind that right of yourn. Now get out there and give him somefink to fink about."

Round three and Griggs' legs were getting wobbly.

"Yer fightin' like a bleedin' tart! Wassamatter wiv yer?" Martin was working furiously on a cut above Griggs's right eye. "You don't start smackin' him, you're outta here in the next round."

Griggs nodded, and as usual, said nothing.

Tommy Martin was right. A big haymaker of a right hand landed in Griggs's face that sent him down for the count. And the toffs in the front row got what they came for.

Blood.

You don't expect to see a young girl's good looks marred by a line of blood across her throat.

Abraham Shapiro stood in his back yard dressed only in his long johns and looked at the five or six rats huddled together around the back door. There was another odour mixing with perspiration and ageing cat crap that wasn't normally present. Shapiro shrugged his shoulders and shooed the rats away but they were contemptuous to his actions.

"*Gai in drerd arein!*" Shapiro yelled at the vermin. He knew that once they got into the sweatshop and began to make nests in the bolts of cloth or scraps, he'd have the Devil's own work getting rid of them so hell was about the right place for them. Mice he could put up with, rats he didn't want. He grabbed the yard broom and attacked the vermin.

"Seven o'clock and already this worry," he muttered.

This was his morning ritual: Up before the family, go into the yard and open up the sweatshop and put on the lights. Then inspect the three treadle machines, checking the cotton threads and belts, that the bolts of cloth were ready to hand and that the basters' bench was clear. He hated it when the workers came in at eight o'clock and had any excuse to delay in getting the day started. What did they think he was paying them for?

Being short and overweight didn't help him any, sweat came easy and rolled down his face. Once he beat the rats away he leaned back against the door and put his bare foot into something sticky and wet. He looked down at the source and his mouth dropped into a perfect O. He shot the bolts and pulled the door open.

At first he thought it was a tramp. The head was resting

against the door and fell back when he opened it. It was a young woman. She still held her purse in her right hand, her clothing was intact but a bloody pool had haloed her head like an obscene caricature of a saint's corona.

"Oi, gevald!"

Shapiro staggered back, shot a hand across his mouth and gulped back the threatening vomit. It was hard not to look at the gaping wound: sickening but fascinating at the same time. He'd seen dead bodies before but none that had been murdered. He guessed she was eighteen or twenty years old and had no wedding ring on her finger. Her hair was thick and tawny, cut like a boy's, swept back from her forehead. Her eyebrows had been plucked to a thin line and penciled over, and a deep purple lipstick had been applied. Far too much for his liking. And her clothes. Now he turned a professional eye over her attire. The sleeveless knee-length chiffon dress was shapeless, the boat shape neckline was edged with red and white plastic beads. The stitching was poor and amateurish. Shapiro noticed that she wasn't wearing stockings and had no doubt she wore a lace bandeau bra lined with net to stop her breasts moving around. A cheap attempt at sophistication. This boyish look was all the rage with the young women. To Abraham Shapiro, she was a *nishtikeit,* a nobody but a gentile. And clearly dead.

"Picture this: that yid, Bert Ambrose and his Orchestra givin' it all they've got at the Embassy Club on Old Bond Street. An' Jimmy here, coming through the tables with two tarts on his arm. Suddenly one of 'em trips and goes arse over tit! She ends up on all fours with her arse sticking up in the air. Jimmy looks down at her and without thinkin' says, 'At least I can park me bike somewhere tonight!'"

The five men sitting around the table burst out in raucous laughter in unison. One spitting out a mouthful of bitter rather than choking. It wasn't a very funny anecdote but when Kruger made a joke, you laughed.

"You dozy git, Tiny," Kruger said. "Can't you hold your drink nowadays?"

"Sorry, Krug. Got me by surprise, that did." Tiny wiped the back of his hand across mouth.

"Dozy git." Kruger repeated quietly. He sat back in his seat and adjusted the trilby on his head.

Tiny said, "What tune was they playing?"

"What?"

"Ambrose. What tune was he playing?"

"Fucked if I know, Tiny. A bleedin' foxtrot for all I care." Kruger was bemused by his muscle man's interest.

Kruger was the first to stop laughing. He let the others carry on, watching them, each man with his own story. Jimmy Gilbert, all bones and sinew, was the best pick pocket for miles around. Tiny Miller, actually six feet five and known to everyone as a gentle giant, providing you didn't get on the wrong side of him. Danny Marks, could speak German and a bit of Yiddish and the quickest brain for figures. And lastly, Lenny Procter, the shortest of the bunch but made up for it by being the most vicious of the gang. All Kruger's men through and through.

They had all been born in the same street. And been friends since childhood. They played on the same side for street football and cricket matches. Went to the same school and all left at the same time. The Millers and the Procters lived in the same house whilst Jimmy Gilbert lived two doors down from Kruger. At the age of seven they formed their own gang, The Black Hand Gang of Shandy Street, getting the idea of the name out of *The Wizard*. They terrorized the local kids, stealing their sweets and comics if they were foolish enough to flash them around. By the time they were in their mid-teens they didn't mind the odd scrap or two. The highlight of the weekend was when they went down to Whitechapel and hung around the top of Thrawl Street waiting to have a dig at the Jews from the tenements. That was where Kruger got in a bit of practice with a cut-throat razor he'd stolen from his Dad's barber shop. And six months in borstal. When he got out, his role as leader went unopposed.

They had all served in the same regiment and saw action in Salonika and Mesopotamia, dodging bullets and malaria. Like so many men returning from war, they came back to a changed Mile End. Physically unaffected by the war, they had seen enemy action and survived the odiousness of life at the front. Returning home to face unemployment and more hardship was not on their agenda so they took to a little light thieving. At first it was just a little housebreaking in a more affluent area, or perhaps a factory or warehouse needing to be relieved of their goods. Soon they were moving up in the world.

Billy Griggs walked between the billiard tables of the Grove Club, keeping his head down. A couple of people recognized him and called out hello, but he didn't look up or acknowledge them. Did they know what he was here for?

Any other time he'd be happy to accept their compliments, the friendly slap across his back and the show boating of mock punches thrown at him and he would smile and give them a big grin. Not tonight. Tonight he felt like shit. Didn't it ever occur to them, he thought, that he wanted to end it all?

He stopped at the back of the club where the billiard tables gave way to a small dance floor area that had wooden tables and chairs placed to one side. The wall mounted gas mantles hissed and spluttered, spreading a ghostly yellow glow. A small bar ran along the side wall; all mirrors, glasses and bottles. Trying to capture the enthusiasm of an American drinking club but failing miserably as only an East End dive could. Leaning against the bar were a couple of men dressed like bookies, hands tucked into their waistcoats, drinking beer with young women who were smoking and drinking outrageous looking cocktails. His instructions were to go to the very back of the dance floor and see the man on the door.

He told him that he'd come on Kruger's request and the door was opened for him. Griggs entered the backroom where the gang operated from.

Kruger was sitting at the table wearing a three-piece lounge suit in herringbone tweed, the soft white shirt was the open collar type with a bold red neckerchief around his throat. He wore a half-sovereign ring that shined in the glare of the overhead light. His trilby was pushed back on his head so no shadows were cast over his face. Around him the laughter was dying.

Kruger asked, "You know how much a boxer earns a year?"

From the back of the room, Griggs said, "You askin' me, Kruger?"

"No, I'm askin' Lloyd fuckin' George! Course I'm askin' you."

Griggs removed his cloth cap and rolled it between his hands and looked over at Kruger. "Don't know about others but I reckon I earn two hundred quid."

"You worth that much?" Tiny whistled. He leaned across the table, holding his hands together as if in prayer, resting them by stacks of neatly bundled five-pound notes as if protecting them from Griggs.

"Really?" It was Jimmy. "That much?"

"A tart earns more than that in four months," added Lenny.

You should know, thought Griggs, you run enough of 'em. But he kept his mouth shut.

"A couple of hundred for a sixteen-year-old. Ain't bad. Ain't bad at all." Kruger pushed his chair back and stood up. Like Jimmy Gilbert he was thin, but unlike Jimmy he was all muscle beneath his dapper suit. A light stubble decorated his lower face and a thin roll up stuck out the corner of his mouth. His nose was bulbous and broken blood capillaries spidered the surface.

"I'm doin' all right, Kruger." He tugged at the striped muffler around his neck.

"Got yerself a nice shiner there, Billy boy. Nose is a bit bust up as well. You done well."

Griggs nodded.

Outside, on Globe Road, the rain began to fall. A sudden autumn shower that would help keep the stench down, and keep the rats off the streets.

Kruger stood in front of Griggs and gave him a light slap on the cheek. The boxer didn't flinch.

He said, "Let's see if I can't help the pain."

He pulled out a wad of notes from his inside pocket and thrust them into Griggs's hand.

"Hundred and fifty quid. Not bad goin' for fifteen minutes' work."

Griggs looked down at the money, then at the man.

"I think – I don't want to . . ."

He thought of all the people he had let down. Men who had lost their week's wages when they betted on him. They were the ones who had to explain to their wives that there was no money that week. How many doorsteps could a woman wash and polish for a pair of kippers just to keep body and soul together? He was frightened to tell his Mum what happened, knowing that she would disown him. He felt dirty. And used.

"What's the matter?" Kruger asked. "Before you open your trap, be smart. So you took a dive, so what? You pocket nearly a year's wage an' I make a bit as well. It was a business deal an' it worked out for both of us. Now do yourself a favour, put the gelt in yer pocket, turn around an' walk out of here."

"I only want to be a boxer."

"I know that."

"I want to fight properly. Nuffin' fixed."

"Oh, right." Kruger put his hands on Griggs's shoulders. "When I say you drop in the third," he said. "You drop."

Griggs nodded.

"You're a hungry young man an' so am I. I'm yer promoter now so don't piss me off. That way you get to stay a boxer, understand?"

Again Griggs nodded.

"An' yer mum keeps her kneecaps."

By midnight Kruger had had enough so he left the others to finish their drinks. He walked onto the dance floor and saw her straight away. She was standing alone at the bar using her reflection in the bar mirror to put on her lipstick.

How far are these women going to go? Kruger wondered.

She saw his reflection in the mirror. He was standing next to her, both hands on the counter and a grin on his face.

"What's the joke?" she said.

"Ain't one."

"Well?" She flicked her hair back with one hand.

"Well what?"

"You gonna stand there all night, or what?"

The rain was still hammering the streets when they stopped outside his house. He opened the door and took her by the elbow leading her through.

"That you, Krug?" A woman's voice called out.

"Fuck!"

A moment later a woman wearing a thin cotton night gown appeared at the top of the scullery stairs. She was small and even in the gaslight she had a pretty face crowned in black sleep-tossed hair. Kruger went towards her but her eyes were on the other woman.

"What's happenin'?" she asked.

"I bought a visitor home," he replied.

The woman put her hands on her head and grabbed fistful of hair, twisting and tearing.

"No. Not again, Kruger. You promised. You promised!"

"Don't get yourself worked up, girl."

She was shaking her head. "No. You said . . ."

"Don't fuckin' go on!" Kruger raised his voice.

"Get that bitch out of our house. Now! I mean it, Krug. What gutter did you find her in?"

Kruger's face reddened and his nostrils flared.

"No one. No one speaks to me like that!"

"For Chrissake, I'm your wife!"

The young girl in the doorway gasped.

"Forget to tell you that bit, did he?"

"You'll do as you're fuckin' told!" Kruger shouted and took a step closer to his wife.

The war had been ended three months when he came calling for her one day. He was dressed in a wool suit and was wearing two tone shoes. They had been courting a little while before he went off to war and all the while he was away she missed him. She gradually realised that she was in love. Mary McCarthy was in love. Then he did something amazing. He said that they were going to get married.

"C'mon girl, we gettin' wed'." Was what he said.

They lied about their age and where they lived, and on the wedding certificate put down that their fathers were deceased. Kruger told her it would be all right, he'd sort it out with them later. Tiny Miller and his sister, Eileen, were the witnesses. Later, a drink in The Fountain and that was it. That was five years ago. Five years: a four-year-old daughter named Ada, one miscarriage and their month-old son, Charlie, dead in her arms one morning.

Now this again. My God, she thought, not again. Never again.

Mary sprang at Kruger, arms outstretched, fingernails ready to take out his eyes. But he was ready for her and simply twisted his body out of her reach. At the same time he pulled out his razor and flicked it open. Mary's momentum carried her past him and then came an unexpected stinging sensation across the whole of her back.

The girl screamed. The screech echoed in the street. She stood there and watched, not lifting a hand to help.

The blood flowed down Mary's back, tracing her spine and soaking into her nightgown. She turned. Now the tears came. She looked at Kruger.

There was a faint smudge of blood on the razor's edge.

Mary whispered something too low to be heard. Kruger ignored the pleading in her eyes and caught her by the wrist and spun her around.

She pulled against him, fighting him.

"You want more?" He waved the razor under her chin. "Go on, give me a reason."

"Krug, don't," she said. "Kruger!" She was screaming now. Screaming at him to stop. She looked at the girl in the party dress for help, but she looked away.

He pressed the blade against the soft fold of her throat. Not hard enough to draw blood but enough to let her know that at any time he could. She smelt the stale odour of alcohol and tobacco on his breath. He gritted his teeth and pushed her away from him. Mary's legs weakened but she didn't buckle.

"'ere, take yer coat an' piss off!"

Kruger shoved Mary's coat into her hands, then bodily threw her out into the street. Once the door was closed against Mary's cries the silence in the confined passageway was eerie. Kruger waited a second to catch his breath and to see if the commotion woke his brother and his family upstairs. But no – nothing. He slipped the razor back into his jacket pocket before taking the girl by the elbow and leading her into his bedroom.

Jimmy, Tiny, Lenny and Danny came out of The Empire cinema into the cold night air. A thin mist shrouded the street and surroundings.

Tiny said, "Did you believe that stunt?"

Danny said, "Bloody amazin'."

"D'you reckon he was up that high?" Jimmy asked.

"What made me laugh," Tiny said, "there he was, hangin' on to that clock for all he was worth an' he still kept his straw hat and glasses on!"

Safety Last with Harold Lloyd had kept them amused for a while. They were at a bit of a loose end before they could make their rounds, so they went to the cinema. The men made their way down Mile End Road, cutting down Bancroft Road, into Stepney Green.

"What's the world comin' to, I ask yer?" Lenny Procter said. Unusually for him, he'd been quiet most of the evening. "Kattie was one of me girls an' gets her throat cut, an' we go swannin' around at the bleedin' pictures!"

Jimmy said, "Lenny, we're goin' to sort out whoever done this."

"Too fuckin' right we are!" Tiny added.

"Some bugger is goin' to pay for this. She was one of me best girls. Good lookin', smart, well-liked. An' one of the best dips."

"It's bloody criminal what 'appened to 'er." Danny agreed. "But it goes with the territory."

"Fuck off!"

"Leave it, Danny," Jimmy suggested.

But Lenny wasn't going to let it go.

He said, "D'you think that just because she was a prossie, she deserved to get topped?"

"I didn't mean it like that."

"Sounded like it to me."

"Maybe the geezer caught her with her hand where it shouldn't be."

"Not on his dick?" Tiny came up with the one-liner.

"If you ain't got anything sensible to say, Tiny, shut yer gob."

"Oi! Don't take it out on me, Lenny."

Jimmy said, "Right, that's enough! I said we'll sort it out, Lenny – all right? An' Tiny, you ain't on the stage, so shut it."

As it was, Jimmy thought Tiny's crack was a good one. But he didn't dare laugh. If he did, he knew that he would spend all night trying to get Lenny to calm down. Or even swapping a couple of punches. But they had to stick together at times like these. So all right, one of Lenny's girl's had been killed. Then it was up to them or the police to get the killer, and he knew they had the better chances. The world was full of snitches and narks, someone would come up with something and pretty quick since she came out of Kruger's stalls.

The strength of the gang lay in that Kruger could fix anything. Unwanted pregnancies dealt with; people on the run, he could hide them; landlord troubles – no problems; bets and loans were his specialities. Everything had its price. And he was smart because he didn't personally get involved. Always saying, "Yeah, I might know someone who could help."

Murdering one of the girls went against the grain. Some were accosted, their money stolen and they might get a thump but murder? Murder was different. Before dealing with that, they had a little bit of business to attend to. Which was why they were out tonight with knuckle-dusters and lead saps banging in their pockets. The bloke they were on their way to see was taking the piss. They'd let Jack Jenkins off with just a slap the last time, when he promised he'd pay back the loan with a bit on top. But word had reached Kruger that Jenkins had been mouthing off that he had screwed over the money lender. Don't people learn?

They caught Jenkins coming out of The Railway. He was three parts pissed and unsteady on his feet. Tiny stepped up behind him and twisted Jenkin's arm up his back until he was nearly crying. Jenkins was a big man, a waterside labourer, but he couldn't move in Tiny's grip.

"Think you're so clever, you mouthy git!"

"Jimmy, please! There's ten quid in me pocket. It's all I got. Take it." His beer-puffed face was pouring with sweat.

"Too late for that. Too fuckin' late."

Lenny swung the sap. It connected with Jenkins's left knee cap and exploded bone and cartilage. He used his left fist to uppercut Jenkins's jaw. His head snapped upright, blood and tears merging. Lenny Procter was enjoying this. Now he could get rid of some of his anger and frustration on the man in front of him. In his mind's eye, Jenkins had become the man who murdered Kattie. The sap descended again.

Strange as it may seem, this was the moment he loved the best. The arc lights, the roar of the crowd and the tension – all gone. Just him on his lonesome. The feeling of elation still coursed through his body. He had knocked out Marsh Cronin, the little Irish lad from Islington, in the third with a beautiful combination ending with a clubbing right hand right on his chin. He'd earned six pounds for tonight's fight. Kruger trying to make up for last week.

Griggs heard footsteps running down the corridor.

Jimmy came in first. His face red with anger, his self-control lost.

"They've nicked Kruger," he said. "The coppers came for him this afternoon."

"What for?"

"Murder."

"You what?"

Jimmy moved into the room and leaned against the wall, looking at Griggs.

"He was in the scullery and they dragged him out. Took six of 'em, mind you."

"I didn't know. Been in the gym all day, an' I hadn't heard a word."

Danny, Lenny followed by Tiny stepped into the room. It was growing claustrophobic in the changing room.

"It's all over the manor," Danny said.

Jimmy said, "Nicked him right in front of his Missus and little Ada."

"It's fight day," Griggs said. "I do a bit of sparrin', a bit of shadow boxin'. I don't go out. No one told me."

Lenny sat on the edge of the table swinging his leg gently back and forth. "He won't be there for long."

Griggs didn't know what else to say and the silence stretched out between the men until Danny said, "Notice he hasn't asked who was murdered."

"Or how," Jimmy added.

"Because the bastard already knows!" Tiny pointed out.

They jumped him before he could draw another breath. He tried to struggle but they pinned him down on the table.

"No! For God's sake!"

Jimmy slapped him around the face. "Feelin' proud of yerself?"

He struck him again. "Get his hand."

Tiny took hold of Griggs's right arm and stretched it in the air.

"What're you gonna do?" Griggs asked.

"First, I'm gonna break every finger on yer right hand," Jimmy answered and yanked back Griggs's middle finger until it snapped. "Then I'm gonna start on yer left." The ring finger was next. "An' then every fuckin' bone in yer body!" he shouted over Griggs's screams.

They brought him around by throwing a bucket of water over his head.

"Why'd you do it?"

Griggs looked up at Lenny through swollen eyes.

His voice was hoarse. "'Cos he threatened me Mum."

Lenny stood back. "You what?"

"The night at the Grove Club, he said he'd break her knees."

"Is that all?" Lenny was dumbstruck.

"Yeah."

Tiny said, "Probably will do now."

Danny said, "He will. He will."

"When we're through with you," Jimmy said. "Never mind being known as 'Fast Hands'; be more like fuckin' 'Slow Hands'!"

They broke the rest of the fingers of his right hand, then those of the left. The second time he came around there was a quiet calmness about him. If they wanted to know everything, then what more harm could they do him? He was finished as a boxer, he wouldn't be able to swing a paper bag, let alone a punch.

Griggs nearly lost his footing, dizzy and eyes a little out of focus, he just about remembered where he was. He had been drinking since two o'clock that afternoon, bitter at first, then a glass of whisky. And then he gave up counting. He should have stuck to the beer. God he wished that now. He walked along the street a gangling, staggering figure.

Then she was walking alongside him.

"Where you off to?" she asked.

"Home." He looked around at the young woman.

"Sure?"

"Hmm?"

She put her arm through his and pulled him closer. "'Ere, do I know you?"

"'Praps. I'm a boxer."

"Yeah, right. Billy Grey, ain't it?"

"Griggs. Billy Griggs. An' you work at the Grove Club, dontcha?"

She nodded. "Well, Billy. Want to show a girl what you can do with them hands?"

They had reached a junction where a small turning on the right led off into the darkness. She pulled him in that direction.

Sixteen years old, a boxer on the up, fifty quid in his pocket and now he was going to lose his load. Griggs thought that life couldn't get any better than this.

They leaned their bodies together and kissed. His right hand slipped behind her and cradled her backside. He could feel her firm buttocks through the chiffon. She did nothing to dissuade him. Now his hand moved over her breasts.

"Oi! Not so fast."

She pulled away, breaking contact.

"Gonna cost you."

Griggs nodded. "Yeah, of course." He pulled out a small bundle of notes and peeled off a single five pound note.

The prostitute smiled and snatched the money from his fingers before he could argue the price. She opened her purse and pushed the note inside. That's when he saw the razor.

"What you got there?" he asked.

She took out the razor and held it in the palm of her hand.

"Don't worry about it. I took it off some geezer so's he couldn't use it no more."

"Let's have a look."

He knew it belonged to Kruger. It had a distinctive mother of pearl handle and a small nick on the razor's edge. The very same one that had been stuck under his nose when he was told that he was under new management.

Griggs couldn't remember the rest. Just a blurred image of the prostitute on the floor, blood pumping out of her throat. He didn't remember putting the razor under her body. Just that he had a chance to fix Kruger.

"How'd you find out?"

Jimmy dragged on his cigarette, exhaled and said, "You stupid schmuck. Ain't even worked that out, have yer? Go on Danny, tell him."

Danny Marks was quiet for a moment, then said. "I spoke to the yid who found Kattie's body. He didn't want to say nuffin' at first but I persuaded him that the Pogrom was nuffin' compared to the grief I'd give him. Seems he took a fiver out of Kattie's purse. That was all she the money she had on her. Thing is Billy boy, it was one of mine. I got a list of all my notes and who they went to. It was one of the forged notes that Kruger gave you. Did you ever stop to think why Kruger was so happy to part with a hundred and fifty quid when you threw the fight?"

Thoroughly Modern Millinery

MARILYN TODD

Somehow the Roaring Twenties and Marilyn Todd are made for each other. Of course we all know Marilyn from her series featuring the cunning vixen of ancient Rome, Claudia Serferus, who first pushed back the sheets in I, Claudia *(1995), and somehow I think Claudia would have loved the Roaring Twenties as well.*

The Pink Parrot was buzzing louder than a barrelful of hornets when Fizzy Potter fluttered her fingers at Lennie the barman, tossed her feather boa over her shoulder and shimmied up the sweeping spiral staircase. Down on the dance floor, the exuberance of the Charleston had given way to pencil-thin couples fusing together for the Argentinian tango, a relatively recent import, but one which seemed destined to remain the chief talking point among the middle-aged and middle-classed for years to come. Sensitive to the dance's stillness and pauses, the conductor of the Pink Parrot Orchestra was milking its suggestiveness for all it was worth.

"I say, Fizzy!" A young man with a moustache that looked like an anchovy on his upper lip waved her over. "Care to join me with a whisky and soda?"

"Sorry, darling," she quipped back, "but with you and me it'll only ever be gin and platonic!"

With his laughter ringing in her ears, she made her way to the corner where her friends had set up their usual Friday night colony. All feathers and beads, cloche hats and silk stockings, Fizzy also happened to own the finest pair of knees this side of the Bosporus. A point which rarely went unappreciated when she sat down, as now, and crossed her long legs.

"Jolly glad you made it, old girl," Marriott muttered across his martini.

Impeccably turned out as usual, and with a crease in his trousers that could slice bacon, he twiddled the yellow rosebud in his buttonhole. Marriott Stokes was the only member of the group who didn't need to go out and earn his weekly envelope, his father having left him a packet several years previously.

"Rather hoping you can do something with old Catspaw," he drawled.

"Yes, I'd noticed he's sporting a face like a vulture whose carrion has just made a miraculous recovery and is now dancing the fandango instead of providing him with a good supper," she said. "What's the matter?"

"Seems Bubbles gave him the raspberry," Foxy Fairfax explained.

Like Fizzy, he was also an illustrator, only instead of working freelance for magazines, Foxy tended to restrict himself to children's books.

"Come off it, chaps, every girl gives Catspaw the bird," she said, sliding her olive off its cocktail stick. "Why should Bubbles be different?"

Anyway, Bubbles was married, and girls like that don't pass up on rich bankers in favour of penniless cartoonists.

"Exactly what I told him," Biff said. "In fact, I seriously advised the old halibut to go and get stinko and forget all about popsies. Like the Mongol hordes descending from wherever it was they used to descend from, girls only bring grief on a chap."

Adding, as Marriott ordered another round of drinks, "I say, Fizzy. Given any further thought about swanning down the aisle with me?"

As a partner in the family firm of purveyors of quality pickles, Biff Kilgannon had no interest in art like the rest of the gang, in fact the nuances of Impressionism, gouache and the finer points of the Neue Sachlichkeit sailed completely over his head. He only tagged along because his sister, Lulu, was an artist and this way he got to mix with lots of Witty Young Things, something one tends not to do in the gherkin and piccallilli department. It wasn't that Biff wasn't a dish, Fizzy mused, especially since playing prop forward had endowed him with muscles of steel. It was just unfortunate that he had a brain to match.

"Sorry, Biff." Fizzy set to powdering the shiny spot on her nose. "The answer's still no.'

The mirror in her cloisonné compact reflected a heart-shaped face with a much-kissed snub nose and big eyes enlarged further by finely plucked brows and heaps of soot black mascara. It was only upon closer examination that one realized that one eye was brown, the other blue.

Fizzy's appointment diary rarely showed a blank spot.

Snapping the compact shut, she slotted a cigarette into its holder. Simultaneously, a battery of clicks produced enough light to power up half of Southern England and quite possibly a chunk of East Anglia, too. Thanking her gallant knights with an all-encompassing smile, Fizzy struck her own match and thought, funny how the entire male section of the Westlake Set was queuing to slip a diamond cluster on the third finger of her left hand – yet every time she pictured the hatload of kids she so desperately wanted, all the little beezers sported the same ski-slope noses, lopsided smiles and floppy fringes of the only man who'd never once jumped forward in a bid to light her gasper.

Damn you, Squiffy Hardcastle. Damn you to hell.

" – don't you think so, Fizzy?"

"Sorry, Kitty, didn't catch that."

"I was just saying, sweetheart, that his work's far too Gauginesque for my taste—"

Fizzy didn't bother asking whose work. "Absolutely," she replied, her mind elsewhere. On a certain painting, as it happened, in a gilt frame . . .

" – Matisse is living in the south of France, I hear—"

" – now does Lulu's stuff reflect Synthetic Cubism with a hint of Purist, d'you think, or pastoralism with a touch of Analytic Cubism?"

Snippets drifted past like ducks on the Thames, while Fizzy contemplated portraits in gilt frames . . .

"Sorry we're late, everyone."

Her train was interrupted as Orville Templeton, Hon.

Member for Knightsbridge & Chelsea, held out a chair for his wife.

"Traffic was an absolute stinker."

"You haven't missed much," Foxy told the newcomers. "Chilton and his protegé haven't arrived yet."

"Traffic, probably," Orville said, shooting his cuffs.

Poor Orville. Noble, worthy, gallant, dignified – a hundred decent men packed into one – and duller than a miner's bathwater. Fizzy exchanged smiles with his wife and thought the same couldn't be said of Gloria Templeton. Fizzy's best friend was five years older than her and a study in understatement, from the simple wedding band to the pale cream silk she always draped herself in. Not half as modish as Fizzy's white cloche, Gloria's broad-rimmed hats were perfect for hot summer evenings like this, flattering her chestnut bob and emphasizing her strong patrician features – though nothing could disguise the permanent sadness in her lovely green eyes.

That was the problem, Fizzy sighed, when one's still in love with one's first husband.

A husband, moreoever, who was handsome and charming, gave one two gorgeous daughters, then betrayed all three of them by getting himself blown to pieces in the very last week of the War. Her blue-brown gaze rested on Orville, looking for all the world like a reject from a second-rate taxidermist's. Poor Orville. The Hon. Member for K&C worshipped his new family. Adored Gloria. Idolized his adopted girls. Would do anything for them, anything at all. Even to accepting that he would only ever come second best . . .

Second best, of course, was a concept far beyond the scope of Fizzy Potter and, along the banquette, Bubbles was slipping her Cartier-encrusted wrist through Teddy Hardcastle's arm.

"I say, were you *really* the youngest captain in the Great War, Squiffy?"

Any closer, dammit, and she'd be a tattoo.

"Too jolly right he was," Marriott boomed. "Gave him a gong for it, too."

Hardcastle spiked his rebellious fringe out of his eyes, but made no effort to prise the limpet away.

"Take no notice of Marriott," he told Bubbles, with a flash of lopsided grin. "By the time I joined up they were running out of men. Another six months and they'd have made a machine gun captain."

"Don't be so damned modest, man," Marriott snorted. "It's the same with his bookbinding commissions, y'know, Bubbs. All that inlaying of coloured leather, gold fillets, those wossnames in enamelled porcelain you mount on the covers—"

"Plaques."

"Plaques, thank you, and that's without him encrusting the whole bloody thing with mother-of-pearl and those other wotnots."

"Cabochons."

"Cabochons, thank you, so don't let him tell you different, Bubbs. They're works of art he churns out."

But Bubbles wasn't interested in Hardcastle's technical aptitude. Rich bankers are dandy when it comes to footing bills at the likes of Chanel or Van Cleef & Arpels, but the trouble is, they *will* spend so much time at the bank. Having given one beau the old heave-ho tonight, she was looking to plug the vacancy fast.

"Why 'Squiffy', darling?"

With a glass of champagne permanently welded to one hand, even Biff could work out how she'd acquired *her* nickname.

"Not what you think, Bubbles," Foxy laughed. "It's from the way Teddy wore his cap at school, and damme if he don't still wear his hat at that angle."

On anyone else, Fizzy thought, it would come over rakish. On Teddy Hardcastle, the pitched brim lent a certain equanimity and she quietly damned ski-slope noses to eternal hellfire and sent lopsided smiles down the piste after them.

" – so this exhibition tomorrow," Orville said. "Is everyone going?"

"Are frogs waterproof?" Foxy Fairfax retorted.

And as though a light had been switched on, the whole group became animated about Chilton Westlake's new prodigy.

"What's the verdict on this, then?" Kitty asked, unrolling one of the posters she'd designed to publicise the exhibition at their friend's gallery. "Have I captured The Great Man, do you think?"

When Doc Frankenstein shot the first electrical bolt through his monster, it couldn't have made so much of a jolt.

"By Jove, Kitty." Biff was the first of the group to recover. "You've got the blighter off to a tee."

And how, Fizzy thought. Lank black hair, olive skin, stubbled chin, the slight sneer to his lips . . . dammit, this WAS Louis Boucard.

"Just as well one can't get scent off a poster," Biff added, wrinkling his prop forward's nose.

"He's French, darling!" Bubbles protested. "And an *artiste*, to boot. Parisians don't think the way we do."

What she meant, Fizzy reflected, was that soap and Louis Boucard were strangers, whereas booze and cocaine were blood brothers. She considered all the other attributes of this artistic genius – his gambling, his womanizing, his debauching of young girls – and wondered exactly how well Kitty Gardener had known Louis Boucard to be able to produce such an intimate representation.

Indeed, how well every other member of the Set had known him, to recognise what they were seeing . . .

"Can't stand the fellow, as y'know, but I do feel his work has an affinity with Chevaillier," Catspaw Gordon remarked, emerging from his doldrums at last.

The Boucard effect, of course, Fizzy mused. The uncombed Parisian touched a nerve with everyone sooner or later, and her thoughts flashed back to that portrait in its gilt frame . . .

" – pronounced Symbolist influence, certainly," Marriott was saying, "with a touch of the new Classicism overlaid with subtle early Cubist House elements and, hmm, maybe the merest smidgen of the draughtsmanship one sees in Migliorini—"

"Tosh!" Foxy Fairfax interjected. 'Boucard's a bounder and a cad who corrupts everything he touches! He's a liar, a conman, a thief and a cheat, and by his own admission, he trawls the gutters to paint –" he adopted an exaggerated French whine " – prozzitutes *et* felons."

"Yes, darling, but there's something so utterly exciting about the demi-monde, don't you think?" Bubbles shuddered delightedly. "I mean, all that naked flesh and loucheness? I find his work riveting. How about you, Squiffy?'

But before Teddy Hardcastle had a chance to venture his opinion on this blight on the moral and artistic landscape,

Chilton Westlake, the gallery owner whose name the Set had adopted for their Friday night get-togethers, arrived wearing a mustard check suit, straw boater and a face like absolute thunder. He was also alone.

"Have you seen these?" His chubby fist pounded the newspapers in his hand. "Have you?" He didn't wait for an answer. "*The Westlake Gallery is holding an exhibition of exciting new Parisian artist, Louis Boucard,*" he read.

"Sounds just about top-hole to me," Orville exclaimed. "You wanted a plug for the old show."

"Plug? PLUG?"

Chilton was in danger of testing medical science's latest advances in cardiac technology.

"*I* was supposed to be one doing the plugging here, matcy. Instead, what happens? Boucard only gives me some cock-and-bull story about needing to borrow the key to the gallery to make a couple of last minute alterations, don't he?"

"Inviting the press for a sneak preview instead, I suppose?"

Trust Gloria to get there before anybody else.

"*Boucard's bold style pushes the boundaries of art deco to a new dimension,* says the London Bulletin."

Chilton tossed the paper on the floor and ground it with his spatted heel.

"*A greater whiff of decadence than a hundred Tamara de Lempickas,* according to the Evening ruddy Witness, and I wouldn't have minded him stealing a march on my show," he said, gulping down Marriott's martini. "But get this."

He hurled the paper at Foxy, who read aloud.

" – *Boucard has promised a work entitled 'Revelation' in addition to the paintings listed in the catalogue. A portrait, the likes of which, he claims, has never before been on public display in this country – a portrait so daring, so scandalous that he's keeping it under velvet until the official opening. Even the gallery owner* . . . Oh, I say, Chilton, is that right?" Foxy goggled. "That even *you* have no idea of this picture's content?"

Westlake glugged down Kitty's drink and even managed to prise Bubble's bubbles out her grasp.

"Couldn't be righter, old man. First I knew about this so-called 'Revelation' was when I read about it in the bloody papers."

His little fat hand lashed out to tip Catspaw's, Biff's and Teddy's drinks down the hatch, his expression brightening only slightly when he noticed a stupendous pair of knees crossed elegantly on the soft leather banquette.

"But the really galling thing," he wailed, "was that Boucard had the cheek to tap me for the fare back to the gallery, and that's not the first time he's tapped for a tenner, either!"

Fizzy's martini was the last remaining casualty and Chilton Westlake was in no mood for taking prisoners.

"I'll kill the little bashtard," he said, his boater rolling under the table as he slid down the table. "Sho help me, I'll shlit his dirty French throat and then I'll pull his bloody gizzards through the hole."

At that stage, of course, no-one actually believed him.

3 p.m. on a Saturday afternoon and the Westlake Gallery resembled more tin of sardines than a preview of an exhibition by a hitherto unknown artist. No invitation had been refused, placing something of a strain on the nosebags and drink trays, since Chilton invariably considered himself lucky if one third of his invites turned up to these dos, most often only a quarter (and those usually only relatives and friends). Today the place was packed to the gunwales and, despite bloodshot eyes and an aversion to bright lights, he wasn't looking half as bad as Fizzy expected. That, she supposed, was because the gallery stood to make a mint from the sensational publicity and give Boucard his due. The Frenchman knew how to play the press.

"Not drinking, sweetheart? Splendid!" Kitty swapped her empty glass for Fizzy's full one. "Stuff's in perilously short supply. Well, chin-chin."

Straightening his purple bow tie, Chilton Westlake mounted the podium and launched into a speech about his exciting new protegé and Fizzy noted the care he took to plug the other artists he'd sponsored, clearly intent on shifting as much stock as possible today. Sadly, though, her little plump friend was better at evaluating works of art than talking about them and her attention wandered in the direction of certain portait in a gilt frame. Entitled "Woman in a Mask", it was typical of Boucard's style in that –

"I'm not convinced Bubbles finds the demi-monde half as

riveting as she'd supposed," a wry baritone murmured in Fizzy's cloche-covered ear.

She followed Teddy's gaze to where the banker's wife was sandwiched between a brace of hard-eyed villains and a group of women in red heels and even redder lips. In another surprise for Chilton, Boucard had mischievously invited several of his "prozzitutes *et* felons", who were swigging champagne and helping themselves to cigars on an industrial scale. Bubbles's high colour showed she was finding it hard to reconcile the fact that, any minute, she'd be seeing these same people sprawled naked across the gallery walls.

Chilton cleared his throat.

" – I now call upon Louis to join us and declare this exhibition open!"

Nothing.

"I said," he repeated, raising his voice, "that I now call upon Louis Boucard to come out from the back room and open the exhibition held in his honour."

Knowing glances rippled round the crowd, as well as one or two giggles. Drink, drugs, you name it, only a relentless optimist like Chilton could seriously have expected the artist to be sober during the daytime. Louis Boucard was a creature of the night. In every respect.

"Haw, haw." Chilton tried to cover the gaffe with humour. "Not sure I'll ever understand you temperamental *artistes*—"

Bubbles seized the opportunity to detach herself from her underworld sandwich to fetch him, but she wasn't alone for very long. The shrill scream and the accompanying crash of crystal said it all.

Louis Boucard was dead.

"And you are, miss?"

"Phyllis Potter, 62 Northwell Mansions, Bayswater." Fizzy's smile was directed straight at the constable, but her glance was slanted at the man standing beside her. "Right between the museum and a gentleman's club, if you must know."

"Thank you, miss. And you, sir?"

"Edward James Hardcastle, 17b Elton Square, Chelsea." He kept his eyes straight. "Too many stuffed shirts and old fossils for my taste."

"Oh, dear. Elderly residents are they, sir?"

"Not exactly, constable. Is that all?"

"For the moment, yes, thank you. But we're asking people not to venture far from the scene, as there will doubtless be other questions we wish to ask. In fact, I understand there's a bar down the road—"

"Jo-Jo's," Fizzy said. "We know it well, constable. Regular watering hole," she added, tossing her boa over her shoulder, but instead of following Kitty and Marriott out into the afternoon sunshine, she took advantage of the milling confusion to slip into the anteroom.

Ugh. Louis Boucard wasn't what one would call classically handsome in life. Grey and waxy in death, he was even more unprepossessing! She took care not to tread in the broken glass from Bubbles's champagne as she approached the desk where he was slumped. Someone, it appeared, had caved the prodigy's head in with a rather sleek black marble panther. The bloodied statuette lay on the desk among enough cocaine – she tasted the powder with a tentative finger – yes, with enough cocaine to supply a small continent for a decade, possibly two.

So then. Not content to take it himself. Louis had been pushing the stuff.

"You realize he was dead before he was beaned?"

Fizzy yelped, half of her livid that she hadn't noticed him leaning against the wall with his hands stuffed deep in his pockets. While the other half was too busy picturing her hatful of kids made in this man's wretched image . . .

"If you're telling me someone frightened him to death," she said coolly, "I'm not remotely surprised."

A muscle twitched at the side of Teddy Hardcastle's mouth. "Boucard, I fear, was more tormenter than tormented."

He feared right. Louis could be facing an army of flesh-eating zombies and he'd con them back to the grave.

"Look."

Teddy lifted a hank of dark hair to reveal a puncture wound in Boucard's dirty neck.

"The ice pick or whatever severed his spinal cord, paralyzing all muscular activity. The lungs stopped functioning, so did the heart, but death, as always I'm afraid, comes slowly."

Fizzy reeled and was immediately caught in a steel net that smelled of ski slopes and pine.

"Never fear, Phyllis Potter of 62 Northwell Drive, Bayswater. Looks like he was unconscious when it happened."

Fizzy disentangled herself from his arms, slightly surprised that bookbinders had so many muscles.

"Why aren't the police swarming all over this room?" she asked.

"Ah, well. It would appear our boys in blue haven't realized that there would be more blood, had Louis been alive when he was brained, and knowing the blunt instrument to be a favourite among the criminal underclass, they rather fancy one of those as the culprit."

Solicitously, Teddy straightened her hat. Fizzy jerked away, hoping he couldn't see the furious blush that had suffused her cheeks.

"What guff," she snapped. "Those girls aren't on the game because they enjoy it. They're dishing out knee-tremblers because they've run out of options, and even if one of them *had* killed Louis Boucard, they'd never leave a fortune in cocaine lying around."

Not when it would buy them their freedom – and no self-respecting thief would dream of walking away empty-handed, no matter *how* pushed they had been to commit murder!

"Precisely the argument I presented to His Majesty's law enforcers," he began, but whatever else he was going to say was overtaken by the door bursting open and Chilton, Orville, Gloria and a uniformed inspector rushing into the room.

"This is an outrage," Chilton was blustering. "An absolute bloody outrage! Why should *I* want to kill him?"

"You have a persuasive line in arguments, Mr Hardcastle," Fizzy muttered under her breath. "You got them to abandon the criminal underclass, so they're pinching Chilton's collar instead."

The inspector shot her a venomous glance and continued.

"You were overheard threatening the deceased in the Pink Parrot nightclub last night," he told Chilton, leaving the assembled company in no doubt as to his opinion of such a den of tangoed iniquity. "Lewis Buckard had given the press an unauthorized showing—"

"For heaven's sake, man, it's *Louis*," Chilton protested, "pronounced Boo-car."

" – and he'd also been holding out on you with regard to a mysterious portrait. To wit, this."

He indicated the easel in the corner draped in black velvet.

"Inspector," Orville cut in, "I have explained how Mr Westlake was in plain view of everyone at all times this afternoon. I don't see how you can possibly follow this ridiculous line of questioning."

In true political style, the Hon. Member then rephrased his argument in fifteen different ways. Somewhere between the fourth and the fifth, Gloria came across and took both Fizzy's hands in hers.

"Are you all right, darling? You look terribly pale."

"Yes, I'm fine, really I am. Just a shock, that's all, seeing death at close quarters."

She glanced at Teddy Hardcastle, who had seen more of it and at far closer quarters, then looked back into Gloria's permanently sad eyes.

They'd been laughing, that was the terrible part. Celebrating because Fizzy had landed her first job with *À la Mode* and Gloria had just received confirmation that baby number two, already well advanced, was healthy and ready to hatch out on schedule. Yes, they'd been laughing fit to burst when that telegram came . . .

Fizzy shivered. "The police don't really suspect Chilton, do they?"

"Darling, if they had a man standing over the body waving a placard written in Louis's own blood which read 'It was me', they'd still think the butler did it."

Gloria glanced at her husband, boring the inspector into submission.

"Orville will set them right," she assured her.

Shouldn't be hard, either, Fizzy supposed. To compensate for his physical shortcomings, Chilton upholstered himself in the loudest checks he could find. Top that with a purple bow tie and spats, and who could miss him?'

"For goodness sake," Chilton snorted. "I'm hardly likely to kill the goose that lays my golden eggs, am I, you clod?"

The inspector, who wasn't entirely won over by being

labelled a clod, didn't take to having his chest prodded, either.

"You're wasting time," Chilton snapped, "and anyway, what about the theft of my picture, eh? Eh? Why aren't you investigating *that*?"

"What picture?" Fizzy asked Gloria.

Patrician eyes rolled. "Wouldn't you just know that while this kerfuffle's been going on, someone would filch one of the exhibits? Of course, it'll be worth a fortune on the black market after today. Chilton's incandescent."

"Nonsense," Fizzy murmured. "He probably snitched it himself, to drive up the price of the others."

"So true, darling. No artist is ever worth so much as when he dies."

Meanwhile, the combination of being branded incompetent, a dim-wit, having a finger poked in his breast bone and being blasted with the notion that theft ranked higher than murder was doing little to enhance the inspector's opinion of Chilton. Especially since the accusations were being made in front of the Hon. Member for Knightsbridge & Chelsea.

"What Mr Westlake is forgetting, sir," he told Orville, "is that apart from Lewis Buckard playing him for a sucker over the publicity, he'd borrowed money from him totalling nearly one hundred pounds, which he apparently had no intention of repaying, and we know he was holding out on him."

He indicated the velvet-draped easel as he read from the press.

". . . *the likes of which has never been on public display before in this country – a portrait so daring, so scandalous that he's keeping it under velvet until the official opening*. 'Revelation', Mr Buckard called it."

With a flourish that could only be described as smug, he whisked off the velvet.

Revelation indeed. Six pair of eyes gaped at the empty frame.

Teddy Hardcastle let out a soft laugh.

"B-but—" Chilton couldn't find words to express what he felt.

"Well, I say!" Orville could.

The inspector rubbed his jaw for what seemed like an hour, pausing only to glower at Chilton in the way a lioness might watch her marked zebra leap the gorge into safety.

"Do you suppose," he asked eventually, "that it was within Mr Buckard's character to pull a fast one to drum up publicity? That there never *was* a scandalous portrait to unveil?"

Five voices responded as one, the verdict unanimous. Such a stunt was *well* within Boucard's capabilities, they replied.

Cue more jaw-rubbing by His Majesty's servant.

"Whoever killed Mr Buckard did so by holding the weapon in this—" he held up one of numerous soft cloths used in the gallery to dust the frames " – to avoid leaving fingerprints. Unfortunately, we have no witnesses to say they saw anyone go in or come out of this room."

"Why would they?" Orville asked reasonably. "We were all facing the podium, inspector, anxiously awaiting the moment when the doors to the exhibition would open and we could be one of the first to see, and hopefully grab a slice of, this new and prodigious young talent."

"There were nearly eighty people crammed into my gallery," Chilton snapped, "and not all of them with gilt-edged invites, I might add. You mark my words, one of those low-lifes killed Louis."

The inspector turned his scowl on Teddy Hardcastle, making it clear who was responsible for diverting precious resources on this ridiculous wild goose chase when the police had had it sussed all along. With a loud "harrumph" he stomped back into the gallery, trailed by Chilton and Orville, with Gloria adding poise to the rear and leaving Fizzy alone with Teddy once more. This time, though, the silence between them stretched to infinity.

"The question," he said at last, "isn't who killed Louis Boucard, is it?"

"No?" Frogs croak louder, she thought.

"No." He let the wall take his weight at the shoulder. "The question is, why should *two* people want to kill the same man."

Turning out of the gallery into the glorious midsummer sunshine, a mischievous breeze whisked off Gloria's hat and carried it halfway down Mayfair. Biff, of course, would have tackled it before it had gone fifteen yards, but Biff was already ensconced in Jo-Jo's Jazz Cellar sinking his second martini and by the time the Hon. Member for K&C had picked up sufficient speed, a

Ford with an unnecessarily heavy foot on its accelerator had flattened Gloria's masterpiece right between the tulle and the rosebuds. Another time and the group would have hooted with laughter. Today, though, a man's life had been taken and the crushing, in an instant, of something so vibrant and bright stood for all that had happened.

On the other hand, it's an ill wind. Fizzy couldn't help but notice the look of gratitude and affection that Gloria shot her husband as handed the battered titfer back to his wife and her heart gladdened. He was a good egg, the Hon. Member, and whilst he wasn't – and would never be – the love of her friend's life, she'd always felt he deserved more than mere recognition.

"Well?" A long stride fell into step alongside her, its fedora angled low over one half of his forehead.

"Any more thoughts?"

In front of them, Orville had offered a chivalrous arm to his wife and although Fizzy had hoped for a similar offer from Teddy, none came. She adjusted her beads, smoothed her drop waistline, tucked her clutch bag under her arm and thought, who cares about floppy hair anyway?

"I mean," he added evenly, "you must know it's one of us.'

"Don't you mean two of us?"

Dammit, Pekingese dogs don't snap that hard, but if Teddy Hardcastle noticed, it didn't show.

"Foxy called him a cad and a bounder," he said, "and not without justification. Did you know Boucard conned him out of five hundred pounds?"

"*How much?*"

To an illustrator of children's books, that was a fortune, and Fizzy calculated that she'd have to work until she was a hundred and twenty-eight to cover that kind of spare cash. Oh, Foxy, Foxy, what have you done . . . ?

"We've already heard the inspector's case against Chilton," Teddy said, stuffing his hands in his pockets.

Pity, because they were nice hands, with just the right amount of crisp, dark hairs on the back, and she'd pictured them tooling, stamping, making intricate mosaics of metal and leather. Perhaps, in his painstaking artisan mind, magazine illustrators came in on a level with doodlers?

"Also, our Parisian friend helped himself to a whole pile of

Bubble's jewels in, quote, payment for services rendered, unquote. He derided Catspaw's cartoons in the press, got Marriott to underwrite an enterprise that didn't exist and – this must go no further, please – he also got Kitty Gardener pregnant. That's the reason she zipped off to Zurich in the spring."

"Not a poster designer's convention, then?'

"There's a clinic that deals with these things—"

She didn't dare ask how he knew.

" – and it's common knowledge that Lulu was engaged to friend Louis until she found him in bed with Bubbles, and you know how passionately Biff feels about his sister's honour. Damme," he added lightly, "if the list ain't just about endless."

"Aren't you're forgetting someone else with a grudge against Boucard?" Fizzy asked as they reached the steps of the Cellar. "Someone, for instance, like you?"

Ahead of them, Orville was tipping the doorman and Chilton was checking in his boater, but Teddy remained behind on the steps.

"You don't say."

"Oh, but I do say." Suddenly the sunshine seemed terribly bright. "I don't know where you gathered *your* gossip from—"

"Information," he corrected mildly. "We called it information in the Intelligence." Adding, in response to her involuntary raising of eyebrows, "There was a lot to sort out after the Armistice."

The hundreds, no thousands, of atrocities committed after the surrender flashed through her mind as it occurred to her that maybe that's what inspired soldiers to become bookbinders. Intricate, absorbing, it makes one forget . . .

She coughed. "Anyway, don't think I don't know that Louis got your kid brother hooked on a certain white powdery substance."

And him only sixteen, poor sap.

"I see," Teddy said slowly. "So which do you have me pegged for? The puncture wound, the blunt object or both?"

Fizzy took a step back up the stairs to meet him square in the eye.

"Louis Boucard," she said stiffly, "was a man with neither scruples nor conscience, but reasons to hate aren't motives for murder, and even if they were, then the killer would surely choose somewhere more private, wouldn't they, where they're more likely to get away with it?"

"Ah, but they are going to get away with it," Teddy replied softly, holding her miscoloured gaze. *"Aren't they?"*

Down in the Jazz Cellar, it looked like a tornado had swept through the place, with the contents of handbags and pockets spilling over every table and chair as the police searched everyone who'd been in the gallery in an effort to find the missing portrait of a young woman wearing nothing but a painted Venetian mask. The sombre mood quickly gave way to hilarity as photographs fell out of wallets showing girls who were definitely not the title-holders' wives along with two cream buns discovered in the kitbag of a woman who constantly bored people rigid with tales of her regimented diet. But no paintings of women in masks!

Having been officially declared a A Snitched-Portrait-Free Zone, Fizzy found a sudden need to sit down. As shaking hands slotted a cigarette in its holder, she found herself met with the usual click of a dozen offers for light and one noticeable absence.

"I say, Fizzy, are you free for the opera on Saturday?" Biff wanted to know. "Well, how about the Saturday after?"

"Tough luck, old man," Marriott cut in, "because I've already got my offer in for a spin down to the seaside in the old jaloppy. What d'you say, old girl? Are you up for it?"

"Excuse me."

She had to pass Teddy to reach the powder room, but managed to do it without meeting his eye, though suddenly, there seemed to be something wrong with her breathing. Just not enough air in the club. Once inside the pink painted sanctuary, she sank against the door, the feathers on her white silk cloche hat fluttering with each tremble that she gave.

"Goodness, darling."

Gloria, a vision in her customary cream silk, stopped abruptly from the business of applying lipstick to her perfect pout.

"You look like you've seen a ghost!"

A hundred ghosts, Fizzy thought, recalling laughter, first jobs, second babies. Telegrams –

Her legs felt like they'd been filleted. There was no blood in her veins. None at all.

"That gust of wind gave it away," she said quietly.

The lipstick in Gloria's hand faltered, but only momentarily.

"In all the years I've known you," Fizzy continued, "you've always worn wide-brimmed hats, Gloria, but the one thing they need that a cloche doesn't is a hat pin."

Not an ice pick.

Louis Boucard was killed with a hat pin.

"And when the wind took yours down the street, I knew."

As did Teddy Hardcastle.

She drew a deep, shuddering breath. "I presume it was because of your affair?"

Gloria swallowed. "I went in to that with my eyes wide open, darling, because whatever other faults Louis might have had, he . . . well, let's just say he didn't have them in the bedroom department."

Fizzy felt it best to let that one pass.

"But he used you as a subject?"

That was his great "Revelation" – and what greater dynamite for an advertising campaign than the wife of a respected politician on public display?

"Like the press said, he only ever paints nudes," Gloria said ruefully. "But the treachery is that he painted me while I slept. I hadn't an inkling until he started blackmailing me – he was always in arrears with the bookies."

"He wanted more, I suppose?"

"No."

Gloria fixed her perpetually sad eyes on her friend.

"Orville's positively swimming in lolly and quite frankly the amount I was paying Louis, Orville didn't even notice. Another frock, another hat – he didn't question it. No, the trouble started once people began to appreciate the genius of Louis's work. You see, the two things my lover wanted most in life were to be rich and famous, and that's when he decided to unveil his masterpiece. To propel himself into the limelight."

She drew herself up to her full height.

"Me, I could have ridden the storm, I've ridden worse, and the girls are too young to understand. But Orville, darling – Orville's a good man, and to see him publicly humiliated as a cuckold . . . Well, he'd have stood by me, no question, but the scandal would have destroyed him. I couldn't let Louis do that.'

"So you did the only decent thing? Stabbed him with your hat pin?"

What little colour was left drained from Gloria's face at the sharpness of her friend's tone.

"It wasn't what I intended, believe me. The idea was to sneak in and steal the horrid thing, but when I slipped into the back room, he was collapsed over his precious cocaine and—" She made a brave attempt at a smile. "Typical Louis. Never did know when to stop."

"Why kill him, Gloria?"

"Why not, darling? If you'd only seen Kitty after she got back from Switzerland! The doctors say she'll never be able to have another baby, did you know that? And then there's Foxy. Five hundred pounds, can you imagine? He'd ruined poor Lulu, was blackmailing Bubbles, had said terrible things about Catspaw, so I thought, what the hell."

Gloria pointed to a spot on the back of her elegant swan neck.

"I read that if you go right between the vertebrae it severs the spinal cord. He was out cold, Fizzy. I swear he never felt a thing, and if you ask me do I regret it, I can honestly put my hand on my heart and say it was no worse than putting a rabid dog down."

Fizzy counted to three.

"Except you couldn't bring yourself to pull the pin out?"

Gloria shuddered. "Could *you*?"

Fizzy doubted she could have driven it in in the first place. But then she wasn't a widow still deeply in love with a dead husband doing the best for her two tiny daughters by marrying someone who worshipped the ground they all walked on. A rich man, moreover, who would do anything to protect them. Anything at all –

"Orville saw you, didn't he? Orville saw you come out of that room, no doubt ashen and shaking—"

"I didn't know." Gloria collapsed onto the stool and buried her head in her hands. "I swear, darling, I had no idea, not until they said he'd been hit over the head with that panther."

It didn't take much working out, really. Orville saw his wife come out of the back room and wanted to know why Louis was upsetting his wife. What went through his head when he saw Louis dead and his wife's hatpin sticking out of his neck? Fizzy swallowed. Not such a dull stick, after all. Quite the hero, in fact, because it was Orville who pulled out the weapon, then disguised the method of murder by bringing the black marble panther down on his head.

"What did you do with the incriminating canvas?" Fizzy asked. "Everyone's been searched."

A hint of colour returned to Gloria's cheeks. "What I planned from the outset." She opened her bag to reveal a pair of nail scissors. "I cut it into tiny pieces and flushed it back to the sewer where it belongs."

Congratultions to Chilton Westlake, Fizzy thought. He'd been very insistent about having all mod cons installed at the gallery!

"What are you going to do now, darling?" Gloria asked.

This time Fizzy counted to ten. Then ten more.

"About what?" she replied steadily. "I only came in here to adjust my suspenders. This left one's digging in like the blazes."

She swallowed two tablets for migraine.

"Is it my fault we ended up talking for ages about what hats we might be wearing for Ascot?"

It was gone midnight when the Set finally tumbled out of the Cellar, leaving Jo-Jo one very happy proprietor, having trousered twice the usual takings. The moon was full and waxy, inspiring stars to twinkle, cats to yowl and Foxy Fairfax to treat Londoners with a loud rendition of *Danny Boy*.

"Fancy putting on the old nosebag with me, Fizzy?" Marriott asked, with a hopeful twiddle of the yellow rose in his buttonhole. "Only there's this little French place I know round the corner that serves up some pretty nifty proteins and starch."

"We could all go," Biff said, elbowing Marriott out of the way.

"If you don't mind, I'll give the roasts and boileds a miss tonight, chaps. I rather fancy an early night is in order."

And besides. There was a cold, twisted knot deep inside that wouldn't let her eat if she tried.

"Don't be a wet blanket, sweetheart," Kitty said, pouring

Bubbles into the back of her car. "There's plenty of room with us girls."

"I know!" Biff nodded towards his convertible parked with its usual insouciance half on, half off the kerb whilst managing to completely block a back alley. "Let's all go to the Kitty Kat Klub!"

"Good idea," Bubbles and Kitty chorused together.

"It won't be the first time you've sat on my knee, Fizzy," Catspaw said.

"No, but it'd be the first time she's sat on mine, so don't be greedy, old man," Chilton retorted.

"Actually," a voice rumbled beneath a fedora set at a rakish (some might say dignified) angle, "the lady's already accepted a lift."

"Dammit, Squiffy, you always get the pretty ones," Catspaw wailed, as Biff revved up the engine. "See you up there, then, what?"

"Twenty minutes," Teddy promised, as the convertible cranked off the kerb with a splutter. Across the way, Orville was opening the door of his Rolls for Gloria and Teddy watched impassively as the Hon. Member settled himself behind the wheel and purred off.

"Happy endings all round, then," he murmured.

"Not for Louis Boucard," Fizzy said.

Teddy pursed his lips, but only briefly. "True, but let's face it, the world's one scoundrel lighter and none the worse for it, and what odds the police make six wrong arrests before they stuff the file in the 'Unsolved' archives and forget it?"

"Is that your definition of happy ending?"

"Ask Chilton. He'll make four times as much dosh with his prodigy dead and how fortunate there was no scandal to come out, that velvet-covered easel being nothing more than a practical joke and all that."

"Oh, that sort of happy ending."

Teddy leaned against the brickwork and stuffed his hands into his pockets. "Actually," he said quietly. "I was rather thinking of Chilton's missing exhibit and the matter of true love running smooth."

"There *was* no portrait, remember?"

"Not under the velvet, no. I meant the one you stole when

everyone was crowding into the room when Bubbles found Boucard's body."

Fizzy reached into her handbag for a cigarette and attached it to the holder with a surprisingly steady hand.

"I don't even like Louis's work," she said. "Why would I steal one of his beastly paintings? Cubist mixed with Symbolist—"

" – and just the merest smidgen of the draughtsmanship one sees in Migliorini. Yes, I know. Ghastly, aren't they? Especially the portraits of masked nudes with one brown eye and one blue."

A lighter clicked in the darkness and suddenly Fizzy's hand was anything but steady.

"I saw it in his studio when I went round to persuade him to lay off my brother. Unfortunately, our French friend was out, so I never did get chance to exercise my knuckles. Shame, that."

"Maybe that was another practical joke," she said evenly. "I mean, we've all been searched. Thoroughly, as I recall."

A soft laugh echoed into the night. "Ah, women! What cunning and devious creatures thou art, is it any wonder we men are in thy thrall? First, Gloria—"

"How did you know it was her?"

"Don't tell anyone, but His Majesty's Intelligence Service relies more on guesswork than they'd like people to think. But in this case, Miss Potter, I know Boucard, I know his type and more importantly—"

Before she'd even realised what had happened, she found herself in his arms.

" – I know how human minds tick. Not to mention," he added an eternity later, "that there are widgets designed to stop ladies' hats from bowling down Mayfair that are called, strangely enough, hat pins."

"And the panther?"

"Who else would cover up another person's murder? I suspect they'll both view each other differently from now own. A rather more balanced relationship, one would hope."

"So that's what you meant by happy endings and true love running smooth."

"Hadn't quite got to that last bit," he said, kissing her again. "Only it strikes me that Fizzy Potter is a nice enough name, whereas Fizzy Hardcastle tends to run off the tongue rather more smoothly, don't you think?"

She couldn't be hearing this right. "Edward James Hardcastle, are you actually asking me to *marry you?*"

"Not tonight. Far too late to knock up a vicar. But yes. That seems to be the general consensus."

But . . . Fizzy pulled away.

"What about the painting?"

"What about it?" he rasped, drawing her back, and when they finally came up for air, he said, "I don't imagine you'll make a habit of stealing. I mean, the logistics of bringing the kids to visit you in the clink would be an absolute nightmare."

"That's not what I meant," she stuttered.

He gave her nose a little tweak.

"Like my kid brother, darling, we all have siblings."

He tilted her chin up to face him.

"The eyes were the wrong way round, Fizzy. Yours," he said kissing them in turn, "are blue on the left, brown on the right and trust me, artists of Boucard's calibre don't get such details wrong."

For the first time in her life, Fizzy knew what it was to be floating on air.

"I suppose I *might* consider marrying you—" she began, though her actual thoughts ran more along the lines of wild horses.

"Very kind.'

" – but what about money? Neither of us earns very much—"

"True," he agreed, "but don't you think this," he whisked off her cloche hat and pulled out "Woman in a Mask", "should get us off to a good start?"

"Do you mind!"

Fizzy snatched at her sister's naked image and stuffed it back under the brim.

"It's worth a fortune on the black market," he rumbled.

"Teddy Hardcastle, you aren't seriously asking me to weigh my sister's morals against cold hard cash?"

She rammed the cloche back over her bob.

"Because if you are, you ought to know right now that I won't use something as tawdry as this to pay my electricity bill!"

She adjusted the cloche and thought, silly cow. Shouldn't have posed for him in the first place.

"A honeymoon, on the other hand . . ."

Teddy's laughter echoed into the darkness. "Which do you fancy, you wicked, wicked child? A fortnight in Antibes? Or would you prefer to see Venice?"

Fizzy snuggled back into his muscular arms. "Don't care," she murmured.

Because with that painting they could afford both.

The Day of Two Cars

GILLIAN LINSCOTT

Now here's a little-known fact. Did you know that the very first public telephone box was set up in Britain in 1921? And not just in cities but in rural areas, areas where city life seemed so far away. That's the scene that Gillian Linscott wanted to explore, where rural and city life met in the 1920s. Gillian is no stranger to the 1920s, or rather the years leading up to them. Her series about suffragette Nell Bray, which began in Sister Beneath the Sheets *(1991) has taken us from the Edwardian period and through the First World War.*

"It was a young woman who found him," the village constable said. "Molly Davitt, the blacksmith's daughter. She thought he was having a conversation on the telephone. After a while when he didn't move she decided something might be wrong."

"After how long, exactly?" the inspector asked. He was a city man and disliked vagueness.

"Half an hour or so, Molly says. Could be longer."

"You mean to tell me this young woman stood watching a man in a telephone box for half an hour or more?"

"There's not much happens round here. And the fact is, Molly's been fascinated with that telephone box from the time they put it up."

It was the spring of 1924 when they came to install the telephone box in Tadley Gate. Nobody was quite sure why. The men from the Post Office travelled from Hereford, 17 miles away as the pigeon flew and half as much again by winding country road. All they knew was that they'd been instructed to erect the standard model Kiosk One, designed to be especially suitable for rural areas, on the edge of the common, in between the old pump and the new war memorial. It was made of reinforced concrete slabs with a red painted wooden door and large windows in the door and sides. In a touch of Post Office swagger, a decorative curlicue of wrought iron crowned it, finishing in a spike that some people assumed was an essential part of the mechanism. Nobody in Tadley Gate (pop. 227) had asked for a telephone kiosk and very few had ever used a telephone. Still, they were pleased. The coming of the kiosk was an event at least, which made two events in eighteen months, counting back to the other new arrival, the petrol pump. The petrol pump belonged to Davy Davitt, Molly's father. A third generation blacksmith by trade, he'd had more than enough of horses and fallen in love with cars. The sign over his workshop said "Blacksmith and Farrier" in the curly oldfashioned letters that had been good enough for his grandfather. Underneath he'd painted, stark and white. "Motor Vehicle Repairs Undertaken." The fact that the parish included 33 horses and ponies and only one motor car limited his scope but he was a resourceful man. Long negotiations with a distant petrol company ended with the arrival of a tank and a pump. The pump was red like the phone kiosk door, topped by a globe of frosted glass with a cockleshell and "Sealed Shell" on it in black letters. The tank below it held 500 gallons of petrol, delivered by motor tanker. In the first year Davy's only sales were five gallons every other week to the colonel from the big house who drove a Hillman Peace model very cautiously, so at that rate it would be nearly four years before the tanker needed to come with another delivery. But as Davy told anybody who'd listen in the Duke of Wellington, that was only the start. He was looking ahead to the arrival of the motor tourer. It stood to reason that as more people bought cars and the cars became more reliable, they'd drive for pleasure far away from cities and into the countryside. It didn't matter that the only motor tourist Tadley Gate had ever seen was somebody who'd got badly confused on the way to Shrewsbury and didn't want to be there.

Davy believed in the petrol pump the way an Indian believed in his totem pole. He was even inclined to credit it with attracting the telephone kiosk to the village. He reasoned that now, properly equipped with both telephone and petrol pump, Tadley Gate was ready to unglue itself from the mud and enter the age of speed. Only the age of speed seemed to be taking its time about getting there.

Molly had no strong feelings about the petrol pump. She didn't like the smell much, but petrol was no worse than the throat-grabbing whiff of burning horn when her father fitted red-hot shoes to horses' hooves. On the other hand, the phone box enchanted her from the day it arrived. She was twenty then and single, having just broken her engagement to a local farmer's son. The second broken engagement, as it happened, and more than enough to get her a reputation as a jilt. She honestly regretted that. She'd quite liked the farmer's son, as she'd quite liked the young grain merchant before him, but shied away from marriage because they were both of them firmly tied by work and family to the country around Tadley Gate. If she married either of them she'd have had to stay there for life and she knew – with the instinct that tells a buried bulb which way is upwards – that staying at Tadley Gate wasn't the way things were meant to be. She'd been away from the village once, for a family wedding in Birmingham where she'd been a bridesmaid. In the days before and after the ceremony she'd gone with her cousins to the cinema, bought underwear in a department store, read the *Daily Mail* and seen advertisements in magazines of sleek women poised on diving boards, leaning against the bonnets of cars, dancing quick-time foxtrot in little pointed shoes with men in evening dress. At the end of the visit she'd gone quietly back to Tadley Gate with a new shorter hairstyle that nobody commented on, an unused lipstick tucked into her skirt pocket and a conviction as deep as her father's belief in his petrol pump that the world must somehow find itself her way. The men who came to set up the telephone kiosk, pleased to find an unexpectedly beautiful girl in such an out of the way place, had been only too pleased as they worked to answer the questions she put to them in her soft local accent.

"So who can you talk to from here?" (She had the idea that a telephone had a predetermined number of lines, each one to a different and single other telephone.)

"Anyone," they said.

The elder and more serious of the two explained that when she went into the kiosk and picked up the receiver, a buzzer would sound in the telephone exhange. Then, in exchange for coins in the slot, the operator would connect her with anybody she wanted, anywhere in the country.

"But how would she know? How would the operator know where to find them?"

"Everybody has their own number," the older man explained. "They're written down on a list."

"So if you had a particular friend," the younger man said, risking a wink at her, "he'd give you his exchange and number and you'd give that to the operator, then you could talk to him even if he was hundreds of miles away."

"So I could stand here and talk to somebody in Birmingham or London?"

"As long as your pennies lasted," the other man said.

At lunchtime she brought them out bread and cheese and cups of tea. At the end of the afternoon as they packed up their tools, the younger man explained about police calls.

"You don't have to put any money in. Just tell the operator you want police and she puts you straight through."

"To Constable Price?"

He was their local man, operating from his police house in a larger village three miles away.

"Or any policeman. Just run to the box, pick up the telephone and they'll come racing along as if they was at Brooklands."

Constable Price only had a bicycle. She assumed a telephone call would bring a faster kind of police altogether. It all added to the glamour of the phone kiosk. When the men had gone she stood looking at it for a long time, went in and touched the receiver gently and reverently. It was inert on its cradle and yet she felt it buzzing with the potential of a whole world. Every day her errands around the village would take her past it. She'd slow down, touch the kiosk, sometimes go inside and touch the receiver itself, trying to find the courage to pick it up. One autumn day, she managed it. The woman's voice at the other end, bright and metallic as a new sixpence, said "Hello. What number please?" She dropped the receiver back on its cradle, heart thumping. She didn't know anybody's number, nobody's in the world. But in her dreams, one day a number would come into her head and she'd say it. Then the operator would say "Certainly, madam," the way they did in the department stores in Birmingham, the phone would click and buzz and there would be somebody on the other end – London, Worcester, anywhere – who'd say how nice to hear from her and he could tell from her voice that he'd like her no end, so why didn't he come in a car or even an aeroplane and whisk her away to a place where she could quick-time foxtrot in little pointed shoes and drink from a triangular glass under a striped umbrella? What was the point of telephones, after all, if they couldn't do magic? So like her father with his petrol pump she waited patiently for it to happen.

"So," the Inspector said, "Miss Davitt decides after half an hour or possibly longer that all might not be well with our man in the kiosk. So she looks more closely and finds Tod Barker with the back of his head cracked open the way you'd take a spoon to your breakfast egg."

Constable Price thought inappropriately of the good brown eggs his hens laid in their run at the back of his police house.

"Yes, sir. Only she didn't know it was Tod Barker, of course. She'd never seen the man before."

"Which isn't surprising, because as we know the only times you'd find Tod Barker outside the East End was when he was on a race course or in prison. And unless I'm misinformed, there aren't any prisons or race courses in this neck of the woods."

"No, sir. He had quite a record, didn't he? Three burglaries, two assaults, two robberies with violence and four convictions for off-course betting."

This feat of memory from the documents he'd read earned him an approving look from the inspector. But Constable Price reminded himself that a village bobby who wanted to keep his job shouldn't be too clever.

"Those are just the ones they managed to make stick in court," the inspector said. "Plenty of enemies in the under-world too. Our colleagues in London weren't surprised to hear that somebody had given Tod Barker a cranial massage with an iron bar."

"An iron bar, was it?"

"So the laboratory men say. Flakes of rust in the wound."

"And nobody surprised?"

"Not that he was dead, no. Not even that he was dead in a phone box. In the betting trade I gather they spend half their lives on the telephone."

"And we know he'd made a call from that box earlier in the day."

"Yes, and since they keep a record at the exhange of the numbers, we know the call was to the bookmaker he works for back in London. So no surprise there either. In fact, you might say there's only one surprise in the whole business."

The inspector waited for a response. Constable Price realised that he was in danger of over-playing rural slowness.

"Why here, you mean, sir?"

"Exactly, constable. Why – when Tod Barker regarded the countryside as something you drove through as quickly as possible to get to the next race meeting – should he be killed somewhere at the back of beyond like Tadley Gate?"

"There's the petrol pump, of course." Constable Price said it almost to himself.

"Does that mean you get a lot of cars here?"

"No sir. We had two of them here on the day he was killed and I'd say two cars in one day was a record for Tadley Gate."

When the first of the cars arrived, around midday on a fine Thursday in hay-making time, Molly was sitting at the parlour table with the accounts book open in front of her, getting on with her task of sending out bills to her father's customers. Men's voices came from outside and the sound of slow pneumatic wheels on the road. She jumped up, glad to be distracted, and looked out of the window. Advancing into their yard came an open-topped four-seater, sleek and green. A man with brown hair and very broad shoulders sat in the driving seat. It moved with funereal slowness because the engine wasn't running at all. Its motive power came from two men pushing from the back. One of them was plump, middle-aged and red-faced. The other – bent over with his shoulder against the car – happened to glance up as Molly looked out of the window. He smiled when he saw her and her heart did such a jolt of shock and unbelief that it felt like a metal plate with her father's biggest hammer coming down on it.

She thought, "Did I really telephone for him after all?"

Then, because she was essentially a good and practical girl, she told herself not to be a mardy ha'porth, of course she hadn't, so stop day-dreaming and get on with it. Her father hadn't heard or seen the car because he was hammering a damaged coulter in his forge out the back. It was up to her to get into the yard and see what they wanted. As she stepped outside the two men stopped pushing and let the car come to a halt not far from the petrol pump.

"Is there a mechanic here? Call him quickly, would you."

It was the older, red-faced man who spoke, in a south Wales accent. The other man, the one she'd have called on the telephone if she knew he existed and had his number, straightened up and smiled at her again, rubbing his back with both hands. He was pretending that pushing the car had exhausted him but Molly knew at once from the smile and the exaggeration of his movements that he wasn't exhausted at all, was just making a pantomime of it for her amusement. She smiled back at him. He was taller than average and maybe five years or so older than she was, with black hair, very white teeth and dark eyes that seemed more alive to her than any she'd seen before. And the smiles they exchanged were like two people saying the same thing at once: "Well, fancy somebody like you being here." But she had to turn away because the red-faced man was repeating his question loudly and urgently.

"I'll get my dad," she said, whirled away into the shadowy forge and shouted to him over the hammer blows. Davy Davitt followed her into the sunshine, still wearing his thick leather farrier's apron and when he saw the motor car by his petrol pump his face lit up.

"Twelve horse power Rover, nice cars, six hundred pounds new," he murmured to himself. Then aloud, "What's the trouble then, sir?"

"Blessed axle gone," the red-faced man said. "These roads are an insult to motor cars, not a yard of tarmac in the last twenty miles."

"Come far, have you?"

"Far enough," said the tall young man. "We started from Pontypridd."

His voice was Welsh too, bright and dancing. The red-faced man gave him a hard look.

"Doesn't matter to him where we started, Sonny. Question is, can he do something so we can get where we're going to?"

"Where's that then?" Davy asked.

"London. And we're in a hurry."

Even though the red-faced man's voice was impatient, they were some of the sweetest words in the language to Davy. In seconds he was horizontal under the car, with the man bending himself double to try to see what was happening. Nobody was paying much attention to the other young man who'd been in the driving seat. He'd got out and was sitting, calm and contented in the sunshine, on the low stone wall between the house and the yard, looking at Molly. And Molly was staring enchanted at the man called Sonny because she'd just heard from his lips some of the sweetest words in the language to her.

"Would there be anywhere here with a telephone I could use?"

Proudly she led him to the kiosk and sat on the step of the war memorial to watch. She always liked to watch on the very rare occasions when people used the telephone, grieved by their hesitations and fumblings. Sonny was different. He didn't pause to read the card of instructions, or drop coins on the concrete floor or fidget with doubt or embarrassment. He simply picked up the receiver and spoke into it as if it were a thing he did every day, easy as washing your hands. She saw a smile on his face and his lips moving and knew he must be giving a number to the distant operator then he must have been connected to his number because his lips were moving again though she couldn't hear what he was saying.

"Blessed car's broken down, back of beyond. No sign of them though. Didn't guess we'd be going this way."

He was speaking to his father, who ran a boxers' training gymnasium in Pontypridd.

"That's where you're wrong, boy. They're right behind you. Left

Cardiff early this morning in a black Austin 20, heading same way as you."

"*How did they know, then?*"

"*Never mind that. Fact is, they do know. Tell Enoch. You at a garage?*"

"*Blacksmith's with a petrol pump.*"

"*Can't miss you then, can they?*"

"*They can't do anything to him, not in broad daylight.*"

"*Only takes a little nudge, you know that. Elbow in wrong place, oh dear so sorry, damage done.*"

"*Enoch and me wouldn't let a flea's elbow near him, let alone theirs.*"

"*You look after our boy.*"

Molly watched as he came out of the kiosk looking worried. "Have you had bad news?"

It didn't strike her that she had no right to ask this of a stranger. He answered her with another question.

"Your father good with cars, is he?"

"Very good."

"We need to be moving, see? Quicker than I thought."

She caught his urgency and they practically ran back to the yard. By then her father was out from under the car and delivering his verdict. Beam axle gone and rear axle just holding together but wouldn't make it to London. Both of them would need unbolting and welding.

"How long?" the red-faced man asked.

"Two or three hours, with luck."

"Make it two hours or less and, whatever your bill is, I'll give you ten pounds on top of it."

Davy's jaw dropped at the prospect of more money in two hours than he usually earned in a week. Then he went under the car with a spanner and Sonny, in his good suit and shiny shoes, went under too. Davy called out to Molly to go and tell Tick to make sure the fire in the forge was hot as he could make it. Tick was the apprentice, a large and powerful sixteen-year-old. Molly found him in the forge along with the other young man who'd been in the driving seat of the car and for an angry moment thought the two of them were fighting. Then she saw it was no more than play, the man dodging and dancing on the trodden earth floor among the scraps of metal and old horseshoes, feet moving no more than an inch or two at a time, but enough to avoid the light punches Tick was aiming at him. A furious bellow came from behind them.

"Rooster, are you bloody mad, boy? Come away from there."

It was the red-faced man.

"Sorry, Uncle Enoch."

Obediently, the young man followed him out to the yard. Molly tried to give Tick her father's instruction but could hardly get the boy to listen. His face was shiny with excitement.

"Did you hear what he called him? I thought he might be, then I said to myself it couldn't be. I'd only see'd him from a good way off and he looks different in his clothes. So I put my fists up, joking like, and he . . ."

"What are you saying, Tick boy?"

"The Rhonda Rooster, that's all. He's only the Rhonda Rooster!"

"What's that?"

"Only the next British middleweight champion, that's all. He'll be fighting for the title in London the day after tomorrow and the money's on him to win it."

"A boxer?"

"Then he'll take on the Empire champion after that. Could be world champion. When I see'd him at Cardiff he won by a knock-out in three rounds against a heavier man even though there was so much blood pouring down his face he could only see from one eye."

Molly was a country girl, not squeamish.

"If he's as good as you say, how come he'd got so much blood on him?"

"He's got a glass eyebrow."

"A what?"

"That's what they call a weak spot. Hard as iron all the rest of him, only he's got an old cut over his left eyebrow and if that opens up it pours with blood so the referee would have had to stop the fight if he hadn't knocked the other chap out first."

It turned out that her father had heard of the Rhondda Rooster too because he got his head out from under the car just long enough to tell Molly to make the gentlemen comfortable in the front parlour and get them something to eat. She rushed round making tea in the good china pot, putting bread, cheese and cold beef on the best table cloth. Sonny had come out from under the car by then and she was conscious all the time of his eyes on her. The Rooster's eyes were just as admiring if she'd noticed, but he was nothing beside Sonny – shoulders and chest too broad for the cut of his suit, one ear a bit skew-whiff, big hands that he kept bunching and flexing all the time they weren't occupied with knife and fork. Under the stern eye of the red-faced man, Uncle Enoch, he had the clumsy good manners of a schoolboy, while Sonny seemed a man of the great world. Occupied with serving them, she missed another milestone in the speeding up of life in Tadley Gate. Another stranger went into the phone kiosk and picked up the receiver. It was the first time since the kiosk was built that it had been used more than once in a day.

The new stranger was small, dark-haired, and twentyish, in a dark suit and cow-dung smeared shoes that hadn't been designed for country walking. He looked round to see nobody was watching and slid quickly into the box as if glad of its protection from the country all around him. The number he wanted was at an east London exchange.

"*Bit of luck. Their car's broken down.*"

"*Have they seen you?*"

"*Naw. We came over a hill and saw them pushing it. So we turned off before they saw us and Gribby and me followed them on foot. Bleeding miles over the fields.*"

"*Where's Gribby?*"

"*Keeping watch. Trouble is, they've all gone inside this house at the garage place.*"

"*They'll have to come out sometime.*"

"*Won't be easy, making it look like an accident.*"

"*You could pay a boy to bung a stone at him.*"

"*You joking?*"

"*With what I'm paying you, don't expect jokes as well. Next news I want to hear is the fight's called off. Understood.*"

"*Understood.*"

In the parlour, Uncle Enoch was restive.

"I'm going to see how he's doing with the car. You stay here, Sonny. Rooster can have another slice of beef if he likes but no more bread and for heaven's sake don't let him even sniff those pickled onions."

There was a tangle of briars and bushes at the back of the garden, clustering around the small stone building that sheltered the earth closet. Two rowans formed an arch over the pathway between the earth closet and the house. They'd been planted in a time when people still believed they kept away witches, all of fifty years ago, by Davy Davitt's grandfather. Davy kept threatening to cut them down but never got round to it, so they formed a useful screen for Tod and Gribby. Tod came back from making his phone call and found his partner lurking in the bushes.

"They still inside?"

"The Rooster and the tall one are. His trainer's gone inside the forge place. What's that you got?"

Tod held out his hand to show him. It was a rusty horseshoe, worn thin and sharp on one side.

"What's that for then? Bring The Rooster good luck?"

"Some kind of luck."

Molly was in the kitchen, washing up. The Rooster was shifting around on his chair in the parlour. Because they'd started so early he'd missed his training run and his internal system was out of rhythm.

"Where's the little house then, Sonny boy?"

"Down the path, back of the house."

The Rooster went down the path, under the rowan arch and into the stone building, latching the door behind him. Tod, watching from the bushes, gauged exactly the height of The Rooster's left eyebrow against the rough stonework of the door frame. As soon as the latch clicked down he crept out and wedged the horsehoe into place between two blocks of stone, sharp side towards the privy, so that a man coming out couldn't help run into it. The loud sigh of satisfaction that The Rooster gave from the inside when his business was done was echoed more quietly by Tod in the bushes.

The Inspector stared out of the window at Constable Price's potato patch.

"So Tod and Gribby were in one car and the British middle-weight champion just happened to be in the other," he said.

"He wasn't that at the time, sir. He didn't take the title until the fight in London two days later. But yes, they broke down in the village."

"Going from The Rhondda to London?"

"Yes sir."

"And Tod and his pal were driving from Cardiff to London?"

"Yes sir."

"And the shortest and best way from either place doesn't go within miles of Tadley Gate, does it?"

"No sir."

"So what in the world were both of them doing there?"

"The statement from The Rooster's uncle says he thought a country route might be calming for him."

"And Tod – was he doing it to calm his nerves as well?"

"No sir. I'd suggest that the presence of both cars in Tadley Gate was not a coincidence."

"So you've got that far too. Go on."

"We know Tod worked for a bookie. We know there was a great deal of money riding on the outcome of that fight. Wouldn't the bookie want to know how The Rooster was looking, the way they watch race-horses on the gallops?"

"So Tod and Gribby go all the way to South Wales and back to spy on him."

"It's one explanation, sir."

"And not a bad one". The inspector gave him a re-considering look. "You've got a brain, constable. If you solved this one, I'm sure you could expect promotion to somewhere quite a lot livelier than here."

Constable Price tried not to let his alarm show. He liked his garden, his hens, his pig. His wife and children were healthy in the country air. He'd been born in a city and now devoted quite a lot of his considerable intelligence to making sure he wasn't promoted back to one.

"So what goes wrong?" the inspector said. "Assume Tod and Gribby are spying. The Rooster's people might be annoyed about it, but not annoyed enough to beat Tod over the head with an iron bar. And remember the Rooster's lot haven't a trace of a criminal record among the three of them, unless you count Sonny Nelson being fined for doing forty-two miles an hour in Llandaff.''

"Yes sir."

"So we come to thieves falling out, then. Gribby's got a record even longer than Tod's and on the evidence you collected, he drove out of the village on his own and he was in a devil of a hurry to get his petrol tank filled."

The Rover was in the yard, with the repaired front axle bolted back in place. Sonny, Davy and Tick were carrying the rear axle from the forge, still warm from its welding. The Rooster had been forbidden to help so was back on the wall chatting to Molly who was sitting beside him but not getting anywhere with her because her attention was on Sonny. All of them were startled by the loud burping of a horn as a black Austin 20 drew up at the pump with a large man in a checked suit at the wheel. After a glance over his shoulder, Davy ignored him.

"He'll have to wait. Get this job seen to first."

They put the axle down by the Rover. Uncle Enoch watched, chest heaving as if the strain of waiting had been too much for him and his face had turned grey. Sonny looked concerned and put a reassuring hand on his shoulder. The horn went on burping.

"Oh, serve him first and get him out of the way," Sonny said. "We can spare a few minutes."

Enoch looked at him doubtfully and Davy hesitated, caught between the allure of repair work and a customer for petrol. An idea struck him.

"Molly, you know how to work the pump. Go over and see to the gentleman."

She got up lightly from the wall and started crossing the yard, passing so close to Sonny that he caught a whiff of the perfume she'd bought herself in Birmingham and not used till then. Following his impulse he leaned towards her and said so softly under the noise of the horn that none of the others even knew he'd spoken: "Delay him, long as you can." She gave him a gleaming glance, the slightest of nods and went on across the yard to the pump. The man in the check suit was out of the car by then with the petrol cap off, quivering with impatience. The sharp smell of his sweat mingled with petrol fumes. Molly fumbled with the hinged panel at the front of the pump. The Rooster seemed disposed to go across and help her but Sonny called to him sharply.

"Rooster, I think I left my wallet on the parlour table. Go and see, would you?"

The Rooster obligingly went back into the house. By then Davy and Tick were both under the Rover with spanners. Sonny took Enoch by the elbow and led him back into the shadows of forge.

"Get a move on please, miss," said the man with the Austin 20 to Molly. She'd managed to get the panel open but was staring at the pump mechanism inside as if she'd never seen it before. Eventually she remembered that the little wooden handle unfolded at right angles and began to wind it slowly anti-clockwise to draw up the petrol. The man wanted to do it for her but she wouldn't let him. When she'd got the first gallon pumped up she turned the handle slowly clockwise to let it down into the tank. The bronze indicator needle by the pump mechanism moved to figure one. She looked at the driver of the Austin.

"Is that it?"

"No, of course it's not. Fill her right up, for heaven's sake."

In other circumstances Gribby would have tried flirting with her because she was undeniably a good-looking girl. Now he could hardly restrain himself from hitting her. Slowly she pumped another gallon up and down, then another, his eyes on her, willing her to hurry. He looked away from her only once and then it was because some movement at the back of his car caught his attention. He swung round and there was Sonny standing there, his hand on the big black luggage trunk. The two men's eyes met. Sonny returned the stare for a few moments then shrugged and moved away, as if he'd been admiring the car. It took Molly the best part of ten minutes to get the indicator to the ten-gallon figure and by that time Gribby was nearly gibbering with anger. He shoved some money at her, not waiting for change, then accelerated out of the yard in a cloud of dust and exhaust. Tick shouted after him as he went, "Hey, your trunk's undone." One of the straps round it was unbuckled and flapping. But the man at the wheel can't have heard because he didn't stop. Forty five minutes later, with Sonny driving, the repaired Rover followed more sedately. Sonny made sure that nobody saw him touch Molly's hand or heard his whispered "Thank you."

The Rover turned on to the road past the common. "We'll stop at the phone kiosk," Sonny said. "Let them know we're on our way again."

He slowed down as they came alongside it, almost stopped then accelerated away so clumsily that he almost stalled the engine. From the back the Rooster said, "What's wrong?"

"Nothing wrong, Rooster. Just there's somebody using it already. We'll find another one further along."

Sonny and Enoch exchanged glances and from there on Sonny drove so smoothly that the Rooster slept most of the way to London.

"So Gribby drives off in a hurry," the inspector said. "Less than an hour later Rooster's lot notice a man in a telephone kiosk. An hour or more after that, Miss Davitt finds Tod dead and her father sends the apprentice to tell you."

"And I got there as soon as I could," Constable Price said. When Tick arrived, breathless on an old bicycle, he'd been at a farm on the far side of his own village, investigating a case of ferret stealing. His wife sent his son running for him and he cycled from there as fast as a man could go on a police bike to the telephone kiosk in Tadley Gate.

"And, judging by your report, you decided at once that whoever battered him over the head didn't do it in the kiosk?"

Constable Price regretted giving in to the temptation to be clever in his report, but couldn't go back on it now.

"There'd have been blood splashed all over the place, sir. As it was, he'd just bled down the back of his suit and onto the floor."

"Yes. So our assumption is that he managed to stagger to the phone kiosk from wherever Gribby hit him with the iron bar, probably intending to call for help."

"You think that's what happened, sir?"

"Speaks for itself. Then there was that trail of blood you noticed from the road to the kiosk, as if he'd dragged himself the last few yards. So they quarrel – probably over the money they're getting paid for spying on the Rooster – Gribby bashes Tod over the head, leaves him for dead and scuttles back to London as soon as he's got a full tank of petrol. Only Tod comes round and has just enough life left in him to make it as far as the phone kiosk but not enough to pick up the telephone."

Constable Price thought about it in his slow rural way. "So that's it then, sir?"

"Yes, but we're never going to pin it on Gribby unless you turn up a witness. So work on it and keep me informed."

The inspector went back to his car – smaller and more battered than either the boxer's or the villain's – and headed back thankfully for the town. Constable Price went to feed his hens. But he couldn't stop thinking about the girl watching a dead man in the phone kiosk.

When the Rover left her father's yard Molly was in a world she didn't recognize any more. Her father and Tick were tidying their tools away, pleased with their day, talking about the Rooster. The murmur of their voices, the small metallic clanks, the lingering petrol smell, should have been familiar but she felt as if she'd been put down in a foreign country. Probably a nice enough country if you got to know it, but nothing that had any connection with her. From habit, she went in the kitchen, put a saucepan of water on the stove for her father to wash, boiled a couple of eggs for his tea since their visitors had eaten everything else. But as soon as she'd finished washing up she let her feet take her towards the common and the telephone kiosk. It was the link between herself and Sonny. She didn't believe that the combined magic of her father's motor mania and the telephone kiosk would bring him here and let him go again as if nothing had happened. The squeeze of her hand surely meant he'd be back – and how would he let her know that if not by telephone? Her heart gave a jolt when, from a distance, she saw a man in the kiosk. But it wasn't Sonny, nothing like him, just a smaller man in a darker suit. Nobody she recognized, but on this day of wonders another stranger more or less made no difference. She sat on the steps of the war memorial, thinking about Sonny while the shadows of a summer afternoon grew long on the grass round her. Then cooling of the air made her realise that time had passed and the stranger was still there in the phone kiosk. Curiosity, then increasing alarm, made her hurry towards it.

Once Tadley Gate knew that the body was a stranger's everybody got on with haymaking before the weather broke. When the news got out that the dead man had been a criminal from London some people in the village implied that it was the fault of the phone kiosk and the petrol pump, which would naturally attract people like that. Once the police had finished in the kiosk a woman who usually did the cleaning in chapel took it on herself to scrub and disinfect it and people went back to not using it quite normally. Davy Davitt and Tick were more interested in The Rooster's chances for the Empire and World titles. Constable Price sometimes discussed it with them. He'd taken to dropping in at the forge quite often these days. One day he had to go to the privy and noticed a rusty horsehoe with a sharp edge lying on the earth outside. It seemed a funny place for a horseshoe, but it was a farrier's after all. Some of the bushes had been pushed back as if something heavy had landed there not long ago, but then you got boys fighting all over the place. Constable Price tried hard, but he couldn't stop thinking. As for Molly, she strolled on the common within earshot of the telephone in the long evenings but apart from that got on with the cooking and accounts like any sensible girl. Then, one day when she was scrubbing a frying pan, two boys arrived running from the common with just enough breath between them to get out the news.

"Miss, you're wanted on the telephone."

She dropped the pan and ran to the kiosk with her apron still on.

"Miss Davitt?" Sonny's voice, distant and metallic but perfectly clear. He had to say it again before she managed to whisper a "yes" into the receiver. He apologized for not telephoning before. He'd had to stay in London with The Rooster and Uncle Enoch but would be driving himself home the next day and wondered if he might call in. "Yes," she said again. For her first telephone call it was hardly a big speaking part, but it seemed to be all that was needed.

* * *

When she got back to the yard, Constable Price was there, sitting on a wall in the sun. His bicycle was upside down and her father was doing something to its chain with pliers. He was looking at a magazine, open at an advertisement for the Austin 20. He stood up when he saw her.

"Hello, Miss Davitt. Will you stay and talk to me?"

Molly didn't want to talk to anyone. She wanted to rush around shouting that Sonny had telephoned, was dropping in. But you couldn't, of course. She sat down on the wall and Constable Price sat back down beside her.

"Nice roomy cars, Austin 20s. Space for a good big trunk at the back."

She nodded, still not concentrating on what he was saying.

"There was a good big trunk on the one the man was driving, the one who filled up with petrol here. Remember? Tick noticed it wasn't properly fastened when the man drove out, only he was in too much of a hurry to stop."

She said nothing, but he felt something change in the air round her, as if it had suddenly gone brittle. "Stop now," he said to himself. But something was throbbing in his brain, like a motor engine with the brake on.

"I suppose nobody happened to open the trunk while he was getting his petrol?"

"You wouldn't." She said it to the sparrows pecking in the dust. "Not to put in petrol."

He noticed it wasn't an answer, felt the brake in his mind slipping.

"So if there'd been anything in the trunk, you couldn't have known?"

She shook her head, still looking down.

"Did he go anywhere near his trunk while you were putting in the petrol?"

She murmured, "No".

"Or did anybody else?"

She raised her head and looked at him. Such a look of desperation he'd only seen before in the eyes of a dog run over by a cart that he had to put out of its misery. He pulled on the mental brake, told his brain it couldn't go along that road. If he persisted, she'd break down, tell him something he couldn't ignore. She was a good girl, didn't deserve trouble. He stood up.

"Looks like your dad's finished with my bicycle."

He waved to her over his shoulder as he pedalled away.

Sonny came next day, in the Rover. He asked Davy if he'd be kind enough to have a look at the electrical starter, something not quite right about it. While he was working on it, Sonny and Molly strolled together in the sunshine on the common.

"A promise I made Uncle Enoch," he told her. "I'd never say a word to anybody, long as I lived, just one exception. If there was a girl I liked, I might have to tell her. If I could trust her, that is."

"You can trust me."

"I know. The Rooster matters to Enoch more than all the world. Anything threatening him, he goes mad. And it was my fault, partly. If I'd done what he told me and not let The Rooster out of my sight, they wouldn't have had their chance. When he came back to the parlour and I told him The Rooster was down at the little house on his own he rushed straight down there, just in time. A second later and The Rooster would have walked right into it. The wickedness of it."

"Yes."

"And we couldn't let The Rooster know. It would have unsettled him. But we couldn't leave the body there in the bushes because it might have caused trouble for you and your dad. So when I saw the other one driving into your yard, bold as brass, it came to me that if we put it in his trunk it would serve both of them right. And you played up to me. Without a word. Just trusted me."

"Yes."

As they walked, the back of his hand brushed lightly against hers.

"Only it went wrong, you see? He must have noticed the trunk strap flapping just after he drove out of your yard. So when he looked in there and saw what he saw, all he could do was dump it in the phone kiosk. Only it happened to be you that found him. I'm sorry about that."

Their hands met palm to palm and stayed together.

"It's all right," she said.

Later, when they'd been married for some time and Sonny was doing well in London as a boxing promoter, she had a telephone in her own home and talked to her friends on it nearly every day. Sonny was driving a Daimler by then with plenty of room at the back for the children and they sometimes used it to pop down to Tadley Gate, where her father had put up a proper garage sign and often filled up as many as half a dozen cars a day on summer weekends. Sometime between one visit and the next the Post Office took away Kiosk One and replaced it with a more imposing model, all bright red paint and glass panels. They gave it a glance as they drove past.

The Hope of the World

MAT COWARD

It's not easy to pigeon-hole Mat Coward, and that's all to the good. There's escape in versatility. He's written science fiction, hard-boiled mysteries, humorous crime (check out his Edgar-nominated story "Twelve of the Little Buggers" in his collection Do the World a Favour*), and reference books on humour, such as* The Pocket Essential Classic Radio Comedy *(2003). Occasionally he delves back into the past, and here takes us to the days before the planned communist revolution. It's a country-house murder with a difference.*

Beneath a monkey-puzzle tree on the west lawn of his seat in Sussex, Lord Bognor and his guests were trying to settle on a date for the revolution. Capital, they all agreed, had clearly had its day; it was just choosing the day itself which was proving problematical.

"Wednesday, September the tenth," suggested Norbert Whistler.

Lord Bognor flicked the pages of his appointments diary. "Wednesday the . . . ah, no, sorry. No good for me, I'm afraid – playing for the Old Boys against the Lord Chancellor's XI."

Diana Lawrence clicked her teeth together in irritation. "Well, couldn't you miss it, just this once?"

Bognor sucked hot July air through a gap in his bottom teeth and compressed his face so that his eyebrows almost met his cheekbones. "Not really, old thing. You see, I'm opening bat – they rather rely on me. If it was any other game, perhaps, but the Lord Chancellor's is a top team. I suppose if it rains . . ."

"Oh look," said Willie Browning, "I spy refreshments."

A butler and two kitchen maids, indeed, were making their unhurried way from the house, carrying between them a variety of large trays. The Special Arrangements Group of the Executive Committee of The Bolshevist League of Urgency adjourned for tea. This was on the afternoon prior to the violent unpleasantness, and it was such a lovely day.

"What exactly *is* a flange-mounter?" asked Diana Lawrence, spraying flecks of seed cake towards Norbert Whistler, who sat on a lawn chair beside her.

Norbert swallowed a gulp of tea. It should have been a sip, of course, in such company and in such a setting, but his throat was dry. "It's rather complicated. Difficult to explain to the layman. It's to do with flanges, you know, and the mounting thereof."

"Of course, silly of me. But we are *so* happy to have you here, Comrade Whistler – representing, as it were, the vanguard of the class-conscious proletariat! If one may put it that way."

"Quite so," said Norbert, trying not to look up her skirt. She wasn't a young woman, and it wasn't a long skirt. At thirty-two, Norbert was the youngest man in the group by at least ten years, and he thought he sensed something hungry in Diana's earnest, avian gaze.

"I know Boggy, in particular, is delighted. You're quite a catch, you know! Being, that is, the – I'm sorry, the Assistant Secretary . . . ?"

"Assistant North-East Regional Secretary of the Consolidated Federation of Flange-Mounters and Correlated Crafts," said Norbert, all on one breath because he feared that if he paused during the sentence he might be unable to complete it.

"Rather! Good show. And *tell* me, Comrade Whistler – or, if I might, Comrade Norbert? Formality is an outmoded bourgeois mechanism, one feels. Doesn't one? There'll be no surnames after the revolution."

"By all means," said Norbert, wondering how that would

work, exactly: no surnames. It'd make telephone directories a bit tricky, surely?

"There! Now, do you feel that the flange-mounters of the north-east are ready for revolution? As a *class*, one means."

Norbert chewed slowly on his scone, and made ruminative noises. When he felt that this device had carried him as far as it might, he cleared his throat. "Aye, well. Happen they are, and happen they aren't. It all depends, I would say, on the objective nature of the circumstances prevailing and, naturally – and, if I may say so, subjectively – on the direction of the leadership."

Diana was clearly more than satisfied with this response, and hurried off to share it with the others. Once he was alone, Norbert produced a small, leather notebook from his jacket pocket.

"Diana Lawrence," he wrote. "Lady of refined type. In her seventh decade, but with the vigour of one in her fifth (and the costume, it might be noted, of one in her third). Introduced to me as 'the celebrated travel writer'. Politically: enthusiastic, but not noticeably well-informed."

Diana's place at his side was soon taken by Willie Browning, an extravagantly thin and modestly bearded man of considerable age. "I wonder," he said, indicating their delightful surroundings, "what old Charlie would have made of all this."

"Charlie?"

The old man chuckled. "That's what we always called him in the old days. Karl Marx, I mean." He looked away, towards the rolling green horizon, as if what he had said was nothing, merely a casual remark.

Norbert did not have to counterfeit an impressed expression; over the years, he had shaken hands with many people who had shaken hands with many idols of working-class history – but, by any measure, this was a bit special. "You *knew* Karl Marx?"

"Oh, my people knew him a bit – they moved in some of the same circles, you understand."

"What was he like?" Norbert knew it was a meaningless, cliched and unanswerable question, but felt it would have been almost rude not to ask it.

"Old, by the time I met him. That's my main memory of the great man – how very old he was. The beard and everything, you know?" He sighed. "Mind you, he wasn't as old when he died as I am now, but in my youth he seemed very old to me."

Norbert smiled. He was trying to place the elderly Marxist's accent; place it by region and hierarchy. Willie spoke with a little too much precision to be truly posh, and his vowels contained the faintest leftover of East Anglia. A collar-and-tie man, no doubt, schooled but never moneyed.

"Very fond of the public house, Charlie was." Norbert couldn't be sure whether Willie's tone was nostalgic or censorious. "A sociable fellow, if he took a liking to you. But he fell out with everyone sooner or later. Didn't have a friend left in the world by the time he died, not counting poor old Engels."

"He perhaps wouldn't have been terribly surprised by what we see here, then," said Norbert, suddenly and uncomfortably aware that his own accent would tell more about him than he might wish told, to the right listener.

"I'm sorry?"

"I mean to say," said Norbert, "it does appear to be something of a characteristic of working men's movements – the setting up of new parties every few years."

"Ah." The old man nodded. "Like prophet, like followers, you think? Yes, you could be onto something there, my young friend. And it can be quite painful, breaking from good comrades. But sometimes it has to be done."

"You speak from experience?"

"I was with the Communist Party for a short while, but I'm afraid it was impossible for me to stay. *Impossible.*"

"Oh, dear."

"Yes, you see the local branch secretary – well, really, he didn't have even the faintest grasp of revolutionary theory. Do you know, he put it to a branch meeting, in all seriousness, that the revolution might break out on a Sunday? A Sunday!"

"A Sunday," said Norbert. "I say."

"Well, quite! Revolutions do not happen at weekends. How can they? The men are not at work at weekends. If they are not at work, they do not constitute a proletariat, and only a proletariat can institute a proletarian revolution. By definition! Revolutions occur during the *week*." He took out a small handkerchief and mopped his face. "Well obviously, I couldn't stay after that."

"Obviously," Norbert agreed. Despite a long association with the revolutionary movement, he was still astonished by the tininess of Willie's ideological dispute with orthodoxy. Days of the week: that was pretty impressive, by anyone's standards.

"A plump man, the branch secretary," said Willie. "Dreadful manners, very informal with the female comrades."

Ah, thought Norbert; yes, that sounded more like it.

Comrade Diana Lawrence had a headache, Comrade Lord Bognor reported to the committee after tea, and had gone for a lie down. "Occurs to me that the date-claiming business might, in any case, be better done once everyone's here, so I propose we adjourn until tomorrow."

Norbert didn't entirely follow Bognor's logic, but was in favour of anything which got him out of listening to further extracts from his noble host's crowded social and sporting schedule, so he raised his hand as part of a unanimous "Yes" vote.

Freed to wander, Norbert wandered. Walking quietly and with purpose was a skill he'd long possessed, and it was in that manner that he made his way along the upstairs corridors of the main house, looking into this and listening to that. He was in a room of unobvious purpose when a voice from the doorway very nearly made him jump.

"I see we share a vice, Comrade Whistler."

The young woman who had been taking the minutes during the meeting on the lawn; he searched for the name. "A vice, Comrade Chaplin?" She had rather delightful hair, somewhat longer than was fashionable. Perhaps, he thought, she was one of those who believed that short hair could lead to baldness in women.

She smiled. "Nosiness!"

He raised his hands. "Guilty! I just couldn't resist. It's not every day you get to look round a place like this, is it?"

"Quite. And then, of course, places like this won't exist for much longer. As private homes, that is."

Her voice trailed off, and her brow wrinkled. Norbert didn't need to look behind him to see what had caused her attention to stray. "Yes, I've been wondering what that thing was, too. In fact, this entire room's a bit odd."

She leaned forward to read the label on the peculiar contraption. "'The Vibro-Vitaliser.' I suppose it's some sort of health and fitness machine. I must say, it looks more like something the Okhrana might have used to extract information from reluctant witnesses."

He laughed. "It does, rather. I'm Norbert, by the way – I don't think I caught . . . ?"

"Susan." They shook hands.

"And what do you make of the proceedings so far, Susan?"

Her face and posture signalled her disappointment. "Well, I have to say, I'm not entirely . . . that is, Lord – I mean Comrade – or rather –"

"Comrade Boggy?"

She smiled. "Him, yes. He does rather seem to view my role on the committee as being largely *secretarial* in nature."

That was what she did for a living, Norbert remembered; and lived with her parents in one of the newer London suburbs. "One of those Tube-station places," he'd heard someone say. Diana Lawrence, probably. "Yes," he said. "I suppose he does, rather."

Her face reddened. "Which seems a little unfair, I have to say. I mean, if a woman can be chairman of the General Council of the TUC – "

"You might hope that self-proclaimed socialists would be a little more post-war in their attitudes, certainly."

Susan nodded. "If not socialists, then whom? You know that the first thing the Bolsheviks did when they came to power in Russia was to declare universal suffrage for everyone over the age of eighteen – both sexes. It's not even as if Comrade Boggy is some reactionary old stick. He can't be more than forty-five, wouldn't you say? And quite youthful with it."

They both jumped, guiltily, when the door creaked open. "'Ullo, me old ducks! 'Ere I am again with me old string bag." Seeing their expressions – which were not so much blank as startled – Lord Bognor added: "Ah, perhaps you two don't listen-in? It's just something one of those comedians says. On the wireless, you know."

"I see," said Susan.

"Awfully funny when she does it." He coughed, smiled, and coughed again. "Well, I was just passing and I heard chatter coming from in here, and wondered if anyone was lost."

"No," said Norbert, "we were just admiring the equipment here. Do you use it yourself?"

There was more throat-clearing; more on-off smiles. "Not, ah – well, no. No, not personally. It belongs to my wife, she's awfully keen on . . . She stays in London mostly, these days. For the theatre and so on."

The only decent response to that seemed to be an awkward silence; Susan and Norbert supplied one.

"I don't know how half of it works, to be honest," Bognor continued, his voice a little hoarse from all the coughing. "My wife calls it her Vitality Room."

"This one, I suppose, is some sort of slimming machine?" said Norbert, lifting a long, thick leather belt which protruded from a metal plate on the wall. "I presume it works by vibration."

"Of course," Bognor replied, "this would all be right up your street, wouldn't it? Engineering, and all that. Tell me, are there many flanges involved in a device such as this?"

"Oh, you know – pretty much the usual number." Norbert was coming to loathe bloody *flanges*, and was very glad when Susan stepped onto the platform of another of the Vitality Room's exhibits.

"But what on earth is this thing?" she said, running her hands over the extraordinary loops and lengths of rubber tubing, metal canisters, valves and electrical wires which made up whatever it was. She read from the manufacturer's plaque in front of her. "What is Galvatronic Therapy?"

"What it is, my dear," Bognor explained, with another less than ecstatic smile, "so far as I can tell, is something designed to maximize the profits of the electricity company." His guests laughed dutifully.

"I imagine," said Norbert, stepping up beside Susan, "you're supposed to put this metal skullcap on your head, and depress that switch in front of you. Though to what purpose, I couldn't guess."

"Ah!" said Bognor. "Anything involving electricity, the ladies lap it up."

"Actually," said Susan, "I think I read about something

like this in a magazine. It's believed that the application of galvanism to certain regions of the head can increase mental capacity, and provide aid to those deficient in nervous energy."

"I also read something in a magazine," said Bognor. "About a chap who's invented a Death Ray." He paused, and barked a laugh. "Let's hope it wasn't the same chap."

Not to be left out, Norbert recalled something he'd read in a magazine; a report by a panel of doctors, warning that young women today were leading such hectic social and working lives that they were becoming dangerously thin and exhausted, relying on alcohol, tobacco and other drugs to keep them going. The unavoidable result, the doctors were sure, would be an unprecedented epidemic of consumption.

He kept the fruits of his reading to himself, however, suspecting that Comrade Susan Chaplin would not take kindly to a gang of male doctors trying to convince her sisters that they'd been happier before the Great War.

"If this is where you switch it on – no, don't worry, I'm not going to," said Susan, "then what are those controls over on the wall?"

"They regulate the dosage, I think," Norbert said, having investigated. "I suppose you set that before you mount up."

To Bognor's visible relief, the sound of the electric doorbell reached them from the main hall. "Ah, excellent – that'll be our penultimate guest. Shall we greet him, Comrades?"

If the newcomer had turned out to be the late Lenin himself, Norbert could not have been much more surprised. Sir Reginald Lloyd was a cotton man, and – even by the standards of that none-too-gentle trade – was reputedly a ruthless competitor, and notoriously anti-union, loathed by his peers and his underlings equally.

"What on *earth* is that dreadful man doing here?" Willie Browning stood at Norbert's elbow, his face displaying astonishment and what appeared to be real distress.

"I cannot imagine," said Norbert. "Perhaps he has seen the error of his ways."

Having been introduced to the beef-faced tycoon, Norbert made his excuses and retired to his room. He spent twenty minutes writing in his notebook and then sat back in the enormous wing chair and closed his eyes, just for a moment. He wondered whether Sir Reginald used flanges in his business, and if so whether he was personally acquainted with the mounting thereof. And then he stopped wondering; in the modern world, there were few silences so deep as that found in the guest wing of a country house, late on a summer's afternoon.

He awoke to the sound of a thousand daddy-longlegs. He reached his bedroom window just in time to see an aeroplane land in a meadow a few hundred yards from the house.

Well, thought Norbert: this really is a different world. He'd be willing to bet that very few flange-mounters, north-eastern or otherwise, had ever seen a sight such as that. Why aye bonny lad, look you, isn't it?

He was admiring the plane – slightly bigger, he thought, than the few he'd seen during the war – when its pilot emerged. It *couldn't* be! It bloody *was*. The young man was wearing motor-cycle goggles and a leather cap, and had a scarf wrapped around his throat and lower face, but never mind – Norbert would know that walk anywhere. It wasn't a swaggering walk or a loping one, let alone a strut. It wasn't anything as vulgar as that. It was effortless; unthreatening, devoid of arrogance, open and confident and friendly. Supercilious *bastard*. It took centuries of careful breeding to condense such an intensity of superiority into so simple an action. Norbert washed his face, changed his shirt and hurried downstairs.

"Ah, here he is," said Lord Bognor, standing in the hall with Susan Chaplin and the pilot. "Giles, I'd like you to meet a most valuable member of our group. This is Norbert Whistler, Secretary-General of the Eastern Mounted . . . Consolidated Secretary of the Mange-Flouters of . . ."

Norbert took a deep breath. "Assistant North-East Regional Secretary of the Consolidated Federation of Flange-Mounters and Correlated Crafts, Comrade," he said, smiling at the pilot and holding out his hand. He hoped handshakes weren't irredeemably bourgeois; it would be so galling to make a faux pas. "Pleased to meet you."

"Quite," said Lord Bognor. "And this young chap is the friend of a son-in-law of a dear old friend of mine – that is, of his late brother, to be precise – and a sterling supporter of our great cause."

The pilot returned the handshake and the smile, doubling both of them. "Giles Macready. A real privilege, I must say, to shake hands with one who is on the front line of the struggle against injustice. Tell me, what *is* a flange-mounter? Precisely, I mean; of course, I understand the concept in broad terms."

Norbert didn't particularly want a cigarette, but – discovering that his fidgeting had caused his cigarette case to appear in his hands – felt that he could hardly put the bloody thing away again without ever opening it. He offered a cigarette to Susan, who declined, and to Bognor, who declined. He then offered himself one, which he was obliged to accept.

"It's a bit complicated," he told Giles, with a still broader smile. "Perhaps later, if you're that interested."

Bognor laughed, loudly; a sign, Norbert knew, that a joke was coming. It had been his observation that the upper-classes always laughed before the joke, rather than after it, as if giving a fox a fair start. "By the way, young Giles isn't a bald Negro, in case you were wondering – he's wearing a flying cap. He's a valiant aviator, you know. In fact, he's brought tomorrow's lunch to us, fresh from France."

"Oh, atrocious manners, forgive me." Giles removed his headgear. "I didn't realize I was still wearing it – these things become like one's own skin after the first few hundred hours of flying time."

"An aviator?" said Norbert. "How interesting."

"Oh, you know, nothing very glamorous." Giles slapped his cap against his thigh, then folded it into a pocket on his leather jerkin. "Just the regular Croydon–Paris passenger run. It's a trade, like any other – pays the bills, until the dawning of the Glorious Day."

"Speaking of the Glorious Day," said Norbert, "how did you come to be involved, if you don't mind me asking, in the historic struggle of the workers?"

"Ah well, as to that." Giles's smile withdrew, delicately, into the corners of his mouth and eyes, and a suitably solemn look replaced it. "As I was saying to Comrade Boggy here, when we met quite by chance in his club last week – I saw a fair few things during the war."

"Yes, indeed," said Bognor. "Quite so."

"Things I don't care to dwell on. I'm not alone – lot of chaps went through pretty much the same, lot of chaps didn't come back to bore on about it, so least said, the best. But I said to myself in 1917, 'If we get through this lot, things have got to change.' "

Bognor nodded, and Norbert noted that without one of his usual repertoire of more-or-less idiotic smiles in place, he looked so sincere it was almost upsetting. "Got to change," said Bognor. "Never again."

"Well, they have changed," Giles continued. "For the worse. And it's up to our generation, Comrade Norris – "

"Norbert."

"Comrade Norbert, it is up to us – "

An astonishing noise shook the walls of the ancient hall, and the inner ears of its inhabitants.

"Ah!" said Bognor, clapping his hands together. "Dinner. It's an electrical klaxon, you know; we don't have a gong any more. Gongs, do you see, are reminiscent of feudalism."

Giles begged leave to remove the rest of his flying togs, and wash his hands, before dining. When he emerged from the lavatory, Norbert was waiting for him.

"What the bloody hell are you doing here?"

The valiant aviator put a fraternal arm around Norbert's shoulder. "Same as you, old chap, I imagine. Shall we go in?"

"Listen to me, you stuck-up little – "

"I see we're not expected to dress for dinner. Splendid, much better for the digestion. Most liberating, you have to admit, this communism business."

"It's called asparagus," Diana Lawrence whispered. "One eats it with one's fingers."

Norbert thanked her. He'd probably eaten more sparrow-grass than the rest of them put together; his uncle used to bring it home for soup, unsold from the market stall.

The conversation at dinner was mostly of a political nature. Willie Browning and Diana were the most vocal, with Lord Bognor restricting his comments to hearty concurrences. Sir Reginald Lloyd concentrated on his food, though he did emerge from his trencher once or twice to "congratulate Your Lordship on your choice of chef."

There was general agreement that the Communist Party of Great Britain had surrendered to reformism, and that only The Bolshevist League of Urgency clearly understood the necessity of naming the Glorious Day without delay. Diana let it be known that, in her opinion, the CPGB contained "very few comrades of real *character*". From the apologetic smile she bestowed on Norbert after delivering this remark, he gathered that she was complaining about the regrettably plebeian nature of the mainstream communist movement.

"We all know," said Willie, as they awaited their fish course, "that the flood of surplus capital from America into Europe which has eased the current crisis of European capitalism cannot furnish but a temporary revival, since the interest on American loans can only be repaid by further borrowing. As soon as the flow of credit is broken, catastrophe will set in. Capitalism will only be able to increase its profits in the following period by a direct and vicious attack on wages and conditions."

"Quite so," said Comrade Boggy. "Direct and vicious."

"The north-east?" Giles Macready asked, effortlessly projecting his voice across the table to Norbert. "Whereabouts?"

"Jarrow," said Norbert.

"Interesting. I thought I caught a hint of the Principality in your consonants; just a hint, you know, at the back of the throat, there . . . ?"

"My grandmother was from Pontypridd," said Norbert. "One of my grandmothers."

"Maternal?"

"Paternal," said Norbert. He took a mouthful of boiled potato, and added: "So now you know, bonny lad."

General mingling was the order of the postprandial hour. Norbert smoked a cigarette in the billiard room, where he learned that Diana was one of the world's leading female players of that game. She dealt with both Bognor and Giles in short order, but was unable to persuade Sir Reginald to pick up a cue. Norbert suspected that her display of simpering and eyelash-fluttering had produced an effect in the businessman precisely opposite to that intended. She had to content herself with beating Willie, while wearing a blindfold.

Susan was prevailed upon to provide a few tunes ("A smile, a song and a piano!" as Bognor put it) in one of several rooms which contained a baby grand. When it became clear that Sir Reginald's interest was more in the shapely shoulders and soft hair of the pianist than in the music she was playing, Norbert contrived to steer him towards the veranda, where a manly cigar school was in full flower. This act of chivalry earned him a grateful look from Comrade Chaplin.

Sir Reginald did not seem to be much of a conversationalist – a mercy, perhaps, given the amount he had drunk at dinner and subsequently – but he did become quite lively concerning his suspicions of corruption and hypocrisy amongst the members of the Labour government.

"They say Macdonald has a car, you know."

"Well," said Giles, "he is prime minister. I daresay he needs to rush from place to place, you know, betraying the working class."

"Yes, but how does he pay for it?" Sir Reginald dropped his cigar, and Norbert picked it up for him. "He has no money – how does a man of that class run a motor? You tell me that."

"His wife has money, I believe," said Bognor, but Sir Reginald didn't seem to hear him.

"You can't run a ruddy car on what a prime minister makes, take it from me."

A little later, Norbert announced that he fancied an early night, and offered to show Sir Reginald to his room. The latter was drunk enough to take this as a courtesy, not an impertinence.

"Have we met before?" Sir Reginald asked, moving his face backwards and forwards in an attempt to focus on Norbert's. "I know you from somewhere, don't I?"

"Quite possible." Norbert had been wondering when this would come up. "I'm a trade union official."

"Are you, by God? I bloody hate trade union officials."

"I hope you don't mind me asking," said Norbert, as they made their lopsided way along the landing, "but what brings a man of your eminence in the industrial world to join Comrade Boggy's group?"

Sir Reginald stopped, looked around him, and gestured untidily for Norbert to come closer. In a voice which he evidently imagined was a whisper, he said: "You've read Marx, have you? Course you have. So have I. You're not the only one. I've read Lenin, too. And he's more to the point. After the revolution – and everyone says it's only a matter of time, half the people I do business with have moved their money to America; moved their families too, some of them – after the revolution there will be a transcription period – "

"Transition period?"

"Sshh! This is between you and me. Even my secretary doesn't know I'm here, let alone my wife. There will be a transmission period, during which the socialist state will work with chosen capitalists. Well now, if a chap happened to be able to *guarantee* that he would be one of those chosen catipalists, he'd be laughing. Laughing, take that from me."

"I see," said Norbert, marvelling inwardly, and not for the first time in his life, at the lengths a Lancashire businessman would go to in order to secure a monopoly. Presumably the real Communist Party had turned him down; hence his affiliation with this unlikely offshoot.

"I delivered the first instalment, in cash, to that grinning fool, Bognor, this afternoon. And I told him – I said, 'There's more where that came from, my Lord.' Plenty more. There are certain things money can't buy, and for which I will pay any amount."

Norbert wished Sir Reginald a "Goodnight, Comrade," then hurried to his room to bring his notes up to date. The corpse was not discovered until after breakfast.

"Nothing like it was before the war, of course," said Diana Lawrence, shovelling onto her plate enough kidneys to process the urine of a small boatload of lambs. "But still, old Boggy does a lot better than most. There's a chef, thank God, a kitchen maid, a scullery maid, between-maid, several chaps in the garden, a groom (for the motor), butler and hall boy, obviously, an odd job man, a carpenter – "

"Good God, there's hundreds of them," said Norbert, dealing himself a third helping of mushrooms to go with his second lot of scrambled eggs. He'd been a bit surprised to discover that breakfast was self-service. It reminded him rather of a works canteen – though with undeniably superior cuisine. "I'm sure I spotted a smithy yesterday. Surely Comrade Boggy doesn't still retain his own blacksmith?"

"Indeed he does. He currently has him making enormous hammer-and-sickle designs, with which to adorn the estate gates."

One by one, and with only one exception, the revolutionaries arrived to take part in the storming of the serving dishes, until most of the food had gone, and that which remained was cold. At that point, Bognor – ever the attentive host – instructed his butler to see that a tray was taken up to Sir Reginald's room. When the butler returned to report that the gentleman was not in his bedroom, nor in his bathroom, a search was instigated. It ended in the Vitality Room.

This was not an image the galvatronic therapy types would be likely to use in their advertisements, Norbert couldn't help feeling, as he gently elbowed his way through the crowded doorway and knelt to check Sir Reginald Lloyd's pulse. The industrialist was even more red-faced than usual, and his tongue seemed to hang halfway down his chest. His hair was scorched, and the metal skullcap appeared almost welded to his head. His hands resembled claws, perhaps because he had tried to free himself from a length of flexible tubing which had become entangled about his neck. Strange place for Lloyd to die, Norbert thought; he seemed hardly the health and fitness type.

"No vital signs," he reported. "I'm no doctor, but – I should say he has been vibrated to death."

"Dear God!" cried Bognor.

"Also strangled."

"Oh Lord," said Susan.

"Electrocuted, too, I think . . ."

"Bloody hell!" said Diana.

". . . and quite possibly boiled."

There was a silence, until Norbert looked up and nodded, to signify that he had finished.

"One way or another," said Giles, "he sounds quite dead."

"Utterly."

"What a beastly accident," said Bognor. "The blasted machine must have gone rogue." He patted his waistcoat absently, as if searching for shot.

"Not an accident, I'm afraid," said Norbert. "The dosage controls over there have been set to maximum – and the off switch here on the machine itself has been disabled."

"He's right, you know," said Giles, after a quick inspection. "Someone's shoved a cigarette card in there. I reckon you'd need a penknife to free it, too. Unless this was an especially peculiar way of committing suicide, then this is undoubtedly a murder."

"But who – " said Susan.

"Any one of us could have done it." Norbert paused; he thought the occasion demanded it. "I don't believe any of us can alibi any of the others for the entire period during which this crime might have been committed. Rising times this morning were various and individual. As for breakfast, we all came and went without formality. Can anyone refute any of that?"

"Could it not have been one of the staff?" Willie asked.

Bognor shook his head. "No, no. They'd have been far too busy preparing breakfast and so on. Besides, any servant who was absent his post would be noticed by the others."

"Unless they were all in it together," said Susan.

Bognor and Diana looked at her in astonishment. "All in it *together*?" said Bognor. "But that would be tantamount to . . ." He couldn't finish the sentence. A particular word hung in the air for a short time, and then, seeing it wasn't wanted, slunk away.

". . . unthinkable," said Diana.

Bognor nodded. "Unthinkable."

"At least we can eliminate one suspect from your list," said Giles.

"Indeed? Who?"

"Why, *yourself*, Comrade Norbert." Giles smiled, and looked around at the others. "After all, you are the detective, Sergeant Whistler – and you can't be the detective *and* the killer. That isn't how these things are done, at all."

The late Sir Reginald Lloyd was removed to an unoccupied bedroom – in the servants' wing, naturally – while the living comrades gathered in the Small Library.

"It was only just now that I remembered where I'd seen Comrade Norbert before," Giles explained. "During the 1919 police strike, wasn't it, Norbert?"

"Is this true?" demanded Diana. "A detective? A policeman? Sent to spy on us, I suppose!"

"Well, yes," said Norbert. "In a word. But never mind that now, there is a killer amongst us and he or she must be identified: that is the priority. I must ask no one to leave the house and immediate grounds until I have determined what happened." The relief of being able to speak once again in his natural, Kentish tones almost outweighed his displeasure at being unmasked as a spy. How the lingually acrobatic Geordies ever managed to produce that extraordinary noise in the first place, let alone keep it up for hour after hour, was beyond him; they must practise constantly, perhaps in front of mirrors.

It was agreed, nem con, that the comrades should occupy themselves upon the tennis courts, while Norbert summoned them individually for interview in the billiard room (chosen for its view over the tennis courts, and its comfortable chairs). He began with Giles.

"Hope you don't mind me letting the cat out of bag, Comrade Norbert," said Giles, settling himself happily in the very chair which Norbert had intended for his own. "But I thought it better to keep this in the family, rather than involve the local coppers. We'd both sooner this matter didn't make the *Daily Mirror*, yes?"

It pained him to do so, but Norbert was forced to agree; there was plenty of potential for embarrassment all round in this messy situation. "Besides," he said, "I may end up arresting you for murder, and I wouldn't want anything to complicate that."

Giles laughed. "My dear fellow, I don't know what sort of things you get up to in the Met, but I can assure you that His Majesty's intelligence services do not go about vibrating businessmen to death in stately homes. It's simply not within our purview."

"You must admit you have a motive. You wouldn't care to see a revolutionary movement getting hold of Sir Reginald's money." Norbert wasn't going to be put off by any quantity of sangfroid.

"Only the precise same motive which you have yourself as a Special Branch officer – and *I* don't accuse *you*."

"Then what *are* you doing here? This organization is absurd, not dangerous."

"I could ask you the same question." Giles sighed, as if Norbert's silliness was at last becoming tiresome. "And I'd get the same answer – they *all* need watching, no matter how absurd they might appear. Brother Lenin was pretty absurd, I daresay, up until the moment he wasn't."

Detective Sergeant Whistler considered this answer, and found it incomplete. With Whitehall apparently convinced that the entire country was on the verge of all-out class war, why would MI5 waste an experienced field man on a bunch of crackpots and misfits like The Bolshevist League of Urgency? He was about to say something along those lines, when Giles added: "Incidentally, old boy: was it your idea to come here, or the Yard's?"

Time to reassert control of this interview; past time, in fact. "All right, what do you make of the others?"

"Are you consulting me, my dear old thing?"

Norbert ground out his cigarette, and gave the secret agent a hard look. "No, Mr Macready, I am interrogating you. As a murder suspect. I should bear that in mind, if I were you."

There wasn't a flicker of uncertainty on Giles Macready's face. There hadn't been such a flicker on a Macready, Norbert was sure, since the Norman Conquest. "What do I think of the others? Well, I would take a close look at Boggy himself. The man is notoriously unstable – this present passion for revolution, for instance, dates most coincidentally from the time of his wife's departure."

"Eccentricity is surely natural in the aristocracy?"

"Certainly, but his previous eccentricities centred on motor cars, aeroplanes, the usual – this is different. And believe me, he's not the inbred, rustic idiot he appears to be."

"What possible motive might *he* have for killing Lloyd?"

"I've no idea – but the way you phrase the question does rather sound as if you've already thought of motives for the rest of us, you clever old thing! It doesn't stop at flanges with you, does it?" Giles stood, signalling that the interview was over. Norbert remained seated, signalling nothing more, he feared, than that he was not standing. "By the way," Giles added, his hand on the doorknob, "a flange is a projecting or raised edge or flank, as of a wheel. It always pays to do one's preparation."

The annoying thing was that Norbert knew full well what a flange was. He'd done his preparation. He always did; it had been the secret of his success throughout what had so far proved to be a quite complicated career.

"Sir Reginald, if you'll forgive my indelicacy, seemed to be taking rather an interest in you last night. An inappropriate interest, I mean." He smiled, hoping to put Susan Chaplin at her ease.

"He was a little predatory, that's true. But I can assure you, Sergeant, that I am well used to such attention from men of his type. I take no notice of it."

Her words sounded like bravado, but then Norbert had no doubt that bravado was an important part of the modern working woman's armour. "You're a typewriter, I believe?"

"I prefer 'typist,' but yes. I'm employed by a secretarial bureau in the West End."

"And have you ever met Sir Reginald before?"

"No." She smiled; the first smile she'd allowed him since the revelation of his duplicity. "I'd never met Sir Reginald – only his kind. In fact, the only person here that I knew already was Diana Lawrence. Our agency handles all her typing. She saw me reading *The Clarion* in the office one day, and we got talking about the revolution and so on."

"She's a friendly woman, you'd say?"

Susan shrugged. "She is to me. I admire her. But I think a lot of men find her rather terrifying."

"Really?"

"Oh yes! Well, that's her reputation, anyway. 'No man dare say her nay!' – that's what my boss told me. Anyway, it was through her that I became involved in the League."

"Were you previously involved in the movement at all?"

Susan's posture stiffened. "I'm sure you could find out with a simple phone call, Sergeant. You keep files on us all, don't you?"

"Not all, Miss Chaplin, no. There are too many of you for

that." This time, she almost answered his grin; he'd have to be content with that.

"I was a member of the Labour Party for a short time. My parents are Labour, keen Co-operators, and so on. They disapprove of communism, of militancy generally – they fear that the bosses will use the Red Bogey to drive Britain back to the right and destroy the Labour Party."

"You disagree?"

"I don't care! We have a Labour government – are we one inch closer to socialism? It's too late for reform. Surely the war taught us that much?"

"So why the League, rather than the established Communist Party?"

"Frankly, I am beginning to ask myself that." She pushed her hair out of her eyes, and made a noise halfway between a laugh and a hiccup. "If I'm honest, I think the fact the meetings take place at the house of a lord influenced me – my parents can hardly say it's not respectable, can they?"

Norbert smiled. "Respectability is important to them?"

"They were both born working-class, Sergeant. They have risen, through great effort, to the very bottom-most rung of the lower middle-class ladder. They cling to it for dear life. But the poverty that's growing in this country since the war is of a severity unseen since my *grandparents*' day. The poor are getting poorer, the working classes are losing their power, and the moderately comfortable are slowly slipping back to where they started. That's why I have no time for reform."

There wasn't much Norbert could argue with in that, even had he wished to, so instead he said: "I think it's time for lunch."

Champagne and sandwiches were served on the terrace. Norbert would have preferred a beer on such a hot day – or even a cup of tea, given the heavy afternoon facing him. He ate a round of cheese and pickle, and then ate three more. The sandwiches were delicious, and as he chewed he worked out why that should be so: the bread, the cheese, the butter and the pickle were probably all made here on Lord Bognor's estate, mostly from ingredients grown on Bognor land.

Bognor. He'd been to Bognor once, on a daytrip. Very pleasant. His aunty had been sick, and blamed the water. Not that this had anything to do with anything, of course.

No, definitely not a champagne day. He took himself off to the kitchen, where he bought one immense mug of tea for a small amount of coppery gossip, and where he was invited to share a sit down on the back steps with a white haired gardener. Norbert employed a conversational opening which he had never known to fail with anyone over the age of forty.

"You'll have seen some changes around here."

"What! What *hasn't* changed, more like. This is a fact, professors of universities will tell you this, what's happened in the last generation – the big estates being broke up, and that – that is the biggest change in land ownership since the Norman Conquest."

"Norman Conquest." Norbert made a noise between his teeth. "Get away."

"That's true. Mechanization. Falling prices. This is getting to be the biggest depression we've had in the countryside since I don't know when."

"Norman Conquest?" Norbert suggested.

"People are leaving the land in their thousands, hundreds of thousands, moving to the cities. Most of those as stay behind are unemployed."

"Don't listen to him," said a young girl – a maid of some sort, Norbert assumed – as she joined them on the steps. "He's all for unions, he is. If you listen to him, he's Noah and it's started raining." She poked the gardener with her foot, almost knocking him over, to demonstrate that her intentions were kindly.

"You met my niece, have you?"

"Charmed," said Norbert, standing to shake hands with the maid.

He was glad he had ten minutes later, when they were alone, and she put her mouth close to his ear. She had very sweet breath, like violets. "You know that lady?"

"Which one?"

"Older one, with the skirts. She's a very light sleeper." She giggled.

"Is she?"

"Don't make any impression on the sheets at all, that's how light she is."

*   *   *

Diana Lawrence, he was told, was up on the roof, sunning. That seemed reasonable.

She'd found a nice spot: a flat area about the size of a suburban sitting-room, sheltered by the humps of windows in the servant's rooms. Norbert settled himself so that the sun was in his eyes. Diana was wearing a bathing suit which, Norbert felt, would have looked a lot better on the gardener's niece.

They discussed roofs for a while. It turned out to be something they had in common. Norbert enjoyed a good roof, though he couldn't claim to share her experience and sophistication in the matter. He had once attended a rooftop dance, complete with an American jazz orchestra, but he'd been on duty so that probably didn't count.

"One can see the future from a good roof. In Italy," she told him, "there is a racing car factory which has a test track on the roof."

"Impossible," he said, although in fact he'd seen pictures of it in a magazine.

"Most extraordinary thing you've ever seen. One drives up, through the factory itself, there are ramps at each floor, and then – "

"You've *driven* on it?"

"Of course. One could hardly visit such a phenomenon, and not go for a spin. Oh, you'd love it, Sergeant! The most extraordinary sensation of flying into space, as if the Alps themselves are an extension of the track."

"Was that how you met Lord Bognor, through an interest in racing cars?"

"It was."

"And you found you shared another interest? In communism."

"Quite so."

"And if you don't mind me asking – how did it come about that you were attracted to the revolutionary position?"

She sighed. "I'm sorry, Sergeant, but it seems such an incomprehensible question. The answer is simple: I've seen the world. Anyone intelligent who has seen more than their own back garden would be communist. Except policemen, I suppose." Norbert said nothing, and after a moment she continued.

"In this country, in America, all over Europe – everything is collapsing. Everything! They are turning prisons into hostels for the homeless. Prisons, meeting halls, even opera houses. How long do you think that can continue before there's another war?"

"And you really believe that Britain is on the verge of revolution?"

"Your lot do! It's all anyone of rank talks, thinks or dreams about – will it be this year, next year, next week? They know their time is up. Workers are organising, established religion is dying away . . . whatever happened to the social unity of the war years? Are you aware that the gulf between rich and poor is actually *increasing*, is actually worse now than it was before the war?"

Norbert was aware of that – of all that – and he was aware that, according to his friend the gardener's niece, Diana hadn't slept in her bed last night. While Susan Chaplin was running from Sir Reginald's embrace, perhaps Sir Reginald was running from Diana's. Perhaps he didn't run, of course, but perhaps he did, and perhaps she spent the night on the roof, brooding about things.

"You're right. How very observant of you." Willie Browning gave a resigned smile. "I worked for Lloyd's when the Old Man still ran the place – Sir Reginald's father. I ended my working life there, indeed. As a clerk." He looked up at Norbert. "You do read Wells, I suppose?"

"I have done, yes."

"Well, there you are then. A junior clerk, in my senior years, and a member of a socialist bicycling group. Actually, that was how I first met Boggy. I still cycle; he doesn't, did it for a few months, bought all the equipment, gave it up and moved on to something else. Cars, perhaps, or aeroplanes or polo."

"And the father was not a sympathetic employer? He didn't approve of junior clerks who bicycled with socialists?"

"Like father, like son, from what I gather." He slapped his hands on his thighs, and began searching his jacket pockets for his pipe. It was in the last pocket he looked in. "So there you are, Comrade Detective Sergeant: there's my motive."

"Indeed. Thank you for your frankness."

"I can afford to be frank. I didn't kill him." Willie stood up, and shook hands with Norbert – for no reason that Norbert could readily deduce. "I didn't kill him, but I did enjoy the champagne at lunchtime."

He hadn't meant to leave Comrade Boggy for last; to do so looked annoyingly deliberate, either deference or studied insult. But that was how it worked out. His Lordship, for one thing, had not seemed to be available at the various times that Norbert had been looking for him. He was informed on eventually by his butler, who was fed up with the master cluttering up his pantry.

In the billiard room, Norbert asked Bognor how he had come to know Sir Reginald.

"Oh, you know how it is – someone at the club whose brother-in-law knew someone's sister who dined with a chap's secretary . . . I don't really remember." But his heart wasn't in it.

"He approached you, didn't he? Rather than the other way about."

Bognor had yet to look Norbert in the eye. He did not do so now. "Well, yes, I think that might have been so."

"And when did you discover that his motives were not pure?" It was a fair guess, Norbert reckoned, if the lack of discretion Sir Reginald had displayed last night was habitual.

Bognor spent a moment or so twisting his features this way and that, in various simulations of a wronged man. "When you first arrived here, I think I told you to call me Boggy. Didn't I? Thought so. I generally do. I can't stand all that *Lordship* rubbish, all that formal nonsense. Even the servants – "

"*Really?*" Norbert couldn't help the interruption.

"Oh, yes. Oh yes, they all call me 'Sir,' I simply don't use the title. But you see, this wretched Lloyd fellow, he would keep *M'lording* me, as if I were a high court judge. It's incorrect, apart from anything."

"How annoying."

"And when I asked him to stop it, he got quite unpleasant – after dinner this was, I think he'd had one too many – and he told me that when *he* had a proper title he'd bloody well expect people to bloody well use it, and that he'd be getting one bloody soon."

"I see."

"Bloody well thanks to me. Do you see? He'd be getting one soon, bloody well thanks to me. Well, that could really only mean one thing, couldn't it?"

"I'm afraid so." The sheer depth of disappointment in Lord Bognor's eyes almost melted Norbert's heart. Disappointment that he wouldn't be leading a revolution after all, and disappointment at discovering that the world was full of scoundrels, whose word could not be trusted.

"Do you know what upsets me, Comrade Norbert? Do you know what *really* upsets me the most? These enormous advertisements they're erecting on the verges all over the place. Have you seen them?"

Norbert, in his days as a walking copper, had spent many hours with madmen and alcoholics. Now he came to think of it, that was the penultimate line of a police canteen joke, but the point was that he was far too used to sudden changes in conversational direction to be thrown by them. "Billboards, sir?"

"That's the chaps. I mean, what is the point of them? They are disfiguring the countryside. There won't be any countryside left, ten years from now. There'll be nothing but billboards and motor buses." He stood up. Sat down again. "Look, this is a bit awkward, but it has to be said. I'm the last one you've spoken to, is that right?"

"Correct."

"And I imagine you have managed to detect possible motives for each of us, in this ghastly matter?"

"I have."

"And if you don't mind telling me – I'm afraid I really must insist, rather – what is your own?"

Norbert blinked. "My own . . . ?"

"Your own motive. You see, I'm wondering if perhaps we shouldn't call the county constabulary in, after all. No offence intended, I assure you, but at the moment – looking at the thing purely from a layman's point of view – the evidence seems to point to you being the killer."

Norbert said nothing. He tried to remember how blinking worked.

Lord Bognor's attention was suddenly taken by the clock

above the scoreboard. "Oh dear, where are my manners. Would you care for a sherry?"

He had been thinking of gathering them all in the library – the main library, this time – and going through all the evidence bit by bit before finally pointing at Giles Macready and saying "Hold him fast!" and telling everyone why Giles had killed Sir Reginald Lloyd. But he didn't really feel like it now. The moment had passed.

Instead he went for a bit of a stroll down past the stables and along the river, and under a sweet chestnut tree he met Susan Chaplin.

"I know you didn't do it," she said.

"That's very kind of you."

"It was Giles, wasn't it?"

"No doubt. I'm not quite sure why, though."

"But it does rather *look* as though it was you, doesn't it?"

"A bit, perhaps." He didn't think it did, especially, even after Boggy had pointed out the supposed clues. But then, he knew it wasn't him, so it was easy for him to see coincidence as coincidence.

"But I think you're being 'framed,' as the Americans say. Giles – he's police too, isn't he?"

"MI5, actually."

"Similar, then. The case against you is that Sir Reginald – I think we should refer to him as Mr Lloyd, don't you? Only crooks get knighthoods anyway – Lloyd obviously knew you from somewhere. He mentioned it to a couple of people, but you didn't say anything about it."

"I was on duty at a Mansion House banquet a few months ago. Lloyd got drunk, and I had to see him home."

"So the idea is you killed him to prevent him blowing your cover. Then of course, it was you who didn't want to call the local police – "

"No it wasn't – it was Giles!"

"Everyone says it was you. But . . ."

"But?"

She grinned at him, and made a show of looking around for eavesdroppers. There was a large dragonfly in the vicinity, but it paid them little notice. "But I know *why* you didn't want to call the police. I've worked it out. I've read the signs, Comrade Norbert."

"Do you?" He lit two cigarettes. After a moment he remembered that one of them was for her, and passed it over. "Have you?"

"You didn't want to give the press ammunition for a new scare: 'Bolsheviks Run Amok In Country House Bloodbath.' Did you? You hoped you could sort it all out nice and quietly on your own."

"I'm not sure quite – "

"Anyway, there were a few other things, which I won't bore you with – they're all obvious enough if you think back. The point is, why would MI5 want to frame you?"

"Well, yes." He coughed, and threw his cigarette away. "That is where the whole thing falls down, isn't it?"

She hugged herself, and drew on her cigarette as if it were a glass of barley water. "I worked that out, too. Equally obvious, once you think about it. You're not *only* a police spy, are you, but also – "

"What do you know about that?" He sat down. He hadn't realised he'd stood up, and he felt a bit of a chump about it, now.

"It was you so obviously knowing Giles that set me thinking."

"Oh. Was it obvious? I thought I handled that quite smartly."

"Well, you refrained from hanging a painted sign around your neck, saying 'I have known and hated Giles Macready for several years in a professional capacity,' so I suppose you deserve credit for that."

"Thank you."

"But the first time you met him, supposedly, you already knew he didn't smoke."

"Oh, bugger," said Norbert. "Pardon me."

"I expect it's true that he knows you from the Police Strike of 1919; but you were on opposite sides then, weren't you? You were with the strikers. And you're still on opposite sides today. Aren't you?"

Norbert's instructions on this matter were perfectly plain: admit nothing, ever. Those who trained him probably hadn't envisaged his being interrogated on a July riverbank by a young female typist from a Tube-station town.

"I imagine you were approached by Special Branch after the failure of the strike, and given the choice of dismissal and blacklisting, like so many of your comrades, or of turning your coat. And when you reported that approach to the CPGB, they urged you to go along with it. You are the Party's man amongst the political police. I wonder whether it was the Party or the Yard who first suggested you come and spy on us?"

He thought he'd better say something, just so she wouldn't think he was dead. "Macready asked me the same thing. I didn't give him an answer, either."

"You must have worked very hard to get Special Branch to trust you. I can only guess at the price you – and, no doubt, the Party – have paid for that trust. But Giles never quite trusted you, did he?"

How odd, Norbert was thinking: the life he led, and yet this long-haired girl who lived with her mum and dad was twice as cynical, twice as matter-of-fact about the world's machinations, as he could ever be. The conclusion she was implying was one that had never occurred to him. "You think Giles killed Lloyd in order to incriminate me?"

"It makes sense, doesn't it? Perhaps he's working on his own, or perhaps he managed to convince MI5 that you were a communist spy."

"Then why not simply arrest me? Or kill me?"

Her hand gripped his wrist. She didn't seem to know she was doing it, so Norbert thought he wouldn't mention it. "Because this way they get rid of you, *and* they get a wonderful red bogey story as a bonus."

"They usually just make up their red bogeys. Or commission the good old *Daily Mail* to do it for them."

"But nothing as good as this one – a communist spy in the police, murdering a defenceless knight of the realm."

Yes, thought, Norbert; and they'd humiliate their despised cousins in Special Branch at the same time. One should never underestimate the contempt which existed between those two organs of the state, or the outrageous lengths which members of each outfit would go to in order to damage the other. Susan's theory wasn't impossible. There again, neither was this . . .

"Your workings out have certainly been most productive, Comrade Susan. I wonder if you can apply the same logic to help me answer another question."

She removed her hand, perhaps seeing from his expression that there was no point in all that, now. "I'll try," she said.

"What do you suppose Lloyd was doing in the Vitality Room in the first place? Does he seem to you the type to take an interest in exercise machines before breakfast?"

"Curiosity, I suppose."

"Initially, perhaps. He heard the noise of one of Lady Boggy's machines, wondered what it was, went to have a nose. But having seen that it was merely that young show-off pilot fellow doing some boring exercises, I'm quite sure Sir Reginald's thoughts would have returned immediately to sausage and kedgeree and black pudding. Unless . . ."

"Yes," she said, and he couldn't quite tell from her lack of inflection whether the word was a question or a statement.

"Something must have lured him in there. Now, what would persuade him to set foot in the room, let alone to step up onto that strange machine? Only a woman, surely? Only a pretty, young woman."

"Yes," she said, and this time her meaning was apparent.

"Just as a matter of interest, where did you learn to fly?" Norbert asked Giles, thinking that life in Intelligence was very different to life in the Branch, where flying lessons were, to put it mildly, not standard issue.

"Fly? Oh, a couple of my pals have their own planes, it's something I mess about with now and then at weekends. I never was much good at croquet, you know, or crosswords."

Of course. A couple of pals. Naturally. "Giles," said Norbert, "I'm thinking of arresting you for the murder of Sir Reginald Lloyd."

"I see. Although, of course, you must know by now that I didn't do it?"

"I don't know who did it, but I'm not sure it matters. I'm confident I can make a convincing case against you." To which, he hoped, MI5 would respond with a thorough whitewash. The whole business would be entombed, and forgotten.

Giles made a sympathetic face. "Wouldn't work, I'm afraid."

Earlier, under the chestnut tree, Susan had told Norbert: "I didn't *lure* him." Clearly this was a matter about which she felt strongly. "Don't say that, please, you make me sound awful."

"I'm sorry," Norbert had replied. "I withdraw the word."

She'd been trying out the equipment, that's all. How could she resist? And one of the slimming machines was having a . . . certain effect on her. Vitalism, you know. Sir Reginald Lloyd watched her from the doorway, watched her a while without announcing himself, which was a filthy thing to do, wasn't it? And then when he *did* speak, and approach, it was evident that he misinterpreted her shortness of breath, her flushed neck. He repeated his advances of the previous night, more forcefully this time, and she suddenly saw an opportunity not to protest and plead with yet another unwelcome man, but for once to teach a lesson.

He was easily persuaded onto the machine; she convinced him of its delights. She didn't intend him real harm: she was going to give him a bit of a shock, make a fool of him, leave him to extricate himself or scream the house down, as he preferred. But the moment she pushed the dosage switch to maximum – Lloyd died. He gurgled, twitched, thrashed, moaned and died. It took, perhaps, five seconds. Maybe the machine was faulty; maybe the industrialist was.

Susan was horrified, naturally. Of course. But when you think about it, one day soon they're *all* going to be dead, aren't they? Every rich man, every exploiter, every capitalist. Did it really matter that Lloyd got his reward a few months early? So Susan had a bath, and then went down to breakfast.

And now, here they were; the policeman and the intelligence officer, discussing motives and the absence thereof.

"Wouldn't work," said Giles. "My lot know I wouldn't kill Lloyd to stop him giving his money to the dear old League of Urgency, because you see – "

"Because the dear old League of Urgency is your creation. Right?"

"Well done. Knew you'd get there in the end."

And *that* was bloody annoying, because Norbert had known for a while that Giles had no motive for sabotaging the League; but he couldn't say so now without appearing childish. "I'm sure Boggy's lot aren't your only unwitting useful idiots. I daresay you're preparing all manner of phantom Bolshevist conspiracies. You intend the first Labour government to be the last, don't you?"

"Dead set on it," said Giles. "This is, my dear Sergeant Whistler, a time for the choosing of sides."

For weeks there had been rumours – he'd heard them at the Yard and in the Party – that a mass arrest of Communist Party leaders was imminent. One way or another, Norbert's double life was nearly over. He wondered if they needed detectives in Moscow. "This murder is a reverse for you, isn't it?"

Giles spread his hands. "A hiccup."

Norbert tried to keep his face from showing what he was thinking, which was, essentially, "How can I resolve this in such a way as to keep Susan Chaplin from harm – because no-one deserves to hang for what she did – and keep me from harm, and land bloody Giles in it?"

He went off for a walk around the fishpond to sharpen his appetite. As he left the room, Giles called after him: "There are many ways of slitting one's own throat, Sergeant, but I'm sure you'll do the right thing."

"Don't worry," said Norbert. "I will." Halfway through his walk, having abandoned his search for the answer, the correct question occurred to him: what did Giles *want* him to do? Keep the killing quiet. Write it up as a mundane accident, or better still a heart attack in the bath. And, since that would broadly serve Norbert's immediate interests as well, that was what Giles *expected* him to do.

Which made the whole thing much simpler.

Giles was asleep when his aeroplane was stolen. Comrade Boggy wasn't, he very much suspected, but he couldn't prove it. He didn't hear it take off, because it was first towed to a field at the other end of the estate by a team of horses.

As luck would have it – luck, or information received – it was officers from the Special Branch who discovered Sir Reginald Lloyd's corpse in the pilot's seat of the aircraft, upon their arrival at Croydon Aerodrome the following day. They didn't openly disbelieve Giles's account of Sir Reginald's death, but when the rest of Lord Bognor's guests were unable to recall the industrialist's presence at the house, there seemed little point in pursuing the matter.

His reputation and career stained to a degree which was downright embarrassing, Giles Macready would very much have liked to discuss the affair, robustly and frankly, with Detective Sergeant Norbert Whistler. This desire was something on which, uniquely, Giles and the Special Branch reached early accord; but by then, Comrade Norbert was thousands of miles away. In a hot country, as it happened, on a roof, taking the sun and looking to the future.

Bullets

PETER LOVESEY

Peter Lovesey has produced an interesting range of historical mystery novels. His first and perhaps still best known are those featuring the Victorian police detective Sergeant Cribb, starting with Wobble to Death *(1970). Equally popular are his novels featuring Bertie, Prince of Wales (and future King Edward VII) as a sleuth, starting with* Bertie and the Tin Man *(1987). His others include a 1920s mystery,* The False Inspector Dew *(1982), set on a translatlantic liner and which won him the Crime Writers Association's Gold Dagger Award as that year's best novel. For the following story Peter turns to the craze for magazine competitions and mottos, which reached new heights in the twenties – the first crossword puzzle to appear in Britain was in* Pearson's Magazine *in February 1922.*

"You can remove the body."

"Was it definitely . . . ?"

"Suicide, I'd stake my life on it," said Inspector Carew, a forceful man. "Single bullet to the head. Gun beside him. Ex-army fellow who didn't return his weapon when the war ended. This must be the third or fourth case I've seen. The world has changed too much for them – the wireless, a Labour Government, the bright young things. All these poor fellows have got is their memories of the war, and who wants to think about that?"

"He didn't leave a note."

"Are you questioning my conclusion?"

"Absolutely not, Inspector."

"I suggest you get on with your job, then. I'm going to speak to the family."

The family consisted of the dead man's widow, Emily Flanagan, a pretty, dark-haired woman not much over thirty; and her father, whose name was Russell. They were sitting at the kitchen table in 7, Albert Street, their small suburban house in Teddington. They had a bottle of brandy between them.

The inspector accepted a drink and knocked it back in one swig. When talking to the recently bereaved he needed all the lubrication he could get. He gave them his findings and explained that there would need to be a post mortem to confirm the cause, obvious as it was. "You didn't find a note, I suppose?" he said.

Emily Flanagan shook her head.

"Did anything occur that could have induced him to take his own life? Bad news? An argument?"

Mrs Flanagan looked across at her father.

"No argument," the old man said. "And that's beyond dispute."

Mrs Flanagan clapped her hands twice and said, "Good one, Daddy."

Inspector Carew didn't follow what was going on, except that these two seemed more cheerful than they should.

"As a matter of fact," Mrs Flanagan said, "Patrick was in a better mood than I've seen him for some time." The ends of her mouth turned up in what wasn't quite a smile, more a comment on the vagary of fate.

"This was last night?"

"And for some days. He was singing *Horsey, Keep Your Tail Up* in the bathroom."

"Bracing himself?" said the inspector. His theory of depression was looking shaky.

"What do you mean, 'bracing himself'?"

"For the, em . . ."

"*Felo de se,*" said old Mr Russell. "*Felo de se* – fellow's sad day."

"Daddy, please," said Mrs Flanagan.

The inspector decided that the old man had drunk too much

brandy. This wasn't a comfortable place to be. As soon as he'd got the essential details he was leaving. "I understand you were both woken by the shot."

"About midnight, yes," the widow said, glancing at her fingernails. She was holding up remarkably.

"You came downstairs and found him in his office?"

She nodded. "He called it his den. And Father came in soon after."

"He'd given no indication of taking his own life?"

"He liked his own life, Inspector."

"What was his work?"

"He was an actor. He was currently playing in *Bulldog Drummond* at the Richmond Theatre. It was only a small role as a gangster, but he did it to perfection. They'll miss him dreadfully."

The inspector was tempted to ask, "And will you?" But he kept his lips buttoned. "*Bulldog Drummond*. I can't say I've read it."

"It has a sub-title," said Mrs Flanagan. "Daddy, can you remember the sub-title?"

"*The Adventures of a Demobilized Officer Who Found Peace Dull.*"

"I knew he'd know it," she said. "Being housebound, Daddy has more time for reading than the rest of us. '*A Demobilized Officer Who Found Peace Dull.*'"

This was closer to Inspector Carew's diagnosis. "Poignant, in the circumstances."

"Oh, I don't agree. Patrick's life was anything but dull."

"So last night he would have returned late from the theatre?"

"About half-past eleven, usually."

"Perhaps he was overtired."

"Patrick?" she said with an inappropriate laugh. "He was inexhaustible."

"Did he have a difficult war?"

"Didn't every soldier? I thought he'd put all that behind him."

"Apparently not, unless there was something else." The inspector was beginning to revise his theory. "Forgive me for asking this, Mrs Flanagan. Was your marriage entirely successful?"

The lips twitched again. "I dare say he had lapses."

"Lapses," said old Mr Russell. "Like lasses on laps."

This piece of wit earned no more than a frown from his daughter. She said to the inspector, "Patrick was an actor. Enough said?"

"Didn't it anger you?"

"We had tiffs if I caught him out, as I sometimes did."

"You seem to treat it lightly, if I may say so."

"Because they were minor indiscretions, kissing and canoodling."

The inspector wasn't certain of the meaning of "canoodling," but he guessed it didn't amount to adultery. "Not a cause for suicide, then?"

"Good Lord, no."

"And how was the balance of his mind, would you say?"

"Are you asking me if he was mad?"

"When he shot himself, yes."

"I wasn't there when he shot himself, but I think it highly unlikely. He never lost control."

"Well, then," the inspector said, preparing to leave, "it will be for the coroner to decide. He may wish to visit the scene himself, so I'm leaving the, ahem, den as it is, apart from the, ahem . . ."

"Mortal remains?" old Mr Russell suggested.

"So please don't tidy anything up. Leave it exactly as it is." He picked up his hat and left.

Mrs Flanagan had barely started her next brandy when the doorbell rang again. "Damn. Who's that?" she said.

Her father wobbled to the door and admitted a fat, bald man in a cassock. He smelt of tobacco. "Father Montgomery," he said.

"Should we know you?" she asked.

"I was Padre to your husband in France. I'm the incumbent of St Saviour's in Richmond. I heard from one of my congregation that he'd been gathered, so I came at once to see what I could do."

"Very little," said Mrs Flanagan. " 'Gathered' isn't the word I would use. He killed himself. That's a lost soul in your religion, isn't it?"

The priest sighed heavily. "That *is* distressing. I know he wasn't a regular worshipper, but he was brought up in the Church of Rome. He professed himself a Catholic when pressed."

Old Mr Russell said in a parade-ground chant, "Fall out the Jews and Catholics."

"Exactly, sir. So I do have a concern over the destiny of poor Patrick's soul. Is it certain?"

"If you call putting a gun to your head and pulling the trigger certain, I would say it is," said Mrs Flanagan, wanting to be rid of this visitor. "We've had the police here and they confirm it."

"His service revolver, I suppose? How I wish the army had been more responsible in collecting all the weapons they issued. May I see the room?"

"Is that necessary?"

"I would like to remove all doubt from my mind that this was suicide."

"You have a doubt?"

His eyes flicked upwards. "I have a duty, my dear."

She showed him into Patrick's den, a small room with a desk surrounded by bookshelves. Her father shuffled in after them.

The body had been removed, but otherwise the room was just as the police had seen it, with the revolver lying on the desk.

"Please don't touch anything," Mrs Flanagan said.

The priest made a performance of linking his thumbs behind his back. He leaned over and peered at the gun. "Service issue, as I expected," he said. "Did the police examine the chambers for bullets?"

"Empty. He only needed the one."

"Where did he keep the gun?"

"In the bottom drawer – but don't open it."

Father Montgomery had little option but to look about him at the bookshelves. There were plays by Oscar Wilde and George Bernard Shaw. "Did he act in any of these?"

"No. He collected them for personal reading. He was a well-read man."

"Well-read," said old Mr Russell. "Oh, essay, essay, essay."

"Father adores his word-play," Mrs Flanagan. "Not one of your very best, Daddy."

The books continued to interest the priest. There was a shelf of detective stories above the drama section featuring works by

Conan Doyle, E.W.Hornung and G.K. Chesterton. Three by the author who called himself "Sapper" were lying horizontally above the others. One was *Bulldog Drummond,* the novel of the play the dead man had appeared in. On another high shelf were some volumes the priest wished he hadn't noticed, among them *Married Love*, by Marie Stopes. But his eyes were drawn inexorably to *Family Limitation,* by Margaret Sanger – not for its provocative title but for the round hole he noticed in the binding.

"Might I ask for a dispensation to handle one of the books?"

"Why?" asked Mrs Flanagan.

"Because I think I see a bullet hole through the spine."

"Jesus, Mary and Joseph!" said Mrs Flanagan, forgetting herself. "Where?"

The priest unclasped his hands and pointed. "Do you mind?" He reached for the book and removed it. Sure enough, there was a scorched round hole penetrating this book and its neighbour, *The Psychology of Sex*, by Havelock Ellis. "Didn't the police remark on this?"

"They didn't notice it. What can it mean?"

"Presumably, that two shots were fired and this one missed. If you look, the bullet penetrated the wood behind the books. Do you recall hearing two shots?"

"I couldn't say for sure. I was asleep. I thought it was one shot that disturbed me, but I suppose there could have been two."

"And this was when?"

"About midnight, according to the clock in my room. Daddy, can you recall two shots?"

"Aldershot and Bagshot," said the waggish Mr Russell.

"It's a puzzle," said the priest, rotating his head, his eyes taking in all of the books. He replaced the damaged volume and turned his attention to the floor. "There should be two spent cartridges unless someone removed them."

"Do you think you're a better detective than the police?" Mrs Flanagan said, becoming irritated.

"No, but I work for a Higher Authority." He pushed his foot under the edge of the carpet and rolled the corner back towards the chair. He couldn't be accused of touching anything; his feet had to go somewhere. "Hey ho, what's this?"

Under the carpet was a magazine.

"Leave it," said Mrs Flanagan.

"We're allowed to look," said Father Montgomery, bending low. The magazine was the current issue of *John Bull*, that patriotic weekly edited by Horatio Bottomley. The number seven was scribbled on the cover in pencil.

"Well, I'll be jiggered!" said old Mr Russell.

"Is that your magazine, Daddy?" Mrs Flanagan asked him. "You said it was missing."

"No, mine's upstairs."

"We have it delivered every Thursday. Father does the competition," Mrs Flanagan explained. "What's the competition called, Daddy?"

"Bullets."

"Right." She gave her half-smile. "Ironic. He sometimes wins a prize. They give a list of phrases and the readers are invited to add an original comment in no more than four words. Give us an example, Daddy."

"'Boarding House Philosophy: Let Bygones Be Rissoles'"

"Nice one. What about one for the church? What's that famous one?"

"'Wedding March: Aisle Altar Hymn'."

"That won five hundred pounds for someone before the war. Daddy's best effort won him twenty-five, but he keeps trying. You're sure this isn't your copy, Daddy?"

"Mine's upstairs, I said."

"All right, don't get touchy. We'd best keep this under the carpet in case it's important, but I can't think why." Mrs Flanagan nudged the carpet back in place with a pointed patent leather toecap, wanting to hasten the priest's departure. "Is there anything else we can do for you, Father Montgomery?"

"Not for the present, except . . ."

"Except what?"

"If I may, I'd like to borrow your father's *John Bull*."

"I'll fetch it now," said the old man.

And he did.

Father Montgomery returned to Richmond and went backstage at the theatre. It was still early in the afternoon and there was no matinee, but some of the actors were on stage rehearsing next week's production.

He spotted the person who had first informed him of Patrick Flanagan's sudden death. Brendan was painting scenery, a fine, realistic bay window with a sea view behind.

"My dear boy," the priest said, "I'm so pleased to catch you here."

"What can I do for you, Father?"

"I've come from the house of poor Patrick Flanagan, rest his soul."

"We're heartbroken, Father. He was a lovely man."

"Indeed. Would you happen to know if he had a lady friend at all?"

"You mean Daisy Truelove, Father?"

"I suppose I do, if you say so. Where would I find her?"

"She's in the ladies' dressing room."

"And how would I coax her out of there?"

"You could try knocking on the door and saying 'A gentleman for Miss Daisy'."

He tried, and it worked. She flung open the door, a flurry of fair, curly hair and cheap scent, her eyes shining in anticipation. "Hello, darling – oh, my hat." She'd spotted the clerical collar.

"Miss Truelove?"

She nodded.

"The friend of Patrick Flanagan?"

The pretty face creased at the name. "Poor Patrick, yes."

"Would you mind telling me if you saw him yesterday evening?"

"Why, yes, Father. He was in the play, and so am I. I'm Lola, the gangster's moll."

"After it was over?"

"I saw him then, too. Some of us went for a drink at the Star and Garter. Patrick ordered oysters and champagne. He said he'd recently come into some money."

"Oysters and champagne until when?"

"About half-past eleven."

"And then?"

She hesitated. "Do you really need to know?"

"Think of me as a vessel."

"A ship, Father?"

He blinked. "Not exactly. More like a receptacle for anything you can tell me in confidence."

"You want to hear my confession?"

"Not unless you have something to confess."

She bit her lip. "We went on a river steamer."

"At night?"

"It was moored by the bridge. It had fairylights and music and there was dancing. So romantic. He ordered more bubbly and it must have gone to my head. We finally got home about four in the morning. I'd better say that again. *I* got home about four in the morning. We said goodnight at the door of my lodgings. There was nothing improper, Father. Well, nothing totally improper, if you know what I mean."

"How was his mood?"

"His mood?"

"Was he happy when he left you?"

"Oh, dear!" she said, her winsome young features creasing in concern again. "I'm afraid he wasn't. He wanted to come in with me. He offered to take off his shoes and tiptoe upstairs, but I wouldn't risk upsetting the landlady. I pushed him away and shut the door in his face. Do you think that's why he killed himself?"

"No, I don't," said Father Montgomery. "I don't believe he killed himself at all."

"You mean my conscience is clear?"

"I have no way of telling what's on your conscience, my dear, but I'm sure you did the right thing at the end of the evening."

Inspector Carew was far from happy at being dragged back to 7, Albert Street by a priest he'd never met, but the mention of murder couldn't be ignored.

"The wife lied to us both," Father Montgomery said as they were being driven to Teddington. "She insisted that the shooting was at midnight, but I have a female witness who says Patrick Flanagan was with her in Richmond until four in the morning."

"So what?" said the inspector. "Emily Flanagan has her pride. She won't want to admit that her wayward husband preferred to spend the night with some other filly."

"She wasn't exactly grieving."

"True. I noted her demeanour. Maybe she's not sorry he's dead. It doesn't make her a murderess."

"There's money behind this," the priest said. "A man who can splash out on champagne and oysters at the Star and Garter is doing too well for a jobbing actor with a wife and father-in-law to support."

"We checked the bank account," the inspector said, pleased to demonstrate how thorough he'd been. "They have a modest income, but two days before his death he withdrew most of what they had, about sixty pounds. And so would I, if I was planning to do myself in. I'd have a binge and a night out with a girl before I pulled the trigger. Wouldn't you?"

"I don't go out with girls and I wouldn't pull the trigger," said Father Montgomery. "Neither is permitted."

They drew up at the Flanagans' house in Teddington. Emily Flanagan opened the door, saw them together, and said, "Holy Moses!"

In the kitchen, the brandy bottle was empty. Old Mr Russell was asleep in a rocking chair in front of the stove.

"No need to disturb him," Inspector Carew said. "This concerns you, ma'am. An apparent discrepancy in what you told me. You said the fatal shot was fired at midnight."

"Or thereabouts," said Mrs Flanagan.

"Our latest information places your husband on a river steamer in Richmond at midnight."

"The heel! What was he doing there?"

"Dancing with an actress until nearly four in the morning."

"I'm not surprised," she said, failing to appreciate what an admission this was. "Which baggage was it this time?"

"Do you admit you lied to me?"

"How could I have known what he was doing in Richmond?"

"The time. You lied about the time."

"'Thereabouts' is what I said. What difference does an hour or two make to you? I guessed he was entertaining some little trollop on the last night of his life, but the world doesn't need to know, does it? Allow me some dignity when I walk behind his coffin, Inspector."

"Did you know he emptied his bank account and treated his actor friends to oysters and champagne?"

"Did he, the rotter?"

"You don't seem overly concerned."

"He left no will. As his nearest and dearest I'll inherit everything he ever owned, including this house."

"Not if you're hanged for murder, madam."

"*What?*" For the first time in all this sorry business, she looked alarmed.

Father Montgomery raised his hands to urge restraint on both sides. "Before we go any further, Inspector, why don't I show you what I discovered in the den?"

Emily Flanagan, muttering mild expletives, followed them into the room where the body had been discovered. The priest pointed out the bullet hole in the books and remarked that it was unlikely that the victim had held a gun to his head and missed. "I suggest that someone else was holding the gun, someone who waited through the small hours of the night for him to come in and then pointed it at him and brought him in here and sat him at his own desk, where it would look as if he chose to die. I suggest there was a struggle and he deflected the first shot, but the second was fired with the gun to his head."

"A crime of passion, then," said the inspector.

"No. Let me show you something else." He rolled back the carpet and revealed the copy of *John Bull*. "You can pick it up," he told the inspector. "Take note of the number seven scribbled on the top right corner. The magazine was delivered to this house as usual. It was Mr Russell's copy, but Patrick Flanagan grabbed it the day it was pushed through the letterbox and hid it here. Now turn to page thirty-eight, headed *Bullets*, and look at this week's thousand pound winner."

The inspector read aloud, "*Mr PF, of Teddington, Middlesex.* That's Patrick Flanagan. No wonder he was out celebrating."

"But Patrick didn't do the Bullets!" said Mrs Flanagan in awe.

"Right, it was your father who provided the winning entry. Being unable to walk more than a few steps, he relied on Patrick to post it for him. Patrick ripped open the envelope and entered the competition under his own name. I dare say he'd played the trick before, because the old man was known to have a flair for Bullets."

"They're second nature to him," said Mrs Flanagan.

"Patrick delayed paying in the cheque. I'm sure we'll find it in here somewhere. He hid the magazine under the carpet so that your father shouldn't find out, but the old chap managed to get hold of a copy."

"He sent me out to buy it."

"And when he saw the competition page, he was outraged. The main object of his life was to win that competition. He'd been robbed of his moment of glory by a shabby trick from his son-in-law. So last night he went to the study and collected the gun and lay in wait. The rest you know."

The inspector let out a breath so deep and so long it seemed to empty his lungs. "You're clever, Father."

"A man's soul was at stake, Inspector."

"Not a good man."

"It's not for us to judge."

Mrs Flanagan said, "What was the winning entry?"

"Well, the phrase was 'A Policeman's Lot'."

"'A Lawfully Big Adventure'," said the murderer with pride, entering the room.

He Couldn't Fly

MICHAEL KURLAND

Michael Kurland has written science fiction (Ten Years to Doomsday, *1964*), *fantasy* (Ten Little Wizards, *1988 – which is also a mystery novel featuring Lord Darcy, created by Randall Garrett*), *mysteries* (The Infernal Device, *1979, featuring Sherlock Holmes's nemesis Moriarty*) *and a wide range of reference books, such as* How to Solve a Murder *(1995) and* The Complete Idiot's Guide to Unsolved Mysteries *(2000). He has also written two novels featuring newspaper columnist Alexander Brass,* Too Soon Dead *(1997) and* The Girls in the High-Heeled Shoes *(1998). Both those books are set in the 1930s, but in the following story we follow Brass back to an unsavoury episode in 1926.*

Late last Tuesday night Brass and I ran into Theodore Finter, better known as the Two Step Kid, upstairs at the Hotsy Totsy Klub on Forty Seventh Street, off Sixth Avenue. In the circles which Brass and I frequent the Kid is a well-known character, but it happens that I've never had the opportunity to speak to him before, although Mr Brass first made his acquaintance many years ago. The Kid is a short, thin, wiry man with an unlined face, even now when he must be well into his forties. His avocation is dancing. His vocation, it is said by those who should know, is murder.

When the set was over, Fletcher Henderson and his boys

retired to the green room, the bathroom, or the bar, and the blonde that the Kid had been two-stepping with went off to powder her nose. The Kid stepped over to our table to have a few words with Brass. They got to talking about the Good Old Days, which, as Mr Brass has told me many times, is anything that happened more than ten years before whenever you're talking. Eventually the conversation got around to the last days of Sammy the Toad Mittwick, and this was a story which I had not heard before. It's quite a tale and deserves retelling, so I went abroad into the world which is New York City and did some checking and some listening, and I wrote it all down here for you.

This happened back in March of 1926, ten years ago now, and five years before I went to work for Mr Alexander Brass, famed columnist for the *New York World*, so I'm telling it based on talks with those who should know, including Brass himself, although he hasn't been as forthcoming as he might. You will see why. My name is Morgan DeWitt, and I am Mr Brass's amanuensis, leg man, bottle washer, errand-runner, and general all-around sycophant; but that's all you'll hear about me because, as I said, all this happened well before I arrived at the *World* building and talked Brass into hiring me. I'm going to tell it like I was there when it happened, looking over Brass's shoulder, 'cause that's the best way to tell a story. But, since I wasn't, some of the dialogue is what I figure they must have said, things being the way they were. Anyway, here's the story.

It started when Jimmy Eisen, from his hospital bed in Brooklyn General, asked to see Brass. They called Jimmy the Canarsie Crusher when he was in the ring. He was a big man, big and powerful. But he was no Dempsey – he was slow. His left jab could do more damage than a 10-pound sledge, and if he ever landed a right, well, you were down for the count and then some. But if you couldn't dodge or block his jab you shouldn't be on that side of the ropes; and as for the right; you'd have to stay awful still for an awful long time for it to reach you. But he could take a lot of punishment while he waited to land that one punch that would put you on the canvas.

The trouble was that, after eight years in the ring, he had taken a lot of punishment. It didn't show in his face much, although his ears were maybe a little flatter than God had made them, but you could see it in his eyes.

His kidneys didn't work too well anymore either. He peed blood. And when he talked there were pauses between his words that God never intended; and sometimes his sentences didn't end up where he thought they would. But by God he could still take it.

Whoever had worked him over the night before had meant business: two ribs cracked, an arm broken maybe – the docs were still trying to figure out whether there was or wasn't a chip out of the bone, the ulna I guess it's called, by the elbow – and one side of his face really messed up. But he still managed a grin when Brass walked into the hospital room. At least Brass decided it was a grin, it was hard to tell for sure what with his face all bandaged up.

"Glad you could get over here, scribbler," he said out of one side of his mouth. "I think maybe I got some info for you."

"Who worked you over, Crusher?" Brass asked, coming over to the side of the bed. "I brought you a bag of oranges. Do you think you can eat them, or should I have someone squeeze them for you?"

"Oranges," said the crusher. "Oranges in March, who wudda thought?"

"Florida," Brass explained.

"Yeah," agreed Eisen. "That too."

"I'll leave them here on the table," Brass told him. "Who did this to you?"

"It was a private dispute," Eisen said. "It took four of them with brass knuckles to knock me off my pins, and they was not without a few bumps and bruises themselves before it was over."

"I'm sure," said Brass. "If you don't want to say any more than that, then you don't. What do you have for me?"

Eisen stared up at Brass with his one uncovered eye. "You remember Lumps Madigan?"

Brass nodded. "Middleweight," he said. "Canvasback. Not but that he didn't try."

"Yeah, well, he's hiding out from the mob boys, and he wants to talk to someone, like maybe buy some insurance."

"What happened, did he make a mistake and forget to fall down in the fourth?"

"Nah, he's quit the ring. He was working for Dutch Schultz as an enforcer, 'cause he's pretty good at hitting those as don't hit back. Not that he's a coward or nothing, but he's got a glass jaw."

"So what's his problem?"

"Seems like somebody told the Dutchman that Madigan and a couple of other lowlifes are preparing to talk turkey to the McWheeter Commission. The Dutchman isn't sure he believes this, but discretion being the better part of valor, he's decided to have them all offed."

Brass's eyes widened (or so I would suppose. I wasn't there but Brass's eyes always widen when he's told something of interest. Okay, okay; I'll butt out now). "What sort of insurance does Lumps think I can buy him, except maybe a bus ticket to California?"

"You'll have to ask him," said the Crusher, "which is the idea what I been telling you – that you should go ask him."

"Why didn't he just call me?"

"'Cause he don't have no telephone where he is at, and he don't want to go outside of where he is at."

"Well then, why didn't *you* just call me?"

"I did," the Crusher pointed out. "But I didn't want to tell you nothing on the phone, 'cause how could I be sure it was you?"

"Makes sense," Brass agreed. Then his eyes narrowed (trust me on this). "Say, did the Dutchman's boys do this to you?"

"You might say that," the Crusher agreed.

"You must owe Madigan a lot, if you'd take a beating like this for him," Brass said.

Eisen shook his head, then groaned and stopped trying to shake his head. "Nope," he said. "I don't care one way or the other, 'cept I hate to see a guy get a raw deal."

"But you didn't give him up."

"It's like this," the Crusher said. "You let one gang of hoods beat something out of you, and pretty soon they'll all be trying it. It's the percentages."

"Right," Brass agreed. "The percentages."

"So you'll go talk to him?"

"Give me the address."

"One-Twelve East Eighty-Eighth, off Lexington in Manhattan. The name over the doorbell is Benchman. Ring twice, then wait maybe half a minute and ring three times, and he'll buzz you in. Don't let yourself be followed."

"Say," Brass said, "what do you take me for, an amateur?"

The Crusher croaked out a sort of laugh, which might have been an answer, and Brass got up to leave, saying he'd be back to see how the Crusher was doing.

"I'll be here for the next little while," the Crusher assured him.

Brass pulled his Auburn 8 Speedster over to the side lane on the Brooklyn Bridge and got out to inspect a front tire. The drivers behind him honked and beeped and swore colorful oaths, but none of them stopped or tried to stay behind him. He crossed Canal Street over to the West Side and went up Broadway to 86th Street, where he crossed through the park back to the East Side, stopping briefly in the park to admire the trees. By now he was sure that no one had managed to follow him, even if they had tried.

One-Twelve East Eighty-Eighth was a brownstone tenement like all the other brownstone tenements on the block. Brass parked the Auburn in front of the house and scanned the sky for signs of rain. The overcast was increasing, but the rain would probably hold off for a while longer, so he trotted up the steps to the front door without bothering to put up the car's canvas top.

He found the button for 2B. Benchman, gave the secret signal, and was buzzed in. The building was old, but respectable. The stairs complained under the threadbare carpet runner, but the railings were polished to a shine.

The door to apartment 2B was cracked open a hair when he reached the landing, and Brass could see an eye peering through.

"Why don't you look through the peep hole?" Brass asked the eye. "It's not quite as obvious."

The door pulled open. "'Cause you can't see nothing through the peep hole, that's why," said Madigan, who stood in the doorway in a gray bathrobe, and oversized black slippers, looking like a giant pouter pigeon. "The mirror or whatever is busted, and all you can see is a little strip of floor right in front of the door. If I could get everyone to write their names on their shoes, then I could use the peephole. You're Brass, right? The newsy?"

"That's me."

"Yeah," Madigan said, squinting at him. "I recognize you from around. Come on in." he stepped aside, and Brass entered the apartment.

The living room was decorated in early French brothel. The wallpaper was some kind of flocked red flower pattern, with an occasional yellow butterfly; the furniture was some dark wood with overstuffed cushions on the chairs and couch; the drapes were red and cream, with heavy red tassels; and the pictures on the walls were Victorian studies of sparsely-draped maidens in heavy gold frames. The only thing missing was an upright piano being played by a short, stout Negro in a red and white suit.

In place of the piano was an oversized Stromberg-Carlson radio with a built in record player on top. At the moment a record was spinning out the sound of a Dixieland jazz band playing something that sounded like "Oh, What a Girl!" but probably wasn't. Lumps went over and turned the music down. "Glad you came, Mr Brass," he said. "I got what you might call a problem."

"So the Crusher told me," Brass said.

"I been working for the Dutchman," Lumps said, "doing a little collecting, and a little persuading, and a little of this and that."

Brass nodded.

Lumps disappeared through a doorway for a moment, and returned clutching a bottle with no label and two glasses. "Have a slug, Mr Brass," he said, pouring a generous double shot into each glass. "It's the real stuff. Canadian. Right off the truck."

Brass took the proffered glass and sniffed suspiciously.

"Say, didn't I tell you?" Lumps said, looking offended. "It's Canadian."

"Your word's good enough for me," Brass agreed, and took a swig. "Well, how nice," he said. "It's been pre-watered for my convenience."

Lumps frowned at this for a second, and then decided to ignore the remark. "Somebody told the Dutchman that I'm planning to sing to the McWheeter Commission," he told

Brass. "Which is not so; and besides I got nothing to sing about even should I choose to warble. But Flegenheimer, the no-good shit – that's Dutch Schultz's real name, you know: Arthur Flegenheimer, the no-good shit – don't bother asking me or nothing, he just puts the spot on me."

"You have my sympathies," Brass said. "But what can I do about it?"

Lumps dropped into one of the overstuffed chairs and waved Brass over to the couch. "I figure I got two choices," he said. "First I gotta tell you that I ain't never squealed on nobody; it ain't in my nature."

The music stopped, and the massive mechanical device lifted the arm from the record, hiccoughed twice, and turned itself off. "I'll take your word for it," Brass said into the silence. "It doesn't much matter to me one way or the other."

Lumps looked at him as though he'd just said he didn't care whether or not the Yankees won the series. "It matters," he said. "If a guy ain't got his integrity, what has he got?"

Brass raised his glass in a silent toast to Lumps's integrity. "Good point," he agreed.

A girl in a fuzzy pink peignoir that almost reached to her knees appeared in the inner doorway. Her overly-blonde hair hung in ringlets framing her oval face, and her overly-large brown eyes were set in rings of kohl. She leaned against the doorframe and peered blearily into the room. "It's too light," she complained. "Turn some of it off, for the love of mike."

"It's the sun, Ellen," Lumps told her. "You can't turn it off."

"Yeah? Well, who asked for it? What's it doing up this early?"

"It's almost noon," he told her.

"Yeah? Well, like I said. Say, who's this?" She leaned forward to try to get a better look at Brass.

"This is Mr Brass," Lumps told her. "He's a reporter for the *World*."

Brass only winced the slightest wince, and decided not to try to explain the difference between a reporter and a columnist.

"Fancy that," Ellen said, "a reporter for the whole world. Ain't that something." She advanced across the room one foot in front of the other, hips swaying, like a tipsy cat, holding her peignoir not quite as closed as possible with her left fist, and extended her right hand to Brass. "Ellen Benchman, your reportership," she said, curtseying and not quite falling over as Brass took her hand. "Want to do a story on an up and coming young actress?"

"She's in the *Scandals*," Lumps volunteered.

"Third girl from the left in the chorus," she said. "But I'm understudying the second girl from the left."

"Is that a step up?" Brass asked, smiling.

"It's two steps to the left," she told him. "'Scuse me now, I've got to shower and like that. I'll be back shortly." And with the slightest hint of a moue and a subtle wiggle of her peignoir, she exited the room.

"Quite a, ah, young lady," Brass commented. "Is she your girlfriend?"

Lumps stared after the retreating pink vision. "And what if she is?" he demanded.

"Then this is the first place the Dutchman and his boys will come looking for you," Brass told him. "The fair Ellen could get hurt."

Lumps thought it over for a second. "Nice of you not to mention what would happen to me," he said. "But as it happens, Miss Benchman is my sister-in-law, which is not generally known on account of my wife don't associate with my professional acquaintances. She is the lady friend of Sammy the Toad Mittwick, who is keeping her in this apartment what he fixed up himself. Ellen, that is. Not my wife."

Brass looked more closely at the room's furnishings and pursed his lips. "Good taste, Sammy has," he said. "Does Sammy know you're here?"

Lumps managed to look insulted. "What are you suggesting?"

"Sammy the Toad is a bagman for the Dutchman," Brass said.

"You ain't telling me anything what I don't already know."

"He might sell you out," Brass said gently. "The notion of honor among thieves is greatly overrated."

"Yeah, well, I know something what you don't," Lumps said. "Namely that Sammy ain't feeling too congenial toward the Dutchman himself. He's got something worth selling to the

Commission, which I don't, and he's thinking of going to talk to McWheeter himself. Only the Dutchman don't know it."

"What's he got?" Brass asked.

"Ask him," Lumps said. "If I knew, then I'd have it too – which I don't."

Brass nodded. "Makes sense," he said. "So, what help can I be to your efforts to disentangle yourself from this situation?"

Lumps thought that over for a minute. "Like I said, I figure I got two choices," he said. "First I can convince the Dutchman that I ain't going to squeal, no way, or second I can go to the McWheeter Commission myself and get protection in return for what I got to tell them."

"Two choices," Brass agreed. "Either swear that you'd never squeal, or squeal."

"Only both of them are no good," Lumps continued. "I got a Chinaman's chance in Hell of making it home alive if I try to see Flegenheimer, the shit, to tell him anything. And McWheeter's going to want something in return for protection, and I ain't got nothing to give him."

"So, what can I do?" Brass asked.

Lumps turned and thumped Brass on the arm with his index finger. "You're my third choice," he said.

Brass looked at him dubiously. "And just what must I do to receive this honor?" he asked.

"There's a little town in Nebraska where the Dutchman would never think of looking for me at. I need for you to help me get there."

"Help how?"

"Maybe to the extent of springing for a couple of G's, 'cause what I ain't got is cash. And in return, I'm going to tell you things that you can write down and use in your newspaper."

"I thought you didn't know anything," Brass said.

"I don't know anything for the McWheeter Commission; they want names and dates and amounts of money and like that. Which I ain't got. But if you want to know how bootlegging works from the inside, how the stuff is shipped in from Canada or England or Cuba, how it's distributed, and that, then I'm your man. And I'll throw in with some great stories about moving the stuff around the city and hijacking and leg breaking and like that. The kind of stories that read good, like that Damon Runyon stuff, but don't get nobody specific arrested."

Brass thought it over. "It might be good for a couple of C-notes," he allowed. "I'll get you to a rewrite man to take down your story, and if it's at all of interest, I'll spring for train fare and a little over."

"Say!"

Ellen was standing in the doorway, wearing a blue skirt that showed just as much leg as a good girl ought to show, but only if she had great legs, and a light blue sweater that was just too tight enough, and white stockings, and it was her "say" that had just stopped the conversation.

"What's that?" Lumps asked.

"If Mr Brass here is going to help you, why then he should help my man. Sammy's in a bind, and he's got a lot more to tell than you, if words is what's gonna help get him outta this mess."

"Sammy's not on the spot," Lumps said. "Nobody's on the look for him carrying a Thompson in a violin case."

"Not yet," Ellen said, "but they're gonna be if he don't figure a way out pretty fast." she turned to Brass. "He's worried, Mr Brass, he's worried for his life."

"He didn't tell me nothing about this," Lumps objected.

"He don't go around advertising it," Ellen said. 'He don't want word getting back to Mr Schultz – that being what he's worried about."

"It ain't likely I'm going to be speaking to Mr Schultz anytime soon," Lumps told her.

"What does Mittwick want," Brass asked, "money to get out of town?"

"Money ain't his problem," Ellen told him. "Or, let me say, money is his problem, but not because of the lack of it."

Lumps stood up, and then dropped back down again. "Don't tell me he's been skimming," he demanded, his voice tight.

"Not exactly," Ellen said.

"Not exactly? Say, I better get outta here. If the Dutchman sends some of his boys after the Toad, they'll find me instead. And that won't be good."

"Hey, listen," Ellen said. "I wouldn't do that to you. Mr

Schultz don't know about Sammy yet – and don't call him 'the Toad,' it ain't respectful.''

Brass stood up. "I could listen to this for hours and hours," he said, "but maybe we all have better things to do."

"Yeah, that's right," Ellen agreed. "I got to get to work. You going to help the Toad, Mr Brass?"

"Hey, that ain't respectful," Lumps mocked her. She stuck her tongue out at him.

"I'll have to know what he wants before I can tell whether or not I can help him," Brass told her.

"Yeah," Ellen agreed, wrapping a fur boa around her neck. "Well, he wants to talk to the Commission, that's what he wants. And then he wants he and I should go away somewhere."

"Yeah," Lumps said. "Like maybe Mars?" He stood up. "I better get dressed so's I can get outta here." And he lumped out of the room.

"Why does Mittwick want to talk to the Commission?" Brass asked Ellen. "And what has he got to tell them?"

"He'd better tell you that. He's meeting me after the show. Come around backstage at around ten thirty, and I'll introduce you. Or if you like, I can leave a ticket for you at the box office."

Brass nodded. "Okay, Ellen. Tell your boyfriend the – ah – Mittwick that I'll see him backstage after the show. But don't bother with the ticket."

"It's a good show," Ellen told him, sounding a little miffed.

"It is," Brass agreed. "I've seen it. And, come to think of it, I remember you – third girl from the left."

"You do?" She brightened.

"Good timing," he said. "Great legs."

"Yeah," she agreed. "That's me."

"Sammy Mittwick's a lucky man," Brass said.

"Yeah," she agreed. "He is." Then a frown line appeared between her carefully-plucked eyebrows. "Only I hope he gets to stay that way. Lucky, I mean."

"I'll talk to McWheeter this afternoon," Brass told her. "See what kind of deal I can make for him."

"That's good," she said.

"Of course it'll depend a lot on what he's got to bring to the table."

"Oh, he's got a lot of good stuff," she said enthusiastically.

"Why he knows who the Dutchman's getting his protection from – that ought to be worth something."

"He does?"

"Oh!" she said. "I wasn't supposed to tell you that, on account of he was holding that back as a bargaining stick."

"Bargaining chip," Brass said.

"Oh, chip – right – chip."

"That ought to be worth something," Brass agreed.

"Three thousand dollars a week," Ellen said, her eyes wide at the idea of that much money. "My Sammy delivers it."

"To whom?"

"They call him 'Mr Big,'" she said.

Brass laughed. "Mr Big?"

"Say, it ain't my idea," Ellen said defensively. "Sammy don't know his real name, but he knows where his office is, and they should be able to get it from that. That ought to be worth something."

"I'll see what I can do," Brass said.

Lumps emerged from the back room wearing pants that were a little too plaid, and a black turtle neck sweater. "I guess I'm ready to go," he said. "Only where am I going?"

"You come with me," Brass said. "You'll be safe in the *World* building on Fifty Ninth Street, telling your story to a guy named Jake. He'll get everything we need. Then we'll see about getting you out of town.

"It's a two-seater, but if you want to squeeze in," he told Ellen, "I'll drop you."

"I don't mind being squeezed between two good-looking guys," Ellen said. "Just be careful where you put your hand when you're shifting gears."

"My honor as a boy scout," Brass said, raising his hand in a two-finger salute.

"Say, was you a boy scout?" Lumps asked.

"Nope," Brass told him.

"Neither was I," Lumps admitted. "I couldn't pass the test."

The ride downtown was uneventful, although Brass couldn't refrain from keeping a worried eye on the rear view mirror. He dropped Ellen off at 46th and Sixth Avenue, two blocks from her theater, and circled back to the *World* building on 59th and Tenth. One of the doormen took the keys from Brass and drove the Auburn off to that curious half world where doormen find parking spaces while Brass and Madigan went upstairs.

Brass told the city editor what was happening, pulled Gus Damici off the rewrite desk, and put Gus and Lumps together in the outer room of his office. Damici was well into his eighth decade and had been a reporter for over 50 years. He was expert at pulling the telling details that made a story memorable from witnesses who didn't know they'd seen anything worth talking about.

"You know the kind of stuff we want," Brass told Gus. "If he gets recalcitrant, remind him that we haven't paid him yet."

"Say," said Lumps. "I ain't re– what you said. I'm here, ain't I?"

"True," said Brass. "Forgive me." He went into his inner office, picked up the phone, and jiggled the receiver until an operator came on the line. "Faye? Oh, Pearl. Listen, get me the McWheeter Commission; you've got the number there somewhere . . . I'll hold."

He stood there drumming his fingers on the desk and listening to the clicks, hums, and hollow silences while the connection was made. "This is Alexander Brass of the *New York World*," he told the secretary who picked up at the Commission. "Is McWheeter in? Can he talk? . . . McWheeter? It's Alexander Brass of the *World*. I've got something – someone – for you. He's Dutch Schultz's bagman . . . That's right. He's ready to talk in return for protection. I'll explain when I see you. I'll be up there in about an hour."

He hung up, adjusted his tie, and skipped down the narrow back stairs, reserved for those who knew it existed. After a quick dish of scrambled eggs, home fries, rye toast, and a piece of apple pie at Mollie's across the street, he headed across town to the offices being occupied by the New York State Commission for the Investigation of Prohibition Enforcement Related Crimes, which was called either the SCIPERC (pronounced Sky-Perk) Commission or the McWheeter Commission, depending on the time of day, the phase of the Moon, and the latitude of the speaker, or some such.

Brass moved fast, it was his nature. Walking relaxed him and helped him think, and the faster he walked the more relaxed he got. He never actually broke out into a run, but I've known those who just about had to trot to keep up with him. Some-where around Central Park south and Sixth Avenue, he noticed that a short, skinny guy in an oversized grey fedora had been staying about half a block behind him since he left Mollie's. Now it wasn't all that far, but as I say Brass moved fast, and it was pushing coincidence for the same person to stay just half a block behind him for more than, say, half a block. Brass turned right on Sixth, went down a couple of blocks, and then headed east again. Sure enough, the skinny guy was still there when he checked.

Morris and Daughters' Delicatessen was just off Fifth, and Brass trotted down the three steps and ducked inside. The back exit let out on an alley, and Brass scooted through it, past a couple of smoking busboys, and doubled around the block, coming up on his tail from behind while the tail was lurking in a doorway two down from Morris's establishment.

"Hello, there," Brass said softly.

The skinny guy tensed up for a second, and then whirled around, pulling a Colt .45 Army model automatic from under his jacket with mongoose-like speed. Brass took a step back and raised his arms in the air.

"Why, Mr Brass," the skinny guy said. "You startled me." The automatic disappeared like a stage magician's dove, and he brushed his palms together. "That's not always a wise thing to do"

Brass dropped his hands. "Mr Finter," he said. "Why are you two-stepping your way into my life?"

The Two Step Kid looked thoughtful for a second. "Why am I following you, you mean?"

"That's it."

"Why, to see where you're going, Mr Brass, to see where you're going."

"And why is that?"

The Kid chuckled. "Listen, Mr Brass, you've got your secrets and I've got mine. Let's leave it at that, shall we?"

Brass sighed and shook his head sadly. "I'm heading for the Feldmar Building," he said. "You want to walk with me, and we'll talk about this and that?"

"No, that's okay," the Kid said. "I'll leave you be for now. Maybe I'll just stop in here for a plate of matzo brei. Sadie –

Morris's younger daughter, is well worth looking at over a plate of matzo brei."

"Fifty bucks if you'll tell me who put you on to me," Brass said, reaching into his pocket.

"Take it easy going into your pockets around me," the Kid said, putting his two hands in front of him like he was trying to stop a streetcar. "I get nervous at the gesture."

"Sorry," Brass said. "But, like I said . . ."

"Mr Brass, you should know better than that. I got my professional pride."

"Just thought I'd ask."

"No hard feelings," the Kid assured him. "See you around, hey?" he tipped his fedora at Brass and descended the three steps into the deli.

Harlan McWheeter had been a judge in the Supreme Court of New York county system for 12 years. He was now a partner in DaSilva Brown Henderson & McWheeter, and had been recommended to Governor Roosevelt by our honorable Mayor Jimmy Walker to head the SCIPERC Commission. He was a tall, bony man with a prominent nose, deep set brown eyes, and a black toupee that looked as though each hair had been carefully glued into place. That day he was wearing his usual dark blue double-breasted suit; the starched collar of his underlying white shirt jutted up so high that it looked as if it was a structural support for his narrow chin. There was a story that a junior associate had once walked into his office and seen the judge with the two top buttons of his jacket unbuttoned. The associate was promptly fired.

Brass was frisked quickly and efficiently before he was shown into the inner sanctum of McWheeter's suite of offices, where five people awaited him, grouped at the far end of the long mahogany table that took up most of the room. The judge, looking stern and magisterial in the center, was flanked by a pair of Commission attorneys in blue suits, a stocky bodyguard in brown, and an elderly male secretary with a steno pad.

"Sit," McWheeter said, indicating the chair in front of Brass, which put him the whole table length away from McWheeter and his cluster.

Brass sat. "If there's anything I look forward to," he said. "It's a quiet, *intime* little tête-à-tête."

"How's that?" asked McWheeter.

Brass raised his voice. "I said I hate yelling," he yelled.

"Stop that," McWheeter said irritably. "No need to shout." He sat down and, as though they were worked by strings, the others sat with him. "Now, just what sort of information is it you have for us, Mr Brass?"

"We should first warn you," said one of McWheeter's minions, giving Brass a steely glare, "that we are not prepared to offer immunity from prosecution unless what you tell us is substantial and can be verified."

Brass smiled. "Blessings on you, little man," he said. "I don't require immunity. But the gentleman on whose behalf I speak may, and he will definitely require protection."

"What sort of protection?" McWheeter's other minion inquired.

"Dutch Schultz will certainly put the spot on him when he finds out he's talking," Brass said. "And he would just as soon not be spotted. As I said on the phone, he's the Dutchman's bagman."

"He collects money for Mr, ah, Schultz?" McWheeter asked.

"Collects and pays," Brass said. "And what he's got to trade, among other things, is the identity of the city official – I assume it's a city official – whom Dutch is paying off for protection."

"Son of a – " the lawyer on the left slapped the table. "Say, that would about put this commission on the map, now wouldn't it?"

"Governor Roosevelt would be very pleased," McWheeter allowed. "Is this man reliable?"

"Well, I'd say he has nothing to gain and a lot to lose if he isn't," Brass told him.

"Does his information sound, ah, plausible to you?" McWheeter asked.

"I don't know what his information is," Brass said.

"He hasn't told you?"

"My understanding is that the Dutchman pays three thousand dollars a week to someone they call 'Mr Big'."

McWheeter sat back and glared down the long table. "Mr Big? Surely you jest."

"Perhaps my informant does," Brass told him. "But I surely do not."

"That has all the plausibility of a Nick Carter dime novel," McWheeter said. "Who is this 'Mr Big'?"

"I don't know," Brass told him. "I'm not sure that Sammy does either."

"Sammy?"

"Sammy Mittwick, the bagman in question. He's willing to testify, but he will want protection, and possibly immunity; although I don't know whether collecting and delivering money is per se a crime. Bank messengers do it all day long."

McWheeter pondered. When he arrived at the Pearly Gates and the recording angel asked him whether he wanted to enter or take the elevator down below, McWheeter would ponder. "All right," McWheeter said finally. "But he'd better come up with something – or someone – we can verify. Something better than merely 'Mr Big'."

"He can show you the place where the transaction happened," Brass said. "And I suppose he could identify 'Mr Big' if you could get him in a line-up."

"It's a start," McWheeter's right-hand minion offered.

McWheeter nodded. "We're putting our witnesses up at the Gotham," he said. "Those who require putting up. I suppose – "

"The Gotham's too public," the left hand law minion objected. "Everybody knows about the Gotham. We'll want this testimony to be a surprise until it's delivered."

"Not to mention that if Schultz hears about it first, he'll never live to testify," Brass added.

"Secret and secure," the right hand lawyer said. "Deputy Commissioner Mapes has a special squad for handling jobs like this. I'll call him. Where is this Mittwick now?"

"I'll have to talk to him first," Brass said. "I'm just the messenger. I can tell him that you agree to keep him hidden until he testifies?"

McWheeter nodded. "You can tell him that," he agreed.

"And what about after?"

McWheeter pondered. "We'll see that he is taken safely to a location of his choosing," he said finally. "Somewhere in the United States. He is to agree to keep in touch with us in case we require his further testimony."

"Okay," Brass said. "I'll pass it on."

"But our responsibility, and our expenses, end there," McWheeter warned. "Don't lead him to expect that we're going to finance his living expenses from then on."

"I think he can take care of himself in that regard," Brass said. "Or so I understand."

McWheeter looked at him doubtfully. "The fruits of illegal activities – " he began.

" – Are not our concern at this time," the left hand legal minion cut in smoothly.

McWheeter thought this over, and nodded. "True," he said. "The harvest of Mammon may be put to good uses. Have this man call us, and we'll arrange matters."

"Here," said the right hand lawyer, coming around the table and handing a card to Brass. "The private phone number of Deputy Commissioner Mapes. I'll tell him to expect your call."

McWheeter looked sourly at his minion. "I suppose that's best," he said. "Well, thank you for coming in, Mr Brass. We have other matters to attend to now." And, with a wave, he dismissed Brass from his thoughts.

The final big production number of *George White's Scandals of 1926* was time stepping its way across the Knickerbocker's wide stage as Brass pushed his way through one of the closed entrance doors. The house manager, who was standing in the lobby with a brace of ushers, recognized Brass and trotted over. "Mr Brass," he said. "You should have told me you were coming. There are some seats in the orchestra. I'll have one of the girls . . ."

"That's okay, Mr Purcell," Brass told him. "You've got, what, fifteen minutes to run? I'll stand in back. I've just come to see one of the performers after the show."

"Ah!" Purcell said. "One of the chorus girls, Mr Brass?"

"As it happens, that's right, Mr Purcell."

Purcell arched his eyebrows. "Any particular one, Mr Brass?" he asked.

"Why, Mr Purcell!" Brass said, his eyes wide. "Shame on you!"

Brass tiptoed his way to the back of the auditorium and tried to spot Ellen on the distant stage. He couldn't look for the third girl from the left, as the chorus line was circling around a large man in a dinner jacket and oversized white bow tie, who was singing "Are You The Girl For Me, Or Have I Been Misinformed?" to each of the chorus girls in turn as she passed him. They all seemed to be quite willing to be the Girl For Him, and he was having an understandably hard time in picking just the right one. Then the girls straightened out their line, faced the audience, and went into their step-step-kick-step routine, and Brass was able to focus on the third girl from the left.

Ellen, Brass was pretty sure it was Ellen, seemed quite beautiful from the back of the auditorium, with long and shapely legs. But then, so did the other 21 girls. At any reasonable distance, all women look beautiful. Men find women in the abstract desirable, as evidenced daily at any maternity hospital.

Brass felt a tap on his shoulder, and a high-pitched voice murmured, "are you looking for me?"

He turned. "Mittwick," he whispered. "Let's go back into the lobby, where we can talk."

"Nah," said the Toad. "Come off to the side over there; there's a hall leads backstage. We can talk backstage."

"It's going to be kind of noisy," Brass objected in a whisper.

"There's a room," the Toad said. "Come."

Mittwick led the way down a narrow corridor lit by bare electric bulbs hanging from disused gaslight fixtures, the brick walls plastered with posters from long-defunct shows. When they reached the backstage area, Mittwick crossed to a circular iron staircase toward the back. "Don't stomp," Mittwick whispered to Brass, "this thing creaks."

"Got it," Brass agreed. "No stomping."

They went up two flights and entered a room full of oversized trunks and folded draperies. "What's in the trunks?" Brass asked.

"Who knows?" the Toad explained.

"Ah!"

Mittwick stretched out on the floor with his head outside the door, and peered down the stairs. A large revolver of ancient vintage had suddenly appeared in his hand.

"What on earth are you doing?" Brass asked.

"Shut up for a minute, will you? I gotta make sure as we weren't followed."

Brass looked sadly down at the prone Mittwick. "You don't trust me?"

The Toad twisted his head around and looked up at him. "Any reason I should?"

Brass shrugged. "I guess not. Ellen trusted me."

"Yeah," Mittwick grunted. "That and a nickel will get you on any subway in the city."

"Sammy!" Brass said. "Your own girl friend!"

Mittwick shook his head. "She's a great girl," he said. "But she ain't got the best judgment in the world. Hell, she chose me, didn't she?"

Brass was speechless.

After a couple of minutes Mittwick stood up and brushed himself off. He closed the door. "So, did you talk to this McWheeter guy?"

"I did."

"What did he say?"

"They'd like to believe your 'Mr Big' story, but they're not convinced. He said if you've got something they can use, and you can prove it, they'll help you."

"Prove it? How prove it?"

Brass shrugged.

"I can show them where his office is," the Toad said. "I can even tell them what he looks like." He chuckled. "He used to do this thing, like out of the dime novels. He'd wear like a black bag over his head with these two eye holes cut out, you know?"

Brass nodded to show that he knew.

"So I got curious. One day I sat in the barber shop downstairs with a hot towel wrapped around my phiz so's he wouldn't spot me, and waited. Sure enough, about ten minutes later he came out. No bag. So I got a good glom at him."

"You didn't follow him to see who he was?"

"I thought of that, but this big limo pulls up and he hops in and splits. So I didn't get the chance. After that I guess I was too nervous to try it again. But I think I got enough to find him. Besides I got the names of all the sports I've been collecting from. Probably half the speaks, gambling dens, and whore houses in Manhattan, and a couple in Jersey."

"It sounds like you've got something saleable," Brass agreed.

"You know it," said the Toad.

"So when do you want to do this?" Brass asked.

"No time like the present," Mittwick said. "They got to come and get me. I got a bag packed downstairs."

"You think you're in trouble already?"

"Listen," Mittwick said. "The Dutchman has this guy working for him; Havasack, they call him. His real name's Berman. Abbadabba Berman. He's a math wizard of some kind."

"This guy's name is Abbadabba, and he has a nickname?" Brass asked.

"Everybody's got a nickname," the Toad said. "Everybody in the rackets, anyway. It's a thing."

"I guess so," Brass said.

"Anyway, this Havasack, he's been working the track. Something to do with changing the odds or something. But he just came back to the city and, to have something to do, he decided to go over the Dutchman's books. That was two days ago. The Dutchman, he was laughing about it. He said anybody that was stealing from him, they'd better watch out. But you may think he was kidding, but believe me, he wasn't kidding."

"So you've been skimming, and you figure that this Havasack is going to find you out?"

"I been taking a little off the top," the Toad agreed. "I figure there's a good chance he's already found out. Like I said, he's some kind of math wizard."

"You're a brave man, stealing from the Dutchman," Brass said.

"Hell, I didn't figure on getting caught," said the Toad.

Brass spiraled down the iron staircase and crossed to the payphone by the stage door. When the operator came on, he dropped in his nickel and looked on the little card for Deputy Commissioner Mapes's phone number. "Canal three-four-three-six," he told the operator.

"That is a local exchange," she told him, each word carefully enunciated, each syllable rounded. "You may dial that yourself."

Brass sighed. "I would, but this payphone has no dial."

"All our payphones without dials are being replaced," she informed him.

"Perhaps," Brass said, "but this one hasn't been yet."

"I will get that number for you," she said in her rolling tones, "but in the future please remember that you can dial numbers on local exchanges yourself."

"Oh, I will, I will," he assured her.

An assistant picked up the phone, but the deputy commissioner came on immediately. "Brass," he said, his gravelly voice booming into the phone. "I've been waiting for your call. What's the story?"

"Sammy's going to sing to the Committee," Brass told him. He filled Mapes in on those parts of the story that concerned him and suggested that he get a few plainclothes men in an unmarked car over to the Knickerbocker Theater as soon as possible.

"I'll issue a subpoena for him," Mapes said. "That way we can hold him in protective custody."

"The more protective the better," Brass agreed. "Pull around to the stage door. Mittwick is edgy, and may have good cause."

Sammy the Toad came slowly down the spiral staircase, Ellen, still in her *Misinformed* costume, hanging on to his arm, her feathered headdress brushing along the underside of the spiral. "You're going to be okay, baby," she said, trying womanfully not to cry. "Let me know where they take you, and I'll come see you right away, I promise."

"That might not be such a good idea, kid," he told her bravely. "When they get me out of here, I'll find a way to send for you. But it'll be a couple of months."

"I don't know if I can wait that long without you, my darling," she sobbed.

A few minutes later a large, unmarked touring car pulled up to the stage entrance and three large men in dark blue double-breasted suits got out, a tommy gun cradled in each of their arms. Sammy spun up the spiral staircase and was in the upstairs room with the door bolted before you could say "subpoena". It took Brass and Ellen together to lure him out.

"Come with us," the officer in charge said. "We'll take care of you."

"Where are we going?" Mittwick asked. "Where are you going to take me?"

The officer looked around. "No disrespect," he said to Brass, with a nod to Ellen, "but it would be better if I didn't say."

"I quite agree," Brass said. "Mittwick, these gentlemen will keep you safe until after you testify. After that, I'll make sure they don't forget their promise to get you away to someplace safe."

"Yeah, well, okay, Mr Brass." Sammy shook hands with Brass, kissed Ellen firmly, grabbed the hefty suitcase he had stashed by the door, and got into the car. "Thanks for what you've done for me, Mr Brass," he said. "I won't forget it." The car pulled away.

Brass sighed. "Come on, Ellen," he said. "I've got my car around the corner. Get into something resembling street clothes, and I'll take you home."

"Say, Mr Brass," she said. "I'm grateful for what you're doing for Sammy, and all. But I don't know if it would be right, I mean so soon – "

"Take you home," Brass said, smiling a sad smile, "and leave you at the door. Honest."

"Oh," she said. "Well, I guess that's okay, then." And if she sounded slightly wistful, neither of them mentioned it on the drive home.

It was three days later that Deputy Commissioner Mapes called Brass at his office. "If I give you something," he boomed into the telephone, "can you keep it under your hat?"

"I have a very large hat," Brass assured the deputy commissioner.

"And when the time comes," Mapes continued, "you'll remember how to spell my name?"

"My word," Brass agreed. Which is, after all, largely how a column like *Brass Tacks* comes to be written: confidences kept and names spelled right.

"Meet me downstairs in ten minutes," Mapes told him. "There should be a large envelope waiting for me at the city editor's desk. Bring it down with you, if you don't mind."

It was closer to twenty minutes before the large open touring car pulled up in front of the *World* building. Brass clambered into the back seat, joining Deputy Commissioner Mapes, a burly man with a round face and a thick black mustache. "Sorry I'm late," Mapes said. "McWheeter kept me with last-second instructions and suggestions. The man can fidget and fuss more than two cats in a kettle." He beamed at Brass and waved the chauffeur onward. "Ready to fight crime?" he asked with a chortle as the car pulled out into traffic.

"Is that what we're doing?" Brass passed Mapes the bulky manila envelope the city editor had given him.

Mapes held the envelope up with his left hand and tapped it with his right forefinger. "In here," he said, "are the photographs of forty-two members of the city government who might be the mysterious 'Mr Big.' We're going to spread them out before Sammy the Toad and see if he is able to point to one and say, his voice ringing with sincerity, 'That is the man to whom I've been paying three thousand dollars a week!'"

Brass took his silver cigarette case from his jacket pocket and waved it in Mapes's direction. Mapes shook his head. "I'm a cigar man," he said.

Brass selected a cigarette from the case with a care that suggested that one was somehow different from the others. He went through the routine of tapping it and lighting it and putting the case away. "McWheeter's not going to be able to put away Dutch Schultz, or Luciano, or Rothstein, or any of the other top, ah, liquor importers; you know that, don't you?"

"Are you suggesting that this is all an exercise in futility?" Mapes grinned. "Then you don't understand its true purpose."

Brass leaned back in the seat cushion. "Enlighten me," he said.

"Roosevelt's going to be running for president this next election, or the one after," Mapes said. "And Walker might be thinking of moving up himself. And the people who vote – even the ones who are in favor of booze – aren't fond of the murder and mayhem that's accompanying its delivery these days.

"This investigation is serving the dual purpose of convincing the voters that Roosevelt is a crime-busting governor, and pointing out to the rum runners that we don't give much of a damn about bathtub gin or Canadian rye, but we don't approve of the killings that go with it."

"At last," Brass said, "an honest and cynical explanation that I can understand."

"Don't quote me," said Mapes.

Brass puffed on his cigarette. "Where have you got the Toad stashed?" he asked.

"Brooklyn," Mapes told him. "Out by Prospect Park. A hotel called the Staunton Arms. We have the whole eighth floor."

"Any problems?"

"Not a hint."

They chatted about this and that as the touring car crossed the Brooklyn Bridge and headed down Flatbush Avenue. As they turned right along Prospect Park Mapes pointed down the block. "There's the hotel," he said, "and – damn! Steve, pull over!"

"What is it?" Brass asked, looking up at the building looming ahead of them as the chauffeur pulled the car over to the curb. There, about two thirds of the way up the side of the building was a figure leaning out of a window. No – he wasn't leaning out, he was hanging out. And then, silently and, it seemed to those watching, in slow motion he fell, disappearing from view behind a shorter building in front.

"Shit!" said Mapes with feeling.

"Sammy Mittwick?" asked Brass, already knowing the answer.

"Any odds you want," Mapes said.

The two of them were out of the car by now and racing toward the hotel. As they ran, they could see heads appearing in the upstairs windows around the wide open one. "Yup, it's the eighth floor," said Mapes. He stopped for a second to stare up at the open window, where the bottoms of the curtains had been pulled outside and were flapping in the wind. "Mittwick could sing," he said, shaking his head sadly, "but he couldn't fly."

Brass and Mapes ran into the lobby of the hotel to find everything normal: bellmen lounging, room clerks scribbling, elevator men staring mutely out of their cages; even one lone cop strolling unconcernedly across the lobby. Mapes pulled out his badge and waved it in front of him. "I'm Deputy Commissioner Mapes," he shouted. "You – " he pointed to a room clerk, "call the local precinct. Tell them somebody was just pushed out of a window here, and to get here in force."

"Who? What? Wha – ?" the room clerk stuttered.

"Never mind, just do it. You – " he pointed to the cop " – take the front door and don't let anybody in or out, especially out. Get someone to cover the back door."

"Yes, sir," the cop said, saluting.

"Somebody's head is going to roll for this," Mapes said, running for the elevator. "I just hope it isn't mine."

Just as Mapes and Brass entered one elevator, another opened and four cops came boiling out. Mapes yelled at them, barking instructions for them to cover all the remaining exits and stay in place until told otherwise. They disbursed and Mapes snapped "Eight!" to the elevator operator.

"I guessed," the man said, slamming the door closed and putting the elevator in gear. "What's going on?"

"A man was shoved out a window," Brass told him.

"No way," the operator said. "With all them cops up there?"

"So you would have thought," said Brass.

The door opened on the eighth floor to a corridor full of moiling policemen. Mapes brought them to order with a couple of shouted instructions and ran down the hall to where an open door led into one of the hotel rooms. Inside were a few more confused-looking cops and a wide open window, the curtains pushed outside and flapping in the wind. "What the hell happened?" he demanded.

Sergeant Dickson was the ranking cop there, and he told the tale. "About an hour ago a call came through from McWheeter's office. Says this broad named Ellen is the Toad's girlfriend, and she has the okay to come by and bring him some clothes and stuff – maybe stay half an hour. You know."

"Of course you checked to make sure the call was authentic," Mapes asked, smiling tightly.

"It had to be," Dickson offered. "Who else knows the guy is here?"

"Okay. And?"

"And she shows up and goes into his room. 'Sweety,' she says, 'I'm here.'"

"And of course you searched her before she went in?"

"Her and the bag she brought with her," Dickson said, sounding aggrieved. "Full of clothing. Like an extra suit for him, and a negligee thing lying on top; all pink and stuff."

"Okay. And?"

"And nothing. And that's it. About ten minutes later we hear this scream and go busting into the room. And it's empty, and the window is wide open. We look down, and there's the Toad lying in the alley, all broken up."

"So where's the girl?"

"That's what I sez, Commissioner. Where's the girl? She was nowhere to be found. We looked in the closet and under the bed and everything."

"No bathroom?"

"It's down the hall. She never left the room."

"This the only door?"

"That's it."

"So she just disappeared?"

"Not only that, she left all her clothes behind."

"How's that?"

Dickson pointed to the bed. There was a skirt and a blouse and a pair of shoes and crumpled up white stockings.

"Shouldn't leave shoes on the bed," Brass commented. "That's bad luck."

Mapes glared at him, and then turned back to the sergeant. "There's people from the local precinct coming," he said. "I want this room gone over from side to side, top to bottom. I want this hotel gone over with a fine tooth comb. Check the identities of everybody in the hotel, staff and guests. I want to know what the hell happened in here."

Sergeant Dickson left the room, and for the first time Mapes and Brass were alone. "If you saw what I saw," Mapes told Brass, his voice pitched so that it wouldn't carry, "I want you to shut up about it."

"You mean when the Toad went out the window?" Brass asked.

"Yeah, that," Mapes said.

"You mean the fact that the hand that let go of him from inside the window came out of a blue sleeve?"

"Yeah," Mapes said softly. "That."

"For now," Brass said. "You've got my word. Here's something you should think about."

"What's that?"

"When you saw him fall, did he scream?"

Mapes considered. "No," he said.

"And the police outside the door busted in a couple of seconds after hearing the scream, and the girl was gone."

"So?"

"So who screamed?"

Ellen Benchman, the only possible suspect, turned out to have an invincible alibi; at the time of the defenestration she was in rehearsal for a Gershwin song that they were switching into the show. And besides, when the cops that had been on duty took a look at her, they agreed that she wasn't the "Ellen" they had let into Mittwick's room.

And there the story lay for ten years.

"It was you, wasn't it?" Brass asked the Two Step Kid that night at the Hotsy Totsy Klub. "You dressed up like a woman and high-heeled your way into Mittwick's room."

"What makes you think so, Mr Brass?" Finter asked.

"You're the loose end," Brass said. "You were following me, so somebody put you onto it. And it was right after I talked to McWheeter on the phone. You didn't follow me to the hotel, because you were there first and I didn't know where it was. But somebody else knew, and sent you."

"Put me in a dress and you can take me anywhere," the Kid said, with a high-pitched laugh. "My only worry was that someone would notice my knobby, and very unfeminine, knees. But I guess those white stockings covered them up pretty well. Let's assume it was me, Mr Brass, just hypothetically. Then what?"

"Hypothetically, I've always wondered how you got out of that room."

The Kid considered. "Well it was, hypothetically, like this. I went into the room with the valise in front of my face so Mittwick couldn't tell I wasn't the fair Ellen, and when he got close I sapped him with this equalizer I had up my sleeve. Then, with him lying unconscious on the floor, I changed clothes."

"Into what?"

"Into a cop's uniform which I had in the valise, turned inside out so the cops couldn't tell if they searched it. But all the guy did was stick his hand in and poke around. I think he was embarrassed by the nightie."

"So that's it!" Brass exclaimed.

"That's it," the Kid agreed. "I dumped the Toad out the window, then got next to the door and let out a scream. The cops come rushing in, and I'm right behind them; except I was coming from behind the door. Then I went down the stairs, and I was outta there. Oh yeah, and it was me you saw in the lobby."

"You were the cop Mapes told to guard the front door?"

"Hypothetically," the Two Step Kid agreed.

The blonde he'd been dancing with had emerged from the powder room and was weaving her way across the room toward our table. The Two Step Kid got up. "I guess I should go now," he said. "This is all between us, right?"

"Who'd believe me?" Brass asked. "How did Dutch Schultz find out where Sammy the Toad was being kept?"

At that the Kid did break out laughing. "He heard it on the radio, Mr Brass, he heard it on the radio."

"What do you mean?"

"It wasn't the Dutchman I was working for, Mr Brass, it was Mr Big."

"So there was a Mr Big."

"Yeah. You knew him. His name was McWheeter."

"Son of a – "

"How true, Mr Brass, how true." And with that the Two Step Kid held out his arm for his beautiful blonde lady and sashayed out to the dance floor.

Well, Ellen moved out to Hollywood and changed her name. You've probably seen her if you go to the movies. The Dutchman got his with the aid of a machine gun in the Palace Chop House in Newark last year, and by a twist of fate Abbadabba Berman was eating with him that night, and became an unintended victim. And McWheeter disappeared about three years ago. Just plain disappeared. Maybe we should ask the Two Step Kid about that one. Or maybe not.

Putting Crime Over

HULBERT FOOTNER

This is the first of three stories I've reprinted in this anthology which are not only set in the 1920s but were also written in the 1920s. I was surprised, when I began delving, how few good whodunnits really reflected the Roaring Twenties. There were, of course, the obvious ones by Agatha Christie and Dorothy L. Sayers, but I didn't want to reprint stories so easily available elsewhere. So many other perfectly good stories were either more Edwardian or even Victorian in flavour (really all Sherlock Holmes or Dr Thorndyke imitations) or were hard-boiled crime stories that had no whodunnit element. Having searched long and hard I've settled on three which I think have a unique flavour and which to me are the essence of Roaring 20s whodunnits written by the people who were experiencing it.

The first is from Hulbert Footner (1879–1944), unjustly forgotten today but in his heyday a popular contributor to the leading magazines. He was born in Canada but lived most of his life in America. He was best known for a long-running series featuring the beautiful Madame Rosika Storey, who was something of a psychologist with an unusual technique in solving crimes. She first appeared in the novel The Under Dogs *(1925) and in several story collections including* Madame Storey *(1926),* The Velvet Hound *(1928),* The Casual Murder *(1932) and* The Almost Perfect Murder *(1933). I'm not aware that the following story was included in a collection. It first appeared in* Argosy-All Story *for 20 November 1926.*

t was owing to the last-minute illness of Mrs Cornelius Marquardt that I had the good fortune to be included in this little dinner of Mme Storey's. Her guests do not often disappoint.

Everybody in the know is aware that the best talk in New York is to be heard around her table. She picks her guests with that end in view, careless of their social position. One may meet a visiting marquis or a tramp poet – the poet more often than the marquis.

Mme Storey herself is a better talker, in my opinion, than any of them, but one would be slow to learn that at her own table. Her object there is merely to keep the ball rolling briskly. She likes to listen better than to talk.

On this occasion the men included Ambrose G. Larned, the brilliant advertising man, who had introduced so many new ideas into his profession; John Durward, the famous English novelist; Harry Evans Colter, our own clever and popular short story writer; and Inspector Rumsey, of the New York police.

Rumsey, the dear little man, is not at all a brilliant person; but he is a perfect compendium of crime, and, since crime seems to be the most interesting of all subjects to persons of every degree nowadays, Mme Storey finds him very useful at the dinner table. When people try to draw *her* out on the subject of crime, she shifts them on to Rumsey.

Foreigners regard us Americans as preeminent in crime; they come over here to see crime; and when we have a distinguished visitor like Mr Durward, Rumsey is pretty sure to be included.

My mistress, as you know, is not enamored of crime, and she managed to divert the talk to other subjects until after we had left the table. When the little company was grouped around the amusing 1850 living room upstairs, it could no longer be staved off, and she let it have its way.

I must tell you that New York was experiencing a crime wave at the moment – but indeed it always is. It is like an ocean beach, with one crime wave falling right on top of the one before.

This was the time of the bobbed-hair-bandit sensation, when many of the smaller jewelers were putting in defensive arrangements of siren whistles and tear gas. These things were always going off accidentally and throwing whole neighborhoods into a panic. The Englishman was all agog as he listened.

Everybody is familiar with Mr Durward's fine head with its silvery hair and delicately chiseled features. He supplied a chorus of "Amazing! Extraordinary! Incredible!" to all the stories that were told.

"In the middle of the day!" I remember him saying. "With crowds passing in the street, these fellows go boldly into your jewelry shops, and point their guns, and take what they please, and get away scot-free! Such a thing would be impossible in London!"

"Not impossible," Inspector Rumsey pointed out good-humoredly. "It has happened even in London. Your police are luckier than we are, that's all. For London streets are narrow and crooked, and the few main thoroughfares are always crowded. It is exceedingly difficult to make a get-away. Now, our streets are broad and straight, and only one of them is completely full of traffic during business hours. You may have noticed that our holdups never take place in the center, but always in busy neighborhoods off the center, where there is enough traffic to conceal the bandits in their get-away, but not enough to stop them."

"Well, what's to be done? Are you just going to submit to this state of affairs?"

"There is a remedy," said Inspector Rumsey quietly, "whenever the public is willing to pay for it."

"And what is that?"

"It is ridiculous and humiliating to the police to be forced to go on foot, when every bandit is provided with an automobile. All patrolmen should be mounted on motorcycles."

"Hear! Hear!" said Mme Storey.

"Even the women are taking to banditry!" murmured Mr Durward. "An incredible country!"

"There's a good deal of nonsense about her," said the inspector. "The newspapers have played up the bobbed-hair bandit so hard that their credulous readers see a bobbed-hair bandit everywhere they look."

"And I notice that the police are advertising in the subway cars," Mr Durward went on. "Cards addressed to the bandits, warning them that they will certainly be caught in the end. Surely that is very naive."

"Well," said the inspector, smiling and firm in the defense of his beloved department, "we must try everything."

Colter spoke up, a young man quick in his movements, with an eager, warm-colored face: "If you're sure to get him in the end, why bother to advertise?"

"It was Mr Larned, here, who persuaded the commissioner to use those cards," said Rumsey.

"Anything can be accomplished by intelligent publicity," said Larned.

He went on to sing the praises of the wonderful new science, of which he was one of the most brilliant professors. A handsome man in his forties, with the full, beaming eye of the enthusiast, we were all sensible of his charm. He was of that type not uncommon in our country, the artist turned business man.

They said his private life was rather scandalous, but I know nothing about that. His new wife was among the ladies present, a pretty woman, but negligible as far as conversation went.

"That's all true," said Harry Colter, when he could get an opening, "but publicity is a two-edged sword which is apt to cut in unexpected directions."

"Take these subway cards," went on Larned. "The idea was that the bandit lives in a world of his own, supported and encouraged by those of his kind, and cut off from all others. It was thought that it would be a good thing to remind him in this unexpected fashion of the existence of the real world which would not tolerate his actions. I appeal to Mme Storey to tell us if this is not sound psychology."

My mistress smiled in a way that told me what her opinion was, but refused to commit herself.

"Harry has something more to say on the subject," she remarked.

"It's a confession of weakness on the part of the police," said Colter energetically. "Mr Durward, with his fresh point of view, instantly perceived that. Irrespective of the effect on an occasional bandit, it certainly lowers the morale of the whole public that rides in the subway. For the public relies on the stern and secret measures of the police in dealing with crooks, and to have them come out in the open like this and beg the bandits to be good cannot help but be demoralizing."

Inspector Rumsey agreed with Colter, though nothing could induce him to admit that the department could be in the wrong.

"It is true," he said, "the stick-up boys have the public
scared. And every story of a successful hold-up that the newspapers print is just that much additional publicity for the
bandits."

"You can't blame the newspapers for that," said Larned.

"I don't. It's their job to purvey the news. But it's too bad
they've got to feature it the way they do."

"That just proves my point," said Larned. "You've got to
have a counter-publicity to deal with it."

I felt impelled to put in my oar at this point. Though I'm only
a humble secretary, Mme Storey expects me to keep my end up.
There must be no dummies at her table.

"But a true counter-publicity would be directed toward
boosting the public morale instead of further depressing it,"
I suggested.

Mr Larned gave me a cold look, as much as to say: Who is this
red-haired female? His eyes quickly passed on to my mistress.

"Perhaps Mme Storey will tell us how she would handle the
situation," he said.

My mistress held up her hands in mock dismay.

"Thank Heaven, I'm not obliged to answer that," she said
laughing. "My job is quite difficult enough. Bandits are a little
out of my line."

II

Some days or weeks after the dinner party, when all recollection
of this conversation had passed out of my mind, I was working
in the outer office of our suite on Gramercy Park one morning,
when a good-looking young man came in. He was a mere lad of
nineteen or so, but his face wore that unnatural look of experience and assurance that suggests a childhood spent on the
streets.

Yet my eyes dwelt on him with pleasure. Though short of
stature, he was beautifully made; he moved with a lithe grace
that suggested the perfect coordination of every muscle.

His round head was set low between his strong shoulders; the
black hair was crisp with health, the black eyes sparkling. I
suspected Italian blood. He was well dressed in a somewhat
common style, and he addressed me with an ingratiating smile.

"Is this Mme Storey's office?" Like the wolf in the old story, he was trying to sweeten his harsh voice.

"Yes," said I.

"Are you her?"

"No; her secretary." I could see that the little wretch was only trying to flatter me.

"Well, is she in?"

"Mme Storey can only receive visitors by appointment," I said. "Will you tell me your business?"

"Sure," he said, with an appearance of the utmost good humor, plumping himself into a chair without waiting for an invitation. His bright eyes traveled around the room, taking everything in. "You sure got a swell joint here," he remarked sociably.

I ignored this. "What can I do for you?" I asked coldly.

I could see from the beginning that he was just stringing me along; but it never occurred to me to suspect he might have a sinister motive. All kinds of people come into the office, and waste my time, particularly when we have been engaged on a big case, with all its attendant publicity.

"I just wanted to apply for a job," he answered.

"A job?" I said, surprised. "What sort of job?"

"Anything at all," he said, grinning. "I read in the papers how Mme Storey employed a whole raft of operatives, private detectives like, in the Harker case."

"It is only occasionally that she is engaged on a criminal case," said I. "And then any operatives that we may require are secured temporarily from a list that we keep."

"Well, put me down on your list," he said. "John Casey, 123 East Broadway."

He was no Casey! However, as the quickest way of getting rid of him, I wrote the address on a pad.

"You got a swell job here, secretary to Mme Storey and all," he said while I was writing. "Somepin' doin' alla time, I guess."

I made no answer.

"Don't she employ no clerk nor office boy nor nothin'?" he asked.

"No," I told him.

"There'd be the job for me," he said.

"Well, let me have a sample of your handwriting," I suggested, pushing the pad toward him. I thought I had him there.

He drew back. "I got a cramp in me hand today," he said without batting an eye. "But say, I could make myself useful here, receivin' callers and runnin' errands and all. And when you needed an outside man I'd be on the spot."

I shook my head.

"And say, when she was out I'd be company for you," he said with a sidelong grin.

The good-looking little wretch was actually trying to vamp me. I was highly amused. His sharp eyes perceived my amusement, and it encouraged him to go further.

"Say, what's your name?" he asked.

"I don't see that that matters," I said.

"Just in case I wanted to write you later to see if there was an openin'."

"I will write to you if there is an opening," I said dryly.

He affected to laugh heartily. "Gee, you're wise, all right! You're there with the comeback!"

He came close to me and smiled insinuatingly. I suppose with a certain type of girl he had found himself irresistible. "Me and you'd get along fine, eh?"

"I dare say," I said coldly. "But you will have to excuse me. I'm busy."

"Is that the door to her room?" he asked, pointing.

I did not answer. He knew that it was the door to her room, because there was no other except that by which he had entered.

"Let me take a look in," he said cajolingly. "I bet it's a swell room!"

"Certainly not!" I said, rising to forestall any move to open the door. "Mme Storey must not be disturbed."

"Oh, I didn't know she was in there," he remarked with an innocent air. "Well, so long, kid," with a final grin over his shoulder. "You know where to find me." And went out.

It did not occur to me to be angry. Indeed, after he had gone, I sat down at my desk, smiling. Such is the power of youth and good looks. I merely put him down in my mind as another fresh kid.

Immediately afterward Mme Storey called me in to take

dictation. We were still suffering from the publicity attendant upon the famous Harker case, and there was a pile of letters six inches high on her desk.

My mistress as a matter of courtesy insists on writing once to everybody who writes to her. Of course if they continue to send in trifling letters they go into the wastebasket. Had we been less busy, I would no doubt have related the incident of my caller just for her amusement, and the whole course of subsequent events might have been changed; but as it was, I did not mention him.

I have on several former occasions described the arrangements of my mistress's beautiful room. There is nothing about it to connote the word office.

Once the front drawing-room of a great house on Gramercy Park, it is now furnished with priceless Italian antiques, and forms a fit setting for Mme Storey, who is herself like a vivid figure out of the Renaissance – but not antique. In spite of all pressure from the outside, she preserves her individuality.

She refuses to organize her genius, nor will she work herself to death either. She accepts the few cases that most appeal to her; all the others are turned down. I constitute her entire office force; and when we feel like it we close up the office altogether, and go for a jaunt.

Mme Storey sits at an immense oak table, black with age, her back to the row of casement windows which look out on the square. At her right hand is the door into my room, and in the same wall near the back of the long room, another door leading directly into the hall.

This door, which is closed with a spring lock, permits her to escape from anybody waiting in my room, whom she may not want to bother with. In the middle of the back wall is a door giving on what we call the middle room, which is used for the multitudinous requirements of our peculiar business – dressing-room, hiding place, temporary jail, and what not. The three rooms constitute our suite.

In taking dictation I sit at my mistress's right hand, with my back to the door from my room. We were in the middle of our work without a thought in our minds except the desire to get to the bottom of that pile of silly letters, when the buzzer sounded that announced the opening of the outer door into my room.

I finished the sentence I was putting down, and rose to my feet. I got no farther, for at that moment the door from my room burst open, and two men ran in, each grasping an ugly automatic.

One was my visitor of half an hour before; the other was a few years older.

What a moment that was! Death itself could not have been worse than what I suffered. My heart turned to water in my breast; I seemed to lose all strength, all control of my body.

How I longed to shrivel up to nothing before those guns! I dared not look at my mistress, who was alongside, and a little behind me. My eyes were glued to those hideous weapons.

"Stick 'cm up!" barked the older man.

My hands went over my head like a shot. They strained away from me, as if desirous of flying up under the ceiling on their own account. I heard Mme Storey drawl:

"I'll put mine on the table if you don't mind. The other attitude is so ungraceful."

I stole a look at her. Good Heavens! What a woman! She was actually smiling. The sight of her smile did not put any heart into me, though.

It gave me a dreadful pang to realize that those worthless youths, the sweepings of the streets, held the life of such a glorious woman in their hands.

"None of your tricks!" growled the leader.

"Bless your heart, I wouldn't think of it!" drawled Mme Storey. "I have a gun in the drawer of this table, but I'm not going to try to get it out. I value my skin too highly."

"Look through those two doors," the leader said to his companion. "I'll keep the women covered."

As silently as a shadow, the younger man ran to the two doors. "This door goes out into the hall," he said at the first; and at the other: "Nobody in this room."

"Do you mind if I smoke?" said Mme Storey, moving her hand toward the big silver box that stood on her table.

"Keep your hands in front of you!" barked the leader.

Taking a step forward, he threw back the cover of the box. Seeing that it contained only cigarettes, he shrugged, and allowed my mistress to take one.

"Won't you join me?" she drawled mockingly.

He helped himself, tossing the cigarette up to his mouth without taking his eyes from Mme Storey's face. She nonchalantly lighted up, and offered him the burning match. He put the cigarette to it, with his eyes fixed on hers.

What a picture! While the first one was merely a good looking boy, this one was infernally handsome. Mme Storey's face still wore the mocking half smile; his was like a mask.

It was perfectly inhuman in its immobility; not a muscle quivered; his very eyes appeared to be glazed. It made a cold shiver run down my spine.

"Hand over your pearls," he said.

Putting down the cigarette for a moment, Mme Storey unfastened the string about her neck.

"I'm sorry they're not my best ones," she said. "Still, they're pretty good." She tossed them over.

"Your watch, your rings," he went on, dropping the pearls in his pockets.

She unfastened her watch with calm deliberation, holding her head on one side to keep the cigarette smoke out of her eyes, and drew off her lovely emerald, and the three diamonds. They followed the pearls into his pocket.

Meanwhile the other man commanded me to hand over my pearls.

"A-ah!" snarled his leader out of the side of his mouth. "They're only fish-skin. Don't yeh know the difference?"

The young man refused my beads then, with an abashed look like a schoolboy. But I had to hand over the watch that Mme Storey gave me, and the little diamond I bought with my own savings.

My heart burned with helpless anger. My little stone had not a fraction of the value of Mme Storey's, but she could replace hers the next day, whereas mine represented years of self-denial. What kind of a world was it, I thought, where such wrongs were permitted.

"Your money!" said the leader harshly to my mistress.

"It's in the same drawer with my gun," she told him pleasantly.

He put a hand on the table, and leaned over, bringing his mask-like face close to hers.

"Get it out," he said curtly, "and let me see you touch the gun, that's all."

"By no means!" said Mme Storey, smiling. "I just wanted to warn you, so you wouldn't shoot at the sight of it."

Pulling the drawer toward her, she picked up her gold mesh bag, and tossed it on the table in front of him.

"Now the gun," he added. "Pick it up by the muzzle."

She obeyed. "I'd be glad if you'd let me have my hanky out of the bag," she said. "I may need it."

"Ah, cut the comedy," he told her with his indifferent air. "Where's your safe?"

"In the outer office. There's nothing in it but business papers. My secretary will open it for you."

"You go with her," said the leader to his man.

I leave you to imagine what my feelings were when I had to turn my back on the gun, and walk out of the room with it following me. I nearly died out of sheer terror. I felt a hundred bullets tearing through my body.

But I got the safe open somehow, and satisfied the young bandit that it contained nothing of value to him.

We returned to the other room. My mistress was smiling still. The young bandit was sitting now, with his chair tipped back in a parade of indifference.

No muscle of his waxen face had changed, but there was a glint in his eyes as he watched Mme Storey. He contemptuously permitted her to see that he approved of her as a woman.

When his man reported that there was nothing in the safe, he stood up.

"Then back out," he said, with a jerk of his head toward the door into the hall.

"Why hurry?" drawled my mistress. "Let's have in tea."

The leader stopped. An open, scornful admiration leaped up in his eyes. The insolence of it was simply indescribable.

"You're a pretty game chicken, ain't yeh?" he drawled, putting a hand on his hip in a swaggering fashion. "You look good to me."

He dropped his gun in his pocket – he knew he had her disarmed – and returned a step or two toward the table. He drew a ring off his finger and tossed it toward her.

"Wear that," he said. In a flash he was gone.

When the door closed after them I collapsed. I could hear myself bawling like a child, without any power to stop it. The next thing I knew I was pulling frantically at one of the casements, so that I might alarm the street.

Mme Storey drew me away before I got it open.

"No good," she said. "They'll have a car waiting. You'll only start a panic among the kiddies in the park."

I could still hear myself crying and carrying on like somebody else. "Why didn't you send for the engineer? The button is there under the edge of your table for just such an emergency."

"What!" she said, smiling at me. "And bring John in here empty-handed to get shot?"

"It's outrageous!" I cried. "Coming in here like that! And you take it so calmly. The way that man looked at you was intolerable."

Mme Storey smilingly quoted the childish couplet, slightly amended:

"Sticks and stones will break my bones,
But looks will never hurt me."

"Such insolence!" I cried. "I cannot bear it!"

"Oh, a shot of heroin will do wonders to buck up a man's self-esteem," she said calmly.

She was sitting there smiling, and examining the fellow's ring with the eye of a connoisseur. It was a handsome carnelian in a wonderful antique setting. Heaven knows from whom it had been stolen.

The sight of her indifference drove me almost into a frenzy. "Aren't you going to do anything?" I cried.

"Oh, surely," she said, partly arousing herself. "Do all the usual things, my Bella; telephone to the police and to the newspapers. But as for me—" she relapsed into her smiling, musing upon the ring "– I intend to have a little fun out of this."

III

With proper management this affair need never have got into the newspapers, since no whisper of an alarm had been raised.

But Mme Storey disdained to conceal it; on the contrary, she informed the press herself.

"It would make such a good story, it would be a shame to keep it from them," she said in her provoking way.

Of course, as I was to learn later, this publicity was necessary to the plan that was even then shaping itself in her mind; but I couldn't guess that in the beginning.

Well, you can imagine what a sensation was created by the news. The famous Mme Storey held up in her own office by a pair of youthful bandits! To come as it did, right on the heels of her brilliant success in the Harker case, when her name and fame was on everybody's lips, gave point to the tale. While the newspapers were still terming her the greatest criminologist of modern times, here she was stuck up by a couple of boys and robbed of her pearls!

It is a weakness of all democracies, they say, that when a citizen is elevated above the heads of the mob, nothing pleases the said mob better than to find an excuse to turn and shy things at the hero. We had to submit to an unmerciful razzing, both public and private. What a chance it gave to the cartoonists!

Mme Storey, I need hardly say, took it all smilingly. Borne up by her secret knowledge of the retribution she was preparing, I think she actually enjoyed it. She encouraged the razzers that her revenge might be more complete in the end.

But it was a bad time for me. I ground my teeth every time the telephone rang. My temper was in a continual state of exacerbation. Not the least of what I had to submit to were the hypocritical condolences of all the old cats in the boarding house where I live.

Inspector Rumsey suffered no less than I did. That his police had allowed Mme Storey to be robbed right under their noses, so to speak, caused the worthy little man almost to burst with chagrin. He wanted to surround us afterward with a whole cordon of police wherever we went, but of course Mme Storey would not hear of anything like that.

What she had termed all the usual things were done, of course, and nothing came of it. We furnished the police with exact descriptions of the bandits, which were sent broadcast. Several of the best men attached to the Central Office were put on the case.

Mme Storey and I went down to headquarters and turned over hundreds of pages of the Rogues' Gallery, without finding the faces we were in search of. Inspector Rumsey was not surprised by it.

"Every year," he said bitterly, "we have a fresh crop of young desperadoes to deal with."

I could not but be sorry for our friend during these days. His difficulties were owing to no fault of his own. After our robbery the crime wave mounted to still greater heights. Nearly every day the police had a fresh holdup to deal with, and on some days three or four.

"The publicity attached to your case has bucked them up all down the line," Inspector Rumsey said bitterly.

Mme Storey herself took no direct measures toward searching for the bandits. One day when I was burning with indignation at the facetious comments of some newspaper or another, I ventured to remonstrate with her on this.

"Oh, our little holdup boys were merely pawns in the game, my Bella," she told me. "I'm after the commanding pieces."

I was relieved to learn that she was not entirely idle in the matter.

One morning when she took off her hat I cried out in dismay upon perceiving that she had acquired a boy's haircut overnight. I must confess that it was very becoming, revealing as it did the beautiful shape of her head and emphasizing the pure line of her profile. Still I hated to see her adopt so extreme a fashion.

She smiled at my distress. "Wait!" she said, holding up her hand, and disappeared within the middle room.

An hour later she called me to her. I stopped in the doorway, aghast. She stood in the middle of the room, striking an attitude.

I say "she", but at the first glance it seemed to me as if my mistress had vanished, leaving a horrible changeling in her stead. The closely cut hair was now silvered, and her face heavily made up, one might almost say enameled.

Around the eyes and mouth it was cunningly shadowed to suggest the hollows of growing age; in a phrase, the fashionable, hard-living woman of fifty.

She was wearing a costume cut in severe mannish lines,

showing a rolling silk collar at the neck, and a Bohemian tie. A little tough hat went with it, and a malacca stick with a plain ivory knob. I'm sure you get the picture: an elderly charmer of the highest fashion, handsome, hard, and utterly reckless.

"Will it pass?" she asked in a throaty voice with a hint of huskiness.

"It is marvelous," I murmured.

"I am Kate Arkledon," she went on, with a half sneer which was fixed in her face; to smile would have ruined the effect. "Have you ever heard of her?"

I shook my head.

"A little before your time, I suppose. Ten years ago Kate Arkledon was one of the cleverest confidence women in the United States. She was famous in her way. Then suddenly she dropped out of sight of all her former associates. As a matter of fact, she is living in respectability and affluence not a dozen doors from me. Once upon a time I did her a service which she has never forgotten.

"Well, with her permission, I am staging a come-back for Kate Arkledon. There is a slight resemblance between us, which I have built upon. It will be good enough at least to deceive anybody who has not seen her for ten years."

I foresaw danger ahead, and my heart sank.

Mme Storey broke off, to study me through narrowed eyes. "Turn around," she said.

"What do you want of me?" I faltered.

"Get a permanent wave," she said.

"But I will look like a Hottentot!" I cried.

"Of course," she said calmly. "They all do when they come out from under the curlers. You will make a very effective red-haired vamp, my Bella. I will dress you and teach you how to make up for it."

"But the make-up is only the beginning!" I gasped. "I could not possibly keep up such a part."

"Certainly you could. It will not be nearly so difficult as the character of Canada Annie, which you carried off so well. You can be a Dumb Dora this time with nothing to do but sit and look unutterable things at men. All you will have to say is 'Ain't it the truth!' when you agree, or very scornfully, 'So's yer old man!' when you disagree."

All this was uttered in the sneering, husky tones of the character she was portraying. It made me shiver.

"What are we going to do?" I asked fearfully.

"We are going to organize a little holdup gang of our own," said Kate Arkledon with a wicked grin.

A cry was forced from me. I could not imagine anybody less fitted for the part of bandit than myself.

"Not really – not really!" I faltered.

"It will be just as real as I can make it appear," she said. "I mean to pull off a stunt or two in the most spectacular style."

I groaned inwardly.

"This is how I figure it out, Bella," she said in her natural voice. "There is certainly an organization behind the crime wave; but it's operating along new lines. It's a very loose and flexible organization, with all the units working independently of each other. Well, my idea is to form a unit of my own which will function so brilliantly that the organization will be forced to make overtures to us. Inspector Rumsey is in the secret."

I tasted in advance the awful excitement that was in store, and my heart was like lead in my breast. But I would have torn my tongue out sooner than protest aloud.

IV

Busy days followed. It was impossible to let our other business slide, and we had to lead double lives.

By day Mme Storey and her secretary, Bella Brickley, worked in the offices on Gramercy Park, taking care to give out an interview to the newspapers occasionally, so that our presence there was regularly established. By night Kate Arkledon and her pal, Peggy Ray, showed themselves in certain gilded resorts on the West Side.

A good many days passed before I got accustomed to the sight of my painted and bedizened self in the mirror. On the whole, though, I had an easy role to play. All that was required of me was to act as a foil for my mistress.

For the purpose of enabling us to change from one character to another and back again, we engaged a room in one of the nondescript warrens on West Forty-Seventh Street, where all kinds of queer little businesses are carried on by all kinds of queer characters. One could enter or leave such a building at any hour without exciting remark.

For Kate Arkledon's regular hang-out we chose a well-known West Side street, once fashionable, and now much favored of the white collar gentry. It often breaks into the news. However, I shall not name it for fear of depressing real estate values.

We rented a four room flat in a pretentious apartment house, where the tenants' reference were not too closely scanned; and here we immediately began to gather our gang round us.

Mme Storey's principal aid in this affair was the man I shall call Benny Abell, though that was not his real name, nor yet the name by which he had become famous in the underworld. If you have read my account of the Melanie Soupert case you will remember him.

His specialty had been sticking up the box offices of theaters, always working alone, and displaying a truly superhuman nerve. Since my mistress had broken up the Varick Street gang he had become re-united with his family, and had gone straight.

Mme Storey needed him now as a sort of liaison officer with crookdom, where his exploits were still remembered. She never had any intention of using him in an actual hold-up, which would have been like a nightmare to the poor fellow who had been through so much.

Abell, when I first knew him, was a small, determined, white-faced man, of an elegant appearance. Trained to a finish by danger, he was like a sheaf of quivering nerves.

Now happiness had caused him to take on flesh, and his face to assume a serene expression. However, he worked hard to reduce for this emergency, and played his part admirably.

Next we took in George Stephens, one of our regular operatives, and the best man we had after Crider. I should have been glad to have had Crider himself at our back, but he has worked for us so long Mme Storey feared the danger of his being recognized. She didn't want to have any more disguises than she could help. Stephens had the advantage of not having been in America long. A young fellow of aristocratic appearance, he soon acquired the soubriquet of English George.

Our remaining man was Bert Farren, a mere boy who has done good work for us on one or two occasions. Mme Storey chose him because boy bandits seemed to be the fashion.

We still lacked a direct, present connection with the world of crooks; but my mistress said we would have to wait for circumstances to furnish that.

Very early in the game the scene of our first exploit was chosen. This was the jewelry store of B. & J. Fossberg, a large and handsome establishment on Broadway not a hundred miles from One Hundredth Street. It is the finest establishment of the sort on the upper West Side.

Inspector Rumsey was acquainted with Benjamin Fossberg, one of the proprietors, and after a great deal of persuasion won his consent to the staged hold-up. His brother was told, of course, but the clerks were kept in the dark.

It was arranged that the guns which were kept in the store for protection should be removed as if for repairs on the day of the stick-up.

Night after night the five of us met in the flat on West — Street to discuss and rehearse our plans. I had no idea that such elaborate preparations were required to stage an affair which would be all over in a minute or two.

By day our three men watched the store until they were familiar with every detail of the business routine. The Fossbergs had not fallen for any of the idiotic safeguards such as tear gas, sirens, etc. They trusted to the imposing appearance of their establishment to overawe gunmen.

It was on a corner, and occupied the space of three ordinary stores. No such big place had ever been attacked.

A detailed plan of the store was drawn out, together with a map of the neighborhood. This we all studied. Each of us was allotted his station, and many rehearsals took place.

To me fell the comparatively easy job of acting as look-out on the sidewalk. Mme Storey was to enter, and ask to have goods shown her. George and Bert were to cover her get-away with their guns, while Abell was to drive the car, which was to be waiting in the side street.

When the business of the evening was over, it was our custom to show ourselves at one or another of the gilded resorts in the neighborhood. Gradually we settled on the Boule' Miche' as our public hangout.

Abell, who had been making inquiries, said that it had become a favorite gathering place of the white collar gangs.

It occupied the site of a famous old New York restaurant on Columbus Avenue, which had rapidly gone down hill after prohibition, and changed its name half a dozen times.

You would never have guessed the characters of its frequenters from their appearance. Everybody looks alike nowadays. In the Boule' Miche' you found exactly the same sort of sleek, showy women, accompanied by sleek and not so showy men, that you would see in any other night club.

It was only when you possessed a key to their occupation that you began to perceive a certain wary look in the eyes of the men; a tendency to glance toward the door every time it was opened. Once in a while strange snatches of conversation would reach your ears. Of course, many perfectly respectable people must have been included among the patrons of the place.

The present proprietor was a dark-skinned gentleman, with a perpetual gleaming smile, and a hard eye that was anything but smiling. His evening clothes fitted him to a marvel. His name was Bat Bartley, and Abell knew him.

He was one of those mysterious New York characters whom everybody knows, and nobody knows anything about. It was the custom of all his patrons to fawn on him, as they always do in such places – I can't tell you why; and while he smiled he scarcely troubled to conceal his contempt of them.

When Abell introduced my mistress to him as Kate Arkledon I saw the wary eyes narrow slightly. Evidently he was familiar with that name. My mistress treated him with cool disdain, whereupon he immediately began to fawn on *her!* Such is human nature!

Upon our first visits to the Boule' Miche' nobody attempted to address us, though, of course, so striking a figure as that of my mistress could not pass unnoticed. People stared at her, and whispered to each other, clearly asking who she was.

No doubt they asked the proprietor, and no doubt he told them – or at least such of them as he could trust. By degrees a tinge of respect and admiration appeared in the glances of the regular habitués. One could almost pick out those who belonged to the fraternity of crooks by the way they looked at the supposed Kate Arkledon.

And then one night we had an encounter which terrified me; I thought our whole elaborate structure was about to collapse.

I needn't have been terrified. I underrated my mistress's superb aplomb.

An old boy with a red face and bulging blue eyes, who had been talking to Bat Bartley, came to our table. His Tuxedo, while of good material, was of an old fashion; an air of having seen better days clung around him. Fixing his bloodshot eyes on my mistress, he asked:

"Is this Kate Arkledon?"

"The same," she said, with an air of cynical indifference she now affected.

"Well, well, well!" he said. "I never should have known you, Kate. And you, I see, have completely forgotten me."

My mistress made believe to study him. "Your face is very familiar to me," she said. "But the name – the name—"

He shook his head mournfully. "To think that *you* should have forgotten me. Remember the St Louis Fair?"

Mme Storey must have had Kate Arkledon's biography at her finger tips.

"Chad Herring!" she said instantly, and offered the old fellow her hand. "But how changed!"

"Ah, don't rub it in!" he said. "I know it! Chad Herring's on the shelf! But you, good Heaven, you're fresh as paint!"

"Paint is right!" said my mistress, with her scornful smile, touching her cheek meanwhile.

He laughed uproariously. "Just as smart as ever, I see! You're a wonder, Kate!"

"Sit down," she said.

I trembled at her temerity. Surely the least slip would be fatal. She introduced us all to him by our underworld names.

"Young blood – young blood!" he muttered, sadly shaking his head. He turned to her with a pathetic eagerness. "Kate, what do you hear of Bill Blandick and Paddy Nolan—" He named a whole string of names. "The old gang."

"All gone," she said, spreading out her hands. "That is, gone from me. I have not heard of any of them for more than ten years."

"What have you been doing, Kate?"

"Leading a godly, righteous and sober life," she replied with a bitter sneer.

"You don't look it," he said innocently.

"Ah, there's nothing like dullness to break you up!" she told him. "I'm done with a respectable life. I've come back."

"Come back?" he repeated almost with horror. "At your age! Remember, I know how old you are."

"Well, you needn't broadcast it," she said sharply.

What a wonderful piece of acting she was giving!

"Come back!" he repeated again. "Do you think you can keep your end up in this day of youth and jazz and high-powered automobiles?"

"And why not?" she demanded proudly. "My nerve is as steady as ever. Look at that hand." She held it out. "And I can teach these youngsters a thing or two. Good God, Chad – think of the opportunities nowadays! There was never anything like it in the old days!"

He looked at her with that same fear. I suppose that the fierce energy she expressed made him feel old and broken by way of contrast.

After a little desultory talk he ambled away. Presently we saw him telling Bat Bartley about it.

"That will help establish our characters," said my mistress calmly.

V

On the morning of the appointed day I awoke in blessed unconsciousness and lay staring at the ceiling. Then the realization of what was before me came winging back, and the bottom seemed to drop out of my stomach. I suppose it was much the same feeling as that experienced by a murderer on the morning of his execution. The worst of it was, our stunt was not to be pulled off until four o'clock, the most crowded time on upper Broadway, and I had all those miserable hours to put in beforehand. My breakfast choked me.

Every detail having been completed the night before, there was nothing for Mme Storey and I to do but proceed to the office in our own characters and attend to our usual business.

During the day that amazing woman, my mistress, gave out interviews, talked over the telephone, and dictated letters as if it was no different from any other day in the year. If she noticed that my hand was prone to tremble and my voice to shake, she never spoke of it. Indeed, no reference of any kind was made to what was almost immediately before us.

At three o'clock she locked the drawer of her desk and said to me casually: "Well, Bella, let's go."

I declare, from the openness of her smile and the brightness of her eye, one might have thought it was a picnic we were bound on. She enjoyed it!

Proceeding by taxi to the room on Forty-Seventh Street, we transformed ourselves into Kate Arkledon and Peggy Ray. I noticed that my mistress, while carefully preserving the same character, toned down her make-up somewhat. For the jewelers' she did not wish to emphasize the hardness, the recklessness that she flaunted in the Boule' Miche' every night.

As it was, the perfection of her plain, smart get-up and her high manner created a figure that any jeweler would rejoice to see coming into his shop. Around her neck she clasped a short string of valuable pearls, her only ornaments.

"Decoys," she said to me with a grin.

Me you must picture with my red hair frizzed to a fare-you-well, and my face made up like the American flag, wearing a showy hat, a smartly cut caracul coat and high-heeled satin slippers. The make-up robbed my face of all character, and I looked to the life the expensive, empty-headed woman that you may find on upper Broadway in her hundreds. But I doubted my ability to run in those high-heeled slippers.

"Then kick 'em off," said Mme Storey. "It will add a picturesque touch to the story."

We continued uptown to the flat on West Street, where we found our three men waiting for us, all smartly rigged out according to the custom of the modern gunman, all cool and smiling. The youngster in particular seemed to regard it as a great lark.

I could almost have hated them all for their unconcern. I wished myself anywhere but there. Mme Storey dealt out guns to all. They were loaded with blanks. Mine went into a specially prepared pocket of my fur coat.

Inspector Rumsey came to us here for a final consultation.

"How about the Fossbergs?" asked Mme Storey. "Do you think they will play their parts satisfactorily?"

"I haven't a doubt of it?" said the inspector dryly. "They

couldn't be in a worse state of funk if they expected to be robbed in earnest. I persuaded them to stay away from the store until just before you came, so their clerks wouldn't get on to anything."

"And the guns?"

"It's the custom of the store to keep four loaded guns in different places under the counter. These were collected yesterday and sent to the makers to be cleaned and inspected."

I thought, with a shiver: How does he know but that one of the clerks may have a gun of his own? However, there was nothing to be gained by bringing that up then, and I kept my mouth shut.

"What are the police arrangements?" asked Mme Storey.

"According to your instructions, I did not attempt to interfere with them," returned the inspector. "I have taken nobody in the department into my confidence. There is a man on fixed post on Broadway two blocks south of the store, and another stationed in the little park three blocks north. These men are far enough away not to interfere with you, but you must be careful not to drive past them, or they might shoot if they hear the alarm.

"In addition there are two patrolmen whose beats meet in the middle of the street alongside the store. You will have to watch for these. After they have met and gone back you can depend upon about twelve minutes before they return. Don't forget that there are many men on fixed post along Riverside Drive."

"We will keep off the Drive," said Mme Storey dryly.

The final arrangements were that we were to proceed to the Fossberg store separately; Abell in the car was to wait in the side street near the corner of West End Avenue with his engine running; the rest of us were to walk up and down, keeping in sight of each other, until the two policemen had met.

Two minutes after the policemen had gone back Mme Storey was to enter the store, and I was to take up my position at the door, glancing up and down the street as if I was waiting for somebody. Abell and Farren were then to be looking in the window. Two minutes after Mme Storey had entered they were to follow her into the store.

"Well, good-bye and good luck," said Inspector Rumsey, smiling. "I must say it seems like a mad scheme to me; but I have had too many lessons in the past to venture to oppose any plan of Mme Storey's.''

A few minutes later four of us were separately strolling up and down outside Fossberg's store. I was thankful for the rouge which covered my pale cheeks. However, we were not in the least conspicuous on the well filled sidewalk.

A policeman passed, swinging his club, without looking twice at us. In the side street, down near the end of the short block, I could see the car waiting; a touring car, with the top down in true bandit fashion. It was a "stolen" car, too, to add verisimilitude – stolen from one of Mme Storey's friends, however.

Broadway uptown is an immensely wide street with grass plots down the middle. Trees used to grow there; but nowadays they would have nothing to root in but the subway.

Both sides of the way are filled in with immense and expensive apartment houses with entrances in the side streets. The Broadway level is given up to shops, not large in size, but nearly all dealing in expensive luxuries.

While it is not a fashionable street, I suppose there is as much money to the mile as in any other street in the world. The people of that neighborhood have a fat, soft look that must be tempting to a bandit.

Fossberg's, as I said before, is the finest establishment in that part of town. Only a few very choice objects are displayed in the show windows. There is but the one entrance, which is cut across the corner; at that season it was closed by a revolving door.

Inside, the four walls were lined by show-cases, the tops of which served as counters; and there was in addition a square inclosure in the middle of the store, surrounded by other cases to display goods. Within this inclosure was a block of low safes, in which many valuable objects were kept.

Well, the two policemen met, exchanged a word or two, and each slowly retraced his steps. The two minutes passed; then Mme Storey with her languid, graceful carriage went through the revolving door, and I took up my station outside it.

At this moment, when I expected to have died with terror, all fear suddenly left me. Explain it how you will, my heart rebounded; all my faculties became preternaturally sharpened; the scene of that street was bitten on my brain as if with an acid;

the towering apartment houses, red electric cars, smoothly moving motor cars, well dressed people drifting up and down.

Stephens and Farren were close by, looking in one of the show windows. The former was carrying an umbrella hanging from his arm. He had his eye on the chronometer exhibited in a corner of the window to inform passers-by of the correct time. When the proper interval had elapsed they followed Mme Storey through the revolving door.

In order not to interrupt my narrative, I will describe here what happened inside while I was waiting outside, poised like an animal ready for I knew not what.

There were eight or nine customers in the store, Mme Storey said, mostly in couples, since people generally like to have a friend along when they are choosing costly objects. There were five clerks on duty. Mr Benjamin Fossberg ought to have been waiting to receive my mistress, but he and his brother were both too nervous to show themselves openly. They watched the preliminaries from their office at the back.

Mme Storey went to the center inclosure. She had waited a moment or two for a clerk. In the meantime her two men entered; Stephens turning to the left, where watches were displayed, and Farren making his way toward a case of jeweled cuff-links.

Mme Storey told the clerk who came to her that she wanted a diamond ring. She affected not to be able to decide whether she wanted three diamonds in a marquise setting, or an emerald with a diamond on each side. We knew that the most valuable rings were kept in a certain safe, and her object was to make him open it. She said her clerk was an exquisite young gentleman like a model for a clothier's advertisement, and it was a shame to frighten him so rudely.

When he had opened the safe and brought a small velvet lined tray of rings to lay before Mme Storey, he found himself looking into the stubby barrel of her automatic. His face turned as white as the starched collar he wore; his eyes started from his head; no sound escaped him but a little throaty gasp.

"Fetch out all the trays from that safe and put them on the counter," said Mme Storey quietly.

Like a man in a dream he started to obey, reaching blindly for the trays while he kept his terrified eyes fixed on the gun. As he put the trays on the counter, Mme Storey, always keeping him covered, with her free hand coolly emptied the contents on the square of velvet which covered the glass counter and put the trays to one side.

So quietly was all this done that several of the trays had been brought out and emptied before anybody else in the store got on to what was happening. Then a woman customer on the other side of the center enclosure caught sight of Mme. Storey's gun. A low, terrified cry broke from her, and instantly everybody in the store took alarm.

Stephens and Farren then slipped forward with their guns out, one on one side of her, one on the other. Standing back to back, they commanded the whole store between them.

"Keep still or I shoot!" growled Stephens.

"If you move a step I'll plug you!" added the boy.

There was no other sound, they said, except the hoarse breathing of the terror-stricken men and women. Everybody was frozen where they stood.

In sheer panic the two proprietors had dropped down behind the office partition. Stephens described to me the semicircle of still, ghastly faces that remained turned toward him.

There was one fat, overdressed woman in a near-seal coat, whose lips moved continually. But whether she thought she was gabbling a prayer or beseeching Stephens to spare her life, he never knew, because no sound escaped her.

There were only three persons on Farren's side of the store. None moved. Mme Storey meanwhile continued to concentrate on the clerk who was serving her.

"Move sharp!" she said, raising the gun a little.

He dumped the remaining trays on the counter in a heap. Mme Storey deliberately emptied them. There was now a glittering, sparkling mound of rings on the square of velvet.

Mme Storey picked up the corners of the square, one after another, and, giving the sack a twirl which confined the contents in a ball, dropped it into her hand bag. She then started to back toward the door, the two men covering her retreat.

During all this I was playing my part outside. Immediately after Stephens and Farren went in a woman entered, and I made no attempt to stop her; but when, a moment or two later two more women came along, according to instructions I attempted to hold them in conversation. I asked for information about vacant apartments in the neighborhood.

It is a fruitful subject, and I detained them without difficulty until out of the corner of my eye I saw Mme Storey backing toward the door. You must remember that all this happened in much less time than it takes to tell it.

I gave the revolving door a push to facilitate my mistress's exit. She came out, the gun already hidden. Farren followed, then Stephens.

There was no appearance of hurry. Stephens slyly dropped his umbrella in such a fashion that the revolving door jammed on it, and stuck. These doors will only turn in one direction, you know.

My last impression was of white faces inside, and fists beating on the glass; and the two foolish women that I had been talking to, vainly pushing at the door to get in. They had no idea of what had happened.

The people inside were shrieking at them, and pointing down toward the jammed umbrella. But the two women never got it; they only looked indignant.

Meanwhile we four walked rapidly, but with perfect sedateness toward our waiting car. There was never any need for me to kick off the satin slippers.

Just as we were getting into the car, the clerks broke out of the store with a roar; but in a jiffy we were around the corner and bowling down West End Avenue at thirty miles an hour. Conditions were just right; there was enough traffic in the street to conceal us, and not enough to hold us up. The pursuit never came within sight or sound of us.

We kept right on down West End Avenue past the point where it becomes plain Eleventh Avenue, and scattered at Forty-Second Street, leaving the "stolen" car to be found by the police in due course.

Such was our first hold-up. I expect you will smile at me, just as my mistress did, but I felt disappointed at the outcome, it seemed so easy. After getting so tremendously wrought up as I did at the last moment I required more excitement to satisfy me.

"It will do for a beginning," said Mme Storey cryptically. "If we appeared to get along too well without outside help, it would only be to defeat our own purpose."

VI

You can imagine with what eagerness I searched the newspapers next morning. Once more I was disappointed.

It appeared that while we were turning our trick at Fossberg's, the famous Bobbed-Hair Bandit had been conducting a sensational raid on the pay roll of a factory in Brooklyn. She got a whole column and a half whereas they only gave us a couple of short paragraphs tacked on to the end of her story.

According to this account which had been given out by one of the clerks, he and his mates had put up a bold resistance, and had succeeded in driving us off with only a trifling loss to the establishment. These lies made me good and sore.

Why, the value of the rings taken by Mme Storey was upward of fifty thousand dollars. I experienced the psychology of a real gunman. I felt that we had been cheated of our due.

Mme Storey was highly amused when I voiced my feelings.

"Oh, never mind the general public," she said soothingly; "if we get credit among our professional friends at the Boule' Miche', it will be more to the point."

That night Benny Abell was sent on ahead to the resort to act as a sort of advance agent for the company. We were to join him there after midnight.

The Boule' Miche' calls itself a "club", of course, though it hangs out a glittering electric sign to the street. Only "members" are admitted upon presentation of their cards. It is not difficult to get one's self elected.

The entrance is ingeniously protected by a series of dressing rooms and lobbies swarming with employees. Beyond is the restaurant proper, consisting of three large rooms, all done in a florid rococo style with slashings of gilt scroll work.

In the center of each room a little fountain throws up a jet of water with colored lights playing upon it. At this time the place was enjoying a wonderful run of prosperity owing, no doubt, to the widespread connections of the genial proprietor.

Pretty soon Bat Bartley would sell out and the Boule' Miche' blossom out under a new proprietor and a new name. For obvious reasons none of these places lasts long.

As soon as we took our seats in the principal room, it became apparent that Abell had done his work well. Those whom we had spotted as the shady habitués of the place bore themselves toward us with an increased respect.

In particular Bat Bartley was even more supple and suave than usual. He came hurrying up to ask with a meaning air if we would like a private room that night.

"I do my best to keep out the wrong sort of persons," he said, "but once in awhile they will get by." He was referring to agents of the police.

"No, thanks," said Mme Storey with her cool smile. "I enjoy watching the crowd. Nobody is looking for us yet."

Bat Bartley laughed as if she had made an excellent joke. As a matter of fact, no descriptions of us had been published; and we had learned through Inspector Rumsey that the clerk at Fossbergs' had been incapable of furnishing the police with working descriptions.

"Well, anyhow," said Bartley with a wink, "have a bottle of cider on the house."

This beverage, which was served from a plain bottle, unless I miss my guess, originated in a cellar of Reims.

Abell did not remain with us continuously, but visited his acquaintances through the rooms as occasion offered. By and by he brought one of them up to our table.

"Meet my friend, Mr Tinker," he said, "you know, Muggsy Tinker between friends."

It was a comical figure. He had the look of a little boy who had become middle-aged without growing up.

He had a boy's curly pate now streaked with gray, and a schoolboy's sheepish smile, though his face was seamed and wrinkled. A large, staring glass eye which matched very ill with its little twinkling mate added to the peculiarity of his appearance.

He was wearing the conventional dinner coat, but would have looked more at home in a rough jacket with a dirty handkerchief around his neck.

"Please' to meet yeh. Please' to meet yeh," he said, grinning affably all around. He sat down and accepted a glass of cider.

"I've heard of you," said Mme Storey. "You and Buck Millings used to work together years ago."

"That's right. That's right," he said, greatly pleased. "Buck and me pulled off many a job together. He was an A-I partner.

They don't make his like nowadays. Poor Buck, he met his end under a freight train in the Joliet yards. To think of anybody remembering them days! We used to hear of you then, ma'am. Oh, yes, you was famous. Way out of our class. You for the classy kid glove work, us for the rough!"

Mme Storey toasted him with her glass.

Mr Tinker, without saying anything plainly, went on to let us know that he had heard of our exploit of the day before, and highly commended it.

"Say, that was pulled off in a real big style," he said. "It was just what you'd expect of Kate Arkledon."

"Just a beginning," said Mme Storey with a casual air.

"Say, the papers gave you a rotten deal on that," he went on. "It made me sore. A brilliant piece of work like that ought to get proper credit."

My heart quite went out to the little man for his sympathy.

"Oh, well, we're not looking for publicity," said Mme Storey.

The little man gave her a sharp look.

"Oh, I don't know," he replied. "Times have changed."

The talk drifted away to other matters. After awhile he said, apropos of nothing that had gone before: "You ought to see Jake."

"Jake who?" asked Mme Storey with an idle air.

"I don't know his proper name. We just call him Jake the Canvasser."

"Whom does he canvass for?"

"Oh, his organization," said Muggsy vaguely.

I pricked up my ears at that.

Mme Storey refused to betray any interest in this Jake; but Muggsy returned to the subject of his own account. "Jake may have a proposition to put up to you. You ought to talk to him. He's an A-I feller."

"What sort of proposition?"

"Oh, let him name it to you himself. You'll find him better than his word. We all deals with Jake. He earns his commission all right, and then some."

"I know these Jakes," said Mme Storey scornfully. "They belong to the family of bloodsuckers. They live off us who do the work and take the risk."

Muggsy wagged his hand back and forth. "No, no," he said, "you get this wrong. Jake ain't no common receiver. He's got a new proposition. Up-to-date."

"Oh, I guess I can run my business without him," said Mme Storey.

An ugly look appeared in Muggsy's face. "You'll find you gotta deal with Jake," he said. "We all do. The service that Jake supplies is for the benefit of all, and all are expected to pay their share. Nachelly, if anybody tried to profit by Jake's service without puttin' up for it, it would make the crowd sore."

"I'll hear what he has to say," said Mme Storey, coolly.

"Times has changed, ma'am," said Muggsy meaningly. "It used to be everything was individuality, but nowadays it's organization. You can't do nothin' without organizing. Eithcr you gotta climb aboard the band wagon, or the wheels will sure go over yeh!"

VII

On the following evening the redoubtable Jake turned up at the Boule' Miche' in person. Bat Bartley brought him to our table. He was as smooth as a well-whipped mayonnaise.

In appearance he was the prosperous business man – well, not quite, for the marvelously cut blue suit, a little lighter in color than men usually wear, the pale pink shirt and tie of a darker hue gave him a sporting character. He wore an immense diamond on the middle finger of his left hand.

He was more the successful theatrical manager or baseball magnate. He had one of these smooth full faces that lent themselves naturally to an unctuous smile; his handsome, dark eyes rolled and beamed mysteriously, and gave nothing away.

His first act was to order up a bottle of "cider". I found that he was always amply supplied with funds. He was driven about town by a smart chauffeur in an elegant new car of the most expensive make. He was liberal, too, in making loans to any member of "the crowd" who was out of luck.

You are not to suppose that he sat down and came out plump and plain with his proposition. By no means. A good hour was spent in laying the foundations for a beautiful friendship.

A second bottle followed the first. He made no secret of his admiration for my mistress, and in that I think he was honest. I believe he was a little astonished by her superb style after the commonplace material he was accustomed to deal with.

He entertained us with pleasant gossip of the great world. He seemed to know everybody worth knowing, and I was greatly impressed until he gave the snap away by bringing in the name of Mme Storey.

"Oh, Rose and I are intimate friends," he said carelessly. "She owes her success to the fact that she keeps in close touch with men like me who know all sides of life. But," he added with a confidential smile, "I don't tell her too much, you bet. I look after my friends. Anybody will tell you that. Rose don't get as much out of me as I get out of her."

I wish you could have seen my mistress's innocent expression while he was getting this off. She looked like the cat who has swallowed the canary.

By insidious degrees he approached the real business in hand. He was careful never to give the plain brutal names to things.

"The organization that I represent," he explained, "has two main objects; first to advertise the business as a whole; second, to see that the individual operator gets proper recognition. You can't rise in any profession without publicity. Look at the mean way the papers used you the other day. That couldn't happen if you were in with us.

"Providing publicity to the nervy boys and girls that live dangerously," he went on, "that's our line." The phrase "live dangerously" was continually on his lips. I wondered where he had picked it up.

"Look where they stand today as the result of our publicity," he went on. "The police helpless, the public terror-stricken. You have only to pull your gat anywhere for every boob in the neighborhood to freeze solid. All due to intelligent publicity; to such stunts as the Bobbed-Haired Bandit. That's our stuff. That's reached such a point that we don't even have to furnish the stories any more. The papers run it spontaneously. They hand it to us."

"So it seems," said my mistress.

"But we don't stop with one stunt," he resumed. "Always something new. It was my people who staged the holdup of Mme Storey awhile ago. That was a wow of a stunt. Just look at the publicity we got out of it. It had a tremendous moral effect. For everybody says to themselves: 'My God! If they can get away with that what chance have *we* got?' And they give up without a struggle!"

Here a certain compunction appeared to attack him, and he assumed a deprecatory tone.

"Of course, I told you just now that Rose Storey was my friend, and so she is in a manner of speaking. I know her well, but she ain't a real friend, like. She only goes with me for what she thinks she can get out of me, so I don't feel under any obligations to her. I just go her one better. That's fair, ain't it?"

"Absolutely," agreed my mistress. "By the way, who pulled off that trick?"

I kept my eyes on my plate during this amazing scene. I distrusted my own powers of dissimulation.

"Two young fellows that I'm bringing out," said Jake. "Falseface Petro and Tony Lanza."

"Falseface? How did he get that name?"

"Because he can make his face like a wax mask. He gives nothing away. It's worth a fortune in our business."

"Sure!"

"Oh, those lads have a future before them," commented Jake. "They're young yet, but they're bound to rise."

"I'd like to meet them," said Mme Storey carelessly. "Perhaps they'd be willing to work work with me."

"They'd jump at the chance," said Jake. "A woman of your reputation. I'll bring them up some night."

"Well, tell them who I am, and what I've done," said Mme Storey indifferently. "I can't be explaining myself to kids."

Jake enlarged upon his organization.

"In addition to publicity," he said, "we have a special advisory department to investigate likely plants and furnish our subscribers with full information. In that case all you got to do is to go and turn your trick, knowing that everything is all right. That costs more, of course."

"I would prefer to investigate my own plants," Mme Storey told him.

"Sure, sure," he said obsequiously; "a person of your experience. We are also prepared to furnish suggestions for big, spectacular stunts, good for a column or more of space, and beside that we run a press clipping bureau."

"Press clippings?" repeated Mme Storey, elevating her eyebrows.

"Sure. Every operator, after he has covered a clever trick, wants to read what they say about it. It's valuable, too, to learn what the police are doing in his case."

"Well, I've been in the game too long," said Mme Storey. "I'm not interested in clippings. What could you do for me?"

"Say," said Jake impressively. "I wouldn't give a person like you no hot air. You're wise. I wouldn't say a word to you about what we could do. I wouldn't ask you to pay a cent, neither. All you got to do is to let me know the place and time where you're going to pull your next trick, and we'll do the rest. The result will surprise you." His eyes gleamed appreciatively.

"Say, with a person of your style and your reputation," he went on, "there's no limit to what we could do! What a chance! What a chance! Why, we'd leave the Bob-Haired Bandit tied to the post!"

"All for nothing?" queried Mme Storey dryly.

"You would agree if you were satisfied with the publicity to pay us our usual commission. Ten per cent of the proceeds. That's all."

"In goods?" she asked slyly.

His face hardened. "In cash. All our dealings are in cash. We don't want to interfere with your arrangements for disposing of the goods."

"I see," said Mme Storey. "Well, look here. I'll tell you what I'll do. You ask your people to furnish me with a suggestion for a sensational stunt that will break into the headlines, and if it appeals to me I'll do business with you."

"Fine!" cried Jake. "You shall have it tomorrow night!"

Shortly after this we went home, it being then about half past two. We left Jake the Canvasser circulating from table to table amongst his customers.

The Boule' Miche' closed officially at the legal hour, but behind its darkened front the privileged guests lingered on until morning. In the midst of a gay party in the outer room I saw the face of Madge Caswell, a young woman who works for us sometimes. She has a faculty for trailing a suspect that amounts to genius.

She was there by Mme Storey's orders, and in a fleeting glance of intelligence my mistress signified to her that Jake was her man. Madge's instructions were to spare no expense in keeping in contact with him, even if it meant hiring half a dozen assistants, but to allow him to slip at any moment sooner than risk letting him suspect he was watched.

The following night found us in our usual places at the Boule' Miche' after midnight, surrounded by the same showy and noisy crowd with flushed faces and glassy eyes. The Boule' Miche' represented a good time to these people, but they were not really having it. They whooped themselves up to it.

What a lot of time and money mortals waste in the constant pursuit of so-called pleasure!

We saw Jake the Canvasser from time to time with one party or another, but he was coy tonight and allowed a good while to elapse before he came to our table. Perhaps he wished to force Mme Storey to send for him. But she was a better waiter than he was, and in the end he had to come of his own accord.

He sat down and entertained us with his anecdotes. My mistress would not deign to question him. Finally he said:

"– Er – I heard from my people."

"Yes?" said Mme Storey, with perfect indifference.

Jake glanced questioningly at the rest of us.

"Oh, you may speak freely," she told him; "these people are in on everything I do."

"Well," said Jake, "the organization suggests that you go back to Fossberg's and turn a second trick. First-rate publicity in that. It will be the last place they'd expect you. If you make your second visit before the clerks have time to recover their nerve, it'll be a walk-away!"

"Not a bad idea," said Mme Storey, with a subtle smile.

My heart began to beat with the same old suffocating fear of the future.

VIII

Next morning we plunged into our preparations again. We already had full information as to the plan and layout of the

Fossberg store, and had now to concoct a new line of approach that would stand as good a chance of success as the old.

Bert Farren, who was sent up to make a preliminary reconnaissance, reported that the revolving door had been replaced with two pairs of swinging doors. These doors swung either way. Also, a carriage opener had been hired to stand outside.

It was obvious that he was a detective in disguise, and armed. This man seemed to me like a fatal obstacle in the way of our success, but Mme Storey smiled when she heard about him.

"It will make the problem more interesting," she said.

We struck another snag when Inspector Rumsey approached Benjamin Fossberg with our proposition. He met with a flat refusal.

It was somebody else's turn to be the goat, Fossberg said; he and his brother had not recovered from the shock of the first hold-up. The inspector was finally forced to bring him down to our office, for Mme Storey to exert her charm upon him.

She finally won a reluctant consent, with the stipulation that both brothers be allowed to absent themselves from the store when the stunt was pulled off. Mme Storey had no objection to this, of course.

Fossberg pointed out that he had now no excuse to deprive the clerks of their guns.

"Then load them with blanks," said Mme Storey. "They'll never know the difference. Let there be an exchange of shots. It will add drama to the affair."

In these preliminary discussions it soon developed that I was to be put forward this time as the principal performer. Mme Storey could not be the first to enter the store without adding a disguise to her disguise, and this she could not do since it was necessary for the success of the affair that the clerks should recognize her in the end.

The realization of what they expected of me almost overwhelmed me, but not quite, for now I was borne up by the secret hope that when the actual moment came I should be able to play my part as well as any of them. In the meantime, though, I suffered all the torments of the damned.

This "living dangerously", as Jake termed it, was not all that it was cracked up to be.

We continued to frequent the Boule' Miche' late at night, and our prestige there was growing. Through Jake and through Bat Bartley we were gradually becoming acquainted with all the "operators" or "adventurers", as they termed themselves. Most of them were incredibly young, and all distinguished by the childish vanity which seems to be inseparable from the modern crook. Among them were several of the girls who alternated in the role of the Bobbed-Haired Bandit.

I understood that there were at least half a dozen bobbed-hair bandits. These youngsters, recognizing a great character in Mme Storey, instinctively deferred to her. She would have made good with them, even without the infernal halo of Kate Arkledon's reputation around her head.

One of the girls quite won my heart. They called her Brownie. She was not strictly beautiful, her mouth being too wide and her blue eyes set too far apart, but she had that indefinable something which is called charm.

Her frank gaiety was irresistible. It was her finest qualities which had driven her into association with these thieves – a hatred of smugness and sham. Under happier circumstances she might have adorned the highest circles.

After it was all over we tried to find this girl, but she had disappeared. Like May-flies they enjoy their brief dance in the sun – then oblivion.

I may say here that none of these young people suffered as a result of Mme Storey's activities in the case. It was agreed between her and Inspector Rumsey that the police must do their own work in respect to apprehending the small fry.

My mistress's interest lay with the cold-hearted man or men who remained in safety in the background, profiting by the recklessness of the young. But of course she always meant to get Falseface Petro and Tony Lanza; that she owed to herself.

My heart gave a great jump when I first saw these two enter the Boule' Miche'. Now for the acid test of our disguise, I thought, glancing at my mistress and at my own reflection in the mirror.

We had been playing our roles for many days now, and they had become second nature to us; there was little likelihood that they would recognize us separately. True, for them to find us together added to the danger somewhat; but we were now in the midst of quite a large party, most of whom were known to Falseface and Tony as "safe".

The two young men had been told all about us, and that is the secret of a successful disguise – *i.e.*, to prepare in advance the minds of those whom you wish to deceive.

Jake brought them up to our table from behind me. I could *feel* them coming. My heart beat thickly as at the approach of a dangerous animal. Fortunately I was playing an insignificant role, and they scarcely deigned to notice me.

Little Tony was hailed by the crowd as a good fellow, while Falseface was greeted with more respect. The latter, though he was not now in action, still maintained his pose of inscrutability.

He stood there with a good-humored sneer, as much as to say he would permit the ladies to admire him. And the worst of it was, you couldn't help but admire him.

Conceited and empty as he was, there was power in his unnatural self-control. In that circle of grinning faces he never smiled.

It was quite thrilling to see him and Mme Storey together. Neither would yield an inch. Each affected to ignore the other; but it was none the less evident that for these two the others at the table simply did not exist.

Neither had much to say. Mme Storey smoked one cigarette after another, and through the haze of tobacco fumes her expression appeared even more cynical and reckless. Falseface Petro gave himself the languid, elegant airs of a celebrated screen star.

We had made room for the newcomers at our table, and the inevitable "cider" circulated. Of course in company like that we never discussed business; the talk was just as empty and meaningless as might have been heard at any table in the place. It was merely a noise.

"Well, what's the good word, Falseface?"

"Nobody's got a good word for you, Butch."

Loud laughter greeted this sally.

"Say, you're so quick you're ahead of yourself. Wait till you catch up, fella."

"If I waited for you, I'd be there yet."

"Is 'at so?"

Somebody broke into song:

>"My gal's a high-bawn lady;
>She's dahk, but not too shady –"

"Where'd you dig that up, Brownie? That song was laid away when mother was a girl."

"I don't care. I like it."

Louder:

>"Fedders lak a peacock, just as gay;
>She's not cullud, she was bawn that way."

"What yeh tryin' to do, compete wit' t' orchester?"

"T' orchester ain't in it wit' me."

Fortissimo:

>"Down the line they can't outshine
>This high-bawn gal of mine!"

". . . Odds of sixty-four to one, and she romped home. I had a tip, too, and I wouldn't play it. I wisht somebody would kick me now."

"Hey, fellas, Tony wants somebody to kick him!"

"That's a good show down at the Booth."

"Yeah. Lee Shubert sent me a box last week."

"Yes, he did!"

". . . They're gonna call it the Sans Sowcy."

"What's 'at mean?"

"Soich me! Vincent Astor and young Morgan and all the big fellas belongs."

"Well, they're nottin' in my life."

There was dancing in the middle room, and the crowd at our table was continually breaking up and reforming in different combinations. When an opportunity presented itself Mme Storey whispered to me to pass the word to our fellows to let us go home alone this night.

It turned out in the end that Falseface Petro was not as indifferent as he seemed. When Mme Storey rose to leave, he got up also in his lordly way and squired us out.

Tony followed after like his shadow.

Falseface signaled a taxi at the curb.

"Can I drop you anywhere?" he drawled.

"I live in – Street," said Mme Storey.

The upshot was that Falseface and Tony accepted an invitation to come up for a last drink and a smoke. By this time we had thoroughly established our characters with them, and there was little chance of a discovery. But the sense of danger was always present; one could not relax for a moment.

How strange it seemed to be hobnobbing with those two sleek young savages!

Arrived in our own little flat, none of us needed to put a curb on our tongues.

"Jake told me about the stunt you pulled off at Fossberg's last week," said Falseface. "That was a damn neat piece of work."

"Oh, I was just getting my hand in after quite an extended rest," said my mistress carelessly.

"What you get out of it?"

"Twenty-five thousand. That was about half what the stuff was worth."

"It's better than I can do. Those fellows are bloodsuckers."

"You're no slouch at the game yourself," said Mme Storey. "That was a nervy stunt you pulled in Mme Storey's office. I like to see a woman like that get it. She's too big for her shoes, she is."

"If you've got the nerve they can't stop you!" said Falseface, pluming himself.

"Sure. That's the principle I've always gone on."

"Me and you ought to be in on something together," he said with an elaborate show of indifference.

"Suits me," said my mistress. "We're going to pull a big stunt next week. Going back to Fossberg's to make a second cleanup. There will be good publicity in it this time."

"Well, Tony and me's got nothing on next week," said Falseface carelessly.

"I could use a couple more men if they were the right sort," said Mme Storey. "I take a third; I'll give you a quarter; and the rest divide what's left. There won't be but six or seven of as in it."

"We're on," said Falseface, without troubling to consult his partner.

"All right," said Mme Storey. "Be here at nine to-morrow

night to meet the crowd and talk things over. We'll go on to the
Boule' Miche' after."

IX

The affair was first set for Wednesday afternoon of the following week. On Tuesday Inspector Rumsey came into our office
in a state of perturbation.

He had just learned that the captain of the precinct in which
Fossberg's was situated had made a shift, and that thereafter
there would be an officer on fixed post in the middle of Broadway, immediately in front of the jewelry store.

"Of course I could have given him a tip to put it off until after
tomorrow," said the inspector, "but you told me most particularly not to interfere with the local police arrangements."

"Quite so," said my mistress. "If you told the captain to
put it off, and then the robbery took place tomorrow, the cat
would be out of the bag. And we're not yet ready to release
that cat."

"But what will you do?" asked the inspector. "You can't
make a get-away with an armed policeman outside the door."

"We'll make a new plan," said Mme. Storey calmly. "Speaking of cats, there's more than one way of skinning them."

"That makes two men outside the door," he said in distress.

"Well," rejoined my mistress, smiling, "there's a back door."

To give us time to discuss the details of the new plan, and to
rehearse our parts, the affair was put off until Saturday at ten
thirty. On Saturday mornings the volume of business is about
the same as the afternoons of other days. On the afternoon of
Saturday we feared there would be too great a crowd for our
comfort.

I was relieved to discover that in the new plan I was not called
upon to play so dangerous a part. We were all to enter the store
simultaneously.

Abell was released from any participation in this holdup,
much to his joy. There was no glamour about it for him. That
left six of us to conduct the actual operation.

The gang was completed by a dandy chauffeur borrowed by
Mme Storey from a wealthy friend. The car "stolen" for the
occasion was an elegant new limousine.

On Saturday morning at nine we met at the flat. I was in a miserable state of funk. I hope I succeeded in concealing it.

Mme Storey served out the guns, and she herself made sure that Falseface and Tony were not carrying any additional weapons. They protested against the blank shells, but our leader stood firm.

"Our object is robbery, and not murder," she said coolly. "If you are obliged to shoot, the blanks will go off with just as much noise and have the same moral effect. And if there is any slip-up in our plans, you won't land in the death chamber."

They appeared to see the force of her argument.

We left the flat separately. It fell to my part to ride uptown in the elegant car with the dandy chauffeur.

But I was in no condition to enjoy all this grandeur. My knees trembled, my hands were clammy, my tongue clove to the roof of my mouth. I wore a close hat which completely hid my red hair, and certain changes had been made in my facial decorations.

On the first occasion the clerks at Fossberg's could not have had but the briefest glimpse of me; still there was a possibility of my face having been photographed on somebody's mind, and we were not taking any chances.

Two blocks below the store I halted in order to make sure that I was not arriving too soon. Mme Storey came to the car door as if to greet an acquaintance.

"All here," she said cheerfully. "Give us two minutes, then drive on, and go ahead with the program. Do not look about for us as you are entering the store."

"How about the two policemen on beat?" I asked.

"You can disregard them today."

When I drove up in front of Fossberg's in my fine car, the door opener hastened to help me out. As I stepped down I made believe to stumble, and allowed a little cry of pain to escape me.

"Oh, my ankle!"

The man caught hold of my arm to support me. "Will you get back in your car?" he asked.

"No, let him drive on," I said. "I will sit down in the store for a moment."

He helped me across the sidewalk. This trick was to draw him inside the store, you understand.

I was half paralyzed with fear. He must have felt how my arm was trembling; but I suppose he ascribed it to the pain I was suffering.

Inside the store, a clerk made haste to push up a chair, and I sank into it. In a glance I saw that the place was fairly well filled, and then things began to happen.

As the door opener left me to return to his post, he found himself facing Falseface, Tony, and young Farren, who had entered behind me, each with a gun in his hand. Instinctively the doorkeeper's hand went toward his pocket; but at a harsh command from Falseface, he thought better of it, and flung his hands above his head.

In a twinkling Tony had disarmed him. Behind them, in the space between the two pairs of doors, Mme Storey was coolly bolting the outside doors, and pulling down the shades. To the glass of the door she affixed a little notice which had been prepared in readiness:

"Closed on account of death in the family."

Stephens had been sent around through the apartment house to cut off the escape of anybody who might try to get out by the rear door of the store. This door opened into the lobby of the apartment house.

For the moment I remained sitting where I was. All fear left me, and I seemed to be able to see all round my head.

Mme Storey joined the three men, and the four of them spread out, and advanced across the store like skirmishers. When they came abreast of me, I fell into line with them.

A strange silence filled the place. Then Mme Storey ordered everybody, clerks and customers, over to the far side out of our way, and they scurried like rats at her bidding.

The human creature is not a pretty object when he is in the grip of terror. Over in the corner they struggled insanely to get behind each other.

Never will I forget the sight. There was one big woman squeaking in terror, and struggling with all her might. In spite of her struggles, one of the men clerks, who had her by the elbows, continued to hold her in front of him.

Another clerk, instead of following the crowd, silently dropped out of sight behind the counter on my left. I knew he had a gun back there, though it was loaded with blanks. I told Mme Storey about him.

"Well, if he sticks his head over the counter, blow it off," she said harshly, loud enough for him to hear.

Nobody but me could hear the faint ring of laughter in her voice. She was enjoying herself.

A third clerk slipped out through the office at the back, but we were not concerned about him. Presently he reappeared, walking backward, stepping high, and holding his hands above his head. Stephens followed, covering him with his gun.

Mme Storey ordered Stephens to dislodge the man behind the counter. As Stephens looked around the counter, the clerk fired.

Low, terrified cries broke from the people across the store. My own heart failed me at the sound of the explosion, though I knew it was all a comedy.

Stephens did not return his fire, but flung himself upon the clerk, and dragged him out of his hiding place. At the back of the store there was a tall safe with the door standing open. Stephens flung his man inside, and closed the door.

Meanwhile Falseface, Tony, and I had made for the safes in the center of the store. Each of us was provided with big pockets inside the skirts of our coats. I had the combination of each of these four safes, but they were not called for since all stood open.

Dropping on our knees, we began to pour the contents of the trays into our pockets. Such a cascade of glittering necklaces, pins, bracelets and rings!

While I worked, I could see Mme Storey out of the tail of my eye, helping to cover the cowering crowd in the far corner. Without lowering her gun, she took a tiny cigar from the breast pocket of her neat jacket, and sticking it in her mouth, lit a match with her thumb nail. I think this display of coolness intimidated our victims as much as the guns.

It took us but a minute or two to empty the safes. We did not bother with the show case stuff.

Coming out from behind the counter we made for the rear door. Mme Storey and the other two men backed slowly toward us.

Then from the midst of the crowd they were covering somebody fired, and instantly pandemonium broke loose. Whipping out their guns involuntarily, Falseface and Tony returned the fire as fast as they could shoot.

Nobody could be hurt, of course; but from the shrieks and yells which rose, you would have thought that every shot had found its mark. Somebody was shoved through a show case with a horrifying crash.

As we backed through the office, a loud pounding was heard on the street door. We had not a moment to lose. Somehow, we found ourselves in the lobby of the apartment house, and got the door closed.

It was quiet there. The door closed with a spring lock, and opened inward toward the store. There was no means of fastening it from the outside; but Stephens had brought a long, thin bar for the purpose. When this was laid obliquely across the door, caught inside the handle, the ends projected beyond the door frame; and those inside were unable to pull the door toward them.

I saw it was quiet in the lobby, and the way clear. The door from the street was locked, and Stephens, upon first entering, had bound and gagged the elevator attendant, and had thrown him in a little office alongside the entrance.

To be sure, the door of one of the rear apartments opened, and a white face showed for a moment, but we had nothing to fear from this direction. The door was quickly slammed again.

We crowded into the elevator. Stephens knew how to operate it. The last thing we saw, as we shot upward, was a crowd of people headed by a policeman turning in from the sidewalk toward the street door.

My knees weakened at the sight of the bluecoat. A policeman is such an obstinate fact to face.

On the top landing a couple of people were waiting for the elevator. They fell back in affright as we poured out. We ran up the final flight of stairs to the roof.

I should explain that this apartment house was one of a pair exactly alike, which occupied the whole block fronting on Broadway. All we had to do therefore was to run across the roof, and descend into the twin house, whose entrance was in the next cross street. The door from the roof was armed with a bolt on the inside, and this we shot as we passed through.

In such a state of excitement, one's instinct was to run right down through the house; but Mme Storey would not permit it. She feared that the noise of our descent might alarm somebody below, and result in our being cut off.

She forced us to wait on the top landing for the elevator. Oh, but it was hard to wait with one's nerves jumping!

The elevator came at last. As we were getting in, we heard running feet on the roof, and fists began to pound on the door we had bolted. The negro elevator boy looked at us terrified, and hesitated.

Mme Storey, smiling, took out her gun, and affected to examine it. The boy's black face turned gray with terror, and he took us down in a hurry. Not a word was spoken.

We issued out of the house without any appearance of hurry. Our elegant limousine was waiting at the door with the engine running. The alarm had not yet penetrated into this street.

We could see people running down Broadway. Mme Storey was the last of us to get in the car.

As she pulled the door after her, the people running down Broadway stopped, and a crowd came pouring around the corner from the other direction. They were headed by a policeman with a gun in his hand. They were not in any too great a hurry, though.

They stopped to reconnoiter prudently. I was looking out of the rear window of the limousine. As the policeman raised his arm I dropped.

We roared away down the street. The policeman sent a couple of shots after us, while I made myself small. However, they went wide. We turned the corner on two wheels; turned another corner and slowed down.

We were safe. Away from the actual scene nobody would ever have suspected that handsome car with its dandy chauffeur of having taken part in a holdup.

When I realized that we were really safe, I suddenly dissolved in weakness. I seemed to lose all grip, all control of myself. Simultaneously perspiring and shivering in an agony of after-fear, I groaned to myself: Never again! Never again!

At Eighty-Sixth Street we turned east, and making our way through the park by the transverse road, abandoned the car in Yorkville, and scattered. As Mme Storey and I made our way decorously down Madison Avenue, all that had happened seemed like a dream. However, the weight of jewelry bumping against my knees reminded me that it was no vision.

My mistress went into a drug store to telephone. With a grin in my direction, she left the door of the booth open a crack, and I heard this astonishing conversation:

"Is this Fossberg's jewelry store? . . . This is the lady who just held you up . . . Held you up, I said: Can't you understand English? I just wanted to tell you, in case you had overlooked it, that one of your clerks is shut up in the big safe at the back of the store . . . Better let him out before he suffocates . . . Oh, that's all right. Don't mention it. Goodbye."

X

By two o'clock the first brief accounts of the affair were on the streets. The late afternoon editions carried the complete story. And it was a story!

As a feature we had no competition that day. Jake the Canvasser had certainly delivered the goods. Mme Storey and I read the newspapers, chuckling.

It appeared that the chief source of information was a customer who happened to be in the store at the time. The clerks, as before, were too flustered to give a coherent account of what had happened.

I shall not give the newspaper story in full since I have already described what happened. The best part of the story was that it was true, except for certain artistic details added by the narrator. As when he said he heard the bandits address their leader as "Duchess".

There was a clever touch! The soubriquet stuck, of course; we never appeared in the newspapers after that but Mme Storey was termed the Duchess, or the Duchess-Bandit.

What a marvelous thing is publicity! Only start it once, and it rolls up like a snowball. Every day some new story of the Duchess's exploits appeared.

People claimed to have seen her here, there, everywhere. Moreover, the newspapers all carried indignant editorials asking what was the matter with the police that such things were allowed to go on. That was good publicity, too.

In that first story every possible detail concerning Mme Storey was played up; her elegant appearance, her extraordinary coolness, the humorous remarks that she addressed to her trembling victims. The fact that it was our second descent on the place was not omitted.

Fantastic were the accounts of the loot we had secured. It appeared that so far as the more valuable part of the stock was concerned, Fossberg's was completely cleaned out. In point of magnitude it was the greatest jewel robbery that had ever taken place in New York.

Two policemen added their quota to the story. Officer James Crear said:

"I was on fixed post at the corner of Broadway and – Street about ten thirty this morning, when a fellow ran over to me, and said there was something wrong in Fossberg's jewelry store on the corner. Said he heard shooting and yelling inside as he passed by. So I ran over there, and I found the store closed, and a notice on the door reading: 'Closed on account of death in the family.'

"I thought this was funny, because I had seen folks going in and out just a few minutes before. I could hear a racket inside, and I rapped on the door with my stick. Pretty soon it was opened by one of the clerks, who was so scared he couldn't tell a straight story. But I understood there had been a hold-up, and the bandits were making their way out through the apartment house lobby in the rear of the store.

"I ran around outside to the door of the apartment house. It was locked. I forced it, and inside I found the elevator boy tied up and gagged. He told me the gang had gone up in the elevator. I ran up the stairs after them. They went over the roof, and down through the adjoining apartment house. They bolted the roof door after them, and I lost more time forcing it. When I got down to the street they were out of sight."

Officer William Rohrback said: "I was patrolling the west side of Broadway at – Street, when I heard Officer Crear rap for assistance. I was two blocks away from his post. When I got there I found a crowd milling around Fossberg's jewelry store. I was told that a hold-up had taken place and that the bandits had gone upstairs in the apartment house, and with the help of Officer Regan, who had also run up, we put a watch at every exit from the house.

"The janitor came up and told me there was a way over the roof into the adjoining house, so, leaving the others on watch, I ran around into the next street. When I turned the corner, I saw a woman getting into a limousine car. It was such an elegant looking outfit I hesitated; but when it started down the street at forty miles an hour or better, I fired three shots in the air. The car failed to stop."

The "customer" in Fossberg's who supplied the real story to the reporter had this to say about the Duchess:

"She was a woman of about forty-five, but well preserved. Must have been a beauty in her youth. In figure still as slender and active as a young woman. She looked more like one of those fashionable dames than a bandit; and more like Park Avenue than Upper Broadway; the real thing. She had the hardest boiled face I ever saw on a woman. I mean by that, she meant business. A desperate character. I wouldn't have thought of opposing her.

"As she was standing squarely in front of me all the time we were herded over at the side of the store, I had plenty of time to size her up. She looked at us as if we were dirt under her feet. The most striking features about her were her eyes, the pupils of which closed up to mere slits, like a cat's eyes in daylight. It gave her a terrible look."

You see how cleverly he blended fact and fiction.

An amusing outcome of the affair was, that two days later a committee of West Side merchants waited upon Mme Storey in her office, and did their best to persuade her to take the job of running down the Duchess. My mistress smilingly declined.

But I am getting a little ahead of my story. On the night of the hold-up we telephoned ahead to the Boule' Miche' asking for a private room. Such detailed descriptions of all of us had been published, it was no longer prudent to appear in the general room. We entered by a side door, and were taken upstairs by a private stairway.

In the "Diamond Room", as they called it, we held a sort of reception, which lasted half the night. Everybody "in the know" – that is to say, every shady character who frequented the place, came up to congratulate us. Our fame was great in the underworld; the Duchess had thrown the Bobbed-Hair Bandit in the shade.

When Jake the Canvasser came to us that night, what an exchange of compliments took place! For once Jake lost his cagey air; enthusiasm carried him away. He held Mme Storey's hand in both of his, and gazed in her face like a lover.

"Finest thing I ever heard of!" he said. "Finest thing I ever heard of! You're the queen of them all!"

"I had A-1 support," she said, including us all in her glance.

"Are you satisfied with the way we handled it?" asked Jake. "Of course, there'll be a lot of new stuff in the morning papers."

"More than satisfied!" said my mistress. "The man who got up that story was a genius!"

"Of course, we put our best man on it," said Jake. "I may say he is a well-known literary guy, who just does this on the side. But at that, he couldn't have done a thing if you hadn't given him the stuff to work on. Say, that notice, 'Closed on account of death in the family,' and the little cigar, and that trick of lighting a match with your thumbnail while you kept the crowd covered; that was better than anything he could invent."

"Oh, I don't know," she said, not to be outdone: "that name he hung on me, 'the Duchess', that was a masterstroke. To a professional person a good name is more than half the battle. And that touch about the cat's eyes; it couldn't have been bettered. I hope your people are pleased with the way we pulled the thing off."

"I haven't had any communication with them yet," said Jake, "but I know they must be. In fact, the affair reflects credit on both sides. It shows that we were just waiting for each other; you feel that, don't you?"

"I'll never make a move without consulting you," she said.

Later, Jake contrived to get all outsiders out of the room, so that he could talk business with my mistress.

"Have you any notion what the stuff is worth?" he asked eagerly.

In respect to this matter, Mme Storey intended to string Jake along as far as she could, of course.

"Not yet," she told him. "I've got good people working for me, and the stuff is all in their hands. But there's so damn much of it it'll take a while for the market to absorb it. They have paid me twenty-five thousand on account. I brought yours."

It was paid, over in twenty-five crisp hundred dollar bills. I may say that this money was not marked. In dealing with men so astute as Jake and his employers, it would have been too risky. But we had the numbers of the bills, of course, and hoped to be able to trace them by that means.

Jake put away the money.

"Well, how about our next grandstand play?" he said, rubbing his hands.

"Oh, give us a chance," laughed Mme Storey.

"Oh, there's no desire to overwork you," said Jake, in his oily way; "no, indeed! But we mustn't miss the psychological moment, either. This thing that we've started will run along for a week or ten days without any help from us. They'll all be workin' to hand us publicity. But when she begins to slack off, that's the time we've got to strike again, and strike hard in a new quarter. And we've got to be ready."

In my mistress's eyes I could read the determination: Not if I can help myself! But Jake could not see that. For all her cool and careless airs, Mme Storey was fully aware of the terrible risks we ran in staging these affairs, and she had no intention of attempting fate any oftener than was absolutely necessary.

"Well, it's no harm to talk over what we're going to do," she said carelessly. "I'm always open to suggestions."

With the lines we had out, we hoped to have Jake and the men who were back of him lodged behind the bars before another such affair could be máde ready. But in this, as you will see, we were disappointed.

XI

In order to avoid repetition, I will combine the gist of several of Madge Caswell's reports into one.

For a number of years, she said, Jake the Canvasser has been a widely-known character throughout the white light district of Broadway. He passes there as Jake Golden, which is his right name. He has two brothers, prosperous manufacturers, and belongs to a widespread family connection, with which he keeps in close touch.

None of these people have any reason to suspect his association with the criminal world. Indeed, so open and aboveboard appears his whole life, that even after watching him for two weeks, I should not have succeeded in turning up anything suspicious, had it not been for the information you gave me in the beginning.

He passes on Broadway as a "sporting character," i.e., a man who makes his living by promoting and backing sporting events and theatrical enterprises. As a matter of fact, he has various small interests in these lines, but not anywhere near enough to support him in the lavish style in which he lives. He has a comfortable apartment in the – Hotel, one of the best in town, that he leases by the year. He has hundreds of friends in every walk of life, who believe that they know him well. The only mystery about him is, where does he get all the money he spends.

In sporting circles individuals come up and disappear with great frequency; men's memories are short, and none of Jake's present associates remember, if indeed they ever knew, that Jake Golden served a sentence in Sing Sing for swindling, some years ago. Previous to that he had been confined in the Elmira Reformatory.

I have three operatives besides myself engaged on this job. We all have a number of disguises, so there is no danger of his being struck by seeing the same face about him day after day. We have been somewhat handicapped by your instructions that we are not under any circumstances to allow him to suspect that he was being followed.

Once or twice we have had to let him slip when we seemed to be about to learn something interesting. However, it probably would not have been definite. He has his tracks too well covered. He does not yet suspect that he is being watched. It is second nature with the man to take the most elaborate precautions to keep his real business secret.

I am prepared to assert that he has not in all this time met his principal. I believe that it is the corner stone of their whole system of defense, never to meet. Every day he drops into some pay station or another to call up his principal. It is always another pay station that he calls up, and every day a different one.

It is usually a call to Newark, Paterson, Hackensack, White Plains, Flushing, Jamaica, *et cetera;* some large town on the outskirts of New York. Once or twice, by getting the next booth, we heard his conversation over the phone, or a part of it. But as the details of the affairs that he reports are already known to you, this throws no fresh light on the matter.

Two of his talks had to do with "Kate Arkledon". He has no suspicion that she is other than she seems. He merely reports what has happened since the day before, and receives his instructions. In speaking over the phone, he never names the man he is talking to. At the end of the talk he receives the number that he is to call next day. He comes out of the booth with his lips moving, as if to commit it to memory. As he never writes it down, there is no way in which we can learn that number beforehand.

On Monday last he called up – Passaic. I sent one of my boys over there as quickly as possible. It proved to be the principal drugstore of the place. Now, as it is somewhat out of the common for a man to wait around a pay station to be called up, one of the clerks happened to remember the incident. The call came in for "Mr Wilkins", and a large, well-dressed, good-looking man of about forty-five stepped forward to take it, the clerk said. He had dark hair, dark eyes, he said; couldn't say if he was bald because he kept his hat on.

Clean shaven; gentlemanly manner; looked like a retired business man. I send you this description for what it is worth. It would fit about one hundred thousand men around New York, I suppose.

On Tuesday Golden called up St George—. This is the municipal ferry station on Staten Island. Got nothing there. On Wednesday it was another drugstore, this one in Flushing. We were there forty minutes afterwards, and a clerk remembered the call coming in.

It was for "Mr Adams". This clerk described the man who received the call as middle-aged and "funny looking". Was unable to explain just what he meant by funny-looking. Thought his eyes were blue, and that he had a heavy mustache, but couldn't swear to it. Yet it was undoubtedly the same man. Very few learn to use their eyes.

However, this clerk added one more item to our store of knowledge. After "Mr Adams" had finished talking he got into a fine limousine car at the door. It had a chauffeur in livery. Of course, he would have to have a car if he's going to get around from Passaic to Staten Island to Flushing day after day.

It was in sending money to his principal that Golden evinced the greatest ingenuity. Golden maintained accounts in four different banks up-town. In each place his credit was high. None of these banks were aware of his other accounts.

By splitting his business into four like this, the volume of it did not appear large enough to excite suspicion. You told me on the night of the twenty-third Golden was handed eighteen hundred dollars in cash at the Boule' Miche' by a man known as Hutch Diver, and you asked me to trace what became of this money, if this were possible.

Well, I am able to report that he deposited the money in the – National Bank on the following morning. He puts all cash in the bank as received, so there is no use trying to get him by marked bills. He may draw it out later.

One of his favorite stunts is to buy American Express Company checks, and mail them to his principal. These checks are being more and more widely used by automobile tourists and others who do not wish to carry cash on their travels. They have to be signed when purchased, and again when cashed; but Golden's unknown principal has no difficulty in making a passable imitation of his agent's signature when he cashes the checks.

A number of these checks have been returned paid to the head office of the Express Company, and I have traced them back, but without results. Anybody will cash such checks without question; banks, hotels, stores, *et cetera*. They are for moderate amounts, consequently the transactions leave no impression on the memories of the parties who cash them.

These checks have all been returned from towns near New York, the same towns, in fact, that Golden calls up on the telephone. Another method that Golden has of transmitting money to his principal is to draw checks to bearer, and have his bank certify them. Such checks are as good as cash anywhere.

Golden mails these checks to his principal by means of the mail chute in the hotel corridor outside his apartment. As it is impossible for me to keep a man on watch in the corridor, I cannot catch him in the act of mailing them, consequently there is no way in which I can recover the envelope and get a sight of

the address. I know, however, that the checks are mailed in
plain envelopes, and that Golden keeps a typewriter in his room
for the purpose of addressing them.

XII

From the foregoing report, which embodies several of the same
tenor, it will be seen that we had been brought to a stand. We
were between the devil and the deep sea. We could neither go
forward nor back.

Consequently, when the suggestion came through from
"headquarters" that we prepare to hold up the Beauvoir Hospital on the day that the payroll was made up, we had no choice
but to agree. Alas for my vow, that I would never do it again! I
could not abandon my mistress. Feeling a sickness of the heart,
I had to go in with the rest.

Beauvoir Hospital! In the mere naming of it you will
perceive what a stupendous task we had been given. Up to
this time nobody had ever thought of holding up a hospital.
And Beauvoir, the great charity hospital which spreads over
several city blocks, was by far the largest and the best known
of them all.

With its psychopathic cases, its accidents, its victims of mur-
derous assaults, it is continually in the news. In fact, it receives
more publicity than all the other city institutions put together.
Beauvoir is an essential part of the fabric of New York life.

Imagine being asked to attack such a place. Why, it is a very
hive of industry, with crowds entering and leaving at all hours;
police bringing in accidents' cases; police sitting at the bedsides
of wounded prisoners. It seemed to me like a bad joke on the
part of Jake's employers.

I wondered if perhaps they had not penetrated our disguises,
and were using this ingenious means of bringing about our
downfall. But Madge Caswell's reports continued to assure us
that they did not suspect us; and Mme Storey, after a study of
the problem, considered that the trick might be turned, though
it was appallingly difficult.

Beauvoir, as everybody knows, is on the East River front. It
consists of an ancient stone building which forms a nucleus for
innumerable more or less modern wings spreading in every

direction. The office of the hospital, which was our mark, is in this old building, just inside the main entrance.

There are other entrances for patients and their visitors. The main entrance is used principally by officials of the hospital, and those doing business with them. Unfortunately for us, the old building fronts on a courtyard, which is overlooked by literally hundreds of windows. The grand difficulty would be to get out of that courtyard with whole skins.

You may gauge the size of the institution when I tell you that the weekly pay roll amounted to nearly seventy thousand dollars. This money was brought to the hospital every Thursday morning by armored car. In the office it was made up into pay envelopes by a force of clerks; payment to the employees was spread over the whole week.

Our attack was timed for Thursday just before noon, when the clerks would have the money spread out in the office in the act of making up the envelopes. The force consisted of a head bookkeeper, three male clerks and two women. No additional guards were employed. I suppose nobody had ever dreamed of the possibility that a hospital might be attacked.

The first thing we had to decide was whether or not to take the hospital authorities into our confidence in respect to the proposed raid. We held several anxious consultations with Inspector Rumsey upon this matter.

It appeared that the cashier, whose name was Tabor, was in full charge of all financial matters, and the inspector volunteered to sound him out. He reported later that Mr Tabor was a testy gentleman, whose whole life had centered in Beauvoir.

He had an overwhelming sense of the dignity and importance of the institution he served, and the inspector said it would be quite useless to put up any such scheme to him. He would certainly have a fit at the bare mention of such a thing.

"Very well," said Mme Storey coolly; "then as far as Mr Tabor is concerned this must be a bona fide hold-up."

"Suppose he puts up a fight?" asked the inspector anxiously. "He's a determined old party. He is almost certain to be armed, and perhaps his clerks also. You have a big enough risk to run from chance shots outside, without facing a point-blank fire inside. I could not permit that under any circumstances."

"Pull the right wires," suggested Mme Storey, "and introduce a man of your own as clerk in the office."

This was done. Inspector Rumsey's man subsequently reported that there was only one gun in the hospital office. This was an old-fashioned revolver in the drawer of Mr Tabor's desk, which had apparently not been shot off nor cleaned in many years. It was not, however, any the less dangerous on that account.

Since Mr Tabor made a point of being the first in the office every day and the last to leave, our agent said it was doubtful if he could secure the gun beforehand to unload it; but he guaranteed to seize it when the attack was made. We let it go at that.

It fell to my part to make the first preliminary examination of the ground. I confess I did not like it at all. Beauvoir Hospital bore too strong a resemblance to a prison.

The entrance was by a triple gateway from the street. The two narrow side gates were for visitors to the various wards, and the center gate, which was double, admitted to the courtyard and the main building.

The three gates were divided by two little buildings where guards, presumably armed, were on duty at all hours. Visitors to patients were provided with cards of admission, and it was the duty of these men to examine the cards, and set the holders on the right path.

If we took our automobile inside the courtyard, the guards had only to close the iron gates to block us. If we left our car outside, we would have to run the gantlet of the guards on foot.

I should say that the windows of the office looked out on the courtyard; the first shout from the clerks would alarm the guards. In short, it seemed to be just about as perfect a trap as could be devised. I did not like it.

There was a doorman on duty at the main entrance; but he was a doddering old fellow, incapable of putting up any serious resistance. Inside, a corridor ran right and left throughout the length of the old building. You turned to the right, and the first door on your right admitted you to the office.

It was an old-fashioned double door of solid wood; it stood open during business hours. The room was about thirty feet long, with an old-fashioned wooden counter running the length of it, topped by a brass grille some three feet high, with several wickets in it.

At one side a door made of heavy brass wire gave entrance to the clerks' inclosure. I noticed that there was no way out for them, except by this door, thence by the door into the corridor.

I had chosen a Thursday morning for this visit, and they were all busy at a long table in the middle of the room putting the money in pay envelopes. Certainly it was tempting Providence to handle their cash practically in public like that.

When I reported to Mme Storey the difficulty of getting out past the guards, she said:

"Well, there must be other ways out of that old warren. We'll study the floor plans."

Inspector Rumsey, who was looking up the police arrangements in the neighborhood, subsequently informed us that since First Avenue had become an important motor thoroughfare, a motorcycle policeman had been assigned to patrol it; and that he spent a good part of his time standing in front of the hospital. Verily, the difficulties surrounding the adventure seemed to be pyramiding against us!

Mme Storey said thoughtfully: "We have a reputation for originality to maintain. We must do something quite new this time. Let us dispense with a car altogether, and make our getaway by water."

XIII

From the New York *Sphere*, January –, 192–.

THE DUCHESS MAKES ANOTHER HAUL

Beauvoir Hospital the Victim; Loss $67,000

Boldest Robbery in History of City

"The Duchess", that most amazing criminal of modern times, played a return engagement this morning. It scarcely seems possible, but she actually succeeded in capping her own exploits; in exceeding her reputation. This time it was no mere jewelry store that was the object of her raid, but Beauvoir Hospital.

Everybody in town is asking: What next? In the teeth of all the orderlies, police and armed guards who are to be found

around the hospital, she and her gang relieved the office force of
the week's pay roll to the tune of sixty-seven thousand dollars,
and made a clean get-away.

The crime had been carefully planned. The bandits displayed
a perfect familiarity with the rambling old building. They made
their way out through the rear to the bulkhead adjoining the
river, and were picked up by a speedy motor boat. One of their
number was wounded in the retreat, but his comrades carried
him off. As usual there is no clew.

Every Thursday morning an armored car brings the money for
the week's pay roll to Beauvoir Hospital. The amount averages
close to seventy thousand dollars. Though the institution has
doubled and quadrupled in size since those early days, the pay
envelopes are still made up in the office in sight of all and
sundry, just as they were twenty-five years ago. In some manner
this reached the ears of the Duchess, and the inevitable
happened.

At eleven forty-five this morning Emerson Tabor, the cashier
of the hospital, and his five clerks were engaged upon this
regular weekly task. In another fifteen minutes the money would
have been locked in the safe for the noon hour. All six persons
were working at a long table in the hospital office.

They were cut off from the public by a stout wooden counter
running the length of the room, upon which is superimposed a
heavy brass grill. The whole structure is about six feet high.
Four of the clerks were filling the envelopes while Mr Tabor and
another checked them. There was no one else in the office at the
moment except Rudolph Glassberg, of 400 West Ninety-Third
Street, who had called to obtain the address of a former
employee of the hospital. It was this accidental witness of the
affair who was able to give the most comprehensive account of
what happened.

Mr Tabor had just told Mr Glassberg that he had no record of
the employee in question, when a tall, elegantly dressed lady
entered the office. At first glance Mr Tabor was struck by
nothing unusual in her appearance, except that she was rather a
fine lady to be calling at old Beauvoir. She had an envelope in
her hand, which she partly extended toward him.

In a low, musical voice she asked him in what part of the
building that person was to be found. As Mr Tabor put a hand
through the wicket to take the envelope, his wrist was seized in a
grip of steel. The woman dropped the envelope, and from
somewhere about her person whipped a pair of handcuffs.

In a trice the cashier was handcuffed to his own brass grill. He
found himself looking into those baleful cat's eyes with the
narrowed pupils which have been so often described.

Mr Glassberg happened to be looking directly at the woman.
He was dazed by the suddenness of her act. So was Mr Tabor.

For a moment there was no sound. The clerks in the rear had no suspicion of anything wrong. Then Mr Glassberg heard the woman say in her courteous, well-bred voice:

"So sorry to discommode you, but I can't let you get to your gun, you know."

The cashier gave a shout of warning, and yanked at the chain; his clerks jumped up, knocking over their chairs. At that moment the rest of the gang entered swiftly and quietly from the corridor.

Mr Glassberg tried to leave then, but was harshly ordered to remain where he was. He frankly confessed that he squeezed into the farthest corner, not daring to make a sound, nor to stir during what followed.

It was the same gang which held up Fossberg's jewelry store last month; four good looking, well-dressed lads, showing none of the obvious marks of the gunman, none of them over twenty-five years old, and one a mere boy; and the showily dressed, red-haired girl who appears to be the Duchess's first lieutenant. The four men, as if performing a well rehearsed drill, leaped on the edge of the counter, and vaulted over the brass grill.

Mr Tabor shouted to his clerk, William Hughes, to get his gun out. Another clerk, Edward Ensor, beat him to it. Ensor had only been working at the hospital for a few days. He snatched the gun out of the drawer where it was kept and fired at the oncoming bandits.

The shot went wild. Immediately two of the bandits dived, and, tackling Ensor low, flung him to the floor. He was disarmed before he could recover himself. Of the two women clerks, Miss Mary Phillips fainted dead away at the sound of the shot, while Miss Gertie Colpas dived under the table, where she kept up a continuous screaming until all was over.

Mr Glassberg said what with the screaming of the woman, the shouting of Mr Tabor, and his frantic efforts to free himself, the noise in the room was deafening. The bandits coolly disregarded it. No sound escaped from any of them.

Two of the men covered the clerks, while the other two producing black silk bags from under their coats, started sweeping up the money and the pay envelopes on the table. All moved as by clockwork.

When the gang entered, the Duchess coolly closed the door from the corridor. She and her woman aid took up their places one on each side of the door, ready for any one who might enter. The Duchess produced the inevitable little cigar while she waited.

Mr Glassberg said she watched what was going on within the clerks' inclosure with a half contemptuous smile, as one might look at a second rate play. There was something about the woman's unnatural coolness that froze his very blood, he said.

As on the former occasion, the Duchess's attire expressed the very acme of elegant simplicity. She was wearing a severely cut costume of brown, which set off her slender figure to perfection. Inside the collar of the coat was wound a gaily colored silk scarf, and a handkerchief to match it, peeped out of her breast pocket.

Her hat was one of those smart little recent importations that closely outline the shape of the head. Her shoes were smart English brogues, and a pair of chamois gloves completed the ensemble.

Within a minute or so the money was gathered up, and the four men as one, leaped back upon the counter, and vaulted over the brass grill. The Duchess opened the door, and they all ran out into the corridor. Mr Glassberg peeped around the door frame to see what became of them, but did not dare to follow.

At the entrance to the building was stationed John Staley, the doorkeeper; but as he was a man of sixty-nine, and unarmed, he could do nothing to stop the bandits. However, six or more of the husky orderlies for which Beauvoir is famous came tumbling down the stairs from the wards above, attracted by the noise.

Though these men were unarmed, they boldly ranged themselves in a line across the corridor to block the bandits. The latter instantly formed a flying wedge with the biggest among them, the one who resembles an Englishman, in the center, and charged, bowling the orderlies over like nine pins.

It was at this point that the bandits revealed their uncanny knowledge of the premises. Instead of turning out of the main entrance, where they would presently have run into half a dozen armed guards, they opened a door under the stairs, and charged down a concealed flight into the basement.

The basement of the old building at Beauvoir is cut up into a multitude of serving rooms: laundry, kitchen, pantries, store-rooms, and the like; nevertheless, the bandits made their way out unerringly, while the orderlies who were in pursuit of them got lost. The bandits burst through the kitchen, bringing terror into the hearts of cooks and dishwashers, and ran out into the open space between the hospital and the river.

In the summer this is a pleasant grass plot. It is surrounded on three sides by tier above tier of balconies, where, in pleasant weather the patients are wheeled out to get the air.

At this season there were few patients on the balconies; but the doctors, nurses, and orderlies ran out to see what was the matter below, adding their shouts to the uproar. Several shots were fired from the balconies at the fleeing bandits, but none took effect.

They made straight across for the bulkhead alongside the river. Here they met with a check, for their boat could be seen stalled a hundred feet or so out in the stream, the mechanic working frantically to start his engine. A shout of triumph went up from the watchers on the balconies.

At this moment it was touch and go with the Duchess and her pals. Six armed guards had made their way through the hospital, and the bandits were cut off between the buildings and the river. The guards did not immediately rush them, but stood close to the building, firing as fast as they could pull the trigger.

The bandits returned their fire without effect. Finally the Englishman dropped, wounded. Heartened by the sight, the guards charged across the open space, firing as they ran.

However, by this time the motor boat had come alongside the bulkhead; the bandits leaped in pell-mell, carrying their wounded comrade, and the boat shot out into the river.

The guards continued to fire after it, but as the occupants all flung themselves into the bottom of the boat, it is not likely that any more of them were hit. In a moment they had disappeared around the end of a long pier.

The motor boat was a rakish, sharp-prowed mahogany tender of great speed. It had the look of a millionaire's playing, and was, no doubt, stolen for the occasion, though no such loss has as yet been reported to the police. Her name had been painted out. All the observers agreed that the craft was not one which customarily frequents the East River.

Police launch A-22 is stationed in a slip immediately to the south of the hospital, and in less than five minutes she was in pursuit. But the bandit craft was already out of sight down the stream. The police launch was no match for her in speed.

They caught sight of her again off Corlear's Hook; but by that time she had been abandoned, and was already awash. When the police reached the spot she had sunk, leaving only a patch of oil on the surface. What happened to her cannot be known for certain; the police hold to the theory that she was deliberately scuttled.

Children playing in the park at Corlear's Hook told the police that they had seen the mahogany launch come alongside a waiting tug, which had presently passed on, leaving the launch to sink. The tug was too far offshore for her name to be read.

The police are questioning the captain and crew of every tug in the harbor, but it is admitted that the chance of picking up a clue by this means is a slender one. Once again the Duchess appears to have vanished into thin air.

XIV

Such was the first account of the affair. Later editions of the newspapers only amplified and elaborated the story. While a conventional horror of the deed was expressed, you can see by reading between the lines that the ultimate effect of these stories was to glorify the daring and successful bandit.

Such is the evil effect of too much publicity. If a man becomes famous enough, thoughtless persons do not stop to inquire into the quality of his fame.

During the days that followed our gang had to lie very close, for the police were roused to a fury of activity by this "outrage". I suspect that Inspector Rumsey had a very difficult part to play, for he was put in charge of the case. Of all the force, only he and the commissioner were in on the secret.

One problem that faced us was how to return the money to the hospital without giving the whole game away. We solved it by having the same millionaire who had loaned us his automobile on a former occasion come forward and donate to Beauvoir Hospital the sum they had lost. He got great credit for this act.

Stephens was carried to a sanatorium up in Westchester to recover from his wound, which was not a dangerous one. Falseface and Tony were sent under care of Abell to rusticate in a camp belonging to another of Mme Storey's friends in the neighborhood of Saranac Lake.

Abell's real job, of course, was to keep them under surveillance until we were ready to order their arrest. Young Farren was sent off to amuse himself down in Florida.

Mme Storey and I were perfectly safe working in our office every day in our own proper characters; but as she was obliged to keep in touch with Jake the Canvasser, we had to disguise our disguises for the evening. Madge Caswell's reports still held out no hope of reaching the principal through Jake, and it was necessary to take other measures.

I donned a black wig, blackened my eyebrows and lashes, made up my face dead white, and wore a pair of horn-rimmed glasses, while Mme Storey, past mistress in the art of disguise, transformed herself into a shapeless old woman dressed in tawdry finery.

On the night following the robbery we telephoned to Bat Bartley at the Boule' Miche', and asked him to save us a private room. It would be better, we said, if we did not receive our friends that night, however safe they were. The risk was too great. But we wanted to see Jake.

Well, Jake came to us there in due course, and was much amused by our disguises. Mme Storey paid over his share of the loot. We hated to see that good money go, but there appeared to be no help for it.

Jake was in great form. I will pass over all his fulsome praises and compliments; for you are already familiar with his style. The Duchess would become as famous as Jesse James, he said, a national hero. The crown of courage had passed to a woman. And so on.

My mistress let him run on until he said something to the effect that all of us would have to do some hard thinking in order to cap the previous day's work; whereupon Mme Storey held up her hand.

"Nothing doing," she declared firmly.

"Hey?" said Jake, with a falling face.

"I'm done!"

"What!" he cried. "Why, we've just started!"

"No," she said. "I've made a nice little stake out of these two jobs. I'm satisfied. As for publicity, I can scarcely better what I've got. Better quit while I'm on the crest of the wave. You may make out in your newspaper stories that I'm a superwoman, but as a matter of fact I'm just the common or garden variety like any other. And if I try to bite off more than I can chew I'll choke."

"Have you lost your nerve?" he asked with a sneer.

"Not my nerve," said my mistress coolly; "it's as steady as ever it was, and my wits are better. But my body is beginning to rebel. After all, I'm no longer young. A woman of fifty-five, even though she may have kept a passable figure, is not expected to run like a gazelle. When I got home yesterday I collapsed. I had to have a heart stimulant to bring me around."

"Well," said Jake smoothly, "we'll bear that in mind when we're planning our next stunt."

"No," affirmed Mme Storey, "I would not take anything safe and easy, either. I wouldn't appear before the public at all unless I could better this show, and as I don't see my way clear to doing that, I think it's a good place to quit."

Jake lost his smooth air. His distress was very real.

"Wait a minute – wait a minute!" he said. "You don't have to decide anything to-night. This is just a sort of reaction, like.

Just let things run along for awhile. You've earned a good rest. Then my boss may have an idea that will appeal to you. He has the most brilliant mind in America today – a soaring mind."

"Just so," rejoined Mme Storey; "but if you keep on flying higher and higher, you're bound to crash in the end. Not but what I hate to give it up, too," she added pensively. "I love the game. I love to match my wits against those who have money!"

"What'll I say to the boss?" asked Jake plaintively. "He's countin' on you. You ought to hear the way he talked about you over the phone to-day. 'Jake,' he says, 'this is the best material we ever had to work with!'"

"Nice of him to say so," said Mme Storey.

Jake did not perceive the dryness of her tone.

"Oh, the boss is never one to hold back credit from anybody," he said.

For an hour longer he continued to argue with her. By the end of that time she had convinced him that she meant what she said.

He was greatly depressed. More than anything else he was alarmed by a suggestion she let fall, that she was just going to drop out of things and travel.

He finally exacted a promise from her that she would not disappear until he had a chance to consult with the boss. When we left he asked anxiously:

"Be here tomorrow night?"

"Oh, I expect so," said my mistress indifferently. "We can't stay shut up in our rooms all the time."

On the following night Jake turned up with an entirely new line of arguments, which had no doubt been furnished him over the telephone during the day. When all these proved to be of no avail he said with an offhand air:

"How would you like a job inside the organization?"

I started inwardly. So this was where my mistress's elaborate comedy had been tending! I had not perceived her drift before.

"What sort of job?" she asked indifferently.

"To run our advisory department."

"What's that?"

"You would investigate likely plants, and furnish the operators with full details. You would think up big spectacular stunts, plant all the details, and coach the operators."

"Yes," said Mme Storey, "and have somebody else take all the credit!"

"Oh, I don't know," replied Jake. "We could keep the Duchess alive in the public mind, though you never appeared in person."

"What would there be in it for me?"

Jake made a magniloquent gesture.

"Oh, there wouldn't be any difficulty about that. The boss is the soul of generosity."

"Sure. But just what would it run to?"

"Well, say fifty thousand a year."

"Liberal enough," said Mme Storey indifferently; "but it don't appeal to me much. I hate to be tied up in an organization. I like to be on my own."

Jake set himself to work to persuade her. Little by little she allowed it to appear that she was coming around. Finally we heard that which we were silently praying for. Jake said:

"The heads of the organization never meet. It's better so. We have other ways of communicating. But you and the boss would have to have one talk to settle the details."

"Plenty of time for that," said Mme Storey carelessly. "We'd better wait until the search for me lets up a little."

"No need for that," said Jake. "Your present disguise is plenty good enough."

"Well, that's up to the boss," she said, shrugging. "If he wants to see me I'm at his service."

XV

Three days later Mme Storey and I started out to keep our rendezvous with the "boss". You can imagine how my heart was beating. I could scarcely believe that we were in sight of the end of our difficult and dangerous job.

I was tormented with anxiety. So much mystery had been made of this powerful boss that he seemed to me to be invested with almost superhuman attributes. I dreaded lest he might slip through our fingers after all.

We were on our way to the Madagascar Hotel, where we were to ask for Mr Peter Endicott. All the arrangements for the visit had been made with the greatest care. Jake the Canvasser was not to accompany us. Jake had wished Mme Storey to go alone, but she had declined to do so. Any offer that might be made to her must include me, she said; and Jake finally conceded the point.

From the moment when the meeting had first been proposed we had been shadowed, as we were quick to perceive; and thereafter we never came out of the characters of Kate Arkledon and Peggy Ray. Our ordinary haunts knew us not. By day we remained shut up in the little flat on West — Street. There was a telephone in the flat, but we dared not use it; the danger was too great that the boys at the switchboard might have been tampered with.

We finally solved the problem of communicating with Inspector Rumsey by taking a leaf out of Jake's book. We wrote the inspector a letter, and posted it in the mail chute outside the door of our flat.

The inspector could not communicate with us and, before setting out, Mme Storey had armed herself with a pair of handcuffs, intending to make the arrest herself if the police failed her.

The lobby of the Madagascar displayed its usual animated aspect. Since they cut off the front to make a row of shops on the street it is always overcrowded. I felt rather than saw that we were objects of interest to several of the prosperously dressed men who were sitting and standing about. These I supposed to be police, and my heart rose. Inspector Rumsey was not showing himself – his face is too well known – but I had no doubt that he was near.

It appeared that our journey was not to end at the Madagascar. As we made inquiry at the desk, a slender, gentlemanly young chap stepped up from behind us.

"Good morning, ladies," he said, smiling. "I was waiting for you."

"Oh, are you Mr Endicott?" said Mme Storey, not without surprise. She had hardly expected to be received by such a stripling.

"His secretary, at your service. I am to take you to him."

I confess I did not like this at all. Mme Storey appeared quite unconcerned.

"Where is it?" she asked.

"Half an hour's drive. I have a car waiting."

He led the way out. I hoped that the police were behind us, but did not like to turn my head to see. We stood waiting under the glass canopy in front, and presently an inconspicuous sedan drove up. Our conductor, always smiling, opened the door for us, and we drove off. I silently prayed that the police might have a car handy also. In the press of traffic it was impossible to tell if we were being followed.

Our route lay over the Queensboro Bridge and out Queens Boulevard. The young man made agreeable small talk all the way. He had all the *savoir faire* of a diplomatic secretary.

On the bridge and beyond it seemed to me that there were more motorcycle policemen than usual about, and I took hope from that. Perhaps they were under Inspector Rumsey's orders.

We drove very fast. Once on the boulevard we were stopped and warned by a policeman. Later, after we had turned to the right in a busy crossroad, another passed us at great speed and came back a few minutes afterward.

We now turned to the left and lost ourselves in one of the amazing new subdivisions that have sprung up so thickly in that district. Picture to yourself rows of little new wooden houses, all alike, stretching on every side as far as you could see. All designed alike, painted alike, the same number of shingles on each roof, I could swear; built so close together there was but just room for a man to walk between; not a tree in sight, and scarcely a blade of grass.

Thousands upon thousands of the little boxes, all alike. To me it was like a nightmare. Consider the numbing effect of this sameness upon the people who lived there! Then another thought came to me: what an admirable hiding place!

We turned right and left; right and left again so many times I was dizzied. All this was unnecessary, of course; the little streets were all laid out at right angles, and we could have reached our destination with one turn.

There were street signs in the usual hap-hazard New York fashion, but we turned the corners so quickly, and the signs were so hard to find, I could rarely read them. And when at last we came to a stop before one of the little houses, no different from thousands of others, I didn't know what the name of the street was. The number of the house was 154.

"Is this Mr Endicott's home?" asked Mme Storey.

"One of them," said our conductor, smiling.

The instant we were out of the car, it whisked out of sight around a corner. We were admitted by a neat, elderly maid servant who looked as if she had seen all and told nothing.

The inside of the house was as standardized as the outside; the furnishings looked as if they had been purchased *en bloc* from an installment shop. But it was comfortable enough.

The servant requested us to follow her upstairs to take off our things. She led us into the front bedroom above.

"As you have so much to discuss with Mr Endicott," she said in her quiet, courteous voice, "and as it would be imprudent for you to leave, and come back again, he hopes that you will remain as his guests here, until everything is settled."

Mme Storey bowed.

"Does that mean we are prisoners?" I asked when the woman had left us.

"Pooh!" said Mme Storey. "They couldn't keep us in this match-box against our will. We could kick our way out."

The front door closed, and we saw the young man who had brought us, making his way quickly up the street. A moment later we heard a motorcycle. As silently as a shadow, Mme Storey ran to the window, but did not succeed in attracting the rider's attention.

"He was clever to follow us so far into this maze," she said.

"But how can he pick out the house now?" I groaned.

"We'll hang out a sign," she said, fishing in her bag for a pencil. "A sheet of paper. Oh, for a sheet of paper!"

It was not forthcoming.

"Never mind," she said, "the upper part of the house is painted white."

We locked the door, and she stationed me beside it to listen for the return of the maid. She threw up one of the windows, and sitting upon the sill, leaned over and began to pencil her initials in big black letters on the white space between the two windows: R. S. In the absolute sameness of that street, it must have stuck out like a sore finger.

We had the window closed, and were standing decorously in the middle of the room, when the maid returned.

"If you are ready," she said.

"Please lead the way," said Mme Storey.

On the floor below the maid opened the door into the rear room, and stood aside to let us enter. I followed my mistress with a fast heating heart.

It was a narrow room with a single window in the corner, looking out on a cement paved space between two kitchen extensions. It was furnished with a "dining suite" and two easy chairs, one on each side of the gas logs. A man stood with his back to us, looking out of the window.

At the sound of our entrance he turned around, and my heart gave a great jump. *I knew that face!* That clever face with the full, dark, beaming eye of the enthusiast; where had I seen it before?

My brain spun around like a teetotum, and then settled down soberly. I remembered. It was Ambrose G. Larned, the publicity genius; and the last time I had seen him was at Mme Storey's own dinner table!

I stole a glance at my mistress. Under the grease paint her expression was very bland.

"So this is the Duchess!" said our host, coming forward with outstretched hand. "And her trusty lieutenant! Sit down ladies, we have much to talk over."

XVI

Well, there we sat, the three of us, in front of the tawdry fireplace, Mme Storey and I in the two easy chairs, and the unsuspecting Mr Larned between us in a straightbacked chair. My mistress was smoking one of the famous little cigars, and Mr Larned waved a cigarette about while he talked.

Each recognizing a great spirit in the other, they mostly ignored me. I was quite content to look and listen.

"We strike in the spot of our own choosing," Mr Larned said enthusiastically; "and with a high-powered automobile at hand, or as in your case a speedy motor boat, the danger of capture is almost non-existent − that is, if the affair has been properly planned. And no policeman can tell in advance where the next blow will fall.

"Just look at our record during the last few weeks. First, the creation of the bobbed hair bandit with the numerous exploits to her credit; then the robbery of Mme Storey in her office; then the double hold-up of Fossberg's; and finally your magnificent raid on Beauvoir last week to cap the climax. What can the police do? What could Mme Storey do with all her boasted cleverness? Why, nothing.

"A vastly overrated woman, by the way," he went on, lighting a fresh cigarette. "I know her. There is nothing much to her. Publicity has made her. Which is a further illustration of my point. Publicity will do anything."

I heard the doorbell sound somewhere in the house. Mr Larned's eyelids flickered, but he kept right on talking:

"Publicity is man's greatest discovery. He doesn't know what he's got yet. There are any number of professors and practitioners and promoters of publicity; but they haven't scratched the surface of their subject."

I noticed that nobody went to the door. The suspense became almost more than I could bear, sitting still.

"Rather a good scheme this of ours, don't you think?" said Mr Larned. "One directing head, and a number of units working quite independently."

"And taking all the risk," put in Mme Storey slyly.

"Surely," he said with the utmost coolness; "and quite right, too. It would not be fitting for the commanders to expose themselves on the firing line. The individual operators must fail sometimes, but the organization goes on—"

The front door went in with a crash. A second later Inspector Rumsey entered the room, with other men behind him. Larned swelled up like a pouter pigeon.

"How dare you?" he cried. "What do you mean by this outrage?"

"Inspector Rumsey of the police department," said our friend coolly. "You are under arrest." Then he recognized his prisoner. "Ah, Mr Larned, so we meet again!"

Larned still essayed to bluff it out.

"You know me," he cried. "Everybody knows Ambrose G. Larned. How dare you break into my private dwelling?"

"It won't go, Larned," said the inspector smiling. "Thanks to the activities of this lady, we know all about you and your organization. Jake Golden is already under arrest."

"Who is this woman?" queried Larned.

"The Duchess," said Rumsey with relish; "alias Kate Arkledon; but in reality, Mme Rosika Storey."

Larned collapsed like a pricked balloon. The sight was both tragic and absurd. He slunk to one side, and dropped into a chair.

Well, that ended one crime wave. If another one rolled up almost immediately afterward it was not our fault. Abell and a plainclothes man brought a chopfallen little pair of bandits back from Saranac next day. I would not have missed the scene when Mme Storey returned Falseface's ring with a smile.

What an extraordinary psychological study Larned was. I believe he was a little mad. Mme Storey and I visited him in jail. Even in his downfall he played the great man, and displayed no rancor toward her.

He still loved to air his theories on publicity. It was his theories which had led him into crime. He explained that having tasted all the possible successes of a regular business career, he craved a greater excitement; and finally yielded to the temptation of wielding this enormously powerful weapon in secret.

Valentino's Valediction

AMY MYERS

*The film stars of the 1920s are still well known today –
Douglas Fairbanks, Sr., Mary Pickford, Charlie Chaplin,
and, of course, Rudolph Valentino. Valentino's death in 1926
saw huge crowds and mass hysteria. Amy Myers uses the
magnetism of Valentino's character as background in this
following short tale. Amy is best known for her series featuring Anglo-French master chef and sleuth Auguste Didier,
which began in the Victorian era with* Murder in Pug's
Parlour (1986), *but has since moved into the Edwardian age.*

Until the Sheikh galloped into her dreams, Ruby Smart had
been happy enough with her husband Harold. After that,
life at 12, The Cedars was never quite the same. A romp with
Harold on Saturday night, however jolly, bore no comparison
with Rudolph Valentino's dark smouldering eyes as he threw
her across his horse, grating out:

"Lie still, you little fool."

She could tell his voice was deep and sensuous, even though
all you saw at the pictures was his lips moving and the words
flashing up afterwards on the screen. The very thought of his
being near her, bare-chested, nostrils flaring, made her shiver in
anticipation. His hypnotic eyes seared right through her, doing
odd things to her body.

She had been a little taken aback when she found out that
they were doing the same odd things to Gladys Perkins, her

chum at No. 16, but consoled herself that it was nice to have someone with whom she could pore over *Picturegoer*, dissect every sentence of Rudolph's autobiography, wallow in his book of poetry, swap photographs and queue up at the Picturedrome when Harold refused to go. Which was all the time now. *And* he refused to wear sideboards like Rudolph, so how could he blame her for going with Gladys, even if it was three times a week?

Last year she and Gladys had actually seen Rudolph, when he came to London for the first night of *The Eagle*. She and Gladys had taken the train to Charing Cross and walked all the way to the Marble Arch Pavilion – they'd had to, because the traffic was at a standstill. The newspaper next day said there were 5,000 people gathered outside, and she was one of them. She and Gladys had fought their way almost to the front, and Rudolph had looked right at her. Gladys said it was her he looked at, but Ruby knew differently. After all, Gladys was a blonde and it was obvious Rudolph preferred dark-haired women like Ruby. Ruby had fainted dead away, and when she got home Harold hadn't been in the least sympathetic. It had been a comedown returning home to Harold with her fish and chips making her gloves all greasy, but in her soul she was still with Rudolph being rescued from her runaway carriage by the handsome Cossack lieutenant, and this comforted her a lot.

"If only Harold had a chest like Rudolph instead of being all flabby and hairy," Ruby had wailed to Gladys.

"I'll tell you someone who has," Gladys giggled.

"Frank?" Ruby couldn't believe that of Gladys's meek and mild husband. He was even plumper than Harold. He and Frank were chums in a way, because they were both commercial travellers. Harold reckoned he had more style than Frank owing to the fact that Frank only dealt in kitchen goods, but Harold travelled in ladies' stockings. It sounded funny to Ruby, the way he put it, travelling in ladies' stockings, but when Harold got red in the face she stopped laughing. He did not like his pride hurt.

"No. Cyril Tucker," Gladys said.

"Who's he?" Ruby asked blankly, not being able to remember any film stars of that name.

"Keep a secret?"

"Of course," Ruby breathed, leaning closer.

"Our milkman."

Ruby was an innocent in such matters. "How do you know, Glad?"

"He obliges."

"Obliges what?"

"When he comes for his money on a Friday, he – well, you know."

Ruby didn't.

"He doesn't mind doing a Valentino for me," Gladys amplified.

"Glad!" Ruby was overawed. "You mean he takes off his shirt for you?"

"More than that, Rube."

Ruby's bow-shaped mouth opened wide in shock. "Oh, Glad!" And when Gladys sniggered, she continued with dignity, "I'm going right home now and pretend you never told me that." She'd never taken much notice of their milkman. He wore the usual blue and white striped apron over his clothes and a cap, and she'd not looked at him much otherwise. When she began to think though, she supposed he was quite good-looking. How Gladys *could*, however. She decided not to see Glad for at least a day.

And so it might have ended, had Harold not complained about having sardines on toast for his tea two days running. It put her in a bad mood, and she told him he was jolly lucky to get any tea at all, considering she'd only just got back from a reshowing of *The Four Horsemen of the Apolocalyse*. What did he expect? she hurled at him.

"What I expect," Harold said pathetically, "is a wife who doesn't have Rudolph Valentino tucked up in our spare room."

"Oh, Harold." Ruby was mortified at this unfair criticism. "You can't deny me that. Here I am every day all alone."

The spare room was her temple – or, rather, her tent, her Room of Araby. It was swathed in yards and yards of white sheeting and curtain net from Woolwich Market, and below it was a divan with a pillow and cover almost exactly like in the film. From the walls Rudolph gazed down at her in adoration as the Sheikh, the Young Rajah, Monsieur Beaucaire (holding a lute in a way which Gladys said looked so *naughty*), and as Julio, the sultry tango dancer. Words from the films adorned each wall, painstakingly typed out on their old typewriter, together with the sheet music of "The Sheikh of Araby", which she thumped out on the piano wistfully when Harold was away. (He said it disturbed his digestion.)

"I don't know why you do it," he said, perplexed.

"I just like him."

"He looks like a pouf."

"A what?"

Harold reddened. "Never you mind."

"I won't have you being rude about Rudolph. You're just jealous."

"I'm not," Harold cried defiantly.

"Oh, Harold." Ruby relented, sighing deeply. "If only you were more masterful."

Ruby was never quite sure what had made her take the final step in providing herself with her own sheikh. She thought it was probably the waste.

Looking round her Room of Araby the day after that conversation with Harold, it occurred to her that her body was crying out for the intimate attentions of a sheikh. Unfortunately Rudolph himself was far away and could not be counted upon for this task. He would never realize how desperately she needed him. She was forced to face the fact that meeting his eyes across the crowd was the nearest she would ever get to him. And Harold wasn't sufficient replacement. When he rolled over, just grunting, "Goodnight, old girl," she was left with a feeling that life must have more to offer her.

She slept alone in the Room of Araby when he was away on his travels, imagining her sheikh by her side, and those eyes staring down at her. Longingly, desirously. In her heart, she was Lady Diana Mayo from the film, not Ruby Smart, and at last she had decided she could wait no longer.

Cyril Tucker, or Rudolph as he was to her, had proved to be everything Gladys had said and more. It was a little hard the first time, as he took off that awful cap, she saw immediately that the sleeked-down dark hair was a considerable improvement. And those sideboards! She had self-consciously led the way upstairs, wondering if her stocking tops were showing under the scallops of her short skirt and trying to pull it down

in case. Once his apron, waistcoat, shirt and vest went, magic
had taken the place of doubts as to the wisdom of this venture.
His manly chest flexed magnificently as he strode meaningfully
towards her.

Ecstatically, she had swooned in his arms, then felt herself
lifted high in the air, then tossed mercilessly on to the divan.
Her body ached for him, but she trembled with delicious fear, as
had Lady Diana Mayo.

"Why have you brought me here?" she uttered the famous
words.

Her eyes closed, then flew open again, so as not to miss a
moment of this rapture. Slowly, silently, menacingly, he bent
over her, eyes fixed desirously upon her person.

"Are you not woman enough to know?" he grated on cue.
Then his hands removed the white jumper Mum had knitted
her last Christmas, he patted her feet, just as Rudolph had in
The Four Horsemen of the Apocalypse, then slowly and sensu-
ously drew off Harold's best artificial silk stockings from her
legs and invitingly stroked Lady Diana's cami-knickers.

"Oh, Rudolph," she sighed, happy at last as she lay back to
accept her fate.

It had become a regular fixture. Gladys had already bagged
Friday lunchtime, and even Rudolph could not manage more
than one Lady Diana a morning so it was arranged that Tuesday
afternoon after he finished his rounds would be a very nice time
to call.

When, at the beginning of August 1926, Harold announced
he had to go to York, up north somewhere, for four weeks,
Saturday afternoon was temporarily added to the itinerary.
After all, she had several weeks to pass before the London
release of *Son of the Sheikh*, and needed something to take her
mind off the long hours of waiting.

Ruby looked up with red-rimmed eyes as Gladys came through
the back door. She too was clad all in black. They had been in
mourning for several days now. It was lucky Harold was still
away up north or he'd have kicked up such a fuss. Frank never
said a word, according to Gladys. He understood. Frank always
did, not like Harold, Ruby thought enviously. How could
anyone not share their grief? Rudolph was dead. Gladys's

and her lives were over. Romance had ended. There would be no more films after *Son of the Sheikh*.

The tragedy had come out of the blue. First came the shock that Rudolph was ill, and had to have an operation for gastric ulcer and appendicitis. Then the relief when it was successful and he was said to be recuperating well. Then came the terrible news that he was dead. It was unbelievable. How could they let him die? Each morning she seized the newspaper to read every tiny detail. She realized that she was not alone in her loss. Women, and men, too, had flocked to Campbell's Funeral Parlour on Broadway, and mounted police had to be called in to prevent the crowds storming the parlour in their grief. Inside lay his – oh she could hardly bear to read it – poor body in a bronze coffin, his beautiful face and shoulders exposed.

"Look, Ruby!" Gladys sniffled, thrusting yet another newspaper under Ruby's nose. "Isn't that Harold?"

"Harold? Glad, don't make jokes at a time like this." Ruby glanced at the photograph of the queue waiting to enter the Parlour. And, yes, it did indeed look rather like Harold. But how could it be? She supposed that could have been his Homburg hat, and that certainly resembled his samples' case of ladies' stockings. Nevertheless Ruby was quite sure it could not have been Harold.

"He's up north somewhere, so it can't be."

"Looks like him, Rube." They agreed it was queer but they had a more pressing problem to consider: Cyril. Was it, or was it not, morally right to continue with Cyril's services, when Rudolph himself was dead?

Gladys was in no doubt that it was. After all, she explained: "It's like his spirit come to bless us, isn't it?"

Ruby found that very consoling. Even so she thought it right to wear a black armband when she saw Cyril on Saturday, and insisted on keeping it on after he had ripped all her clothes off, even her rubber corsets, and had her shivering helplessly before him. Cyril had sniggered when he saw it, and she reproved him.

"Don't laugh, please." Sometimes it occurred to her that Cyril was a little common.

"Whatever you say, Ruby. You're the boss."

"No, *you* are, Rudolph."

Cyril had belatedly remembered his role, picked her up and thrown her on the divan most satisfactorily. (On one terrible occasion he had missed and it had been most painful.) His eyes smouldered and if only she could ignore his flashy new combinations, the illusion would be complete. What did he think she had provided all the proper costumes for? She had given him Don Alonzo's gaucho hat, his matador's jacket, Monsieur Beaucaire's wig, his Sheikh's turban complete with tassel, and the Young Rajah outfit. Finally, the offending combinations were removed.

"Lie still, you little fool," he whispered, looking almost as handsome as Rudolph himself.

Even though Rudolph was dead, it was a great comfort to Ruby to know that he lived on at 12, The Cedars.

"Yes, it's probably me." Harold gave a cursory look at the newspaper picture on his return on the Monday evening.

Ruby, who had assumed by now that the man in the photograph could not possibly have been her husband, was flabbergasted. "But you said you were going to York."

"*New* York, I said."

Ruby tried to take this in, and fastened on the one salient point. "But why go to the funeral parlour? You didn't even like Rudolph." Then a warm glow spread through her. "Oh, Harold, did you do it for me?"

"No, Ruby. I killed him, you see. Then I thought I'd take a last look at my handiwork."

Ruby didn't understand. "What do you mean, killed him?"

"I murdered him."

With this pronouncement, Harold sat down with the *Daily Mail* as though he were asking for a cup of tea.

"Who?" she shrieked.

"Your precious Rudolph Valentino."

"Don't make fun of me, Harold."

"I'm not, Ruby. You said I should be more masterful, so I went out there and murdered him."

The room spun around her. "You'd never kill anyone."

"I never wanted to before." There was a touch of complacency in Harold's voice. He was smiling in a most peculiar way, and Ruby felt quite uneasy. The newspapers said Rudolph died of complications after the operation, so were they covering something up? If so, what was it? And if Harold had murdered him, what was her husband doing safely back home instead of being locked up in Sing Sing like in the films?

Then she realised this was all nonsense. Harold was pulling her leg. "He died of complications after a gastric ulcer and appendicitis," she said scornfully, "and anyway he was in hospital when he died."

"Recuperating on the ninth floor of the Polyclinic Hospital. Armed guards all around."

"There you are then. You couldn't have murdered him." Not that Ruby had *really* thought he had, but all the same it was a relief to know he couldn't possibly have done so. But why was he still grinning at her?

"Ah, but it wasn't a gastric ulcer, was it? It was arsenic," Harold informed her.

"Arsenic?" she shrieked. "That's poison."

"Yes and it doesn't half do nasty things to your stomach."

"How could you get close enough to Rudolph to poison him?" Ruby hardly dared breathe his sacred name in company with such an outrage.

"It was easy. He was taken ill at a party, and I was there."

"How did *you* get to a party with Rudolph?" She couldn't believe it, no, she couldn't.

"I met this fellow in the hotel, who told me he was a chum of your precious Rudy. He said he was off to a party in an hour of two being given for him by a friend of his, Barclay something or other. So I told him my wife was a fan and she'd never forgive me if I let an opportunity to meet him slip by." Harold giggled. "I got this rat poison easily enough, and poured it into this drink I handed him." Ruby gave a faint cry. "When the party broke up, I followed the Great Lover back to his hotel and waited outside for a while. Sure enough, an ambulance was called an hour or two later and off he went to hospital. I bet he didn't look so handsome then." He glanced at her stupefied face. "Shall I show you the tin? Would that convince you?"

"Harold," she moaned, backing away from him. She was already convinced. There was his picture in the newspaper and he knew details the papers hadn't revealed. She, Ruby Smart of Blackheath (well, Woolwich really, only it was nearly Blackheath) was responsible for the death of Rudolph Valentino. There'd be a trial. She'd have to give evidence. She would call it Blackheath then. All these thoughts raced through her mind and then her brain clarified.

'I'll have to go to the police."

Harold looked serious. "Of course, Ruby. I'd expect you too. It's only right. I'm ready to face the consequences like a man."

Feeling the whole weight of the world on her shoulders, Ruby put on her best dress next morning, and took the 11.18 train to Charing Cross. This was too serious a matter for the Woolwich police station. She had to go to the top. She walked self-consciously to Scotland Yard on the Embankment. She wasn't even nervous. She was doing this for Rudolph, sacrificing her own husband for justice.

The gentleman at the desk was very polite when she said she'd come to report a murder. Had it just happened, he asked? No, she explained, about two weeks ago in America. She was asked to wait and another gentleman came almost straightaway, though he wasn't in uniform, which rather disappointed her.

Ruby sat primly on the chair, smoothing her skirt down. It would never do to display too much thigh here. It would be letting Rudolph down.

"You tell me about it, Mrs Smart," the policeman said encouragingly. "Who's dead?"

And so she explained everything.

"Rudolph Valentino, eh?" was all he commented.

To her great indignation, she could see he was trying not to laugh.

"Well, Mrs Smart, I think your husband is having you on, don't you?"

"No," she replied said truthfully. "He wouldn't do that." But then she wondered whether perhaps he was right. After all, she had been so sure it was York Harold was going to. The policeman then sent for someone to make her a nice cup of tea, and assured her, as he ushered her out, that he would make enquiries with the FBI in America.

That sounded right to Ruby, but she ventured to ask, "When will you arrest Harold? I'll have to pack something for him, you see."

"We'll let you know," he replied gravely. "It'll be out of my hands, Mrs Smart.'' Greatly relieved, Ruby had her tea and left. After all, Harold knew she was coming here, so she wasn't worried about getting home quickly – even though she suddenly realized it was Tuesday and she'd forgotten to cancel Cyril's visit. Harold must have been at work, though, and even if he were home early Cyril would have thought up some excuse. When she got back home, Harold was indeed there, however. He was watering the tomatoes. A keen gardener, was Harold.

"I've done it," she announced, just a little uncertain of her reception.

"Oh good. By the way, Ruby, I've put a little memento from New York for you in the spare room."

She flew upstairs, half expecting to find Rudolph's dead body, maybe even something personal to him. Heart aflame, she could see just a single red rose, very withered – as one would expect if Rudolph had handed it to Harold two or three weeks ago. Underneath, however, was a little note from Harold:

"Ha, ha, I was joking, Ruby."

She didn't know whether to be furious or relieved. She decided on fury for tonight and then she'd relent tomorrow.

The next morning she duly relented. First of all, she'd found the receipts from his hotel while he'd been away, and that had been in York, not America. So it was a joke, although one in very poor taste. Never mind. Perhaps since he was disappointed yesterday, her very own Rudolph in the form of Cyril would come this afternoon instead. After all, she and Gladys had agreed Valentino was immortal, and so she could mourn him through Cyril. That's what Gladys was going to do, anyway.

Strangely, no milk had been delivered that morning. It didn't arrive until lunchtime, and was then delivered by a new unknown milkman. "Where's our usual man?" Ruby asked, trying to sound as if she didn't care.

"Don't know, missis. Didn't turn up for work."

Now that *was* unlike Cyril. Perhaps he was ill, she thought, although he had certainly been in the pink of health last week. He'd danced the tango with her, she swathed in a sheet, he barechested. It was a preliminary to a most exciting sequel, when he steered her to the divan, whipped off her sheet, and proceeded to treat her very masterfully indeed.

"What's up, Ruby?" asked Harold, who had belatedly told her he had the week off.

"Our milkman's ill," Ruby said, trying not to go pink.

"He's getting quite a reputation round here," Harold observed.

"For not delivering milk?"

"With the ladies. So Frank says."

Ruby was instantly alert. "I haven't heard."

"You wouldn't." Harold replied darkly. "Wouldn't be surprised if some jealous husband hadn't done him in."

No milk? Frank involved? Ruby couldn't wait for Harold to go out so she could run round to Gladys's. At last, he went, and the minute Gladys saw Ruby she burst into tears.

"Rudolph's dead," she moaned.

"Well, I know that, Glad. It's awful but Rudolph's in heaven now."

"Not him. Our Valentino. Cyril."

"*Cyril?*" Ruby went white. What was this all about?

"Strangled with a stocking, he was," Gladys continued. "Found in the woods at Shooter's Hill."

"I can't believe it," Ruby gasped. "Not Cyril."

Even as she said it, though, she thought of Harold being alone in the house when Cyril would have called yesterday. Thought of what Harold had said about jealous husbands, and wondered if by any terrible chance Harold knew about Cyril somehow. But how could he? They'd been so careful, she and Gladys. There was no doubt there was something odd about Harold yesterday though. Yet how would Harold have got the body to Shooter's Hill? Almost instantly she realised how he could have managed it. Behind The Cedars was a back alleyway which the dustmen used. Cyril used to leave his horse and cart there out of sight when he called as Valentino. All Harold would have had to do was hide the body amongst the churns and bottles, put Cyril's cap and big apron on and drive off. He liked driving horses and carts. He'd told her once it all came of having an auntie who lived out Dartford way in the country.

Ruby's imagination worked overtime.

"What kind of stocking was it?" she blurted out the question without thinking how odd this sounded.

"How would I know?" Gladys shrugged.

When Harold came back with the evening papers, it was all over the front cover. "That's our milkman," she said to him, as he hung up his coat and handed it to her to read.

"That's right," Harold said in his jolly tone.

"It says he was strangled with a silk stocking."

"Two, actually."

"Two?" Ruby wailed. "How do you know?"

"One stocking is strong, so I tell my ladies," Harold carefully explained. "But it's not that strong. Our milkman was a big man, Ruby. Bigger than Valentino. But then you'd know that, wouldn't you?"

Ruby couldn't speak for fear at first, then she managed to say, "What can you mean, Harold?"

"I said some jealous husband probably did him in. It was me. I've been jealous of him for some time. He would keep leaving his blessed turban in the spare room. I couldn't stand it, Ruby. I was joking about the first Valentino, but I decided to murder this one for real. I got the idea in York. There was an American newspaperman in the hotel who got all the details about Valentino's death, more than the papers here carried. So I decided to act. Do you know, Ruby, I believe I'm becoming very masterful indeed."

Ruby let out one long wail, as Harold went on to describe exactly how he'd killed Cyril Tucker and how he'd got the body to Shooter's Hill – just the way she'd thought. He even considerately described a birthmark on Cyril's chest for her, just in case she should be in any doubt.

"I suppose you'll have to tell the police, otherwise they'll suspect all the other husbands around here," Harold said, using his jolly voice again.

"All?" Ruby repeated faintly.

"Oh yes. Our Rudolph was quite a Casanova. Quite a Valentino in fact. He had a day for each of you. You weren't the only one. I wonder what you'll all do now?"

Ruby suddenly found her voice. "I'm going to tell on you. You killed my very own Rudolph."

"I'm glad you believe me, Ruby. I did bring his *Monsieur Beaucaire* wig with me to convince you. I found it in the cart."

Ruby screamed. Sobbing, she ran from the room. She had to get back to Scotland Yard to tell them the terrible truth. She didn't even stop to put her best dress on this time, and she ran all the way from Charing Cross to the Embankment. She was quite out of breath by the time she finally panted up to the front desk.

"It's me again, Mrs Ruby Smart," she told the man.

He grinned at her. "I'll take your statement, madam."

"No, I must see the policeman I saw yesterday."

She had to wait some time on this occasion, and when he appeared she wasn't taken to another room, but had to tell him the awful truth then and there.

"My husband did it. Rudolph Valentino, no, I mean the milkman in the woods. He's Valentino. My husband murdered him." She saw the disbelieving look in his eyes, and struggled on desperately. "It was really Cyril Tucker, well you know that, but we call him Rudolph Valentino, and my husband—"

"Now, Mrs Smart, we've already arrested a man in connection with that. Frank Perkins, I think he lives further up your street."

"Frank? But he didn't, he couldn't. Oh no, you've got it all wrong."

"We had good reason to arrest him, Mrs Smart. You'll see it all in the papers tomorrow no doubt, so I'll tell you. He had all the Valentino kit in his study, poor fellow. Wigs, turbans, whips. Round the bend with jealousy. So you go home and have a nice cup of tea, Mrs Smart."

She wasn't even entitled to receive one here today. Frank couldn't possibly have been involved. It was obvious Harold was trying to blame it on Frank and now they weren't even listening to her, and Harold would go scot free. Perhaps it was all a joke. Perhaps Frank really had done it, but somehow she knew that couldn't be true. Anyway, she'd done her best, and it wasn't her fault they wouldn't listen. She put her key in the lock and turned it. As she kicked off her shoes inside so as not to dirty the desert-coloured carpet (her choice), she could hear voices from upstairs which was odd. And odd sounds too. Thumps and giggles.

Coming from the Room of Araby.

Indignant and terrified at the same time, she raced up the stairs, as she heard the grating sound: "Lie still, you little fool."

It must be one of her gramophone records. It must be. Heart pounding she threw open the door.

Rudolph Valentino in sheikh's outfit, minus the top half, but including a whip, didn't even look up. Below him Lady Diana Mayo sighed in ecstasy. Gladys had found another sheikh.

"Harold! What are you doing?" Ruby moaned.

Harold grinned before he turned back to his captive: "Are you not woman enough to know?"

Skip

EDWARD MARSTON

You may have already noticed that boxing has been a recurrent theme in several of the stories, and in a few more to come. It takes centre stage in this story. World champion boxers became amongst the first superstars in the 1920s. The match between Gene Tunney and Jack Dempsey on 23 September 1926, brought in the largest ever crowd for a championship fight. What better place for a whodunnit.

Keith Miles, who writes as Edward Marston and, for that matter, as Conrad Allen, Martin Inigo and Christopher Mountjoy, has written many historical novels, perhaps the best known being the Domesday Book series which began with The Wolves of Savernake *(1993). His architectural mysteries, featuring Merlin Richard, are set somewhat closer to the 1920s and include* Perspective *(1997) and* Saint's Rest *(1999).*

Philadelphia, 1926

When the cops arrived at the scene, there wasn't much left of the body. If you choose a locomotive as your murder weapon, you can rely on it to do the job properly. Most times, they bring a coffin to carry away the corpse. All they needed on this occasion was a sack. It was one of the worst crimes ever perpetrated in Philly. Who on earth could do such a thing?

I never met a guy who was as smart as Skip Halio. He had a mind like a razor and a tongue that could talk a bird out of a tree.

Skip didn't get either of them things out of book learning. No, sir. He hated school like the plague. Got expelled at least three times for activities that were not considered to be either scholarly or, for that matter, entirely wholesome. At least, that's the way Skip tells it and he's the sort of man who somehow makes you *believe* him. For a time, anyway.

His real name was Elmer Duane Halio but everyone called him Skip. I thought it was because of his walk – a funny, skipping action on tiptoe – but that wasn't the reason at all. Skip was a gambler who worked exclusive in the field of sport. He'd take bets on anything. Usually, he made a profit. When he didn't, and when angry punters were demanding their winnings, Skip just skipped town. Apart from a wad of money, the most important thing in his pocket was a railroad timetable.

As I was driving him in my cab that morning, he talked freely. You can learn a lot about a guy on a long journey. I'm a good listener. I find that I get bigger tips that way.

"Always know how soon you can beat it from a place," he told me. "Choose a hotel near the station in case you wear out your welcome. When you have to skip – skip fast!"

"I'll remember that," I said.

"The thing is, Walter – I'm telling you this as a friend – that you can always go back in the fullness of time. Get me? Tempers cool, memories fade. At the racetrack in Saratoga, I was making big bucks by offering the kind of odds that a betting man just can't refuse. One day," admitted Skip, pulling on his cigar, "an outsider comes in at 100-1 and I don't have enough dough to meet my commitments. So what did I do? I skipped town. I high-tailed it out of there with a dozen guys baying at my heels. Coupla years later – listen to this, Walt – I go back there, wearing a new suit and a new mustache and not a soul recognizes me. That means I can work Saratoga once more."

"So what are you doing in Philly?"

He laughed. "You need to ask a question like that?"

"Ain't no races on this week, Skip."

"There's something far better than a string of horses pounding their way round a track, Walter. Two men, filled with ambition and darkness, thirsting for blood, ready to kill each other."

"The big fight," I said, catching his drift. "Dempsey versus Tunney."

"That's it, my friend," he agreed, stretching forward to slap me on the shoulder. "William Harrison Dempsey, Heavyweight Champion of the World, against James Joseph Tunney, the challenger."

"I thought it was Jack Dempsey versus Gene Tunney."

"Those are just the names they fight under."

"Oh, I see."

"Though Dempsey is also called the Manassas Mauler."

"What do they call Tunney?"

"Ask me after the fight."

"Who's going to win?"

"I am," he said, flashing me that grin of his. "I am, Walter."

Skip's confidence was amazing. It sort of oozed out of him. You could see it in the way he dressed, hear it in the way he talked. When he came into a room full of strangers, he skipped in like he owned the place. Within minutes, he'd be on first-name terms with just about everyone. But it was when it came to women that Skip was really in his element. Don't ask me what his appeal was. All I know is that it worked.

I mean, it's not as if he was handsome. He was short and fat with one of those squashed tomato faces that make you feel sorry for the guy. Then you'd notice the suit he was wearing, and the rings on his fingers, and that huge gold watch he liked to fish out of his waistcoat pocket. You'd smell the smoke from his Havana cigar and know you were in the presence of money. Okay, he was flashy. He liked to brag. Skip Halio had the air of a veteran carpetbagger. But women – some women – fall for that kind of thing.

Millie Eberhart was one of them. She worked at the hotel.

"What time d'you get off, Millie?" said Skip.

"Why're you asking me that, Mr Halio?"

"I told you – call me Skip."

"We're not allowed to get too friendly with the guests."

"So what're you gonna do – punch me on the nose instead?"

Millie giggled. She had a wonderful giggle. Her face lit up, her head was tossed back and those two big, round, succulent breasts of hers bobbed up and down for the best part of a minute. Skip couldn't take his eyes off them. Leaning across the bar counter, he lowered his voice to a seductive whisper.

"You on duty this evening, Millie?" he said.

"No, Mr Halio."

"That mean you're open to offers?"

"I'm afraid not, Mr Halio."

"Ah," he went on, noting her tone of regret, "in other words, you wish that you *did* have some free time. That correct?"

"I'm not saying."

"Hey – don't be coy with me, honey. There's only two of us here."

"I know, but I'm supposed to be working."

"Entertaining a guest *is* working, Millie. And you sure as hell are entertaining me. I just hate to think that the most exciting thing that's gonna happen to you today is to serve me a glass of lemonade."

Millie Eberhard was a full-figured woman in her late twenties, one of those pretty gals who can look almost beautiful when you see them, in a flattering light, all gussied up. She'd been working behind that bar for over five years now and was used to customers trying to hit on her. Most of the time, she pretended that she didn't even hear their brash propositions or their sly innuendoes. Millie had certainly never taken up any of the invitations that routinely came her way. She had standards. Until, that is, Skip Halio turned on his charm.

"I'm new in town," he explained, beaming at her. "All I need is a guide, for a couple of hours, to show me the sights of Philly."

"I'm sorry, Mr Halio. I can't help you."

"Would you like to, Millie?"

"I don't think I should answer that, sir."

"Why not?"

"Because I'm married."

"So am I," he said, pointing to one of the rings on his left hand. "That means it's perfectly safe. We pick up a cab, hit a few nightclubs then I deliver you back to your husband without a fingerprint on you. Where's the harm in that?"

"It won't work, Mr Halio."

"How do you know if you don't try it?"

"I've got plans for tonight."

"Then how about tomorrow?"

"Look, Mr Halio—"

"Millie," he interrupted, putting a gentle hand on her arm, "don't be frightened of me. I'm not suggesting that we run off and commit bigamy. You're happily married and so am I. All I want is the pleasure of your company for a while. You're my type. I could tell it at a glance. "Come on," he said, squeezing her arm softly. "Gimme a chance, will you? What can you lose?" He released her arm. "Or, to put it another way, when was the last time a guy was ready to buy you a meal for a hundred bucks?"

Millie's eyes widened in surprise. Nobody had ever spent that kind of dough on her. She lived in a world where a two-dollar tip was the most she could expect. Yet someone was prepared to lay out fifty times that amount to show his appreciation of her. Millie was tempted. Skip Halio clearly had money to burn.

"Think it over," he suggested.

Millie was uncertain. "I don't know. I really don't."

"Sleep on it tonight."

"What do I tell my husband?"

"That's up to you, honey. Though my guess is that you got nothing to worry about. Your husband trusts you. He knows you're not in the habit of going out with guests."

"That's right, Mr Halio. I'm not."

"Then I'm the exception to the rule."

"I haven't said that I will yet."

"But you promise to give it every consideration?"

"Maybe."

"I'll settle for that. Goodbye, Millie."

"Goodbye, Mr Halio."

"Ah-ah," he said, wagging a finger. "The name is Skip."

"Okay, then – goodbye, Skip."

Millie giggled again. She was hooked.

Until he blew into town, I hadn't taken much interest in gambling. I hate playing cards for money and I've never placed a bet on a horse in my life. Mind you, I've met dozens of guys who have, real suckers, always down on their luck, always boring you with stories of how they almost cleaned up, always trying to borrow those few bucks that they're convinced they can turn into a fortune. Dreamers, all of them. It ain't never going to happen. Why? Because they're up against the pros like Skip Halio, seasoned experts, smooth-talking jaspers who live on their wits and who make sure that they live well.

The only way you can hope to make a killing is by getting to know one of these privileged insiders, hard-nosed masters of their trade who seem to have a telepathic relationship with every horse that runs, every baseball player who picks up a bat, every golfer who steps on a tee in a major championship, and every boxer who puts his life on the line. In short, with someone like Skip Halio. Sniffing the chance to make some real money for once, I did my best to befriend him.

"Hi, Skip," I said. "Just bought me a ticket."

"Didn't know you was a fight fan, Walter."

"I'm not, but something tells me this bout is gonna be special."

"Oh, it is," said Skip, chuckling. "I can vouch for that."

I bumped into him outside the Sesquicentennial Stadium, the only place in Philadelphia big enough to host such an event. After queuing for hours, I paid my money and made my own small contribution to what turned out to be a two million dollar gate. Lots more dough would be generated by betting. Skip was clearly determined to have his share of it.

"I been reading the newspapers," I told him.

"So?"

"Most of them reckon that Dempsey is clear favorite."

"Then why not stick your money on Jack?"

"I got my doubts, Skip."

"What d'you mean?"

"Well, it seems that Dempsey hasn't had a fight for three years."

"Except with his wife," he said with a chuckle.

"The guy must be outa condition."

"Don't you believe it, Walter. The reason Jack has kept the title on ice for three years is that he can make more money out of the ring than inside it. Last year, he notched up half a million bucks as a vaudeville and movie star. Everyone loves a champ. But he has to *look* like a champ," he added, adopting a fighting pose. "That means he has to keep in shape. Jack's trained hard for this fight. He'll get into that ring real mean."

"You backing him to win?"

"I'm offering odds of 4-1 on Tunney."

"But he's had over sixty fights with only one defeat."

"That's because he's never been tested. Look at the guys he's been in with – second-raters and no-hopers. Besides, they weren't all victories for Tunney. Some of those fights ended with no decision."

"They say that Tunney can move like lightning."

"Then how come someone as slow as Harry Greb beat him? Okay, Tunney's a good-looking guy who can prance around a ring like a ballet dancer but he hasn't got the punch to finish off Dempsey. Jack will split him in two."

"You advising me to bet on Dempsey, then?"

"It's your choice, Walter."

"Can't you just give me a hint?"

"I've told you the odds I'm offering. How big a hint do you need?"

"Sounds to me as if Dempsey is a cert."

"Nothing's certain in the fight game," warned Skip. "Look at Jess Willard. Six foot, five inches, weighing near on three hundred pounds. When he took the title from Jack Johnson, everyone said he'd hold it for a decade or more. Then along comes this unknown from Colorado, this hobo by the name of Dempsey. Nobody gave him a chance."

"Yet he beat Willard to a pulp in three rounds," I said. "At the start of the fourth, someone threw in a blood-soaked towel from Willard's corner." I smiled quietly. "I been reading up on Dempsey's career."

"Enough to make you put money on the guy?"

"Not yet."

"What's holding you back?"

"I always got a soft spot for the underdog."

"Underdogs go under."

"Dempsey didn't go under against Willard."

"Jack is one in a thousand, that's why?"

"What about Tunney? I like what I've heard about him."

"In that case – if you promise to keep this between the two of us – I'll give you odds of 5-1. Just think, Walter. Give me ten bucks and you could walk way with fifty."

"Unless you get to the railroad station first," I pointed out.

He laughed. "Oh, I don't aim to skip town this time."

"You sure?"

"Dead sure. I got the betting rigged so I can't lose. Besides," he said, airily. "I got personal reasons for staying around for a while. Philly is growing on me. Tunney wins, you get your dough. That's a promise."

"Okay," I decided. "Let's shake on it."

Millie Eberhard had also decided to trust him. The first night she went out with Skip Halio was a revelation. Prohibition was keeping most of the restaurants in the city dry but he knew exactly where to take her to get the very best champagne. Millie had never tasted food like it or danced to the music of the finest band in Philly. Being with Skip was exhilarating.

"You never told me where your wife lives," she said.

"Let's not talk about her. Tonight is a night when my wife and your husband don't even exist."

"I just wondered. Is she far away?"

"Far enough," he said. "She's in Chicago."

"I've always wanted to go there, Skip."

"Who knows? Maybe you will one day."

Millie giggled. "You gonna invite me, then?"

"We'll see."

"Will you be coming to Philly again soon?"

"Now that I've met you, I'll have a job keeping away."

It wasn't just the delicious meal in the luxurious surroundings that excited Millie. She was being given a glimpse into a world of the elite, the freemasonry of the wealthy and powerful. Skip pointed out the more celebrated diners to her with the ease of a man who'd rubbed shoulders with Presidents.

"That's Andrew Mellon," he said, knowledgeably, "and the guy on the table behind him is Joseph Pulitzer. I reckon you never been in a restaurant before with a Biddle, a Rockefeller and a Roosevelt, have you? Not to mention the greatest baseball player of all time – Babe Ruth. See him in the corner? He's the big fella, chewing his food like he's got no table manners."

"What are they all *doing* here?"

"Hoping to take a peep at Millie Eberhart."

"Don't tease, Skip. I'm nobody special."

"You are to me, honey."

"So why are all these bigwigs in Philly tonight?" she asked.

"They've come for the same reason as that guy," he said, indicating the dapper figure, being shown to a table with a young woman on his arm. "They're all fight fans."

Millie goggled at the newcomers. "That looks like Charlie Chaplin."

"It is Charlie Chaplin."

"Wow! I'm in the same restaurant as a movie star?"

"Correction. A movie star is in the same restaurant as the prettiest gal in Philly," Skip told her, taking the opportunity to stroke her thigh. "You got class, Millie. You belong in a joint like this – not serving behind that bar. Glad you decided to come out with me?"

"Very glad."

"Skip Halio knows how to treat a lady proper."

"Charlie Chaplin," she sighed, still gazing at the little man in wonder. "I don't believe it. Thank you so much for bringing me here. This has been the most wonderful night of my life."

Skip smiled complacently. "And it's not over yet."

When the cab dropped her off at her home, Millie Eberhart was relieved to see that her husband was not back yet. He always had a night out with the boys on Thursday. True to his word, Skip had given her an unforgettable time before returning her safe and sound to her modest house in the suburbs. Head still swimming, Millie hugged her memories to her breast like the children she could never have. There was only one drawback. She could never share her secret with anyone else, especially with her poor sap of a husband who thought she was visiting a friend.

That, in a sense, was true. What she would never dare to tell him, of course, was that the friend in question was a certain Skip Halio, a guest at the hotel where she was employed. Her husband would be deeply hurt. He was a good man, kind, loving and hard-working but the romance had long been drained out of their marriage. It had taken an evening with Skip Halio to prove that to her. She was realistic about her new friendship. Skip would soon move on and she might never see him again, but that didn't matter. He'd opened her eyes in every way. He'd shown Millie her true potential. And before he did leave Philly, he was going to take her to the Big Fight.

By the time her husband got back, Millie had washed off the smell of Skip Halio and the stink of his cigar. Tucked up in bed, she didn't even feel someone climbing in beside her to plant a farewell kiss on her cheek. She was too busy dreaming about Charlie Chaplin.

To anyone interested in the noble art, the return to the ring of the world champion was like a Second Coming. Jack Dempsey was an American hero, a teak-hard, no-nonsense fighter who'd learned his craft in a hundred bars, hobo jungles and mining camps, taking on all-comers in brawls that had no room for such niceties as boxing gloves, referees or rests between rounds. In that dog-eat-dog world, there was only one long, unrelenting, blood-covered round. The papers kept harping on about the contrast. Inside the ring, they said, Dempsey was all muscle and iron determination. Outside it, he was gentle, quiet and shy.

The more I read about Dempsey, the more I wondered if I should've put my money on him. Except that I couldn't raise a big enough stake to make a sizeable profit. Ten bucks was all I could afford. For guys like me with slim billfolds, Tunney was the better option. If, by a miracle, he actually won, we'd go home real happy. In order to convince myself that he stood a chance, I found out everything I possibly could about the challenger. I was encouraged.

On the night itself, 23 September 1926, the biggest crowd I'd ever seen converged on the stadium. Hundreds of cops were on duty. Bodyguards made sure that celebrities got safely to their seats. The air of anticipation was almost tangible. I was pushing my way towards the entrance when I saw the man who'd first sparked my interest in the contest. He was checking that big gold watch of his and looked as if he was waiting for someone.

"Don't you try to skip out on me, Skip," I cautioned.

"No chance of that."

"I want to collect my dough."

"Only if Tunney wins," he reminded me, "and that's not exactly on the cards. Tell you what. I'm a fair-minded guy. You want to switch your money to Dempsey, that's okay by me."

"I'll stick with Tunney."

"Then you're in the minority, Walter."

"There'll be two of us in that stadium at night who believe that Jack Dempsey will lose," I declared. "Me and Gene Tunney."

"You're crazy. Tunney will be shitting his pants."

"Oh, no. He's been waiting a long time for this chance."

"He won't even last the first round."

"You got inside information?"

"I got eyes, Walter. I got instincts."

"Well, so have I, Skip," I said with conviction. "While Dempsey was taking a rest from the ring, Tunney trained or fought every single day. He's battle-hardened and he's pickled his hands in brine to make them like lumps of stone. For the champ, this is just one more fight. For the challenger, it's everything. Tunney will win because he's *hungrier*."

Skip grinned broadly. "Thanks for your ten bucks, Walter," he said, punching me playfully in the chest. "You're a brave loser. There's no way your man will win." He stood on his toes, to look over the heads of the people who were thronging past. "I gotta go. Friend to meet. Enjoy the fight – and don't say I didn't warn you."

"Tunney," I said defiantly.

But he'd seen the person he was waiting for and skipped off.

If you really want to know what the Roaring Twenties was all about, you should've been there in the Sesquicentennial Stadium. It was like walking into a zoo when all the cages have been opened. Most everyone there seemed to be liquored up and ripe for action, especially the women. The noise was deafening. In the mad scramble for seats, I had to fight to get mine, then put up with the reek of stale sweat and the stench of cigar and cigarette smoke. Stuck at the back, all I could see of the ring was this tiny canvas square that blazed with light. People like Charlie Chaplin, William Randolph Hearst and all the other people who mattered were down at the ringside. Skip Halio would be somewhere close to them.

The other fights on the card were simply there to warm up the crowd, to turn decent, law-abiding citizens into bloodthirsty morons who were on their feet as soon as the first punch was landed. By the time that we reached the main bout, I was part of this seething mass of humanity that roared like angry lions and that could only be appeased by the sight of ritual slaughter. I was frightened yet I was only in the audience. How must Gene Tunney be feeling?

Well, to his credit, he looked fairly calm during the preliminaries and didn't seem to mind that Dempsey got a much bigger cheer when he was introduced to the howling mob. In the general pandemonium, I didn't even hear the bell but it must have been rung because they came out of their corners with their guards up. Even from that distance, I could see that Tunney was wary, conscious of the champ's reputation. He held back, as if afraid of Dempsey, ignoring the ear splitting jeers from all sides of the stadium and biding his time.

Jack wanted to get it over quick. Charging in with both fists flailing, he tried to floor his opponent by sheer, raw, animal power but his over-confidence let him down. Tunney had kidded him. To show that he didn't really fear the champ at all, he hit Dempsey with a perfectly timed right that sent him reeling backwards and all but knocked him out. Weaker fighters would have been stopped there and then, but Dempsey had the strength to come back. The trouble was that Tunney now had the upper hand. He was fitter, faster and landed much the cleaner punches. Dempsey just couldn't seem to get through his defense.

Unable to knock the champ out, Tunney simply wore him down, round by round, until Dempsey was sweating like a pig on a spit and panting for breath. He was also bruised and bloodied whereas Tunney seemed to be unmarked. He was fighting the crowd as well as Jack Dempsey. They wanted Tunney to slug it out, toe to toe with their hero, to be smashed into oblivion by the famous fists of the Manassas Mauler. Instead, they saw a courageous fighter being out-foxed and out-boxed by a tall, skinny guy from nowhere. After ten rounds, they were both still standing but there was no doubt who won the contest. Gene Tunney had become the first man in history to take the title on a points decision.

The stadium was like bedlam. Arguments started, fights broke out and the first few chairs were used as weapons. All I was interested in was my fifty bucks from Skip Halio. Shoving and shouldering my way down the aisle, I got close enough to the ring to recognize some of the famous faces who'd watched their hero slowly crumble before them. It took me a while to find Skip but I eventually spotted him, making for the exit and having an argument with a woman who was trying to hold his arm. With a sudden movement, he shrugged her off, slapped her hard until she backed away in pain, then vanished through a doorway. In a flash, I realized what he was doing. Unwilling to pay all of us who'd bet on Tunney, he was falling back on his favorite trick.

Skip Halio was trying to skip town.

Most boxers who'd just won a world title would have celebrated all night and drunk themselves into imbecility. But not Gene Tunney. He was a modest, clean-living young man. After a shower, he got dressed and went off to a hotel to have several pots of tea. How do I know that? Because it was in all the papers, underneath a picture of the new champ. But even Tunney couldn't dominate the front pages in Philly the next day. The big story was spelled out in a banner headline – MURDER AT THE RAILROAD STATION.

It seems that a bookie named Skip Halio was violently attacked by a local man. In the course of the struggle, Skip was deliberately hurled across the track, seconds before a train came steaming into town. Iron wheels ploughed on regardless, mangling the body beyond all recognition and ruining an expensive gold watch into the bargain. The killer made no attempt at escape. He gave his name as Walter Eberhard, a cab driver from Philadelphia.

"It wasn't really the fifty bucks," I told them. "It was the way I saw him treat my wife at the fight. Nobody hits Millie like that and gets away with it."

The Broadcast Murder

GRENVILLE ROBBINS

The early 1920s saw a Radio Craze in Britain and America. The first commercial radio broadcast began in 1920 from Station SMK in Detroit, and the BBC began broadcasting over Station 2LO in London in 1922. And this story, written and published in 1928 is, so far as I know, the first radio murder mystery – certainly the first "locked room" one. Robbins was a newspaperman who wrote for The Times. *He was also a writer for radio, and though he had no books published (leastways, not under that name) he had several unusual stories in the popular magazines of the 1920s and 1930s, several of which I hope to resurrect in later anthologies.*

The Oxford voice from the wireless loud speaker, to which I had been listening, suddenly stopped in the middle of a word. There was silence for a second, and then a terrifying yell rang through the room. It came from the loud speaker. I jumped up and gaped at it in frozen astonishment.

"Help!" gasped the voice. "The lights have gone out. Someone's trying to strangle me. I—"

There was another terrible shriek, an agonizing gurgle, and then all was silence. There seemed no doubt whatever that the announcer, whoever he was, was either unconscious or dead. And the whole thing had not taken more than a second. He had been strangled, alone, and with no one to save him, while hundreds of thousands of people, who were unable to help him, had been listening to every sound.

While I was still gaping at the loud speaker, I heard the sound of a scuffle come from it. Then there was a crash, as though the microphone had been upset, and then there was the sound of someone coming into the room. Help had come at last and, from the ominous silence, it had come too late. Then the machine went "dead", and I knew that the apparatus had been cut off.

I turned off my set almost automatically.

And that was how I came to be in at the beginning of the great "Wireless Murder". "Great", not because the crime and its unravelling were so out of the ordinary, but because the circumstances were so exceptional.

It was certainly the first time that so many people had been present at the beginning of a crime of this kind. Thousands and thousands of people knew about it at the very moment of its being done. Thousands knew about it before even the newspapers could tell them. Thousands, in short, had listened in to a new kind of programme, such as even the newly constituted Government Broadcasting Corporation had not contemplated.

For some months before this there had been a great outcry as to the need for more "reality" in the wireless programmes. They had given us reality this time with a vengeance.

I was sitting in my lodgings at Birchester, when the thing happened. What Birchester thinks today, as everybody knows, London thinks tomorrow, or never thinks at all, which is sometimes just as lucky for London. Anyway, Birchester is one of our largest provincial cities and is not slow to be proud of the fact.

I, "James Farren, 33, hazel eyes, florid complexion, scar over –" and so on, as the police might say if advertising for me, was in a nice, comfortable position on its leading newspaper. And everyone knows that the *Birchester Mercury* makes papers like *The Times* and the *Manchester Guardian* look like poorly produced pamphlets.

I was single then, and, as I was still living in lodgings, had turned on the loud speaker while I was having a lonely early dinner before I turned out to start my evening's more or less honest toil, which was usually devoted to misinforming the minds and inflaming the passions of the inhabitants of Birchester. Throughout the meal, the immaculate Oxford voice at the other end of the loud speaker had been droning on methodically. It was the time of the local news bulletin. We had already had the weather from London with its local depressions. Now we were hearing the local woes from the local studio.

A Mrs Jones had apparently mislaid a baby while shopping. "Would anyone," the voice was saying, "who finds the lost child, restore it to its parents at—"

It was there that the voice stopped and the scream rang out.

Now, I am no wireless "fan" myself, but I knew that most of my readers were, and that they would all want to hear more about this unusual crime on the morrow. So I rang up the office at once and had a couple of my sprightliest young men put on to it, to go into the matter as deeply as they could for the edification of the public.

A second telephone call, preceded by an unmannerly altercation with the exchange, who informed me that my number was engaged before I had mentioned it, got me in touch with the chief police station, and in another minute I was on my way there in a taxi.

I must say that I was very lucky throughout all this business in having a friend at court. He *was* a friend, too, in spite of being a relation. William Garland, the gentleman in question, was some vague kind of a cousin – and a jolly good fellow to boot. He was also a jolly good detective, although he was never called anything so obvious as that. He had a kind of roving commission in the Birchester police force.

I knew that, if he were about, he would be the first to be sent by the police to the scene of the crime, and, when I rang up, he was just off in answer to an urgent message from the broadcasting people. He told me to buzz round to the police station at once. I took his advice and "buzzed".

He was standing on the pavement when my taxi got to the police station, and, ordering it to go on to the broadcasting studio, which was about a mile away, he jumped in and we were off again.

"Not in the way, I hope?" said I politely.

"Not more so than usual," he answered, and I knew that he was glad to see me.

"You might even be some faint help," he went on, puffing at

his pipe. "You newspaper men are so used to inventing things that you might be able to invent a solution to a crime. Were you listening in?"

"Yes."

"So was I, as it happened. Horrible row, wasn't it? Sounded as if he were throttled to death."

"Who was it?"

"Name of Tremayne," he answered. "Their principal announcer. Didn't know him myself, except by his voice, and that wasn't anything unusual."

"How is he?" I asked.

"I don't know," he answered.

"Didn't you ask?"

"Yes."

"Well. Why don't you know?"

"Because they didn't know," he answered placidly.

"Don't be a fool," I said impatiently. "They must know."

"Don't be silly," he answered. "They don't."

"But don't you even know if he's dead or not?"

"No. He's vanished."

"What?"

"Yes, vamoosed from a hermetically sealed studio."

"Good God!"

"And after being strangled pretty thoroughly, too."

"They must be all mad," I said.

"I wonder," he said, thoughtfully puffing at his pipe.

A policeman was already stationed outside the door of the studio when we arrived, and he saluted us when he saw who my companion was. Inside the vestibule a youngish man was fidgeting. We soon found out that this was the chief of the studio. Stephen Hart was his name. He was a comparative newcomer to the establishment, and I had not met him before, but he struck me very favourably. He was probably thirty-two or thirty-three years of age, and was not only good-looking but also obviously endowed with a good deal of intelligence.

When he saw us, he came forward eagerly.

"Mr Garland?" he said with a quick smile. "I am the chief here. I rang up the police station directly the – thing – happened. I've heard of you, sir. I'm so glad you were able to come."

William introduced me, and we all shook hands.

"I suppose," went on Hart, "that you'd like to go straight to the studio. Nothing's been touched, except the telephone, and I answered that when the poor chap's wife rang up. Naturally she was very frightened. I told her to stay at home, in case the police wanted to see her. Was that all right?"

"Quite," answered Garland. "There's a telephone actually inside the studio then, is there?"

"Yes. It's not often used, but occasionally, when the broadcasting isn't actually going on, we want to get in touch with someone in the studio."

"I see. Well. Shall we go straight up?"

Hart led the way. We mounted a couple of flights of stairs and passed through an open door into a typical broadcasting studio. In the middle of the room was the overturned microphone and by it an overturned wooden chair. That was all the furniture. The place was brilliantly lighted, and otherwise was quite bare. The lights were high up in the middle of the ceiling, and were turned on and off by a couple of switches just by the door. On the other side of the door was the telephone. In one corner was a thing rather like a telephone box. It was, I gathered, soundproof, and, when necessary, it was used to check the performance that was going on in the studio. There was no furniture inside it. Nothing but a pair of earphones. On the floor of the studio was a thick carpet. The walls, which were bright yellow in colour, were covered by thin curtains. That was all.

"Would you mind shutting the door?" said William to Hart. He did so. It closed automatically with a spring lock and fitted flush into the wall.

"You have a key, of course," went on William.

"Yes, and there are two or three others belonging to the staff. It is shut like that to prevent the possibility of any stranger barging in in the middle of a performance. Of course, it's not likely—"

"It seems to have happened tonight all right," said the other dryly.

"Yes," agreed Hart. "I can't understand it."

"Well, Mr Hart," said my friend, after he had had a quick but thorough glance round the room. "Do you mind if I ask you a few questions?"

"Of course not."

"We both of us heard what happened from our end of the wireless. I suppose that was Tremayne's voice all right?"

"Yes."

"Did you see him come in?"

"Yes. He came in about ten minutes before he started doing the local announcements. My office is just outside, you know. He came in to say good evening, and left his hat and coat there as he usually does. They're still there."

"And then he went into the studio?"

"Yes. We chatted for a few minutes. I gave him the announcements that were to be read and then he came in here."

"The lights were on?"

"Yes. I came in with him. The place was just the same as it always is."

"I see. And then you left him here alone?"

"Yes. With the average performer we have someone in that box through his performance. Either I or poor Tremayne used to do that, to keep a check on the performance, but, of course, we've never done it with our own announcers. We always assume that they'll be all right."

"Does Tremayne do all the announcing?"

"He *used* to do most of it. In fact, he did it all, unless he were away on holiday. It's not a big staff here. It's mainly a relay station, you see."

"I see. And so you left him in here alone?"

"Yes. When I went out, he was sitting at the microphone. I left him there and shut the door behind me. Then I went to my office to do a bit more work. It's the end of the month and I was in rather a rush. I had been in my office most of the day."

"And what happened then?"

"Well, I had the loud speaker in my office turned on, as usual. It provides another check on the performance. I get so used to it, too, that I scarcely pay any attention to it. At least, until today."

Here he was obviously overcome by emotion.

"After a few minutes," he went on at last, "I heard exactly what you and everyone else heard."

"I see. You heard Tremayne call out that the lights had gone out and that he was being strangled?"

"That's it."

"You couldn't hear it directly, of course?" went on the detective.

"No. The studio's absolutely sound-proof. I dashed to the door at once. It was still locked. My own door was open, and I can swear that no one had opened the studio door, come out, and closed it behind them. I'm sure it would have been quite impossible. Then I found that in my excitement I had left the key of the studio door on my table in the office. I dashed back and got it, opened the door – and found the place in darkness."

"That's curious," commented Garland.

"It was," said Hart. "There wasn't the slightest sound. I groped for the switch at the door. It had been turned off. I switched on the lights and they came on all right. I thought at first that they might have fused and that Tremayne had had a kind of fit. But even that wouldn't have explained his — Oh well! And that's all I know. The room was just as you see it now. Absolutely empty."

"Extraordinary!"

"It is. I do hope you can do something. I'm terribly worried."

Here he broke down altogether.

"Cheer up," said Garland. "There must be some explanation. I'll just have a bit of a look round. I wonder if you would mind getting his hat and coat from your office. I'd like to have a look at them. By the way, was there anyone else who would have seen him coming to work tonight?"

"Yes. Sergeant Jones, the commissionaire at the front door."

"Oh, yes. Would you mind sending him up? I'll see the rest of the staff later. How many are there?"

"About a dozen."

And with that he went out, looking thoroughly miserable.

When he had gone we both had a thorough search of the room. We found absolutely nothing. The walls were solid everywhere. The only opening was the door. The floor under the carpet we soon found to be made of solid concrete. Any entrance or escape through the ceiling was out of the question. Even if there had been a trap (which there wasn't) no one could have dropped through, strangled Tremayne, and got back again (even if he had had a ladder) in the time between the crime and the entrance of Hart.

"Very baffling," said William, with a queer smile.

"Very," I agreed.

The commissionaire at the front door came in at that moment. A typical army man was Sergeant Jones.

Yes. He had seen Tremayne come in earlier in the evening. He arrived at his usual time. He would know him out of a thousand. Very peculiar walk he had. Coat collar turned up as usual. Glasses? Yes, everything quite ordinary and as usual.

He was dismissed with a benediction.

A clerk was then produced who had passed him coming up the stairs. He, too, was dismissed with thanks.

Sergeant Jones, recalled, said that, even supposing a body *had* been carried past Mr Hart's office without being noticed, it would not go into the street without him, Sergeant Jones, seeing it. Most indignant he was about this. Of course, the thing was impossible. He was there to watch people coming in and going out, and, if he didn't notice a body going out, he wasn't worth his money.

"Why," he went on, "I could tell you every movement of every member of the staff today."

And he went on to enumerate a long list, finishing with Tremayne, who had come in at 5.30, and Mr Hart, who had come in at noon, and not left the office since.

Garland scratched his head thoughtfully at this information, and decided that he had learnt enough here.

"I'm going round to see Mrs Tremayne," he said to me. "And I'm sure that one's enough for an interview with an hysterical woman who's probably a widow. You run back to your office. I'll give you a ring if anything else happens tonight."

With that he left me, and I walked thoughtfully back to my office.

He didn't ring me up that night, and when I went to bed I was still as puzzled as ever by the mystery. My two reporters, good boys both, had done their best, and produced some very readable stuff, but they had not been allowed much scope by the local police, who knew their job much too well. All the newspapers could get was a very little fact and a great amount of conjecture.

And it was not an easy case to conjecture about. I, for one, was hopelessly baffled. The wife of the vanished announcer had been interviewed by my reporter as well as by the detective, and she swore that it was her husband's voice she had heard from the loud speaker. And there was no doubt that she ought to know.

It was really most amazing. Tremayne had been attacked in an empty and unapproachable room, and then had been spirited away – all in a space of less than two minutes.

No wonder that next day all the newspapers were full of it. One after another they gave the case flaring headlines. Some went so far as roundly to declare that the whole thing was due to magic.

The thing was so surprising that it might have been considerably more than a seven days' wonder; but the newspapers this time were not to have a long drawn out mystery, for by the following evening Garland had drawn the net tight and all was over, bar the shouting – and the scaffold. It made the story even more surprising but, as a journalist myself, I could not help thinking regretfully of the cleverness of this relative of mine, which had so soon ended the newspaper sensation of years.

I was down at the office that afternoon when the telephone bell rang. It was Garland. He wanted to see me, and I told him to come along. In a very few minutes he was shown in. He looked tired – and, to my trained eye, immoderately triumphant.

"Well?" I asked.

"Very," he answered. "I want to relieve my brain, so I'll talk to you for a few minutes. You will admit, won't you, that it's impossible for a man to be strangled in an empty sealed room, and also impossible for him, when he's been strangled, to vanish from that room?"

"Yes. But was the studio sealed?"

"We examined it ourselves. The police have been over it again today. A fly couldn't have walked out of it without being noticed. The walls are solid, the ceiling is solid, the floor is concrete. How on earth was the victim removed?"

"The only way was through the door."

"That certainly seems the only way, but you must remember this – Hart was in his office all the time with his door open. He was bound to hear and see anything being taken past his door.

And, even supposing that he hadn't noticed anything, there was the commissionaire downstairs."

"He may have been bribed."

"Possible, but not very probable. Besides, there wasn't time for anything to be carried away between the strangling and the opening of the door. Hart was in the room, he says, almost as soon as the deed was done. There's proof, too, because you could hear someone coming into the room over the wireless."

"Did his wife tell you anything?"

"Nothing directly. She's very attractive. No children and no sign of trouble. Husband happy at the studio. On good terms with his boss. Hart, she confided, had even condescended to come to tea once. A tremendous honour, I gathered. She's very distraught, of course, but convinced that her husband's alive and kicking somewhere."

"But the thing's impossible," I cried. "The thing's positively eerie. He's simply vanished into thin air."

"That's certainly what it *seems* like, but things you see, as Gilbert once observed, are not always what they seem."

He yawned, and then went on:

"Would you like to be in at the death?"

I started.

"Of course. Is it a matter of death, do you think?"

"I don't think. I'm sure. There's been a particularly heartless murder; but murder will always out. It's a thing that – given a little intelligence on the other side – is bound to be discovered. Take this case. There aren't any clues. What then? Why, the very lack of them is significant. That was what got me started on the right track. Lack of clues plus logic plus (possibly) a little luck. That was the formula. And in an hour the whole mystery will be exploded. It seems rather a shame, because it was all very clever and artistic."

"It baffled me anyhow," I said.

"It baffled me for nearly twelve hours. I got quite puzzled, until I began to think of human nature. Then everything was moderately simple."

With that he looked at his watch.

"Well," he said, "if you want to be in at the death, follow me, O fourth-cousin-twice-removed."

And he led the way to a waiting police car.

He was very quiet during the journey, and my feeble attempts to make conversation soon fizzled out. Luckily, it was not a long ride. We soon stopped at a large detached house on the outskirts of the city. On the pavement were a couple of constables. After a whispered consultation, they took up their positions just inside the gate.

"Do you know who lives here?" said Garland.

"No."

"The widow of the murdered man."

Our ring was answered by a trim maid.

"Tell your mistress," he said, "that the detective's back again and wants to see her."

The maid returned in a second and we were ushered into a sitting-room. In a corner was seated an attractive woman of about thirty. She was very pale, and obviously stricken with grief, and, when she saw us, she seemed involuntarily to shrink back from us. I could sympathise with her, and I was about to murmur my condolences when my companion spoke.

I had never heard him use such a tone before, and I was not surprised that he was the terror of criminals.

"Excuse the intrusion," he rapped out. "But I wanted to talk to Mr Hart in your presence. I asked him to come here at seven. It's just that now."

At these words she turned so pale that I thought she was going to faint. She did not say a word, but motioned to us to sit down, and at that moment Hart came in. The maid did not announce him. At any other time I should have been surprised, but now there were too many other matters of surprise for me to think of that little detail.

He smiled at the pale woman in front of him, went over to her, and stood by her side.

"Well?" he asked.

"Sorry to worry you like this," said Garland; "but there are one or two questions I want answered, and I thought that I'd better ask them here. I like doing things on the spot."

At this the man went as pale as the woman.

"Well?"

"I wish it were," answered the other gravely. "Now, don't let's beat about the bush. I'm not a fool. Why did you do it?"

"Do what?" gasped the man.

"And," went on Garland, ignoring the question, "where—?"

At this query both of them looked instinctively towards a French window leading into the garden beyond. The look was only the matter of a fraction of a second but Garland noticed it.

"Ah! I thought so," he said. "Well, is there any need to go on with this farce any longer?"

"I'm afraid I don't understand you," said the man in a self-possessed voice.

"You're sure?"

"Quite."

"Right," said Garland, turning to me. "Go and fetch those two policemen. There are some tools in the car. Tell them to wait for me in the garden just outside the window. Our friends here will be able to watch what they're doing nicely."

I turned to the door, and at that moment the woman let forth a scream such as I never hope to hear again. The man held her in his arms and tried to soothe her, but it was too late and, do what he could, he could not stop her from sobbing out the whole miserable story. And what a miserable story it was!

How Garland had guessed the truth I could not imagine; but he had, and now that his theories were vindicated, he looked as miserable as the two unfortunates he had trapped.

It was the old, old story. The eternal human triangle. The murdered husband had neglected his wife. The other had consoled her. Things had got worse and worse until the husband had actually begun to ill-treat his wife. Then they resolved to get rid of him. They had – but the sequel can best be told in Garland's words.

The last I saw of those two unfortunate creatures caught up in the web of their own crime was as they were led out by the two policemen. They had no eyes except for each other, and each was trying to help the other. It was pitiful. There was true love there, if there had ever been true love in the world. And they were going inevitably to the scaffold!

The body, of course, was buried in the front garden. When Garland had finished all the unpleasant formalities connected with the arrests and the digging up of the body, he came round to the office.

"Life's a rum business," he said, flinging himself into a chair. "Those two would have made a model married couple.

As two sides of a human triangle, they were nothing less than fiends."

"So I see; but when did you begin to guess? I'm still as baffled as ever I was."

"I was at sea at first. I almost got to the point of thinking something supernatural had happened, and that's no way for a detective to think. It was obvious that there must be some material explanation of the entire disappearance of a man who, if one's ears are to be trusted, was either unconscious or dead. We examined the room pretty thoroughly. It was as solid as a coffin."

I shuddered.

"Yes. But that's just what it wasn't. No body could possibly have been taken out of that room without the knowledge of Hart, and I was soon convinced that no body could have been taken out of the building at all. The commissionaire's evidence was good enough, apart from anything else. And there were other people about. No, the thing was impossible. It couldn't have happened."

"But it did."

"I know it did, but not there. All that took place was that an idea that it happened there was projected to us through one of our senses. A clever fellow, Hart, to contrive that touch. He knew it was impossible to hide a murder altogether. So he made it appear that the murder should take place at a spot which would baffle everyone. The studio was only a red herring. No body had left the building. There was no body in it. What, then? There never was a body there at all."

I nodded.

"But," I objected, "What about his voice over the wireless?"

"Yes. That was a good bit of psychology, too. I suppose you've heard the voices of a good many announcers in your time. Very Oxford, aren't they? And, even if you knew the men, I bet you'd find it darned difficult to tell the difference between one and another. These two, Hart and Tremayne, used to interchange the announcing work occasionally, and I soon found that there was no one in Birchester, who could swear that there was any violent difference in their voices. Announcers are like leaders in *The Times*. They're all anonymous and all alike."

"Yes, that's all right," I said. "Their voices when they are actually making announcements may be all alike, but what about the scream? I can't imagine two men screaming alike."

"That's all very well, but who has heard either of these two men scream? People aren't in the habit of screaming in public. The only real evidence that that scream came from the dead man was the evidence of his wife. She swore it was his scream. She certainly ought to know, if anyone could, but I doubt if even many wives have heard their husbands scream. That was what first aroused my suspicions. She was so sure that it was his scream. And I wondered if it was possible to be as sure as that."

"I see."

"So that the only evidence that the voice over the wireless was actually his was provided by the wife and his chief. I was now convinced that Tremayne had never been to the studio at all, and things began to narrow down very considerably."

"But," said I, "what about the commissionaire? He *saw* Tremayne coming in, and swore to its being him."

"Pardon me. He swore to seeing a man come in with a limp, with Tremayne's coat, and so on, but he only *thought* that it was Tremayne. What easier disguise could there be? A limp, glasses, coat collar turned up. Good God! The thing leaps at one. Someone had impersonated Tremayne for reasons of his own. Only one man could have done it. That was Hart."

"But he was in his office all day. That was corroborated."

"Oh, no. It was proved that he came in early and was not seen to leave again. That was all. Did you notice, by the way, that there was a telephone by Jones' cubbyhutch in the front hall?"

"No."

"Well, there was. What could be easier than for Hart to arrange for a call to be put through at a definite time, say by an accomplice, say by the wife in the case, and to slip out while Jones was answering it? That is precisely what did happen. I found out that there had been an exasperating wrong number just before six, and, mark you, Hart had given orders that he was not to be disturbed between 5.30 and 6.30. He was working behind closed doors then, too. Are you beginning to see now?"

"Yes."

"He left the building then, put on Tremayne's hat and coat, which he had secreted round the corner, and then came in again to act his little piece. The murder had been done already. The body was buried in the garden there. You see, if the dead man were missed from his home, suspicion was bound to fall on his wife. If he were to disappear from the studio, on whom could suspicion fall?"

"Dashed clever!"

"It was. When Hart returned he did that clever little piece of acting, and then reappeared in his own fair form. It might have succeeded, you know. No one would have thought of looking at his house for a crime that was obviously committed a mile away. Well, I've no doubt, from the sound of him, that the husband deserved all he got. But I'm afraid they'll both hang, poor devils. They found the body all right. Sack over the head and the head battered in terribly. Horrible mess! I found that Tremayne was away for the night that night. He was at Stanport on business. The wife sent him an urgent telegram to come back by a particular train, and they struck him down at the very second he entered his house. The maid, I need hardly add, had a nice night off. Terrible! Terrible!"

That should have been the end of the story but it wasn't.

I was sitting in my office the next afternoon when a man called on what he announced to be very important business.

He was shown in. He was about thirty-five, well dressed, and of pleasant appearance – until you looked at his eyes, and they were about the most evil that I had ever seen in a human face.

"Your name, sir?" I asked.

"Mr Tremayne. Charles Tremayne," he said, giving the name of the murdered man.

"Please, don't joke on unpleasant subjects," I said.

"I was never more serious in my life," he went on. "I've just been reading your excellent account of the Wireless Murder. I can tell you something else now. Charles Tremayne was not murdered at all. Here he is. I am he."

I simply gaped at him.

"Yes," he said, with an evil smile. "I had an idea that those two were anxious to get rid of me, but I honestly never thought that they were going to do it so crudely as that. When I went to Stanport that day, I had decided never to return. I saw a lawyer there to arrange for a divorce, and I had asked him to call on my wife that night and lay the situation before her. When I got her telegram I asked him to get the train she mentioned, so as to let her know why I was not returning. In fact, he kept my appointment. And, moreover, he was bearing the news that my wife would soon be free and that the two turtle doves would be free to be married. I'm very much afraid it was the lawyer who was killed in my place. He was about my build and they must have got the sack over him in the dark. Just like that scene from *Rigoletto*."

"Good Heavens!" I gasped. "What irony! He was actually carrying those two the message that they would be free to marry, and they killed him. And now they will both have to die."

"Yes," he said with a chuckle. "It's all very amusing, isn't it?"

And that was the last I saw of a very unpleasant gentleman. He was quite right. They had murdered the wrong man, and within a month they were both hanged for their crime. I wonder if they obtained any grain of consolation from the fact that "in death they were not divided"?

For the Benefit of Mr Means

CHRISTINE MATTHEWS

*Christine Matthews is the partner of Robert Randisi, who
also appears in this anthology. Together they write the
mysteries about book-dealer sleuths Gil and Claire Hunt
that began with* Murder is the Deal of the Day *(1999).
Her short stories have been appearing since 1989 and many
will be found in the collection* Gentle Insanities and Other
States of Mind *(2001), a title that seems equally suitable to
describe the Roaring Twenties.*

*Devotees of cinema history will know well the cause célèbre
of 1921 when the popular film star, Roscoe "Fatty" Arbuckle, was accused of raping and causing the death of the
young actress Virginia Rappé. He had done no such thing
and was found not guilty, but the case had ruined his career
and he was blacklisted by Hollywood. He later directed
films, but had turned to drink and died at the age of only
46 from heart failure – Buster Keaton said it was of a
broken heart. In the following story we see the real Roscoe.*

YOU ARE CORDIALLY INVITED
TO JOIN LILY ARMSTRONG-SMITH
IN CELEBRATING HER TWENTY-FIFTH BIRTHDAY
ON THE FOURTH OF SEPTEMBER
ONE THOUSAND NINE HUNDRED and
TWENTY SEVEN
EIGHT O'CLOCK IN THE EVENING

AT HER BENTON COVE ESTATE
NEWPORT, RHODE ISLAND

gifts required

"If I told ya once, I musta told ya fifty times – you'll be swell."

Irma bit her red fingernail. "But I don't know all the words. Not like Peggy does."

"If ya get into trouble, just give us a nod and we'll cover ya."

Cal turned toward Johnny Long and nodded a signal. Johnny reached up to straighten his bow tie and then played the first six notes solo before the rest of the band joined in.

Cal shoved Irma toward the microphone. "Just remember – smile!"

It was the caliber of people in the mansion that got the butterflies flapping in her stomach, not being up there on stage. She'd been singing most of her eighteen years . . . that was the easy part. And what God had cheated her out of in talent, He'd made up for by loading up the charm.

She sang the first three lines of the song and then hesitated for a moment. Raising her eyebrows and then her small hand, she waved as Harold Lloyd entered the room. Now, why had she done that? Like she knew the man, geepers! But the guy was a real gentleman and bowed slightly, even waved back before continuing through the crowd. "The man I love . . ." Piece of cake, she thought. If I can just keep from going gaga every time one of them hot shots looks at me, I'll be fine.

"There's three of them. All perfectly matched. I heard Lillian had those chandeliers made in France. Mustn't be outdone by the Astors!"

The woman's companion looked up at the pale lavender ceiling, then inspected the crystal lights evenly spaced across the expanse of the great room.

"You can bet your Aunt Sally they cost more than Lillian's dearly departed father plus his father made in their entire lifetimes – even throwing in that haberdashery her brother runs up in Providence," he said.

"And just how would you know that, if I may ask?" she asked.

"I was her accountant years ago."

"Do I detect a tiny smidge of bitterness in your tone?"

He laughed.

A man with a grudge. The evening was going to be fun! "And now?" She leaned in closer. "You work for her in some other capacity?"

"No, she has an entire office – hand picked – just to handle her affairs." More bitterness. "Men highly qualified to run at the drop of her imported hat."

Now it was her turn to laugh. After composing herself, Zelda Fitzgerald pressed on. "Twice divorced! That's our Lily. I bet that would require more than one lawyer indeed."

He gulped down his martini. "She's become quite an expert at the fine art of matrimony but when it comes to divorce, Madam Curie couldn't keep up!"

"Will you look at that carpet! Really look at it!" the newcomer said loudly as he interrupted the two guests. "Hand stitched. Custom made! Exquisite. Simply exquisite."

Before Zelda could get rid of the obnoxious intruder, her accountant friend walked away.

"Well?" Dorothy exhaled the word, slowly. Smoke from her second cigarette of the evening hung above her head in a halo. "Where is our birthday girl? Is she decent yet?"

"If she were, she wouldn't be giving herself another birthday party."

"Now, Bill – be nice."

He looked at her with disdain.

"You have to feel sorry for poor Lily. Three birthdays in one year. And twenty-five? How on earth did she come up with that laughable number? A bit eccentric or pathetic, I haven't quite figured it out yet," she said.

"Keep at it, old girl, I'm sure you'll come up with something."

This time it is was she who scowled.

"Why, you're W.C. Fields, aren't you?" A round, balding man stood in front of the group seated on a long divan covered in velvet the color of burnished pewter. "I've enjoyed you on

Broadway . . . oh, and of course, the films. Yes, I've spent many enjoyable hours laughing at you and Chaplin . . ."

"*He* sir, is not an actor. I'll thank you to never mention him in my presence."

The man looked puzzled.

Fields continued, "Chaplin is a goddamn ballet dancer, nothing more." Picking up the book that lay in his lap, he resumed his reading as if he were the only person in the room.

"Don't mind him," the woman said. "He's just a cantankerous old man."

The stranger shifted his weight, unsure how to proceed until his ego kicked in. "Allow me to introduce myself. My name is Means. Gaston Bullock Means." He waited a moment for some sort of reaction. When she didn't say anything he elaborated. "I'm the author of *The President's Daughter*."

"Oh." She withdrew her hand. "Of course I've heard of you. Who hasn't?"

Fields huffed. "You, sir, are a hack — a gossip monger who happened to luck into a scandal. Now Mrs Parker here is a writer."

Fields had enough of the boorish crowd and stood up. Without a nod backwards, he walked across the room to the bar.

"Gin. And keep pouring, my good man, until I pass out," he said to the bartender.

"Sure thing Mr Fields."

The band was getting ready to wrap up "Someone to Watch Over Me", as two couples danced slowly.

"Have you seen Miss Armstrong-Smith?" he asked the bartender.

"Gee, Mr Fields, can't say as I have."

With a glass in each hand, the actor made his way to a large seating group in the middle of the room. The sweet young thing singing with the band caught his eye. He raised a glass and blew her a kiss.

She tried concentrating on the words, but he was W.C. Fields — in the flesh! She stopped to return his kiss and Cal leaned over.

His tuxedo didn't fit as well as it could have but the call to play for the party had come at the last minute, it being a Saturday and all. His regular suit was at the cleaners so he borrowed his brother's tux and scrambled to replace Peggy with

Irma. Irma Levine, what a mixed-up dame! But so far – so good. And Mrs Armstrong-Smith paid well, had a lot of parties at the Cove and he wanted to get in solid with her. Now, baton in hand, he tapped on the music stand propped in front of him and asked Irma, "Need some help?"

"What? Oh, sorry, no, I'm fine."

As she sang, she never lost eye contact with Fields. "I hope that he, turns out to be . . . someone to watch over . . ." Ramon Novarro walked into the room and she lost it again.

In contrast to the glamorous, inviting atmosphere downstairs, the air on the second floor was charged, like a storm ripping through a Kansas town.

"Where are Mrs Smith's pearls?" the maid asked, panicky. "If we don't find them, there'll be hell to pay, I can guarantee you that! She's out for blood tonight."

"Alice!" Lily's voice boomed down the long hallway. "Hurry! Alice!"

"So, tell me my good man," Gaston Means said, "what is the source of your supply and will I die of alcohol poisoning later this evening?"

The bartender studied the pompous little man for a moment and then decided to take his comment as a joke. "Don't worry, sir, it will be a most pleasant death. Mrs Armstrong-Smith only serves the best."

"Then I'll have a brandy." The man patted the bar, happy with his decision. "Yes, brandy."

After carefully pouring, the bartender slid the crystal glass toward the man. "There you go, sir. Napoleon, the best we have. Enjoy."

He swirled the amber liquid around in the snifter. After a moment spent inhaling, he finally sipped. "Ahh, yes, excellent."

Truth be told, Mr Means couldn't tell bad brandy from good. As he stood there, surveying the room, he watched the parade of celebrities pass by and felt confident he belonged. A gentleman came and stood beside him, recognizing the voice, he turned. "Mr Crosby." Means held out his hand. "I'm a great fan of your trio, The Rhythm Boys. Allow me to introduce myself."

Bing Crosby started to shake hands until he heard the name Gaston Means, then quickly withdrew his hand. "Sorry, I don't associate with swindlers or spies."

"I beg your pardon?"

"You and your kind make me physically ill."

"But . . ."

"I've read all about you, Mr Means. How you sold information on Allied shipping to the German embassy, were fired from the FBI, got yourself involved with that Ohio Gang scandal. Then without missing a beat, rolled around in the dirt with that Nan Britton woman."

"She hired me to investigate her husband . . ."

"*The President's Daughter*! You expect the American public to believe that a President of the United States fathered an illegitimate child?"

"He was a senator at the time . . ."

Crosby wasn't interested in anything Means had to say. "You, sir are a coward, benefiting from people's delusions . . ."

"But I assure you Miss Britton's claims are true!"

"Why don't you try doing something useful with your life?" After taking a minute to stare at Means with disgust, Crosby walked off.

It wasn't embarrassment that swirled around in Means' brain, no, it was disbelief. Hadn't H.L. Mencken written favorably about *The President's Daughter?* Right there in the *Baltimore Sun*? Who the hell was this Bing character anyway? What did some lousy crooner know about politics? Literature? Means shrugged and headed for the buffet table.

"Gee, Cal, when are we gonna get a break?" Irma asked. "My feet are killing me in these shoes." She pointed down to her new red satin pumps that had been custom-dyed to match the roses stitched across the black velvet of her chemise. While the band played, Irma fingered a spit curl which curlicued across her left cheek. "Come on, Cal, I need to sit down a minute," she whispered. "Be a pal, will ya?"

The last note of "Lady be Good", ended when Cal brought his baton down. "Ladies and gentlemen, thank you for your enthusiasm. We're going to take a short break but don't worry, we'll be back to play more of your favorites in fifteen minutes."

A few people applauded but most seemed not to notice.

"There, are ya happy?" he asked Irma.

"Yeah, thanks." It wasn't her feet that were hurting – it was her heart. She had to go meet Ramon Novarro. What a dream boat! As she hopped off the bandstand, her long string of pearls bounced in time with the matching earrings that hung almost to her shoulders.

Judy McKeon hated her employer. If she could have gotten away with slitting the throat of that obnoxious cow, she would gladly have done so. But then she'd not only be out a big fat pay check each week, but have to clean up the mess as well.

"Juuudith! Come here this instant!"

Ordinarily, Judy would have run to help Lily (Mrs Armstrong-Smith insisted she call her Lily). But this particular evening she wasn't feeling very helpful. As she rushed past the bedroom door she kept her eyes down and her mind set on escape. The party had started, the guests were sucking up the free hooch and one of the maids could surely tend to their demanding mistress.

"Gaston Bullock Means," he said as he shook the man's hand in almost a violent manner. He was sick and tired of being looked down on. "Author of *The President's Daughter*. You must have heard about the book. It's almost certain to become a best-seller."

The poor fellow had been in the middle of a conversation with the beautiful woman next to him when this imbecile interrupted him. His anger forced the truth to erupt from inside like a volcano. "I, sir, would never soil my hands let alone my intellect with such garbage. Besides, I thought that piece of trash was written by a woman."

"Well yes, Nan Britton and I did collaborate."

"Maybe you should mention that next time you introduce yourself. By saying you're the author gives the impression you had an original idea – did all the difficult work of writing yourself. Maybe next time . . ."

Means walked away.

A large man sat in the corner, alone. Means headed toward the loner to introduce himself. This time he would leave out the part about writing a book. All he wanted to do now was get drunk. The booze was free, the food exceptional. If he just kept his mouth shut he could have a good time.

After twenty minutes, Cal went looking for Irma. Aside from the ballroom and library, the first floor of the mansion was quiet. Walking through the French doors, he scanned the pergola which had been strung with red and gold lacquered Chinese lanterns. A few couples stood admiring the view of Narragansett Bay. The air was cool and clean, the grass slightly damp. Even though an additional bar had been set up outside, the evening was too chilly to have many takers.

The bartender waved across the expansive lawn to the Band-leader.

"You seen Irma anywheres?" Cal shouted.

The man pointed toward the water.

Cal walked across the lawn, wondering why on earth Irma would be out in the cold. He could hear water slapping against the rocks and as he wandered away from the artificial light of the lanterns, his pace slowed a bit while his eyes adjusted to the darkness beyond.

Finally, he was able to make out two figures. One, short – female, and one considerably larger – male. He stood there, conflicted. Not wanting to intrude, not wanting to walk any further in the dampness and dark. But even more anxious than ever to find his girl singer.

He started to shout out to the pair but was interrupted by the low bellowing from a nearby lighthouse. He waited, then shouted, "Irma!"

The female turned toward him. "Just a sec, Cal. I'm kinda busy here."

"No, Irma. You're on my time now, break's over!"

"Okay, okay!"

He turned and headed back to the house.

The crowd seemed to have grown considerably in the short time he had been outside. His men sat waiting impatiently for their instructions.

"Come on, Cal," the trumpet player complained. "Are we playin' or ain't we?"

"Quit your gripin'. You're gettin' paid, aren't ya? Whether you play or just sit back on your rented tails, you're gettin' paid."

Looking away, in the direction of the drums, Cal stood waiting for Irma, silently daring the musician to say another word.

The drummer, oblivious to the situation, stared out across the crowd.

"Fascinating Rhythm," Cal finally said. "And ah-one, ah-two." Bringing his baton down, he continued, "ah-three."

The band had only gotten a minute or so into the number when Irma appeared. Frantically, she scrambled across the small stage. Cal was too angry to notice the long tear in her dress.

"I'm sorry," she whispered.

Cal ignored her.

"Gee, give me a break, will ya?" she asked. "It was only a few minutes. So I got a little carried away. Come on, Cal, I said I was sorry. I promise it won't happen again."

Before he could respond, a woman pushed her way through the crowd. The bandleader couldn't make out what she was shouting until she got closer.

"Mrs Armstrong-Smith is missing!"

The musicians froze, conversations hung unfinished in the air.

"What do you mean by 'missing?'" W.C. Fields asked.

"I'm sure she's around here someplace," an older woman said. "You know how fond Lily is of surprises."

"She was upstairs in her bedroom just a moment ago."

"And who might you be?" Gaston Means asked.

The hysterical woman looked around, unsure who had asked the question and even more unsure if that person was speaking to her.

"Young woman," he started again, "calm down. And please, tell us just who in Sam Hill you think you are, coming in here shrieking like a banshee, ruining our—"

"Judith McKeon. I'm Mrs Armstrong-Smith's personal secretary, sir, that's who the hell I am! And would you be so kind as to tell me why you're standing here wasting my time instead of helping me look for Mrs Armstrong-Smith? She's vanished – maybe been kidnapped – or worse. We have to find her!"

Means approached the woman. "Surely your employer couldn't have just disappeared."

"But I saw her less than ten minutes ago. Well . . . I didn't see her . . . with my eyes. She was in her room, dressing and wanted her . . ." That's when Judith's eyes settled on the sapphire clasp of Irma's pearls. Wide-eyed she pointed and screamed. "Those pearls! You stole them! They belong to Mrs Armstrong-Smith!"

Irma was mortified. Clutching her throat she shook her head violently. "I didn't steal nothin'. These are mine!"

"What did she say?" someone asked.

"What's happening?" a lanky man sporting a pin striped suit wanted to know.

"Should we call the police?" one of the maids who had been serving hors d'oeuvres asked, after swallowing the small toast point and last bit of caviar she had swiped.

"No!" The large man standing near the French doors shouted. "No police!"

Everyone's attention turned. As he walked into the room, a unified gasp rose from the crowd.

"I can certainly understand your concern, Mr Arbuckle," Judith began, "but I don't think . . ."

"Fatty Arbuckle?" Gaston Means asked. "*The* Fatty Arbuckle? The man who killed that Rappé woman?"

"He was acquitted," Judith snapped.

"And if your memory is good enough to dredge up that poor woman's name after six years, then I'm sure you remember I was exonerated twice."

"Hey! He told me his name was William Goodrich," Irma explained to Cal. "He said he was a director."

Cal whistled through his teeth. "Yeah, honey, and I bet he told ya he could get ya in the moving pictures." As he spoke, Cal noticed the rip in Irma's dress. "Was he the one who did that?"

"Well . . . yes . . . but not like you . . ."

Cal walked to the microphone. "Miss McKeon, I suggest ya detain Mr Arbuckle. He attacked my singer, here."

"What?"

"I did no such thing," the large man said. Sweat broke out across his forehead; his round face was slowly turning a deep crimson. "I would never do that!"

"He's right." Irma was now talking into the microphone. "Mr Arbuckle and I was just talking. He was a perfect gentleman. And then we spotted the . . ." Irma stopped abruptly. Her eyes slammed shut and she stood there, head down, staring at the floor.

"Spotted what? What did you see?" Cal asked.

"Sorry, Mr Arbuckle. Sometimes I can be a real dope."

Fatty had hoped for enough time to take care of his "situation". But when she had started to run for the house he had to stop her, grabbing for her arm. She was younger and quicker and all he had managed to do was rip her sleeve. The thing that had upset her the most about this incident was the damage to her dress. When he promised to not only replace it but throw in another with matching shoes and evening bag, she agreed to give him half an hour to take care of things.

"I think I know where Lily is," he slowly told the crowd.

"Well, for God's sake tell me," Judith demanded. "I've spent days putting this party together and now, maybe, some of the evening can be salvaged."

"If one of the men will go with me," Fatty suggested, "we can escort Lily . . ."

"Anything. Do whatever you want. As long as she's not been kidnapped."

"No, I can assure you she hasn't," Fatty told her.

"Fine, then." Judith McKeon pivoted around on the heels of her practical shoes, annoyed, and marched out of the room. "Just like that old cow," she muttered to herself. "Selfish, ungrateful . . ."

"Mr Means?" Fatty said. "If you would be so kind as to come with me."

"And just what are the rest of us supposed to do?" Bing asked.

"Eat, drink and be merry. Isn't that why we're here?" Fatty asked.

"I suppose it is," the crooner answered. Then, turning to Cal, he said, "Play something light. How about a Charleston?"

"Sure thing, Mr Crosby."

As the music started up again, Means and Arbuckle headed through the ornate doors. When they had crossed the patio and stepped into the plush grass, Means asked his companion, "Why me?"

"Because we are two of a kind, I suppose."

"How can you say that? Before tonight, we've never met."

"Not face to face, you're right about that. However, I am very well acquainted with your reputation, Mr Means. We both have scandalous backgrounds. And it's that fear of being disgraced again that puts us on our best behavior."

Means stopped dead. "So, if each of us in on his best behavior, then it stands to reason we are the most honorable of all the men – or women – here."

"Exactly. Now, follow me. I want to show you something."

The men continued walking in the direction of the jagged shoreline. The only light guiding their way came from the full moon.

"There." Arbuckle pointed. "See her?"

Means studied the area he was being shown. After a moment he was able to differentiate between rock, sand, water and a human form. He gasped. "Is that? No . . ." He leaned as far as he dared. "It can't be."

"I spotted her while talking to that girl with the band. Of course she went all hysterical. She even started to run back into the party. Well, I wasn't even sure it was Lily down there . . ."

"And you couldn't afford another scandal, now, could you, Mr Goodrich?"

"Come on," Fatty said, removing a cigarette from a silver case. "We both know I can't use my real name if I want to work in the movies. The Hays office saw to that."

"Cleaning up Hollywood. There's a good one for you," Means said. "The town's crawling with hookers and drugs, bootleg hootch—"

"Men like William Randolph Hearst who flaunts his mistress, men who think nothing of the lives they ruin. No, nothing matters to them except money," Fatty said with contempt. "You certainly are aware of the kind of diseased vermin making huge profits in the film industry, Mr Means. So you can certainly understand why I tried delaying Irma's exit."

Means nodded. "Well, I guess we should get down there and see if that is in fact our hostess before worrying about what decisions need to be made."

"How do we do that without causing a riot?" Arbuckle asked. "You're the investigator. The ex-FBI man. What do we do?"

"We're not alone in our need for propriety, Arbuckle. Why, just from the misfortune that has befallen the two of us, every single person in that house knows how easily their careers can tumble down around them and their families. We have to go back in there and stoke that fear."

It was as if they had all forgotten about Lily completely. When the two men entered the grand ballroom, not one guest turned to ask them what had become of her. The music was loud, the glasses were full and the majority of voices were competing for attention. Gaston Means walked the length of the room alone without attracting one glance.

When he had come to what looked to be the library, he was met by a butler.

"May I help you, sir?"

"Please get Miss McKeon for me."

"Certainly, sir." The elderly man bowed and slowly, as if each step caused pain, walked out of the room.

She must have been just down the hall, because Judith McKeon returned within a moment.

"Well? Where is she?"

"I assume Lily . . . Mrs Armstrong-Smith has a gardener on the premises? A caretaker?" Means asked.

"Yes, William. He lives in the cottage up the road."

"Call him. I need his help."

"May I ask . . ."

"You may not. Call him and tell him to meet me by that dead evergreen near the cliffwalk. Tell him to bring a lantern and a rake."

"Fine."

"Oh, and Miss McKeon," he said, looking up at the tall woman, "I'll need you to stay close by."

She glared down at him as if he were an imbecile. "I live here, Mr Means. Where else would I go?"

"That's her, all right," William said as he watched Means drape Lily's body with a tablecloth. "I kept telling Mrs Armstrong-Smith that she should put a fence up along here. But she'd just laugh. Told me it would detract from the 'wildness' of this place. Can you believe that?" he asked, eyeing Arbuckle as he approached. "Wildness? After all the money she poured into this property? After the landscapers and architects, builders, fancy artists? There ain't nothin' wild left out here except maybe that water down there."

"Thank you, William," Means said when Arbuckle was standing next to him. "Please, don't say anything to alarm the staff. We'll have Miss McKeon send for the doctor who will in turn, no doubt, send for the police."

"Whatever you say, Mr Means. But I want it on the record that I warned her many times. She was very headstrong; she didn't listen to many people."

Means nodded, watching Fatty bend over to lift the cloth from Lily's face. "I'll make sure the authorities are made aware of your concerns."

"That's all I'm asking, Mr Means." William removed his cap from his jacket pocket and pulled it down over his thinning hair. "That's all I'm asking." Satisfied that he was blameless, William quickly walked back to his cottage.

Fatty stood up. "She fell, then? But I don't understand why . . ."

Means waited until William was out of sight. "That's what I thought at first. And that's exactly what I want William to believe. At least for the time being. But if you'll look closely at her neck, you can see the bruises."

Fatty slowly lowered his hefty frame again. Means held the lantern closer to the body. "Well, I'll be. You can see the imprints of hands, right there, plain as day."

"The person who did this had to be very strong."

Fatty wheezed as he stood up. "How do you know that?"

"Well, not only did they strangle Lily but they dragged her body all the way out here. How do you suppose they did that? Without being seen?"

"What makes you so sure she didn't come out here on her own? Maybe she just wanted some fresh air."

"Not likely. She'd be getting ready for her party. You know how much she looked forward to these productions of hers. Besides, did you happen to notice she only has on one shoe? And her stockings are worn away only on the heels."

"So? Maybe she didn't have new stockings for the party. And her other shoe probably came off when she was thrown into the water."

"No, if I'm not mistaken, that's it over there."

The two men walked toward the object Means pointed out. Holding the lantern close to the ground, it was easy to see a black velvet pump half buried in the soft earth.

"Whoever killed Lily had to be strong enough to drag her out here."

"I don't like the way you're looking at me, Means." Fatty was angry. "I thought we were in this together."

"Relax, I didn't mean that to sound like an accusation. I'm just thinking out loud."

"So what do we do now? We have to go back in there."

Means looked toward the mansion. "And we have to convince everyone to trust us enough so they don't leave until we can figure out who killed Lily."

"Why does everyone have to stay for us to do that?" Fatty asked.

Means brushed off his jacket. "Because, Arbuckle, what we both fear the most will happen quicker than you ever imagined. If you thought you had troubles before, wait until you see what they do to you now. Both of us have been put through the grinder, had our reputations ruined. But somehow, we managed to make lives for ourselves again."

"Yeah, things are a helluva lot better than they were a few years ago."

"And I have the new book," Means said. "But this, getting our names connected to a murder? This would bury us alive! There'd be no coming back . . . ever."

Fatty didn't understand what Means had planned; all he knew was he was scared. "Okay," he said, "just tell me what to do." He reached in his pocket and pulled out a large handkerchief to blot the sweat.

"What time is it?" Means asked.

"I don't know." Fatty shrugged.

"But you have a pocket watch. There," Means pointed to the chain hanging from Arbuckle's gray flannel vest.

Arbuckle looked down, embarrassed. "That's just for show. I had to hock the watch years ago."

Means didn't care about his companion's sad financial state. "Well, I imagine we've only been out here for twenty minutes – half an hour at the most. From the sound of things inside, I don't think we've even been missed."

When Irma saw Arbuckle enter the brightly lit room, she immediately thought of Lon Chaney. The way he'd contorted his face – his whole body – when he played the Hunchback of Notre Dame had given her the willies for days. His eyes bugging out that way. Poor Fatty, she thought. He looked so ill-at-ease that she felt deeply sorry for him. The lights made his skin look waxy. She stopped singing without realizing she had done so. And when she stopped, the band stopped. And when the musicians broke off so abruptly, everyone in the room froze.

It was Zelda Fitzgerald who came to life first. "So," she giggled, apparently drunk, "where is our little Lily? Our precious little flower? Our lovely, lost Lily?" Her laughter embarrassed practically everyone in the room.

Gaston Means walked onto the dance floor. "Gather around," he said. "I have an announcement."

"Oh, a game! We're going to play a game!" Zelda clapped her hands together.

"Hush," someone shouted.

"You wouldn't talk to me like that if Scott were here." She took another gulp of her drink and then retreated into a pout.

"But he's not, so kindly hush up," the same person told her.

Satisfied he had their attention, Means began. "First off, is Miss McKeon here?"

"I certainly am," she said as she walked over to stand beside him.

"Good. What I am about to tell you is very upsetting but I want you all to remain calm and quiet until I've finished."

Judith straightened her back and folded her arms across her chest. "Just tell us, Mr Means, we're not children."

"Our hostess is . . ."

"Dead! I knew it!" Irma said.

The crowd ignored the singer and continued staring at Means as if she hadn't spoken.

"She's right, I'm afraid. Lily must have fallen. We found her body down in the water."

"How terrible," Judith said.

Disbelief ricocheted around the room, hitting each guest in their gut, then their heart. Shock, then commotion. "Dreadful!" "Unbelievable." "How very awful." "Poor Lily."

Fatty looked at Means, confused.

Means motioned for him to remain quiet. Then turning to Judith, he asked, "Do you have a guest list?"

"In my office. I'll go get it."

Several people asked the butler for their coats. Means hurried over to the servant and told him to stay where he was. "Listen. Please. No one can leave here yet."

"The party's over, as they say, old chum," Bing said, slapping the man on the back.

"The police have to be called," Means said. His words quieted the room.

"Then we should clear out so they can do their work. Write up their reports. Whatever it is they do." Dorothy Parker walked to the bar and sat her empty glass on a coaster.

Judith returned with the list and handed it to Means. He held it over his head. "I have the names of every person in this room and I'm going to check to see if we're all here."

An elderly woman wearing a diamond choker timidly asked, "But what does that matter? Lily had an accident and . . ."

"It wasn't an accident!" Arbuckle shouted from his side of the huge room.

"Is this true?" Judith asked.

"Well, possibly. Maybe. I believe her death was caused by someone other than . . . herself."

Fatty came closer. "He means she was murdered."

"I have to get out of here," W.C. Fields said. "I can't be associated with any of you. Look what happened to ole Fatty there. No, no, this would definitely ruin me. Excuse me, but I must be on my way."

"Sorry, Mr Fields. That is precisely why you should not leave. We must all stay here and be accounted for. There is strength in numbers. If we all remain calm and vouch for each other, we're safe."

"Then tell me, my good man," Fields asked, looking down at Means with disgust, "why did you tell us Lily succumbed to an accident when in fact she was murdered?"

"I'll tell you why," Fatty said, "because he was a hot shot with the FBI, then a private investigator after he got involved in one too many scandals. Now he's looking to solve a murder – make the headlines and a new name for himself. Think all will be forgiven, Mr Means? Think you can write a brand new book about the murder of Lillian Armstrong-Smith?"

Means was the confused one now. "No, why would you ask me that? I thought we had an agreement? An understanding of sorts."

"I did too until you lied to me out there, when you showed me Lily's shoe."

"What do you mean?"

"Oh, I know you think I'm just a big, fat, dumb clown. Everyone does. But I'm real good at what I do. I spent years practising falls, tumbling, figuring out where arms and legs land when you chase someone. Hell, I did nothing else for hours at a time with the Keystone Cops. I'm a professional, Mr Means, and damn good at what I do – did.

"The shoe you showed me was dug deep into the ground. If someone dragged Lily, as you assumed they did, her shoe would have slid off and fallen away – not pushed down into the soil. For the shoe to end up where and how we found it, would have meant one of three things: someone pushed her forward, she walked to that place willingly, or she was running away from her attacker. However, it was you who found the shoe, in the dark. Odd, considering I had been out on the grounds in the yard – on that very spot – earlier and missed it. Imagine! In the light of the full moon, I missed a silver object the size of a shoe, sparkling there – like a spotlight. Therefore, I can only assume you planted it yourself, Mr Means."

Means fell down into a plush club chair forcing it against the wall. "All right, I admit I put the shoe there, but only after I'd stumbled over it earlier."

"Why would you do such a thing?" Judith asked, stunned.

Embarrassed to look the woman in the eye, he spoke slowly. "I needed to be believed."

"You mean admired," Fatty said. "You thought this was just the opportunity you needed to regain some credibility."

"Is that true?" Bing asked.

"Yes," Means said, still too cowardly to look up. "I worked

for the FBI. I had respect, a position close to the President of the United States. The most powerful man in the world."

"And you brought disgrace down upon yourself," Bing ranted. "You brought disgrace to your office and your country. There is no one to blame for your misfortunes except you, sir."

"I know. Don't you think I know all that?"

"So," Judith said, "let me see if I understand this. You took Mrs Armstrong-Smith's death as an opportunity to benefit yourself?"

Dorothy Parker sniffed. "Typical man, you'll always land on somebody's feet."

Judith McKeon shook her head. "Poor Mrs Armstrong-Smith."

"Oh come now, you hated her . . ." Arbuckle's fat hand swiftly clamped over his mouth.

Means' head jerked upward to look at the secretary. "You did?" And then shifting his eyes to Arbuckle he asked, "How would you know something like that? Have you met Miss McKeon before this evening?"

"Well, yes, and . . ." He looked to the woman contritely.

"It's okay, Roscoe, I'm not ashamed of our friendship."

"Friendship? This is all so cozy I can't stand it," Parker quipped.

"Miss McKeon wrote me several letters while I was going through my ah, trouble."

"Fan letters?" Means asked.

"It started out that way," Judith told them. "I was infatuated with . . ."

"A star. It happens all the time," Crosby said. "But the papers, magazines, they were full of stories. All the gory details. Weren't you afraid you were corresponding with a murderer?"

Judith looked at Fatty adoringly. "Oh, no. I could tell Roscoe would never hurt anyone. He's a gentle, kind, sensitive soul."

"And you could tell all of this from . . . what?" Bing asked. What ever led you to believe you knew this man so intimately . . . unless . . ."

"No! Don't even think it! Nothing happened between the two of us."

Means studied the guest list he had gotten from Judith. "I

notice here that your name is not among those invited, Mr Arbuckle."

"And if you look closer, Mr Means, neither is yours," Judith pointed out.

"I don't understand."

"*I* invited you – both of you. It was easy just to slip in a few extra guests, being responsible for the invitations and all. Mrs Armstrong-Smith never saw what went out in the mail or what I didn't want her to know came back."

Dorothy Parker finished her martini, held the empty glass up to attract a waitress. "So why the invites?" she asked.

W.C. Fields laughed. "Life is certainly a stage and how we all do strut. Our little lady here set us up. We were all here for her entertainment. Isn't that so, my dear?"

"No. I just wanted to see Roscoe. I knew he'd never consent to meet me otherwise. So I spoke through Mrs Armstrong-Smith. But it wasn't as if she would have appreciated a man like you," she said to Arbuckle. "Truth is, she always thought you were a killer."

"So knowing what her reaction would be at the very sight of me, you wanted to shock her? Upset her?" Arbuckle's face fell into a soft frown.

"It's terrible," Judith admitted, "I know it's unforgivable but, Lord help me, as much as I wanted to be with you, I wanted to see her uncomfortable more. I wanted to see her frightened."

Cal walked over, Irma trailing behind. "Miss McKeon, should I tell the boys they can pack up and go home? Or do we have to wait around for the police?"

Judith was glad for the interruption. "What do you suggest we do, Mr Means?"

"Why in Sam Hill are you asking that imbecile?" W.C. Fields wanted to know.

"Because he's the closest thing we have right now to any kind of law."

"Law by association? That's rich." Parker laughed.

"Tell your band to hang around," Means addressed Cal, ignoring Dorothy.

"Sure thing." Cal turned to leave and Judith spotted the necklace around Irma's neck.

"Hold on a minute, you." She grabbed Irma by the arm. "Just where did you get those pearls?"

Means stood up and advanced on the woman, hoping to frighten her into an answer.

"Cal gave them to me. Honest! I ain't no thief, I'm a good girl!"

The bandleader started for the French doors. Means chased after him.

A group of drinkers sitting in lawn chairs laughed as Means shouted for help. It was Novarro who ended up tackling the man.

"Get offa me!" Cal shouted to the actor. Then to Means, "I found them. Honest, Mr Means. Over there. I swear! Just go ask that guy." He pointed to the bartender stationed under a green awning.

"Bring him over here," Means told Novarro.

Grabbing the man by the collar of his tuxedo jacket, the actor dragged Cal across the lawn.

The bartender smiled, oblivious to the commotion. His attention had been focused on one of the attractive waitresses. "What'll it be, gentlemen?" he asked when he saw them.

"The gentleman here," Means said pointing to Cal, "claims he found a strand of pearls out here and that you can vouch for his story."

"Name's Howard Pearson, sir, and no, I'm sorry but I never saw any such thing. I'm afraid he's lying to you."

Cal's shoulders went limp. Novarro released his hold but stood close. "Come on, Howard, tell them how I found those damn pearls right over there." Cal pointed to a spot near the cliffwalk. "Ya saw me. I showed ya them. Ya acted like you didn't know where they came from, that ya'd never seen them before."

Howard rubbed his chin, the stubble looked like dirt stuck to his face. "Sorry, Cal."

Before anyone could stop him, Cal lunged across the bar and grabbed the bartender. "I thought we were friends here, Howard. Ya told me if I covered up for you, I could have the pearls for Irma. Ya told me . . ."

"Get him off me," Howard grunted.

Hearing the commotion, Judith McKeon came running, leaving the rest of the party inside, watching the scene as if it were a moving picture. "Howard," she said jerking to a stop. "I didn't know you were here."

"Isn't he one of the bartenders you hired?" Means asked.

"I called the agency and they sent over some people. I've used Howard in the past. There's never been any trouble before. We have a good working relationship."

Howard pushed himself away from the men. "Working relationship? Judith, we both know it was a hell of lot more than that."

Before she could speak, Means addressed the man. "Tell us how you would define your relationship with Miss McKeon."

"I have connections, know what I mean? I'm very popular with the upper crust, especially in these difficult times. Understand what I'm saying here? I can get alcohol – illegal hooch. High quality and lots of it. I've helped her out on more than one occasion."

"That's true," Judith said. "Mrs Armstrong-Smith is very demanding and when she wants something I either accommodate her or I'm not only out of a job, but as she has threatened many times, never going to find work in this country."

"It's a big world out there, Miss McKeon," Means said, "and I'm sure an intelligent woman such as yourself . . ."

"You don't understand how influential Mrs Armstrong-Smith is . . . I mean was. And excuse me, Mr Means, but you of all people should understand how difficult it is to start over with a questionable reputation. It follows you everywhere. I've watched it happen over and over again."

Means nodded. "You're right; I do understand." Turning to Howard he asked, "So you've done some favors for Miss McKeon from time to time, and worked as a bartender at a few parties. That's all there is to it, then?"

"Yes," Judith answered. "That's all."

"And when did you last see the pearls?" he asked her.

"Days ago. In fact, Mrs Armstrong-Smith was still looking for them earlier this evening."

"Cal, do you want to stick to your story or are we calling the police now? I think we can drum up a burglary charge if not murder."

"Okay, no police. I swiped them – so what? I didn't know they were hers. I didn't know who they belonged to."

"Explain," Novarro said, anxious to hear the man's story.

"I got here earlier this afternoon to check things out – set up. I saw the pearls on the floor in the hall. I picked them up, put them in my pocket, and gave them to Irma. Thought maybe I'd get lucky after we were done tonight."

"And if Irma got caught wearing them, she'd be the one in trouble, right?"

"To be honest, I never thought that far ahead. I had other things on my mind."

Arbuckle joined the group in the middle of Cal's story.

"Let's go back inside," Judith suggested. "It's getting cold out here."

Means stood fixed in thought. "You never saw Mrs Armstrong-Smith leave the house?" he asked Judith.

"No, I told you, the last I heard she was getting dressed in her room."

"What side of the house is your room on?"

"The opposite side."

"Why? Wouldn't she want you close by?"

"Yeah, you were always telling me what a tyrant she was," Fatty said.

"Precisely, that's why I insisted I be in the other wing. I needed some privacy. I do have a personal life."

"I'll say," Howard laughed.

Everyone turned.

"Shut up, Howard!" Judith snapped.

"Shut up! Go away! Be quiet! I'm sick of your orders, Judy. You can't treat me like that anymore."

Means saw his opportunity and sympathetically asked the man, "Like what, Howard? Does she treat you badly? Women can be so . . ."

"She's a bitch! She lies to me; she treats me like a dog."

"But you love her anyway, right?" Means asked.

"Yes, but she loves someone else."

Means turned to Arbuckle. "Did Miss McKeon ever confess her love for you in any of her letters?"

"Well . . ."

"Come on, man, no one can hold you responsible for what another person writes."

"Occasionally she would say something along those lines."

"And you told me you loved me, too," Judith said. "Tell them. Tell everyone now how much you love me and how we're going to be together. Forever! That's what you said . . . forever!"

"And just how did you expect that to happen, girlie, when you was with me?" Howard shouted. "All the time telling me how that bitch boss of yours was the only thing keepin' us from being together and now I find out you was writing this fat man, planning to be with him. But I was the one who got rid of . . ."

Silence.

"Continue, Mr Pearson," Means insisted. "You were the one who got rid of who?"

"No one."

"Call the police," Means told Judith.

She didn't move. It took a moment but when she spoke, she erupted. "You, Howard? You killed Mrs Armstrong-Smith?"

"For you, Judy. For us."

Howard jumped over the bar and started for the cliffwalk. Arbuckle and Novarro were on his heels. The smaller man tripped him and Arbuckle pinned him to the ground.

Judith ran inside for the phone.

"Gaston Bullock Means," he told the reporter. "M . . . e . . . a . . . n . . . s."

"I've heard that name before. Wait a minute. Don't tell me." The pretty young thing was anxious to get all her facts straight.

"I used to work with the President; I was with the FBI." He beamed.

"And now you've solved a murder!" she said.

"I guess I was just born to be of service to my fellow man."

"Well jeepers, Mr Means, I can't thank you enough for talking to me. None of the other people at Mrs Armstrong-Smith's party will give me the time of day."

"Don't mention it, my dear. Don't mention it."

Without Fire

TOM HOLT

*Tom Holt's best known for his comic fantasy novels, which
began with* Expecting Someone Taller *(1987), but he's
written much else besides including historical novels, such
as* Goatsong *(1989) and* The Walled Orchard *(1990) and
the continuation of E. F. Benson's Mapp and Lucia books,*
Lucia in Wartime *(1985) and* Lucia Triumphant *(1986),
which brings us back to the Roaring Twenties.*

I was dragged out of blessed sleep by a ghastly thumping
noise outside my cabin.

At first I assumed it was just the unspeakable Brindesley-
White woman again. She had barged in the night before, an
exotic but fairly monstrous spectacle in a beaded and fringed
evening dress that for some reason reminded me of a Crusader
on a church brass; waved a half-empty champagne bottle under
my nose and told me, superfluously and with bad grace, that I
wasn't Bunny Delahey. I'd acknowledged the truth of her
accusation and pointed out that Major Delahey's cabin was
number 106, next door. She had peered at me sideways, just to
make sure I wasn't the major trying to be funny, and drifted
unsteadily away; that she eventually reached safe harbour, so to
speak, I deduced from the wail of a portable gramophone
reverberating through the cabin wall ten minutes later.

On this occasion I was feeling distinctly fragile, on account of
broken sleep and sundry other factors, and in no mood to cope

with inebriated females. Accordingly, I lay still and waited. A moment or so later, a man's voice called out my name. "Are you there, sir?" he added, which ruled out Major Delahey as well; I'd only spoken to him once, and he'd addressed me as "old son".

I grunted inarticulate permission to enter, and my tormentor took shape before me, a stocky figure in a white jacket with horribly shiny brass buttons.

"Sorry to disturb you, sir," the purser said, "but the captain would like to see you right away."

For a moment, I thought the poor fellow was talking a foreign language, because he wasn't making any sense. Why would the captain want to see me, in the middle of the night?

I fumbled my way into a dressing gown and followed him out down the corridor. "Quickest way's through the cocktail lounge, sir," the purser said, "if you'd care to follow me."

As it so happened, I knew where the cocktail lounge was; in fact, I'd spent rather more time in it than was good for me since we'd cast off from Liverpool. That in itself was remarkable, since it was a singularly unattractive place; slightly smaller and less ostentatious than St Mark's in Venice, painted white with pickled wood panelling, littered with those awful chrome bar-stools covered in red leather; whenever I see them, I can't help thinking of Mr Wells' Martian war-machines. As I trailed through like a prisoner under escort, a long, bald fellow in a white dinner jacket was crouched, almost hiding, behind the piano, valiantly singing the very latest hit while nobody listened. I winced at his performance but couldn't help a vestigial salute to the dexterity of the lyrics; one tradesman acknowledging another.

As we left the room, a man and a girl blocked the doorway, coming in as we were leaving. He was stout, pudding-faced, evening-dressed and gripping a bottle like a 'keeper dispatching a wounded pheasant; she was shingled and practically skeletal, her jewelled headband slipping down over one eye in the manner favoured by the pirates in the storybooks of my childhood. Neither of them was looking particularly well; he was bright red and she was pale green, so they clashed unforgivably into the bargain.

"Don't want to go out there, old man," the youth told me. As it happened he was quite right – I wanted to be in bed, asleep, back in dear old England where the floor stayed still – but I wondered how he knew; intuition, I supposed. He weaved past me, towing the girl by the wrist like a coal barge, and lunged into the scrum of black mohair backs and bare, fish-belly-white shoulders. It was like watching bees returning to the hive, because a moment later the two of them had been absorbed into the swarm, and I don't suppose I could've told them apart from their peers if my life depended on it. My brother in arms the pianist had finished with "Let's Do It!" and embarked on "Bye, Bye, Blackbird." I shuddered from head to toe. There are few sights more revolting to a man with a delicate head than the scenes of joy and youthful exuberance he left four hours ago with a view to sleeping it off.

We carried on up onto the boat deck (uncharacteristically deserted), through an undersized steel door, down one flight of confoundedly awkward steps and up another. I have precious little sense of direction at the best of times (a failing which, on one notable occasion during the War, both endangered and saved my life) and it wasn't long before I was hopelessly lost. Fortunately, the purser paused from time to time to allow me to catch up.

The captain's office was smaller than I'd anticipated, but rather more magnificent; a pleasant contrast, to my old-fash-ioned eye, to all the chrome and smoked glass with which the rest of ths ship was festooned. The panelling was a rather splendid dark wood, possibly teak, and the desk wouldn't have looked out of place in the lair of some American merchant prince. The captain was a short, round man with cropped white hair and bright blue eyes. He was, he told me, frightfully sorry to have troubled me, but he needed my help.

The mystery again. "That's perfectly all right," I lied. "What can I do for you?"

The captain shuffled, as if painfully aware that everything was somehow his fault. "I regret to say," he said quietly, "that's something rather dreadful has happened. A woman's been murdered."

"Good God," I said. I was still, of course, two thirds asleep. In fact, I was reminded of an unfortunate occasion when I was a boy, and had the misfortune to doze off in the middle of a maths lesson, to be woken by the crisp, harsh voice of the maths master repeating my name and a problem in mental algebra. The helpless, frustrated feeling of panic as I struggled to apply to the problem a mind still furred up with sleep came back to me at that moment with most unwelcome vigour. "I'm terribly sorry to hear it," I said, "but what possible help can I be to you?"

The captain frowned, as though I was being deliberately obtuse. "It's quite simple," he said. "As I told you, a woman's been killed. But we have no idea who did it, and clearly it's of the utmost importance that we find the killer as quickly as possible. For all we know, there could be a homicidal maniac loose on the ship, and obviously we must make sure he doesn't kill again."

I was about to say, "Then why in God's name don't you call the police?" but mercifully I managed to stop myself in time. We were at that time three days' out of Liverpool bound for New York.

"I take your point," I said. "But what can I do? I'm not a detective."

The captain may have sighed, very faintly. "Of course not," he said. "But I've checked the passenger list, and I have to say, you're the nearest thing to one that we've got."

"Nonsense," I said. "I'm nothing of the sort. You must be confusing me with someone else."

"I think not."

This was ridiculous, and I fear my manners were beginning to fray. "Does your precious passenger list happen to tell you what I do for a living? I'm a writer. I write song lyrics for musical comedies."

The captain frowned. "It says on your passport," he replied, "that you're a barrister."

That deflated me a little bit. "Used to be," I corrected him. "Before the War, actually; I was in practice for about six months. If I remember correctly, my entire earnings amounted to a shade under five pounds."

I could see myself tumbling a degree or two in his estimation, not that I cared unduly. "Nevertheless," he said, "a trained legal mind – "

"My field was Chancery work, not criminal cases," I said. "And I was hopeless at it, too."

"Even so," the captain said, sitting up a little straighter.

"Your military service; a captain in the Gloucesters, and the DSO – "

I sighed. "Let me tell you about that," I said wearily. "Having been ordered to lead my men back from the front line to prepared positions, I lost my way. It was raining, murky but not dark, and I set off in entirely the wrong direction. I found what I took to be my assigned destination, only to find it was full of Germans. Fortuitously, they were even more surprised than we were. With respect, if you want someone to help you find something, I think you've got the wrong man."

The captain was starting to look worried, but I could tell that he'd already made up his mind. "There's nobody else on the ship even remotely qualified to investigate the matter," he said sadly. "Furthermore, we know for a fact that you couldn't possibly have done it. You can see the relevance of that for yourself."

That aspect of the matter hadn't even occurred to me. "I'm delighted to hear you say so," I said.

The captain smiled thinly. "At the time the murder took place," he said, "you were – excuse me – in no fit state to harm anyone, except possibly yourself."

"Ah, yes," I said. At least that helped me put things in context. Earlier that evening, a very kind and polite steward had helped me make my way from the bar to my cabin. "Seasickness," I explained.

"Quite," the captain replied. "The point is, you can be eliminated as a suspect straight away. I can also eliminate myself and eight members of the crew, who were with me on the bridge." He scowled; keeping his patience was plainly costing him a good deal of effort. "Well, will you help me or not?" he said. "If you positively refuse, of course – "

"No, of course not," I replied, sounding perhaps a little more resigned than was polite under the circumstances. "If you believe I can help you, I'll certainly do my best. I hope you won't be disappointed."

He declined to express an opinion on that score. "Come with me," he said.

You'll have gathered that I earn my living in the theatre. The truth is, I'm what's known as a play doctor. A musical comedy is put into production, at great expense; at the eleventh hour, it becomes painfully obvious that the music is adequate but the words aren't, and they send for me. I spend ninety-six hours in a darkened room, poisoning my system with nicotine and coffee, and with luck the show is saved. It's a pretty grim sort of existence, but I'm good at it. I can rhyme "gadabout" with "lad about" and "yes, sirree" with "Tennessee" as well as any and better than most, and like a bull terrier, I won't let go until my prey is dead. Nobody has ever heard of me, but I've saved the money and reputations of a good many household names. Accordingly, when it finally dawned on Mr Ziegfeld that his latest extravaganza was little short of an affront to human dignity, he cabled me with an offer no sane man could refuse and ordered me to New York by the first available ship.

It's understandable, therefore, that I tend to see things in theatrical terms; positions on the stage, exits and entrances, a stratified cast of characters. In the melodrama that unfolded as the captain explained the situation, the unenviable role of victim fell to Lady Julia Harkness. Actually, there was a certain sweet irony in that, since Julia Ormerod (as she then was) made a name for herself in the mid and late 1990s as the most perfectly adorable victim ever to grace the West End. She was reviled and snubbed by Shaw's hypocrites and Barrie's insensitive husbands, turned out into the snow by Maeterlink, driven mad by Ibsen and hounded into decline and the grave by Lewis and Pinero. After a decade of this unceasing abuse, she quit the stage to marry Sir George Harkness, shortly after he made his first million selling spavined horses to the cavalry during the South African war, and settled down to a life of refined tranquility in Berkshire.

Why she was sailing to America nobody could tell me; the general view seemed to be that a wealthy and respectable widow didn't need a reason. As far as we knew at that point, she died her last death shortly after lighting a cigarette on the boat deck, in company with a group of other ladies, not long after dinner. The witnesses all agreed that she lit the cigarette, inhaled deeply, choked violently and fell over; after a few ferocious convulsions she became still, and by the time the ship's doctor arrived at the scene she was already dead. Almost immediately, the doctor diagnosed the cause of death as cyanide poisoning.

Here the mystery began. According to witnesses, including the captain himself, at whose table she had dined, it was impossible for the poison to have been in her food. Her appetite had been poor, on account of seasickness; she had taken a little soup and a few mouthfuls of salmon, and drunk maybe half a glass of wine. Everyone else who had had soup from the same tureen, salmon from the same dish and wine from the same bottle was still very much alive. The cigarette could also be ruled out; one of the young ladies in the group had handed round her cigarette case, and four others had smoked from it. The doctor had recovered the body to his surgery and was carrying out a post-mortem, though he couldn't vouch for the conclusiveness of his results given the rather basic facilities at his disposal.

As for a possible motive, the captain had nothing to offer. Lady Julia was, he said, not the most pleasant person he'd ever met; she seemed to have a low opinion of many people and little compunction about sharing it with anybody who'd listen. On the other hand, the captain said, if that sort of thing was enough to provoke murder, the first class lounge would've been two-thirds empty before we were out of sight of Ireland. As for specific grievances against her, he didn't know of any. She was rich, of course, but a few discreet questions among the passengers she'd been keeping company with revealed that her heirs were three nephews, all at home in Berkshire. Her circle aboard ship were all slight acquaintances or people she'd met for the first time on the voyage. If robbery was the motive, she'd been killed for nothing, since her pearl necklace and the Harding sapphires were still in place when the doctor took away the body, and were currently in the ship's safe.

As far as the means for the crime were concerned, there were over five hundred passengers, quite apart from the crew, and a small quantity of cyanide would be easy to smuggle aboard. For obvious practical reasons, he didn't propose to search the ship unless it was absolutely essential.

"Well," I said, when the captain had finished his summary, "at least we know one thing."

He looked at me. "Do we?" he said, rather hopelessly.

I nodded. "Whoever killed the wretched woman must've

planned to do it before he left England. People don't tend to carry doses of cyanide about with them on the off-chance that it might come in handy along the way." The captain's expression tightened a little; I suppose I was being rather flippant. "As far as I know," I went on, "the only thing cyanide's any use for is killing people, or killing things, at any rate; so we can rule out the possibility of someone having it with them for a legitimate reason and subsequently deciding to use it as a weapon. This can only be a premeditated murder, which leaves us with two possibilities. Either the killer is a lunatic killing at random, or the crime was deliberate and premeditated, and therefore designed to achieve something. Occam's razor –" The captain raised an eyebrow, but I ignored him. "Occam's razor argues against a millionairess being the victim of an indiscriminate maniac. Either there's a personal grudge involved that we don't know about – which is far from unlikely – or she was killed for her money."

The captain shook his head slowly. "As far as we know," he said, "nobody on this ship stands to profit from her death, and the people who were in a position to give her the poison were all relative strangers." He rubbed the tip of his nose against the back of his hand; I knew a lieutenant in France who used to do that when he was puzzled about something. "Are we looking for a hired assassin, do you think? I have to say, that seems a bit far-fetched to me."

I pulled a face. "It's one of those confounded puzzles that gets worse the more you think about it," I said. "And I don't think we're going to make any progress sitting here, more's the pity. I suppose we'd better go and have a look at the place where it all happened; and then we'd better begin talking to people. To be honest with you, the most we can hope to achieve is to keep everything pretty much as it is until we reach New York, and hand the whole business over to the authorities there."

"I suppose so," the captain replied. "But I was hoping we could resolve matters before then. There's still the distinct possibility that whoever did this could kill someone else."

He was looking at me again, and I didn't like it. In my life I've had to take responsibility rather more often than I'd have liked, and usually very little good has come of it. My career record as a failed barrister and an inept infantry officer didn't strike me as sufficient justification for entrusting me with the safety of five hundred people; particularly when I was feeling distinctly fragile, and still wearing my pyjamas. "I really wish you'd find someone else to look into this," I said. "Pretty well all I'm qualified to do with the evidence you've given me is turn it into verse and set it to music, and I don't think that'd help matters very much."

He looked at me some more. "Perhaps you should go back to bed for a while," he said.

I don't know how real detectives can stand it.

Perhaps if I'd ever met a real detective, I might have a better insight into the way they cope. I haven't, of course, and what little I know about them derives from the theatre, the movies and sensational fiction. My understanding is, however, that they somehow contrive to spend hours at a time interviewing witnesses, and still remain calm and positively civil – British detectives, anyway – in the face of unremitting vagueness, deviousness and affronted dignity. After four hours the next morning asking what I thought were perfectly reasonable questions, politely expressed, my admiration for the professional guardians of the law knew no bounds. For my part, I wanted to strangle somebody.

A wise man knows his own breaking point. I sent a steward to convey my apologies to the last three people on my list; I was running behind schedule, (a lie) and would therefore be obliged if their appointments could be deferred for half an hour. Then I got out of the poky little cabin I'd been using as an interview room and headed for the fresh air.

To legitimise my truancy, I made for the boat deck, scene of the crime, of which I had so far made only a cursory examination. Fictional sleuths, I knew, made a great performance of examining the *mise en scene*; they crawled about on their hands and knees like Boy Scouts following a spoor, peered through lenses, picked up hairs and fragments of cigar ash and packed them carefully away in clean envelopes. My head was still a bit too delicate for crawling about on decks, but there was one thing I knew I had to look for; something obvious and fundamental, which ought to provide the key to the whole affair.

It wasn't there, of course.

This meant that I had to ask a steward to take me to the bridge (no, I explained, I didn't know the way), and when I arrived, I learned that the officer I needed to see had gone off duty ten minutes before I got there. Another long walk; he was in his cabin, getting ready for bed. Fortunately, he was able to answer my question with a single word. Largely for the sake of appearances, I went back to the crime scene and made a show of looking round. I didn't get down on my hands and knees, but I did lean over a few times, and even stooped to pick something up (I should have been looking for it all along; but attention to detail was never my strong point, as my old master in chambers would be delighted to confirm); the rest of the time I spent leaning against the rail looking thoughtful and broody. I don't suppose I fooled anybody. I may mix with actors in the course of business, but I've yet to master the art of protective mimicry.

My brief furlough over, I went back to that miserable little cabin and waited for the next witness to arrive. Before she showed up, the captain bustled in, looking very pleased with himself. He asked how I was getting along, and didn't wait for an answer.

"I think we may have a lead," he said excitedly. "One of the stewards – Brewer, a most reliable man – came to me a few minutes ago and told me that shortly before the tragedy took place, he noticed a passenger on the boat deck acting in a most suspicious manner."

I nodded gravely. "Promising," I said.

"I believe so," the captain replied. "Luckily, Brewer is a most observant fellow, and happened to notice that the suspect –" my expression didn't change, although people tell me I'm a hopeless poker player – "was wearing a rather unusual and distinctive hat, a fedora is the term, I believe; the latest thing in New York, but hasn't caught on yet in England."

"Excellent," I said. "So we're looking for an American."

The captain nodded, pleased by my ready grasp of the evidence. "Furthermore," he continued, "Brewer described the individual as tall and thin, by his movements young or at most in early middle age. I consulted the passenger list with the help of Mr Standish – the purser, you know."

"We've met."

"Of course, yes. Anyway, only three passengers fitted the

description, and two of them had reliable alibis. Accordingly, I've sent three stewards to look for the third man and bring him to my office as soon as possible. I'll let you know as soon as he arrives, and you can take it from there."

I smiled warmly. "Splendid," I said. "Though really, I don't suppose you need me there. I mean to say, you appear to have the whole thing under control, so – "

He shook his head. "I'd rather you conducted the actual interrogation," he said. "Your barrister's training, and so forth. If you don't mind, of course."

I made a graceful gesture of acquiescence. "My pleasure," I said.

He left; and my next interviewee hadn't shown up yet, so I slipped back up on deck and poked about around the lifeboats for a moment or so, until I'd satisfied myself on a couple of points. By the time I got back, my witness was ready and waiting.

"So sorry to have kept you," I said. The woman – I forget her name – didn't bother to acknowledge my apology, so I sat down and steepled my fingers on the desk in front of me.

"First," I said, "I should just like to reassure you that we have no grounds whatsoever to suspect that you had anything at all to do with this dreadful business."

"So I should hope," the woman replied; but I couldn't help noticing that she seemed to deflate very slightly, like a leaky tyre, and the red glow faded gradually from her face as the interview went on. "Nevertheless," I continued briskly, "it would be most helpful if you could just answer a few simple questions, to help us build up a picture of what happened. Would that be all right?"

"I suppose so."

"Splendid. Now, then." I tried to remember how proper barristers went about it; but that was a long time ago, and I was never paying much attention at the best of times. "The other witnesses I've spoken to have given me a fairly good idea of what happened, but I'm hoping there are some points you can corroborate for me. We're reasonably confident that however Lady Julia came to harm, it couldn't have been in the dining room or the first class saloon; and the doctor informs me that if cyanide in any effective form had been administered before dinner, it would have taken effect long before Lady Julia went out on deck. Accordingly, we believe that the fatal act – what we lawyers call the *actus reus* – must have taken place on the boat deck."

I paused, mostly to congratulate myself on remembering the Latin tag. It's pretty much all I do remember of my criminal law. She said nothing, so I went on.

"As I understand it," I said, "at approximately a quarter to eleven, you were standing at the rear of the boat deck, quite close to the rearmost lifeboat derrick."

She frowned. "I'm sorry," she said, "I'm not familiar with nautical jargon."

"The steel crane arrangement that the boat hangs from."

"Ah," she said. "In that case, yes, I was."

"Very good. Now, three other witnesses have confirmed that during the relevant time – approximately a quarter to eleven until the moment of death, something like ten minutes later – nobody passed them coming down the boat deck from forward – I'm sorry, from the front end of the ship; and I was hoping that you can tell me if anybody came past you from the back end going forward."

She frowned, clearly wrestling with the mental geometry of the thing. "You see," I went on, "if that's the case, we can be pretty sure that the person who administered the poison must've been one of the four ladies who were standing chatting with Lady Julia just before her death. But if anybody else was passing by during the relevant time – "

"I see," she interrupted. "No, nobody came past me, I'm certain of that. I was waiting for my husband to join me, he'd stopped in the bar to talk to some people and said he'd meet me on the deck, and I was looking out for him; he'd been rather longer than I expected."

Quite, I thought. "That's fine," I said. "Most helpful. May I ask, did you see Lady Julia collapse?"

She looked rather embarrassed. "I'm afraid not," she said. "As it happened, I was looking the other way. Of course, as soon as that woman screamed – "

"Thank you," I said. "No further questions."

She took the hint and pushed off (just like a particularly stout, well-feathered old Welsummer hen that used to belong to my aunt Stephanie in Gloucestershire) and I had a moment or two to assimilate what I'd learned from her before the next exhibit turned up.

As I think I mentioned, I'm something of a student of mystery fiction. My guess was that next guest was, too; accordingly, I altered my manner a little.

"Sit down," I snapped, as he shut the door behind him.

He gave me what I suppose he thought was a cool, insolent look, and slid into the chair. "Sure," he replied. I'm not the world's best at accents, particularly American ones, which can be so hard to pin down; but even I could recognize a native New Yorker.

"You aren't wearing your hat," I said.

He frowned. "Pardon me?"

"Your hat," I repeated. "A particularly foul blue-grey fedora. Sears Roebuck, at a guess, but I don't claim to be an expert."

"I got a fedora," he replied, more puzzled than anything. "What about it?"

"Where is it?"

He shrugged. "Damnedest thing. Blew right off my head into the ocean, just now."

"You mean," I said, "you deliberately threw it over the side, to get rid of it."

He opened his eyes wide. "Why would I do a thing like that?"

"Oh, several reasons." I shrugged. "Vestigial good taste, for one. Or maybe—" Here I leaned forward a little. Basil Rathbone does it rather better. "Maybe you didn't want to be recognized."

He shrugged again, took out a cigarette and lit it. "Sorry, mister," he said, "I don't get you."

Well, I'd had my fun. I yawned a little, then leaned back. "So," I said, "what sort of stuff do you deal in? Scotch?"

He took it pretty well. "Mostly" he said. "Also brandy, some wine. Classy stuff."

"Naturally," I replied. "The sort of thing you can't just buy in Canada and lug over the border in a truck. Still, it's a lot of trouble and expense to go to, isn't it? Hardly worth your while, after expenses."

He smiled. "It was a whim," he said. "I'm telling the truth, I had to go to London on business – other business, nothing to do with you know what – and well, it seemed a shame to go home empty-handed, you know? So – "

"Quite," I said. "Just out of interest, how did you get it on board?"

He chuckled. "Easy as pie," he said. "I had a few fellows row out one night when the ship was in dock, before we set out. We climbed up the side with a rope, hauled up the booze and stashed it. Nobody gave us any trouble. Couldn't get away with that in the States, not without you bribe a lot of guys. You people don't know security from nothing."

I thought for a moment, then nodded. "Fine," I said. "That's all, for now." He stood up, warily. "By the way," I added, "the captain's got some stewards out looking for you."

He looked at me. "Is that right?"

I nodded. "You were seen lurking round the lifeboats just before the murder. He's bound to ask you why. You may care to get a few answers ready for him and – well, make a few arrangements."

His eyes narrowed. "I might, at that," he said. "Thanks." He paused. "You're being mighty helpful," he said.

"Thank you."

"Why?"

I smiled. "Enlightened self interest," I said. "You see, I'm going to be spending a bit of time – weeks, possibly a couple of months – living in your fair city, and as I understand it, there's a degree of difficulty about getting hold of certain home comforts – I wonder," I added, "do you happen to have a business card or anything like that?"

He grinned, and produced one. "Just ask for Johnny," he said, and left.

I'd saved the next interview till last, partly because after coping with all those strangers, I needed to see a friendly face; and unless you're of an age to remember the likes of Emily Fowler and Jessie Bond, no friendlier face has ever graced the London stage than that of my final witness.

"Hello, Jill," I said. "Darling," she replied, registering pleasant surprise. "I didn't know you were on board."

I shrugged. "It was all terribly last-minute. A royal summons." I lowered my voice. "Ziegfeld."

"Oh, dear." She pursed her lips. "Putrid?"

"So I'm told," I replied, "though of course I've yet to view the body, so the extent of the putrefaction remains to be seen. But it must be pretty rotten, or he wouldn't have sent for me."

She nodded. "I'd heard rumours," she said. "But you hear that sort of thing about every big show."

"So you do," I said. "You're not in it, are you?"

She laughed. "Heavens, no," she said. "Nothing so splendid, I'm afraid. Just some run-of-the-mill old thing that Jerome and Plum and Bill are putting together, and which'll probably close in Newark."

"I doubt it," I said, politely. "Anything good for you in it?" She shook her head. "I bounce on in the middle of the first act clutching a tennis racket," she replied, "and it sort of goes downhill from there. There's supposed to be a nice dance routine somewhere in Act Two, but it'll probably be cut by some interfering play-doctor."

"Those brutes," I said sympathetically. "Still, it's America. Splendid chance to bag a millionaire or two."

She gave me a look. I rose above it.

"Seriously," I said. "Sooner or later, one of those goofy-eyed young exhibits I'm always seeing clustered round the stage door is going to wear you down by sheer force of persistence, and then who am I going to write smart soubrette patter-songs for?"

She thought for a moment. "Jessie Matthews," she said. "No, really," she added, "she's much better than people give her credit for. Excellent diction."

I shrugged. "I hope you're right," I said. "It's hard enough as it is without knowing that your words are going to be chewed up and swallowed by some lisping half-wit who never learned how to breathe."

She smiled. "Don't worry," she said. "I have no plans to retire just yet. But come on," she added briskly, "aren't we supposed to be talking about this dreadful business with poor Julia?"

"I suppose we should," I replied. "England expects, and so forth. Very well." I sat up straight, just the way my mother would have liked. "You were with the deceased on the boat deck at approximately ten forty-five last night?"

"Yes, officer."

"Known her long?"

"Oddly enough, no," she replied. "I may have bumped into her at parties, but I don't remember saying two words to her before we met up on this boat."

I nodded. "How about the other three harpies in your little throng?" I looked down at my scrap of paper. "Cynthia Berry, Diana Butler and Jane Armitage. I spoke to them all just now, of course, but I couldn't tell 'em apart if you paid me. Who are they?"

She smiled. "Nobody much," she said. "People's wives, I think. Let's see; I played baccarat with Diana and Jane the night before last, and Julia played bridge with Cynthia and Jane two nights before that." She sighed. "That's the hellish thing about being on a boat," she said. "You're cooped up with people, and can't just remember a prior engagement when they want to be your friend."

"Dire," I agreed. "So, all five of you, chance acquaintances." I paused. "You've got a gold Cartier cigarette case."

"Had," she replied with a frown. "That tiresome captain made me give it to him, which means I've had to smoke beastly Sullivans all morning. Do you think you could be terribly sweet and get it back for me?"

"It might be possible," I said. "In fact, here it is, hiding under my notes."

"Angel," she said, and reached for it; but I held it back, and opened it.

"Help yourself," she said.

"Not just now, thanks," I replied. "You will please remember that I'm still on duty, and therefore not at liberty to accept offers of refreshment from members of the public. This was the case you handed round last night?"

She nodded. "Julia had run out, and the other three are all the most frightful cadgers, but one must be polite."

I glanced down at the open case. There were ten cigarettes on the right side; the left side was empty. "And the other three – Diana and Cynthia and whatever her dratted name is – they all helped themselves and no ill effects."

"And me too," she pointed out.

"And you too." I looked at her. "So it'd have been impossible for some horrible murdering person to have slipped a poisoned cigarette – cyanide, for instance – into this case, on the slim chance that Lady Julia would pick that particular cigarette, smoke it and die."

"Well, of course." She raised her eyebrows at me.

"That clears that up, doesn't it?" I sniffed the cigarettes, then closed the case and slipped it into my pocket. She watched me, but didn't say anything.

"The problem is," I said, "that we've got a dead body, and what looks depressingly like a murder, but not the faintest whiff of a motive. Can you think of one, Jill, dear?"

"No," she said. "But of course, I don't know the first thing about her."

"You'd never met her before this voyage," I replied.

"That's what I just said." A slight pause; then, "Don't you believe me?"

"Of course I believe you. But." I hesitated. After all, it really was none of my business. It was the most infernal liberty on the captain's part, conscripting me to be his master sleuth when all I want to do with what's left of my life is earn a little money and spend it pleasantly. One has a duty, of course, to society; but I maintain that I discharged that duty for good and all, one foggy morning in 1917, when my hopeless sense of direction led me astray in a muddy hellhole in France. Death did well out of me that day, and I owe him no more lives.

Nevertheless; "But," I repeated, "I have an idea that you did know Julia Harkness quite well. At second hand, I mean; by report."

"Not really. She'd retired by the time – "

"Quite so. She retired, I think, in '04 – wasn't the last thing she did that Pinero revival? – and married her fabulously wealthy war profiteer, the way you wonderful actresses do, and suddenly came over all respectable; and although her husband died relatively young and their union was never blessed with issue, I seem to remember reading or hearing somewhere that there's a couple of nephews – young fellows, about your age – who stand to inherit, of course, now that the old lady's popped off."

"Is that so? I don't – "

"I believe so," I said. "Which would be a stroke of luck for them, I suppose, if either of them was contemplating what my dear mother used to call an injudicious marriage; you know, someone a bit shady, with a reputation, an actress or something of the sort. I suppose it's the old poacher-turned-gamekeeper thing, but I'd heard that Lady Julia had a positive horror of the family money falling into the paws of some wretched little gold-digger. Imitation, presumably, not being the sincerest form of flattery, in her view."

"I have no idea," she said coldly, "what you're talking about."

"Of course not," I said. "But another thing I remember, just a snippet of silly gossip; some fool was telling me that you'd been seeing rather a lot of young Bertie Allsop, and wasn't his mother – ?"

She gave me a look I won't forget in a hurry. "Mary Ormerod, yes," she said. "What a memory you have, to be sure."

"Only for the trivia of my profession," I replied. "From memory, the Ormerod sisters started off in the Gaiety chorus in eighty-something, but Mary married a solicitor or something awful like that, and it was Julia, always reckoned the plainer of the two, who went on to make a name for herself." I laced my fingers together, rather too tightly for comfort. "May I take it that congratulations are in order?"

She was quiet for a long time; then she laughed. "Splendid, darling," she said. "And you're quite right, Bertie and I were secretly engaged at Christmas, but of course we didn't dare tell the old hag about it, she'd have cut Bertie off without a shilling. So yes, I couldn't be more pleased that wretched Julia dropped dead, positively at my feet, like a scene out of one of her dreadful melodramas. And of course," she went on, "you're thinking that perhaps I had something to do with it."

"The thought had crossed my mind," I confessed.

"In that case," she said sweetly, "you might care to tell me how I did it."

"You poisoned her," I said. "Cyanide, which you'd brought with you from England, in a cigarette."

"Really." She looked at me as though I was a poor idiot child.

"And maybe you can tell me how I contrived matters so that she got the poisoned one, rather than me or Cynthia or Jane or – what was that stupid woman's name?"

"Diana," I said. "Actually, I can, and it's really rather simple. At first," I went on, "I wondered if the other three were in it with you, but I scrubbed round that pretty quickly; they genuinely were perfect strangers to you, and it could have messed things up dreadfully. Fortunately, they were women of excellent taste, and so everything was all right."

"Please don't talk drivel, darling. It's giving me a headache."

"I'm sorry," I said. "I'm quite prone to headaches myself, as it happens. For instance, I always get a headache when I smoke those revolting Turkish cigarettes that are so popular these days. Honestly, I don't know what people see in them."

"Neither do I."

"Of course. But," I went on, "lots of people adore the filthy things, which is why the pleasant custom has grown up of filling one's cigarette case with Turkish on one side and Virginia on the other. Curiously, according to the maid who cleaned her cabin, Lady Julia only ever smoked Balkan Sobranie – such a misleading name, because of course they're as Turkish as the Blue Mosque. Which made me wonder; what if there was a cigarette case with plenty of Virginia on one side, and just one solitary, sad little Turk on the other? Assuming, of course, that the other ladies in your circle have the good taste to smoke God's own Players."

"Rather a big assumption, don't you think?"

"Lucky guess," I replied, "but also borne out by the maids who empty their bedside ashtrays. I give you full credit for high-class fieldwork, by the way; watching who Lady Julia spent time with, taking note of what they smoked."

She was looking me straight in the eye. It was like staring down a deep well. "What a simply wonderful imagination you have," she said, "and such a pity you don't use it in your work. I suppose you have something by way of proof of all this?"

I sighed. "That's awkward," I replied. "I'd hoped to find the cigarette itself, of course, but no luck at all. I searched, but it wasn't there. The captain said it probably fell overboard when Julia keeled over; but quite by chance I found the match she used to light it with. All you fashionable things have lighters, of course, but Julia preferred a good old-fashioned lucifer. Anyway, judging by where she fell, if the match was still there, I'd have expected to find the cigarette as well. There was always the chance that the ship had tilted over, the way they do, and the silly thing had rolled off into the sea. So I went to the trouble of having a word with the chappie who steers the boat, and he told me the sea's been as calm as a millpond since early yesterday evening. I can only conclude, therefore, that some wicked person took care to kick the dratted thing over the side when everyone else's attention was distracted."

She smiled beautifully at me. "So," she said. "No proof."

"No proof," I agreed sadly. "Well, actually, I tell a lie. Now," I went on, "this is a rather curious story, so bear with me. It so happens that aboard this ship we have a genuine American bootlegger, a charming gentleman whose name I won't bore you with. Now he took it into his head to plant thirty cases of rather good Scotch in one of the lifeboats, shortly before we left Liverpool. He thought he was being terribly clever, but what the silly fellow failed to realize was that safety procedures on a ship like this dictate that the lifeboats have to be checked regularly throughout the voyage. Must've come as rather a shock to him when he found out; and as soon as he heard about it, he hurried down to the boat deck in the hope of being able to shift at least some of his hoard to a better hiding-place before some officious swine stumbled across it. He'd got as far as untying one of the tarpaulins, but then you and Julia and your crowd came butting in, and he had to abandon operations and wait for you all to go away. It was sheer bad luck that when you kicked that horrid cigarette off the deck, it landed in the curl of the tarpaulin; worse luck that the sea-spray inside put it out before it could burn away; and the final touch of insult to injury when the captain told me to investigate some mysterious American who'd been hanging about the scene shortly before the crime took place. If he hadn't, I wouldn't have gone poking about in the tarpaulin," I said, reaching into my top pocket and taking out two thirds of a wet Sobranie, "and found this."

The Austin Murder Case

JON L. BREEN

*I was very tempted at the outset to include several parodies
and pastiches of famous 1920s sleuths, especially Poirot and
Wimsey, but decided better of it. However, I was then
reminded of the following story by Jon L. Breen. The
biggest-selling writer of detective fiction in the 1920s, bar
none, was S.S. van Dine with his books featuring the dilettante amateur sleuth Philo Vance. He appeared in* The
Benson Murder Case *(1926), the first of twelve novels of
which perhaps the best – certainly the most complicated – is*
The Bishop Murder Case *(1929). So popular were the
books that there was an instant parody with* The John
Riddell Murder Case *(1930) by Corey Ford, writing as
John Riddell. Van Dine wrote no short stories featuring
Vance so, forty years later, mystery aficionado and Professor
of English, Jon L. Breen, decided to rectify that omission.
Breen has written other parodies of famous detectives, and
you can find them in* Hair of the Sleuthound *(1982). Apart
from his own novels, he has written several indispensable
reference books of the mystery field including* What About
Murder? *(1981) and* Novel Verdicts *(1984).*

Of all the curious and inexplicable crimes that came to the
attention of Philo Vance during the incumbency of his
friend John F.-X. Markham as District Attorney of New York
County, there is wide disagreement as to which one was the

most bizarre, which one permitted the greatest exploitation of his deductive powers. Perhaps because of the brevity of the investigation and the speed with which Vance was able to put his finger on the guilty person, the murder of Jack Austin, or as it was often called in the press, "The Talkie Murder Case", has often been ignored in such discussions. But some feel, among them Vance himself, that his exposition of the vital clue in this case was one of the most dazzling strokes of his career.

Our connection with the Austin murder case began, as did so many of Vance's exploits, with a visit from District Attorney Markham. But this time it was not a worried Markham, puzzled over some unfathomable crime, but a more jovial District Attorney, passing along an invitation to a social engagement.

"It's a little masquerade party, Vance, at the home of Jack Austin, a week from Thursday night. He thought that you and Mr Van Dine, both of whose works he admires very much, would like to come."

"Most ingratiatin' of you to extend the invitation, Markham old chap, but to tell you the truth I don't find the idea altogether thrillin'. I can find better things to do with my time, don't y'know, than to dress up and go to a costume party at the digs of a most annoyin' and irritatin' vaudevillian. Thanks anyway, old dear."

"Mr Austin will be most disappointed. I dare say you're the only person in the city of New York who would turn down an invitation to Jack Austin's last party before he leaves Manhattan."

"Actu'lly leavin' ol' New York? Not altogether distressin' idea, y'know, but may I ask where he's goin'?"

"Hollywood. To make talking pictures."

Vance puffed his *Régie* and sniffed disgustedly. "If one of the talkin' cinema's first accomplishments will be to allow that chap's nasal off-key singin' to be heard by millions of people throughout the world, it's just another proof of the mistake the film industry's makin' in desertin' true cinema."*

* A devotion to the silent film was but another feature of Vance's many-faceted personality. He was the author of *Epistemological Symbolism in the Films of William S. Hart; Elmo Lincoln, the Renaissance Man*; and *Broncho Billy Anderson and Aristotelian Tragedy* – all highly regarded by film scholars.

"Quite so, Vance. Since you have such an enthusiasm for the silent film, though, perhaps you'll find the party more intriguing than you had at first thought."

"Might I?" rejoined Vance languidly. "And why might that be?"

"Each guest will come as his favorite movie star. I, for instance, am going as Tom Mix. Judge Peter Hawley will be there as Henry B. Walthall. Austin himself will impersonate Charlie Chaplin."

Vance turned to me. "'Pon my word, Van, it might be an inter'stin' time at that I have always wanted to become Douglas Fairbanks for an evening, and here an unprecedented opportunity presents itself. Respectin' your desire to remain inconspicuous, we might find a less dynamic star for you to impersonate – Jack Mulhall, Donald Keith, or one of those chaps."*

"Sporting of you to accept, Vance!" Markham exclaimed. "I'll relay your response to Jack Austin."

A week later Vance and I made our appearance at Jack Austin's stately Manhattan mansion. The first person we met as we entered was Stitt, the Austin butler, who set the tone for the evening's proceedings with his Keystone Kop costume.† As soon as we entered the mansion's immense ballroom, decorated in a motion-picture soundstage motif, Jack Austin himself rushed over to greet us. His costume of battered hat, baggy pants, cane, and old shoes, together with the small moustache and duck-like walk he had affected for the occasion, gave us the sensation that it was Charlie the little tramp himself who cordially held out his hand and said, "Mr Vance and Mr Van Dine! How good of you to come!"

"It's wholly our pleasure, y'know, Mr Austin," Vance drawled. And, as if further inspired by his surroundings, he

* We finally settled on Malcolm McGregor.
† Sitt's natural reticence prohibited his playing this role to its best advantage, but some of the other Kop-costumed servants, hired especially for the occasion, presumably from a casting bureau, gave a more uninhibited performance. Additionally, Austin had found a brace of serving men who bore startling resemblances to the comedy duo of Stan Laurel and Oliver Hardy.

leaped over a chair and turned a double somersault with an agility I hardly knew he possessed, as if the Douglas Fairbanks Black Pirate regalia gave him an athletic ability he otherwise lacked. Austin and his guests laughed delightedly, particularly a lovely red-haired flapper-type, quite obviously designed to represent the vivacious Clara Bow, with the beauty and personality of the original.

Austin performed the introductions. "Mr Vance, this is Miss Molly Hawley." Vance smiled and bowed to the waist in the best Fairbanksian manner. "And I am sure you are acquainted with her father, Judge Peter Hawley."

Judge Hawley, a slight, distinguished-looking man of late middle age, was known to both of us. But we hardly recognized him as the judge, he so resembled Henry B. Walthall in his greatest role, that of the Little Colonel in *The Birth of a Nation*.

It occurred to me as we met the other guests how strangely appropriate their costumes were. For example, Arletta Bingham, a society flirt with many broken hearts (and homes) in her wake, was well cast as the vamp Theda Bara. Markham, in white ten-gallon hat and flamboyant cowboy garb, made a perfect Tom Mix. Indeed, much of the same kind of personal magnetism that had made Mix a star had led the voters of New York to put Markham into office.

Sergeant Ernest Heath of the Metropolitan Police, a frequent participant in Vance's previous cases, was among those present, rather surprisingly. In Heath's case no costume was necessary, since he bore an uncanny resemblance to the humorous character actor Eugene Pallette.*

Broadway playboy Roger Kronert impersonated country-boy hero Charles Ray – he appeared at the party in bare feet, blue jeans, checkered shirt, and wide-brimmed straw hat, a fishing pole over his shoulder.* The most amazing and startling figure was struck by Broadway producer George Gruen, known as "the new Flo Ziegfeld". It was appropriate that the creator of incredibly elaborate stage shows should turn up with the most elaborate disguise of all, an incredibly faithful imitation of Lon

* The reference here, of course, to the portly Pallette of his later years. The more svelte-figured Pallette, to whose heroics in the French tale of *Intolerance* audiences of 1916 thrilled, would never have been mistaken for the good Sergeant Heath.

Chaney's famed Phantom-of-the-Opera makeup, which has precipitated feminine screams of terror in movie houses throughout the world. Aside from the makeup, Gruen's costume consisted of traditional evening dress and an all-enveloping black opera cape.

It was a highly successful evening, made so not only by the inventive clowning of the host but by the astonishing vigor with which Vance threw himself into his swashbuckling role, doing everything like Fairbanks short of swinging from the chandelier. Only on a few occasions, in the early part of the evening, did any discordant notes introduce themselves, but those few incidents certainly foreshadowed the tragedy that was to strike before the gay festivities ran their course. It appeared that while all of the guests were wishing Jack Austin good luck, a few of them were not really on the best of terms with their host.

It was no secret, for one thing, that Arletta Bingham was being summarily cast off by the departing Austin, and Miss Bingham was far more accustomed to rejecting than to being rejected. As the evening wore on, and drink loosened her tongue, her gay veneer began to slip away and a hidden bitterness to show itself.

"You're a big man, aren't you, Jack?" she slurred. "Going to be a big talking, singing, dancing movie-talkie-singie star. Well, ain't that swell?"

"It's such a wonderful thing!" exclaimed Molly Hawley. "To be seen by millions of people all over the world in one performance, where on the stage you can display your talent only to a few hundred at a time."

"I feel it's a great opportunity," said Austin, with feigned humility. "I hope I'm worthy of it."

George Gruen entered the discussion suddenly. He, like Miss Bingham, was beginning to wobble on his feet. "Talking pictures are just a fad, Jack! They'll never catch on with the public. They go to movies to sleep – to be stimulated, they go to the theatre. And talkies will neither stimulate them like the

---

* In mid-evening Kronert made a startling costume change, suddenly appearing in full evening dress, thus illustrating the recent change in Ray's screen character from country boy to man about-town. Kronert's feet remained bare, however, symbolizing the unfortunate Ray's failure to make a completely successful transformation.

legitimate theatre nor let them rest like the movies. Jack, take my word for it, you're making a terrible mistake."

"If that is so, George, I shall come back to Broadway, and I'm sure you'll be glad to give me a job." Austin drifted away to join another group of guests, and the conversation quickly became more openly bitter.

Arletta Bingham cackled drunkenly, "Broadway forgets fast. In three or four years his name won't mean a thing. He'll be a forgotten has-been. He won't even be able to get a job."

"And you'll still be a living legend in every bed on Broadway," said Roger Kronert, raising his glass in facetious salute. The vamp snarled sullenly and took a gulp of her drink. As Kronert passed, she aimed at his bare toes with a vicious thrust of her heel and narrowly missed.

George Gruen was talking to his drink more than to those around him. "He's a welsher, that Jack Austin. He's a dirty welsher."

"Come, come, George," replied Monty Baby, a well-known Broadway agent, wearing the familiar hat, vest, and glum expression of Buster Keaton. "You let him out of his contract like a gentleman. Why spoil it now?"

"He had no right," the quasi-Opera Phantom moaned. "He's a welsher. He wants to ruin me on Broadway." It was well-known that with so many of Broadway's top stars heading west, Gruen was having trouble finding a star for his new show, reportedly a weak vehicle that would take the artistry of an Al Jolson, an Eddie Cantor, a George Jessel, or a Jack Austin to put it across. Austin's leaving the cast had been a well-publicized blow to the producer, but Gruen had been very sporting about it – at least in the theatrical pages.

Another bad moment came when one of the waiters, elaborately moustached in the manner of lead-Kop Ford Sterling, spilled a tray of drinks on Jack Austin. It was a comical incident, as the waiter's fumbling and Austin's reaction had the style of a well-planned Hollywood "sight gag". However, it soon became clear the incident was not planned and Austin was surprisingly angered by it. "You idiot!" he said between clenched teeth. "Get out of here!"

"But, Mr Austin –" the unfortunate servant began.

"Get out of here!" Austin iterated. Then he virtually chased the serving man back toward the kitchen. Recovering his composure, he returned to his guests in the comical tramp walk.

"What a temper," said a startled Clara-Molly Bow-Hawley, who had been looking on in shock.

Another young woman, dressed in the homely garb of the perpetual ingenue Mary Pickford, replied, "You needn't know Jack Austin long to find out about that. I know. I loved him. Once."

Shortly, the latter-mentioned lady, a New York debutante named Edna Stuyvesant, was cavorting with Vance and Austin in a manner reminiscent of the United Artists partners, Pickford, Chaplin, and Fairbanks.* This entertainment served to get the party back to its previous quotient of merriment, and it remained so until eleven o'clock.

At that hour, with most of the guests at the height of their enjoyment and many of them more-or-less intoxicated, it was suddenly realized that their host had not put in an appearance for some time.

"What can have happened to him?" asked Molly Hawley.

"He's dropped out of sight," Roger Kronert observed.

"I remember him steppin' into the library around nine-thirty, and I don't believe I've seen the boy since," said Vance. "I'll see if he's become ill or something." And he strode toward the door of the library, hurling the huge punch bowl on his way. Markham, Heath, Stitt the butler, several other guests, and I followed him, though walking around the punch bowl. What we saw when Vance opened the library door was enough to bring the festivities of the evening to an abrupt halt.

Jack Austin lay dead on the floor of the library, near the fireplace. His tramp costume was covered with blood, his Chaplinesque moustache pitifully askew. He had seemingly been stabbed several times, and the apparent weapon, an ornately chased Oriental letter opener, lay near the body.†

* The fourth partner, D. W. Griffith, was not represented at the party. It was hoped that Griffith himself might be present, but the motion-picture pioneer had sent his regrets at the last moment.
† Vance had several penetrating observations to make about the origin, design, and artistic merits of the weapon. Were this a full-length novel, I would reproduce those remarks here, since they would undoubtedly be of interest to collectors. Unfortunately, the short-story form offers less latitude for the introduction of such peripheral matters.

"He's done away with himself," said Roger Kronert.

"Quite impossible, old chap, judging from the placement and multiplicity of the wounds," said Vance.

"Then he's been murdered!" exclaimed Sergeant Heath.

"Deucedly penetratin', Sergeant."

"Who could have done this?" Judge Hawley whispered.

"Virtually anyone here, I should think," replied Markham grimly.

"Or an outsider," offered Heath, indicating the open window.

"It must have been a prowler," Hawley said shakily.

Vance, kneeling beside the body, had made a discovery. "I think the old boy's tryin' to tell us something, Markham. Look at what he's clutchin' in his right hand."

"A pair of cheaters!" exclaimed Heath.

"But Austin didn't wear eyeglasses," said Judge Hawley.

"You'll notice," said Vance, "that they are of the large, round type affected by the motion-picture comedian Harold Lloyd. If one of the guests here to-night had come as Harold Lloyd, we might regard this as a most rewardin' clue to the miscreant's identity. However, I don't recall anyone wearin' such a costume."

Stitt, the butler, suddenly spoke up. "Harold Lloyd sent his regrets, sir. He could not come."

Vance rose. "Ah. Then there was to be a Harold Lloyd here tonight?"

"Yes, sir. Mr Archie Belmont."

The name brought several gasps from the group. All the guests, suddenly sober, were now gathered around the body.

"Why, he hated Jack!" Arletta Bingham exclaimed.

Roger Kronert supported this contention. "He was supposed to get the part in that talkie they signed Jack Austin for. He hated Austin's guts."

"Seems a likely suspect, Vance," Markham said.

"It's possible," Vance murmured.

"Open and shut, if you ask me," said Heath. "I'll call the lab boys. Show's over now, folks," he added, dispersing the crowd. "Let's give this corpse some air."

"Vance and I will have to talk to this fellow Belmont, see what sort of alibi he has," said Markham. "You can hold the fort here, Heath. We'll want to question everyone later, so no one may leave."

Several protests came from the assembled guests.

"Save your breath, folks!" Heath said. "This is a murder investigation. It's not a party no more."

"In that case, Mr D.A.," said Arletta Bingham tauntingly, "hadn't you better get out of that cowboy outfit before you carry this any further?"

And suddenly we all realized how absurd we looked. Markham in his Tom Mix regalia, Vance in his Black Pirate apparel, Judge Hawley in a Confederate Civil War uniform, Roger Kronert barefoot in a tuxedo, Gruen in his opera cape and hideous makeup. With all merriment vanished, we looked rather pathetic and comic and even, taken in conjunction with the brutally murdered little tramp figure, somewhat terrifying.

I shall never forget that macabre scene. With Austin's murder, Charlie Chaplin, Douglas Fairbanks, Mary Pickford, and Buster Keaton had all vanished, leaving only their outward habiliments behind. All of their merry spirit was washed away by the destructive tide of violent, unanticipated death.

"Yes," said Markham, "I think we should change into street clothes. Inconveniently, Mr Vance, Mr Van Dine, and I all arrived in costume, but I think those of you who donned your costumes here could be allowed to change. Then, Sergeant Heath will want to take your statements. Carry on, Heath."

"But, Mr Markham, if you leave now, you'll miss Doc Doremus."*

"So we will. Well, if he says anything really funny, write it down. Mr Van Dine may be able to use it in a footnote."†

Stitt provided us with Belmont's address, a plush Park Avenue apartment, and soon Vance, Markham, and I were in a taxicab on our way there, glad to leave the horror of deflated dreams behind us at the now-somber Austin mansion.

"All that blood," Markham, still in the all-white uniform of a wild west "good guy," was saying, "The murderer had to be spattered with it, Vance! And so I don't see how it could be someone who was at the party. Any of them could have slipped

---

* The Chief Medical Examiner, who had figured in several of Vance's previous cases.

† He said nothing worth footnoting on this occasion.

into the library unseen, but how could they have gotten out and rejoined the party without being covered with enough blood to give them away to the other guests?"

Vance did not attempt to answer the question.

"I'm sure Belmont is our man, Vance. It appears the simple, uncomplicated product of a diseased, insane, vengeful mind. Don't you agree?"

Vance said sorrowfully, "Markham, old dear, I make it a practice not to jump to conclusions about people whose psyches I have not probed. Belmont may prove to be psychologically incapable of this murder. I will know soon enough."

Markham snorted. "If you had to present a case to a jury, Vance, you'd be more interested in hard-core evidence."

"Quite so, but I am an amateur in crime detection. Once I find a murderer, I have no taste for mountin' him in a big album like a prize postage stamp. I'm not int'rested, y'know, in your stupid courts and your silly rules of evidence. That's your department, my dear chap, and the people of New York pay you handsomely for it."

Markham grunted in reply. That was the extent of our conversation en route to Belmont's quarters.

We found Belmont at home alone. He greeted us affably enough. At first glance, it seemed unlikely he had been out that evening. He appeared to all the world like a man spending a quiet evening at home.

"We expected to see you at Jack Austin's party to-night, Mr Belmont," said Markham.

"What a bore that would have been! He sent over a costume for me to wear – a Harold Lloyd getup. I sent my regrets. I hope I never see that ham again."

"You probably won't," remarked Markham heavily. "Have you sent the costume back?"

"No, it's still here. Why? What's this all about?"

"May we see the costume, please?"

"Yes, of course. What's happened anyway?"

"Jack Austin was murdered tonight, Mr Belmont. He had a pair of Harold Lloyd glasses clutched in his hand when we found him."

Belmont looked up with a start. "Murdered? Say, you surely can't think that I –"

"We understand that you hated Jack Austin because he was chosen for that part in the talkie picture."

Belmont laughed. "Look, that's one of those things that happen. It would have been a great opportunity for me, but I've lost parts before. I was disappointed, but I'd hardly commit murder over it. As for hating Austin, I'll admit I was no fan of his. He was an insufferable egotist, an impossible man to work with, and an utter cad, a one-hundred per cent wretch. Whoever killed him deserves a medal. But I am not the man."

"Mightn't you get that part now that he's dead?" inquired Markham.

"A possibility. But it hadn't occurred to me until you just mentioned it."

Markham's expression indicated he doubted the statement. In the meantime, Belmont had found the box the costume had come in. The familiar Harold Lloyd glasses, however, were absent.

"I don't understand it," muttered Belmont. "I must have mislaid them."

"Perhaps you mislaid them at Jack Austin's home, Mr Belmont. Perhaps, during your struggle, he grabbed them off your very nose."

"Mr Markham, why would I wear the Harold Lloyd costume at all, if I wasn't even going to the party? That doesn't make any sense!"

"I don't pretend to understand the mind of a cold-blooded murderer. Mr Belmont, by the authority vested in me by the people of New York County, I arrest you for the murder of Jack Austin and remind you that anything you say may be used against you."

"Tut! Tut! Markham,"* said Vance softly. These were the only words he uttered while we were in Belmont's apartment. They were enough to show Markham that Vance felt the District Attorney was proceeding too hastily, and Markham seemed uneasy after the arrest was made.

Back at the Austin mansion, we found that Heath had been hard at work taking statements from the guests.

---

* Egyptology was yet another of Vance's many so-called "dilettante" interests.

"I think they can go home now, don't you, Vance?" Markham said hopefully. "I imagine we can consider this investigation as good as closed."

"Not quite, Markham," Vance replied. "I am not convinced that Mr Belmont is psychologically capable –"

"Psychology again!" Heath exclaimed disgustedly. "Mr Vance, I know you've done some good work in the past, but you can't take every case like it's a page out of – who's the fellow?"

"Freud, you mean? My dear Heath, a psychological approach is suitable to any problem of crime. And there are other people far more psychologically capable of committing this crime, people in this house now."

Before the discussion could continue, Stitt approached us, still ludicrously dressed as one of Mack Sennett's Keystone Kops. "Mr Vance," he said stiffly, "I think there is something you should know."

"What is that?"

"Those glasses that Mr Austin had in his hand are not the same pair that were sent to Mr Belmont."

"They weren't, eh? Then there were two pairs?"

"Yes. The pair that Mr Austin had in his hand were given him by Mr Harold Lloyd himself. They occupied an honored place on the mantelpiece in the library."

"I see. Then they were always here, not brought in by someone from outside. That puts a pos'tively different light on matters, y'know. He grasped 'em not from the nose of his murderer, as Mr Markham has postulated, but from the mantelpiece."

"In an effort to tell us the murderer's identity," said Markham.

"Quite so. Changes matters a bit, eh what?"

Markham appeared exasperated. "But, Vance, I honestly don't see how this development changes anything. I still would put the same interpretation on the clue, wouldn't you? That is, as an indication of the guilt of the man who was to impersonate Harold Lloyd – that is, Archie Belmont."

"No, indeed, Markham. Austin's message to us is a bit more subtle than that. In fact, I might not have been able to read it, had I not linked it with a couple of other pertinent clues."

"Do I understand you to mean, Vance," demanded Markham, seeming near apoplexy, "that you claim to have solved this case?"

"Oh, quite, old chap."

"And Belmont is not the murderer in your redoubtable estimation?"

"'Fraid not, old boy."

"Then who did it?" demanded Heath.

"Gather the guests in the ballroom and I'll tell you all about it," Vance promised, puffing his *Régie* nonchalantly.

Markham complied, though too upset to speak above a strangled whisper. A few moments later, Vance was telling the assembled group, "A most entertainin' comedy, y'know. I rather fancy it would make a fine picture, non-talkin' of course. Archie Belmont, who somehow mislaid his big round glasses, was accused of a crime in which his big round glasses didn't really figure at all. Amusin', what? Quite so."

Few of the tense gathering appeared very amused. In strained silence, they hung on Vance's every syllable.

"It's all extr'ordin'rily simple y'see. The real murderer is here, among the people in this room. A person capable of bitterness and vindictive hatred. One capable of plannin' a darin' and complicated crime."

He paused dramatically and looked at each face in turn – the pale, beautiful visage of Molly Hawley; the ashen, haggard face of Judge Hawley, her father; the handsome, uncharacteristically serious face of Roger Kronert; the scowl of George Gruen, his Lon Chaney makeup removed; the sneering, now unlovely features of Arletta Bingham; the impassive countenance of the butler, Stitt.

Which of these was guilty, we all wondered – all but the one who knew.

"The murderer was one whose costume allowed him to cover up any annoyin' blood with which he might have been spattered – cover it up with a handy black opera cape!" Suddenly, all eyes were on George Gruen, who began to rise out of his chair but thought better of it when he felt Heath's beefy hand on his shoulder. "A man who hated Jack Austin for leavin' him on the brink of financial disaster. A man who is noted on Broadway for colossally elaborate musical productions with countless chorus girls and expensive, intricate sets, a producer of – in short – *spectacles!*"

With breathtaking suddenness, Gruen produced a dagger from under his cloak and plunged it into his own heart. The drama was over.

And so ended the famous Austin murder case. To me, I confess, it is more memorable than any of Vance's other cases – and for reasons apart from Vance's great detective skill.

Though you may have difficulty in believing it, we were men, Vance and I, not mere cardboard figures. I admit here for the first time that during the course of this investigation I fell in love for the only time in my life – in love with Miss Molly Hawley, the judge's red-haired daughter. Of course, I could say nothing, for to do so would be to break one of my own rules.*

I could have composed long paragraphs celebrating her Titian locks, her flawless white teeth, her dimpled cheeks, but I had long ago vowed never to lose my equanimity in the manner of Dr Watson and other narrators of detective tales who have allowed themselves such indulgences as romance.

By being true to the rules, I consigned myself to a life of loneliness. And seeing every Clara Bow movie I possibly can has not significantly abated that loneliness.

---

* S. S. Van Dine's "Twenty Rules for Writing Detective Stories," Rule Number 3. "There must be no love interest in the story."

The Man Who Scared the Bank

ARCHIBALD PECHEY

Here's the last of the stories I have reprinted from the 1920s. Pechey (1876–1961) was scarcely known under his own name. He wrote all his best known books and stories under two pen names, initially as Valentine during the 1920s and later as Mark Cross. He was as well known in the theatre as the literary world, collaborating on writing the lyrics for, amongst other musicals, The Maid of the Mountains *(1917). Pechey's longest-running series featured Daphne Wrayne and the Adjusters. Wrayne was a beautiful, rich society girl who served as the front (and often the brains) behind a group of four individuals who were known only as the Adjusters. Their identities are never revealed to the public, though the reader is let in on the secret. Pechey struck a rich vein. The stories first appeared in* Pearson's Magazine *in 1928 before being collected in* The Adjusters *(1930), all under the Valentine alias. Pechey then changed persona and, as Mark Cross, penned another forty-six novels in the series, from* The Grip of the Four *(1934) to* Perilous Hazard *(1961). The series ended only with Pechey's death in 1961. The following is the first story in the series.*

Pechey, by the way, may be remembered for one other production: his daughter – the TV cook, Fanny Cradock.

The Editor of the *Daily Monitor* rang his bell.
"Send Mr Mannering to me at once," he said when the boy appeared.

He sat drumming on the table with his fingers and frowning at the letter in his hand until a knock sounded on the door. Then:

"Come in, Mannering. Read that letter!" thrusting it at him.

The other took it, scanned it, whistled softly.

"I know the Duchess, sir," he said.

"Exactly. That's why I sent for you. Go up and see her at once. Find out all you can about this story. Maybe she'll get you an interview with these 'Adjusters' people. Hitherto no one's been able to get one. Get hold of every bit of news you can lay your hands on . . . The moment we publish the fact that they've recovered her necklace the public will be on its toes to know who and what they are. It's over three months since the necklace was stolen from Hardington House, and the police have owned themselves beat."

For four weeks the Adjusters had been intriguing public curiosity. Who and what they were no one seemed to know. Four times had a full-page advertisement appeared in the *Daily Monitor:* –

IF THE POLICE CANNOT HELP YOU

THE

ADJUSTERS

CAN.

179, CONDUIT STREET, W.

Just that and no more. Interviewers and reporters had called, but had come away empty-handed. All that they could say was that the Adjusters occupied the whole of the first floor at 179, Conduit Street, that a stalwart commissionaire – an ex-army man with a string of ribbons across his chest – replied to all callers that "Miss Wrayne could see no one except by appointment, and no Pressmen in any circumstances whatever."

Now he gave the same reply when Mannering presented his card. But Mannering merely smiled and produced a letter.

"Perhaps you will be good enough to give that to Miss Wrayne," he said. "It's from the Duchess of Hardington."

Five minutes later the commissionaire came back.

"If you will come this way, sir, Miss Wrayne will see you," he said.

The next morning the *Daily Monitor* brought out flaming headlines announcing that the Duchess of Hardington's world-famous pearl necklace had been recovered by "The Adjusters of 179, Conduit Street". But it was what followed that made the public rub its eyes in astonishment –

"Armed with a letter of introduction from the Duchess of Hardington I succeeded yesterday in gaining an interview with Miss Daphne Wrayne, the secretary of the Adjusters. To comment on that interview is impossible. I can merely state what Miss Wrayne told me and leave the public to judge for themselves. Probably they will be as bewildered as I was – and still am."

Followed then an account of a lavishly furnished suite of offices and a beautiful young girl who called herself the secretary, who declined to give the names of her associates, but who said that the Adjusters came into being for the "Adjustment of the inequalities that at present exist between the criminal and the victim." Asked to explain this a little more fully, Miss Wrayne said that where the police were chiefly interested in the capture and punishment of the criminal, the Adjusters were solely concerned with the restoration to the victim of the money, or property, out of which he or she had been defrauded. She added, furthermore, that they had unlimited money behind them and charged no fees whatsoever! Then the *Monitor* man went on:

"But, frankly, to me Miss Daphne Wrayne is the most amazing part of this amazing firm. It is well-nigh impossible to believe that this singularly lovely girl, barely out of her teens, who looks as if she had just stepped out of a Bond Street modiste's, is really in control of an enterprise of this kind. I say, 'in control' for even if she is not, she is, on her own statement, the only one whom the public will see, and behind the very up-to-date exterior, with its dainty Paris frock, silk stockings, etc., there is obviously a brain out of the ordinary.

"I was bewildered at the rapidity with which this pretty, laughing-eyed school-girl who smoked cigarettes and used slang, changed into an earnest young woman, with the criminal life of London at her slim fingers' ends.

"I came away from Conduit Street trying to tell myself that it was foolish, impossible, ridiculous. And yet there is Miss Wrayne herself. I can still see those clear hazel eyes of hers, and hear her final words: 'Is it so strange that some who have unlimited money and brains should want to help their less fortunate brethren?'"

One week later, when Sir John Colston – the interview had been arranged that morning by telephone – was ushered into Daphne's private room, he was conscious of a slight sense of annoyance. To discover that he, Sir John Colston, the head of one of the biggest banks in London, had to lay his difficulties at the slim feet of a lovely, hazel-eyed girl hardly out of her teens – a girl who coolly waved him to a chair as she lighted another cigarette – it was almost preposterous!

"Well, Sir John, what can we do for you?"

Just as if he were nobody and his affair a trivial matter!

"I understand from the Duchess of –" he began stiffly, but Daphne Wrayne's eyes narrowed a little as she cut in on him.

"I know, and you're surprised at finding me so young." She leant forward suddenly in her chair. "Forgive me for saying so, but you're a little behind the times. You are obviously in trouble or you wouldn't be here. If you want my services they are at your disposal. But in that case it will be very much better, both for you and for me, if you will forget that I am a girl and not yet twenty-one. You will excuse my plain speaking, won't you?"

A little smile curved her lips, but her eyes were steady on his.

"You're not the first, you know, Sir John," she went on. "It's a bit of handicap sometimes, being a girl!"

His resentment vanished from that moment. Her ingenuousness disarmed him.

"I'm sorry, Miss Wrayne," he said. "I'm an old man – a bit old-fashioned, I'm afraid, too. You – this place," he waved a hand, "rather took me by surprise."

"Of course," sweetly. "Now, let's get to business. You, I take it, are the head of the Universal Banking Corporation of Lombard Street?"

"I am. I have a client of the name of Richard Henry Gorleston."

"The bookmaker?"

"I begin to see that what the Duchess told me about you was true," he smiled. He was becoming more impressed now every minute.

"I have a good memory for names," she replied.

"He has been a client of mine for nearly three years. His father, I may tell you, left him £50,000. The son has banked with us ever since, and until this week has been a trusted client.

"I must tell you," he went on, "that ever since he opened an account with us it has been his habit to draw out large sums of money in notes and to replace them within a few days. He told me from the start that he lived by gambling.

"On numerous occasions he has presented cheques for five or ten thousand pounds, and drawn the money out in notes. Then a few days later he would come and pay it all back, perhaps a little more, perhaps a little less.

"Ten days ago he called at the bank and came into my private room – nothing unusual in that, though. He often does. Now, the moment he came in I noticed that he was wearing horn-rimmed spectacles, a thing which he has never done before. I commented on it and he said that he'd had trouble with his eyes, and had been to an oculist."

"Mention his name?" casually.

"He did. James Adwinter, of Queen Anne Street."

Daphne Wrayne made a note of it.

"Please go on, Sir John."

"I asked him if he was drawing out any money and he said he was – would I tell him what his balance was. I sent out and found it was about thirty thousand pounds. In front of me he took his cheque book and wrote a cheque for £25,000. I sent for one of my cashiers and we paid it over to him in thousand-pound notes. Now comes the amazing part of the story. Two days ago he came into the bank and presented a cheque for £15,000. The cashier told him he hadn't got it, and reminded him of the £25,000 one. He indignantly denied it – said he'd been out of town for nearly a fortnight, and he could prove it. Declared that someone must have impersonated him. This morning we received a letter from his solicitors threatening us with an action."

"But the signature, Sir John? If it was Richard Henry Gorleston's usual signature with no irregularity—"

"That's the trouble, Miss Wrayne. This," handing her a cheque, "is his usual signature. This," handing her another, "is the disputed cheque."

Daphne Wrayne's eyebrows went up as she scanned it.

"How did you come to pass this cheque without comment?" she queried. "The difference is not very great, I admit, but still —"

"Miss Wrayne, I put it to you! You have an old client whom you know well. He comes in, sits down and talks to you, writes out a cheque. You send for your cashier who knows him equally well. You've seen him write the cheque. You're satisfied. You cash it without question."

"Oh, I know. But will the law exonerate you?"

"I'm afraid it won't," a little ruefully.

"Tell me, Sir John," after a slight pause, "had you any shadow of doubt when this man presented that £25,000 cheque but that he was Richard Gorleston?"

"Not the faintest, Miss Wrayne."

"When he came in two days ago was he wearing spectacles?"

"He wasn't. He said he'd never worn them in his life, and never heard of Adwinter."

"What was his manner like?"

"Oh, he was naturally very upset, but he quite appreciated our position, though he said, of course, that we should have noticed the difference in the signature. He went on to say that he'd known for some time that he had a 'double', but he'd never been able to run him to earth."

The girl wrinkled her forehead thoughtfully.

"He told you he'd been out of London all the time. Did he say where?"

"Yes. He gave me his address. 'The Golden Crown, Port-worth, Tavistock' – trout fishing. Incidentally I have verified this by one of our local branches. He was there the whole time."

"Well, Sir John, in about a week's time I'll report to you. In the meanwhile say nothing to anybody."

"What am I to tell my solicitors to do?" a little perplexedly.

She laughed merrily.

"Oh, come, Sir John, you don't want to throw in your hand yet! Instruct 'em to say that you repudiate all liability.

After all, if you have to climb down – still, let's hope you won't!"

In a comfortably-furnished room in the Inner Temple four men sat round a table talking. Just an ordinary room, but certainly no ordinary men, these four. Actually, you could have found them all in *Who's Who*.

The big, tanned, curly-haired, merry-eyed giant, who sat next to the empty chair at the head of the table, was none other than James Ffolliott Plantagenet Trevitter, only son of the Earl of Winstanworth – Eton and Oxford, with half a page of athletic records added. Next to him, lounging a little in his chair, thin, lean, bronzed, almost bored-looking, with his gold-rimmed monocle, sat Sir Hugh Williamson, most intrepid of explorers. Opposite to him, elderly, grey-haired, almost benevolent-looking, Allan Sylvester, the best-loved actor-manager in England. And lastly, leaning forward talking, a smile on his clean-cut handsome face, Martin Everest, K.C., the greatest criminal barrister in England.

And these were the four Adjusters . . .

The clock on the mantelpiece chimed out the hour, and as it did so the door opened and the four men rose to their feet, as Daphne Wrayne stood in the doorway.

"Well, Peter Pan!" exclaimed Sylvester.

"Well, you dear Knights!"

Very lovely she looked as she came forward, and her eyes were for all of them. But it was Lord Trevitter who, as if by tacit understanding, helped her off with her cloak and put her into her chair. Very naturally, yet quite openly too, she slipped her hand into his and let it stay there. But the other three only smiled indulgently – though their smiles spoke volumes. You felt, somehow, that they had known her from childhood – looked on her now almost as a beloved child. That even if she had signalled out Trevitter – as indeed she had – she loved none of them less dearly for that.

"Oh, it's great to be here!" she exclaimed with shining eyes. "I can still hardly believe it's true."

"It's a wonderful stunt," murmured Everest thoughtfully.

"We've been lucky, Martin," answered the girl. "If it hadn't been for the Duchess's pearls—"

"And then you giving an interview to the *Monitor*," chimed in Lord Trevitter. "That was the master stroke, Daph."

"Well, it was just the right moment, Jim. Having had a big success, it seemed to me to be the very wisest thing to do."

"By Jove it was, my dear," chuckled Sylvester. "It couldn't have come at a better time. If you'd given it before, the public would only have scoffed. But as we had recovered that necklace they couldn't afford to scoff."

"Incidentally," remarked the girl, "the Duchess sent us a cheque for £500."

"Good for her," said Lord Trevitter. "I suppose you've –"

"Oh, of course, Jim! Anonymously, needless to say."

"Quite right," murmured Everest. "Well, what's the big idea this evening?"

"How do you know I've got one?"

"Listen to her!" exclaimed Williamson. "Breaking off a dance at twelve o'clock and keeping us out of our beds—"

"But it's rather a puzzling one, Hugh," interrupting him. "We shall want all our ingenuity to get home this time."

"Splendid! Let's have it, my dear."

Leaning forward in her chair, slim hands clasped, Daphne Wrayne outlined the story to them. Then, as she came to the end:

"But I can add a good deal to this. It seemed obvious to me from the start that there was no double at all – it was just a ruse, carefully planned."

"Particularly why, Daph?" queried Lord Trevitter.

"The signature, Jim, alone. In a forgery of this size your forger never makes a mistake with the signature. It's miles too risky. Besides, assuming that it was Gorleston himself, look at all there is to support the idea? If they detect the flaw in the signature they can't collar him – it's merely a slip. But if it gets by, what happens then? Why the bank's in the cart and they're liable for carelessness."

"You're a true woman, my dear," smiled Everest. "Jump to a conclusion first and fit your facts to it afterwards."

Daphne pouted adorably.

"I hate you, Martin," she said. "Still, I was right."

"You're sure?" demanded Williamson.

"Absolutely. All the same, as my legal friend here will tell you," laying her hand on Everest's arm with a smile, "it's going to be very difficult to prove. However, let me first give you all the facts I have."

She paused for a moment to light a cigarette, and they all waited eagerly.

"I sent Rayte up to interview Adwinter," she went on, "and established pretty satisfactorily that a man wearing glasses and answering in all other descriptions to Gorleston called there recently in the name of John Elwes, of 124, Unwin Street, Bloomsbury. He wanted new glasses and got them. So to Unwin Street, where apparently John Elwes has had a bedroom and sitting-room for over a year. Now, according to his landlady he is a man of no occupation who used to come once or twice a week and stay the night there. He turned up there, on the day the forgery was committed, at 2.15 in the afternoon – note the time – stayed a few minutes, during which he told his landlady he was going to the bank, got into his taxi saying he'd look in in a few days' time. He has never been near there since."

She paused a moment to relight her cigarette, which had gone out. Then she went on.

"Now as regards Gorleston. Gorleston's been stopping, as he declared, at the Golden Crown, Portworth, two miles out of Tavistock. Every morning he's breakfasted at eight and gone out, with his lunch, till ten o'clock at night. Now on the day that this forgery is supposed to have been committed Gorleston swears he was fishing all day. But the curious fact turns up that a ticket collector at Tavistock – who is a fisherman himself, and who had apparently seen Gorleston fishing there that week – swears that he saw him on that particular day going up to London on the 9.11. The booking clerk can't help us, but it's funny that there was only one return ticket to London issued that day. Funnier still that the return half should have been given up that evening, and funniest of all that Gorleston should have come in on that night – the only one – to say that he had had a blank day."

"How can you fix the day, Daph?"

"It was a brilliantly fine day, Martin, and the people at the Inn remember it as strange because two other men staying there had had big catches."

"And the trains? How do they fit in?"

"The 9.11 gets to town at 1.56. A taxi would take him to Bloomsbury at 2.15 a.m.; would get him to the bank at 2.30 – the time we know he was there. While another one would give him the 3.16 to land him at Tavistock at 8.41."

"If you could only find the taxi man who drove him –" began Sylvester, but Daphne cut him short.

"Oh, I have, Allan! He remembers it well. Described his fare as tall and thin, wearing horn-rimmed glasses. Drove him to Unwin Street and waited a few minutes. Then to the bank, where he was given a ten-shilling note and dismissed."

"Seems to me," said Lord Trevitter, "that you've proved it up to the hilt."

But Everest shook his head.

"Circumstantially, Jim," he said, "it's excellent. But it's not a good case to go to a jury with. Brief me for Gorleston and I'll find a hundred flaws."

"I was afraid you'd say that, Martin," said Daphne, a little ruefully.

"I don't want to say it, dear, but I must. Mind you, I haven't the slightest doubt from all you've told me that John Elwes has never existed, but I'm equally certain that even with the evidence you've got, it's going to be hard to establish. You see, who's going to prove that the taximan's passenger was Gorleston from Tavistock? It might have been John Elwes from, say, Surbiton! Frankly, it's a very clever fraud that has got home and looks like staying home. He's got overwhelming evidence that he *was* at Tavistock, and all that we can produce is a ticket collector who's only seen him once or twice. While he, Gorleston, can produce a hundred intimate pals who will swear that he has never worn spectacles, and a thousand or two cheques all bearing his accurate and original signature. No, no, it won't do!"

"Of course there *is* another way," murmured Daphne thoughtfully, "but the question is, will you agree to it?"

The four men exchanged glances.

"It's one of Peter Pan's very choicest, right off the ice!" smiled Sylvester. "Now I'll lay anyone a quid—"

"Oh, Allan!" laughing and blushing. "Don't be a beast! All

right, I'll tell you then. You can laugh at me afterwards."

But there was little laughter in their faces as she talked.

When she had finished Lord Trevitter threw back his head and laughed like a schoolboy.

"Daphne, you're a marvel!" he exclaimed. "My dear, how *do* you think of these things?"

"Is it good, Jim?"

"Good?" echoed Everest. "It's glorious, magnificent! Of course, he *may* not fall for it, but if he's guilty I believe he will. If, on the other hand, he's innocent, well – we're no worse off than we were before."

"I'm in this, mind!" exclaimed Williamson.

"We're all in it, the four of us!" answered Lord Trevitter, with his boyish laugh. "Another success for the Adjusters!"

"Oh, I'm so glad you like my idea!" exclaimed the girl. "Let's thrash it out!"

Richard Henry Gorleston was entirely pleased with himself. As he sat in a West End restaurant eating his dinner he smiled complacently to himself. Twenty-five thousand pounds for nothing, he told himself, was the finest day's work he had ever done. His solicitors, furthermore, had hinted to him that the bank, rather than court publicity, would settle with him. He signed to his waiter and ordered himself another bottle of champagne and a Corona.

"Have you any objection to my sitting here?"

A suave, smiling, elderly gentleman with white hair and gold-rimmed pince-nez was standing at the table, hesitating, but Gorleston answered his smile cheerfully.

"Not a bit in the world. Crowded here to-night."

"Somewhat. I don't know my London well. I'm from the country – North Wales. My annual trip to London. I come up once a year, I see all the sights. And," with a smile, "I have a little opportunity to indulge my pet hobby – billiards."

Gorleston was interested in a moment.

"Funny that," he said. "It's a particular hobby of mine, and –"

They were hard at it in a moment. Finally, when the stranger, who volunteered his name as Professor Lucas, called for his bill,

Gorleston ventured to suggest that he and his new friend should adjourn for a game.

They played several games. The Professor was charmed with his new acquaintance and pressed him to dine with him the following evening. Gorleston accepted with alacrity.

The following evening they met again, but soon after the meal had started the Professor was claimed by three friends of his. He expressed extraordinary surprise at seeing them, introduced them to Gorleston, and insisted on their dining with him. It was a merry dinner, and a considerable amount of wine was consumed. Later on the quintette adjourned – this time it was to a pet place of the Professor's. They had a private room there, and Gorleston trounced the Professor soundly. Then, in boisterous mood, he took on his three friends and administered severe hidings to each of them. So pleased was he that he sent for two magnums of champagne and after trying ineffectually to play with the rest, which he had previously chalked, he subsided gracefully on to the couch. Eventually Gorleston, hopelessly drunk, was assisted into a taxi. The Professor gave the driver the address of 124, Unwin Street, Bloomsbury –

Inside the taxi the behaviour of the four men was a little strange, for they proceeded to extract a good many things from the drunken man's pockets. They also carefully placed a pair of horn-rimmed spectacles on his face!

"Capital!" murmured the Professor as he gazed at the unconscious man. "John Elwes, surely?"

"We'll hope so," replied one of the others. "We'll knock up his landlady and if she greets him as such we're home."

"When will he wake up?"

"About eleven to-morrow," replied the other. "I got that drug from the natives on the West Coast, and I know it backwards. Still, we'll be on the safe side and turn up at ten o'clock tomorrow."

One hour later the landlady, profuse in her thanks for bringing Mr Elwes home, showed the four men out of 124, Unwin Street. In a quiet street they proceeded to remove beards, moustaches and wigs – the Professor becoming Allan Sylvester and his three companions – Martin Everest, Sir Hugh Williamson and Lord Trevitter!

"It was a brain-wave of Daphne's!" chuckled Everest as he lit a cigarette. "We know he's Gorleston, he knows he's Gorleston, but his landlady and Adwinter are prepared to swear he's John Elwes. Besides, he's in Elwes' rooms in Elwes' bed, all his clothes are marked with Elwes' name, and even his cards are in the name of John Elwes. If I were on the bench," thoughtfully, "I should have to come to the conclusion that he *was* Elwes."

"Of course, the amusing thing to me," said Williamson, "is that we've done it so carefully that even if he can prove he's Gorleston, he's in a worse mess. For that establishes definitely that he's been runnin' a dual personality in order to defraud the bank."

"Ah, but his attitude to-morrow morning will decide that. If he refuses to give in, we may be wrong. But he won't. He'll throw up the sponge. You see if he doesn't."

When Richard Henry Gorleston awoke the next morning he stared dazedly round the room. Then with a startled cry he leapt out of bed. But he stopped short, for at that moment the door opened and two men, complete strangers to him, came into the room, and locked the door.

"Well, John Elwes – the game's up!"

"W – w – what d'you mean? My name's not John Elwes!"

"Really! Then may I ask what you're doing in John Elwes' room, sleeping in John Elwes' bed?" He took a quick step forward, picked up a coat which lay on a chair, glanced at it. "And how come you to be wearing John Elwes' clothes?"

The other gasped.

"John Elwes' – clothes?"

"See for yourself! Name in coat – name on the shirt – name on the collar – card case here on the dressing-table" – he took it up and examined it, "with John Elwes' cards in it! If you're not John Elwes, perhaps you'll not only tell us how you come to be in possession of all his things, but who you are and how you are here."

For a space of seconds Gorleston glared at him like a rat caught in a trap.

"My name's Gorleston," he blurted out desperately. "Richard Henry Gorleston. How I got here I don't know."

The taller of the two men smiled pityingly.

"Come again, sonnie," he answered. "We're acting on behalf of the Universal Banking Corporation who are rather interested in getting hold of John Elwes for forging Gorleston's signature to a £25,000 cheque. Adwinter, of Queen Anne Street, will swear to you anywhere, and so will your landlady."

Gorleston moistened his dry lips.

"It's going to trouble you to prove I'm Elwes," he said.

"It's going to trouble *you* to prove you're not," laughed the other easily. "We've got your four pals of last night who swear that while you were drunk you let out the whole story."

"It's a plant!" Gorleston muttered at length. "A frame-up! You know it!"

"Try that on the magistrate," smiled the other. "Of course, it's always open to you, when you get to Bow Street, to subpœna Gorleston himself. If there is such a strong likeness between the two of you, you might get off that way."

"My dear Allan," chimed in his friend sarcastically, "do think of what he's told us! He *is* Gorleston. Though if he can prove it, then Heaven help him, because we can quite easily establish that he is Elwes as well. So all the bank do is to charge him with trying to obtain twenty-five thou' by means of a trick."

"Well, hop it and call a policeman," replied his friend. "I'm sick of all this cackle."

But as the other moved over to the door Gorleston sprang up trembling.

"Can't we – can't we settle this?" he exclaimed desperately.

The man at the door smiled.

"There's Gorleston to be considered," he replied.

"I tell you I am Gorleston."

The other strode back, his hands clenched.

"Yes," he snapped, his voice like a whiplash, "and John Elwes as well! Don't you dare to interrupt me!" as Gorleston made as if to speak. "What about the 9.11 up to London from Tavistock on the day the forgery was committed? What about the chauffeur who drove you here the moment you arrived so that your landlady could prove that John Elwes was in town that day? What about your telling her that you were in a hurry to get to the Universal Bank to cash a cheque? Excellent corroborative evidence, eh, that John Elwes was a real live person? And then you drove on to the bank, gave the chauffeur ten shillings and walked in as Richard Henry Gorleston – and caught the 3.16 back to Tavistock, picked up your fishing rod en route to Portworth and walked into the hotel and said you'd had a blank day. Want any more, you lying devil?"

But evidently Gorleston didn't. He fell back in his chair the picture of absolute rage and despair.

"I – don't know – who on earth you are—"

"And you won't!" interrupted the other. "Now, then, which is it to be – the police, or a confession?"

"A con – con – confession!" stammered Richard Henry Gorleston.

Once more Sir John Colston sat opposite Daphne Wrayne in her private room.

"You will probably agree with me, Sir John," she began in her cool little voice, "that if Richard Henry Gorleston decided to drop his action, gave you a written undertaking to that effect, agreed furthermore to accept the loss and never proceed against you on the same count – you would then, I think, be quite satisfied? In other words, you would sooner let the matter drop – providing your bank didn't suffer – rather than he should get, say, seven years, and the public should know that although you had been swindled, you had been just a little careless?"

"Why, of course, my dear young lady. Publicity is the thing we're most anxious to avoid. But you don't mean to say that Gorleston will do that?"

Daphne Wrayne unlocked a drawer in her table and drew out a paper.

"Please listen to this, Sir John," she said:

"I, Richard Henry Gorleston, of 849, The Albany, London, W., being of sound mind, do declare as follows that the cheque for twenty-five thousand pounds, cashed under my signature at the Universal Banking Corporation, of 99, Lombard Street, in the City of London, on June 15th, 1927, was written by me, and that the error in the signature was made wilfully by me with intent to deceive. Furthermore, that the name of John Elwes was invented by me, and the person and identity of John Elwes was no other than myself—"

"Great Heavens! May I – may I see it?"

"Sir John!" Daphne Wrayne leant forward in her chair and her hazel eyes were earnest on his. "You have perhaps a right to ask to see this paper, but I am going to ask you as a gentleman not to exercise that right. This paper bears the signatures, as witnesses, of two men whose names are household words for uprightness, and integrity, throughout England – two of my colleagues – the Adjusters!"

Just for a moment silence, while he gazed at her spellbound. Then she went on:

"In asking you not to insist on seeing this paper I know that I am asking you a favour. But so that there shall be no uneasiness in your mind, I will give you a letter which will no doubt satisfy you equally."

Daphne took out of her drawer a sealed envelope and handed it to him. He slit it open. Then:

"Do you know what is in this letter, Miss Wrayne?"

"Well, I think I do," with a smile.

"It is from Gorleston's solicitors! In it they say that he has discontinued his action against us, that he exonerates us from all liability, and that no further proceedings will be taken over this matter."

"And you can go on cashing his cheques, Sir John," she added sweetly, "and can henceforward reckon him the most scrupulously honourable client – so far as you're concerned – whom you have on your books. You see, he knows that if he tries such a thing again – well, we produce this paper!"

For some moments he gazed at her, too bewildered to speak.

"Miss Wrayne," he said at length, "words simply fail me. How on earth have you managed this?"

For answer she lay back in her chair, merriment dancing in her hazel eyes.

"Ever play poker, Sir John?"

"Why, certainly, Miss Wrayne," surprised.

"Ever been bluffed out and induced to chuck in a good hand?"

"Afraid I have once or twice," he admitted, "and been a bit mad afterwards."

Smiling she put out a slim hand to him.

"Oh, Sir John," she exclaimed merrily, "if Richard Henry Gorleston ever knows what a good hand he threw in on, he'll be a million times madder than you've ever been!"

A Pebble for Papa

MAX ALLAN COLLINS
& MATTHEW V. CLEMENS

*I hardly know where to begin when introducing Max Allan
Collins. His output is phenomenal, both in quality and quantity.
He is probably best known for his graphic novel* Road to
Perdition *(1998) which was the basis for the powerful 2002
film directed by Sam Mendes. Collins has adapted many film
novelizations including* In the Line of Fire *(1993),* The
Mummy *(1999) and* NYPD Blue: Blue Beginning *(1995).
Perhaps his best known character is his private eye, Nate Heller,
who first appeared in* True Detective *(1983). These stories are
set mostly in the 1930s. Collins is known for the depth of his
research, none better exemplified than in his series of disaster
mysteries, which began with* The Titanic Murders *(1999).*

*Matthew V. Clemens is the author of the regional best-
seller,* Dead Water: The Klindt Affair *(1995), a true crime
work that led him into assisting Max Allan Collins on the
forensics and plotting of the popular* CSI *novels.*

*The following is more of a whowilldoit than a whodunnit. I
reckon you'll soon work out the victim, but who's going to be
the perp?*

The winter of '28 had refused to release its frigid grip on
the city's throat, so the crowd dining at Papa's Ristorante was sparse. From the outside Papa's looked no different

than a dozen other hole-in-the-wall restaurants in Little Italy.

Couples were scattered here and there, some huddled over their table gazing into each other's eyes, others ate spaghetti and drank wine. None of the patrons were paying attention to each other; no one noticed the big man in the brown fedora and cashmere overcoat enter.

The diners had no idea that this was the head of the Irish mob, though one look into Lou O'Hara's dead black eyes would have told them that something about this guy was not quite . . . right. Without even a glance toward Papa's other customers, O'Hara stomped through the restaurant and flung open a door at the far end of the dining room.

His hat and coat were taken from him by an attendant, and he was shown to a chair at the long oak table that dominated the center of the room. Around him were most of the other crime bosses of the city. O'Hara ignored them except to nod toward Raven Milhone, who occupied the chair on his left. The leggy brunette beauty had a crimson-nailed finger in everything from blackmail and prostitution to murder.

She was O'Hara's kind of woman.

The door to the private banquet room opened and Giacomo Ghilini, "Papa" to most everyone in the city, took his rightful place at the head of the table. A powerfully built, thick-chested man, Papa was angry but he didn't let it show. Not even when his hooded brown eyes fell on the reason this dinner hadn't yet been served – Lou O'Hara.

Papa saw it as a lack of respect to start the meal before all his guests were seated. O'Hara, head of the biggest independent outfit in the city, was really nothing more than a two-bit strongarm who had made it to the top through cruelty, callousness, and an uncanny ability to remain standing when those in line ahead of him had fallen. Though O'Hara's late arrival showed flagrant disregard for his host, Papa was not going to allow himself to be dragged down to this thug's level.

He bestowed O'Hara a smile, almost a grin. "We didn't want to start without you, Lou."

O'Hara nodded non-committally, mumbling something about having some business to take care of, but made no attempt to apologize for his tardiness.

"Vito," Papa said motioning to his son and chief lieutenant who sat on his right, "pour Lou a glass of wine."

Vito nodded and did as he was told. Papa noted the contempt in his son's eyes as Vito handed the glass across the table to O'Hara. A good boy, Papa thought, but he must learn to mask his feelings better. He still thought of his third son as a boy, his student, his protégé, though Vito was pushing forty and already graying at the temples.

O'Hara accepted the wine without thanks and gulped down nearly half before he set the glass on the table in front of him. Uncouth, Papa thought. A pig.

Papa studied the faces around the table. O'Hara was on his left, the Irish mobster's white shark's teeth drawn into a grin for Raven Milhone. Beyond them were Deng Chou Lo, leader of the Chinese Tongs, coldly impressive in his traditional silk, dragoned garb; and the ragu-nosed Lawrence Rafferty, city councilman bought and paid for with Ghilini money. Next was another Papa purchase, police Lieutenant Adam Maynerd, in a gray suit that matched his complexion, and finally past him sat Wa Tse Wang, head of the Triads, in a natty three-piece suit whose only Chinatown touch was a many-blossomed tie.

Papa trusted none of them.

Rafferty and Maynerd were allies, but once a man had been bought, Papa believed that sooner or later he'd be bought again. Both Wa and Deng had met privately with Papa recently and he had been forced to work out new accords with each to keep them from going to the mattresses. Raven Milhone seemed far too ambitious to settle for the arrangement she had with the Ghilini family, and O'Hara? Well, O'Hara was just plain nuts.

On the right side of the table were the attendees that Papa considered his allies. Vito of course, Josef Freidkin, aging head of the Jewish gang, Papa's secret grandson Toshiro, Rabbi Seidelman, a close friend for many years, Papa's adopted daughter Beatrice, and Leonard Ford, editor of the *City Times*. At the opposite end of the table was Monsignor John Rossi, priest to the Ghilini family, and most of the rest of the mob as well.

Silent waiters in white jackets and black bow ties served the group their dinner. Though Papa claimed to be nothing more than an honest restaurateur, those seated at this table, unlike the diners in the other room, knew that wasn't true. He was, instead, the man who held the city in his palm.

Papa received his plate last. As the waiters made their exit, Papa looked down the table to Monsignor Rossi. "Father, would you like to lead us in grace?"

The priest nodded and rose. The Confessor, as he was known within the mob, was a compact man of moderate build whose shoulders seemed to sag a little from the heavy weight they bore. His longish silver hair was combed straight back away from a face that seemed far more ancient than his sixty-one years. He clasped his hands, bowed his head.

"Oh, Heavenly Father, we thank you for your blessed bounty we are about to receive and for the kind hospitality of our host, Papa Ghilini. We are grateful to you for all good things. Amen."

Papa broke off a piece of bread and offered it to O'Hara who accepted it without thanks and wolfed it down along with his salad.

"I want to express my gratitude to all of you for coming," Papa said as they ate. "It is good to see that we can all get along again, even after – ."

"So why the hell d'you call us all here?" O'Hara interrupted.

Papa glared at O'Hara and just as quickly smiled. "As I was saying, even after this recent . . . unpleasantness, it's good to see that we can still get along. It is my hope that this dinner can serve as the glue that binds the peace we have negotiated."

"Peace serves the best interests of us all," Councilman Rafferty piped in. "The pie's plenty big for everybody to get a piece."

O'Hara shot Rafferty a withering look. "How the hell would you know? You don't dip into shit. You take exactly what Ghilini hands you and leave it at that."

Rafferty looked down, suddenly very interested in his plate.

"Lou, Lou," Papa said mildly, patting the air. "Mr Rafferty is merely . . ."

"Full of shit," O'Hara finished for him. "Deng," he went on, "how big a percentage are you paying to the Ghilinis?"

The leader of the Tongs glanced quickly at Papa, then turned his eyes to O'Hara. "Our relationship with Mr Ghilini has proven to be quite profitable for both of us."

"Has Papa supported you in the sale of opium?"

Deng leapt to his feet. "We do not sell drugs."

Grinning, O'Hara said, "Why is that, Deng? Is it 'cause you don't wanna make money . . . or 'cause Ghilini here told you he'd put you out of business if you did?"

Deng said nothing as he slowly resumed his seat.

"Lou," Papa said, his voice rising only slightly. "I've told you before, we will not sell drugs in this city. There we draw the line."

Papa hated narcotics and the trouble they brought. He had seen what that vile poison could do, and it was a thing he was loathe to see again. Sure, he made his living from people's weaknesses, but drugs were different. Where gambling and prostitution were activities men partook of their own volition, narcotics were like a whirlpool. They swept you up, then they swept you under and you drowned before you even knew you were in trouble.

O'Hara was glaring at him.

"The issue is closed," Papa said, fighting to keep his voice even.

"Like hell it is," O'Hara exploded. "I'm tired of you tryin' to tell me where and how I can make my money, old man. If I want to sell drugs or whores or fucking red-white-and-blue iceboxes, it's none of your goddamn business and you and your combo of Chinks and petty grafters ain't gonna stop me."

The others were eyeing Papa as he carefully wiped his mouth with his napkin. This was not how this meeting was supposed to go. Papa had sent out the invitations for this meet the previous Sunday, to assure that the heads of all the gangs would be here when he announced his retirement. It was to be a celebration of his stepping down and Vito's ascension to his throne.

And here was O'Hara throwing a fit like a child, challenging his authority in front of the others. Papa felt he could count on most of the others to fall in line with whatever he ordered. After all, they always had before. The course of action he was considering was dangerous, but Papa felt it was the only way to amicably stave off O'Hara's challenge.

He tried to read the faces of the others before he spoke. They were guarded, waiting to see what action he would take. Only Papa felt suddenly weary. He wondered if his decision was coming a year, even six months too late. He drew in a deep breath and let it out slowly.

"Lou," he finally said, reasonably, amicably showing the bastard far more respect than he warranted, "this is not a dictatorship as you would have the others believe. We have made business decisions together. And we have prospered because we have stood by those decisions."

O'Hara was twisting his napkin between his fingers. His knuckles were white, but he said nothing as he continued to glower at his host.

Papa continued: "To prove to you that we are all involved in the decision-making of this organization, we'll put this drug issue to a vote of the board. The decision will be final. And I'm confident, after this vote is taken, we'll have no more talk of drugs in this city."

O'Hara swiveled on the rest. Their eyes fell away from the Irishman's dark stare and Papa was sure he had O'Hara right where he wanted him.

Papa said, "Vito, you will cast the ballot of the Ghilini family."

Vito cleared his throat. When he spoke his voice sounded shaky. "You . . . you all know that the Ghilini family has been against drugs since the beginning. We will not change now."

Beatrice, unable to wait her turn, jumped in. "I'm with Papa too. As I'm sure Toshiro is as well."

All eyes turned to Toshiro who shifted nervously in his chair. "I'm here representing the Yakuza," he said. "You all know that. You also know that when the Yakuza first came to this city, it was Papa Ghilini who found a place for us. Back then, he was the one who helped us thrive when he could just as easily have squashed us like a bug. We are forever in his debt and we vote to follow the current policy."

Papa's eyes darted to O'Hara who seemed about ready to tear his napkin in half. It was all Papa could do to keep his smile to himself. "Josef?"

Freidkin cleaned his gold-rimmed glasses with his napkin. Papa noticed that the man's hand was shaking ever so slightly.

"Papa, you put me in a difficult position. You know that my partners and I are basically law-abiding businessmen these days. Over ninety percent of our holdings are now completely legal. I feel as if I am being asked to vote on an issue that does not concern me. I'm afraid I must abstain from this ballot."

Papa's eyes met Freidkin's and the old Jew looked away quickly. A quiver ran through Papa's gut.

Deng spoke up. "Papa, though it grieves me to agree with Mr O'Hara about anything . . . I'm afraid on this issue, he is correct. Though Councilman Rafferty rightly points out that the pie is large, there are so many pieces being meted out that the Tongs are getting barely a sliver. It is possible that opening the drug market could give us the larger piece we feel we deserve."

Wa echoed the opinion of his countryman.

Due to Freidkin's abstention, the count would now be close. Even if it had come down to a tie, Papa would have the deciding vote. But with only Raven and O'Hara himself left, Papa was suddenly feeling sick to his stomach. If Raven Milhone didn't side with him, it would be a stalemate, and the one thing he had fought to keep out of the city might well become a reality. With each passing thought, another jet of acid shot into Papa's stomach.

He did not feel at all well.

O'Hara rises, his maniacal grin a malignancy spreading over his face. From nowhere, a machine gun appears in his hands. Papa watches in mute horror as fire leaps from the barrel. The stream of bullets rips through Vito even as he rises. Papa feels his mouth drop open as he sees only a red mist hanging in the air where Vito had been standing. O'Hara turns the weapon on Freidkin, the hot steel rain decapitating the Jew. Papa struggles to rise from his chair, but he is somehow glued to it, frozen in anguish as he watches O'Hara mow down Toshiro and Beatrice. He cannot scream, or move, or even whimper, though he feels hot tears rolling down his cheeks. Finally he breaks the spell and heaves himself up. He dives for O'Hara . . .

Papa, bathed in sweat, awoke to find himself sitting up in bed. Mama was sleeping peacefully next to him, blissfully ignorant of the thrashing that had been going on next to her.

"Jesus," he whispered, crossing himself in the darkness. This had not been the first nightmare of the night. He had gotten blessed little sleep since last night's meeting and the few times he had dozed off had been punctuated by these turbulent, violent dreams. Slipping his feet over the side of the bed, Papa bowed his head, and for the hundredth time went through the events of the meeting.

He had known that he was taking a chance calling for the vote on selling drugs, but he had figured the odds were on his side. His whole career had been built on playing the odds and this time, this one time, he had been woefully mistaken in his calculations.

Now instead of handing over the reins of the biggest operation in the city to his son, Papa was left in charge of a family that was considered, for the first time, as vulnerable. What had taken him a lifetime to build had been put at great risk, if not destroyed, over dinner. A voice inside him wanted to blame Raven Milhone and the others who had sided with O'Hara, but he shook his head and drove it away.

It was his fault, his own ego that had caused his error. He pounded a hammy fist into his thigh and swore under his breath. Regaining control, he peeked over at Mama to make sure she was still asleep. He then looked at the clock on the nightstand next to him.

Five o'clock.

Two more hours and The Confessor would be at the church. Papa accepted counsel from very few people, but Monsignor Rossi was a man on whom he could depend for sound advice, perhaps the one man who could help him avoid the war that now seemed inevitable.

Pushing himself to his feet, Papa padded to the bathroom. He cleaned up and dressed in a brown suit, his favorite. His white shirt felt a little snug at the collar, but Papa ignored it. Being careful not to wake his wife, he crept through the bedroom and downstairs to the kitchen. After he brewed the coffee, he sat alone at the table, contemplating the steam that rose from the mug.

The Tongs and the Triads would probably stay in line as long as they were sure that he remained in charge. And though Raven Milhone had secured her position at the table by being an independent thinker, it was clear to Papa that O'Hara was the wild card in the deck. He hoped that between Rossi and himself they could come up with a plan that would allow this to truly be a Good Friday.

He sipped from the mug and worked to clear his mind. Over the course of his reign, Papa's ability to dispassionately view a situation had been the key to his survival. No matter what the circumstances or the people involved, Papa never let his emotions get in the way of making the right business decision.

His son, Paulo, had been proof of that.

O'Hara, though, was making that a difficult proposition. Papa's gut was telling him to have the crazy Irishman whacked, the consequences be damned, but his head told him that there had to be a another way.

Papa took a deeper swallow of coffee. The heat felt good as it trailed down his throat, taking away the chill of the kitchen. He needed to get through today, just today, then he could rest over the weekend. Even O'Hara wasn't crazy enough to start anything on Easter weekend. Papa would talk to Father Rossi, get some rest, then make his decision with a cool head and a clean soul. Unencumbered by his anger at O'Hara, Papa knew he could come up with a plan that would keep his business in order and maintain the peace.

Rising, Papa shuffled to the front door. The morning newspaper was on the porch. Papa picked it up, took a moment to stretch his stiff back, then returned to the kitchen to read the paper over his second cup of coffee.

He barely glanced at the front page before turning to the editorial section. After O'Hara had stormed out of the meeting last night, Papa cornered Leonard Ford and called in a favor owed him by the newspaper editor.

"I think," Papa had told the jittery little man, "that the *City Times is* due for an editorial on the growing drug problem, don't you?"

"I was thinking that myself," Ford said with a grin. "I was even thinking that it might be a good time for the paper to take a stand against organized crime. Maybe do an expose on O'Hara? You know, the city's biggest racketeer sort of thing?"

Papa shook his head, no.

Ford nodded. "Might cloud the issue. Later on, perhaps . . ."

Papa had nodded back. It had been that simple. He grinned slyly as he read Ford's editorial. First Ford praised the police for keeping drug use to a minimum in the city, then in the next breath railed against them to not allow junkies and drug sellers to proliferate the streets.

Swigging his coffee, Papa re-read the final paragraph.

"And let us not forget the warning of the noted Irish judge John Philpot Curran who said, 'The condition upon which God has given liberty to man is eternal vigilance.' Words for our intrepid police department to live by."

Papa wondered if O'Hara was reading the editorial even as he was. Though O'Hara would know that Papa was behind Ford's rantings, there was nothing the Irishman could do about it. And Ford had outdone himself. His editorial would have people talking all weekend. Papa made a mental note to speak with his friends within the clergy. Easter weekend might be the perfect time for a scathing rebuke of drug use from the various pulpits of the city.

His plan was simple. Turn the city against drug use before O'Hara and the others could get the product to the streets. Simple economics might well succeed where Papa had been unable to. The size of O'Hara's supply would be inconsequential if there was no demand.

Noting the time on the kitchen clock, Papa finished his coffee, laid the newspaper on the table, and reached for his overcoat. Monsignor Rossi would be at the church by now. It was time for Papa to make his confession and confer with the family priest.

His driver, Sonny, had not yet arrived so Papa decided to walk the half-mile to Sacred Heart Cathedral. The late March wind whistled in from the north, whipping Papa's overcoat around his legs. Heavy dark clouds announced Old Man Winter's intention to lay one more load of snow on the city before abandoning it to spring.

Despite the temperature, Papa did not hurry. Winter, which signified a state of hibernation to so many others, invigorated Papa Ghilini. His body didn't adjust to the cold as easily as it had when he had been a young man, but he still enjoyed a winter walk as much as he ever had.

He passed few people as he made his way toward the cathedral. It wasn't just because of the weather. Papa knew, through his friendship with Monsignor Rossi, that although the city had a rich, storied Catholic history, many of the younger people considered it the tired religion of their grandparents.

Perhaps that was part of the reason that His Eminence Cardinal Vincenzo Micelli would be presiding over tonight's celebration of the Lord's Passion service. Nothing like having a Cardinal in the church to drag the parishioners out of the woodwork.

The frosty air nipped at Papa's ears and nose. He looked up and could see the cathedral looming two blocks ahead. It was a stately brick building rising three stories, dwarfing the houses and duplexes of the old residential neighborhood. Papa was approaching from the east. On his right was the former rectory, a two story brick house, that now served as offices for the parochial school. A concrete portico connected that building to the side of the cathedral. Two black street lamps flanked the sidewalk that led to the front doors. Each was draped in purple ribbons that signified the season of Advent.

Papa's shoulders hunched inside the overcoat; he looked like a turtle drawing its head inside its shell as he trudged up the walk. The wind had turned even more biting. The large doors were at least twice Papa's six foot height, but they moved easily as he tugged on the handle. He stepped into the vestibule and shook off the chill. Maybe, he thought, it was time to reconsider his feelings about winter. Though the walk had done him good, the cold seemed to have penetrated to the bone.

The church was quiet as a mausoleum as Papa stepped to the door of the sanctuary. On either side of the door were sculpted angels. Each angel's face reminded Papa of the Madonna. They were beautiful women in blue and white robes. Each was kneeling and holding a punch bowl-sized ceramic clam shell that normally contained the holy water; however during this week they stood empty, representing a world without Christ. Papa made the sign of the cross.

He entered the sanctuary and glanced toward Rossi's confessional. The door was closed; someone was with the priest. The vaulted ceiling of the cathedral rose thirty feet over Papa's head. Gilded conical shaped lights hung from the open rafters; stained glass windows depicting the apostles lined the sides of the church. Between the windows, engraved in marble, were scenes portraying the stations of the cross. The pews were divided into four sections separated by three aisles that led to the altar. Papa looked toward the fifteen-foot wooden cross that hung behind the altar. Shrouded in purple satin, it would remain so until Easter Sunday.

Just behind the last row of pews, on a small table, sat a bowl filled with pebbles. Each had a black cross painted on it. The bowl of stones replaced the holy water during Lent. Papa picked up one from the bowl and kneaded it between his fingers as he took a seat in the last row.

He noticed a few parishioners praying silently in the pews nearer the altar. An old woman was in the front corner of the sanctuary lighting a votive candle. Papa watched as the crone blew out the match and made the sign of the cross. She folded her hands, prayed silently for a moment, then genuflected toward the altar before she started up the aisle in Papa's direction. As she approached, Papa hoped that she wasn't coming back to take confession. He needed to speak to Rossi as soon as possible, but he knew that if the old woman sat down in one of the pews he would allow her to go first. Manners and respect, he told himself, these were still important things, whether Lou O'Hara and his mob thought so or not.

As she finally neared Papa, she smiled and nodded. He didn't recognize her, but he returned the greeting. She paused for a moment next to his pew, caught her breath, then left the sanctuary.

Papa's attention had just returned to the large cross on the wall at the far end of the church when he heard the confessional door open behind him. Papa turned his head slightly and from the corner of his eye saw his neighbor Tomasino LaPaglia come out. When Tomasino, bent and aged, saw Papa, a grin formed on Tomasino's wrinkled face and a twinkle appeared in his rheumy eyes. The men shook hands and exchanged brief greetings. Tomasino complained about the cold weather and how it angered his Lombago, then exited as Papa entered the confessional.

Papa closed the door and sat down, still worrying the pebble between his thumb and middle finger. "Bless me, Father, for I have sinned. It's been . . ." his voice trailed off. Papa ran a hand over his face, and was startled by the looseness of his withered flesh. "It has been . . . a long time since my last confession."

"That's all right, my son."

Having his old friend on the other side of the screen made Papa feel more at ease.

"Go ahead, my son."

"I come . . ." Papa hesitated, feeling a catch in his voice. He swallowed and took a deep breath before continuing. "I come to you today, Father, with a heavy heart."

Monsignor Rossi remained silent.

"Over the years I have confided many things to you, my friend. But there are many more things that I have kept to myself." Papa strained to see the priest through the screen separating their cubicles. All he could make out, though, was Rossi's shadow. "Last night's meeting, for instance. I intended to announce my retirement."

Papa waited for a response. There was no movement in the far cubicle.

"I thought if I stepped down, and Vito took over, that things would . . . even out. I know that O'Hara and some of the others think I am getting weak. I don't believe that to be true, but I thought that perhaps they still had enough respect for Vito's strength that he could ascend and maintain the position of the Ghilini family. I see now that I misjudged."

The priest said nothing for a moment, then finally, "We are not young men anymore, old friend. Those running things today, they don't understand respect. All O'Hara and his kind understand is greed."

"There is more to life than money, Father. This much I have learned from the church."

Papa could see the priest nodding.

"Of course," Rossi said. "But it isn't just the money. O'Hara is greedy for power. And who has the power?"

The question hung heavy in the confined space. There was no need for Papa to speak – they both knew the answer.

Monsignor Rossi continued, "Maybe it is time for your way of doing business to change." He paused, giving Papa a chance to digest this before he went on. "Look at our friend Freidkin."

"Freidkin," Papa blurted, louder than he would have liked, the pebble tight in his fist. He regained control, and said, "It was Freidkin who helped put me in this position. If he had supported me last night everything would be right in my world. Vito would be running the Ghilini family and there would still be peace."

"Do you not see why Josef made the decision he did?"

"Yes. He is losing his nerve."

Behind the screen, the priest was shaking his head. "I don't think the answer is that simple, Giacomo. Josef is an honest businessman now. And like all honest businessmen, he is worried what will happen if things with O'Hara get out of hand."

Papa rubbed the pebble between his hands. "And by not supporting me last night he has all but assured a war between O'Hara and my family."

"That is one possibility," the priest said patiently. "Another is that O'Hara will bring narcotics into the city and the authorities will stop him."

Papa shook his head violently. "O'Hara will attack me then, thinking that the police are acting on my orders."

There was a long silence before Rossi said, "Not if you step down first."

"Surrender?" Papa exploded. "Walk away from all I have worked for over the years? And what do I receive in return?"

And in the gesturing palm Papa stretched out, toward the shadowy shape beyond the screen, lay the pebble.

The priest's voice was quiet but assured. "What I am saying, old friend, is that if you are not seen as being in charge, there is no reason for Lou O'Hara and the others to come after you."

Papa's stomach constricted. He felt bile rising in his throat. He thought last night had been the ultimate betrayal, but now here he sat in the one place he thought he would receive solace, understanding, and the one person he thought capable of giving him those things sat on the other side of this flimsy screen trying to convince him that the betrayal of others was the best thing that could happen to him. Forgetting he held the pebble, Papa's touched his heated brow, against which the tiny stone felt cold indeed. Beads of sweat slithered down his face and he struggled to shrug out of his overcoat in the tiny space.

When he spoke again, his words were measured. "Father, do you remember the last time someone tried to bring drugs into the city?"

"Yes."

"What happened?"

"Your son, Paulo, was killed trying to stop them."

Papa's voice became very quiet. "Yes, Paulo was killed."

"Do you want that to happen again? That is why I am counseling you to get out now, old friend. You have lost one son to drug runners. Do you want to risk another?"

"You know," Papa said wistfully, "you were never privy to the whole truth about that event."

"They killed Paulo, and I assume that he was avenged."

Tears mixed with the perspiration on Papa's face. "That is not quite the truth, Confessor."

"No?"

"It was Paulo who tried to bring the narcotics into the city, against my wishes. He knew that I wouldn't tolerate that poison coming in, so he did his best to hide what he was doing from me. He didn't hide it well enough. Do you know what I am telling you?"

He could see the priest shake his head, whether a gesture of ignorance or incredulity, Papa did not know.

"What I am saying is that I had my son, my own flesh and blood, killed for disobeying me."

Papa heard the sharp intake of breath beyond the screen. Papa was shaking now. He clutched the tiny counter in front of him trying to regain control of his emotions, the pebble tumbling from his fingers to make a tiny clatter on the floor of the booth.

"I have shed the blood of my own son in order to keep this sin from entering the city, and now you tell me to allow this demon to do that very thing?"

"I . . . I did . . . didn't know . . ."

"Nor does anyone else . . . I pulled some strings out of town."

"H . . . how could you?"

Papa's voice was a whimper now. "I tried. Don't you think I tried? I did everything I could to get Paulo to stop, but he wouldn't listen. He thought he knew more than his father. He thought he was stronger than the family. I couldn't allow him to spread that poison into the city. I've seen it in other places. It starts with the weak, but eventually it also swallows the strong and the children. How someone, *anyone*, could sell bottled death to the young was more than I could comprehend. I wouldn't have stood for it if it had been one of the other gangs. There was no way I could stand by and let someone in my own family contaminate the future. Now I must take a stand with O'Hara as well."

"That was years ago, Giacomo. The times are different. O'Hara is a powerful enemy with many allies."

"I have allies of my own," Papa said.

"O'Hara has Raven Milhone as well as both the Tongs and the Triads."

"I have the Yakuza."

"Do you think that you can trust Toshiro and the Yakuza?" Papa's voice was cold steel. "Yes."

"How can you be so sure?"

"Do you remember Giuseppe?"

"The son you disowned?"

"Yes. Have I ever told you why Giuseppe was sent away?"

"No."

"In the war, Giuseppe took up with a Japanese woman." Papa paused. "The fruit of this illicit affair was a child."

"Yes?"

"If Giuseppe hadn't abandoned both mother and child, he would still be part of my family. That child was Toshiro."

"Toshiro is your grandson?"

Papa nodded. "When Toshiro came to this country it was I who arranged it. I paid for his education. He earned a degree in business and it was my hope that he would be the first of the Ghilini family to go legitimate . . . A fitting, if ironic, fate for my bastard grandson. That was not to be. I found out that he was fencing stolen art, using his business as a front. I decided that if he was going to enter the business anyway it would be best if he did it in such a way that I could keep an eye on him. It was under those conditions that he was sent to join the Yakuza. Though they are heavily into narcotics in Japan, the Yakuza has been restricting its activities in the city to extortion and prostitution. And now with Toshiro entrenched as one of their leaders, they will be a formidable ally. One, I'm sure, that O'Hara thinks will move to his side. That mistake may well be his last."

"I thought I knew you, Giacomo . . ."

"Even with what I have told you today, Confessor, there is still much more you do not know. But I thank you for your time. Whether you know it or not, you have been of great assistance to me today. I now know what I must do."

"I have done nothing but listen."

"That," said Papa, pulling his overcoat on, "is an important quality to find, Father. It is hard these days to find a good listener."

Rossi started to say something, but Papa didn't hear him as he stepped from the confessional, without having taken time to receive forgiveness for the worst sin he'd ever brought to The Confessor, not noticing the pebble he crushed under his heel.

The bell in the steeple was ringing, calling the parishioners to worship. The Good Friday service, the Celebration of the Lord's Passion, was one of Papa Ghilini's favorites. As Papa and his family made his way into the sanctuary, he crossed himself. He looked at the shrouded cross above the altar, then glanced around the congregation as he moved toward the front of the church. Toshiro was sitting with Beatrice in the back row. Papa gave his grandson a curt nod and continued down the aisle. He smiled to himself. They were a handsome couple. A few rows in front of Toshiro sat Police Chief Harry Hammons and his family. The chief glared at Papa who nodded back, forgiving the copper his sins, if only for tonight.

Papa, Mama, and the rest of the Ghilini family made their way to the front of the sanctuary. Papa and Mama sat in the front row while the others took up most of the next four rows.

Papa felt the warmth of Mama's hand as her fingers entwined in his.

Monsignor Rossi stepped forward to deliver the Liturgy of the Word. As the priest read the words, Papa's mind turned back to his meeting with Vito earlier in the day. Papa and Vito lunched together nearly every day. Today had been no different except they hadn't eaten. Both men were fasting in commemoration of Good Friday, so they had sat down over coffee in the back room of Papa's Ristorante.

"You look pale, Papa. Are you still worried about O'Hara?"

Papa shook his head. "Just tired, my son. O'Hara concerns me, but I am not worried."

Vito's brow furrowed. "I don't understand."

Papa's smile was sad, exhausted. There was still so much for Vito to learn. "Women worry, Vito. Men may be concerned about a problem, but it is our job to solve it. Worrying is wasted energy."

His son nodded.

"We are correct to be concerned about O'Hara and his cronies. They are dangerous people."

Again, Vito nodded.

"With the plan I am about to outline for you, you will defeat them. After that, the Ghilini family's position will be assured."

Papa had outlined his strategy for Vito who grasped the subtlety of it even faster than Papa thought he would.

Glancing down the pew, Papa studied his son for a moment and permitted himself a private smile. Vito was going to be just fine. Papa could step down now, knowing that the empire he had spent his whole life shaping would live on for years after he was gone, in good Ghilini hands.

Cardinal Vincenzo Micelli stepped forward to lead the Veneration of the Cross. Though Papa usually paid close attention to the sacraments of his faith, again he found his mind wandering.

Vito had been astonished to find out that Toshiro was his nephew. Losing both his brothers had been difficult for Vito to endure. To find out now that he had family he was unaware of invigorated his son like nothing Papa had witnessed before. But it also seemed to knock him off balance.

"And you never told anyone he was your grandson?" Vito had asked.

"To tell anyone that Toshiro was family would have put him in danger. Don't you see that?"

Vito shook his head. "I'm your son. If you can't trust me, who can you trust?"

"It's not a matter of trust, Vito. If I had told you about Toshiro before this moment, your behavior, no matter how minutely, would have changed toward him. Someone might have been able to figure out why, and that would have placed Toshiro in mortal danger."

"I would have protected him."

Papa did not argue. "And now you will. Until today it has been my job to protect Toshiro, and the rest of our family as well. Now, my son, that job will fall to you. I'm stepping aside. You will oversee everything from now on."

Vito had been as shocked by that pronouncement as he had of learning of his new nephew. Papa had only smiled at his son's surprise.

"Don't be concerned, Vito. You are ready."

The words still rang in Papa's ears. He believed what he had said to his son this afternoon. Vito was ready to take over the family.

Cardinal Micelli stepped to the altar. His voice carried to the far reaches of the church, even though it seemed, to Papa at least, that His Eminence was speaking in a conversational tone. "We are gathered here today to give thanks to our Holy Father for his gift to man. The Lord so loved his creation that he gave his only begotten son to sacrifice himself for our sins."

Papa glanced at Monsignor Rossi who stood to the Cardinal's left. The priest was listening patiently. That talent was, Papa decided, Monsignor Rossi's greatest gift.

"It was on this holy day," the Cardinal continued, "that Pilate washed his hands, leaving the mob to decide the fate of Jesus."

Papa bowed his head.

"The soldiers stripped Jesus, put upon him the scarlet robe, then placed upon his head the crown of thorns."

Unconsciously, Papa ran a hand through his hair.

"They placed a reed in his right hand, bowed before him, and mocked him, saying, 'Hail, the King of the Jews.' Then they tore the reed from him, spit upon him and beat him."

Papa felt a single tear slide down his cheek.

"Then they tore off the robe and led Jesus into the streets. They bade him to bear his own cross, then marched him through the streets to the jeers of the mob. Then, along with the thieves, he was crucified. The soldiers cast lots for his garments. Above his head hung a sign that read, 'This is Jesus, King of the Jews.' Even the thieves tormented him, saying, 'If thou be the Son of God, come down from the cross.' But he did not."

As the Cardinal went on, Papa could feel himself shaking. No matter how many times he heard the story, it never failed to touch him. Papa turned to look at Vito again. His son's eyes bored into him as Papa heard the Cardinal say, "My God, my God, why hath thou forsaken me?"

Then Vito smiled at him and Papa felt a warm glow that had

not coursed through him for a long time. Not since before Paulo died. Papa's plan was in place, and the threat of O'Hara seemed about to be neutralized. As Papa made his way to the steps of the altar to accept his communion, he realized that the radiance he felt was, of all things, happiness.

As the choir sang the hymn, Papa moved to the communion rail, eased himself to his knees, and clasped his hands in front of him. Father Rossi stood just across the rail. An altar boy placed the paten under Papa's chin and he accepted the host when the priest laid it upon his tongue. Praying silently as he heaved himself back to his feet, Papa made his way to the outside aisle and back to his seat.

He noticed the Cardinal was sitting in a straight back chair near the altar. The man appeared to be weary from the performance of the service. Papa turned his attention to the line of worshipers creeping up the aisle to the rail. As one group rose and moved away, others took their places and knelt. Papa noticed a thin, balding man in a dark suit. As the man rose and moved to Papa's left, Papa thought he saw the bulge of a gun under the man's jacket.

Papa watched the man make his way to the outside aisle on Papa's left. He was sure now that the man was wearing a shoulder holster. Papa studied the man's deep-set eyes, framed by high cheek bones; beak of a nose, what little hair he had left slicked down at the back of his skull. Papa watched from the corner of his eye as the man took an aisle seat in the smaller outside pew two rows behind Papa's.

Vito looked toward his father and Papa tilted his head toward the gunman. He watched as Vito turned to eyeball the guy, then glanced back at Papa and shrugged. His son had not seen what Papa had.

The bald man packing a gun was not one of their soldiers, nor was he anyone that Papa recognized from O'Hara's bunch.

As the Cardinal rose and moved to the front of the altar, Papa continued to watch the gunman from the corner of his eye. His stomach churned as he tried to decide what to do.

The Cardinal, hands folded across his stomach, said, "Lord, send down your abundant blessing upon your people who have devoutly recalled the death of your son in the sure hope of the resurrection."

Alarm bells clanged in Papa's head as he saw the bald man's hand easing under his jacket.

"Grant them pardon; bring them comfort."

The man was slowly rising now, and Papa wanted to yell but no sound would come out of his throat. His mind was screaming at him. *It's a hit! It's a hit!* But as Papa looked at the man's eyes, he realized he was not the target. The assassin's eyes were locked on the altar. Papa couldn't believe what he was seeing. Someone was going to whack the Cardinal!

"May their faith grow stronger and their eternal salvation be assured."

Papa was on his feet now as well. He felt Mama's hand on his arm, but he didn't look down at her. His eyes saw only the assassin and the gun coming out the hitman's jacket in what seemed to be slow motion. There was no way Papa could get to the assassin before the man could get off a shot. There was only one other course of action possible.

Hurdling the rail with an agility even he found surprising, Papa leapt toward the altar.

"We ask this through Christ our Lord . . ." The Cardinal's words trailed off as he saw Papa sprinting toward him.

"Amen," the congregation said as one.

"What are you . . ." the Cardinal bellowed, his eyes wide with fear.

Monsignor Rossi was moving to intercept Papa. The look on the priest's face told Papa that the man thought he had gone insane. The Cardinal took a step backward toward the cross as Papa shoved Rossi to the ground, a gunshot exploding from behind Papa as he knocked the Cardinal to the floor, echoing through the vast chamber.

Papa felt a tremendous jolt in his back. He'd been shot before and instantly knew that the assassin's bullet had found him instead of His Eminence. The impact drove him past the Cardinal and face first into the cross. He grabbed the shroud of the crucifix as he started to topple and the cross wobbled precariously. Realizing what was happening, Papa let go of the shroud but it was too late.

He heard the chorus of screams erupt as he fell backwards. Looking up, he saw the cross coming toward him and knew there was no way to avoid it. As the huge wooden crucifix tumbled, Papa turned his head and saw the Cardinal cowering on the floor, a look of utter disbelief etched on his face.

When the cross finally struck him, a whole world of color bloomed in Papa's eyes. There was a burst of pain, then suddenly no pain at all. His head lolled to one side and the blossom of color disintegrated as he watched the assassin retreating toward the door of the church. Papa's eyes fell shut. He was surprised at how much effort it took for him to open them again. As he did, he made out Police Chief Harry Hammons running toward the doors at the far end of the cathedral with his gun drawn.

"Help him," Papa heard someone whimper.

Forcing his eyes to stay open, he saw Monsignor Rossi bending over him. The priest was holding someone's hand, and though it looked a great deal like his own thick hand, Papa couldn't feel the cleric's touch.

Someone yelled, "Get the damn cross off him!"

Papa could see that several men, Vito among them, were lifting the cross off his chest. He was unable to understand why there was no difference in feeling when the weight was removed from his body.

"Is it bad, old friend?" Rossi asked.

Papa shook his head. The warm, sweet taste of blood filled his mouth and he coughed it up.

Rossi didn't leave his side, but turned to the altar boy. "Get my sacraments," he commanded.

"No time," Papa said, his voice a hoarse whisper.

Tears were running down the priest's face. "You should have the Last Rites," he said.

Papa tried to squeeze his friend's hand but could not. "It's all right, John. I'm at peace with myself – and with my God."

Mama squeezed in on the other side and hugged him. Her cheek was wet and warm, but he felt no other part of her against him. That was all right, he told himself. He'd had the pleasure of her in his arms so many times before and that would be enough to carry him to whatever eternal judgment awaited him.

From outside the church came a sound that might have been a car backfiring, but wasn't.

His mouth was close to Mama's ear now. "I will always love you," he said.

Vito appeared above him. His son's face was clouded with anger and hate. "I'll get O'Hara for this, Papa. Don't worry."

"No. I was not the target. Don't forget your promise to me. That is what is important." Papa's body was wracked by another spasmodic cough and he felt more blood dribble onto his chin. When he could finally speak again, he said, "Only your promise. Remember, that is all that matters."

The edges of his vision were growing dark. From that blackness, Papa thought he saw Paulo moving toward him. His eyes fell closed and behind his lids Papa could clearly see Paulo coming toward him with his arms outstretched.

From that other place Papa heard Rossi say, "You saved the Cardinal, old friend. He is all right. You saved . . ."

Paulo embraced him.

"I'm sorry, my son."

"It is I who am sorry, Papa."

Papa kissed his son. "I love you, Paulo. I always loved you."

"I know," Paulo answered.

Then there was silence.

Thus did a man of violence die in peace, unaware of the masquerade his son Vito had arranged, involving a hitman who now lay dead in the street, shot by a Ghilini soldier . . . a son (*a brother seeking vengeance for a slain brother*) who would bask in the posthumous glory of his martyred father who had, so predictably, thrown himself between God and a bullet. A terrible gang war would simply not have to happen, because this great out-of-date figure had given his life for the Cardinal.

And in the great cathedral, toward the back, a mother was gathering her two children, to remove them from this scene of horror. She tugged hard at the hand of her youngest, a boy who had lagged to pick up a small stone.

Beyond the Call of Beauty

WILL MURRAY

Will Murray is an expert in the history of pulp magazines, and especially those hero pulps such as Doc Savage *and* The Shadow. *He's been able to convert his passion into his job as he has written over 50 books, including 40* Destroyer *novels and eight* Doc Savages *based on Lester Dent's uncompleted stories. He has also contributed to the* Executioner *and* Mars Attacks *series, as well as numerous anthologies. His novel,* Nick Fury Agent of Shield: Empyre *(2000) predicted the operational details of the 11 September 2001 terrorist attacks on America more than a year before they occurred. Most of Murray's fiction has been hidden behind various house names, so it's time he stood out for himself, in the following homage to Dashiell Hammett.*

I heard her voice before I saw ever her face. She was murdering "Freddy the Freshman":

> *Who's wrecks all the parties?*
> *And turns them upside down?*
> *Fanny the Freshman*
> *The freshest gal in town!*

It was a smoky basement speak on Washington Street. A grimey bar. A few tables. Sawdust on the floor. A three-piece band. The granite block wall wasn't enough to keep out the intermittent thunder of the Elevated trains shuttling in and out of Green Street Station, but they cut it down to a tolerable rattle.

As I took a corner table, the red-hot number on the stage kept belting out her inane ditty.

> *She plays the ukelele*
> *She plays the saxophone.*
> *And all the pretty babies*
> *Just won't leave her alone!*

It was the usual crowd. Kids and co-eds from Harvard and Boston College. A sprinkling of more mature patrons. But collegiate types predominated. Hard to believe only ten years after the armistice a fresh crop had already sprung up. They had never known war. If the graybeards were right, they never would.

> *Who got bounced at Harvard*
> *Princeton, Yale and Brown?*

Inebriated laughter rippled and tinkled off the walls.

At one big table a gaggle of co-eds were living it up. A fresh-faced couple were going at it so hot and heavy that when they finally came up for air, I couldn't tell which one was the male of the species. The sleek-haired boy in the vicuna coat and over-sized pince-nez came away with so much lip rouge on his mouth that he might have been a girl.

I gave my attention to the evening entertainment.

Spooky Spookins – I didn't for a minute think that was her real name – was up on the low stage dressed like Clara Bow impersonating Lindbergh. A sheepskin-collared leather flyer's jacket bundled her superstructure. The leather cap and goggles covered every strand of bobbed hair.

> *Boola, boola, boola*
> *She goes to school-a.*
> *Just to foola,*
> *She loves to foola!*

> *Sasparilla, sinfronella*
> *She's a swell-a, swell-a fella!*
> *Rah! Rah! Yah-ta-ta!*
> *That's her college yell!*
> *Baggy pants, crazy dance*
> *It's Fanny, can't you tell?*

The crowd roared its applause. Spooky Spookins bowed once and flounced away. She was all legs and silk stockings as the beaded curtain swallowed her.

I ordered gin, traded a dime for a pack of Spuds from the cigarette girl and thought back to what had brought me to this dim hole.

Donal Reynolds of the Reynolds Construction Company had come up the hard way, laying down one brick at a time until he had built himself up a formidable empire. He still carried his lunch to work in a galvanized pail – but in the back seat of his chauffeured phaeton now, not by streetcar.

He had amassed a sufficient fortune to send his only daughter to Harvard, but didn't like the company that she had fallen in with. They had a row over it, and she had disappeared.

Old Man Reynolds had some choice words for the future cream of Boston society. Spoiled college girls. Inflamed youth. Heathen saloon singers. He was long on indignant invective but short on names. But when he wanted her back hard enough he put some heavy coin behind it.

I'd exhausted every contact in Harvard and Cambridge. All I'd been able to uncover was that no one had ever known the Reynolds girl to have a steady beau. So now I was hunting wayward co-eds at the end of Washington where the sun never shone.

The big table looked promising, so I moseyed over.

Laying down a snapshot of the missing girl, I said, "The name's Norris. With the Weld Detective Agency. I'm looking for this girl."

The merriment subsided like I had delivered a downpour from my hat.

No one volunteered a word. The sleek-haired lad did his best to look in every direction but mine. There was something about him I didn't much care for.

"I recognize her," chirped a turbaned blonde. "Helen Reynolds."

"She's been missing four days. Her father wants her back."

"I think she eloped," said a brunette whose headache band had begun drooping over one lazy eye.

"Yeah, she was talking about eloping with that guy. What was his name? Gosh, I'm so smashed I can't work my little brain."

"You can't work your brain, potted or not," snapped the brunette.

The sleek-haired lad had buried his face in his date's strapless shoulder.

I addressed him. "Anything you'd care to add, Little Bo Peep?"

His voice was so soft I thought he must have been fresh out of high school. "Spooky might know. She knows everyone."

"I'll talk to Spooky," I said, retrieving the snap.

"Yeah. But will Spooky talk to you?"

"Kit, you're a positive scream!" the blonde burbled.

The table busted out in raucous laughter as I walked away.

It was such a swanky joint there was no one to stop me as I knocked on what passed for a dressing room.

"Miss Spookins?"

A smoky voice called out, "If you're a Stage Door Johnny, kindly get yourself lost."

"Detective," I returned.

"City or agency?"

"The latter."

The door opened.

Sans goggles, Spooky Spookins had the kind of eyes you hear about but never meet. They were a deep violet. I thought I detected silver specks, but that might have been the way the light hit them. Lines on her oval face told me she'd been around.

I put the Kodak up to her retroussé nose. "The missing girl liked to hang out here. They say you might know her."

"I know everyone."

"They said that too," I said.

Spooky Spookins seemed to stare at the photo for a very long time. I couldn't read her expression.

Finally, she let me in. Taking a seat at an old deal table, she returned to what looked like a game of Solitaire.

Carefully laying out cards, she said, "I think she ran off with a guy."

"Talk out there is she eloped."

"Yeah. That's it. She eloped with a guy. Rags, they called him. Rags Raglan. A Brown boy. Son of a Texas cattleman."

"What did he look like?" I asked.

Spooky shrugged. She seemed more interested in her cards than in me. Her voice was thin and distant. "Burly. Thick hair. Had a big brush mustache. Made him look like an English lord."

"Tall or short?"

"Short. Very short."

"Rags come equipped with a first legit name?"

"Probably. Don't all cowboys? He wasn't a Rah-rah type, if you know what I mean. I think that's why she fell for him."

"Either of them leave a forwarding address?"

"Not with me. Helen didn't run with our crowd much. A little prim and proper, but not so you couldn't take her."

I handed her my card. "If you see or hear from her, there's a reward."

"O.K. Thanks."

As I walked away, I waited for her to ask "How much?" When she didn't, I knew she had been holding back a few cards. I also knew I'd be interviewing her again.

Out on the sawdust floor, the sorority sisters and their dates had cleared out. The crowd was down to singles and doubles. I made the rounds anyway. Not much resulted.

The barman wasn't too friendly when I made his acquaintance.

I opened with, "What's the singer's real name?"

"What the hell's wrong with Spooky Spookins?"

"It's what you'd name a pet, not a person," I countered.

"I only know her as Spooky. Are you thinking or drinking?"

I slid a shiny Eagle coin across the bar. "Will that buy me her legal name?"

"It would if I knew it."

I showed him my snap. "What can you tell me about her?"

He shrugged. "Nothing to speak of."

I retrieved the coin and made my exit.

The next day I took the train down to Providence and conferred with Brown University's Dean of Students. He was to the point.

"I have no student by the name of Raglan. Nor any student on my rolls who can claim Texas as his natal state."

That seemed definitive, so I took my leave. The local constabulary had nothing on Rags Raglan or Helen Reynolds, either.

On the train back, I decided to look into Spooky Spookins. No one tells lies where they don't have a personal interest in the truth.

This time I slipped a Double Eagle gold coin to the barkeep.

"Will this buy me Miss Spookins' home address?"

He didn't have to think twice. "Sixty Woodlawn St. Jamaica Plain. You didn't hear that from me."

Outside, red and gold Autumn leaves scraped and swirled along the gutters, propelled along by an unusually bitter October wind. Winter was early.

I climbed the iron stairs of Green Street Station and grabbed a Forest Hills train, riding to the end of the line. A short hike down Hyde Park Avenue brought me to Woodlawn. It was a dead-end street, but otherwise presentable. On the right, three-deckers stood high on individual granite embankments. Over on the left, the houses were down at street level and less imposing.

That's where I found Number Sixty. It was a yellow two-story frame dwelling left over from the days before they built the Elevated and Jamaica Plain was a streetcar suburb of Boston. Two towering evergreens flanked the front porch and a clean gravel driveway let to a two-car garage that had once stabled horses. Probably built before Woodlawn Street had a name.

It was dark enough for me to take a peek through the garage door windows. I saw a Jewett Brougham, model 1926. Fancy for a cellar speakeasy singer.

The front door nameplate said "Diamond". I rang the bell anyway. When I got no response, I walked away.

Luck in my business is like iron filings. If you walk around thinking you're a magnet, you'll attract your share.

I happened to spot an old pal getting out of a black Studebaker sedan. He wore blue and gave his nightstick an expert twirl when he heard my voice.

"That you, MacIntyre, you old flatfoot?"

"Norris! You visiting or peeping?"

I jerked a thumb at the yellow dwelling. "Who lives yonder?"

"Now how would I be knowin' with the hours I keep? Let's ask the Missus."

Mrs MacIntyre served tea instead of coffee. I made do.

"A woman," she was saying. "Lives alone. Keeps to herself. I haven't made her acquaintance. I don't know anyone who has."

"Anything unusual about the house or occupants?"

"They have their visitors. Mostly during the day."

"What sort of visitors?" MacIntyre growled.

"All sorts."

MacIntyre and I exchanged glances.

"Couldn't be a house of ill repute," he muttered. "Not with those hours."

"Maybe drugs," I suggested. "I'm looking into a missing Harvard girl. Donal Reynolds' despoiled daughter."

"You're welcome to the attic."

A minute later, MacIntyre was unlocking the door into the attic. It was a moonlight cavern. A few odd pieces of bric-a-brac crowded the rafters. An old Victrola sat gathering dust. The front window looked far down into the street. If I stood off to the left, I had a clear view of the yellow house on the low side of Woodlawn Street.

"I'll take it," I said. "Starting now."

MacIntyre left me with an old pair of field glasses, a stack of ham sandwiches, and a thermos jug of tea. With only my camelhair coat to keep me warm, I hunkered down to what promised to be a long and dusty night.

A sedate sedan pulled into the driveway. It was a Hupmobile, a typical machine for the neighborhood. As it slipped into the garage, I wondered what it was doing keeping company with the Brougham.

In the murk, I couldn't tell if that was Spooky Spookins going in, but the house lights went on and then they went dark again. It was two p.m.

I slept on the dusty floor that night and was back at the window again by the time the sun was up.

I counted six visitors as the day lengthened. They stayed an average of 30 minutes. One came out after an hour. I was coming back from the corner lunch counter, my belly awash in coffee, when Number Seven was pulling out in a new Chevrolet convertable Cabriolet. The Jane behind the wheel looked like she would make sense if you talked to her, so I played a hunch.

Doubling back, I tried not to look suspicious as I hailed a Yellow Cab.

"Follow that rambler," I told the driver.

The driver stayed with the Cabriolet as it ducked under the Forest Hills Elevated and raced past the Jamaicaway where the homes went from wood to brick, the Fords and Essexes gave way to Willis Knights and Imperial Landaus, and the people looked to have come up in the world.

The Cabriolet parked before a converted carriage house. I debarked from my cab.

She was unlocking the front door when I accosted her. She looked like the level-headed Bryn Mawr type so I took the polite route.

"Excuse me, Miss. I need to speak with you. Norris. Weld Agency." Her eyes looked surprised. There was no fear in them.

"I'm investigating a disappearance. Helen Reynolds. Know her?"

"No. Never."

"She's connected with Miss Spookins."

Her "Who?" was so open and natural I took it for honesty. But I've been fooled before.

"I followed you from that yellow house," I said.

Now fear detonated in her gray eyes.

"What? Why?" She was more indignant than frightened.

"We shouldn't do this out here," I suggested.

She hesitated. I grabbed her elbow and escorted her into the vestibule and on through a large parlor with a nice bay window.

A huge gray Persian cat met us at the door. He had a wide masculine face decorated with a big white blotch on his upper-lip. It made him look as if nature had modelled him after a mustachioed British officer.

"Scat!" The cat scattered.

We took substantial mohair chairs.

Miss Bryn Mawr shook her marcelled head negatively at my picture of Helen Reynolds. "I don't know her."

"What is your business at the yellow house?" I pressed.

"That is entirely my affair." Her voice was now a cool contralto.

A small black Tuxedo cat with white paws minced in to lay out in front of the dormant fireplace.

"That house is under police observation," I said flatly. "Suspicion of dope peddling."

"What? It's nothing of the kind. I go there for . . ."

"Yes?"

Her shoulders sagged in quiet defeat. "Spiritual counseling."

I'm sure I looked as blank as I felt.

"Madame Diamond," Miss Bryn Mawr clarified. "She counsels the . . . lovelorn."

"She's a fortune teller?" I blurted.

She winced. "Call it what you will. It is none of your concern."

Suddenly I understood the two cars. There was a fortune teller operating out of that yellow house. Probably Spooky Spookins' mother.

"Do you know a woman with violet eyes?" I inquired.

"Yes. Madame Diamond."

"Must run in the family," I muttered. "Do you know her daughter?"

"No. I never met a daughter. We are not social."

I nodded. I was at a dead end. I rose to go.

The gray tomcat was back. He was eying the black like it was a mouse. His tail twitched back and forth. The other cat slept on, blissfully unaware of the impending upset.

I brushed past the Persian, muttering unacknowledged apologies.

I was bowling down street when a not-unexpected snarling spitting cat-commotion reached my burning ears.

The Bryn Mawr contralto ripped back. "Stop it! Stop right this instant!"

I was deciding whether to hail a cab or walk to the Arborway streetcar line when a fresh cry arrested me in mid-stride.

"Rags!"

Doubling back, I flew through the door like a torpedo. Miss Bryn Mawr had the black cat tucked protectively under her arm.

"Do you know a Rags Raglan?" I demanded. "Where is he?"

She looked at me as if at her great-grandfather's ghost. "What?"

"You heard me."

"That is he. Raglan. I call him Rags for short." She was indicating the gray tomcat, now nonchalantly licking its disorderly fur.

I stood staring at the big gray Persian like it might turn into a man-eating lion. It took a few moments for my brain to rearrange itself so that the world made sense. Short. Burly. Thick hair. Brush mustache. He fit the description to a T. Except that he probably never studied at Brown.

"This Madame Diamond of yours," I said. "How old a woman?"

"I would judge 29 or 30 . . ."

"Would her first name be Spooky?"

"No . . . that is the name of her cat."

"Her cat?"

"She fancies cats. We discussed our pets several times."

"I thought you two weren't social."

"We are not. But we do converse."

"Thank you for your time," I said, exiting.

I caught a cab on the fly and found myself at the Boston Public Library. A City Directory gave me the name Dolly Diamond as the owner of Number Sixty Woodlawn Street. No occupation was listed.

Because I needed to think, I walked to the *Daily Record* Building. I knew a reporter there. I know reporters on all the city papers, but if you want to hit paydirt, look to the tabloids first.

Lowery was what passed for the *Record*'s theatre critic. He was wearing a champagne grin when I found him wandering the halls.

"What's new?" I asked.

"Everything," Lowery grinned. "Raymond Huntley as Dracula is scaring them so hard over at the Hollis, they have nurses in attendence to catch 'em as they faint. Over at Loew's State, they've packin' 'em in with their first talkie, *Our Daring Daughters*. Joan Crawford, you know. This old town is starting to hop. And we owe it all to to the new generation of Flaming Youth. May they dance the Charleston till their arches drop."

"Dolly Diamond. Know the name?"

"What's she done now?"

"I gather she has a reputation," I said dryly.

Lowery took me down to the Record's morgue, and handed me a sheaf of clippings.

The most recent was dated less than a year ago. Torn from the front page, it showed a wraparound-skirted flapper in one of those cloche helmets that pass for a ladies hat these days. Under the picture was a legend:

DOLLY DIAMOND IN HER HEYDAY

I read the clipping with interest.

Dolly Diamond, Ex-Hub girl, given name, Mary McNulty, "a Roxbury girl who made good in the city", is divorced. To the world, she is Mrs Carmine Novelli. In the cafés and night clubs and the late-lighted places of New York, Paris and London, however, she will never be known by any other name than Dolly Diamond. Announcement that she has obtained a Mexican divorce from Carmine Novelli, restaurateur, was made in New York by Eduardo Roldan, Mexican attorney.

He said the woman who left her home beneath the Elevated station near Egleston Square a dozen years ago to marry wealth and fame, charged the Greenwich Village restaurateur with mental cruelty.

It is only a bit more than seven years since Dolly Diamond, then Mary McNulty, daughter of a mail carrier living in Dimock Street, Roxbury, came to fame by eloping to Providence, Rhode Island, with Jack Diamond, Junior, Brown student and son of a wealthy Houston cattleman. Papa Diamond waxed exceedingly wroth over his son's plunge into matrimony and cut his allowance from $500 a month to $5 a week. The romance ended 3

years later with a divorce. She married Carmine Novelli in
1925.

"Where is she now?" I asked Lowery.

"Search me and keep the change. Last known address was
Jane Street, Greenwich Village."

I studied the photo. It resembled Spooky Spookins in a
general way. I realized I had yet to glean the hue of her hair.
"She have a sister or a daughter that you know about?"

"Never heard that she did. But you know that set. Woman
has a brat and it's either with the nanny or foisted off on a
boarding school."

I nodded. "Thanks, Lowery. Watch that giggle water."

"I count every bubble as they go in," Lowery quipped,
patting the flask in his hip pocket.

I was on the next train back to Providence. The Dean of
Students was surprised to see me back, but he took it with
aplomb.

"Jack Diamond is an alumnus," he reported. "Or I regret to
say, was."

"Was?" I asked.

The Dean consulted what appeared to be an obituary.

"Deceased, according to our records. Mr Diamond died in
Paris, the apparent victim of an Apache attack. The year was
1924."

This was getting interesting. I jotted down the essential
particulars, thanked him and left.

At the Agency office, I burned up the trans-Atlantic cable
wires. The Parisian gendarmes were kind enough to supply
further details.

While strolling along a disreputable part of the city, Mr
Diamond was accosted by person or persons unknown. Cause
of death was given as multiple stab wounds in the vicinity of the
heart. The autopsy indicated that the weapon used was one
favored by the notorious Apaches of Paris, an abbreviated
folding knife called a *lingue*. Motive was believed to be robbery.
His wallet was found beside the body, empty of everything
except his identity papers. The murder took place some three

years after Mary McNulty, the former Dolly Diamond, had divorced Mr Diamond, but before her second marriage to the restraurateur, Carmine Novelli.

I spent a few minutes with the chief. He was kind enough to sketch from his vast experience a *lingue*. It resembled a pocket knife, but with a peculiar cat's claw blade that folded into a matching handle. Exactly the kind of thing you'd use to slip between a man's ribs – if that was your trade.

A little more research brought out the fact that Mr Diamond had initiated the divorce, stating as his grounds the old dodge of mental cruelty. Evidently Dolly Diamond profitted from the experience in more ways than one, inasmuch as she used that excuse on her second husband.

I would have liked to have known what Mr Diamond felt constituted mental cruelty from a wife. That charge was normally a woman's prerogative.

I had developed an interesting picture of the woman again calling herself Dolly Diamond, but it was only a house of cards if it didn't lead me back to the missing Reynolds girl.

I decided to revisit Patrolman MacIntyre's attic. Spooky Spookins had deliberately sent me on a wild goose chase. It was high time I unearthed why.

From my coign of vantage, one of Mrs MacIntyre's warm egg salad sandwiches filling my mouth, I trained my field glasses on the yellow frame house.

Lights were on all over the place. It was dusk. I wondered if Spooky Spookins was singing tonight. I wondered also who she really was. Most of all, I wondered where the Reynolds girl was keeping herself these days.

Around seven, the front door opened. I trained my glasses on the wedge of yellowish light. I caught a fleeting glimpse of a parting kiss. Who kissed whom was beyond my present powers of observation. Then someone came skipping down the piazza steps.

I didn't recognize the figure strolling down the street. I recognized his coat. Vicuna. The pince-nez perched on the bridge of his nose was more comical than even a pince-nez had a right to be. A pork pie hat covered his sleek black hair.

I intercepted the college boy, and without any unnecessary

preliminary remarks, hauled him into a narrow walkway between two asphalt-shingled triple-deckers.

"Hello, Kit. How's tricks?"

I squeezed his arm so hard he squeaked like a caught mouse.

"Just had your palm read? Or was this visit personal?"

"I – Um –" Kit was trying hard not to look me in the eye. If he tried any harder, he'd have to hide his head in his pocket. From what I make out of his face, a razor had never touched those rosy cheeks.

I took a fistful of dimpled chin and pointed his upturned nose at mine. The sissified pince-nez dropped free. That's when I got a good look at him.

Surprise made me let go. "I'll be damned! A doll!"

"Let me go, Mister! I done nothing to you!"

"What's your name, tin Lizzy?"

"K-Kit–Kitty. What's it to you?"

I was starting to wonder. I searched her soft features for any resemblance to the missing Helen Reynolds. The commotion caused windows to go rattling up on their sash cords.

Kitty saw her chance and bolted. I pounded after her like Red Grange after the old pigskin. Would have had her too, but when I was on the brink of nabbing her, she shed the vicuna coat. My big Brogans got tangled up in it. I took a header.

Crossing the avenue, Kitty sprinted into the concrete tomb that was Forest Hills Station. But I was hot on her heels. The case was starting to unravel, and I wanted my hands on every strand.

I was taking the escalator steps two at a time when I heard the train doors snap closed. Just as I gained the empty platform, the train was pulling out. I muttered some choice words about the excessive efficiency of the Massachusetts Transportation Authority. That got me nowhere.

There was nothing to do but return to my post and ponder recent developments. In the high dim space, I re-examined the snap of Helen Reynolds until I decided any resemblance to the mannish Kitty was general, not specific.

The hours crawled toward midnight.

Lights began winking out all over the house. They followed an orderly pattern. First the downstairs, except for the parlor.

Then the upstairs. Before the top floor lights went out, a solitary window up under the eaves came on for a long minute.

I spotted what I took to be the shadow of a person, but while I fiddled with the focusing screw of my field glasses, the pane went black. When I thought about it, I decided I'd been looking at the shadow of an old dressmaker's dummy.

The parlor light extinguished, a female form retrieved the Hupmobile from the garage. I watched it slither down the narrow street between the kerb-parked machines of the garage-less.

I waited a good long while before I slipped down to the street and picked the rear door of the Number Sixty.

I was greeted by a very black cat who went "meow" when I asked if its name were Spooky. I took that to be a "yes".

The house was in good order. Furnishings were modern but not quite up to Boston Brahmin tastes. The curtains were Chintz. There was a new Atwater Kent cabinet radio in the living room. Gas fixtures had all been converted to electricity. Over all, the house was the kind you'd expect of a two-bath-room Irish household, so I gathered that the erstwhile Mrs. Jack Diamond had either come down a bit in the world, or was laying low for reasons of her own. There must be a reason she preferred the Hupmobile to the Landau.

I noted a card table in a corner of the kitchen, covered with a lavender velvet cloth. Beside an unopened pack of London Life cigarettes, a deck of well-worn playing cards stood neatly in an open cedar box. The table was tucked into a corner, with only two straight-backed chairs in place. Bridge and Whist were not played here. This smacked of a fortune teller's layout.

I moved on upstairs. I expected two bedrooms, but found only one. It was the smaller of the two. The larger room was furnished in fancy damask cushions strewn about the floor haphazardly. No furniture. Portraits of Hollywood actresses ripped from movie magazines were tacked to the walls. I didn't know what to make of it. With the pink-bordered floral purple wallpaper, it made me think of a Caliph's seraglio – minus the harem girls.

An abbreviated flight of steps led up to a dark attic door. Padlocked. I wondered why people in this neighborhood did that.

I debated over picking the lock. Curiosity got the better of me. I tinkered with it until it surrendered.

The light switch was the turn-of-the-century kind that rotated like a rheostat. I twisted it the wrong way and the switch unscrewed and rolled off somewhere. I gave up looking for it, and let my eyes adjust to the lack of light.

The dressfitter's dummy began to resolve itself amid the shadows. I felt a chill. It was partly the cold, and partly the size of the dummy. It must have belonged to Paul Bunyan's wife, it was so tall.

Using it as a marker, I stepped in, wincing when every floorboard creaked. It was colder than MacIntyre's attic, a regular ice box.

A fast-shifting pattern of light followed by the even-uneven crunch of tires on gravel made me freeze. My blood froze, too. I got a good look at the dummy. Not good enough to scare the daylights clear out of me, but enough to send them temporarily scattering.

I stood in the darkness and waited, my breathing even and measured, cold breath steam drippling out between my lax lips.

The laughter of women came floating up into the chill beneath the rafters. I counted three distinct voices. But there might be more.

"Spooky, where do you keep the wine?" a raucous voice cried.

"There's a choice bottle of Malagua in the pantry."

I waited for them to get settled. The night was still young. And they'd feel the attic draft soon enough. I couldn't take my eyes off the outline towering not four feet in front of me.

The wine flowed freely. Jazzy strains squawked from the cabinet radio. I heard dancing. I didn't detect a single male voice, so I wasn't worried about the awkwardness of my position. Or my future.

"Spooky, why are you acting so strangely?" a young voice wondered.

"Are you talking to me?" asked the smoky voice I knew as Spooky Spookins.

"No, sugar, the tabby. She's jumpy and nervous. Look at her."

"What's the matter, baby?" Spooky Spookins asked her namesake. "Cat got your tongue?"

Another voice wondered, "I feel a draft. Is there a window open upstairs?"

"No. All the windows are closed." Worry troubled Spooky Spookins' voice. "Keep drinking. The night is yet young."

She was coming up the stairs. That was it. I knew what to expect next. The curtain was about to fall on the whole matter.

She had steely nerves. She stopped suddenly. I caught a sharp intake of breath. No cry, no strangled choke or sob. I knew she knew the attic door was open. I let the knowledge sink in to the pit of her stomach.

Then I took a careful step backward. A floor board creaked, as I knew it would.

"Who's up there?" Spooky Spookins hissed.

"Maybe it's the ghost of Jack Diamond," I said evenly.

She didn't favor me with a reply. But I tracked the creak of floor boards coming toward the short flight of steps, up the stairs and into the cold confines of the attic. She fumbled for the light switch, found the bare mounting screw, and muttered something under her breath.

She waited and I waited.

We perceived one another's outline at about the same time.

"Do I know you?" she asked, cool as steel and soothing as a rasp. She had nerve. Ice water was in her veins.

"No. But I know you, Mary McNulty. Alias Spooky Spookins."

"You're that agency dick. I saw you coming back." Her voice was thin.

I said nothing.

"In the cards, I mean," she added.

"How did it happen?" I asked nonchalantly. "To Helen, I mean."

Her voice was just as blase in return. "It was just one of those things."

"What things?" I pressed.

"One of those sad broken-heart blues numbers. Young girl falls in love for the first time and falls too hard for her own damn good. You might say Helen went beyond the call of beauty."

I said, "I might believe that. So might a jury. Maybe. If it weren't for Jack Diamond."

"You act like you know things."

"Maybe," I allowed. "I know someone stabbed him in the Place Pigalle section of Paris, employing an Apache knife."

In the dark, she lit a cigarette. Her hair was a smouldering copper.

"I read that, too," she said softly.

"But the murderer who took his money left his wallet," I went on. "A French Apache wouldn't do that. He wouldn't risk the few seconds it would take to separate leather from greenbacks. He'd walk away with the billfold and safely dispose of it later. The robber wanted Jack Diamond identified beyond any question. And the way his heart was jugged repeatedly suggested a personal grudge, not common robbery. A woman spurned might do it that way, for instance."

She pinched the cigarette dark. Her tone of voice blurred. "Why don't you come downstairs for a drink? We can talk about it over a bottle of Xerxes wine."

"Sorry. It's not in the cards."

She lunged in that moment. I was ready. There was a chair beside me. I had moved it into place beforehand. I flipped it up by the back, and jammed the legs toward the low shadow coming at me.

She hit it hard. I heard a sharp thuck of a noise. When I twisted the chair hard, the stuck blade came with it.

Then and only then did Spooky Spookins shriek.

I expected to be mobbed. Instead, the house simply cleared in a stampede of unsteady heels. Maybe my yelling "Vice squad!" turned the trick.

And that was all there was to it. Except for fighting a pair of handcuffs onto the erstwhile Mrs Jack Diamond's struggling wrists. One after the other, I managed it. She scratched and clawed and snapped her white teeth at me with every exertion. She nipped me once, but it was worth it to hear those steel teeth catch.

I dragged her from the attic, not caring how I did it. Behind us, the dressfitter's dummy swung in the emptiness, swung on a length of clothesline wrapped around the broken neck that no tailor's dummy should ever have . . .

"Mary McNulty was leading the damnedest double life you could imagine," I told the Chief next morning. "Two names, and an appropriate auto for each of them. She read cards as

Madame Diamond, and sang in saloons under the name of Spooky Spookins. Between those occupations, she vamped suggestible college girls for her Sapphic love cult."

The Chief was a worldly man. But I had him stumped. He was examining the Apache *lingue* I'd taken off Dolly Diamond the night before. The thin curved blade was snapped off.

"Dolly Diamond was what they're calling a tin Lizzy now," I explained. "Otherwise, a dyke. I imagine the late Jack Diamond was the first to uncover the truth. So he divorced her, citing mental cruelty to cover his profound embarassment at having married a gold-digging daughter of Sappho."

The deepening furrows on the Chief's freckled brow told me the picture was starting to develop. "You're certain this woman stabbed Jack Diamond?"

"As certain as you can be when you know you'll never prove it in a court of law," I admitted. "The Diamond wren got her hooks into this Carmine Novelli. He was professionally known as a Bohemian restaurateur, but that was just a blind. He operated a tea room down in Greenwich Village. Still does, as a matter of fact. Served tea and light lunches while canny young things read the cards of school girls, blue-haired matrons and the odd social lion. Did a roaring business. Dolly stabbed Jack Diamond so he wouldn't expose her past and thereby gum up her marriage plans. Once she learned all she could from Novelli, Dolly ditched him and returned to Boston to set up shop for herself. She took the stage name Spooky Spookins to conceal her jaded past and make a new name for herself with a fresh generation of good-time gals."

"Where does the Reynolds girl fit into this?"

"Like her father said, she fell in with a bad crowd. Spoiled daughters of privilege who know no bounds and respect no laws, natural or manmade. Maybe Helen Reynolds met Dolly Diamond the fortune teller, or maybe she was first introduced to Spooky Spookins, the jazz singer. It doesn't really matter. One way or another, she found herself in that pink and purple harem room, lubricated by bathtub gin, and drowning in the kind of perfumed bacchanale where you and I would never be welcome."

The Chief actually shuddered. Well, he'd come of age long before the days of Flaming Youth and Jazz bands. It was a new era. Besides, he was long married to the same loyal woman.

I resumed my report. "Somewhere along the way, it all got to be too much for Helen Reynolds. Personally, I'd like to think she had a sober moment and couldn't face what had become of her. She slipped off during an orgy of unconventional love-making and hanged herself in Dolly Diamond's attic, too ashamed to face her iron-handed Irish father, and knowing how large an inconvenience her body would be to her corrup-ter."

"What is the Diamond woman saying about the affair?"

"That Helen Reynolds fell madly in love with her and couldn't abide all the other women and drinking and carousing. But that might be pride talking. Her story is that she was so shocked to find her chum swinging from an attic rafter that she got drunk and stayed that way until she could figure out who to call about the corpse. Either way, she's facing a nice variety of morals and other felony charges – being an unlicensed fortune teller among them – which should keep the up-and-coming generation of Harvard co-eds on the straight and narrow for a good long while."

The Chief sighed deeply. "I will have to find a tactful way to break the truth to our client."

I had given that particular conundrum some overnight thought. "Tell him that his daughter hung herself in the passionate throes of unrequited love. Only leave Dolly Dia-mond out of it. Tell him it was a Harvard boy out of Houston named Kit Ragland, known to his drinking companions as Rags. Paint him as a tender-cheeked son of Texas who affects a pince-nez and vicuna coat, a whiz with the ukelele who is currently struggling to raise his first moustache. Old Man Reynolds won't like it, but he'll get over it in time. And since he's bound to pull the expected social strings to keep his daughter's suicide strictly out of the papers, it should all stick."

"What about Dolly Diamond? Eventually, she might talk."

I picked up my hat to go. "Dolly Diamond is looking at a long stretch at the State women's reformatory. Knowing her, she should make out very well up there."

The Problem of the Tin Goose

EDWARD D. HOCH

Among the fads and extremes that typify the 1920s, such as marathon dancing and flagpole sitting, were the aerial stunt-pilots, or barnstormers as they came to be known. These really "took off" in the 1920s, with such pilots as Clyde Pangborn and Pancho Barnes. Ormer Locklear started one of the original flying circuses in 1919. By 1927 new safety regulations had limited the death-defying stunts and the fad began to fade. Not before, needless to say, Edward D. Hoch's famous doctor of the impossible, Sam Hawthorne, finds himself facing another bizarre mystery. You'll find more Dr Hawthorne stories in Diagnosis: Impossible *(1996).*

"What was I goin' to tell you about this time?" old Dr Sam Hawthorne asked as he poured two brimming glasses of sherry and then seated himself in the worn leather armchair. "Oh, I know – it was the flying circus that visited Northmont. That was a wild time, I'll tell you, with murder committed in what could be called a flying locked room. It all began, I suppose, with a romance that blossomed quickly between a barnstorming pilot and a local girl . . ."

It was a hot, cloudless July afternoon (Dr Sam continued) when I strolled over to the offices of the *Northmont Bee* to place a classified ad in their weekend edition. I was trying to sell my tan Packard runabout that I'd owned for a little over two years. It was a fine car but it had never replaced my beloved Pierce-Arrow that was destroyed by fire in a botched attempt to kill me back in February of '28. Now I'd been lucky enough to purchase a beautiful 1929 Stutz Torpedo, almost like new, from a doctor in Shinn Corners who'd lost a bundle in the stock-market crash. The Packard would have to go, so I decided to run an ad offering it for sale.

"That's sixty cents," Bonnie Pratt told me as she finished counting the words. "This sounds like a good deal. I should come out and take a look at it myself."

"Why don't you?" I urged her. "It's over at my office now."

"Oh, I've seen you driving it," Bonnie said. She was a pert young redhead who'd been working at the *Bee* since she'd dropped out of college when her father died about a year before. The Pratts were good people, and though I didn't know Bonnie well she was the sort of pretty girl who got noticed in a town as small as Northmont. "But maybe I will come over later," she added.

Because I enjoyed chatting with her I lingered a while after I'd paid my sixty cents. "What's the latest news, Bonnie? Give me a scoop."

She returned my grin and said, "You have to buy the paper, Dr Sam. You don't give out free diagnoses, do you?"

"No," I admitted, "but can't I have a peek at the headline?"

"Oh, all right." She relented and held up the afternoon edition. "It's all about the flying circus that's coming to town on the weekend."

"We don't have an airport," I protested. "Where are they going to land?"

"At Art Zealand's Flying School. Look at these pictures. There's a Ford Trimotor, the one they call the Tin Goose because of its all-metal body. They'll actually be taking passengers up in that one, for a twenty-minute ride across the county and back. And this is their stunt biplane. They'll take you up in that too if you're brave enough – five dollars for five minutes. They've got the Ford Trimotor and two of these biplanes in the circus. It's quite a show."

"Those barnstormers have been popular for years," I said. "I wonder why they never came here before."

"Because Art Zealand didn't have his flying school till now," she answered reasonably. "They had no landing field. But aviation's the coming thing. People are flying across the country. I have an aunt who traveled from Los Angeles to New York last year in forty-eight hours! They flew by day and transferred to trains at night because it's too dangerous to fly after dark. She was on the maiden flight and Charles Lindbergh himself piloted the plane."

"You're really excited about this, aren't you?"

"I sure am," she conceded. "They're going to let me interview Ross Winslow for the *Bee*. He's the head of it. Look how handsome he is."

The head of Winslow's Flying Circus was an attractive fellow with curly black hair and a pencil-thin mustache. Looking at his picture on the front page of the paper I was struck by the notion that men like Ross Winslow were the forerunners of a whole new world. They were the ones that girls like Bonnie Pratt hankered after, not dull country doctors like myself.

"I'd like to meet him," I said. "The only experience I've had with fliers was back in '27 when they shot part of a moving picture here."

She nodded, remembering. "I'd just gone off to college. Look, if you're interested you can come with me Friday to meet him. They're flying in around noon."

The idea intrigued me. "Let's see how things go. If Mrs Haskel doesn't have her baby I should be able to get away for a few hours."

So that was how I happened to accompany Bonnie Pratt out to the Zealand Flying School on Friday noon to watch the big Ford Trimotor and the two smaller planes settle down for perfect landings on the grassy field. Art Zealand was there to greet them himself, of course, looking like his idea of a World War flying ace with a white silk scarf wrapped around his neck. Art was in his mid-thirties, about my age, and like me he was unmarried. He'd moved to Northmont a year or so earlier to start his flying school and there were unconfirmed rumors of an abandoned wife and children somewhere down south. He was pleasant enough when the need arose but kept to himself much of the time.

"Good to see you again, Sam," he greeted me as we drove up in my new Stutz Torpedo. "The doctoring business must be pretty good these days," he added, patting the car's shiny black fender. The body itself was tan, the contrasting red upholstery on its twin seats matching the red wheels. It was a flashy car for a country doctor, but it was my one extravagance.

"I figure I need something good for these bumpy country roads," I replied.

"I'll bet you could buy an airplane cheaper than that car."

We went off across the field to welcome the barnstormers. Ross Winslow was easy to spot climbing down from the lead plane, waving and walking forward to shake hands. Bonnie Pratt was highly excited as she introduced herself and me. "Hope we don't need your services, Doc," Winslow joked, shaking my hand with an iron grip. "But then I don't guess we will. If I fall off a wing up there, you won't be able to do much for me."

Art Zealand had met Winslow before and he pointed out the area where the three planes should be parked. There was some discussion about the crowds that might be expected and a low-keyed conversation about Winslow's share of the gate. Apparently Zealand guaranteed him a flat sum of a few hundred dollars plus anything he earned from the plane rides.

I turned my attention to the other members of Winslow's Flying Circus, who seemed to be three in number. Two were men a bit older than I – a blond fellow with a scar on his cheek, whose name was Max Renker, and a short jolly fellow named Tommy Verdun. But my real interest centered on the fourth member of the team, a long-haired blonde named Mavis Wing who gave me a slow smile like nothing I'd ever seen in Northmont.

"I can't imagine women barnstorming and walking on wings," I said when I'd found my tongue.

"Oh, we do it, Dr Hawthorne." The slow smile was back. "Lillian Boyer has her own plane with her name in big letters on the side. That's what I'm aiming for. My name's really Wingarten, but that wouldn't look good on the side of a plane, would it?"

"You could just use your picture. That would be enough," I replied gallantly.

"Oh, come now, Dr Hawthorne – you're something of a flirt, aren't you?"

Before I could pursue the subject, Winslow gave them instructions for parking the planes and Bonnie and I went off with him for the interview. Art Zealand had provided a table and chairs in the hangar, where Bonnie took rapid notes as Winslow spoke.

"Max and Tommy both flew in the war," he explained, "so they're a leg up on me. I took pilot training but it was all over before I ever got to France. The three of us got together nearly ten years ago and decided to try barnstorming. You've probably read about Sir Alan Cobham, the famous European barnstormer. His circus has performed all over the Continent and we hope to do the same thing on this side of the Atlantic. There's a lot of competition, of course, and we try to outdo each other dreaming up wild stunts."

"What about your planes?" Bonnie asked without looking up from her notes.

"In this country we all use Jennies, those little biplanes with the double set of wings. They're JN-4D trainers the Army built near the end of the war. By the time they were finished the war was over and the government started selling thousands of 'em for as little as three hundred dollars each. A lot of us who flew in the war, or who trained to fly like me, went out and bought ourselves a plane. Max and Tommy and I started with three Jennies but last year we traded one in for that Ford Trimotor transport. We found out that after watching our stunts the crowd was really ready to fly. We'd have thirty or forty people lined up for a five-minute ride in a Jennie, so we decided that if we could take up ten at a time, for a slightly longer flight they'd still pay five dollars and we'd make a lot more money."

"Tell me about your stunts," Bonnie urged. "That's what'll get the people out."

"Well, we start out by buzzing the town with the two Jennies while Max and I walk out on the wings. Then Mavis does her wild act, actually hanging by one arm from a wing while I fly the plane. That's been known to make people faint. Tommy Verdun is our clown and he's liable to do anything. Sometimes he dresses up like a woman and waits in line for a ride in one of the Jennies. The pilot gets out and Tommy gets in and pretends the plane is taking off with him at the controls, out of control. It's guaranteed to get screams out of the spectators. Then I wind things up by transferring from one plane to the other, either using a rope ladder or walking across, wingtip to wingtip."

"Do you make good money at this?"

Ross Winslow snorted. "Hell, no. We do it because we love it. Somebody said the most dangerous thing about barnstorming is the risk of starving to death, and he's right. We were going to give it up this year, but they say the country's heading into a depression and where would we find jobs? We figure if we can keep at this for another year or two, till the airlines really get established, they'll take us on as commercial pilots. Then maybe we'll start making real money."

"What about Mavis Wing?"

"She's great. Wait till you see her up there. Mavis joined us last summer and business shot up right away. There's nothing like seeing a girl hanging from that plane to get the crowds cheering and biting their nails. I make her keep her hair long so they know she's a woman from a distance, and she wears knickers so they see a little bit of leg."

"It sounds like a great show," Bonnie said. "I'll be here bright and early tomorrow."

As we were preparing to leave Winslow asked her, "What's there to do in this town at night? Got any good bars?"

"With Prohibition?" she asked in mock horror.

"Come on – I'll bet you know the places to go."

"There's a lunch counter where you can get a shot of whiskey in a coffee cup. Will that do?"

"For starters. Will you go with me?"

She hesitated only a second. "Well – sure, I guess so."

"Fine. Can I pick you up at your office?"

"In your plane?"

He chuckled. "Art said I could use his car while we're in town."

So it was decided. I drove her back to the *Bee* office in my Stutz, amazed that Ross Winslow had gotten a date with her so easily and wondering why I'd never thought to ask her for one myself.

The *Northmont Bee* was published on Monday, Wednesday, and Friday afternoons, with the Friday edition being designated for the weekend. Of course, back in those days most people worked at least a half day on Saturdays, but the Friday edition still had the most readers of the week, which is why I'd run the ad for my car in it. Friday evening brought several interested callers, and one of them – the son of the town banker – came by on Saturday morning to close the deal.

With the car sold I felt I could relax for the weekend. Mrs Haskel's baby still hadn't made it into the world and showed no signs of doing so before Monday, so I decided to close the office early and take my nurse April out to the flying circus.

"You mean to say I'll get to ride in your new car?" she asked. I think that was a bigger treat for her than the prospect of seeing the barnstormers.

"It's the only car I've got now," I told her. "I sold the old one this morning."

"If I'd had the money I'd have bought it myself. You take good care of your cars, Dr Sam."

She was thrilled by the ride in the Stutz, holding down her hair as the wind whipped through it on the way to the flying school. When we arrived a little before noon, I saw that the adjoining field was already crowded with parked wagons and automobiles. Their noise made the horses nervous, but as the planes flew back and forth in their opening salute the crowd roared its approval.

"Everyone in town must be here," April said.

Sheriff Lens and his new wife Vera were there, and I was pleased to see them. Married life had made the sheriff almost a stranger, though I was glad to see he was still his old self. "Doc, Vera was just sayin' the other day we gotta have you over for dinner some night. We been back from the honeymoon six months and the only time we seen you was at that church social in the spring."

Vera took up the urging. "How about next week, Sam? What evening is best for you?"

I knew Vera was still working at the post office and I was reluctant to force dinner preparation on her at the end of a working day. "Maybe Sunday would be good. A week from tomorrow?"

"Perfect," she agreed. "Do I get a ride in your new car?"

"Of course."

April tugged at my sleeve. "Look, Sam!"

The two Jennies had landed but now one had taken off again, and I saw a figure with long blonde hair, a white blouse, and knickers edging out on the wing. It was Mavis, beginning her act. I left April with the sheriff and Vera and walked around the fringes of the crowd for a better view. I'd reached the hangar area, nodding now and then to familiar faces in the crowd, when I encountered Bonnie Pratt standing beside Ross Winslow. He was wearing a short leather flying jacket and had his arm lightly around her waist. "Hello, Bonnie," I said.

"Hello, Sam." She edged free of his arm.

"That was a nice opening," I told Winslow. "I thought you'd be up there flying for Mavis."

"Max is flying her today. After Mavis does her stunts I'll take some passengers up in the Tin Goose."

Zealand came into the hangar, looking troubled. "Can I see you alone, Ross?"

They walked back to the office together and I said to Bonnie, "So you showed him the town last night. Did he enjoy it?"

"I think I'm in love with him, Sam. He's so handsome and dashing. I feel like he's a war hero. The local boys just don't compare to him."

"He's only here for the weekend, Bonnie. Don't get your hopes too high."

"He talks about settling down, maybe here in Northmont. He says he may have had enough of flying."

I wondered how many girls in how many towns had heard that same line over a weekend. But I said simply, "I hope it works out for you, Bonnie."

Zealand and Winslow returned, and I heard the school owner mutter, "I didn't know what I was getting into when I booked your crew." Winslow didn't reply but flashed his familiar smile when he saw Bonnie.

"Will you be going up again?" she asked him.

He nodded, glancing at the sky. Mavis was hanging from the plane by one arm as the crowd screamed its delight and apprehension. "She'll be finishing soon. Come on, I'll show you the inside of the Trimotor." The invitation seemed to include me so I tagged along with Bonnie.

It was a big plane by any standards I knew then. The body was covered with corrugated metal and the high wings supported two of the three engines, the third being at the front of the plane. Inside were two rows of wicker-backed chairs separated by an aisle. I sat down in one of the chairs. It felt about like a lawn chair. "Not too comfortable," I commented to Winslow.

"The wicker saves weight, but the airlines are deciding the same thing. Comfort is important. We were able to get this plane fairly cheap because they're phasing it out in favor of a new Douglas aircraft. These things are noisy, and if you fly too high they're cold."

"When will the new planes be flying?"

"Not for a few years, unfortunately, but when they are they'll probably put Ford out of the flying business completely. Ford owns the Detroit airport, you know, but Henry Ford won't allow it to be open on Sundays." He patted the side of the metal craft affectionately. "Still, this is what we've got today and it gets you where you're going most of the time. Would you like to go up for a spin?"

I wanted to, very much, but I felt guilty going without April. "I should take my nurse along," I explained. "We'll go later."

"How about you two?" he asked Bonnie and Zealand.

"Sure," Art Zealand answered. "Let's go up. I want to see what the customers get for their $5."

I left the plane as Winslow went up a few steps into the cockpit and closed the door behind him. He called out the window to a ground crewman to move the blocks from under the wheels and then started all three engines. I watched him slide the window closed and taxi out to the grassy runway. Then he gunned the motors and the plane shot ahead, lifting its wheels from the ground with ease.

I glanced up and saw the Jennie still circling the crowd. Mavis had lifted herself onto the wing again, and was climbing back into the front cockpit. The second Jennie was still on the ground and I wondered what had become of the other team member, Tommy Verdun.

I strolled back to where April still stood with Sheriff Lens and Vera. "Were you on that plane?" April asked. "I thought I saw you."

"I just took a look. Winslow is taking Art Zealand up, and

Bonnie Pratt from the *Bee*. When he lands they'll start taking paying passengers."

"I'd like to go up," April said.

"I figured you would."

The spectators were pointing toward the sky again and I saw that the Jennie piloted by Max Renker had moved into position quite close to the larger Ford Trimotor. They were flying almost wingtip to wingtip, and Mavis waved to the crowd as she started walking out on the Jennie's upper wing again.

"What in hell is that gal goin' to do next?" Sheriff Lens wondered.

"I think she'll try to walk over to the other plane's wing," I said, remembering what Winslow had told us of their stunts.

And that she did, stepping over as easily as she might cross the street. The crowd cheered as the planes flew overhead, so low I could see Bonnie's face at one of the Trimotor's windows, straining for a view of the wing above her head. "The passengers are missing the performance," Vera remarked.

Then Mavis hurried back, hopping onto the wing of the Jennie, and the two aircraft drifted slowly apart. I watched her climb into the open cockpit of the Jennie as it circled one more time and came in for a landing at the far end of the field. The Trimotor landed right behind it, taxiing to a stop near us.

We waited for the door of the passenger compartment to open, but nothing happened. I couldn't see Winslow through the cockpit windows, although there was movement inside the passenger compartment. Finally, after another few moments, the passenger door was shoved open and Bonnie's head appeared. "Dr Sam!" she shouted.

I trotted across the trampled-down grass of the field, already sensing that something was wrong. "What is it, Bonnie?"

"Ross is still in the cockpit with the door locked. We've been calling him and he doesn't answer. I think something's wrong!"

I climbed through the door and hurried up the aisle between the wicker seats. Art Zealand was pounding on the cockpit door, shouting, "Winslow! What's wrong? Open up!"

"Should we put a ladder up to the cockpit window?" Bonnie asked.

I tried the door myself. "If it's something like a heart attack every second counts. This feels like a flimsy lock." I glanced at Zealand for permission. "Should I force it?"

"Go ahead."

I hit the cockpit door with my shoulder and the door started to give. Once more and it sprang open.

Ross Winslow was visible at once, toppled from the pilot's seat onto the unused copilot's seat next to it. I saw the blood and heard Bonnie's high-pitched voice from the aisle. "What? – What is it?"

I took a deep breath and told Zealand, "Get her out of here, off the plane. Right now." Then I stepped forward and bent over the pilot's seat examining the body. There was no doubt that he was dead.

"What is it, Doctor?"

I turned as Mavis Wing stepped into the cockpit, still wearing her stunt clothes. "Ross Winslow is dead," I said.

"*What?*"

"He's been stabbed to death. Go get Sheriff Lens for me, will you? He's a stocky man over at the edge of the crowd."

Sheriff Lens merely shook his head and stared at me. "What you're sayin' is downright impossible, Doc. Winslow was stabbed to death while he was alone inside this locked cockpit and you're trying to tell me it wasn't suicide?"

"It wasn't suicide," I repeated. "Look at where the knife went in – between the ribs on his left side, toward the back. No suicide would stab himself there. It's an almost impossible angle, certainly an unnecessary angle. Besides, when would he have done it? He landed the plane, remember, and taxied up to the crowd. Are we to believe he suddenly decided to kill himself then, by stabbing himself in the back at a nearly impossible angle?"

The sheriff stroked his chin, thinking about it. "Well, that leaves only one other explanation. Zealand and Bonnie Pratt got him to open the door and they killed him together."

"Zealand and Bonnie barely know each other. Why would they conspire to kill Winslow? Besides, you're forgetting the cabin door was locked from Winslow's side. I had to break it in with my shoulder."

"Yeah," he answered glumly.

"We'd better talk to them," I decided. "Whatever happened in that cockpit, they must have heard something."

They were both waiting in the hangar. I spoke with Bonnie while Sheriff Lens questioned Zealand separately. "I didn't hear a thing from the cockpit," she assured me. "You can barely hear yourself *think* in that plane, Sam! It's the noisiest contraption imaginable! Art Zealand told me that on commercial runs they give the passengers cotton to plug their ears."

"The landing seemed smooth from where we stood."

"It was smooth. There was nothing at all unusual until the plane came to a stop and Ross just didn't come out the door." Her composure cracked on the last word and she started to sob.

"Bonnie," I said softly, "I have to ask you this. How serious was it between you and Winslow? You only met him yesterday."

She turned her tear-streaked face to me. "I'd never known anyone like him, Sam. I never believed in love at first sight, but I guess that's what happened to me."

"Did it happen to him too?"

"He said it did. We – we spent the night together."

"I see."

"He told me he wanted to settle down in a town like this, give up barnstorming and raise a family."

"Maybe he told that to lots of girls, Bonnie."

"I don't think so, Sam. I believed him." She wiped her eyes.

"But if you came out here this morning to watch the circus and then discovered he'd lied to you, it might have made you want to kill him."

"Do you think that?"

"I don't know what to think, Bonnie."

She collected herself and dried her eyes. "Well, suspect or not, I still work for a newspaper. I guess I'd better go write this up for Monday's edition."

I left her in the hangar and went in search of the sheriff. When I found him he told me Zealand's story agreed with Bonnie's. The noise of the plane had kept them from hearing anything unusual from the cockpit. "What now?" Sheriff Lens asked, gazing uncomfortably at the cluster of townspeople still waiting at the edge of the field. They'd been told there was an accident and the show had been cancelled, but most of them refused to budge even after the ambulance from Pilgrim Memorial Hospital came and removed the body.

I thought the best thing I could do then was stop Mavis Wing before she took off with her two companions. I told Sheriff Lens what I had in mind and he trailed along. Mavis and the others were in Zealand's office, staying clear of the crowd. I took her aside and asked, "What was your relationship with Ross Winslow?"

She stared hard at me. "I don't know that I need to answer that. You're not the police, are you?"

"No, but I am," Sheriff Lens told her. "Answer the question."

"Maybe I should clarify it," I continued. "Winslow spent the night with a local girl. Might that have made you jealous enough to kill him?"

"Certainly not. And you're forgetting I was up in the sky at the time."

"On the wing of his plane," I reminded her. "He could have slid open the cockpit window to call to you and been killed by a knife you threw, then managed to slide the window closed before he died." I saw the sheriff make a face as I spoke. Even he could see the impossibility of that theory.

"You can't see into the cockpit from the top of the wing," Mavis told us. "Try it if you don't believe me. Besides, I was on the wing for only a few seconds, and visible from the ground. No one saw me throw anything. Throw anything! I was too worried about keeping my balance."

"We'll try it," I assured her, but I knew I was on the wrong track. I turned to Sheriff Lens. "Have you identified the knife?"

He nodded. "Zealand says it was a utility knife from the hangar. Anyone could have picked it up."

"Did you see anyone with a knife?" I asked Mavis Wing.

"No."

"Did you see anything unusual while you were on the wing of the plane?"

"No."

"All right," I said with a sigh. "The sheriff may want to question you again later."

"What about the other two?" Lens asked as we left the office. "Renker and Verdun?"

"Renker was flying Mavis's plane up there, right next to the Trimotor. Verdun was somewhere on the ground. Maybe Renker threw the knife from his cockpit."

"Oh, come on now, Doc – you know that couldn't 'a happened. First of all, that knife's not balanced for throwin', especially not up in the sky with the wind blowin'. And the wound was in the side, around toward the back, and slantin' upward. No knife thrown through the plane's window could have hit him there."

"Of course not," I agreed readily. "I realized that as soon as I said it to Mavis. And that lets Renker off for the same reason. But let's talk to him anyway."

Max Renker was in his mid-thirties, and his blond hair and the scar on his right cheek reminded me of German war aces with university dueling scars. He answered our questions directly, but added little to our knowledge.

"Did you actually see Winslow in the cockpit of the Trimotor?" I asked.

"Sure, I saw him. I waved to him, even. He was alive and well them – but of course he'd have to be, to fly the plane."

"I want to go up on the wing, like Mavis did," I said suddenly.

His eyes widened. "You mean up in the sky?"

"No! On the ground. Can you get me a ladder and help me up there?"

"Sure."

Renker went first and then helped me up onto the wing, some ten feet off the ground. Although the front of the cockpit could certainly be seen, Mavis was right – the angle of the glass prevented a view of the pilot's seat. "That's what I wanted to know," I said. "Let's go back down."

"Wing-walking on the Trimotor is more dangerous than on the Jennies," Renker explained as he helped me down the ladder. "The smaller planes have cables on top we can cling to or brace our legs against. You can't see them from below but they're a big help."

I reached the ground and walked around to the front of the plane. "What's this?" I asked, pointing to a small metal door beneath the cockpit windows on the right side.

"Compartment for luggage and mail sacks. We use it for tools."

"Is there any opening from here to the cockpit?"

"No. Take a look and see for yourself."

I went back inside the plane, walking up the slanting aisle between the rows of wicker seats, then up the few steps to the cockpit door I'd battered open. I checked the windows and noticed each had a little inside latch that was firmly in place. "We modified the cockpit area to our own needs," Renker explained over my shoulder. "The door is placed a bit differently than in commercial planes, and we added those latches so kids wouldn't be climbing through the cockpit windows when the plane's parked overnight at some hick airfield."

"So the door and the windows were latched on the inside," I mused. "And no knife could have been thrown from outside even if a window was open." I turned to Renker in the cramped cockpit. "What about it? You must have some idea how he was killed."

He leaned against the wall next to the door. "Sure. Art Zealand and the girl stabbed him. Ross staggered back into the cockpit, latched the door to keep them out, and died. I hear people can do things like that, even with a fatal knife wound. Isn't that so, Doc?"

"Yes," I agreed. "But it's hard to believe they're both lying. Besides, I don't see any blood by the door, only right by the seat here, as if he was stabbed sitting down."

"Then what are you left with? Suicide?"

"I don't know," I admitted. "Suicide isn't very likely either."

"Well, I sure had no reason to kill him. Ross was the star of the show, he and Mavis. Tommy and I are nothing without them."

"I'd better talk to Tommy," I decided. "He was on the ground – maybe he saw something the rest of us missed."

Tommy Verdun was a small man with short dark hair. He sat in the office wearing a long white duster pulled around him as if to ward off a chill. "I don't know anything about it," he grumbled. "I sure didn't kill him."

"Where were you at the time it happened?" Sheriff Lens asked.

"I don't know when it happened," he answered evasively. "You think he was killed in the air or on the ground?"

"He had to be alive to land the plane," I pointed out.

"Yeah. Well, I was over in the back of the hangar, making sure the kids stayed away from my plane."

"Anybody see you?"

"I suppose not," he admitted. "But then nobody seen me kill Ross either."

"Did you kill him?" I asked.

"I told you I didn't. You don't listen good."

"Aren't you supposed to be the clown of this outfit? You're not very friendly for a clown."

"Got nothing to be friendly about, with the boss dead."

I went back outside with Sheriff Lens. "I don't like that fellow," I told him.

"Neither do I, Doc, but that don't prove he killed anyone. We still don't know how it was done." He thought for a moment. "But I got an idea. Maybe there was some sort of mechanical gadget that stabbed him when he sat down in the pilot's seat."

"You're forgetting he took off, flew a dangerous stunt almost touching that Jennie's wingtip, and then landed again. He couldn't have done any of that with a knife in him."

"I guess not," the sheriff agreed glumly. "But what about this guy Verdun? If he was a clown wouldn't he be foolin' with the kids instead of tryin' to chase them away from his plane?"

"A good point," I admitted. "But if he's lying about where he was at the time of the murder —" I stopped, suddenly remembering an earlier conversation. "Let's find Zealand."

The owner of the flying school was in the hangar with Bonnie, seated opposite her and holding her hands. They broke apart as we entered. "Hello, Sam. Bonnie and I were just having a chat."

"So I see. Art, before the killing you asked to see Winslow alone and I heard you say you didn't know what you were getting into when you booked his crew. What was that about?"

Zealand shifted uneasily. "This morning I got a phone call

from a friend in Ohio. He told me Winslow and his crew got drunk and smashed up a town out there. Winslow and his wife spent the night in jail."

"His wife?"

"Sure. He and Mavis were married."

Bonnie Pratt flushed deeply and turned away. "Did you know this?" I asked her.

"Art was just telling me. I didn't know it before."

"So there's our motive," I said. "The oldest motive there is."

"Maybe we got a motive, Doc," Sheriff Lens said, "but we still don't have the killer. And you've ruled out every way Winslow could have been stabbed in that locked cockpit."

"Every way but one, Sheriff." I glanced out the hangar door and spotted Tommy Verdun walking quickly across the field toward his plane. "Come on!" I shouted.

I ran out, calling to Verdun, but he broke into a run, perhaps sensing my suspicions. "Try to head him off," I called to the sheriff.

His long white duster billowed out behind him as he ran, and it seemed to slow him down. Finally I was close enough to grab the coattail and I yanked him to the ground. Then the sheriff and I were on top of him.

"So he's our killer," Sheriff Lens said, reaching for his handcuffs.

"No, Sheriff, you don't understand," I said, "Didn't it seem strange to you that Mavis's plane landed at the far end of the field after her act, when the crowd was up here?" I pulled upen Tommy's duster to show the white blouse and knickers underneath. The long blond wig was stuffed in his pocket. "Mavis wasn't on that plane. Tommy walked on that wing in her place while Mavis was in the cockpit of the Tin Goose killing her husband."

I told it all once, after the sheriff had arrested Mavis and taken down her statement. I stood in the center of the empty hangar feeling a bit like a lecturer, and said, "It was really quite simple – so simple I nearly missed it. After I battered in that cockpit door and sent Bonnie and Art for the sheriff, I bent to examine the body and Mavis suddenly appeared behind me in the doorway. Because I thought she'd been on the wing of that other plane, I never asked what she was doing there, or how she'd made it from the far end of the field so fast. I accepted her presence without even wondering how she'd gotten on the plane ahead of Sheriff Lens.''

"How did she get on board?' Bonnie asked. "I didn't see her outside.''

"Of course not, because she was on the plane all the time, hidden in the cockpit. Winslow didn't shout for help when he found her there because he never expected she'd kill him. She'd probably had Verdun take her place on other occasions. Winslow told us Verdun sometimes dressed up like a woman for his act, and at that distance the crowd could only see the long blonde hair and the outfit Mavis always wore.''

"But why did she hide in the cockpit?''

"To confront her husband with the fact that he'd spent the night with Bonnie. Isn't that right, Mavis?''

She shifted on her chair. "He was always doing it," she answered dully. "I told him I'd kill him if he didn't stop.''

"So you hid in the cockpit and confronted him. You probably argued during the flight, with the noise of the plane covering your voices. You stepped behind his seat and brought the knife up into his side. Then you took over the co-pilot's controls and landed the plane yourself. When I broke the latch and pushed in the door, you simply stood flat against the wall behind it where I couldn't see you. When I bent over you stepped into the doorway as if you'd just come on board.''

"I'll be damned," Sheriff Lens muttered.

"It wouldn't have worked if Zealand or Bonnie had remained on board, but you were improvising. It was your only chance.''

"But Renker and Verdun musta known she did it," the sheriff said.

"They strongly suspected it, of course. But they'd already lost one star act and if they turned her in they'd have no jobs.''

Verdun shook his head. "I didn't know what she was plannin' when I took her place. I'd done it before as a joke. I didn't know she'd kill him.''

The crowd had all gone home by the time we finished, except for April and Vera. They were standing out by the Tin Goose, waiting for us to finish. I was sorry April hadn't gotten the plane ride I'd planned for her.

"– And that was the story," Dr Sam Hawthorne concluded. "It was the last flying circus that ever came to Northmont. The era of the barnstormer was just about over. It ended about as quickly as it began. It ended that day for Ross Winslow, one of the great ones.

"In the fall of that same year my folks visited me in Northmont to see how their son the doctor was getting along. It was during hunting season, and their visit was almost spoiled by an impossible killing during a deer hunt.

"But that's for next time."

I'll Never Play Detective Again

CORNELL WOOLRICH

Cornell Woolrich (1903–1968) is so closely associated with nerve-racking suspense, such as The Bride Wore Black *(1940),* The Night Has a Thousand Eyes *(1945, as George Hopley) and the story that formed the basis of the film* Rear Window *(1954),* "It Had to be Murder", *that it's easy to forget that he started out as an imitator of F. Scott Fitzgerald with several Jazz-Age novels. He remained a frustrated jazz-age writer for some while. His biographer, Francis M. Nevins, speculates in* First You Dream, then You Die, *that the following story may well have been written in the 1920s and failed to sell, so was rewritten when Woolrich established his pulp market. The version reprinted here first appeared in* Black Mask *in May 1937, so there are a few post-1920s references (see if you can spot them) but otherwise the story is pure Roaring 1920s.*

I sat there with my top-hat over one eye, listening to him whistle like a canary off-key while he struggled with his white tie. His engagement to Marcia had just broken in all the papers, and her people were throwing a party at the Park-Ashley to celebrate it.

"Give up," I kidded as he fumbled his tie for the fifth time, "you'll never get those two ends to meet."

The telephone started-in again. "Another reporter?" he groaned.

But she didn't sound like it when I got over there. "Tommy darling, is it really true? Let me be the first to—"

I doused it against my shirt-front and wagged him over. "Somebody wants Tommy darling. Just wait'll I tell Marcia this."

I could joke about it because he wasn't that kind at all. We'd been rooming together ever since the days when we only had one dress-suit between the two of us, and whoever happened to wear it, the other guy had to stay home in bed.

I went in to get a spare collar; parties like those last all night. When I came back he'd hung up already.

"I'd have been just as pleased without her good wishes," he told me, going down in the elevator. "That was that Fortescue gal just then."

She'd developed rather a bad case of it the year before, before he met Marcia. The minute he found out about it, he started to dodge and duck and go into reverse; her nature was too explosive to have around the house. She'd even tried to have him beaten up by gangsters, probably so she could nurse him back to health, only he fractured the jaw of one and chased the other to the corner of First Avenue and Fifty-fourth Street, where he lost him in the traffic. Tom couldn't prove it was she, of course, but he'd had his suspicions. After that she'd given up the job as hopeless and we hadn't heard any more of her – until tonight.

"Funny thing about it," he went on, while we were waiting at the door for a taxi, "is the big change in her all of a sudden, saying maybe it was all for the best. Wonder how much of it she really meant?"

In the cab he suddenly snapped his fingers. "Forgot all about it! I should have sent Marcia some flowers."

We stopped by at a florist and he went in. I waited where I was.

"Where are they?" I asked when he came back empty-handed.

"He's rushing them down there by special messenger. Some of the swellest red roses you ever saw, kind they call American Beauties. She must be tired of orchids by now."

It was a three-ringed circus when we got there. The Park-Ashley was seething with debs, sub-debs, post-debs, Princeton and Dartmouth undergrads, dowagers, men-about-town, the whole social zoo. The party was supposed to be on the second floor but it was spilling over in every direction.

Tom and I hired a room together to change collars in later on, before breakfast. We had a highball apiece to see us through the first eighty dances, then we went downstairs and reported for duty. We found Marcia standing next to her mother on the receiving line.

"Almost thought you were going to renege on your own party," she smiled.

"Did you get my flowers?" he asked under his breath, like a fellow in love will.

She looked blank for a minute, then began to laugh. "You must have forgotten to put a card in, in your excitement! Whole carloads of them have been coming all evening."

"I bet I find 'em!" a crystalline voice piped up. Marcia's kid sister was standing there, eyes alight with excitement. "I know his taste."

"Red roses," I said behind the back of my hand, to help her along. She turned and ran outside.

Tom began to dance with Marcia, and just as I was girding up my armor to step into the fray, the kid came darting back again. "I see you found them all right," I said. One was pinned to her dress and she was holding a smaller one, a bud, in her hand.

"Here, this one's for you." She reached for my lapel and drew the long stem through the buttonhole, then snapped it off short. "Ow!" she complained, and put her thumb to her lips for a second.

"See, that's what you get!" I grinned.

We started to dance, but before we were halfway around the room she was leaning against me in a funny sort of way all at once, as if she were tired out. I put my hand to her chin, tilted her head back, and looked into her face. Her eyes were just drooping closed. "Tired," she murmured. "Dick, I – can hardly stand up any more –"

Suddenly she crumpled and would have toppled over if my arm hadn't been around her waist. I managed to half-carry and half-lead her over to the door, and no one noticed; it looked like one of those crazy new dance-steps. As soon as I got her outside I picked her up from the floor altogether and made for the nearest elevator with her. She weighed less than nothing, just somebody's baby sister.

"What do you feel, kid?" I breathed, "What hurts you? Old Man Dick'll take care of you."

She opened her eyes just enough to show two slivers of white, like crescent moons. "Old Man Dick 'n' Little Girl Jean," she sighed. Then she sort of passed out altogether. The elevator-slide opened and I snapped, "Hurry up, take me up to wherever their suite is! And get hold of a doctor!"

The Planters seemed to have taken a whole floor for the occasion. I stumbled through three rooms with her before I got to anything with a bed in it. Flowers everywhere; they were all going to be distributed to hospitals in the morning. A pert-looking number with a lace handkerchief cocked over one eye was sitting reading *Ballyhoo*, legs crossed way up to *here*.

"C'mon, get your thrills later," I ordered. "Help me with Miss Planter."

She squeaked like a mechanical mouse and got the expensive covers at half-mast.

A distinguished-looking man with a silver goatee miraculously found his way in to where we were without a road-map; shoving a bridge-hand into his breast-pocket. He swept aside his dinner-tails and sat down beside her. "Turn the other way," he said to me and began to undo the shoulder-straps of her dress. Something fell across one of my patent-leathers as he tossed it aside, a huge cabbagy red rose; I kicked it out of the way. "This child is dead," he said, in the same tone of voice he would have said "Three spades." The French maid squeaked again, then covered her mouth.

I picked up the pale-green telephone and asked them to page Tommy Nye in the ballroom. I acted as hard as a callus on a mailman's foot but I was crying away inside of me; too much Princeton won't let you show what you feel. There was a long wait and the music from down-stairs came over the wire clear as a bell and out into the room, almost like a radio tuned very soft – that damned waltz of Coward's, *Nevermore*. Her first party and her last, she'd never dance again. I made a face and muffled the thing against my shirt-front. "Tom," I said when he got on, "better take Marcia and her mother back to their house, give them any excuse at all, only don't let them come up here –"

"What's up?" he said worriedly.

"The kid just died up here. Don't let it get around, you can break it to them when you get them home. Get back as quick as you can, will you?" He hung up without a word, I couldn't tell how he was taking it; but then how would anyone take a thing like that? I told the maid to take the Planters' wraps down to them, and then go home with them; she was too frilly for a death-chamber.

That society doctor, meanwhile, had gotten in my hair. He'd telephoned in his notification to the authorities all right, and exerted himself to the extent of tipping one of the pale-green sheets over the poor youngster's mouth. But the next thing I knew he was back at the phone again, had some other suite on the wire, and was bidding in his hand in the game that was awaiting his return. I'd seen some cold-blooded things in my time but that topped them all; I suppose he thought I wasn't listening. "– in that case my partner and I will double," he was saying, "you can begin leading, I'll be right down."

"Let me help you get there even quicker!" I blazed, and hurtled him through the three adjacent rooms with one hand at the back of his neck and the other at the opposite end of him. He stumbled when I let go of him, and by the time he had recovered and turned to puff himself up like a pouter pigeon, I had slammed the door in his face.

I paced back and forth for half an hour amidst the chrysanthemums, gardenias and sweet peas while the medical examiner was busy in the inner room with her. A policeman with hay-fever was sneezing his life away at the outside door. And down below they were still dancing, I suppose, and drinking fizz all over the place. Tom showed up very pale around the gills. "God, what a ghastly experience! They both went all to pieces, had my hands full –" The inner door opened and the examiner came out and went by without a word – or would have but Tom got in front of him and blocked his way. "What's the score?" he asked in a husky voice. Behind him the other two showed up who had come in with him; I hadn't identified them yet, all this was new to me. But they weren't leaving yet, far from it. I could tell by the way they strolled out and took in everything; they were there for the night – and maybe then some. The examiner tried to side-step Tom, but the latter wouldn't let him, snagged him by the lapel. "I'm engaged to her sister – I have a right to know – the whole thing was too sudden – what's it all about?"

One of the two watching us spoke up, in a slow drawl dripping with some sort of hidden meaning. "Funny you should say that, about it was too sudden. You seem to be ahead of us. How come you know it wasn't all jake, when we haven't told you yet? You a mind-reader by any chance?" His eyes never left Tom's face.

"Anyone would say the same thing – she was only seventeen – to drop that suddenly –" Tom broke off. "Who are you, by the way?"

"Homicide squad, by the way," the drawl came back. He snapped off a bud from a sheaf of long-stemmed La Frances and drew it through his buttonhole. We both of us sort of tensed at that. That word, ominous-sounding. He nodded to the examiner. "Go ahead, tell him, if he wants to know so bad. Then maybe after that it'll be our turn, he'll tell us one or two little things."

"Tell, hell," snapped the examiner, "I don't get paid for overtime."

"Poetic, aren't you," I murmured. "You really should be rhyming couplets for tombstones."

"She was killed in a poetic way too," he tossed back just before he closed the door after him, "like this was medieval Italy. Killed by a rose. A rose whose stem was sprayed with something deadly, a rose whose thorns were impregnated with it whatever it was. She pricked herself on it separating it from its mates. The ball of her thumb tells the story. We're having an autopsy –"

"That ain't all we're having, either," observed the more truculent of the two detectives. He scanned the cardboard lid of a box he'd brought out with him, then asked for The Fernery, Incorporated, on the wire. "Every floral piece in these three rooms has a card stuck in it – except the bunch that red rose came from. We're having a talk with the florist delivered 'em –"

I gave Tom a look, but he was staring down at the floor, I couldn't catch his eye. I hadn't seen him select them, but the kid had claimed she'd found them, and Marcia had said something about his having forgotten to send a card with them; it sounded an awful lot like his. The horticulturist who'd grown them must have made some ghastly slip-up, sent them on to the florist without realizing that death lurked along their stems –

But then why didn't Tom speak up, I wondered, save them the trouble of checking with the florist? It would only look worse if they got the information that way. What did he have to hide? *He* had had nothing to do with it, an accident like that could have happened to anyone. But then maybe he didn't realize even yet that they were the ones he'd sent.

I cleared my throat, said "Sounds a lot like the ones –." And then looked at him, to let him finish it himself.

He wouldn't meet my eyes, kept staring down at his feet.

Meanwhile the detective had gotten through to The Fernery and it was too late to do it the easy way. "Evans, Homicide Squad," he snapped. "You the manager? You deliver two dozen American Beauty roses to Miss Marcia Planter at the Park-Ashley Hotel this evening? That ain't what I asked you, I didn't ask if you delivered 'em personally or sent 'em by messenger! What I wanna know is, did they come from your shop? Well, who ordered 'em? . . . Didn't write out any card, eh? Well, would you know him if you saw him again?" His eyes flicked over at Tom and back again, as he put the question.

I shrugged violently at him, gestured with both hands, meaning in pantomime, "Why don't you tell him, what are you standing there mum like that for?" He just looked at me and smiled a little, with the left half of his mouth.

The dick, Evans, hung up. "Any objections to accompanying us – and the flowers – up to the shop for a couple of minutes, Mr Nye?" But it wasn't exactly a question, it was an order.

Tom saluted with one finger at his brow, turned toward the door without saying a word.

"Me, either," I said.

"Who's the echo?" the second detective wanted to know. "Ain't it about time we were finding out?"

"If you'd taken the trouble to ask, you'd have found out long ago," I remarked uppishly. "The name is R. Walsh, Princeton '32."

He didn't pop any collar-buttons over it. "Well, meet B. Doyle, P. S. 62," he said, without offering his hand.

I thought I'd kid him a little. "Howju?" I said gravely,

ducking my chin. "I'm this chap's flat-mate and slated to be his best man. Anything else you'd like to know?"

"Liking," he said, "has nothing to do with it, Trained Tonsils. I'd like never even to have seen you yet, much less heard of you, but this is business. So pop open your trick hat and tail us."

"Tail you?" I said, "What am I, a collie?"

"Oh," he protested coyly, "now don't pin me down *that* closely!" and went out after Tom and Evans. I caught up with them at the elevator, which I suppose is what he meant by tailing in the first place. The last thing I heard, at the far end of the corridor, was that poor policeman with hay-fever still sneezing his brains out back there.

The four of us got in a taxi – technically Tom was accompanying them voluntarily, there was no question of an arrest – and went up there to where he'd bought the flowers, which Evans had brought along, box and all, under his arm.

The proprietor was a silly-looking duck wearing a morning-coat. "Ah, yes," he said, taking a peep under the lid, "these are from my shop. Is there something wrong?" And he washed his hands without soap or water.

"That," said Evans bluntly, "is none of your business. The main idea is, who bought 'em?"

"Why, this gentleman did, of course." He turned to Tom, and even asked for corroboration from that quarter. "Didn't you, sir?"

Tom said quietly, "I bought two dozen roses from you and told you to send them where these were sent, yes. But I hardly think these are the same ones you brought out of the case to show me – or else there's something wrong with your stock. You see, they say one of them killed my fiancée's young sister." And he looked down at the floor again, like he seemed to be doing all evening.

The florist went "Ip!" and jumped back about a foot from the box Evans had been holding under his nose.

Doyle said, "Yeah, let's see the rest of 'em he picked these out of."

Evans gave Tom a dirty look. "Why don't you let us do the talking? We'll tell him anything we think he needs to know."

He didn't answer, so I chipped in: "What's so secret about it? She did die, didn't she, or are we having hallucinations?"

Doyle, who seemed to have it in for me – inferiority-complex probably – growled softly out of the corner of his mouth: "One more twenty-five-cent word like that outa you, and I'll send you home with a note to your mother."

The florist shoved back a glass slide all sweaty with steam and showed us triple tiers of long-stemmed roses. They had a blue light shining on them – why blue I don't know, either to make them look pretty or ultraviolet rays to take the place of sunlight. "They came out of here," he said nervously, "but I'm sure you won't find anything the mat –"

Doyle reached in, said: "Mind if we take a few samples for the research lab on Poplar Street? Nothing like making sure. And don't sell any more of them till we get the results – that's a police order!"

The poor florist acted like he wanted to break down and cry. "They'll be a total loss, you're quarantining one of the most perishable items I carry in stock!"

"Watch it," Evans advised his pal, who was pawing at them clumsily, "don't get a puncture like she did."

"In which case," I murmured softly to no one in particular, "the poor rose'll probably be the one to curl up and die!"

Doyle blew up, violently and completely. I seemed to have that sort of effect on him. "This cake-eater," he yelled at his partner, "is getting in my hair! He must think he's out on a party! Do we have to have him along, what's he doing here with us anyway?"

"Slumming," I said nastily.

Evans didn't seem interested in this side-feud. "How is it," he drawled indifferently, "you didn't put a card with them when you bought them, Mr Nye?" But he was looking straight at the florist and not Tom as he asked it.

"I didn't have one with me, and I was in a hurry to get down there, we were late as it was. It was my engagement party, after all."

The jittery shop-owner, whom Evans was watching, didn't seem to have any control over his eye-, eyebrow-, or lip-muscles; they all moved simultaneously. Evans didn't wait for the signs to become audible. "Meaning he did write out a card – or what? You told me over the phone he didn't!"

"N-no, he didn't." He stumbled over it, and yet he seemed to mean it. "Did you, sir?"

"You're talking to us, not him!" Doyle jumped down his throat.

Tom was standing over by some kind of a potted plant, idly poking his index-finger into the soft mould around the bottom. I could see him getting sorer by the minute, a pulse in his jaw started bobbing up and down. He looked hard at the florist, then at them. "I didn't," he said irritably, coming back again to where the rest of us were. "What's all this business about a card, anyway? I bought two dozen roses in this shop – without even putting my hands on them, just pointed at the ones I wanted! I didn't take them down there with me, didn't even lay eyes on them again, until you two men brought them back here with you just now! Am I supposed to have doctored them up or something? With what object? To – to endanger the girl that's going to be my wife?" His voice was shaking uncontrollably, which showed me – if not them – how deeply affected he was by the tragedy.

Loyal-friend-like, I gave them a dirty look, most of it for Doyle. "They've got to make a mystery out of it, that's what detectives are for," I said scathingly. "You and I, Tom, we're just laymen. It'd be obvious to us, or to anybody else for that matter, what must have happened. Some sort of spray or insecticide was used on them and wasn't properly removed afterward. That's all there is to it, just a frightful accident. But of course that isn't enough for our fine feathered friends here, they've got to go around wanting to know why you didn't send a copy of your birth-certificate down there with them!"

Doyle threw down the flowers, stepped up close. "I don't like your face," he said, "and haven't all evening! Here's where I change it around a little!" And he swung back, in good old 1890 style.

"Fine!" I said agreeably, "but not in here where there's so much glass. There's a perfectly good sidewalk outside –"

"Not there or anyplace else," said Evans, getting in between the two of us. "Grow up, Doyle." And to me he remarked less than affably, "You're excused, Mr Walsh. We can get along without your company, if you don't mind. We're just a pair of ignorant dicks, I know, and you could carry out our routine much better; that's why we're being paid and you're not. The police-lab will tell the story; shoot out there with those roses, Doyle. Keep the two bunches separate."

"Lounge-lizard!" Doyle was muttering throatily in the background, "Ice-cream destroyer!"

"You'll never get to meet the right people that way," I warned lightly over my shoulder as I went out.

Tom and the two dicks got back in the cab and left me behind, sort of persona non grata. Evans wanted to ask him a few more routine questions at Headquarters – again it was a request, not an order.

"See you up at the place later," he said to me. "Leave the key under the mat if you turn in before I get home."

"And don't forget to brush your teeth like a good little boy!" was Doyle's insulting farewell out the cab-window.

"Come back and I'll brush yours with my foot," I promised.

The last thing I saw was the two of them holding him back by main force from jumping out then and there and taking me up on it.

It had been warm in the flower-shop and I'd taken off my neckcloth and crammed it in my pocket while we were in there. Also my gloves. When I started to put them on again, I saw that one had fallen out, I'd lost it. I turned around and went in again abruptly.

The proprietor, who evidently hadn't gotten over the effects of our visit yet, gave a jittery jump when he saw me show up like that again. I wouldn't have thought anything of it, but he happened to be standing close to that potted plant when he did so.

"I dropped a glove," I said, but I let him look around for it. I looked, instead, at the finger-holes Tom had absent-mindedly punched into the mould around the plant that time when that card-business was going on.

"Here it is, I've found it," he said. He meant the glove, but I suited my action to his words, pulled a hundred-dollar bill, rolled into a cylinder, out of one of the finger-holes. He promptly dropped the glove a second time – and a lot of complexion with it.

"What was he slipping you this for?" I asked quietly.

"Why, why I'm sure he didn't mean that for me! He must have dropped that in there by m-mistake –"

"Oh no," I said tonelessly. "He gave you a hard look just then, I saw him. I thought he was sore at the time, but it was a signal it seems. Not to tell – what?"

He didn't know, hadn't any idea, and all that sort of stuff.

"You're not thinking hard enough," I chided coldly. "I'm his friend. Wouldn't you prefer to tell me and keep it sort of en famille? Or suppose I page those two missing links and let them start the whole thing over again?"

I wouldn't have dreamed of doing it, because this didn't look so hot for Tom. They'd gone already, anyway, but he didn't know that.

Since then, people have said to me, Why didn't you butt out? Why be nosey? I mean, what business was it of yours whether your friend had left a century-note in a florist-shop or not? Well, that's just the whole point. If he'd been only an acquaintance, I certainly wouldn't have snooped. He was like a brother to me; either you get the idea or you don't.

He gave in, rather than face the detectives again. "I'm really not absolutely certain what he meant by it myself," he stammered, and possibly he was telling the truth, "but I judge, I imagine, he didn't want the second two-dozen roses mentioned – in front of them. So I didn't."

He evidently hadn't, if there'd been any such, because he'd neglected even to mention them to me. "I imagine so," I agreed, as though I'd been in on it all along.

He wasn't sure I had been, though, I could see that; the mere fact I'd cross-questioned him about the bribe made him wonder. "You know about the other young lady of course?" he said hopefully.

I did now. And it wasn't in character at all. I nodded noncommittally. He shrugged, trying to appear sophisticated. "I know how those things go, young fellows about town like you. But if I'd told *them*, right away it would have been in the papers – one of those gossip-columns maybe – how he sent flowers to his ex the same night he was getting engaged. Get him in hot water. That's why I caught on and shut up about it."

I'd been racking my brains. But there wasn't really much of a list to check. "Fortescue?"

"Yes, on 54th, over by the river."

"You don't have to tell me," I assured him. I was remember-

ing the year before. How often he'd come away from there with
bites on his neck. "Same messenger take them to both places?"

"Yes, he stopped off there first, then went on the Park-
Ashley."

I locked my teeth. "Why, that devil!" I thought "Is it
possible she snagged them away from him – the second bunch
– long enough to do something to them, hoping to harm Marcia?
She must have caught on whom they were for, no trick to that at
all; pumped the kid." I walloped my gloves viciously against the
edge of the case. "I'm going down there," I said to myself,
"now – right now! Dirty little murderess!"

I speared my finger toward him, with the century curled
around it the way it must have been curled around Tom's when
he stuck it into the mould. "Well, this is yours," I said dis-
approvingly. "He seemed to want you to have it – and it's his
money, not mine." It would have to come out, anyway, if she'd
really done what I thought she had – Tom or no Tom.

He took it all right; I would have collapsed if he hadn't.
"D'you think I'll get in trouble?" he wanted to know, though.
"They didn't *ask* me point-blank, you know –"

I wasn't interested. "See you around," I said, and went out.

I got in a cab and went down seven blocks to 54th and over
five to the river. I thought: would that torch-bearer be capable
of doing a thing like that? But how had she known ahead of time
he was going to send her flowers? How had she managed to have
– whatever it was – ready? Was she a modern Lucretia Borgia or
something? And yet it didn't seem possible she'd kept the
messenger-boy waiting there any length of time, Marcia's
flowers had gotten down to the hotel ahead of us, and we'd
had just a straight ride in a taxi.

I vowed, I'll knock all her front teeth out with my own little
fist, if I find out –! And *that* sap – I thought he knew his way
around! That's what comes of picking up loose odds and ends at
Twenty-One on rainy Fall nights!

But the sight of Third Avenue through the cab-window
seemed to bring out the good old-fashioned qualities in me,
the sense of fair-play and even a vestige of chivalry that I hadn't
known was left any more. She hasn't brains enough, I told
myself. Her speed would be to try to have him beaten up, like
she did once before. Why jump at conclusions? That's what

comes of associating with detectives, even for half-an-hour! Simply an accident – and what's more, if one bunch was tainted, then the whole consignment was, and she's in danger of having the same thing happen to her if she fools around with them! So between wanting to sock her in the teeth and wanting to save her from a fate worse than death, I was in a hurry to get over there.

"Get across, get across there!" I prodded the driver.

"That pretty color up ahead," he said sarcastically, "is red. They put it on just to make the street look nice. It don't mean a thing. This your first time in a New York cab?"

"Did I ask you for a civil service examination?" I flared. "You've talked yourself out of á quarter tip."

"You were just looking for an excuse to welsh, you probably haven't got one," he let me know. "Just for that you can open the door yourself. No tip, no service."

I didn't seem to get along with anyone tonight. I got out, bent down, and put sixty cents on the curbstone just out of reach. "You can get out and pick it up if you want it!" I said.

A bedecked janissary inside the Taj Mahal (the décor suggested that, with just a dash of the Colosseum and a touch of the Kremlin) wanted to know who was calling on Miss Fortescue. For which bit of red tape she, I mean Somebody, paid $5 a month extra on her rent.

"Mr Tom Nye," I said unblushingly.

It was all right, it seemed, for Mr Tom Nye to go up. Whether it would have been just as all right for Mr Dick Walsh, I misdoubted me. She'd never bit me on the neck that I recalled – and I have a very good memory for those things, the twice it's happened.

I read into his look that Mr Tom Nye carried an aura of something as far as he was concerned – interest, without friendliness – but since he obviously didn't know him by sight, I couldn't get it. Had the lady spoken out of turn when she was being poured home drunk once or twice?

I tipped my hat elaborately – upstairs. Well, at least *her* roses hadn't played a dirty trick on her. "Hi, Fritzie," I greeted her.

Her face dropped down to her scanties nearly – and there wasn't very much interference in between, I assure you.

"What's the idea?" she said huskily, "Don't you know your own name any more?"

"I know how it is," I soothed her, "a nickel's worth of last-minute perfume behind the ears shot to hell! And all the sofa-pillows punched together for nothing! Wouldn't I do for a stand-in, at least?"

"Don't get so wise," she said sultrily. "You're jealous 'cause you never got to first base, that's all."

She never poisoned anyone, I told myself; just a child of nature. I walked past her as though I owned the place. "My, what nice flowers," I said. "And some tastefully arranged too. Some guys get flowers. When I call anywhere I seem to get grocery-bills." I sat down, flattened my hat with my elbow. Pop!

She took something out of the folds of her negligee, stuck it under one of the pillows, sat back against it. I caught a flash through her fingers, though.

"Mmm," I said, "so he *was* going to get flowers – in a different way, without being able to smell them. I thought you liked him."

"What's on your mind," she said wearily. "Do I have to sit here all night and listen to you talk like Noel Coward?"

She had one pinned to the shoulder of her gray negligee. There was another spray of them arranged in a flat blue bowl near me. I pulled one out – with a wicked webbed thorn sticking up from its stem – started to play around with it. Prod it gently with my thumb, watching her. Not hard enough to break the skin, I assure you.

Judging by her look, she didn't seem to give a rap whether I lived or died – not even if it happened right there on her premises. So I quit doing it, because *I* did give a rap. I pitched the thing over my shoulder.

"Why did you figure you'd need a gun if he came here to see you tonight?" Doyle couldn't have done it any better. "What'd you done to make you afraid of him? What was on your mind?"

She looked hostile, rather than frightened or guilty. "What'd *I* done?" she yapped. "That's a good one! What've I ever done to make me afraid of him? When haven't I been afraid of him?"

Which didn't make sense to me. "Well, when haven't you been?" I parroted.

"Not since after I first found out –" Then she let it down easy. "A few things about him."

There was a tap at the door. One of those prearranged taps, I somehow got the feeling. She went over and opened it and the janissary was standing there. He didn't say anything, just looked at her.

"No, it's all right," she said, "it wasn't Mr Nye." So she'd coached him over the house-phone before she let whom she thought was Tom in, "Look in on me in a minute or two, I might need you!"

Meanwhile I switched the gun to under my own pillow.

She came back and said to me virtuously, "You know, I ought to go to the police. I should have long ago."

I knew how she meant it, but I distorted the meaning. "You ought to," I agreed. "And maybe you will yet before the night's over."

"If he comes near me again I will."

"No, it's not a case of his coming near you. You know, a young girl died down there tonight –"

She took it big. Closed her eyes and let her head loll back and put the back of one hand between her eyes. "Oh my God!" she shuddered, "Oh, that poor girl – I should have phoned – oh, if I'd only had the courage to phone down there! I was afraid, oh I was so afraid –!" She got up and did a couple of half-turns, this way and that. "I've really killed her – I'm to blame –!"

"Now Dickie," I said softly to myself, "we're really getting somewhere. And Doyle thinks he's so hot! Why, there's nothing to it!"

"I've got to have a drink!" she shivered, and poured herself enough to launch a battleship in.

"Have one on me too," I encouraged when she'd downed it without stopping to breathe. "And then I suppose it'll be up to me to call the police or something. Although I hate to be a snitcher. Maybe I'll let them do their own dirty-work." She looked at me and I looked back at her. "So you should have phoned!" I mimicked. "That and a couple of other little things. I'll tell you what you should have done! You should have let those g.d. flowers alone – then there wouldn't have been any-thing to phone about. You'll probably get away with it at that.

'Beautiful love-slave mad with jealousy. I didn't know what I was doing, I didn't want her to have him.'"

The second drink fell out of her hand and parted over her satin slippers like a gold wave. "What are you talking about?" she said in a stifled voice. "Flowers –" She gestured vaguely at the ones scattered around. "– what've they got to do with it?"

"You put something on them, didn't you, and then sent them on to her from here."

"I!" She screamed it. "I got them from him!" She glanced in horrified fascination down at the one on her shoulder. "Is that how – what happened to Marcia Planter anyway?"

"Not Marcia, her younger sister. But at least you admit whom you intended it for – which is no news to me. Why ask what happened? Something deadly on their stems got into her blood-stream –" I snapped my fingers. "Or didn't you intend to go quite that far – did you just want to give her prickly-heat and spoil her beauty? Amateurs shouldn't experiment with poisons –"

But she had no more time for words. I think, woman-like, my latter suggestion had frightened her even more than the thought of death itself. She was afraid to take the thing off her, the one pinned to her negligee, or touch it with her fingertips in any way, so she started pulling and tearing the whole flimsy off her shoulders. And as she did so, she kept giving little bleating wails and side-stepping around in a macabre sort of rhumba.

It should have been excruciatingly funny; it wasn't of course anything of the kind. "Stand still!" I ordered and caught at her. "You'll make it happen twice as quickly that way! I'll get it off for you, I'm not afraid of it –"

I was too, but, well I wasn't afraid enough *not* to try and help her. I pulled the pin out carefully, and the thing dropped of its own weight and I kicked it away with my foot.

"So you didn't – have a hand in it," I said, breathing hard and sitting down again. What else was there to say – after what I'd just seen? Tallulah Bankhead would have been just as convincing, but not ad lib without a rehearsal or two.

She was all in, reached up and pushed her hair out of the way. "But why *before*?" she said. "Why *before* – tonight was only the engagement, wasn't it? I thought it was after their marriage that – that she had to worry about."

She poured us each a drink this time – to make what she had to say go down, perhaps.

"There are two sides to the story," she said, when she was down to the ice-cube in her glass. "Mine – and the one you've heard from him, or gathered from what he'd let drop. I know about that, because he's said to me 'Dick thinks I'm off you. All the better, let him think so.' I can just about imagine what his side of it is – that he cooled off, that I've been running after him ever since, that I even sent some friends of mine out to beat him up. Now listen to my side of it – and it's not a pretty story."

I chewed ice with my back-teeth, noisily.

"I did go for him, I was sold on him. Then one night a year ago we were sitting here eating apples. I'd given him a fruit-knife to pare them with. All of a sudden without any warning he had me pinned down here in a corner of this same sofa we're sitting on, was bending over me with that knife aimed at my throat. No rational reason, no jealousy, nothing like that – just a sudden urge. One look at his eyes, and I knew enough not to struggle. I just lay there limp, talking to him quietly, saying 'You don't want to do that – wait'll tomorrow night –' Oh, anything and everything that came into my head. Dick Walsh, it was a solid hour before I got him to put it down and take up his things and leave. When I got the door locked, after him, I fell in the most beautiful faint you've ever seen – just behind it.

"It happened once again, about a month later. Not quite as bad. I was laughing and had my head back. 'Gee what a soft little neck you've got,' he said, and closed his hands around it, sort of measuring it. He didn't put on any pressure, and I distracted his attention by pointing to something behind him.

"I bought this gun the next day, and I've never received him without it since. Walsh, I knew then and I've known ever since – that your friend has a latent streak of homicidal mania in him. He's probably fighting it, but it's growing stronger all the time, and it's going to come out some day –"

"I've known him since we were both in school," I said. "You're talking through your hat!"

She said bitterly, "A man can go through college with another man; room with him for years, be slated for best-man at his wedding, but when it comes to knowing that other man, the hidden recesses of the mind, the dark quirks revealed in unguarded moments, it takes a woman."

"Why didn't you drop him then?"

"I was afraid to. Afraid he'd turn on me and get me for sure if I antagonized him in any way. I couldn't face it, the thought that he might be lurking downstairs by the door some night when I came home plastered, or get himself admitted up here and wait for me hidden in a closet. I told a couple of small-time racketeer friends of mine about it, and they went out to beat him up. That was their own idea, not mine. That scared me even worse, I begged them to lay off, let me handle it."

"Why didn't you go to the police, then?"

"Walsh," she said drily, "a girl like me has no social standing, she has to take her own chances. Besides, he never actually threatened me, it was just that I never knew from one visit to the next when the thing was going to pop through the veneer of sanity that's hidden it so well from you and everyone else.

"When he first started going with Miss Planter, all I could think of was that meant an out for me, I'd finally get rid of him. I wanted to ring bells and blow whistles. But it was still there, only it had switched over to her. I'm a nice comfortable sort of person; other guys don't hide much from me, I guess I had the same effect on him. He started in by saying that he still liked me better than her, but that he'd have to marry her, because she had all kinds of dough. Then pretty soon he was saying that he'd come back to me and show me what he really thought of me, once he got his hands on that dough. Leaving it sort of indefinite what would happen to her. Then finally it became less indefinite and less indefinite, until I couldn't help knowing what he meant. He didn't say so in so many words, but you couldn't mistake his meaning – he was going to get rid of her some fine day –"

I got my own drink this time. She was getting under my skin, but every pore was fighting her.

"That's bad enough," she said, "that set-up. But there's something worse to it, something worse than that. The real horror of it is, he doesn't *really* want Marcia's money, he doesn't *really* want me. He just wants to kill someone. He's sick in the head. Oh, I looked into his eyes for sixty minutes that night, with a sharp knife at my windpipe, and no one can tell me different! If it isn't her, it'll be someone else, sometime, some-where –"

I looked at her like I hated her for doing this to me. "Proof," I said huskily. "Proof. I've got to have proof. You've destroyed my confidence in him forever, damn you. But still I only have your say-so, your suspicions to go by. I'm with him day and night, I've never noticed anything. I've fallen between two stools now. You can't leave me like this."

"I'll give you proof," she said. She got up and looked frightened, like she was trying to get her courage up for some-thing. "I called him up once tonight. You were there. You didn't hear what he said to me, though, did you?" She went over to the hand-set and dialled Butterfield 8–1200, our number. I read the slots over her shoulder.

"Don't ever tell him," she breathed. "For God's sake, don't ever let him know about this – or I'm finished."

She sat down on the bench, and I sat down on it the opposite way with my head affectionately on her shoulder. We weren't thinking of love, we were both listening to the same receiver. I was shaking a little.

He got on and she said, "Hello, Tommy dear. Did I get you out of bed?"

"Who is this, Fritzie? No, I just got in," he told her. "I've been down at Police Headquarters until half an hour ago. Did you hear what happened?"

She looked at me quickly and I shook my head; it mightn't be in the papers yet. She said no, and he told her. He told her that the report from the chemical lab had come in while he was there, some kind of experimental stuff they'd been trying out for a weed-killer at the hot-houses had got on them by accident; they'd gone down there now to destroy all the rest of the bushes, and were sending out a warning to the various florists around town. "Walsh said that from the beginning," I heard him say "but for a time they had me feeling damned uncomfortable."

She gave me a look, but I didn't call that proof. "And will this delay your wedding?" she led him on.

"Not if I've got anything to say about it," he answered.

"So it looks like I've got to lose you after all," she crooned trickly.

"I'll be back at your door in six months, darling – a widower," he whispered. An electric current went through me. Her eyes met mine; hers were frightened, seemed to say "I told you so"; mine were horrified, incredulous.

"You don't really mean – those things you've been saying all along," she said, to spur him on.

But he was too cagey. "I don't want to talk any more over the phone," he said. "See you soon."

The more we drank, the less able to get drunk we both seemed to be. "Proof enough?" she shivered, gorging on hers.

I drew my hand across my mouth, as though I had a bad taste.

"It's in him," she said. "And if it isn't her, it'll be somebody el—"

"Wait a minute! Wait a minute!" I breathed it as though afraid of the sound of my own voice. "D'you remember when that Andrea girl was killed about a year and a half ago – that case that was never cleared up – did you know him then? He got all excited, dwelt on it, that was all he could talk about for days –"

"Yes, yes!" she agreed. "I noticed that too. He came to see me the night after it happened. He brought in three papers with him, not one, and sat and read every word in them aloud to me. His face was all flushed, he seemed to get a thrill –"

"You scratched him too, didn't you, that night – no, it was the night before that he came home from here all marked up, I first saw it that morning, and he laughed and told me how 'emotional' you'd gotten –"

She put an ice-cold hand on my wrist, so cold I jumped at the touch of it. "He wasn't with me the night before. By all that's holy I swear it! I was out at a bar with another man when the news of the Andrea girl came over the radio. I didn't give him those marks. I noticed them myself the second night – he told me they came from improperly manipulating one of these new electric razors he'd just bought – 'burns' he called them –"

I said it so low it's a wonder she could hear me. "He's never owned one, never brought one into the place from first to last –"

We were awfully quiet, awfully scared. We were both thinking the same thing. We didn't want to know for sure; I had to go back and sleep under the same roof with him, she had to receive him the next time he took it into his head to drop in on her. We didn't want to know for sure.

I left there at three that morning. I left an entirely different girl than the one I'd called on before midnight. I'd called on a slinky, jealousy-crazed vamp, who had pursued the life out of my room-mate and wasn't ready to give him up even yet, not if she had to murder her rival.

I came away from the flat of a girl who was no plaster saint, who wouldn't have thought of refusing a "present" from an admirer when it was offered in the right spirit, but who, far from pursuing Tom, had been living under the shadow of death's outspread wing for the past year or more, had never received him without having a gun handy, ever since she'd found out –

I came away with that gun of hers on me; she had urged me to take it with me herself. "I'm going to get out of here," she said. "First thing in the morning! He'll find out sooner or later I told you –"

"No he won't," I said. "He won't come near you again, don't worry."

"What are you going to do?" she asked.

"I don't know," I said. "He's – my friend."

The janissary came up with the car. I liked him; he didn't want to kill anybody. I gave him fifty bucks downstairs in the lobby. He nearly sat down on his fanny. "You're a good guy," I said. "Look after – Miss Fortescue, will you? She's a good guy too."

Her "What are you going to do?" followed me away from the place. I didn't know what to do. He hadn't poisoned those flowers, he hadn't done anything. He was *going* to do things – some day. Fritzi and I both knew that. An accident that looked like murder had revealed – a real murder, far in the future, not yet committed. That and a suspicion of murder already committed, far in the past.

I couldn't go to the police; he hadn't done anything they could hold him for. I couldn't just sit by either, and watch Marcia Planter or some other girl drift slowly to her doom. I had my own life to live, but I'm funny that way. I couldn't have gone through the months and years with that hanging over me, not knowing when –

It would have been better not to know. But I knew now. And I didn't know what to do.

The latchkey was under the mat when I got back. That riled

me for some strange reason. I felt he should have cowered behind a locked door, away from me and what I'd found out. I made faces while I unlocked, closed the door again after me. Faces like a guy going into a place where there's vermin.

I gave the foyer the lights, took off my topper, shied it into the dark living-room, not caring if I ever saw it again. I went in through the open bedroom-door and gave that the lights. He was sound asleep, a long cylinder under the covers, on the bed nearest the window. I stood there looking at the place, looking at him. A fistful of change and crumpled bills on the dresser, where my jack always went too at nights. How many times we'd had a friendly row the next morning, trying to separate the two. "That fin was mine, y' highway-robber! You only had singles!" Each feeling at the same time that the other guy would have given him the shirt off his back.

I'm not trying to be stagey, but put yourself in my place. A thousand pictures flashed through my mind, like a shell-shocked newsreel. The two of us in the Varsity Show. At proms. Trying out for football. Boning for exams. Getting chased in a second-hand roadster by a State motorcycle cop and piling it up against a tree. Standing together on the stag line at a hundred deb-parties, both going for the same wows and both dodging the same clucks.

And now, here he was. Showing a rotten spot, like an apple. Not showing it, rather, but having it in him. It didn't make me want to break down and cry, it had just the opposite effect, made me sore as blazes – because it was such a dirty trick on me, I guess.

"Get up," I growled. "Get up, you!" My voice rose as I went along. "Get up and get out of here! Murderer! Warped brain! Get out of this flat, before I –!"

He was awake then, startled, stiff-armed against the bed, blinking at me. "What's the matter with you, one too many –?!"

"Get out of here – beat it, quick!" My mouth felt all lopsided. "Dirty murderer!"

"You've gone crazy," he said. "What happened to those flowers was an accident, I waited down there till they had a full report on it –"

"Yes," I said bitterly, "that's the joke of it. An accident came along, and through a chain of circumstances, revealed a murder

– in the making! A murder that hasn't happened yet – and that I'm going to see doesn't happen!''

I sloughed a chair around, sat down heavily on it, back to front, took out Fritzie's gun and broke it open. I took out a bullet and put it in my pocket.

He made a move toward his pants. "No, wait!" I said. "You'll go back to her, won't you, that poor little Fortescue hustler, and you'll do her in – for telling me!" I took out a second bullet. "Or you'll go to Marcia Planter and you'll say, 'Let's get married right away, let's give them all the slip and leave town.' And then some fine day she'll have an accident, won't she, fall out of a window or be swept overboard from a ship – or any one of a million things?" I took out the third bullet and put that away. "No she won't! She loves and trusts you, she deserves a better break than that."

"That lying little tart –" he said.

"You spoke into my ear over the phone an hour ago." I took out the fourth bullet. "And it isn't even that – I'd steer clear of you maybe, but I'd be able to understand – if it was just the money. But it's killing for the sake of killing, that's got you. I saw how you ate up the papers when the Andrea girl was throttled. I don't know if you did that or not, and I don't want to know." I took out the fifth bullet, and I clicked the gun closed.

I saw how pale he'd gotten at the name, and how he shrank back a little.

"Whether you did or not, one thing's sure. The insulation had already started to wear in by that time. And now there's not very much left. It's going to be someone – real soon. Maybe someone you haven't even met yet. The guy that I went through school with, that I've roomed with all these years, wouldn't want that to happen – even if you do. Only Fritzie and I know." I stood up and looked at him, and he looked back at me. "And she's – nobody. And I'm – your friend. Still your friend. Think it over." I pitched the gun away from me on the bed. My own bed, not his.

I turned and I went to the door. "Think it over," I said, without looking at him any more. I closed it after me and I went out.

It hit me awfully quick, I'd hardly gotten halfway through the small-sized foyer outside when it hit me. Seemed to hit me in the back, and lift my heels clear of the floor. A boom that rattled the closed bedroom-door on its hinges.

I didn't look around at it. I went over to the phone and dialed Headquarters. I asked for Doyle, why I don't know. I guess I wanted to talk to somebody I knew, no matter how slightly, rather than just some stranger.

He was still there and they got him for me.

I said dully, "This' Dick Walsh, I don't know if you remember me or not, from the Park-Ashley and the florist-shop tonight —"

He liked me as much as ever. "Sure I do," he said sarcastically. "The amateur detective!"

"My friend just had an accident, better come around." Something like a sob popped in my throat without my meaning it to. "You can have your job. I'll never play detective again. You find — crawling things under the stones you turn up."